THE ANTHEM

THE ANTHEM

Other Books by Noel B. Gerson

FICTION

Francis Marion, the Swamp Fox
Give Me Liberty
Yankee Doodle Dandy
The Slender Reed
Old Hickory

NON-FICTION

Light-Horse Harry
Kit Carson
The Last Wilderness

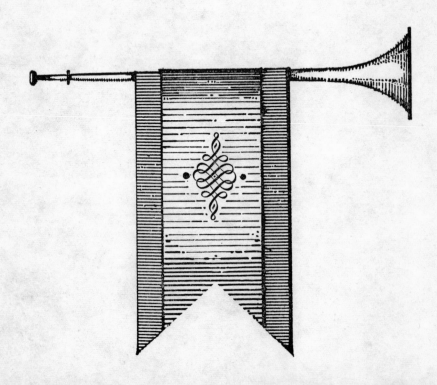

THE ANTHEM

By Noel B. Gerson

Published by
M. EVANS AND COMPANY, INC., NEW YORK
and distributed in association with
J. B. LIPPINCOTT COMPANY
Philadelphia and New York

Copyright © 1967 by Noel B. Gerson
All rights reserved
under International and Pan American
Copyright Conventions.
Library of Congress Catalog Card Number 67–15786
Manufactured in
the United States of America
Designed by Wladislaw Finne

For Noel-Anne

For Noel-Anne

The anthem of hate chanted by the godless makes inaudible even the sounds of angels, but the anthem of love shall prevail.

SERMONS—
HENRY KING (1591–1669)
BISHOP OF CHICHESTER

BOOK ONE

BOOK ONE

E cumenism," Bishop Charles de Montauban said, tugging at the sash of his cassock and stretching his thin fingers toward the logs burning in the hearth, "is undoubtedly the most overworked word in every tongue on earth. Pope John said it so much more simply and directly, you know. He had a real genius for that sort of thing. 'All men are brothers and have one Father, no matter what the different names we may call Him.'"

He glanced at a portrait, above the fireplace, of a stern-faced man in a seventeenth-century helmet and breastplate of iron-reinforced silver, and laughed softly. "It's good of you to have me here, Philippe."

"I'm delighted you could come." For an instant Philippe de Montauban looked up at the portrait, too, and smiled. "Even we heretics have read enough of the Council's sessions to know how tiresome they must have been. You need a rest, Charles, and you won't get it in your own diocese. None of your monsignors will think of looking for you in Paris, and in this, of all houses."

The Bishop was shaking his head, and a lock of graying hair fell forward across his forehead. He brushed it back impatiently. "At no time was the Council tiresome, Philippe. Exhausting, yes, after our exhilaration."

"And your in-fighting, Charles?"

"How our ancestor on that wall would applaud you

11

for that, Philippe. Grant that the Council Fathers opposed to change are men of principle——"

"No offense meant. It's just that Protestants have become so accustomed to the idea that the Roman Church is a solid block of unyielding marble that we've been stunned, you might say, by the spectacle of cardinals and bishops squabbling with each other like fishwives. As a matter of fact, Cardinal Doepfner's speech on Indulgences made remarkable reading. I had the distinct feeling that Martin Luther himself would have approved of every word. Have another aperitif before dinner."

"I'm quite comfortable, thank you." The Bishop turned away from the fire and clasped his hands behind his back. "If you'd care to look through my copy of the entire proceedings, I'm sure you'll find a great many addresses similar in spirit to Cardinal Doepfner's."

Philippe nodded, and his left hand crept up to the rosette of the Legion of Honor in the button-hole of his jacket; he seemed somewhat reassured as he touched it. "I intend no discourtesy to you, of all men, Charles. Ever since you agreed to spend a portion of your holiday here, I've regarded it as symbolic of ecumenism that the two branches of our family should be reconciled under this roof."

Bishop de Montauban accepted the apology with a slight inclination of his head.

His cousin removed the stopper from a crystal decanter and refilled his glass. "You have us at a disadvantage, you know. We Huguenots feel rather embarrassed, and I dare say the Jews are in the same state of mind. You Romans have beaten at us for so many centuries and have rebuffed our gestures of conciliation so often that we don't quite know how to react when you voluntarily hold out your hands to us." He sipped his wine slowly, with relish.

For the first time a trace of acidity crept into the Bishop's voice. "If you'll study the record, you'll find that we haven't done all the beating, not by a long chalk."

They walked in silence to the high-ceilinged dining room, where silverware and wine glasses stood in formal array at two place settings.

"Would you care to say grace, Charles?"

"Not if it will disturb you. Or do I carry politeness

too far?" The Bishop chuckled and, not waiting for a reply, bowed his head and murmured a short prayer.

A maidservant in black, starched uniform appeared with two plates.

"Savory pastry puffs, Charles. I tried to tell my chef about the dish you served me in Rheims—soon after the war, it was, and I believe you were a monsignor then. Delicious! I hope he's succeeded."

The Bishop plunged his fork into a miniature soufflé, sniffed the steam and tasted the dish. "Superb. Far better than we had at Rheims. Eggs and butter were in short supply in those days, and our housekeeper could buy only inferior cuts of stringy beef. Rome has been wrestling with the same problem for centuries. The loss of the Eastern Churches and of the faithful who abandoned us for Protestantism have left us with too few ingredients to make a spiritual soufflé that will nourish the whole Christian world."

"Are you suggesting that the ultimate goal of ecumenism is our reconversion?"

"Old suspicions die hard, eh, Philippe? I certainly won't deny that we'd welcome a return to the fold of any group that wanted admission. But no man can predict the future on earth."

Philippe shook his head. "My tailor, who happens to be a Calvinist, is disturbed because his daughter wants to marry a boy who is Catholic. He and the boy's parents have formed a secret alliance to break up the romance. Don't tell me you're so ingenuous you believe there is no prejudice left in this world just because twenty-five hundred bishops have prepared some documents on the relations of men to each other and to God."

"Hardly. But the doors have been opened, as you say, and the dialogue between peoples has begun. On all sides there will be doubts and fears. For every centimeter we move forward toward understanding, we'll retrogress a few millimeters. The Vatican Council has set forces in motion that are more powerful than any the Church has known since the introduction of monasticism in the fourth century. You accuse us of being autocratic, but I don't agree. The time was ripe for the beginning of a reconciliation of faiths, and Pope John had the genius to recognize a universal human need."

"Let me be the very last to deny his genius, Charles.

There has been no religious leader of his stature—in any denomination—since the founding of the Montauban line. Your mistake, I think, is that you're too eager to assume there will be a growth in tolerance."

"All of us are already more tolerant, Philippe. You confuse factual details with human ideals and spiritual aspirations." The Bishop took a little wine, and obviously liked it. "Look here. Why do you keep the seventeenth-century panels that the old Chancellor installed in this room?"

"Because they're magnificent, of course! I couldn't replace them for fifty thousand francs."

The Bishop hid a smile behind a serviette of heavy double-damask linen. "And that outrageously ornate Louis XIV chandelier?"

"I'm accustomed to it. I grew up with it in this room. Besides, it's been completely modernized. My father had electric wiring installed in it sometime after the first World War. I can't recall the year offhand."

"But it seems rather incongruous, don't you agree, looming over that new carpeting of nylon pile?"

"The Oriental rug that the first Paul de Montauban brought back with him from the Ottoman Empire finally wore out two years ago. Think of it, after all these centuries. And I wanted to replace it with something that might last as long."

"You confirm the very point I'm trying to make, Philippe." The Bishop no longer bothered to conceal his amusement. "Your home resembles the shelves of a bric-a-brac shop, but you've spent your life with this hodge-podge. You rationalize the anachronisms, and you find ways to reconcile each contribution to the decor with the others. How much more strongly do all of us cling to the religious teachings of our childhood—and to the prejudices that were instilled in us. I plead guilty to your charge of optimism, my dear cousin, but I am also a realist. It may take many generations to tear down the walls of hatreds and opposing doctrines.

"But all mankind is at last marching toward the same meeting place. We go by different routes, and at different paces. But we are moving toward it, all of us. Never in all human history has there been such a march. You and I, Philippe, are privileged to be watching the inauguration of the last crusade."

14

book one

Men willingly believe what they wish.
—JULIUS CAESAR

1593

"Get that woman out of my bed!"

The baritone roar echoed through the high-vaulted stone corridors of the Hereditary Ducal Palace at Chartres. Knights, squires, common soldiers and servants hurried to the third landing, some dressed and armed, some in their nightshirts, a few carrying torches that had been immersed in beech oil and emitted thick clouds of pungent smoke.

Standing outside a bedchamber, his small, pointed black beard quivering, was a tall, slender man of thirty years, fully dressed in his usual somber black, with a silver chain and his heraldic insignia of Judge Advocate-at-Arms to Henry of Navarre hanging from his neck. Inexplicably, he was barefooted, and although his toes were a pale shade of blue, he seemed unaware of the icy stones on which he stood.

The men ran toward him, then halted and backed away. It was evident that Count Philippe de Montauban was very angry.

He pointed a thin, accusing finger at a young knight, more insolent than the rest, who was unable to hide a wide grin. "Is this your doing, Fontaine? No? Then perhaps your master is responsible. My compliments to His Grace of Montmorency, and tell the Duke to take the trollop into his own damned bed! I've ridden to Paris and back today, and I'm in no mood for one of Montmorency's pranks!"

The knight quickly sobered. "Montmorency couldn't have put her there, milord. He returned only a quarter of an hour ago from an inspection of our forces outside the town walls."

Philippe grunted and glared at the others. "Well? Speak up! That—that painted, perfumed wench couldn't have found her way into my bed by accident."

A servant wearing the faded gold crests of France and Navarre on his worn livery cleared his throat. "If you please, milord, she's the King's. Mademoiselle d'Estrées arrived unexpectedly this evening to join His Majesty."

Some of the men tittered, and Philippe's glower became blacker. Now he understood what had happened and, thanks to the servant's indiscretion, the whole Huguenot army of French volunteers and Hessian mercenaries would soon know that Gabrielle d'Estrées, Henry's official mistress, had surprised him when he was with one of his

15

other women. Within a day or two Paris would hear the story, and the Catholics could claim, with some justice, that Henry was up to his old, dissolute tricks.

It was too late for regrets, and in any event Philippe was tired. "Where is the King?" he demanded.

The rebuked knight appeared to be the only one who knew. "In the library above the great hall, milord, hearing Montmorency's report."

"Then he'll hear a few other things as well." Philippe started toward the stairs.

The servants fled, the soldiers vanished and even the knights decided to take themselves elsewhere. No one wanted to be nearby if de Montauban had another of his quarrels with the King. There was always hell to pay later.

Fontaine managed to hold his ground, however, and pointed at the Count's feet.

Philippe grimaced and turned back into his own chamber. Paying no attention to the wide-eyed girl who was clutching the bed clothes, he pulled on his stockings and his mud-spattered boots. He started toward the door, halted and as an afterthought strapped on his smallsword. Henry would like nothing better than to create a diversion by reminding him of a royal decree ordering all senior officers— including a lawyer who never rode into battle—to carry weapons in his presence.

Only the sentries in their shabby uniforms of musty wool were in the corridors as Philippe made his way to the second landing. He paused for no more than a moment outside the door of the chamber that the King had converted into a library because he had found the Roman Catholic chapel too ornate for his taste. Unfortunately, in a land that had been torn by civil wars for more than thirty years, few books were available, and the shelves stood empty.

Henry IV, King of Navarre and the rightful but unacknowledged and uncrowned ruler of France, was forty years of age and looked older. Of medium height and painfully thin, he sat before the hearth, his weight resting on the base of his spine, his booted feet thrust toward the flames. His face was heavily lined, and showing beneath the open throat of his coarse cotton shirt was a jagged scar, one of many that bore witness to his lifelong struggle for his rights and his throne.

But, in spite of the late hour, Henry was cheerful and energetic. No one could ever remember having seen him when his energies were depleted. "Our good General de Montauban. Join us, Philippe, and tell us the news from Paris."

Henry de Montmorency, the premier Protestant duke of the realm

16

and deputy commander of the King's army was an amiable young giant not noted for his perceptivity anywhere other than on the field of battle. But he and Philippe had grown up together in the Protestant "inner citadel" in southern France, near Toulouse, and he knew his friend was in a cold rage. He glanced quickly at the nearer door, then the farther, wishing himself elsewhere. But there was no escape, and his smile of greeting was wan.

"Well, did you see our enemies? What of Mayenne? And the Spaniards? What's their reply to my offer?" The words poured out of the King so rapidly when he became tense that he spoke with a slight stutter.

Philippe replied in measured tones. "It was so late when I arrived that I assumed you'd gone to sleep, and I planned to see you early in the morning. In fact, sleep was on my mind, too. But I find my bed occupied by one of your strumpets."

For an instant Henry looked blank. Then he laughed, loudly and a trifle coarsely, and slapped his stained leather breeches. "It's Marie." Still laughing, he turned to Montmorency. "I had a close call tonight, I can tell you. I remembered Marie from our visit to Chartres in November, and early this evening I sent for her. Less than an hour later Gabrielle and her aunt arrived, so I packed Marie off to Philippe's room, not expecting him before tomorrow."

"You put her there," Philippe said. "You get her out."

Pinpoint lights of merriment danced in Henry's eyes to the tune of the leaping flames in the hearth. "Be reasonable, Philippe. And generous. Share your bed with Marie. It's the coldest night of the winter, and I guarantee she'll keep you warm."

"I've had one of the most wearing days I've ever known. My only interest tonight is sleep."

The King's delight increased. "Oh, Marie is a lively wench, take my word for it. She'll provide the entertainment, and then she'll sleep like an infant."

Philippe remained wooden-faced, obdurate.

Henry's ponderous sigh was exaggerated. "My God, de Montauban, you're more straight-laced than old hellfire-and-brimstone John Calvin ever was. I know of no Commandment in Holy Writ that forbids a bachelor the pleasures of simple fornication."

Montmorency came to his friend's rescue, afraid that Philippe's temper had been strained to the bursting point. "Share my room for the night, Philippe," he urged. "I'm using the chamber that Catherine de Medici, that Papist harlot, built for herself and her lovers when she was Queen Mother. My bed is big enough to accommodate a half-squad of pikemen."

Philippe accepted the offer with a half-bow.

The King realized he had gone a little too far, perhaps, and tried to make amends. "You must be hungry after your journey." He reached toward a bell-rope.

"No, thank you." Philippe realized the offense hadn't warranted such great anger, and tried to speak politely. "I ate a joint of beef and a half-loaf of roundbread in the saddle."

"Then you were in a hurry to get here. For God's sake, man, tell me your news!"

In lawyer-like fashion, Philippe marshalled his facts. "I reached the south gate of Paris as the church bells were chiming like mad. It was one of their confounded canonical hours in the breviary, I can never remember which. When I told the officer of the watch I was your emissary, you'd have thought I'd announced I was Beelzebub himself. What a commotion. It was a full hour or more before I was finally taken to the Louvre."

The King almost fell off the bench in his anxiety. "Then you saw Mayenne?"

Philippe's voice became dry. "The great Duke himself received me—in the presence of what must have been the full council of the Catholic League. How they must mistrust each other. I recognized three other members of the de Guise family, and that stupid General von Neustern who commands the Holy Roman Emperor's corps. There were two cardinals and an archbishop there, too. One of the cardinals spoke only Spanish and Latin—"

"Santisi," Henry interrupted softly. "The envoy of Phillip of Spain."

"I wasn't presented to any of the clergy by name. They behaved as though they'd have been contaminated if I had touched them. But I'm sure the Spaniard was Cardinal Santisi."

"Precisely what did you tell them?"

"Precisely what we worked out yesterday. That His Majesty, Henry, now controls seventy-three walled cities and towns. I reminded Mayenne and his colleagues that since our capture of Burgundy they hold only Lorraine and Britanny—"

"And Paris," Henry murmured. "Don't forget Paris."

"I didn't, and neither did they. I created a real stir when I showed them the pledge of fealty to you that fifty-seven Catholic lords of the realm signed and sealed. They sent me away while they conferred in private, and they took so long that I would have starved if the captain of Mayenne's guard hadn't brought me some barley soup and cheese."

Montmorency stirred. "Barley soup and cheese—in the Louvre?"

"I gathered," Philippe said with a slight smile, "that General Biron's siege of the city is progressing nicely."

"You told them, I hope," Henry said in a rush, "that I've finally raised enough money to double the size of my forces. I trust you made it clear to them that I don't stand alone any more."

"Oh, I did, Henry, I did. I showed them the letter from Elizabeth of England offering you half her navy, a corps of twenty thousand men and a loan of eighty thousand gold ecus."

"Which she'd guarantee," Montmorency said under his breath, "by ordering her troops to occupy Normandy for a few generations. No thanks."

"I also told them," Philippe continued, ignoring the interruption, "that the Dutch have already sent you three regiments of their arbelests, the finest steel crossbowmen in Europe. The point lost some of its dramatic impact because they'd already learned the news. But they hadn't heard of the troops from Geneva, Berne and Savoy who are marching to join you. That startled them."

Henry clasped and unclasped his thin, almost absurdly small hands. "In God's holy name, de Montauban, don't keep me in suspense any longer."

Philippe drew a deep breath. "I informed His Grace of Mayenne, as president-general of the Catholic League, that His Majesty, Henry, is willing to grant a personal amnesty to every Frenchman, lord or townsman or peasant, who has at any time borne arms against him. I informed him that His Majesty has only one peace condition—that the troops of Spain and the Holy Roman Emperor be withdrawn from French soil. Most of all, Henry, I emphasized your desire to spare the people of Paris a longer siege—and the bloodshed that is sure to drench the city when we storm it."

The King rose slowly and planted his feet far apart, bracing himself.

"Your offer was refused. Cardinal de Pellevé acted as their spokesman when they called me back——"

"Pellevé rather than Mayenne," Montmorency said scornfully. "Pellevé gives the orders, and Mayenne—Duke of Lorraine and head of the house of de Guise—tugs his forelock like a peasant and does what he's told. There's proof for you that the priests are the real masters of the League."

He was proud of his ability to reach an independent conclusion without help, but his face fell when the King stared at him in cold disapproval. "Through the reigns of the two Popes before this new man, Clement, it's been the worst kept secret in Europe that Vatican Hill is supplying the funds, the intelligence and the initiative for the League. Pellevé is the spokesman for Pope Clement, and not even Philip of Spain himself would dare to defy his word in the League's councils."

"We come now to the heart of the matter," Philippe said. "We assumed—or, at least, it was our hope—that Cardinal Pellevé would refer our offer to his master in Rome. But it appears he has standing instructions to accept no terms of any kind from us. He told me in so many words that we'd have to burn Paris to the ground and kill every Catholic in the city before we can occupy it."

Montmorency whipped a poniard from his boot-top and threw it toward one of the empty bookshelves. The blade buried itself in the wood, and the silver hilt quivered. "My conscience won't keep me awake nights. If that's what they want, they shall have it. We'll level the town and let our troops do whatever they please. How those Hessians will love a day or two of free looting!"

Philippe realized that Henry had fallen silent, and was looking with unseeing eyes at the fire. "We were afraid this would be the League's reply. Surely you aren't surprised."

The King shook his head.

Montmorency was unaware that his monarch's mood had changed. "I'll reinforce the siege corps with two regiments of musketmen and one of arquebusiers."

Philippe knew relatively little of military matters, but the proposal seemed sound to him. The arquebus was a cumbersome, old-fashioned firearm, effective only at short, point-blank range, and therefore would be useful in helping to disperse street mobs in the country's largest city.

"I can spare six or seven squadrons of cavalry, and I'll send all my artillery to Paris," the deputy commander continued. "With luck, I can reduce the city in three months. I insist on taking command of the siege myself. Biron wasn't in Paris on St. Batholomew's Day, and he's inclined to be too soft."

"No." Henry's voice was barely audible.

Montmorency was indignant. "I tell you, Biron will spare every historic building in the town if we give him the chance. He doesn't understand the principles of a war of total annihilation."

"Transfer the regiments," Henry said, still speaking very softly, "but don't increase the pressure of the siege. We'll simply use it as an extra lever for bargaining purposes."

Philippe and Montmorency exchanged covert glances of bewilderment.

"My fight will have been in vain," the King murmured, "if I take possession of a ruined capital. The injured will lick their wounds, mourn their dead and wait for a chance to strike back. No, I'd be playing into the League's hands, and Clement is wise enough to know it. He may be counting on me to reduce the city to rubble. He refuses to take my word at face value, but I insist on ruling all the people of France in peace and friendship."

His subordinates became even more confused, and Philippe, bone-weary after his long day, felt a twinge of annoyance. "Stop talking in riddles! If Paris won't capitulate, we've got to take it by force. We may increase the resentment of the Catholics, it's true, but there won't be enough of them left in the city to matter after Montmorency's cavalry and pikemen have flushed them out."

Henry smiled gently, and his manner was that of a schoolmaster chiding a bright pupil who had made a minor but significant error. "Do you recall the last visit you and I paid to Montauban, Philippe?"

"Naturally. What in particular do you want me to remember?"

"You expelled every Catholic from the town before I arrived, and I told you I thought it was a mistake."

"It was," Montmorency said harshly. "He should have hanged them."

"We've had no troubles of any kind in Montauban for twenty-six months," Philippe said hotly. "There's no one in the town to cause problems—except the Jews, of course, and they know better than to leave their ghetto."

"I think of you as intelligent, even wise," Henry replied, "until you start talking like a court jester. You know I intend to abolish the ghettos after I'm crowned."

Philippe shrugged and Montmorency sighed. Sometimes the King's ideas were too weird and unorthodox to grasp.

"You make no issue of the matter," Henry went on, "because there are so few Jews in France. Granting them a few privileges—except for the right to hold office, of course—can't do any harm. Very well. But you made homeless refugees of one-fourth the population of your county capital when you expelled the Catholics from Montauban."

"Yes, and their places have been filled by Huguenots from other areas. Never in all its history has the town been so prosperous!"

"Your short-sightedness astonishes me." Henry started to pace up and down before the fire. "The Catholics of Montauban have scattered all over France. And even though you assure me that none was mistreated before leaving——"

"We treated them royally. Each family was allowed to take one cart of household goods and two ecus in gold. Have you ever known them to show Huguenots the same consideration when the shoe has been on the other foot?"

"All people love to dramatize their sufferings. It's a common failing. Wherever they've gone, the Catholics of Montauban have told sad stories to wring the hearts of the charitably inclined. And you can be certain that every man who has heard their tales of woe has sworn by all his saints that he'll die before he'll allow a heretic to mount the throne of France. Hatred breeds hatred."

"Perhaps," Philippe said acidly, "Pastor de Lesseps can deliver one of his sermons from a tower outside the gates of Paris. He'll preach such love that the citizens will welcome him with a shower of flower petals."

Montmorency laughed with him. Pierre de Lesseps, the King's personal chaplain, hated Catholics more vehemently than did any other man in the Huguenot army.

"You young hotheads never listen to me when I tell you there's more than one way to roast an ox," Henry said, still smiling.

"First, though, you've got to slaughter the ox!" Montmorency retorted.

"That's where you're mistaken. I've been giving this problem all my attention since we opened the siege of Paris, and I've finally found the resolution of the question. It's quite simple." Henry poured some wine from a bottle into two battered pewter mugs for his companions, then mixed a little with a generous quantity of water for himself. "My friends, you've devoted your lives to my cause, and I hope that before too long I can show you my gratitude. Right now I need greater devotion than you've ever given me. And what I say to you must be repeated to no one."

Philippe was pleased that the King showed his complete trust by not asking them to swear an oath of secrecy.

"De Montauban, I want you to undertake the most delicate of missions for me. I've already sent two emissaries to Vatican Hill, but the cardinals who surround Clement have put doubts in his mind. He believes I'm trying to trick him. You're known to be one of my closest friends, and I'm certain he'll accept you as my personal emissary."

Philippe was too stunned to speak or move, and Montmorency drained his cup, gulping his wine as though parched.

The King calmly refilled it. "See no one but Pope Clement himself, and insist on a private meeting with him. Ask him if he'll disband the League and officially recognize me as King of France if I accept conversion to Catholicism."

Montmorency's cup fell to the stone floor with a clatter. "You're joking!"

"No, you've gone mad," Philippe said. "Either that or you've allowed the d'Estrées woman to soften your mind." He knew he was treading on dangerous ground, that Henry never tolerated criticism of his favorite mistress of the moment, but this situation was too critical to remain silent. It was unthinkable that the successor to Henry VIII of England as the Protestant champion of Europe could even allow himself to think of becoming a Catholic. "I've been afraid of her influence ever since she paid her first visit to the army. A devout woman who travels with her own confessor and uses that confounded rosary of diamond beads to help her pray day and night is a vicious traitor to France!"

Henry had been known to banish a man from the portion of the realm he controlled for insults less violent, but now he remained serene. The King was still married to Marguerite de Valois, who had been banished to his castle in Auvergne. He could of course divorce her whenever he chose, but until he found a princess with whom it would be profitable to make a new alliance, it was convenient for him to remain a married man. Although a slur directed at a royal mistress of the moment was really of no consequence, it could, nevertheless, be dangerous.

"Gabrielle," Henry said, "offers me solace of body and the illusion of domesticity, which is important to a man of my age. She knows nothing of the state of my soul, and even less about affairs of state."

"Then you really mean it." Philippe's legs felt weak, and he sat abruptly on the bench, where Montmorency was crushing his pewter cup between his hands in impotent rage.

"I've never been more in earnest. Clement knows my claim is legitimate, and it's the perfect answer for him, too. I'm sure he'll find other uses for all that money he's been giving the League. And how can he possibly resist the opportunity to make France a Catholic nation again merely by signing the certificate of my baptism? What a blow to the English, the Dutch and the Swedes! I tell you, lads, they'll build bonfires in Rome that will cast their light all over Europe."

Montmorency was still too distraught to reply.

Philippe spoke with great care, as he always did when replying to a legal argument. "I hold no brief for the damned English. They're greedy, and I don't trust Elizabeth. The Swedes can look after themselves. I feel a little sorry for the Dutch, but they're not our concern. What of your own forces and the people who have supported you all these years? How can you dare to let yourself turn against them? The St. Bartholomew's Day Massacre will be repeated, again and again, in every city and town in France!"

Henry put a restraining hand on his arm. "Do you have so little faith in me?"

The blunt demand compounded Philippe's bewilderment. He wanted a full, candid explanation, but the King was being subtle, and when he was in that frame of mind, it was a waste of time to question him. Nevertheless the effort had to be made. "What guarantees do you offer the Huguenots, Your Majesty?"

Henry became solemn. "Trust me," he said.

There was a painfully embarrassing silence. "On the day that I was graduated from the school of law at Geneva, I offered my unrestricted services to Your Majesty," Philippe said stiffly. "As proof of my sincerity I made a public oration to the people of Montauban, telling them that henceforth they were your subjects."

"The occasion hasn't been forgotten." There was a hint of irony in Henry's tone. "The Catholics still refer to it."

"Unfortunately, some Papists were killed in rioting before my constabulary could restore peace. I trust Your Majesty realizes that the fighting in Montauban and the violence that spread to Toulouse the next day has been exaggerated out of all proportion to the truth by sly priests who are trying to incite their flocks against us."

"I'm well aware of the methods Rome uses to achieve its ends, thank you."

Montmorency looked up eagerly; this sounded like the Henry of Navarre he knew and had long followed so blindly. "I knew it! This is another of your pranks!"

"If the Pope will recognize me as King of France—and send a cardinal from Vatican Hill to place the crown of Louis XI on my head, I shall gladly accept baptism in the Roman Church."

Philippe clicked his heels and bowed from the waist. "I regret to inform Your Majesty I cannot accept your suggestion that I carry your message to the Pope!"

Henry's eyes narrowed. "Suggestion, de Montauban? I gave you an order."

The alternatives were obvious: Philippe could either obey or leave Henry's service and go into exile. "When do you want me to leave for Rome?"

"Tomorrow, after I've prepared a letter of introduction to Cardinal de Gonde." The King looked hard at Philippe, then at Montmorency, and stalked out of the library.

The two friends stood for a few moments, glancing uncertainly from each other to the fire. They were silent because neither knew what to say as they walked heavily through the damp, dark corridors of the palace to the bedchamber they would share.

"I wouldn't want this repeated in my own diocese," Florent, Cardinal de Gonde, Bishop of Paris said, "but Rome is the most majestic city on earth. Don't you agree, milord Count?"

Philippe felt slightly ill. It was bad enough to be strolling through the piazza in front of St. Peter's toward the Vatican Hill apartments of the Pope, accompanied by a cardinal in conspicuous crimson, but it was too much, even for the sake of politeness, to pretend he enjoyed visiting a town filled to overflowing with priests and monks, nuns and brilliantly attired high-ranking Church dignitaries. "From the little I've seen of Paris, I prefer it," he replied curtly.

"Ah, yes." Cardinal de Gonde spoke archly. "One forgets that your few visits there have been, ah, circumscribed. Cardinal de Pellevé sent us a most interesting description of your brief meeting with him there."

Philippe bit back a sarcastic reply that would serve no useful purpose. After spending seventy-two hours in Rome, waiting to be received by Pope Clement, he was heartily sick of the place, and the fact that he was at this moment going to the rendezvous did nothing to relieve his mood. The way the supposedly proud Romans fawned on a cardinal was positively sickening. An expensively dressed woman accompanied by two servants had actually halted her carriage in order to ask de Gonde's blessing, and horsemen, from nobles to merchants to military officers of the Papal Guard, had saluted him with a flourish.

The poor either scurried respectfully out of his path or, pulling off their hats, dropped to their knees on the garbage-littered cobblestones while he made the Sign of the Cross above their heads. Even the beggars, more of them than Philippe had ever seen in his travels, stopped chanting in the high, whining voices they affected. It was the only time since his arrival, Philippe thought, that they had given him a moment's peace.

St. Peter's itself looked impressive enough, at least from the outside, if one was impressed by Papist churches. But Notre-Dame in Paris and the cathedrals in Chartres and Rheims were far more attractive. No other people had the French talent for expressing beauty, and even the French Catholics were better artists and architects than those of other lands.

A massive metal door opened at their approach, and Cardinal de Gonde tried again. "I hope you find your quarters satisfactory."

Philippe refused to admit he had been almost overwhelmed by the grandeur of the suite assigned to him at the Hostel of St. Anthony, an adjunct to a monastery where guests of The Holy See were lodged. His sitting room opened onto a private garden where peach and pear trees grew, and the floor of his bedchamber was inlaid with a spectacular panorama of the Crusades in tile. One of the innumerable monks who spied on him day and night had told him it had been transported to Rome from Byzantium three hundred years earlier and reset, tile by tile. Even a lawyer who knew virtually nothing of art was awed by a portrait of the Madonna done by Raphael that was hung over his bed, and Philippe had refused to use the shaving mug provided for him when several of the monks had assured him it had been made by Benvenuto Cellini.

"I have no complaints," he replied curtly.

They followed a priest, an officer of the Papal Guard and an unidentified gentleman in a suit of yellow silk down a corridor and up a flight of stairs. "I can understand your feelings," Cardinal de Gonde said smoothly. "When one is abroad, one often yearns for home."

Philippe glanced at the corpulent little man and decided that if he was hinting, this was the moment to spare him no illusions. "Any one passing through our siege lines outside Paris must carry a pass signed by a member of King Henry's war council and countersigned by me."

De Gonde refused to accept the rebuff. "Ah, the usual precautions of men at war. I know nothing of these things." He paused delicately. "I dare say that a pass signed by Henry of Navarre would also be honored?"

"His Majesty has no time to spare for such trivial matters. He places his complete trust in the judgment of his lieutenants." Philippe felt a mild surge of satisfaction as he watched the Cardinal try to hide his disappointment. Not until Henry and the Pope reached an understanding would de Gonde be allowed inside the gates of Paris. And even then he would be barred until he publicly retracted the inflammatory advice he had given the students of philosophy at the University of Paris on the day of his departure for Rome, only two weeks before the opening of the siege.

"The Holy Spirit," de Gonde had been reported as saying, "will protect that man among you courageous enough to drive a knife into the heart of that barbarian scourge of Christendom, Henry of Navarre."

Henry had laughed when he heard of the address, which was typical of him. He invariably refused to fear threats against his life. But Montmorency had quietly redoubled the honor guard assigned to protect the King from harm. And no member of the council would forget the remark, no matter how Henry himself felt. De Gonde would have Satan's own time trying to get back to Paris.

They reached an anteroom, where several other priests were standing, conversing in low tones, and the Cardinal suddenly asked, "Do you speak Italian, lord Count, or Latin, perhaps?"

"I've had no reason to learn Italian, and my Latin is that of the law courts." Too late Philippe saw the trap.

"In that case," de Gonde said, "you'll undoubtedly want me to serve as an interpreter between you and the Holy Father."

"As I informed you on the day of my arrival, I have been commanded to speak with Clement alone. If anyone else is there, I'll have nothing to say, and will leave at once for France."

Philippe had spoken more loudly than he realized, and was a trifle embarrassed when everyone in the anteroom looked at him. The officer of the Papal Guard suddenly reached out and caught his arm. "You carry arms!" he shouted.

Philippe used a trick General Biron had taught him. Placing a foot behind the officer's, he shoved violently, and the man's grip not only broke, but he staggered backward, landing with a crash against the far wall.

Everyone started shouting, and the babble increased as a door to a chamber beyond the anteroom opened. An elderly man in black breeches and a worn padded jacket of the kind used by Italian peasants in winter stood in the frame. Everyone tried to tell him what had happened, so Philippe assumed he was a servant on the Pope's personal staff.

A hint of amusement appeared in the elderly man's tired blue eyes. "I feel sure," he said as the crowd became quiet, "that the Holy Father has nothing to fear from King Henry's dispenser of justice. Won't you come in, lord Count?"

Philippe walked toward the inner chamber. Cardinal de Gonde started forward, too, but the door was closed in his face.

"De Gonde has never been able to cure himself of curiosity. It's a priest's duty to be curious, and a monsignor's privilege. But it can be a distinct liability to a cardinal. Sit where you please, sir."

Philippe laughed as he moved toward a comfortable, cushioned chair. He had no idea how much longer he might have to wait, but the room was furnished in simple, good taste, the view of the piazza through the high windows was pleasant, and it was a relief to be rid of de Gonde.

The elderly man threw a fresh log onto the hearth and brought the flames to life with a bellows. "This is the coldest winter Rome has known in years." He turned, wiping his hands on the sleeves of his padded jacket. "Perhaps you'd like a glass of brandywine to help you ward off the chill of this old place."

Philippe shook his head, wanting nothing to mar his judgment in the conference ahead. "Not at the moment, thanks," he said, stretching his feet toward the fire in an unconscious imitation of Henry.

"Very wise. We can relax more easily at dinner after we've talked."

Philippe sat upright.

Clement VIII chuckled as he took a nearby chair. "Did you expect me to be sprouting horns and a tail, young man?"

Philippe grinned sheepishly and examined his host more carefully. Clement's seeming insignificance and the "tired" expression in his eyes were deliberately cultivated. He had a quality akin to Henry's. Clement was a man of unbounded energy, which he held in leash through tight self-discipline. Behind the drooping eyelids lurked one of the sharpest, most incisive minds ever to grace the papacy, and the set of his jaw, combined with his deceptive ease, indicated that perhaps he could be as ruthless as Henry, too, when he wanted to impose his will on others.

His attire seemed to indicate that he was a slovenly, even a lazy man, but Philippe appreciated the subtlety. Clement was purposely wearing the most unostentatious of non-clerical garb as a compliment to a Huguenot guest.

"You'll have to forgive my stupidity, lord Pope." Philippe found it impossible to address him as "Your Holiness."

"It's an old habit of mine, catching visitors off guard. I was impressed by your refusal to accept a drink. Or was it prompted by a fear that we poison heretics here?"

"Oh, I'm sure my smallsword will protect me from harm," Philippe replied with a straight face.

They roared with laughter together, and the anteroom door opened to reveal several anxious faces peering in, with Cardinal de Gonde craning his neck as he tried to peer over the shoulder of the tall equerry.

"Go away," Clement said.

The door closed again.

Philippe found he liked the man, and was sorry. It would be so much easier to deal with someone he detested, and he had to remind himself that the modest old gentleman opposite him was the most powerful of all the earth's absolute monarchs.

"I've told my chef," Clement said, "to prepare a currant sauce mulled in dry wine to eat with the duckling, and he tells me it will be spoiled if we aren't prompt. Shall we get down to the business of your reasons for coming to this horrendous place?"

Philippe blinked at him. He could have sworn that no one except Diana, who had died in his arms, had ever known of his fondness for currant sauce with duckling.

"I see to it that I'm kept well informed about my guests," Clement said modestly.

Hereafter, Philippe thought, he would believe anything he was told about Vatican Hill's intelligence operations. But there was one thing the Pope didn't know, and it would be almost pleasant to watch his reaction when he learned of Henry's proposal. Philippe leaned forward in the chair and repeated the King's message in a dry, hard voice.

Clement's face remained unchanged, and he continued to rest easily against the cushions of his chair. "Do you intend to follow your King into the Church, young man?" he asked at last.

"I do not, sir!"

"Every man is privileged to seek salvation or damnation in his own way," the Pope replied politely. "May I ask your reasons?"

"I don't want to bore you with the whole story, lord Pope. This is neither the place nor the time for it."

"You forget that my first duty is to help those whose spirits are wounded. Permit me to guess." Clement leaned forward, fingers interlaced in his lap. "You were reared as a Calvinist, of course, but you showed little interest in matters of faith until a young lady was stoned to death in a tragic display of barbarian horror."

So the old man did know about Diana. "I was betrothed to her, sir, and she was stoned by a raving crowd of your people who were just coming out of a church. She had done no harm to anyone, and her only crime was that she was a Huguenot."

"The sins committed in the name of Almighty God have caused so much suffering that I'm tempted to believe hell is here, not somewhere in the hereafter." Clement paused, and there was a slight, indefinable change in his manner. "I've had no intentions of arousing painful memories, Philippe de Montauban. You've suffered grave injustice, and you've repaid it in kind on the innocent. But all that is irrelevant. I've known of King Henry's desire to become converted to Catholicism for many months. But I don't know what lies behind the façade of his offer. I can't believe he's seeking the security of his soul."

"No, lord Pope, Henry isn't a spiritual man," Philippe said honestly.

"Then I assume he's made a private agreement with you and his other Calvinist supporters. He's offered you guarantees in order to induce you to remain in his camp."

"He offers us nothing, and asks us to trust him," Philippe said bitterly. "Does that satisfy you? Would you have him turn on us and drive us out of France once you've taken him into your fold?"

"My realm is spiritual, not temporal," Clement replied instantly. "I'm incapable of accepting most of the so-called miracles that are reported to me, and I hear of new ones daily. But, if Henry can reconcile and harness his Catholic and Huguenot lords, that will be the greatest miracle of our age." He paused, and the expression of sleepy exhaustion vanished from his eyes. "Do you believe him, lord Count? Do you trust him?"

"I must. I have nowhere else to turn."

"Let me ask just one more question. Suppose you and I are mistaken. Suppose Henry will become a truly devout Catholic. Suppose he listens to fools like Cardinal de Gonde who would inaugurate an Inquisition on a vast scale in France—if I allowed it. If Henry turns against the Huguenots, what then?"

Philippe had asked himself the same question many times, and knew there was only one answer. "I can't find it in my heart to believe that Henry of Navarre is two-faced. But if he should raise his hand against the Huguenots, we will take up arms against him. All of us—Montmorency, Biron, Sully, Nevers. We'd fight against him as we've fought for him, to the last drop of our blood. And we'd win. Because we know him, you see, as you Papi—as you Catholics don't. We know how his mind works. The generals understand his battle tactics before he explains them. I'm familiar with the legal quirks he wants for escapes. Sully is his *alter ego* in matters of finance. If he should be unfaithful to us, we'd show him no mercy."

"I sometimes find it difficult to believe I live in a supposedly Christian world." Clement stood, smiling. "You've told me what I want to know, young man. Henry wants me to crown him, so that he'll have France and I'll have peace. If I refuse him, no one shall have France, and this infernal war I've inherited will drag on for another generation or two. Let's go to dinner, shall we? The currant sauce mustn't curdle, you know."

The dangers of drowning or of capture by Saracen pirates were ever-present in the Mediterranean, but no ship could have been sturdier or better prepared for trouble than the barque *Emmanuel,* a vessel of more than one hundred tons, with three sails, two of them square-rigged and the third fore-and-aft rigged. She was Portuguese owned, and her master, Dom Pedro Ruiz, who had spent more than thirty years at sea, was a member of the minor Portuguese nobility. He knew his business, keeping a sailor on watch in the crow's nest at all times, with the crews of his two guns and three catapults sleeping near their weapons on the main deck. Like most of his countrymen, he was a devout Catholic, yet felt no hatred for the French Huguenots; his own land was under the rule of Philip II of Spain, and he could sympathize with men who were at war with the tyrant.

Some of the crew were Portuguese, and others were Flemish, residents of the Spanish Netherlands, stolid men who energetically unlimbered their catapults and cannon in twice-daily drills, but showed no interest in any concerns other than their own, and carefully avoided the passengers. They were veterans of the sea, like Dom Pedro, and attended to their duties with a minimum of confusion and noise.

In a sense, Philippe de Montauban was grateful to Pope Clement for providing him with relatively pleasant transportation from Ostia, Rome's port, to Henry of Navarre's new naval base at Toulon, on the French Mediterranean coast. After he landed there he would travel through areas under tight Huguenot control and rejoin Henry at the siege camp outside Paris. There were far fewer risks in such travel than in riding north through The Papal States and independent duchies of the Italian peninsula, all of them fiercely loyal to The Holy See and frankly menacing in their attitude toward Calvinists.

The amenities of life on board the *Emmanuel* were palatable. Philippe's cabin was incredibly tiny, but he had privacy, a roof over his head and found he could sleep in the canvas sling suspended from the bulkheads. In the years of Henry's long and often discouraging fight against the Catholic League, he had often spent his nights in the open or beneath the cover of a leaking tent. The food was an unvarying diet of salt pork, even more heavily salted fish and hard biscuits infested with weevils, but the fare was no worse than Philippe had known in the field, and only in the past eighteen months had he been able, on occasion, to enjoy the culinary delights he had known in his childhood.

Clement had done him a favor by making the *Emmanuel* available to him, not for his own sake, of course, but to make certain that Henry received the Pope's reply at the earliest possible date. Not until the day Philippe had sailed, however, had he realized he would have to pay a price for the convenience of the voyage. Only two hours before the barque had sailed he had been asked to take a niece of Florent, Cardinal de Gonde and her entourage under his personal protection. It was a request that no gentleman could have refused, even though the Dame Louise de Longueval was a nuisance and an embarrassment.

She was attractive enough as a traveling companion, Philippe freely admitted. A widow of twenty-three or thereabouts, who could read and write, with green eyes, wavy, dark-brown hair that the sea air made curlier and a figure of which he was not unaware, she was still not his ideal choice of a person with whom to be forced into a close association for more than two weeks at sea and another twenty days on the road, when he would deliver her to the home of her brother, who owned a château near Orléans.

For one thing, she was the devoted niece of the Papist Bishop of Paris. Equally distasteful was the fact that she was the daughter-in-law of Chevalier Philippe de Longueval, a cousin of Henry's latest and most influential mistress, the Catholic Gabrielle d'Estrées, whom the King's supporters hated and feared. Philippe took what nourishment he could from a few cold crumbs of comfort, the knowledge that the Longueval clan were stern moralists and had refused to acknowledge Gabrielle's existence since she and Henry had become lovers.

The worst of Philippe's problem was that circumstances forced him to spend most of his time in the company of Dame Louise. Her cabin was as cramped as his, her dignity and position made it impossible for her to associate with her three maidservants, and Philippe was not only charged with her welfare but was the only other passenger on board the *Emmanuel*.

A man who had known few women in the twelve years since Diana's death, even a man of high Calvinist ideals, found it difficult to maintain an objective distance from an uncommonly pretty and intelligent young lady who had been close at hand from early morning until long after sundown every day for a little more than a week. Philippe was alarmed by the discovery that occasionally he felt increasingly tender sentiments toward the girl, and his only consolation was his conviction that she had no knowledge of his growing involvement. It would be far better to emulate Henry and take harlots as mistresses than to become romantically attached to a lady of high moral principle who was a Papist. Certain disaster would result from any such relationship.

A heavy fog blanketed the *Emmanuel* on the seventh morning of her voyage as, for the first time, she sailed far out into the Mediterranean, away from the comforting shores of the Italian coastline, which Dom Pedro had been careful to keep in sight. The ship's master, like Philippe, was anxious to be rid of his passengers at the earliest possible moment. His sailors considered women on board as omens of bad luck, and Philippe suspected that Dom Pedro himself was not entirely free of the ancient superstition.

In any event, the barque had altered her course a short distance below Livorno, and was heading almost due west across the Ligurian Sea toward Monaco, but would turn seaward again before reaching that small principality because of the insistence of the rulers of that tiny outpost of the Holy Roman Empire that any ships sailing within two and one-half-leagues of her shores had to pay outrageous tolls to the captain of the port.

The sea was gray and calm, with only a slight breeze partly filling the sails of the barque, but Philippe felt the need for exercise after spending the night cooped up in his cell-like quarters. He shaved and washed in water brought to him by Dom Pedro's servant, dressed quickly and, after an unappetizing breakfast of salted codfish from the New World's Newfoundland banks and biscuits from which he was learning to tap the weevils with the nonchalance of an experienced seaman, he drank a cup of watered wine and went out onto the main deck.

Although spring was approaching, the dampness was chilly and penetrating, but Philippe didn't care. As anxious as he was to reach Toulon in another five or six days, he dreaded what would follow. The mere thought of Henry's conversion still made him sick at heart and filled him with foreboding. This interlude at sea, cut off from the world and all its problems, was a welcome respite, and he hated to see it end.

Light footsteps sounded behind him, and he turned immediately, having been listening for them. Dame Louise de Longueval was coming toward him and, as was customary for one of her station, was dressed with as much brilliance and attention to detail as she would have been when attending a formal reception at a royal court.

Her curls were piled high on her head, and above her low cut gown of deep green silk she wore a magnificent necklace of matching emeralds and a pair of diamond and emerald earrings of the same shade. Her dress fell in simple folds to her ankles, beneath which were a pair of green satin slippers, and over her shoulders she had flung a cape of crimson silk, lined in white silk. She would have looked devasting anywhere, and Philippe was dazzled.

He bowed low, removing his hat with a flourish, and then sprang forward when she started to reply with the deep curtsy that was obligatory in noble social intercourse. "Here, now," he said. "None of that. The planks are too wet today." He caught hold of her shoulders and raised her to her feet.

Louise was aware of an exceptionally attractive dimple that appeared on the left side of her face when she smiled, and had long ago learned to use it advantageously. "You're impetuous, milord, but I'm in your debt. This gown is really too fragile for wear at sea, but I was too impatient to send my girls below for another after they stupidly brought it to me."

Philippe looked at her admiringly, wishing he had the glib tongue of a courtier. But he was afraid that, if he tried to tell her how lovely she looked, he would plunge into deeper waters than were safe for a man wanting to avoid entanglements. "The air is raw after you've spent a few minutes out here," he said gruffly, and in awkward pantomime indicated that she would be wise to close her cloak.

Louise did her best to conceal her amusement. She obediently closed the cape and then thanked him for his thoughtfulness.

"Would you care to stroll with me for a time?" He was so eager that his formal words were nearly shouted.

"I'd be delighted." She put her hand lightly on his arm and they moved up and down the deck at a sedate pace.

For years Philippe had been so ill at ease in the presence of ladies of quality that he hadn't known what to say to them. But, to his surprise, he had been reacting in a totally different way to Dame Louise de Longueval, even though he knew she had enjoyed the company of sophisticates and wits since her infancy. She had spent her childhood at the court of Henry II, and his younger sons, who had later become Charles IX and Henry III, had been her playmates. Through her uncle, Bishop of Paris for more than a decade, she had met many of the world's great, and there had been a stir, prior to her marriage, when she had visited Madrid. There had been rumors that she would become the bride of a Hapsburg archduke, and Cardinal de Gonde, who had been her guardian, must have been disappointed when she insisted on marrying the second son of an unpretentious country baron.

In the past year, following her husband's unexpected death in a hunting accident, she had been packed off to Rome by the ambitious de Gonde, but whatever his hopes, she had not fallen in with them, and was returning to France a widow. The thought pleased Philippe, and he told himself that what made him happy was the realization that the Cardinal had been thwarted.

His own reactions to Louise confused him, and he spent a great deal of time each day trying to reassure himself that he wasn't in love with her. His romance with Diana had been wildly exciting, a breathless adventure that had robbed him of all desire for food and sleep. But with Louise he was at peace, and could spend long periods in her company without feeling a need for conversation. She seemed to respond to him in the same way, and he reasoned that their almost serene tranquility could not be love, either as he had known it, read about it or observed it in others.

He glanced down at her, trying to look at her without her knowledge, and suddenly realized they were being observed. One of Louise's maidservants, a homely Gascon wench, was staring at them from the entrance to the saloon, the vessel's one public dining and lounging room that was shared by the officers and passengers. The woman's face was wreathed in a fatuous smile, and her thoughts were so obvious that Philippe felt a twinge of sharp irritation.

Then the serving woman glanced past them, and suddenly her expression changed to one of utter fright.

At that moment the lookout in the crow's nest shouted in a frightened voice, "A sloop off our starboard bow, sir. I think she's a Corsican."

Philippe wheeled, and saw a menacing shape looming only a few yards away across a patch of foggy, open sea. Even before he caught sight of the cannon on the sloop's deck aimed at the *Emmanuel* and the men lining her rail who were carrying a variety of weapons ranging from knives and old Crusaders' double-edged swords to curved Saracen scimitars and heavy pistols, he knew the meaning of the cry, "Corsicans!"

The island of Corsica, located directly below the Ligurian Sea in the Mediterranean, was a dreary, mountainous land with unproductive soil. It was claimed by a number of nations, among them France, Savoy, the Grand Duchy of Lombardy and the Holy Roman Empire, but none thought it worth the effort to land troops there and take possession.

The natives were poor farmers and fishermen, some of them of French origin, some Italian, and from time to time refugees from the Ottoman Empire sought safety there. The desolate coastline, with its many tiny harbors, made it an ideal hiding place for bands of pirates, smugglers and thieves, many of whom had lived there for years in peace and security with wives and children.

Philippe was conscious of the fact that Henry of Navarre had not pressed his claim to Corsica, although he could have occupied it without too much difficulty, because its people, virtually without exception, professed to be Roman Catholics.

Henry had often said that Philippe's mind operated at its best in moments of crisis, and he reacted now with speed and determination. First he hauled Louise to the deck and, behind a raised hatch cover that concealed them from the view of the men on the sloop, rolled her on the wet planking, pulled off her necklace and earrings, which he hid under a length of coiled line, and whispered urgently, "Pull down your hair so it will look like a fishwife's! And smear tar on your face."

Before the stunned girl could obey, he jumped to his feet again, ran to the rail and leaped up onto it. He knew he made a perfect target, and carefully refrained from drawing his smallsword. Inasmuch as he was wearing no armor, he was taking a grave risk, of course, but it was better to gamble against odds than to meet certain death when a mob of cutthroats swarmed aboard the barque.

"In the name of His Holiness, Pope Clement the Eighth, I order you not to board this ship," he called, and the resonant voice that had stood him in good stead in so many courtroom disputes rolled across the open water to the sloop. "Anyone who dares to disobey will be excommunicated by His Holiness and will suffer the tortures of the damned for all eternity!"

The corsairs were hesitating, Philippe saw, and he pressed the scheme that was forming in his mind. "Where's your captain?" he demanded imperiously. "Let him come forward."

A burly, heavily bearded man with a scimitar in his hand and two pistols pressing against his jerkin above his belt shouldered several of his comrades aside. "I'm in charge," he shouted insolently.

"When you speak to me," Philippe told him in a cold voice, "you may address me as 'Your Eminence.' Dom Pedro, will you be good enough to join me?"

The master of the *Emmanuel*, who had been giving frantic, futile orders from his quarterdeck in an attempt to place his ship in a state of adequate defense, hurried down to the main deck. He had heard the exchange, and decided there was nothing to be lost by playing Philippe's game. "Yes, Your Eminence?" He made sure he spoke loudly.

The two ships were cruising side by side now, propelled at an agonizingly slow speed by the most gentle of breezes, and the men on the sloop were able to take in every detail of the scene aboard the barque. Some were crestfallen, others were dubious, and the head of the company, shrewder than the others, was weighing the situation carefully. The speaker at the railing could be a cardinal as he claimed. His doublet and breeches of unrelieved black, together with his somber shoes and stockings, might be the sort of clothing a prince of the Church would wear at sea. Not if he were Italian, but this man spoke French. The captain of the band thought it best to await a further explanation.

"I am traveling on a mission of the greatest importance to His Holiness," Philippe said. That much was the truth, but he knew the story would need embellishment. "I am acting as his emissary, and have been granted extraordinary powers to perform as his viceroy. As the Holy Father's deputy, and in the name of Our Lord, I shall instantly separate from the body of the Church any who dare to violate the sanctity of this ship."

He paused to let his words sink in. "I can't and don't ask you to accept my word. Dom Pedro, be good enough to bring me the commission from His Holiness."

Dom Pedro hesitated for an instant, then turned and hurried off to his cabin. The word "commission" was the key to his errand. It was true that the *Emmanuel* was sailing under a warrant issued by The Papal States, and that the paper bore the seal of Pope Clement's secretariat, as did scores of commercial documents that were signed every day of the year.

As soon as the panting Dom Pedro returned, Philippe leaned down to snatch the parchment from him and, unrolling it, scanned it quickly. It was useless as "proof" of a papal mission, to be sure, but was written in Latin, which he very much doubted the captain of the pirate band could understand. Fortunately any man could see the document's most impressive feature, its red seal, almost as large as the palm of a woman's hand, with the print of a Crucifix plainly visible in the center. Below it, in letters large enough for the semi-literate to identify, was the legend, *Clementus VIII.*

Philippe weighted the parchment scroll with Dom Pedro's dagger, and threw it across to the deck of the sloop, where the leader of the corsairs took it from the man who had caught it. Either the chieftain could indeed read or was a good enough actor to join one of the companies of strolling minstrels that regularly visited the castles and manor houses of wealthy nobles. He studied the document for some time, frowning intently, and his manner was grave. Finally he turned to his companions.

"It's all right here, just like the Cardinal says." He fingered the rich silver hilt of the Portuguese dagger before wrapping the parchment in it and throwing it back to the barque. "Will you give us your blessing, Your Eminence?"

Philippe grasped a line with his left hand to steady himself, and raised his right. He could think only of an inappropriate quotation from the works of Livy, but assumed what he hoped was a convincing clerical pose, and intoned the words. "*Civitas ea in libertate est posita, quae suis stat viribus, non ex alieno arbitrio pendet.*" It meant, "That state alone is free, which rests on its own strength, and does not depend upon the will of another." He would remember to cite it to Henry, who was leaning on the Pope now, and might find himself in Rome's debt if he didn't watch for hidden pitfalls.

The pirates were still kneeling, their heads bowed, so Philippe hastily added, "Amen," and made the Sign of the Cross.

The men on the deck of the sloop shouted their thanks, their captain gave an order, and a few moments later the ship veered sharply away from the barque. Dom Pedro murmured his thanks and returned to his quarterdeck in order to put as much distance as he could between the *Emmanuel* and the pirate ship.

Philippe continued to stand on the rail, smiling benignly until his jaws ached. Not until he was certain the corsairs had vanished far into the thick fog did he jump down to the deck. The barque had changed course, sailing west by northwest rather than due west, and the crisis was past.

Dame Louise de Longueval continued to crouch uncomfortably behind the open hatch cover. Her dress was water-soaked, her hair was indescribably tangled and streaks of sticky seaman's pitch on her face, throat and arms gave her more than a passing resemblance to a chimneysweep's assistant.

Philippe offered her a hand.

Louise struck it aside and struggled to her feet unaided. "You took the Lord's name in vain!" she said furiously.

"Did I?" Philippe was annoyed by her illogical attack. "We weren't boarded, not a single shot was fired, and no one was robbed or murdered."

She chose not to hear him. "You committed blasphemy, you fooled those men into thinking you were blessing them—which is a sin— and you impersonated a cardinal. I suppose you feel proud of yourself, milord!"

"As it happens, I do." The members of Henry's council would roar with laughter when they heard the story, but it might be wise not to repeat it to the King. It was impossible to guess how a future convert would react. Right now, however, there were more immediate concerns on Philippe's mind, and his anger expanded. "It may be that I saved you a great deal of inconvenience." As always when he felt himself losing control of his temper, he spoke very softly.

Louise would not be appeased. "My gown and cloak are ruined, and it will take the rest of the day to scrub off this dreadful tar."

Philippe's anger exploded. "Madame, you're the most stupid woman it's ever been my misfortune to meet." The words poured out in a low, steady stream, and for an instant he thought of what the crazed mob had done to Diana so long ago. "What's a gown worth, or a cloak? Does it matter that your skin will be tender for a few hours? I wonder if you have any idea what those scum would have done had they found a lovely and desirable girl on board this ship! By God, I ought to beat some common sense into you!"

Henry chose the church in Saint-Denis for his conversion because the little town was closer to Paris than any other community, and because so many kings of France were buried there. His siege had been reduced to a meaningless formality, and citizens of the capital had begun to arrive in Saint-Denis before dawn. They continued to appear by the thousands all through the morning, and the narrow, twisting streets were so choked with solid masses of celebrating humanity that troops of the King's household cavalry regiment had been forced to clear a path, gently, for the parade to the church.

Henry provided the Parisians with the most dazzling of theatrical spectacles for the occasion. He rode a white stallion, and was dressed from neck to toe in gleaming white satin, but, for reasons he hadn't deigned to tell anyone, carried his familiar plumed, black hat. Gabrielle d'Estrées followed in an open carriage, magnificently gowned, and strung out behind her were the coaches of the King's princely relatives, many of them his battlefield foes until this day. Cardinal de Bourbon, Henry's elderly cousin, led a delegation of prelates, which included two other cardinals, three archbishops and more bishops than anyone cared to count. There were so many high-ranking Catholic nobles in the line that some couldn't crowd into the church itself and were forced to listen to the ceremony from the vestibule.

Anything that might remind the people of the long civil war had been omitted by the marshals of the parade. Huge tapestries were hung from balconies, as were copies of Henry's personal crest, hastily drawn on huge sheets of parchment by artists recruited for the purpose. Garlands of flowers extended across the town's two main thoroughfares, forming arches, and flower petals were strewn on the streets. In the same spirit, garbage had been cleared from the gutters.

Now, at noon, it was very quiet. The doors of the church had been closed for the ceremony itself, and the huge throng that waited patiently under a hot July sun was orderly and restrained. Vendors of chestnuts, hot meat pies and cool wine advertised their wares in low tones, and the pikemen of the King's First Infantry Regiment, who were standing guard, had literally nothing to do.

The silence in the room on the second floor of the town hall that faced the square was different, and had a brooding, ominous quality. The windows were open, admitting heat waves that danced in the sunlight, but no one looked out at the crowd or the church. Eleven of the fourteen members of the King's council had crowded into the office, and each was occupied with his own thoughts. Montmorency leaned against a wall, staring hard into space. The dapper Biron, the only member of the group who was wearing his dress uniform and medals, occasionally sipped brandywine from a flask he carried in a convenient pouch hanging from his sword-belt.

General de Brissac, long the terror of Papists, cleaned and pared his fingernails with a poniard, and the Count de Montpensier, the royal chamberlain and reputedly the finest Huguenot scholar in all Europe, absently watched him. Soldiers and administrators, generals and dukes and counts behaved like men in a stupor.

The portly Sully, who would at last receive the title of Minister of Finance if the King-turned-Papist didn't discharge him, sat at one corner of the mayor's desk, playing chess with Philippe de Montauban, who would become Chancellor of the realm if Henry didn't send him into exile. Neither payed more than perfunctory attention to his game.

Suddenly the bells of the church began to peal, and the belfries of the town's smaller churches came to life, too.

"It's done," Montmorency said savagely.

A jubilant roar from the crowd in the square caused the portrait of Louis XI above the cold hearth to tremble.

A corps of trumpeters and drummers began to play a triumphant air, but not one of the men in the office went to the windows.

The shouts became louder, more sustained, and built to a frenzy so intense that it became evident to the Council members that the King had emerged from the church. De Brissac gouged out a chunk of the floor with his poniard, then replaced the knife in his boot-top.

The lugubrious silence was broken when the door burst open and Henry of France and Navarre stood in the frame. He was unescorted, and drops of the scented oil used in his baptism still clung to his hair. His subordinates rose to their feet, and he closed the door behind him.

"Shut the windows," he shouted above the commotion.

Two generals hastened to obey.

"That's better. Now we can hear each other." Henry smiled, but no one addressed him.

"It would be a mockery, of course, to expect congratulations from any of you."

Again there was a heavy silence.

"Montmorency," the King said, "your wife was there, sitting with my sister. She seemed to enjoy the whole ceremony enormously."

"My wife," the deputy commander of the French armies replied, choosing his words with care, "is a Papist. Under the agreement we made with each other when we were married, she attends religious functions as she wishes. There is no need for her to get my permission."

"Meaning, of course, that you wouldn't have granted it had she asked you." There was a glint of secret amusement in Henry's intense eyes.

Montmorency was one of the few men allowed to turn his back on his monarch. He went out of his way to exercise the privilege.

"And you, de Montauban," Henry continued. "I saw your lady there, in the third pew. You'll be pleased to hear she was sitting with the Burgundians rather than with her addle-headed uncle."

Philippe felt everyone looking at him. "If it please Your Majesty," he said glacially, "the Dame Louise de Longueval is not my lady."

"Oh? My informants tell me otherwise." The King laughed silently.

"Not that the subject is the concern of anyone but myself, sire, but as Your Majesty has elected to discuss the business in the presence of my colleagues, I would like to make my position clear. I find myself incapable of proposing marriage to a woman from the enemy camp, no matter how high my personal regard for her."

"Am I also your enemy now, Philippe?" Henry asked.

"I have not broken my vow of fealty to Your Majesty, nor will I, unless the requirements of Your Majesty's new faith force you to turn against those whose belief in God is similar to mine." Philippe spoke bluntly, seeing no reason to hide his feelings when the King was going out of his way to learn them.

The others shared the same sentiments. There was a general murmur of approval, and de Brissac declared in a loud voice, "Well said, lad!"

Henry's mood changed, and for a moment it appeared that he might weep. Instead a hard sheen came into his eyes. "My friends," he said, "you're imbeciles." Very deliberately he threw his black hat onto the floor in the center of the room.

Sully and one of the generals involuntarily started to bend down for it.

"No!" Henry commanded in a ringing voice. Picking up the hat himself, he gazed at it for a moment. "The symbol of Protestant resistance to the Church of Rome, eh? That's what the Dutch call it." He began to twirl the hat on the forefinger of his left hand, and everyone saw his new ring, a carved emerald the size of a walnut, that Pope Clement had sent him as a personal gift.

The slow-spoken Montmorency roused himself. "Henry," he demanded, "must you denigrate your brothers? Have you forgotten when we and the sixteen hundred volunteers we managed to muster—and paid out of our own pockets until we were bankrupt—were your only supporters? Have you forgotten we alone stood with you to challenge the power of Catholicism in France?"

"I have forgotten nothing, my brothers, and you shall have your rewards when we go to Paris next week." Henry displayed deep emotion for the first time. "Montmorency, you shall wear the gold sash and become First Marshal of the armies."

There was a stir, and each man glanced at the other uncertainly. The gold sash was, by tradition, the symbol of the highest office in the land under the King, that of Constable, and the significance of the appointment escaped no one. The Catholic nobles would be certain to protest vehemently when they learned the post was being given to a Huguenot.

"Biron, you shall have your Marshal's baton, too, and I want you to begin building a navy. We'll find our admirals in due time. De Brissac, you're promoted to the rank of full general. Sully, you've already been serving as my Finance Minister. Now you'll operate in a larger sphere. De Montauban, your first task as Chancellor will be to reorganize the judicial codes and see that I'm served by impartial judges who fear no man—except me." The King spoke to each man in turn, giving him promotions and honors.

A few beamed self-consciously, but the others remained sullen, and the tension was unrelieved.

Henry professed surprise. "Are you so insensitive to the glories of high places, gentlemen?"

Montmorency tried to express his thoughts, failed and turned to Philippe for help.

The King was feeling the first twinges of irritation. "Ah, yes. Let milord Chancellor speak for you so your collective reply will be balanced, good-tempered and free of any hint of treason."

Philippe stood erect, and removed the silver chain with its insignia of Judge Advocate-at-Arms from his neck. This was the breaking point, and the issue had to be faced squarely, without subterfuge. "I speak only for myself, Your Majesty. I can neither accept the post of Chancellor nor hold my present place if you intend to silence me with bribes. I know my duty to you, but it shouldn't be necessary, in this company, to say that I stand wholly with Calvin. My first obligation is to know and do the will of God. My conscience bows to no king or pope."

The others spontaneously applauded, and Henry listened with an expression that revealed nothing.

"You have joined a Church, Your Majesty, that requires all men to obey the word of Rome. That is your privilege and right. But you're no ordinary man, as you know even better than we. If you must bend your knee to Clement, then we, your servants, must prostrate ourselves before him—indirectly—when we obey your commands. I can't." Philippe held out the chain.

Henry refused to accept it. "Well said, my friend. I've chosen wisely in naming you Chancellor." He walked to the door. "Gentlemen, places are being held for you at the banquet this afternoon. Mayenne is paying for it out of his own pocket, and we're lucky that Lorraine has been a prosperous duchy in spite of the war. None of us has eaten such fine food in years."

De Brissac, a cavalryman who had never flinched in battle, even when fighting against great odds, sobbed aloud. He tried to remove

41

his sword belt so he could lay both the blade and its scabbard at his monarch's feet, but tears blinded him.

Henry sighed, then very slowly clamped his black hat on his head. The emblem of Protestantism tilted so it rode at a rakish angle.

Sully gasped, and the others stared at the King open-mouthed.

Montmorency was the first to recover. He raced to the door, enveloped Henry in a bear-hug and exuberantly lifted him off his feet. The King did not seem to object to the indignity, and laughed when everyone started talking and shouting simultaneously.

As the commotion subsided, the members of the Council became conscious of a chant in the square outside. "Hen-ry! Hen-ry!"

Montmorency released the King, who straightened his white satin suit and, as he walked to the windows, carefully removed the black hat. Philippe and de Brissac hurriedly opened the windows for him, and he walked onto the balcony to acknowledge the cheers of the vast throng.

Montmorency smiled foolishly, and Philippe shuffled his feet, hooked his thumbs in his belt and stared down at the floor. A revived de Brissac smoothed his doublet, and Biron couldn't resist following the King onto the balcony so the crowd could see the splendor of his eight decorations, the largest number accumulated by anyone in the service of France and Navarre.

At last Henry came back into the room and made his way to the door. "Are you satisfied at last, gentlemen?" He paused with one hand on the latch. "I think you'll agree that Paris is well worth a Mass."

To the horror of architectural purists and the intense personal dismay of the noble gentlemen, courtiers and clerks who either worked or lived at the Louvre, two new wings that dwarfed the main structure were being added to the official Paris residence of the kings of France. In summer, for reasons that could not be explained by the scientists who taught in the philosophy department at the Sorbonne or by Gabrielle d'Estrées' staff of astrologer-wizards, who had become official members of her household, the palace retained heat. In fact, the knights, equerries and aides-de-camp to the country's leaders, who lived on the top floor, insisted that it was impossible to sleep in their cubbyholes before October.

Then, as King Henry himself pointedly remarked one day, when the English ambassador asked for a premature repayment of a loan, the Louvre proved herself as fickle as a woman. Overnight she became as cold and draughty as an old barn facing the Atlantic on the shores of Brittany or Anjou. Private chambers were always frigid, no matter how large the fires built in their hearths, and the public rooms were even worse.

Most of the Huguenot newcomers to the palace, not yet acclimatized to her caprices, were afflicted with tenacious cases of the ague early in October, and sneezed, blew their noses and coughed through November into December. The ladies of the court made fewer complaints, but suffered even more intensely than the gentlemen, chiefly because they were obliged to follow the fashion lead of Dame Gabrielle and the King's sister, both of whom had an unquenchable fondness for low-cut gowns.

No one knew or cared how the servants felt, but the poor wretches were miserable, thanks to an order issued by Henry himself, who directed that only limited quantities of inferior wood be burned in the tiny grates that graced some of the servants' rooms. The staff of chefs was reduced, too, as were the bills of bakers, fishmongers and butchers. Henry was living up to his reputation for parsimony in small matters.

In public affairs, however, he was spending so freely that the nation's landowners, were becoming increasingly concerned. He appropriated huge sums for the establishment of a navy and, anticipating its completion, set up a bureau to supervise the expansion of French colonial interests in the raw wilderness of the North American New World. Sully was ladling out government funds for the strengthening of the glass-making, tapestry and silk industries, as there was a demand in other European lands for these goods. Owners of farm estates were granted special privileges in order to encourage agriculture.

The army was being reorganized, even though Philip of Spain had refused to follow the lead of Pope Clement and was still at war with France. Engineers were planning and digging an intricate series of inland canals that would link the entire country by water. And architects were hard at work on sketches for a new City Hall, a series of bridges connecting the Right and Left banks of the River Seine, and a magnificent new square to be called the Place Royale.

No one was idle, and no one was warm. Philippe de Montauban, Lord Chancellor of France, Navarre and Burgundy, Lieutenant General the Judge Advocate of the army, and Supreme Justice of the civilian law courts was frenziedly busy and, he was convinced, half-frozen. His private office was a handsome room on the second floor of the main gallery of the Louvre, a chamber twice the size of his infrequently visited château at Montauban. There were two hearths on adjacent walls, but icy winds cut through the room in spite of them, and Philippe had installed a wood-burning stove that stood a few yards from his desk. Unfortunately, papers were piled so high on the desk that the feeble heat of the little stove afforded him little warmth.

One morning in mid-December he sat hunched at the desk, wearing his heaviest doublet and breeches of Norman wool, with a thick scarf wrapped around his throat. Other members of the court were acquiring the habit of encircling their necks with ruffles of starched silk, but Philippe considered the fashion ludicrous, uncomfortable and impractical.

He reached with numbed fingers for a hot mug of watered wine, heavily spiced because he disliked the taste of even a mild Bordeaux too early in the day. Then he finished signing a stack of documents, leaving their sealing to Sir Andre Fontaine, who had been transferred from Montmorency's staff to his as an equerry. Reaching for a parchment roll, he shivered and then became immersed in his reading.

There was a tap at the door, and Fontaine, handsome in brown and yellow velvet, came into the chamber without waiting for a reply.

These days Philippe invariably was short-tempered before noon. "What do you want?" he snapped.

"You have a visitor, milord Chancellor."

"I see qualified petitioners between three and five in the afternoon. Send him away."

The equerry, after years of service with the blunt and usually even-tempered Montmorency, didn't quite know how to deal with a waspish superior.

"Are you deaf, Fontaine? And please close the door on your way out. The chill becomes intolerable in here when air comes in from the rest of the suite."

"Dame Louise de Longueval has asked to see you, milord," the aide stammered.

Philippe muttered an oath and brushed Fontaine aside as he hurried toward the anteroom. "Why didn't you say so, idiot?"

Louise, wickedly demure in an elaborate hair arrangement and a square-necked gown of pink silk decorated with rosebuds of a deeper silk onto which pearls had been sewn, made a deep curtsy the instant she saw Philippe.

Courtesy required him to reply with an equally formal, low bow. "I'm delighted to see you," he said, and meant it, even though they hadn't been in touch with each other since his arrival in Paris more than four months earlier.

She allowed him to escort her into the office, and after showing her to the most comfortable visitor's chair, he closed the door.

"So this is the highest court in France," Louise murmured, looking at the parchment scrolls, sheafs of papers and books piled on the desk and several tables.

"No, we have other buildings for that purpose. This is where I try to supervise the preparation of a new law code."

"It's very impressive," she said without conviction.

Philippe tried not to gape at her, and wished she were less attractive. The realization that he had avoided her for months made him feel uneasy and guilty. "Would you care for a cup of morning-wine made from a recipe that the Montauban peasants use?"

"I thought I smelled herbs." She wrinkled her nose and declined.

He wanted to tell her she needed protection from the ague, particularly with so much bare skin exposed to the air, but thought she might resent such intimacy.

Louise gathered the strings of the embroidered pouch that contained her rice powder and mirror. Placing it firmly in her lap, she braced herself. "I'm not here on a courtesy visit. I know you have too much to occupy you."

"My work can wait," Philippe replied.

"I've wanted to see you for several weeks in order to have a frank talk with you, but until now I've been reluctant." In spite of her resolve she was embarrassed.

He was afraid he knew what was coming, and didn't want to face the issue. "You've been in Orléans."

"I went to my brother's château because I couldn't stand staying on in the city. Now I've come back for only one purpose—to see you."

Not knowing quite how else to respond, he inclined his head.

"You and I, milord Chancellor, came to know each other rather well in our last days on board the *barque* that brought us to France from Rome. We even enjoyed certain intimacies."

Philippe felt his face burn. "I apologize for my advances," he said lamely, not really meaning a word.

She saw through the hollowness of his reply, and brightened for an instant before sobering again. "Not at all, sir. I welcomed them, and could have curbed you had I wished. I accept my share of responsibility. However, that is minor. We established a rapport, I thought, or so you led me to believe. I, at least, enjoyed our journey from Toulon—"

"So did I!"

"And during the week before the King's conversion, we saw each other constantly in Saint-Denis. I felt, or thought I had reason to believe, that you were courting me. My brother, in whom I've confided, tells me he gained the same impression."

"It was accurate, madame." He knew he couldn't side-step, and decided to meet candor with candor. "Your brother wasn't the only one who saw that I had fallen in love with you."

Color rushed to Louise's face, too.

"King Henry mentioned my feelings before almost the whole Council only a few minutes after his baptism."

"It was that very day you changed!" She began to twist the loop on her embroidered bag. I can't really charge that you snubbed me at the banquet. You were polite enough, but you had withdrawn. And the next day you vanished without a word or even a note."

"I knew of my promotion to Chancellor, and went back to Chartres so I could organize and recruit the staff I'd need. I had only a week before the court moved to Paris."

"And here you were busy, too, I know. So busy that you could only bow to me from a distance in the corridors. If I did something to offend you, I believe it's my right to know it. If you had a change of heart, that is your privilege. Perhaps I ask too much, but I've been humiliated. I don't give my affections to casual strangers, and I feel I've been snubbed. I know the whole court has been talking about us, and with so many new people, so many new faces, I cringe at the very thought of appearing before them."

Philippe felt as though the scarf around his throat was choking him, and tore it away. "I don't value your affections lightly, and I have greater esteem and respect for you than for any other woman alive. I had no desire to fall in love with you, madame. You want the truth, so here it is. I fought myself. I had suffered one tragedy, and didn't want another. But my discipline was wasted. I did fall in love with you, and I love you still."

Louise looked composed as she stood, but her voice trembled. "Then why have you run from me?"

"You're a Papist."

"True. And you're a Huguenot."

"Your uncle is a cardinal."

"He presented you to me on the deck of the *Emmanuel* the day we sailed, and made no secret of the fact that he is my uncle."

Obviously she didn't or wouldn't see his point, and he shrugged helplessly.

"We're the same man and woman we were that day, and my faith is no different. Your views haven't changed, either, I'm certain. I'm told you attend worship services every Sunday at Constable Montmorency's palace."

"Of course I do!"

"Philippe, stop hedging! You knew I was a Roman Catholic when you fell in love with me, just as I knew that you were a Calvinist."

Her attitude, combined with her words, indicated she loved him, too, and Philippe's throat ached. Their situation was even more dismal than he had imagined possible. "It's because of the difference in our beliefs that we have no future together."

"I wonder if it's you who are narrow—or we." Louise took a single step toward him. "Are you afraid I'd corrupt your love of God?"

46

"No more than I'd influence you." He made an attempt to present his arguments logically. "Neither of us has pretended to be anything other than honest. I fell in love with you in the full knowledge that you're a Roman Catholic. And I'm aware of how great your own struggle must have been before you gave yourself to me."

"There was none," she said. "I fell in love with a man, not his theological convictions. There, I've said it, and you may think me a wanton, if you please."

"Never." He could feel himself slipping, and reason deserted him. "There's been too much hatred and ugliness and spilled blood in the past seventy-five years for us to find happiness together. How many of your relatives have persecuted mine? How many of mine have rioted against yours?"

Louise stood motionless. "Milord Chancellor is said to be engaged in a project that will change the law courts of France for all time. My uncle has talked of little else since he returned from Rome. He thinks it's an outrage—and a venial sin, too, I believe—for the ecclesiastical courts to lose jurisdiction over the King's subjects in everything but cases of ecclesiastical law. You're changing our whole civilization, yet you try to hold yourself apart from it. Aren't you being inconsistent, Philippe?"

"No." He ran a hand through his prematurely graying hair. "I make no pretense of liking your Church or anything it represents. I gather from you that Cardinal de Gonde thinks I'm trying to destroy the temporal power of the bishops. Well, he's right. If a subject of the King commits murder, or steals a purse—or becomes involved in a dispute over property boundaries with his neighbor, for that matter—he should be tried in the King's own courts, regardless of whether he's a Catholic or a Huguenot. I say the bishops and their monsignors have no jurisdiction over him."

"How would you feel if he were tried by a Calvinist court?" She seemed to be goading him, but there was neither rancor nor irony in her manner.

"There are none," Philippe said. "In fact, there are no Huguenot judges in the civil courts, such as they are, except in the towns of our own inner citadel. You may forget that we're a tiny minority, outnumbered by more than six to one by you Papists. But we can't afford to forget it for an instant."

"What is it you're really trying to achieve?"

"Ultimately I want to see religion banished from the royal courts. A judge should be appointed by the crown solely because of his knowledge of the law and his ability to deal wisely with the problems of people. His religion should be his own business, irrelevant to his appointment."

"My uncle insists you want to fill the courts with Huguenot magistrates."

"Your uncle, with all due respect, is an even bigger ass than I suspected. Every decision rendered by a Huguenot justice in favor of a fellow Calvinist at the expense of a Catholic will bring the country that much closer to a new civil war. The King is trying to establish a France that's united, and there will be none if the rights of the Catholic majority are curtailed. I seek equality for Huguenots, and to get it I must clip the bishops' wings, but it would be madness to curtail a Catholic's rights because of his religion. I'll gladly tell Cardinal de Gonde to his face that he's mistaken, as usual."

"I wonder if you really know what you've been telling me. You believe yourself opposed to Rome——"

"I am!"

"——yet you're devoting your life to the establishment of a new legal system that will guarantee the rights of Catholics as much as it will those of Huguenots."

"Of course." Philippe thought the room was stifling, and wondered why he had believed it chilly. "All men must be judged equally and receive the same protection under the law, or justice has no meaning."

"Such idealism. And what of women?" Her rising laugh was a prelude to tears.

Louise's loss of control put the full burden on Philippe, and he found himself capable of thinking logically again. Although it was true he despised the Roman Catholic Church and its clergy for their inhumanity and bigotry, it would be stupid for him, while trying to establish an equitable code of justice for all France, to deny his love for a woman who had been given no choice in her faith from earliest childhood. It would be absurd to hold Louise responsible for the massacres of Huguenots, the civil war or the present attempts of the clergy and their associates in the nobility to block his reforms.

Now he could understand Montmorency's marriage. Until now, it had always seemed inexplicable to him that a Huguenot champion regarded second only to Henry himself in England, the Lutheran states of Germany, Sweden and Holland could be happily married to a Catholic.

If, as he believed, true faith depended on an individual's personal relationship with his Maker, established through a choice freely made of one's own will, then he was denying Louise her fundamental human prerogative if he demanded that she accept the dictates of his conscience rather than her own. Inasmuch as she was granting him that same choice and not insisting that he believe as she did, their problem seemed to be resolved.

Louise's crying continued.

Fontaine opened the door, peeked in and withdrew again very quickly.

48

For a moment Philippe looked at her helplessly. Then he went to her. As he kissed her, the last of his doubts vanished. She clung to him, and his lonely torment of recent months disappeared.

He held her more firmly, and they pressed closer to each other. Louise's lips parted and Philippe's desire for her mounted. They lost sight of the fact that they were standing in an office at the Louvre until the sound of voices in the antechamber reminded them they were not alone. Philippe's hold slackened, Louise drew away from him, and they looked at each other in newly-discovered wonder.

"We'll be married at once," he said. It was a statement, not a question.

She nodded, and it was plain that she agreed.

"I'll build a house worthy of you on the other other side of the palace gardens," he declared; and there was no doubt that he would.

"You won't mind," she asked a trifle timidly, "if we're married at Notre-Dame?"

"Of course not!" His joy made him reckless. "In fact, we'll have two ceremonies, one in the cathedral and the other in the Huguenot chapel in Montmorency's palace."

Only in the far reaches of his mind was there a disturbing note: it was so unfair that, in all of Paris, there was not one Protestant church where a marriage ceremony could be performed.

1598

King Henry straddled the rustic bench, leaned his elbows on the table of rough-hewn pine and looked around at the old friends he had summoned to the newest of his innumerable retreats, a lodge deep in the forests of Brittany. "Why the frowns, my friends? De Montauban, you and Villars found the trout biting this afternoon, I hear. And we can smell the roasting of the boar that Montmorency speared. Delicious! Only Sully refuses to take advantage of a sojourn in the country."

The Finance Minister, who grew heavier each year, smiled sourly.

"You should dress simply, as the rest of us do, Maximilien," the King told him in mock reproof, hoping to draw a laugh from the others. It was a standing joke at court that if a stranger walked into the throne room at the Louvre he would immediately believe the brilliantly attired Sully to be the King.

No one smiled, and Villars, a Huguenot duke who had won

increasing favor with Henry since the part he had played in the final defeat of the Spaniards at Amiens a few months earlier, acted as spokesman for the group. "This is the third time in seven weeks you've called us away from Paris. We find it very difficult to do our work when we're constantly being interrupted."

"I find it very hard to change the habits of a lifetime," Henry admitted. "I get a restless feeling if I'm cooped up in one place for more than a few days."

"You'll have to accustom yourself to longer stays in Paris," Montmorency told him. "Now that Philip of Spain is signing a peace treaty with you, there's no excuse to be riding from town to town, rallying the people."

"You're younger than I am, all of you, so you aren't faced with the need of refusing to accept middle age. Besides, I'd think you'd welcome a chance like this to get away from home. Philippe excepted, of course."

Philippe flushed as the others chuckled, but he knew they meant no offense. After four and one-half years of anxious waiting, Louise was at last bearing their first child, and he hated to be away from her side, even though three physicians and the midwife who had assisted at the birth of Gabrielle d'Estrées' children by the King had all assured him there was nothing to fear.

"I wouldn't have asked the Chancellor to join us if we didn't need him here. My friends, this is no whim of mine, and no ordinary conference. Now that the country is finally at peace, I can take some steps I have been wanting to for a long time. Tell them, Philippe."

"For the past six months I've been working on a secret project. Nothing I say to you now, milords, must be revealed—to anyone— until Henry decides the moment is ripe." Philippe rose, clumsy in the thick peasant's boots he had worn when fishing in the trout stream, and went to a leather pouch hanging from a peg in the corner of the room.

Everyone watched him as he returned with a sheaf of papers, which he spread out on the table before him.

"We come into our own at last, gentlemen," he said, and a grinning Henry nodded approvingly. "This will be known as the year the Calvinists of France finally gained recognition as the equals of the Catholic majority. I've been drawing up and refining a series of royal decrees."

"Which I intend to issue as a single edict," Henry interjected.

Philippe picked up the first paper. "This may be the most important of them. Huguenots will have the right to build and hold Divine worship services in at least one town in every *baillage*, or shire, in France."

There were grunts of approval, and the fiery young Villars muttered, "High time."

"You can examine these in detail after I've finished, if you wish," Philippe said, and reached for the next paper. "Every Huguenot landowner will have the right that until now has been restricted to those of us in the higher nobility. Each landowner will be allowed to hold Protestant services in his own home, at his own pleasure, and may build a chapel there if he wishes."

"On his property?" the corpulent Sully asked.

Philippe shook his head. "Inside the four walls of his manor house."

There was an angry mutter, and Henry raised a hand for silence. "Don't be too greedy, my friends. As you shall see, the Huguenots are going to get a great deal. We want to hold down Catholic resistance to a minimum. I urge you not to forget that strategy. Go on, Philippe."

"One moment." Sully was privately called "the bulldog" by his colleagues, and with good reason. "I want to go back to that first decree for a moment. Do you actually believe the Papist clergy will accept a Huguenot church in Paris? They'll fight us like besieged Spaniards at bay."

Philippe exchanged a quick glance with the King, and when Henry nodded, he said, "If necessary, we're prepared to give up the right to build a church in Paris, but we'll use that as a bargaining point in the negotiations."

Sully's sigh of resignation seemed to hang in the silence that followed.

"I suppose," Montmorency said, "that we'll also be asked to stay out of every city and town that a bishop uses as his capital."

Philippe had discussed and argued the point at length with the King, and could only say, "We'll have to face that problem when it arises. If it does."

"I'm damned if we're getting equal rights," Villars said angrily, and brought his hand down on the table with such force that a pitcher of mead teetered perilously before righting itself.

"When a man has fought this battle as long as I have," Henry said wearily, "he's content with a half-victory at a time. Tell them the rest, Philippe."

"Huguenots will enjoy all civil rights, and no privileges whatever will be reserved for Catholics."

The nobles gathered around the table looked a little more pleased.

Philippe reached for the next paper, and raised his head proudly. "No Huguenot will be barred from any office in the land, civil or military, because of his faith."

"By God, that's more like it!" Montmorency shouted.

"No student," Philippe continued, "will be barred from any

university, college or school in France, including those institutions owned and maintained by the Roman Catholic Church, because of his faith."

Villars brushed aside the deep bangs that covered his forehead and laughed scornfully. "Really, Philippe! What Huguenot lad with any sense would go to the Sorbonne and listen to Jesuit lecturers in philosophy when he can study under the finest minds on earth at Geneva!"

Montmorency agreed. "That decree is a waste of parchment and ink. The sons of Calvinists know better than to spend their money listening to speakers who'll fill them with Papist half-truths and evasions. Those who can afford it will go to Geneva. For those who can't there's the free university at Berne. Last year I bought a chalet as a house for the new students, and just this month I donated fifty ecus to establish another chair in theology."

"I'm sure," Sully said, "that all of us have supported the university at Berne generously."

Henry toyed with the tassels at the neck of his leather hunting shirt and gazed innocently out of the window. Since his conversion, all of his gifts to Huguenot institutions and causes had been made through subordinates, and he took scrupulous care never to express himself on such matters in the presence of more than one person at a time.

"Milords," Philippe said patiently, "I'm afraid you miss the principle of this decree. Whether a Huguenot student actually attends a Catholic university is irrelevant. A law from the reign of Charles the Ninth specifically prohibits such attendance, and therefore the Huguenot student is being subjected to discriminatory practices. Catholics are privileged to attend our schools, and we must have the right to walk through the gates of any Papist college in France."

"If you insist." Villars walked to a quarter of roasted venison hanging from a hook near the hearth, and cut himself a slice of meat with a knife which he then wiped on the side of his breeches.

Henry saw the gesture and smiled. Nothing better illustrated the nation's new prosperity. In the time of Francis I the heavy, ribbed material used to make Villars' breeches had been so expensive it had been called the cloth of kings, but now, thanks to the increased production in factories established with royal funds, a man could afford to treat the material casually.

"In my opinion," Villars continued, pouring himself a cup of mead, "the principle of Huguenot attendance at Catholic schools is a quibble."

"In mine," the King declared, "it's a principle."

The others subsided, and Philippe reached for the next paper in the sheaf. "We also think it wise to legalize and guarantee the permanence of a reform already in effect. In every royal court, duchy court and county court there is now at least one Huguenot justice sitting on the bench. This decree will make it mandatory for a king, duke or count to insure that in all his courts there is a minimum of one Calvinist justice for every five thousand Calvinist subjects."

"Is that really necessary?" Sully wanted to know. "It seems to me we're only calling attention to a situation that—thanks to your skill, Philippe—has created very little controversy."

Henry's mind was elsewhere. "I still have no legal heir," he said, reaching for the mead, the only alcoholic beverage he enjoyed.

Philippe felt sorry for him. Henry's sons and daughter by Gabrielle had been made legitimate by a royal decree that no one had questioned, as the children had been baptized as Catholics, but neither of the boys could inherit the throne. He sympathized deeply with the King, knowing how frustrated he himself would feel if his and Louise's as yet unborn children should be automatically barred from the inheritance of his titles.

Realizing Henry would become sour and disgruntled if allowed to brood too long, which would mean a miserable evening for the whole company, Philippe quickly went on to the next decree. "Finally, milords, we're providing Huguenots with the means of protecting themselves against the possibility of future massacres. The Constable has given me a list of one hundred and four Calvinist towns in France that, he assures me, can be defended effectively if their garrisons are manned by Huguenot troops under Huguenot commanders. The decree grants us the right to establish such fortifications in these towns."

Villars, who had been too young to take part in any of the campaigns except the siege of Amiens that had brought the war with Spain to a close, smiled broadly and drained his cup of mead. "There's a decree I approve!"

"The question," Sully said quietly, reaching for a bowl of the chestnuts soaked in brandywine that he always carried on his travels, "is whether the Catholic nobles will accept them."

Montmorency was astonished. "Any man who doesn't—no matter what his rank—will find the Constable's troops at his door. I've had some new cells built at the Bastille for traitors—they're four feet wide and only five feet high, and I can promise you that any lord who spends a few months in one of them will sing a different tune when he's released!"

"That's precisely what we don't want to happen," the King said. "There must be no arrests, no troop movements, no show of force. We must use reason."

"I can think of no argument that would be effective," the Constable retorted.

"I believe you're wrong," Philippe said. "That's our great gamble.

I've been making some discreet inquiries in the past six months, and I think I know the Catholic mind."

"You invite too damned many of them to your house," Montmorency grumbled. "My wife tries, too, but I keep telling her that Papists aren't welcome at my table, and that's the end of it."

Philippe couldn't help laughing at him. "I don't enjoy their company any more than you do. But I've had an assignment from Henry, and I've tried to carry it out."

The Constable thought hard for a few moments, understood and inclined his head. "My apologies. I meant you no insult."

"I accept," Philippe said promptly. "Milords, the Catholic nobles are as anxious as we to avoid a new civil war. The country grows more prosperous every year, and all of us are benefitting, even though Maximilien keeps nipping at our purses with his new taxes."

Sully looked pleased with himself as he popped another brandied chestnut into his mouth and licked his fingers.

"So far," Philippe continued, "we've given them no active cause for alarm. Now, before Henry issues an edict, we intend to test the Papists."

"How?" Montmorency believed it absurd to use diplomacy when the strongest army in the history of France would obey any order he gave.

"I'm planning to show the decrees to a number of Catholic lords. Their reaction will determine the course we take."

"I've approved the scheme," Henry said. "We have nothing to lose, my friends, and there's much to be gained if we can persuade them to be sensible. I've told Philippe to talk to them one at a time. If we keep each of them isolated from the others while we tell them our intentions, only the bravest will dare to oppose me. Then, before they can organize their opposition, we'll present them with the accomplished fact. It's a tricky procedure, and there are obvious risks involved, but the end is worth the means."

"If we beat the Papists with Jesuit tactics," Sully added, "they might make Philippe general of their Order."

Philippe joined in the laughter, but was unable to relax with the others. The cause of Huguenot freedom depended on his skills and persuasive powers.

Louise, Countess de Montauban, looked angelic in the four-poster bed, a silken coverlet thrown over the lower part of her body, a gauze-like peignoir framing her head and shoulders as she rested against a mound of pillows. But she was far from sweet-tempered at the moment, and Philippe's concern mounted.

"The physicians have told you that you mustn't excite yourself." He tried to stroke her hand.

She pulled away from him indignantly. "Not even all the saints in the Church could be calm after what I've learned."

"Then I'm sorry I told you."

"If you hadn't, I'd never have forgiven you."

He became stern. "You're not permitted to leave your bed, and you know it. I forbid you to stand, walk or leave this chamber!"

Louise refused to be cowed. "I have no choice. I'm needed downstairs."

"Nonsense. Do you want to injure your own health and the baby's? Do you know so much more about medical science than the physicians that you'd dare to spend several hours on your feet? Remember what happened to the Countess de Ribes because she was foolish enough to leave her bed three months before her baby was born!"

Tears welled in Louise's eyes. "Then why must you entertain Charles of Lorraine, that gourmand, Mayenne, here?"

"This isn't a social occasion," Philippe said wearily, tired of repeating the same tune. "I have business of state to discuss with him, business of the utmost urgency."

"Then you should see him in your office."

He laughed humorlessly. "One simply doesn't summon a man of Mayenne's stature to the Louvre, unless one happens to be the King, He'd feel grossly insulted, and with good cause, if I invited him to meet me at my office."

"What state business could be so urgently important that you must bring Mayenne into our house on a few hours' notice? If you serve him ordinary food, he won't eat it. You know how particular he is about every dish that's placed before him!"

Philippe had no intention of telling her anything about the Huguenot decrees. "The whole staff is working on the meal. The chef has borrowed two assistants from Henry's household——"

"If the King has allowed you to borrow two of his servants, this must be a very extraordinary occasion indeed! And I'll be disgraced forever if the Duke refuses a sauce."

"Mayenne may be a great gourmet, but he's a man of sufficient intelligence not to expect perfection in the household of a woman who is going to have an infant in about ten weeks. He's eaten enough meals here—and enjoyed them—to appreciate your talents as a hostess." Philippe thought it wiser not to add that when Mayenne learned of the impending decrees he would lose all interest in what had been served.

"All the same, he hates inferior dishes."

Philippe wanted no more of the conversation. He needed to organ-

55

ize his thoughts for the opening clash in the most vital battle of his lifetime, and his wife's stubborn concern with feminine irrelevancies was a distraction. "Madame," he said, "you'll obey your husband, as you swore to do in two marriage ceremonies. The subject is closed."

Louise began to weep.

He stood, half-paralyzed by her tears, knowing that nothing he might say would mollify her and that she would become furious if he tried.

There was a gentle tap at the door, and when he went to it, Fontaine stood in the corridor. "The Duke's outriders are coming into the courtyard, milord."

"Thank you." Philippe cast a single, agonized look at Louise, then made an attempt to put her out of his mind as he followed his equerry to the ground floor.

A gilded coach was just pulling to a halt in the cobbled inner courtyard when he reached it and, as a good host should, he opened the door of the carriage and bowed before stepping back and letting Mayenne's servants help their master to the ground.

The task was not an easy one. Charles de Guise, nominal master of Mayenne and Lorraine, weighed three hundred pounds, and was further encumbered by a suit of the heaviest silk, encrusted with pearls, rubies and semi-precious stones. It was rumored that some of his suits weighed more than one hundred pounds, and Philippe didn't doubt it as he watched four brawny men in the Mayenne livery growing red-faced as, two on each side of the Duke, they pried him through the door of the carriage, and while pretending to help him down the two steps of the coach, actually lifted him to the ground. Then one placed his cloth-of-silver cloak around his shoulders, another fastened his sword-belt of gold, a gift of a pope, around his enormous waist, and a third put his broad-brimmed velvet hat on his head.

Mayenne, after five minutes of being subjected to the ministrations of his household staff, was ready to return Philippe's greeting. "Milord Chancellor," he said, "it's my pleasure to be here. I'm a father, too, and I know how confounded lonely it can be to eat alone when one's wife is confined to her bed."

"I hope, Your Grace," Philippe replied, apprehensive because of the scene Louise had made, "that you'll find the luck-of-the-pot to your liking. We eat so simply here."

A quarter of an hour later the two men were ensconced in high-backed chairs at a gleaming mahogany table, inlaid with the coats-of-arms of France and Navarre in rare woods. The day was too warm for a fire to have been laid in the hearth, yet was too cold for the windows facing Louise's flower garden to be opened. The tapestries that ordinarily covered the windows had been removed, however, and only those hanging in front of the paneled walls were still in place.

Philippe and his guest sipped wine from silver goblets, but neither spoke as the de Montauban servants went through the solemn ritual of presenting each dish to the host and his guest in turn before placing it on its own mat of lined linen on the table. As was customary, each servant carried only one dish.

The first presented a mousse of river pike, and directly behind him was one who brought the vegetables simmered in wine that were to accompany it. Because of Philippe's southern origin there was a huge toureen of shellfish, cooked in a beef broth and redolent of garlic and herbs. This peasant dish had been virtually unknown to the Catholic nobles of the north prior to Henry's coronation, but so many of the Huguenot lords served it that it had become popular with almost everyone of standing. Mayenne's appreciative sniff indicated that Louise's fears had been ill-founded.

As the meal was informal, there were only three kinds of fowl, chickens that had been cooked inside roasting suckling pigs, wild ducks that enterprising farmers hunted in the marshes north of Paris and brought to the city's markets at dawn, and pigeons boiled in rich Burgundy wine and then crisped on a spit while being basted with a syrup-like fig brandywine.

The chef himself, followed by his principal assistants, brought in the roasts for inspection, and returned at once with the meats to the kitchen, a separate building just past the far end of the dining chamber. There the main courses would be kept hot until Philippe and his guest were ready to eat them. There was a saddle of venison, legs and chops of young lamb wrapped in wild boar's bacon, mutton that had been marinated in wine and herbs for twenty-four hours before being placed on the fire and, as the supreme dish, a quarter of roasted beef.

Mayenne used his own pearl-handled knife to cut a round loaf of bread into two parts to use as trenchers, and the meal began. It would have been impolite to converse, and there was silence at the table, broken only by an occasional deep murmur of approval, a conventional gesture expected of guests, and equally brief, equally vague sounds expected of hosts. They ate a pudding of wild strawberries, the particular delight of which was a custard made of cream skimmed from mare's milk, a fig and currant cake and a variety of cheeses, among them several from Lorraine as a compliment to Mayenne.

The five or six wine glasses the servants had refilled with each course were cleared away, and when a decanter of brandywine was placed on the table, the time for serious talk had come. Mayenne belched with a gusto greater than custom demanded, and Philippe, who had eaten sparingly, was able to muster only a weak belch in reply. Then, after pouring the pungent brandywine into two miniature goblets, he explained the King's pending decrees.

It was said that most men, if they ate the quantities of food consumed by Mayenne, would be drugged and incapable of coherent thought. But the Duke was surprisingly alert. He twirled his goblet in his thick, pudgy fingers, and an occasional gleam appeared in his heavy-lidded eyes. But he did not interrupt, and when Philippe finished his recital, appeared lost in thought for some moments.

"It strikes me," he said at last, "that a number of our Catholic nobles will wonder whether His Majesty was sincere in his conversion."

"I dare say that's a matter between the King and his confessor," Philippe countered.

"I suppose so." Mayenne drained the tiny cup, reached for the decanter and refilled it. "You realize, milord Chancellor, that there's certain to be resentment among the more pious Catholic nobles."

"I can't imagine why." Philippe spoke seriously, but with a faintly deprecating air. "They'll lose no rights, no privileges, and no standing."

Mayenne refused to deal on a surface level. "Come, Chancellor. You know as well as I that hatreds run deep."

"I do, Your Grace, and that's why I want to see them ended. I know of no reforms less sweeping than these decrees that will satisfy the Huguenots."

"What do you suppose they'll do if the new rights aren't granted?"

Philippe was prepared for the question, and shrugged. "I can only speak for myself, Your Grace. As I'm the country's chief legal arbitrator and law enforcement officer, I'd be derelict in my duty if I used other than strictly legal means of redress. I assure you I'd continue to press for the adoption of the decrees by all legitimate means."

The Duke nodded soberly. "And the other Huguenot leaders?"

Again Philippe shrugged. "Some of them," he said, "have known only violence for many years. The Constable has sheathed his sword only a short time ago, and Marshal Biron's army is still in the field, keeping watch on the Spanish frontier. Biron," he added, "has always been such an impetuous man. I sometimes wonder if even the Constable could restrain him if he thought he was being denied his fundamental rights."

Mayenne tried with only partial success to conceal his alarm. "Surely," he said, "Marshal Biron would obey His Majesty's command not to take up arms in a new civil war!"

"There were times when we were fighting your armies, Your Grace, when it was almost impossible for anyone, even King Henry, to control Biron. And in this situation it would be even more difficult. He could claim he was fighting to uphold the King's decrees."

Mayenne bristled, his chins quivering. "Are you threatening me, Chancellor?"

58

"Certainly not, Your Grace," Philippe lied. "I'm merely trying to present you with a factual, realistic picture."

The Duke subsided, but was so uncomfortably tense that he belched repeatedly. "There are hotheads on my side, too, you know. This problem is explosive."

"That's precisely why I asked you here today, Your Grace. Perhaps you and I, between us, can dampen the fires. This house was built to my specifications, and I'm very fond of it. I'd grieve if a Catholic mob burned it to the ground. I'm sure you wouldn't want Huguenot troops ravaging your estates and looting your castle in Lorraine. And no matter what the outcome of our talks, I urge you—privately and unofficially, of course—to station some guards at the tapestry factories you've bought here in the city. It's common knowledge that you own them, and if the Huguenot regiments stationed at the Louvre should believe—even unjustly—that you're trying to prevent the promulgation of these decrees, they might go wild."

Mayenne shuddered. "Do they know of the decrees?"

"I hope not, but I can't be certain. A few lords of high rank are familiar with them, but I can't promise that they're keeping quiet. Secrecy in a matter this important to so many people is difficult almost beyond belief to keep."

The Duke stuffed a handful of sugared dates into his mouth, then washed them down with the peppermint-flavored brandywine. "The mere thought of another civil war spoils my appetite!" he exclaimed.

Philippe thought it likely that he was winning the first round. "You and I are standing together, Your Grace," he lied.

"Do you suppose the Constable might be persuaded to transfer his Huguenot regiments elsewhere? The situation might be calmer if only Catholic troops were stationed in Paris."

The Duke's motives were so transparently thin that Philippe hid a smile. "Montmorency is a very proud and touchy man. I'd be very reluctant, myself, to make any suggestion to him concerning something that's his responsibility."

Mayenne bobbed his head glumly and tugged at a rope of sapphires and emeralds that encircled his throat. "The Constable and I are polite to each other. But after leading opposing armies for so many years, it would be impossible for us to achieve a real friendship. No, it wouldn't do for me to speak to him. That leaves me with just one alternative. I'll have to go to the King."

"Before or after he signs the decrees, Your Grace?" Philippe made the question sound innocent.

"By the armor of St. Anselm of Rheims, I'm caught in a vise, Chancellor! There's nothing I can do!"

"But there is," Philippe said firmly. "You can work with me to help the whole country accept these new laws in a spirit of good will to all French subjects."

Mayenne wilted. "At my age the thought of going into the field again makes me ill. I've carried Christ's banner into battle often enough in my day. I deserve the fruits of a few peaceful years."

Philippe could only hope, fervently, that enough Catholic lords shared the Duke's feelings. "I'll depend on you, Your Grace, to help me prevent a tragedy."

Relatives were expected to rally at a time of crisis, but the birth of a baby was of primary concern only to its parents, and Philippe heartily wished Cardinal de Gonde elsewhere. His own tension was so great, his worry about what was happening in the upstairs bedchamber so intense that the very presence of the Bishop of Paris irked him. To make matters worse, de Gonde had chosen to flaunt himself in his scarlet robes and a ridiculous skullcap that made him look like one of the Jews from whom the King had borrowed money during the years before he had won his throne.

Henry didn't appreciate the Cardinal's presence, either, and Philippe felt certain he wouldn't have come to help an old friend through a difficult hour if he had known de Gonde would be there. Now, unfortunately, there was no escape, even though the insensitive, rotund little prelate chose this most inopportune of moments to discuss affairs of state.

"To be completely frank with you, Your Majesty," he said, "I couldn't believe the rumors when I first heard them. I simply told myself that a devoted Catholic who loves God and submits himself to the authority of the Holy Church would not promote the cause of heretics whose alleged faith is a mockery of Christianity. But the stories have persisted, and I must ask you to confirm or deny them."

"Florent," Philippe said, "let me give you another glass of mulled cider."

"Cider, eh? Is that what I've been drinking?" The Cardinal screwed up his face. "That apple brandywine of the Normans is a peasant drink, my dear boy. I must teach you to improve your taste."

"I'll have another glass, Philippe," the King said quietly. "No, don't bother to get it for me. Run upstairs again, if you like."

Philippe drifted indecisively toward the stairway beyond the open door of the library, then halted. "No," he said, "the physicians insist I'm in the way, and I can't stand seeing Louise in such pain. They'll let me know when there's anything to report."

"All women suffer a mild discomfort at a time like this," de Gonde said.

Henry glowered at him and, in a gesture that invariably indicated

60

he was in a belligerent mood, rubbed the palm of his hand across the hilt of the poniard that protruded from his old, worn leather belt. "A mild discomfort? Sometimes I think you priests have mountain water in your veins. Gabrielle has given me three children, and each time she's suffered the tortures of the damned!"

The Cardinal opened his mouth to say that the King's mistress was damned because of her affair with him, but changed his mind. Old Cardinal de Bourbon, Henry's own cousin, had been requested to leave the palace when he had said something mildly critical about the affair. "I think, Your Majesty, that our train of thought was interrupted."

"What you mean, Your Eminence, is that I haven't nipped at the bait you've thrown me. Very well, you shall have your answer. When the time is ripe, and I don't intend to wait much longer for the approval of the Catholic nobles, I shall sign my edict and make it public."

De Gonde's hands fluttered in horrified protest. "Have you corresponded with His Holiness on this matter?"

"Certainly not! Does he consult me before he issues a papal bull?"

The Cardinal was shocked. "Your situation and his, Your Majesty, are far different."

"They are, in many ways. France has a population of more than twelve million, and my army is the most efficient in Europe. There are less than a million people in The Papal States, and Clement's so-called regiments are manned by untrained peasants led by pleasure-loving Italian gentlemen who have never led a cavalry charge, directed an artillery bombardment or commanded a line of pikemen, much less infantry equipped with firearms!"

Philippe thought he heard someone coming down the stairs, and darted out of the room. But he saw no one, and could hear no sounds coming from Louise's bedchamber. Returning to the library, crestfallen, he heard the end of what seemed to be an impassioned speech that de Gonde was making.

"——you encourage the spread of heresy when you grant rights to infidels. Your Majesty! Look at the superb example of Spain. She has remained pure because the Inquisition has rooted out sinners."

"It may not have come to your attention, Your Eminence," Henry replied in a dry tone that his subordinates had learned to beware, "that I'm not very fond of the Spaniards. I don't know how many lives or how much money Philip has cost us in the past five years, and I don't mind admitting that I've found it a great satisfaction to beat him to his knees!"

The Cardinal's retreat was even hastier than that of Philip's legions after their final, crushing defeat. "I wasn't for a moment suggesting you emulate King Philip, Your Majesty!"

"Good, because if you're familiar with French ecclesiastical history, Your Eminence, you know that French Catholics traditionally have accepted no earthly masters except their own consciences, and that their spokesmen have been their kings. When Italian popes tried to force us to act against our own interests, we established our own popes at Avignon."

De Gonde was on the defensive, but he tried to hold his own. "Schisms in the Dark Ages that grew out of mutual misunderstandings have no bearing on a more enlightened age."

Suddenly Henry's manner changed. Delicacy vanished, and so did his faintly impersonal air. "I hope," he said brutally, "that the Church of Rome will follow policies throughout my reign that posterity will consider enlightened. And by posterity, I mean my direct descendants, who'll follow me on the throne."

The sharp attack left the Cardinal at a loss for words.

"You've criticized me for the edict I intend to issue," Henry continued. "Were you speaking for yourself, Your Eminence, or for Pope Clement?"

"I—I doubt if His Holiness has had time as yet to receive the letter I've sent him on the subject."

"You had no direct access to the decrees, so anything you wrote was necessarily hearsay." Henry gripped the handle of his poniard. "For your information, milord Bishop, I myself have done Clement the courtesy of sending him a copy of my edict by special courier."

The revelation was startling, but the Cardinal made a rapid recovery. "His Holiness is sure to disapprove of any extension of privileges to Huguenots, Your Majesty."

"I haven't asked his opinion. I knew a great many warped things would be said and written by the half-informed, so I preferred to give a colleague the facts of the situation."

De Gonde turned almost as red as his silk cloak. Never had he heard anyone refer to the supreme pontiff as a colleague. "Your Majesty," he said solemnly, his voice almost breaking, "it's my duty as your pastor to warn you that you may be endangering your immortal soul."

Henry's expression reminded Philippe of the time the King had ordered three traitors drawn and quartered.

"I'm positive," the Cardinal went on, "that His Holiness will be opposed both in principle and practice to your decrees. I'm equally positive he'll order you not to publish them."

"I sincerely hope he won't be that short-sightedly stupid!" Henry retorted. "I require the Church to pay no taxes on her many properties in France, but if Clement were foolish enough to meddle in affairs of state that are none of his business, I'd have to reconsider my generosity."

The naked threat increased the already brittle tension in the li-

62

brary, and Philippe was torn. He didn't want to miss any of the debate, yet kept peering out toward the staircase.

De Gonde fought with more courage than either the King or his Chancellor thought he possessed. "Let me remind you, Your Majesty, that His Holiness becomes directly concerned when you make it easier for heretics to preach their false doctrines and corrupt the faithful."

Philippe decided to intervene. "It was my impression of Pope Clement, after spending a stimulating day with him, that he is convinced of the truth of Roman doctrine. Like any great man who believes passionately that his cause is right, I can't imagine his fearing that exposure to Calvinism will cause Catholics to leave their Church."

Henry's chuckle made Philippe realize that he hadn't eased the situation, but had goaded the Cardinal.

Certainly de Gonde was furious. "Satan finds many ways to snare a man's soul! The Church must always be vigilant to protect its lambs."

"Then let the Church act as a spiritual shepherd," Henry said, "provided my grain fields aren't trampled. I need the approval of no one to extend to a devoted group of my faithful subjects the basic rights I believe essential to human dignity."

The Cardinal had only one more card to play. "You accepted the authority of the Church when you were baptized of your own free will, Your Majesty."

"I expected the Church to be concerned with my soul when I'm no longer among the living. I permit no one to tell me how to govern France. If Clement excommunicates me, the Church will be the greatest sufferer. But why do we even speak of such unpleasantness? Clement is an educated man, and I'm quite sure he knows to a sou the heavy price that Rome paid when The Holy See tried to meddle in the state affairs in England. My namesake there created a national church not so many years ago—1534, I believe it was—and made himself its head. Sometimes a man in my position feels tempted to follow his example."

The threat was so explicit that de Gonde, who had been disarmed by artillery heavier than his own, was speechless.

"Now," Henry said, "you really have something to put into a letter to Clement."

The thin, piercing wail of a newborn infant made Philippe forget the verbal duel, and he bolted from the library, not bothering in his haste to request the customary permission to leave the King's presence.

Henry's booming laugh followed him as he mounted the stairs two at a time.

A physician in shirtsleeves awaited Philippe in the anteroom adjoining Louise's bedchamber, and a beaming midwife stood beside him, holding an object wrapped in the voluminous folds of a silk-edged, unbleached woolen blanket. "Meet your son, milord," the physician said, "the future master of Montauban."

Philippe paused long enough to stare at a tiny face that, for the moment, filled him with dismay. The baby was as red as a man who had been working for hours in the outdoors, thin fuzz sprouted from the top of his head, and he was so wrinkled that he resembled the senile ancients who dozed in the sun on the stoops of Montauban's houses. "Very handsome," he murmured, and pushed past the pair into his wife's room.

Two physicians were standing over a basin at one side of the chamber, cleaning instruments that made Philippe think they had been borrowed from a Spanish Inquisition torturer. And a maidservant was busily removing a number of heavily bloodstained sheets.

But Louise, lying drowsily on a mound of silken pillows, seemed at peace with herself and the world, and her slow smile of greeting was more reassuring than anything the physicians might tell her worried husband.

Philippe dropped to one knee beside her, and covered her thin, pale hand with his. "You're—all right?"

She pressed his hand gently, still smiling.

His anxiety lessened, and ignoring the presence of others in the room, he muttered, "Louise, I never knew until today how much I love you. I was so afraid that——" He broke off abruptly.

"Women have been having babies for thousands of years," she whispered. "I'm not clever, or exceptional—or unique."

He refrained from mentioning to her that although peasant women seemed to enjoy extraordinary good luck in childbirth, a recent census made at Henry's direction—the first in the long history of France—revealed that four out of ten ladies of the upper nobility died before, during or immediately following the birth of their infants.

"Have you seen him?" she asked. "Isn't he beautiful?"

"I've never seen a more impressive child," Philippe lied, and hoped he sounded properly enthusiastic and sincere.

"I have such wonderful plans for him that my head is spinning." Louise dropped off to sleep, the smile still lingering.

One of the physicians touched Philippe on the shoulder. "Let her rest for a time, lord Count. She'll need sleep in the next few days."

Philippe stood, nodding, and suddenly remembered his obligations. He dug deep into his purse and gave a gold ecu to each of the physicians, a silver half-ecu to the midwife and then, seeing Fontaine in the corridor, emptied the purse of small coins to be distributed to the household staff.

It felt strange to be a father, and Philippe tried to accustom himself to the fact. Suddenly he felt a great wave of sympathy for the King who had no legitimate children. Every princess in Catholic Europe was being offered to Henry as a bride, but Catholicism was responsible for the King's reluctance to take a wife. As a nominal member of the Church he would be expected to marry a lady of the same faith. And their children would be Papists, just as Henry's two sons and daughter by Gabrielle d'Estrées had been baptized in Roman ceremonies so glittering they were reminiscent of the pagan rites of the ancients.

Philippe realized he had good cause to be grateful to the Almighty for sparing him such an ordeal. The thought of rearing his own children as Papists was intolerable, and he was relieved beyond measure that he would never be forced to live with the dilemma. He went quickly to the bedchamber he was occupying until he and Louise could sleep together again, and closed the door behind him.

Bowing his head, he silently offered a prayer of thanks to God for giving him a Calvinist son.

Philippe-Emmanuel de Mercoeur, Duke of Brittany and through his wife heir-presumptive to the duchy of Luxembourg, was already so wealthy that the thought of increasing his financial holdings had no appeal. He was haughty, lazy and set in his opinions, all of them unfavorable to the regime, but even Montmorency paid him grudging respect. Mercoeur had proved himself the most able and courageous of the Catholic Legion's leaders during the civil wars, and frequently had disregarded his personal safety to ride into battle at the head of his cavalry.

He had been the last of the great Catholic lords to swear allegiance to Henry of Navarre, and the Huguenots still mistrusted him. For one thing, he was the brother of the Dowager Queen Louise Anne, whose sons had succeeded each other on the throne of France during its most turbulent years as Francis II, Charles IX and Henry III. Even more significant was the fact, denied at the miniature court Mercoeur maintained at his ducal capital, Nantes, that he kept his own personal envoy, a monsignor who had once been his confessor, at Vatican Hill. The King's efficient espionage service not only knew that the monsignor lived inside Vatican Hill itself, but frequently intercepted Mercoeur's messages and quietly copied them before allowing the couriers to proceed on their way.

Philippe, riding through the streets of Nantes toward the ducal castle, had never been given a less welcome assignment. His son, now miraculously blossoming into as beautiful a baby as Louise believed him to be, was only six days old, and the proud father wanted to be in Paris with his wife and child. What was more, he thought the trip a waste of time. Mercoeur wasn't the sort who would respond to either blandishments or bluff, and Henry should have come here himself to force Mercoeur's acceptance of the Huguenot decrees.

The small party of archers clattered across one of the many bridges built over the rivers that formed the estuary of the Loire River, and approached the island that formed the heart of Nantes. Six calavry outriders who formed the advance guard wielded the flats of their swords dexterously, scattering pedestrians without causing injury to anyone except a boy of about thirteen, who insolently refused to get out of the company's path and was given a lump on his head for his boldness.

There were few visitors to Nantes from Paris, and housewives leaned out of their windows and crowded onto balconies overhanging the narrow streets. Men emerged from shops, fish-drying shacks and the new factories that made soap from fish-oil, established with royal funds over the Duke's violent protests. According to Montmorency, who had visited Nantes when Mercoeur had capitulated to Henry, there were only two inns in the town that served edible food. The patrons of both establishments came to the entrances and spilled out onto the cobbled streets to watch the procession, too. Judging by their appearance, one group was made up almost exclusively of ships' masters and officers engaged in the trade that Henry was encouraging with the natives of the New World; the others were identified as members of the tiny but influential merchant class by their ornate cloaks and doublets, fur-trimmed in spite of the balmy April weather.

Virtually no one recognized the pennants being carried by Phillippe's personal standard-bearer. He would have been surprised had anyone in Brittany known the de Montauban crest, but it was astonishing that men should stare blankly at the banner emblazoned with the official insignia of the royal Chancellor, a flaming torch guarded by a crouching lion. Loyalty to the Crown was not encouraged in the duchy of Philippe-Emmanuel de Mercoeur.

Philippe sighed quietly, and Fontaine, riding beside him, ventured an observation. "The stench in this place is ghastly, milord."

"Unbearable," Philippe replied, but refrained from pressing a scented handkerchief to his nose, a practice that men who had lived in the field with Henry of Navarre believed effeminate.

"The Bretons are a filthy people."

"They're no worse than anyone else." Philippe half-stood in his saddle as he made a broad gesture. "Look about you, Fontaine. Nantes must be made up of as many islands as Amsterdam. Or Venice, although I've never been there and have no desire to go. People use these little branches of the river to carry away their garbage, and when the Loire happens to be trifle sluggish, they pay the consequences."

"They don't seem to notice," the equerry declared.

Philippe smiled sourly. "This isn't the most enlightened of towns, you know. It's been under Papist influence so long and so completely that its citizens live in almost total ignorance. Do you see the cathedral up ahead?"

"A new building, milord?"

"Hardly. Sully tells me it was built more than four hundred and fifty years ago, but no one has ever bothered to complete it."

"That doesn't sound like pious Papists, milord."

"They're required to offer greater devotions to their dukes than to the Holy Trinity. What's the most impressive sight you see, anywhere in the town?"

"The castle that stands between the cathedral and the main body of the river, milord!"

"Precisely. The dukes of Brittany look after themselves. Montmorency tells me that Mercoeur added those four big turrets when he was contemplating standing off a Huguenot siege."

"I wish to God," the knight said fervently, "that he had tried to oppose us in the field. We'd have been rid of the bastard."

"No," Philippe said, "it's far better that he bent his knee to the King without making a stand. The Bretons might have regarded him as a hero if he'd challenged the strength of a ruler who had united all the rest of France. Mercoeur could have caused us trouble for years if he'd shown a little moral as well as physical valor."

The equerry agreed, but reluctantly.

"That's our biggest problem right now. If he refuses to accept the Huguenot decrees, lesser Catholic lords who have been afraid to express their real feelings will rally to him. Mayenne's refusal to oppose Henry destroyed the will to fight of the Catholic moderates, and a great many others have been waiting for the Pope to express himself—which he won't."

"I can't understand why he hasn't acted, milord."

"The King," Philippe said with a grin, "has sent him a number of private messages through one source and another, all of them saying the same thing, in different ways. And Clement is a wise man. He prefers a half-loaf of bread to starvation." His smile faded. "You've been a soldier, Fontaine. Is that castle as impregnable as it looks?"

"No, milord!" the equerry said emphatically. "As recently as twenty-five years ago it might have held out for months, even years, in a siege. But the Constable's new technique of mixing grape and other small shot—including high explosives—with the concentrates of tar used in Greek fire will cause any defending force to surrender in a very short time. It was the combination of exploding metal and intense fire in our artillery bombardments that forced the Spaniards to give up Amiens, and those troops were professionals accustomed to every hardship of battle. Even if the Bretons are as ferocious as they like to think themselves, and no people could be that brave, a few catapult shots into those towers would melt everyone inside them as effectively as a burning wick melts tallow."

"I wonder," Philippe said, speaking as much to himself as to his aide, "whether Mercoeur realizes he's that vulnerable to our artillery."

"He must, milord. Three of his colonels served as observers on de Brissac's staff at Amiens."

"We'll soon find out," Philippe replied as they followed the cavalrymen toward the lowered drawbridge of the huge castle.

A company of pikemen trotted out of the stone guardhouse on the inner side of the moat and formed a solid line across the drawbridge. At a command from an officer they raised their steel-tipped weapons, and the Chancellor's escort was forced to halt.

Philippe immediately rode forward through the ranks of his own men, Fontaine close beside him. He was positive in his own mind that the gesture was a deliberately calculated insult. Even if no one else in Nantes recognized his insignia, it was the duty of nobles on Mercoeur's staff—who had undoubtedly been watching his approach from the ramparts—to know every crest and distinguishing pennant in the country.

"Why do you bar me?" he demanded.

The officer, a dark-skinned man with black eyes, regarded him insolently. "His Grace of Brittany admits no one who seeks shelter here until the visitor has identified himself."

Philippe had no intention of submitting to petty humiliations, and was tired, dusty and hungry, which did not improve his mood. But he kept his temper, and said quietly to his standard bearer, who was directly behind him, "Unfurl the royal ensign."

The page hoisted the banner of gold lilies on a white field, and the pikemen eyed it uneasily.

"In the name of your liege, Henry of France and Navarre," Philippe thundered, "withdraw these men instantly or stand liable for prosecution on grounds of treason!"

"If you please, milord," the officer stammered, "I'm just obeying orders."

"Fontaine," Philippe said in a clear voice, "take the wretch's name. I'll sign the order for his arrest and removal to Paris after I've taken care of more pressing considerations."

The officer hastily disbanded the company of pikemen and fled into the castle.

Philippe and his party moved forward, slowly, and the equerry reached for his sword.

"No signs of force, if you please," Philippe whispered. "They'd love to make the excuse that we started a brawl."

Fontaine nodded, and fell a half-pace behind as they drew up at the main gate of the castle, where a nobleman in silks stood with one hand resting on the hilt of a long sword. "Antoine de Vedelle," the man said, but did not bow.

Philippe knew that Baron de Vedelle was one of Mercoeur's principal supporters, and a former stalwart in the infantry of the Catholic Legion. Studied insults had to be returned in kind, so Philippe dismounted and did not bother to introduce himself. "See to it," he directed curtly, "that suitable quarters are assigned to my men, and have our horses given the best of treatment in the stables. As for me, provide me with a guide who will take me at once to the Duke."

If Baron de Vedelle had any thoughts of using delaying tactics, Philippe's imperious air changed them. "I'll take you to him myself, lord Chancellor," he said, thus admitting that Philippe's identity was known. He gave rapid orders to several knights in the shadows behind him, and they busily began to provide the necessary hospitality for the party.

Philippe's men were anxious to accompany him, but he indicated with a faint frown that he wanted strict compliance with his wishes, and only Fontaine walked beside him as he followed Vedelle down a corridor and up a flight of worn stone stairs to the great hall of the castle.

More than three stories high, the hall appeared at first glance to have been carved out of a single block of hard, gray stone. The walls near the entrance to the chamber were bare, and a few rushes were scattered on the floor, a custom no longer considered civilized in other parts of the country.

But the far end of the great hall more nearly resembled a royal throne room. Superb tapestries concealed the stone walls, and splendid Ottoman rugs woven in Constantinople yielded gently to the pressure of the visitors' boots. Scores of the most expensive, smokeless tapers provided illumination, although it was mid-afternoon, and fifty or more servants lined the walls, all of them stiffly erect in green and yellow livery, the colors of Brittany when it had been an independent duchy and now, theoretically, banned.

The most astonishing spectacle was a raised dais at the extreme far end of the great hall. On it were two green and yellow thrones, and seated on one, silently watching the approach of his visitors, sat Philippe-Emmanuel de Mercoeur, with a large group of his nobles gathered on either side of the dais.

The Duke had acquired a reputation as the most handsome, dashing gentleman in Europe, and lived up to the role. The sable collar above his steel corselet matched his eyes and long, carefully arranged hair; his suit of cream-colored silk, which was studded with diamonds and pearls, emphasized his height and muscular frame; his calf-high boots of soft leather were decorated with tassels of ermine-tails, a fur specifically reserved for royalty.

He leaned on one elbow, his face expressionless, and the members of his court, obviously under instructions, neither moved nor spoke.

Mercoeur's rudeness was doubly insulting. Any host, if his rank was below that of a reigning monarch, was expected to rise and come forward to greet a noble guest. Even more significant, a member of Henry's Council was entitled to be received with honors only slightly less elaborate than those that would be accorded the King himself. Philippe was prepared, however, after the incident at the drawbridge, and knew the best defense was a swift attack.

He deliberately refrained from bowing or removing his hat, courtesies to which a man of the Duke's rank was entitled, and as he approached the dais he said in a voice that every courtier in the great hall could hear, "I'm overwhelmed by the warmth of your reception."

Mercoeur remained wooden-faced. "What brings you here?" he demanded.

"The Lord High Chancellor of France and Navarre," Philippe replied in an even tone, "is in Nantes as the official representative of the King, to whom everyone in this hall has sworn fealty." He mounted the dais and stood near the Duchess de Mercoeur's empty throne.

His boldness and refusal to compromise made it unnecessary to spell out the threat. The Breton nobles had no desire to incur the wrath of the King, who pursued his enemies relentlessly, and one by one they uncovered their heads, knelt and did not rise until Philippe, watching them with grim calm, gave them a signal.

Only Mercoeur himself made no gesture of compromise or amicability, and kept his seat.

On sudden impulse Philippe seated himself in the empty throne of the Duchess de Mercoeur, and pretended not to hear the courtiers' gasps.

Fontaine hesitated for no more than an instant, then followed Philippe to the dais and took his place at the far side of the throne. It was almost impossible for him to resist the temptation of drawing his sword, but he could feel the Chancellor's disapproval, and had to content himself with placing one hand on the hilt of his blade.

"King Henry," Philippe told the Duke, "has directed me to confer with you in private on a matter of importance to the entire nation."

"I keep no secrets from my friends." Mercoeur had the feeling he was being outmaneuvered, and didn't like the sensation.

"Very well. I shall speak as candidly in their presence as I would if we were alone. A few days ago you received copies of a set of decrees that will be issued this spring."

70

"I've been familiar with their contents for weeks, and I disapprove of them."

"Your approval isn't being sought," Philippe declared. "The King directs. His subjects obey. You're his subject."

"Suppose my conscience forbids me to obey?" Mercoeur asked, trying to match Philippe's quiet tone but inadvertently blustering.

"It isn't my place to offer you advice on how you should reconcile yourself to your sworn duty." Philippe looked at the uneasy noblemen, and gestured in the direction of a middle-aged gentleman whose robes identified him as a bishop. "I suspect that His Grace, who has undoubtedly had a great deal of experience in dealing with such problems in his diocese, is better able to counsel you."

The Bishop of Nantes had no desire to be drawn into the controversy. "His Holiness has taken no official position on the matter of the Huguenot decrees, milord Chancellor," he said quickly. "Unless he does, I wouldn't take responsibility for advising any man to defy the King's will."

"Very wise, Your Grace." Philippe smiled, but his eyes remained cold. "Everyone is entitled to speculate as he pleases, of course. It's my opinion that Pope Clement will make no attempt to interfere in a matter beyond his jurisdiction. The relations of the French state with the King's Protestant subjects are not Vatican Hill's concern."

"I've made them mine," Mercoeur said.

"If I send a messenger to King Henry today, telling him you refuse to accept his decrees, the Constable will march on Nantes with fifty thousand men."

"And if I detain you here so you can't send off a courier?"

It had not occurred to Philippe that the Duke might be ready to go so far in his intransigence. Perhaps he was only bluffing; there was only one way to find out, no matter what the personal risks involved. "In that event, one hundred thousand will march with the Constable, and every building in Nantes, including this castle, will be demolished."

The Duke smirked, but the first uneasy sign of doubt flickered for a moment in his eyes.

"Anyone who takes up arms on your behalf," Philippe continued, "will be treated as a traitor. As for you," he said, rudely jabbing a forefinger at Mercoeur, "I offer you a personal guarantee in the presence of these witnesses that your titles will be forfeited, your lands and property will be confiscated by the Crown, and you yourself will be hanged in the rubble of your own courtyard."

No one had ever dared to treat the first lord of Brittany with such brutal contempt, and the nobles stared in fascination at their pale-faced Duke, expecting him to fly into a rage.

But Philippe had no intention of yielding to another speaker.

"Milords, King Henry wants peace within his borders. You should know it better than most. Every last one of you has received his forgiveness for bearing arms against him. If you'll look at your pardons, you'll see they carry my signature and seal as well as his. I prepared them, and I assure you they weren't issued lightly. Anyone who breaks the peace will be executed. There will be no exceptions, and no one will be given still another chance. If it proves necessary for the King to set an example by sending one of the highest nobles in his realm to the gibbet, he lacks neither the courage nor the will to do it."

Mercoeur thought it best to temporize. "I'll need time to consider this situation."

"What you mean is that you want time to rally an army." Philippe shook his head. He had come to Nantes prepared to negotiate and, if necessary, give ground in several of the decrees, but he realized that any concessions he might make now would be regarded as signs of weakness. There appeared to be only one language the Duke understood. Hating theatrical gestures, which he regarded as lawyers' tricks, he nevertheless felt this was the appropriate moment to use one. "Philippe-Emmanuel de Mercoeur," he said, speaking in a resonant voice that echoed against the walls of the great hall, "do you agree to accept and uphold the Huguenot decrees of your liege lord?"

There was long, tense silence.

Philippe's manner was still unyielding, but he felt qualms he didn't dare display. Henry, as he well knew, would be extremely reluctant to use arms in order to force Mercoeur's obedience. The intricate negotiations and meetings of recent weeks had been conducted for only one purpose, the peaceful acceptance of the new laws by the Catholic majority. He held his breath as he awaited a reply.

It was not easy for a proud man to bow his head, but Mercoeur had the grace to admit defeat when he was backed into a corner from which there was no escape. "When a civilized man is threatened with annihilation, he does what he must to preserve the lives and property of his people, which are more important to him than anything else in this world. I accept the King's orders, milord Chancellor." It was the first time he had addressed Philippe by title since the interview had begun.

"Then our business with each other is concluded." Philippe stood and descended from the dais.

"So it is." The Duke belatedly remembered his manners. "Now let us relax together." He beckoned a servant. "Bring us a jar of wine from my private cellar."

Philippe had never been intentionally rude to any gentleman, but he could not accept Mercoeur's hospitality. "I'm not thirsty," he said.

72

"Fontaine, assemble my escort. We'll repair to an inn and wait there for a reply to the message I'll send to His Majesty this afternoon."

Mercoeur was distressed, knowing his reputation as a host would be damaged at every court in Europe. "I beg you to reconsider, milord Count. I can't permit a man of your standing to sleep at an inn fit only to receive common folk. Please don't interpret a stand based on my principles as a personal insult to you."

"No other interpretation is possible," Philippe said, releasing his own anger. "You'll do anything in your power to prevent Calvinists from acquiring the rights they deserve as subjects of France. I, milord Duke, am a Calvinist, and I can't break bread or drink wine at the table of a man who is being prevented by sheer force alone from plunging this country into another bloody religious war." He started toward the far end of the great hall, then stopped as another thought occurred to him. "Jesus Christ, for whose sake you profess to suppress Huguenots, offered food and drink to all men without inquiring first whether they believed in Him or in what way they believed."

Twenty-six thousand of Henry's best troops were stationed in or near Paris, and when the King read Philippe de Montauban's long report he ordered half of the regiments to prepare immediately for a march into Brittany. He had no intention of making war on a recalcitrant subject, however, and made it plain that the expedition was for purposes of celebration. All of the great lords and ladies of the realm were invited to accompany him, and only Louise de Montauban, who was taking her first tentative steps after leaving her bed following the birth of her child, was compelled for reasons of health to decline.

All the cardinals in the French hierarchy were asked to make the journey, too, and were urged to bring their entire retinues with them. Cardinal de Bourbon, hoping his kinship with the King would exempt him, pleaded old age and illness, but Henry thoughtfully provided him with a comfortable royal carriage and assigned a royal physician to attend him. Arnaud Cardinal d'Ossat, Bishop of Rennes, thought of making a journey to Rome instead, but changed his mind when General de Brissac, who brought him the invitation, expressed the certainty that Henry would be grievously disappointed if His Eminence weren't on hand to enjoy the festivities. Cardinal d'Ossat had no wish to disappoint the King, and neither did Cardinal de Gonde or the other three princes of the Church, who resigned themselves to the inevitable.

The Constable rode in battle armor at the head of the column of troops, which was his privilege, but the other nobles wore soft hats instead of helmets and carried no weapons except their smallswords.

Biron, Villars and the other Huguenot leaders tried to make themselves inconspicious in the assemblage, and only Sully traveled with his own staff of chefs and fourteen carts laden with delicacies that had become essential to his happiness.

It was not accidental that the gentlemen who made up the King's personal guard of honor were Roman Catholics, led by Mayenne.

The column reached Nantes on May 4, 1598, and Philippe de Montauban rode out to meet his monarch. Everyone waited while they conferred privately for a quarter of an hour, and then Henry gave the surprising order to pitch the silken pavilions and tents of the company in the wheat fields beyond the town walls.

The mortified Mercoeur arrived while servants were raising the tents, and begged for the privilege of housing the King and the more distinguished of the company under his roof. But Henry told him, "There are too many of us, even for your castle, and the great men are so numerous that some would be forced to remain behind. They'd be insulted, and you'd make enemies, so I'm thinking of you, Mercoeur. You simply can't afford new foes."

Apparently relenting later in the day, however, the King agreed that he and all of the ladies and gentlemen would dine at the castle the next day, following a brief ceremony he intended to conduct in the courtyard.

At noon on May 5th the King rode into Nantes behind two companies of household cavalry, surrounded by his Catholic nobles and attended by all five cardinals and eight bishops. Places had already been assigned in the courtyard to most of those who had come with the King from Paris, and everyone stood under a hot sun waiting for Henry to appear.

The members of his personal staff had brought his throne with them from Paris and had placed it on a platform in the center of the courtyard. Made by carpenters since his coronation, it was a faithful copy of the eighth-century throne used by Charles the Great when he had been crowned Emperor of the West. It was upholstered in the customary purple velvet, a cloth and color so easy to produce in the new textile factories that a special royal decree had been issued prohibiting its manufacture for anyone except Henry and his immediate family. The platform itself was covered with a rug of ermine.

The Constable followed the King onto the platform and took up his usual place at Henry's right. Both were somberly dressed in doublets, breeches and hose of dark silk, and Montmorency wore the diamond sunburst that was his badge of office. Henry, as always, had not bothered with decorations.

There was a slight delay as several servants and equerries tried to hoist Mayenne onto the platform, too, and the dignity of the occasion was temporarily marred when the King and his Constable gave their hands to the Duke and pulled him up beside them. He was unruffled, and appeared completely poised as he moved to the left of the throne and tugged his bright blue doublet into place, smoothed the watered silk ribbon of the sash of Lorraine that swept down across his bulging stomach and, suddenly aware that his plumed hat had been knocked askew, straightened it.

Philippe stood at the rear of the crowd beside de Brissac, and neither called attention to himself. Sully, Biron and Villars soberly attired, were equally unassuming in manner. Their work was done, and this was not an occasion to exult.

A young officer of household cavalry who happened to be a cousin of Gabrielle d'Estrées raised the lily standard of the King on a pole behind the platform, and a squad of trumpeters played a flourish that rang through the courtyard and echoed against the massive walls of the castle. The crowd immediately became silent, and no one moved.

Henry stood, and took his time as he looked at the throng. His gaze lingered for a few moments on the cardinals gathered directly in front of the platform, and he seemed particularly interested in the three young dukes of the de Guise family. He nodded to his cousin, Louis de Bourbon, who had just returned from a sojourn at Vatican Hill in order to claim his inheritance, the duchy of Orléans, and to be invested as premier duke of the realm.

There was a faint but distinct stir as the King, face hardening, stared at Philippe-Emmanuel de Mercoeur, who finally gazed down at his diamond-buckled shoes.

Then, very calmly, Henry began to speak. "We have chosen this time and place to make known our will to you, our faithful servants and deputies, and to command your obedience to it. We hereby publish an edict that, from this day forward, becomes the inviolable law of France." Resuming his seat, he began to read the Huguenot decrees that Philippe had worked so hard to prepare.

The significance was lost on no one. Henry could have issued the edict from the Louvre, as he did most decrees, and certainly there had been no need for him to make a six-day journey to Nantes accompanied by a huge entourage. But he had elected to dramatize the granting of religious freedoms to Calvinists by announcing his edict in the provincial capital of the man most bitterly opposed to his reforms. The warning to Mercoeur—and to all who shared his views—was explicit.

Most of the higher nobles and Churchmen were already familiar with at least the substance of the decrees, and their reading was accepted in resigned, almost sepulchral silence. The cardinals and other bishops exercised self-discipline and were stony-faced. Mayenne, whose reactions could be seen by everyone, set an example for the Catholic lords in general and his de Guise relatives in particular by gazing unblinkingly at a fixed point on the farthest tower of the castle. Mercoeur, who had already caused himself enough damage, kept his head down so no one could see his face.

Only the new Duke of Orléans, who might be in a position to claim the throne if Henry sired no legitimate children, was foolhardy enough to indicate by a subtle squaring of his shoulders and tightness around the mouth that he disapproved of the decrees. None of the Catholic peers dared to indicate they agreed with the Duke, however. They knew that Henry planned to marry when he found a queen he considered worthy of becoming his consort, and it was no secret that he had been shopping in the royal courts of the Continent for a year. He had added fuel to the fires of speculation, too, by telling numerous visitors that he hadn't spent his adult life fighting for the throne in order to hand it down to a kinsman unfit to reign. "No one but my own son," he had said repeatedly, "will rule France."

At last the King completed the reading of the decrees. Mayenne handed him a jar of ink, a quill and a dish of sand. No one had remembered to provide a table for the ceremony, and rather than wait for one to be fetched, Henry balanced the ink and sand on one knee and used the other as a desk. The Constable heated a small cylinder of purple wax over a taper, twice burning his fingers as he performed the unfamiliar task, and Henry sealed the document with his signet ring.

The Edict of Nantes was now incorporated into the basic law of France, and the Huguenot minority could worship openly.

Some of the younger nobles who were anxious to win the King's favor applauded, and everyone else half-heartedly followed their example. The Calvinists, however, deliberately refrained from displaying elation.

Henry descended from the platform, the Constable at his heels, and both of them turned to help the panting Mayenne. All three led the way into the great hall, where Mercoeur's chefs were waiting to serve a fifteen-course meal to approximately four hundred guests. Mercoeur saw Henry, Montmorency and Mayenne to their places at the head table before taking his own beside them, and they were joined by the other dukes and the cardinals.

Others were seated strictly according to protocol, and no special recognition was granted members of the Council or high-ranking military officers who had not been given duchies. Philippe found himself at the fourth table, where other counts were also seated, but was not in the least concerned that the author of the decrees should receive no honors for his labors. It was enough that he had succeeded, that the edict had been issued without causing fresh violence, and that members of both Catholic and Calvinist factions were eating a meal together.

There were no speeches, but Cardinal de Bourbon offered the Lord's Prayer, and everyone present bowed his head. Then Henry said something to Montmorency, and the Constable stood. There were very few Huguenot clergymen in France, and not one pastor was present in the great hall, so the Constable, as the senior Protestant noble of the realm, also intoned the Lord's Prayer, taking care to enunciate clearly when he came to that portion which the Calvinists had added to the Catholic version: *"For Thine is the kingdom, and the power, and the glory, for ever."*

Those thirteen words, Philippe thought, were the most significant ever spoken at a formal royal gathering in France, and perhaps in all of Europe since Martin Luther had posted his Ninety-five Theses on the door of the castle church at Wittenberg in 1517. Total equality for Protestants had not yet been achieved, and there were other reforms that needed to be pressed in the years ahead, but for all practical purposes the Reformation had taken legal root in France and the Huguenots had won a lasting victory.

For an instant, as Philippe raised his wine cup, he caught Henry's eye, and the King lifted his own goblet to his lips. Together they had achieved a feat that, only six years earlier, no man would have considered possible of achievement. Now, and for all time, religious freedom would endure in France.

Louise de Montauban awaited her husband in their private sitting room on the second floor of their Paris house, since it would have been unseemly to exchange a warm greeting in the presence of Philippe's staff members, the troops of his escort or their servants. She had regained her lithe figure, which she was pleased to show off to him in a form-fitting gown of white silk, and she looked ravishing as she stood in the center of the room, her hands at her sides.

Philippe threw aside his riding crop and cloak, let his swordbelt fall to the floor after unbuckling it and went to his wife. They embraced hungrily, and then Philippe released Louise with a somewhat apologetic laugh. "You're wearing a new gown, and I'll ruin it. I'm still covered with the dust of the road."

"Does it matter?" She continued to smile, but was studying him carefully. "You look tired."

"I don't recommend Brittany for a holiday," he said dryly.

"Did everything go as you hoped it would?"

"Better. The joints in Mercoeur's nose are still tender, but he's been tamed. He's lost his chance to fight, and the Breton nobles won't go to war over the edict."

"The King issued it?"

Philippe nodded proudly. "Five thousand copies are being printed and posted in every township in the country. And it will be read from the pulpit at High Mass in the churches this coming Sunday."

"Won't that be likely to stir up trouble?"

"Henry," he said simply, "has ordered it read." That disposed of the question. "Anyone who didn't know you would think you're a bride, not a mother."

"I'm a mother," Louise said, "and I've never been happier in all my life."

They beamed at each other. "Your last letter reached me at Tours," he said. "The baby is still well?"

"You won't know him!" She led the way into their bedchamber, where a wooden bowl of steaming water and scented towels awaited him. "I'll send for him the moment you're ready."

Philippe washed quickly but thoroughly, and changed from his doublet into a loose-fitting silk shirt, one of Louise's thoughtful gifts to him that he privately considered an extravagance. "Did you get the letter I wrote you the night before the edict was signed?"

"The one in which you said you want to name the baby after the King? It came four days ago."

"And you agree?"

"Of course, dear. Henry de Montauban. It has a good, clear ring."

"The King will be pleased, naturally."

"We must ask him to become the baby's godfather."

Philippe paused, a hairbrush of enameled porcupine quills in one hand, and faint frown lines appeared between his eyes. "I don't want to embarrass him. He might be criticized for attending a Huguenot ceremony, even a private one in Montmorency's palace. Of course, now I have the right to build my own chapel here in the house, but that will take a little time. On the other hand, there's no real rush. A christening ceremony for infants isn't that important in our theology."

Louise looked bewildered. "I don't know much about the rules in these matters, but I very much doubt that a second christening ceremony will be permitted. After all, baptism is a sacrament."

"So is marriage, and we had two weddings on the same day."

"Baptism is different. Actually, I've discussed it with Father d'Arcy, and although he hasn't gone to Uncle Florent for a final ruling, he's positive the Church won't tolerate two baptismal ceremonies."

"Uncle Florent," Philippe said with a grin, "may go to Hades—and take Father d'Arcy with him."

Louise made no reply, and her mouth became set.

He studied her more carefully and his grin vanished. "If there must be a choice, my son will either be baptized as a Huguenot or won't be baptized at all. We can wait until he's thirteen or fourteen, old enough to make his own confirmation of faith and confession before men. Some of our pastors prefer it that way, after a boy has studied theology and understands his beliefs in a combination of faith and reason. Calvin himself often favored that approach."

Louise returned his stare. "In the Holy Roman Church, a baby must be baptized. There's no alternative, no excuse. My son will be baptized at Notre-Dame. I'd prefer a public ceremony, but I'm willing to be amenable if you'd rather we hold it privately. I'd like Uncle Florent to officiate, but I know what you think of him, so I wouldn't feel in the least hurt if you perfer Cardinal d'Ossat. Father d'Arcy tells me he's going to be in Paris for several weeks, and I've often heard you say you admire him."

"I've said I think he's as clever as a Jesuit." Philippe's voice was harsh. "That's not the same as admiring him."

"I'm trying to be reasonable, dear. What more can I do to comply with your wishes?"

He tried in vain to keep his voice down. "Are you trying to tell me you want to rear our child as a Papist?"

"I must! I'd be guilty of sin if I didn't! Even Uncle Florent's influence couldn't save me, and I might be excommunicated." Louise shuddered. "The thought of spending all eternity in Hell is unbearable."

A cold chill moved very slowly up Philippe's spine, and he began to perspire at the same time. "It has never occurred to me that our children might become Catholics."

"It's never crossed my mind they wouldn't. I—I'd be denying the essence of my faith in God if I allowed them to become anything else."

"One of us must be mad." Philippe said. "Do you think I could allow my own son to deny the validity of everything I've worked to achieve?"

Louise would not allow herself to back down. "You've won your battle and may worship as you please in public. Now grant our child the same freedom."

"Damnation, that's sophistry! If he's baptized as a Catholic when he's only a few months old, and if he's indoctrinated in Catholicism from earliest childhood, what choice will he have?"

"His choice is that of eternal salvation or the damnation you just mentioned." There was a tremor in Louise's voice, but she gripped a bedpost to steady herself and continued to stand erect. "I swore before God that I would obey you when I became your wife, and I've kept my vow. But if you put me in a position of denying our Lord, I can't heed your orders. You're my earthly master, but my first duty is to Him."

"Do you mean," Philippe asked incredulously, "that you'd defy my command to postpone the boy's christening until he's old enough to submit himself to a pastor's examination?"

"I mean, milord, that a priest of the Holy Roman Church will baptize our son in the one true faith. If you command otherwise, I must disobey you. I've never lied to you, but in this I would. If it were necessary to have the sacrament performed in secret, without your knowledge, I'd have it done. For the sake of our son's immortal soul—and my own—I will do whatever is required of me. The will of our Father, His only begotten Son and the Holy Spirit must and shall be done on earth as well as in heaven." She bowed her head and, murmuring an inaudible prayer, crossed herself.

Her intransigence, as stubborn as it was unexpected, numbed Philippe. His wife's insistence that their child be baptized and reared as a Papist sickened him, but he was helpless, unable to enforce his own desires. It was within his rights as a husband to send Louise to his manor house at Montauban and have her kept under constant guard there, but it would be impossible to keep the act secret. Sooner or later the news would become public, and so would his reasons for sending her away.

Her relatives would become furious and, from their point of view, with justification. Cardinal de Gonde was shrewd enough to make a national issue of the matter, and other Catholic prelates would be quick to see and seize the advantages of attacking him, too. The Chancellor of France, author of the Huguenot decrees, was in a vulnerable position, and through him the whole foundation of the Edict of Nantes could be assaulted by the Papist majority. Even the King would find it difficult to defend a man who put away a lovely wife because of her devotion to her faith.

Therefore Philippe could preserve the freedom of his son to elect Calvinism as his religion in later life only by endangering the precarious base of peace on which the Edict of Nantes rested.

"I salute your cunning, madame," he said bitterly. "Have the boy baptized at Notre-Dame, but don't expect me to attend the ceremony. I congratulate you on your victory."

Louise began to weep, and buried her face in her hands.

Philippe turned and rushed out of the chamber before he lost his temper completely and said things he might regret. Louise was still his wife, and they would have to live together, as best they could, in a new atmosphere of mutual suspicion and uneasiness and hostility.

Servants who saw the Count's dark face cleared out of his way as he stamped down to the dining hall and, completely contrary to his habits, poured himself a goblet of brandywine.

His mistake, Philippe thought, had been basic. He had been wrong to let himself fall in love with a Papist, wrong to marry her. His conviction that she was open-minded, even tolerant on the subject of an individual's faith was an illusion. And his private hell was compounded by the realization that he, in his own way, was as unyielding, as unwilling to compromise as Louise.

1600

The Hôtel Saint-Paul located in the eastern portion of Paris and consequently a considerable distance from the Louvre, had been the official residence of Charles VI, but had fallen into a state of ever-worsening disrepair after his death in 1422. Only someone as wealthy as the Constable of France could have afforded to restore the old palace, and Montmorency had given it a quiet grandeur that reflected his own modest tastes and those of his equally unpretentious duchess.

The tapestries that covered the walls were made of the finest weave of wool and silk, but the scenes they depicted were bucolic and, according to some guests, a trifle dull. The Ottoman rugs that covered the floors had been purchased for warmth rather than decoration, and were less expensive by far than those that graced the homes of mere barons. The problem, as the duchess sometimes explained, was that hundreds of tapestries and scores of rugs were needed in a palace the size of the Hôtel Saint-Paul, and the annual repair bills alone would have bankrupted a man of lesser means than the Constable.

Montmorency's private sanctum, from which he commanded the French army and navy, appeared at first glance to be as barren as the tent in which he slept when he lived in the field. His desk was plain, and lacked the leather top and gold scrollwork much in vogue, but close examination revealed that it had been fashioned by master craftsmen of matching panels of West Indian mahogany. His massive chair had been reinforced in hidden places to bear the weight of a strong, restless man, and so had the Spartan, unadorned visitors' chairs. The rug that covered the entire floor had no pattern, but was thick, and the heavy drapes that hung from two banks of windows were solid, light gray in color and made of the purest silk.

The wood in the fire that crackled in the hearth had been brought to Paris at considerable expense from the Huguenot inner citadel in southern France, as the Constable contended that the pines from his own forest lands gave off more heat than did those from other parts of the country. No one would have guessed, either, that the soot-blackened andirons were the only pair of their kind in existence, having been made of gold mixed with brass.

Montmorency took a silver jar from the mantel and poured two small cups of the Norman apple brandywine known as *calvados*. He handed one to his visitor, and both men drank carefully. Philippe de Montauban was particularly cautious, knowing that several hours of work still awaited him when he returned to his own office at the Louvre.

"We were very pleased to see Louise at Villars' dinner the other evening," the Constable said. "Both of us thought she looked particularly well."

Philippe saw no reason to be less than frank with his oldest friend. "We've reconciled our differences," he said. "Or, at least, we've declared a permanent truce. The strains were becoming intolerable, and with the new baby on the way, I felt I had to compromise. Even though," he added, trying unsuccessfully to stifle his bitterness, "it will mean another Papist in the family."

"I've had the same problem." Montmorency heaved himself into his chair, which creaked in protest. "Catholics, especially the women, are fanatics. They'd rather be burned at the stake than see their children reared in any other faith."

"So I discovered."

"A man who marries one of them is faced with a basic problem. Either he takes the children away from her in their early years, or he hands them over to her—and to her priests."

Philippe thought it odd that the Constable should be dwelling at such length on the matter. Surely there had been state business on his mind when he had sent a message to the Louvre, asking the Chancellor to call on him. He sometimes found it difficult to express his thoughts clearly, however, so it was best to let him develop them in his own way.

"Now that my sons are growing old enough to begin thinking for themselves, I'm trying to teach them something about Calvinism. But it isn't easy. If they're like my daughter, I'm wasting my breath. Only a few weeks ago she actually told me she was thinking of entering a nunnery. I refused to permit such insanity, of course, and whipped a little sense into her. But it gives you an idea of how completely the priests dominate children. Who was it said that bishops produce bigots?"

"I did, I'm afraid. At the time I didn't realize how true it is."

"You and I," Montmorency declared, "aren't the only ones to suffer." He stared gloomily out of the window at the cold rain pouring down onto the cobbled street outside the palace, and sighed heavily.

A wave of apprehension went through Philippe.

"The very worst thing that could have happened to France," the Constable said, "was Gabrielle d'Estrées death just before Easter last year, right on the heels of Henry's divorce from Marguerite. I had no love for Gabrielle and would have hated to see her become queen, but her death was a catastrophe."

Philippe was inclined to agree. "She was a harmless wench, and Henry seemed very fond of her. I certainly preferred her to the trollop he brought in to replace her. I may be mistaken, but I often feel that the d'Entragues woman would meddle in government affairs if she could."

"Forget her," Montmorency said. "She's interested only in money, and she'll quarrel with Henry as soon as he's given her enough to keep her in comfort for the rest of her days." The Constable pulled himself to his feet and walked to the windows, where he stood for a long time, gazing down into the street. "I wish," he said absently, "that there were some way of developing an oiled wool cloth. Sentries' cloaks are useless after a few hours of weather like this."

Philippe became impatient. "You haven't asked me here to talk about Henriette d'Entragues or sentries' cloaks."

Montmorency forced himself to leave the window and walked to the silver jar.

"No more *calvados* for me, thank you."

"I appreciated Gabrielle for a valid reason. Henry cared enough about her to postpone all thoughts of marriage while she still lived. Oh, he made the usual diplomatic inquiries, but he wasn't serious about taking a queen."

"What's happened?"

"He'll tell you officially at a Council meeting tomorrow. Until then, anything I say to you is confidential. He had a private talk with me after we inspected that new cannon foundry today. He doesn't quite know how to break the news to the Council. I sent for you, my friend, to see if we could find some way to stop him, but I'm afraid it's a lost cause."

Philippe mentally ran through a list of eligible princesses, and found no reason for alarm. The three Austrian archduchesses were harmless enough, and so were the daughters of the ruling electors of several German principalities. He felt confident that Henry would avoid Spanish infantas who were members of the immediate family of Philip II. Furthermore, Henry had made himself secure enough on the throne that there was no need for an alliance with the house of de Guise or other prominent French families.

"The contracts have been signed," Montmorency said. "He's going to marry Marie de Medicis."

Philippe felt as though someone had struck him a hard blow across the face. "On second thought, I believe I'll have that *calvados* after all."

The Constable refilled his cup, and they looked at each other bleakly. The de Medicis were the rulers of Tuscany, no family was more prominent in Catholic affairs, and it had been Catherine de Medicis, Marie's aunt, who had been Dowager Queen of France in 1572 and had been personally responsible for instigating the St. Bartholomew's Day Massacre of Huguenots.

The power of the de Medicis at Vatican Hill was enormous. Two of Marie's cousins had been popes, Clement VII and Leo X. Two of her uncles currently were cardinals and close advisers of Clement VIII, and three of her cousins were also cardinals. It was incredible that Henry of Navarre should take such a woman as his wife.

Philippe downed his drink in a single gulp. "Has he suddenly lost his wits?"

"He looked and sounded sane to me."

"Then, in God's name, why?"

"That's what I asked him. You know Henry and women. Clement sent him her miniature. It intrigued him, so that wily bastard in Rome sent him two more."

"No woman could be that beautiful. What can he be thinking? She's a de Medicis!"

Both men found themselves at the windows. "I'm not as clever as you," Montmorency said, "but Henry had answers to all my arguments. He told me this is a master stroke."

"What's his reasoning?" Philippe demanded.

"The marriage will satisfy every Catholic noble in France. Even Mercoeur will be pleased, so the silent opposition of the Papist lords to the Edict of Nantes will melt away."

Philippe tugged savagely at the chain of office around his neck.

"He's convinced that internal peace in France is assured for generations to come."

"Damn him, he's rationalizing. There's never been a de Medicis yet—man or woman—who has failed to stir up trouble. This marriage will give Vatican Hill a direct line of communication to the Louvre."

"I know," Montmorency said, clenching and opening his huge fists.

"If this is a purely political move," Philippe muttered, "there's at least the hope that we can persuade him to break the marriage contract, even if it strains relations with Clement for a time. How badly is Henry smitten?"

"He says," the Constable replied, "that he's fallen in love with her portraits, and that no woman has ever written more charming letters."

"All of them composed, I'm sure, by Clement's council of cardinals and bishops. But no matter. If Henry imagines himself in love with her, there's nothing we can do. Our cause is lost."

Montmorency brooded for a time. "The Papists almost deserve to win."

"I thought we had taken every possible precaution, but Vatican Hill has found the weak spot in our armor." Philippe raised his hands, then let them fall in a gesture of utter despair. "They'll wait a year—or ten—or fifty. They never change their goals. They lose battles, they lose campaigns, but they win every war."

"What can we do?"

"What we must. We'll try to hold Marie de Medicis' influence to a minimum while we work doubly hard to insure that the Edict of Nantes is being obeyed everywhere. I think I begin to understand how the Jews must feel. I know that God is on our side, but I wish He'd give us a few more positive demonstrations of His favor."

BOOK TWO

BOOK TWO

prologue—two

The base of a good onion soup," the Count said, dipping the ladle into the silver bowl, "is a beef stock that has simmered on the back of the stove for days."

"Not too much cheese in mine, please," the Bishop said. "It disagrees with me."

"The secret of ecumenism is equally simple," Philippe continued.

"Is it? You speak with the enthusiasm of Cardinal Bea."

"No, I'm a pessimist. The stock of desire for an understanding must simmer for a long time before the soup is really ready. And that's where you Catholics have made your greatest error. You've assumed that we've been anxious for a rapprochement. There are few genuine miracles, if any, that have been performed in this world——"

"Quite right. This soup is delicious."

"You astonish me, Charles. I thought all priests believe in miracles."

"I'll forgive your ignorance. God is capable of performing any miracle, as He pleases, of course. But I'm not prepared to say that if an individual has sufficient faith, he'll either witness, participate in or be the object of the miraculous."

"If I didn't know better, I'd suspect you were an apostate, Charles."

"Perhaps we should define the miraculous."

"Agreed. When Christ walked on water, if He did——"

"He did."

"That was a true miracle. Agreed?"

Bishop de Montauban nodded. "Where we may differ is on ground that too many non-Catholics misunderstand. My doctors pronounce me incurably ill, let's say. But my faith in God is so firm that I recover.

Philippe studied his soup spoon. "It would be my opinion that the doctors were mistaken in their original diagnosis."

"You're evading the issue. We must assume that the diagnosis was confirmed by X-rays and other clinical evidence."

"As a rational man, I would be forced to conclude that the evidence could not have been conclusive. But, according to your standards, a miracle would have occurred."

"It would not. That's my whole point," the Bishop said. "It would be another demonstration of the blessings that God bestows on those whose faith in Him is strong. No record has ever been kept of such events, but they happen every day."

"To Protestants as well as Catholics?"

"Your question is tricky, Philippe. I'm qualified to speak only of the Catholic's relationship with God."

"We're far more permissive than you. We say there are many paths to God. We prefer our own, because we believe it to be the most direct and true, naturally. But we're willing to admit that the Anglicans, for example, can find Him in their own way."

"A subtle cut, Philippe. And you accuse Rome of clinging to the past. Let me remind you that our attitude is no longer what it was at the time Henry VIII formed his own church. Judge Catholicism in today's light, not that of a past age. Your Calvinism has changed, too, you know."

"I accept the rebuke. But I still don't know what you consider miraculous."

"We read a report in the press that the wounds Christ received during the Passion and Crucifixion, appeared on a statue of Him in a small church located in a southern Italian village. The phenomenon was observed by twenty persons, including the local priest."

The Count stopped eating his soup and made a

derisive sound. "That, Charles, is where the Protestant and Catholic part company. And right there is one of the irrevocable splits that will make it impossible, for all time, to reunite all Christians under one roof."

"When I've read of such incidents," the Bishop said calmly, "I've considered them a manifestation of hysteria, nothing more."

Philippe de Montauban was astonished.

"The Church takes no official position on such so-called miracles. Those who wish to accept them are free to do so. Those who prefer to reject them, in toto, are equally free."

The Count had the last of his soup. "It may be that we aren't as far apart as I've always thought," he said at last.

book two

Denn alle Schuld rächt sich auf Erden.
(All guilt is avenged upon earth.)
—JOHANN WOLFGANG VON GOETHE

1618

Fresh snow, white and heavy, hid the slush, ice and frozen garbage that littered the cobbled streets of Paris. But it was pleasantly comfortable in the master bedchamber on the second floor of the de Montauban townhouse, where fires of knotty pine and aromatic spruce burned in both hearths. It was so warm, in fact, that the comforters had been thrown aside, and only a silk sheet remained. Louise de Montauban wore a thin, rather frivolous jacket embroidered with tiny pearls that had been a favorite for many years, and was engrossed in arranging a small table with legs six inches high on the center of the bed, between her and her husband.

Philippe, more somberly attired in a nightshirt of dark wool, watched her in morose silence as she ladled a clear soup into his bowl and fished several chunks of chicken from an earthenware pot that was still simmering. "Don't give me the leg," he said at last.

She ignored his protest. "You like it."

"I have no appetite any more." He passed a thin hand through his white hair.

"All the more reason for you to eat." Louise remained firm. "I had supper served up here so you'd relax and rest."

He stared gloomily into space. "I have no need for rest. I do nothing from one day to the next."

"Eat." She placed his bowl before him.

Philippe obediently picked it up and drank the broth, then took a piece of chicken and began to nibble at it.

"You've been brooding again."

"I suppose."

"You've mourned King Henry's death for eight years. That's seven too many."

"I become ill every time I think of him being cut down like a wild boar. Hanging was too good for that madman. What a joke on France, on the whole world. The one man capable of forcing people of every faith to live together." He dropped the bone into his bowl with a small splash, and absently reached for the silk sheet.

Louise anticipated him, and handed him a hot, damp square of linen, from which she hastily shook several crushed rose petals.

"The rest of us might as well have been killed, too. When I think of Sully in retirement on his estate, writing volume after volume of his memoirs, and Montmorency rotting away on his farm, not even allowed to visit Paris—"

"Every regime has a right to name its own ministers. You've said so yourself." She pulled a bell-rope at the head of the fourposter.

Philippe roused himself. "If Louis behaved like a king, I wouldn't mind. But he's no more the ruler of France than either of our sons. That damned Italian woman listens to no one but Bishop Richelieu, who spends his days—and probably his nights—conniving and scheming to win himself a red biretta. And King Louis, may the Lord forgive me for calling him by so exalted a title, is a minstrel's puppet in the hands of Cardinal de Rochefoucauld. Yes, and what does the Cardinal do? He fences with Richelieu and blocks his advancement."

"The doctors have told you not to get too excited."

"If I knew nothing of seventeen-year-old boys, I'd say that one of these days Louis will come into his own. But he won't. He's a slave to his own cardinal and his mother's bishop. My God, Louise, look at the difference between him and our sons. Charles is only a few months older than Louis, and he stands first in his law class at the Sorbonne. And Henry earned his secretaryship in the foreign ministry. No one at the Louvre hands free gifts to a de Montauban these days."

Two maidservants came into the room, and while one deftly removed the tureen and bowls, the other placed on the table slabs of rare beef, which rested on trenchers of bread.

Philippe paid no attention to their presence. "I swear to you, if Louis weren't King Henry's son, I'd be up in arms against him."

Louise nudged him.

He was too angry to heed her warning. "Not even in the days of the religious wars was France ruled by so many half-men in skirts. Rochefoucauld, Richelieu, Cardinal Aubert—all of them dance to Vatican Hill's tune. Thanks to Marie de Medicis, France is becoming nothing more than another Italian auxiliary of The Holy See."

The door closed behind the silent maidservants.

Philippe glowered at his wife. "Let them report me to the Louvre. It won't be the first time. And stop worrying. Not even Marie has the courage to throw Henry of Navarre's Chancellor into prison for saying what he believes."

"The meat will grow cold." Her expression and tone were resigned.

"Oh, sorry." He reached for his knife, which was hanging on the bedpost beside him, and holding the meat and bread with one hand, neatly sliced the food into small squares with the other. Then, before attacking his own dish, he gave Louise a smaller knife, which was blunter except for its lance-like point.

Louise quietly speared a chunk of meat and began to eat.

"All right, I was wrong," Philippe muttered. "Neither Rochefoucauld nor Richelieu will place any charges against an old fool who's going to die any day, but it won't do Henry and Charles any good. I honestly know better."

She pressed a bit of meat into a square of bread until the latter was soaked with juice, then ate them together. "I wish," she said, "that you'd stop speaking and thinking of dying. It does you no good."

He poured Bordeaux wine into two goblets, and drank a considerable quantity from his own before replying. "Physicians are as blind as kings' ministers and clergymen," he said with labored humor. "All of them are so convinced of man's immortality they can't see the truth under their noses." He paused, and made an attempt to smile. "Not a very good jest, was it? I don't know how you've stood me all these years."

Louise turned to him, tears in her eyes.

Philippe reached for her.

"You'll upset the table!"

"Damn the table!" He kissed her, and a little wine spilled over the lip of her overfull goblet.

She freed herself with difficulty, but the tears were gone.

"Nineteen or twenty years ago I wouldn't have thought it possible that you and I would be able to find so much satisfaction in living together," Philippe said. "Although I still resent it when Henry and Charles go off to confession."

"I know."

"They're circumspect, thanks to you. Your Papist fast days and feast days are cleverly disguised. And last winter, when Henry gave up brandywine until Easter, I wasn't fooled by his excuse of a distressed bile sac. That boy can eat more heartily than anyone I've ever seen. But I've been grateful for your diplomacy."

"I wonder if it would make you any happier to know I've come to agree with many of your views." Louise said. "I dare say that's what happens when a woman lives long enough with a man she admires and respects."

Philippe suddenly felt uncomfortable; her praise was rare.

"For years you preached that France would be in danger under a Catholic king. I couldn't agree. I was rearing my sons in my faith, and I thought Queen Marie had the same right. Perhaps there should be different rules for royalty. I—I honestly don't know. But when I see Rochefoucauld and his priests in power at the Louvre, and Bishop Richelieu and his priests traveling everywhere with Queen Marie, I know your predictions have come true."

Philippe anchored his knife in a thick chunk of unsliced beef.

"That wasn't easy to say. Thank you. What's more, you obviously believe it."

"Of course I do! It makes me ill when I think of the royal decree forbidding you to visit Montauban. I've never known anything so absurd."

He shook his head, and a hint of shrewdness appeared in his eyes. "If I were one of Louis' clerics, I'd do the same thing. Sully is content to live with his wealth. Montmorency must stay in the south and is barred from Paris. I'm a prisoner in Paris. The others have all been immobilized in one way or another. It's very clever—and damnably efficient."

"But why, Philippe?"

"An order like the Edict of Nantes doesn't guarantee a religious balance for all time. As long as King Henry lived, the country was safe. Now the Papists are greedy again——"

She tried to interrupt.

"No, hear me out. I've learned through the years, too. Most Catholics in this country—including the majority of the great nobles—are patriots. They put their love of France ahead of their worship of God."

"That couldn't be true!"

"But it is. Most men pay lip-service to the Almighty, no matter what their church. I've learned something else I might as well confess. I don't really believe Vatican Hill is pulling the strings for minstrel-puppets. Rome has been burned too often in this past century. The trouble lies with ambitious clergymen, like Bishop Richelieu. Rochefoucauld is a fool, and Richelieu knows it. With the help of a woman like Marie de Medicis, who was born a sly, conspiring Italian bitch, he's determined to rule France. He smells power, and there's no scent on earth more alluring."

Louise continued to eat her meal. "I still get confused. If Vatican Hill isn't responsible, why blame Richelieu just because he's a bishop?"

"For one thing, Rome won't be unhappy when there's a priest in control of France. They'd be rejoicing right now if Rochefoucauld weren't such a bumbling old ass. But even more important is that your priests are compelled by their vows to work against Huguenots. It's their duty to convert sinners and stamp out heresy." He pushed away the food. "Calvin is supposed to have said he doubted he'd meet one Papist in that part of the afterworld reserved for heretical sinners. It's an amusing idea, you know. It depends on whether the Almighty is Protestant or Catholic, I suppose."

"Philippe!"

He grinned wryly. "I won't offend you much longer. Personally, I

95

hope Calvin was wrong. In the unlikely event that there is an afterworld, and the even unlikelier one that a portion of it is reserved for Huguenots, I'd be very lonely if I had to spend all eternity not seeing you again." He covered her free hand with his.

"There were Ottoman fruits on sale at the market today. A convoy from Constantinople put in at Brest. So I've had a pomegranate and fig pudding made for you."

He sighed. "Later, perhaps. Puddings don't tempt me as they once did. Never fear, though. Our son Henry will eat my share as well as his, and if Charles brings home some of his University friends again this Sunday, there won't be a crumb left in the larder." He gripped her hand more firmly. "There's just one thing I ask of you."

"Of course."

"Wait until you hear it before you commit yourself. When I'm no longer—when Henry succeeds to the title, I want him to go to Montauban."

"Have you said anything to him?"

"Once or twice. He's a fine lad, and I couldn't ask for more in a son. But he's spent all his life in Paris, and he doesn't understand that a count has obligations to his people. I'd be in Montauban right now if those swine at the Louvre would give me a passport to leave the city."

"What did Henry say to you?"

"He was vague. And uncomfortable. He mumbled something about his duties at the palace and Aubert being a hard taskmaster. The boy's trouble is that he sees others—counts and dukes and even princes—who never visit their titular seats. It's this new generation's custom to stay close to the throne, apparently. They want to be nearby when Louis and his mother have another squabble, so they'll know which way to jump."

She knew he was right, and could only nod.

"But the people of Montauban have a right to see their count. They're entitled to present their grievances to him, in person, and hear his judgments. I haven't been home in three years, and there must be scores of cases waiting to be heard."

"Didn't you explain all this to Henry, dear?"

"I tried, but the pains in my back were gnawing at me, and I wasn't very persuasive, I'm afraid. Besides, he had other things on his mind. Not that I blame him, you understand. He's a man now, and he knows what Aubert requires of subordinates. Sons always think their world has changed, and that they understand it better than their fathers know it. They don't realize it's the same world."

"I'll speak to Henry."

"Not now. You'd be wasting your breath. I've added a codicil to my will, explaining to him that the nobles will lose their basic rights unless they exercise them. That may help—when the time comes."

"I give you my solemn word, Philippe," Louise said, "that Henry will go to your county seat when he inherits the title."

1621

Count Henry de Montauban stood erect and bareheaded in the courtyard of the Paris townhouse, unmindful of the cold, steady downpour of rain that soaked his blonde hair and trickled down inside the collar of his upturned cloak. He was as motionless as a sentry on duty in the presence of royalty. His lips were set, and only his eyes showed his pain as he watched the eight retainers in household livery lower the bronze casket containing the last remains of his father to a temporary resting place in the cellar.

The task was completed, and the men looked at Henry for further instructions, but he remained silent.

Lord Charles de Montauban, a half-head shorter than Henry, with a physique that more nearly resembled Philippe's, spoke for his brother. "You'll find meat pies and ale waiting for you in the kitchen."

The men nodded their heads and hurried away.

Charles took a square of linen from his pocket, wiped his own dark hair with it and settled his broad-brimmed hat of black velvet on his head. "We can go in now."

Henry appeared not to hear him, but crossed himself and abruptly turned away. The dining hall was crowded with funeral guests eating boiled fresh-water lobsters and spiced cakes, and judging from the noise they were making, they had already consumed large quantities of mulled wine. The group was predominantly male, and although the occasion was a solemn one, most were dressed in vivid silks, brilliantly colored capes and fur-trimmed hats which, according to custom, gentlemen wore indoors as well as out. Rather than face the guests, Henry went to another entrance and started toward a staircase that led to the private apartments.

Charles touched him on the shoulder.

The older brother was mildly annoyed. "Join them if you wish. I've already accepted their condolences, and I prefer to see how Mother is feeling."

They mounted the stairs together. "She's been very calm for the past few days," Charles said. "His final illness lasted so long she had time to prepare herself."

Henry sounded like Philippe when he became crisp and somewhat withdrawn. "There are several matters I find it urgent to discuss with her."

"Today?"

"Now."

The door of the second-floor sitting room was open, and Louise, attired in unrelieved black, was sitting before the fire, quietly drinking a cup of steaming, watered wine. "Is it done?" she asked, not looking up.

It was Henry's place to reply, but it was Charles who spoke. "Yes, Mother."

She turned to them and smiled slightly. "Change your clothes before you catch the ague."

"We'll dry fast enough here," Henry told her, taking up a place before the hearth. "Mother, I must say some things that are on my mind."

Charles became apprehensive.

But Louise remained tranquil. "Your father and I always encouraged candor in both of you."

"The funeral service in that cold, barren room that he called a chapel was a travesty on religion. And the mere thought of burying him in the unhallowed ground of that Huguenot cemetery west of the city gates is too much. It would be a sacrilege."

She had known what was coming, and raised an eyebrow. "What would you suggest?"

"I'm sure we have enough influence to get a dispensation and have him buried in a Christian plot on the Ile de la Cité."

"It would be a mockery of every principle your father ever held."

When Henry clasped his hands behind his back it was a sure sign he would become pompous. "We must think of the living and their relationship with God."

Charles tried to interrupt.

His brother turned on him. "I'm the head of this family now, and I will make the ultimate decisions."

Louise's voice hardened. "Your father made his peace with God in his own way, and I won't allow his memory to be defiled. Have you read his will?"

"Yes, this morning."

"Then you know he urgently wanted you to pay a visit of several months to Montauban."

The young Count gestured impatiently. "At the best of times it would be difficult, and right now it's impossible."

"Why?" The softness of her tone made the question devastating.

"If you must know, the King and his mother are working out a new reconciliation, and it's certain that Richelieu will be given a cardinal's hat."

She stirred in her chair. "What possible connection——"

"Let me finish. The King and Richelieu are in complete agreement that the Huguenot minority must be made to understand it has Christian obligations in a Christian country. Every town in France pays a Church tax—except the Huguenot towns. That day is ended. They'll be required to pay, the same as all the rest. The Ministry of Finance is sending out tax collectors in the next few days. There's certain to be a little resistance—and a great deal of resentment—in the Protestant towns. So this would be a particularly embarrassing time for me to visit Montauban. I'm not a servant in the Ministry of Finance, and I don't want to be regarded as one."

Louise was silent for a long time. "I decided many weeks ago," she said at last, "when your father slipped into his last sleep, that there is only one appropriate place to bury him—Montauban."

Henry stared at her.

"I intend to leave as soon as the arrangements can be made."

"Mother, you can't make a journey alone through the country."

Charles moved a step closer to her. "If you wish, I'd be honored to escort you."

"No, Charles," she said. "I'm grateful for your offer, but your education has been interrupted too often. Nothing pleased your father as much as the knowledge that you intended to follow him into the law, and you can't leave Paris when you'll be taking your final examinations in a few weeks." She turned to Henry. "I'm hoping you'll come with me."

He made a supreme effort to keep his temper in check. "You're trying to trick me into visiting the place!"

Louise stood, and although her son towered over her, the scorn in her eyes made him flinch. "Whether you come or not, I've made up my mind. I'm going."

His frustration was greater than his anger. "You offer me no choice!"

Montauban looked like a score of other towns in the low-lying valley drained by the Garonne River. It stood on the right bank of the Tarn, one of the Garonne's major tributaries, at its meeting place with an even smaller river, the Tescou. Perhaps its most distinguishing feature was an extension of its high stone wall jutting out over the Tarn to enable men on its parapets to halt all traffic on the waters in time of need. This architectural freak had been necessary in the twelfth century, when river pirates had been a scourge of the whole area, and since that time the people of Montauban had taken their wall for granted. In fact, when strangers commented on the extension over the Tarn, they were usually both surprised and pleased.

Most of the houses were very old and small, and the streets were so narrow and twisting that only two were paved. One led to the main square, where a modest Huguenot church and a new town hall built with funds supplied by Count Philippe had been erected at the spot where an angry mob had razed the Catholic cathedral in 1560. The other cobbled road, long in a state of disrepair, extended from the main gate at the riverfront to the one imposing structure in the town, a castle built on the only hill in the area. This massive structure had been started by one of the counts of Toulouse early in the thirteenth century, and various members of the de Montauban family had added to it from time to time.

Each section had been built according to whim, without relation to the rest of the castle, and the total effect was jumbled, confused and something of an eyesore. It was also a thoroughly uncomfortable place in which to live. "I've slept in seven chambers," an exasperated Henry de Montauban told his mother at the end of their second week in his county seat, "and not one of them is fit for a civilized man. In most of them the wind is so icy and persistent that I can't sleep, no matter how many old tapestries I take from the cellars and hang over the walls. In one the hearths belch smoke back into the room, and the stupid masons and sweeps just shrug and say, 'But milord Count, it's always been this way.' And in the chamber I tried last night, the floor creaked. How in the name of Saint Anthony stone floors can creak I don't know—but they do."

Sleeping accommodations were the least of the problem, however. The kitchens were located so far from the great hall, and servants had to walk such a great distance in the open to reach the main building with food that it was impossible to eat a hot meal. Louise made a makeshift arrangement with the owner of the one commercial inn of any distinction in the town to send some of his assistants to the castle and prepare meals for her and her son over the largest of the hearths in the great hall itself.

"This place reeks of garlic and onions," Henry complained, but even he had to admit that the food was now palatable.

It had been his intention on the journey south to spend only a few days at Montauban, but soon after he and his mother arrived he realized he had to revise his plans drastically. Louise herself was responsible for one of the major causes of delay. The churchyard on the castle grounds had been looted by vandals through the centuries, and only the graves of Philippe's parents were untouched. Headstones,

100

statuary and other ornaments were strewn about the ground, and the place was in such shambles that she burst into tears when she first caught sight of the place where she wanted to lay Philippe to rest.

Henry was forced to take charge, and through Antoine de Mercé, a member of the minor nobility who had held the post of mayor for more than twenty years, he obtained the services of more than a dozen laborers and as many craftsmen. All of these men refused pay for their services, insisting that they owed it to the memory of the late Count Philippe to restore the churchyard. Louise was touched, but Henry soon discovered that there was a disadvantage to volunteer labor. The men worked in their free time, and as they were conscientious wage-earners, they could come to the castle only when they finished their regular tasks. All were strict Calvinists, which meant they considered it immoral to work on the Sabbath. Henry estimated that the complete restoration of the churchyard would, therefore, take them at least eight weeks to complete.

He quickly discovered that, no matter how long the workmen took, he himself would be busy for a far longer period. "I wish," he wrote to Charles, "that you had come here as my surrogate. Every farmer in the county, and there are thousands of them, has a claim of law against another. Why they cling to their feudal ways and bring their disputes to me instead of going before the royal courts is beyond my understanding.

"They're a close-mouthed, suspicious breed, and all they'll tell me is that in the courts they can obtain little justice. I've tried to explain that they can expect still less from me, as I'm almost totally ignorant of the law. But they won't listen. I am the Count de Montauban, and they demand that I settle their arguments.

"When the cold in this absurdly old-fashioned place awakens me early in the morning, I look out of my windows and see a long line of them already waiting for me outside the keep. Most of them have come long distances, many have walked, and without exception they smell of the dung-heap. I am heartily sick of them, and yet cannot refuse to see them.

"I know now why our father studied the law. He did so in self-defense. Never have I missed you as I do now, dear brother. It takes me hours to unravel questions of justice you could solve in moments. I know at last what makes these peasants 'mine.' They consume me from morning until late at night, and give me no rest. If the truth be told, they are the masters and I the serf."

There was one subject, however, which no one in Montauban would discuss with the new count. Two days before Henry and his mother had arrived, three tax collectors from the Ministry of Finance had held a long meeting with Mayor Antoine de Mercé and a delegation of the town's leading citizens. At the end of the day the visitors had departed, and everyone had returned to his normal, quiet pattern of living.

When Henry learned of the meeting, he assumed the Church tithe had been collected, but no one, including the mayor, would confirm the fact. He had no reason to pursue the subject, but little by little, over the weeks, gleaned that something out of the ordinary had taken place. Occasionally a peasant or produce dealer made a vague, sly reference to the subject while presenting his legal claim, but fell strangely silent whenever Henry tried to learn more.

Late in April it became apparent, even to a Parisian who knew nothing of rural ways, that something strange, perhaps sinsister, was brewing. Each day scores of men arrived in Montauban, all of them armed with pikes, ancient swords or firearms that looked as though they would fall apart if discharged. These newcomers were absorbed into the homes of the townspeople with a calm that was itself extraordinary. And each day wagons loaded with grain, smoked meats and other durable foodstuffs rolled through the town gates and were driven to the Huguenot church, where they were unloaded.

Henry's sense of uneasiness increased, but no one mentioned the unusual activities to him for more than a week after they had begun. Then, one evening, after he had dined late with his mother and she had retired, one of the servants announced that the mayor wanted to pay his respects.

Antoine de Mercé, a broad-shouldered, heavily tanned man, was virtually indistinguishable from the peasants of the county. Even though he was a hereditary knight and the owner of several hundred acres of wheat and grape producing land, he wore the common people's ill-fitting breeches and shirt of unbleached wool, his hands were work-roughened and his hair was cropped. His one concession to gentility was his old-fashioned, square-crowned hat, and he knew so little of current customs that he removed it as he came into the great hall.

Henry invited him to sit, poured him a cup of wine and thought of apologizing for the stale odors of cooking that clung to the beams overhead, but on second thought changed his mind. The man probably wouldn't know the difference.

De Mercé, obviously ill at ease, sipped his drink for a moment or two and then placed the cup on the table beside him with a crash that would have damaged it had it not already been battered. "I'm here on a matter of serious business, sir," he said, and like many who had known Philippe, refrained from addressing the new count by his title. "It's important that our late master's dear lady leave Montauban in less than two days."

The request was so abrupt that under ordinary circumstances Henry would have laughed. "Nothing would please me more, I assure you, but she won't go until she can bury my father in what she considers a fitting ceremony."

"She must go," the mayor said stubbornly. "Tell her, please, that I bring her a message from the old Duke. He would have come himself to warn her, but he's under guard at his own castle."

Henry blinked. "Montmorency is under arrest?"

"Only a surprise visit of royal cavalry prevented him from taking charge of our defenses himself."

Henry jumped to his feet. "What defenses?"

"The truth can't be hidden from you any longer, not when the Countess Louise's life might be endangered." De Mercé stood, too, and twisted his hat in his hands. "The King has sent an army under General de Bertram against us. It will arrive at the gates in two days' time."

"Why, in the name of Saint Michel?" Henry was shouting.

"King Louis is a rash young man who listens to the wrong counsel. He sends Bertram with eight regiments to force the Huguenot counties to genuflect to Rome, but we won't do it."

"Speak more plainly!" It was obvious that the man wasn't joking, and Henry was alarmed. Bertram, he knew, was the most ruthless and ambitious member of a branch of the de Guise family noted for its loyalty to the Church. Two of the general's brothers were cardinals, one living in France and the other a member of the Curia in Rome, and it was said that the youngest of the brothers, who had been made a bishop at nineteen, would be given his red hat before he reached his majority. If the Louvre had indeed dispatched General de Bertram to the inner citadel of the Calvinists, the Crown meant business.

"Not one of our towns will pay the Church tax," the mayor said proudly. "They won't squeeze an ecu from us for the Pope. No, not a copper. Louis hopes to punish Montauban—and teach the rest a lesson. But we've been warned. We've been reinforced by—well, by enough men to hold them off."

"You're mad."

"If you please, sir, I know your views and I'm sure you know mine." De Mercé was ruffled, but spoke with quiet dignity. "I've brought the old Duke's warning to your mother, and wish you'd tell her we'll provide her with an escort as soon as she's ready to leave."

"As your liege lord I order you to obey the King's command!" Henry vaguely knew he looked and sounded ridiculous, but was too angry to care.

"With all due respect, sir, you're not in a position to give orders. You know the castle too well, so we're forced to hold you as a hostage."

Henry automatically reached for his sword.

103

"If you please, sir, no violence. For your mother's sake, we'd like to conduct this unpleasant business in a manner worthy of gentlemen. Our lads have taken possession of the castle this evening, and I give you my own pledge you won't be harmed. On my own authority I'll grant you parole if you'll give me your word you won't try to communicate with the enemy."

The reference to royal troops as "the enemy" was insane. "This is civil war."

"We aren't starting it, sir, and if they'll leave us in peace, we'll do them no harm. May I have your word?"

For an instant Henry hesitated, but it occurred to him that a promise given to traitors who were deliberately defying the authority of King Louis was worthless. "I give you my solemn promise I won't communicate in any way with—His Majesty's forces." Henry wondered if he could smuggle himself out when his mother left, but supposed that would be impossible.

De Mercé bowed. "I'll return at noon to do the bidding of the Countess de Montauban."

A moment later Henry was alone, and a sense of helpless rage overwhelmed him. Nothing in his experience had prepared him for this wild nightmare, and he knew only that both sides were wrong. He and Charles had been reared in a house that was part-Catholic, part-Huguenot, and although he could recall periods of coolness between his parents, they had lived together in mutual understanding and love for many years.

If a man and woman had been able to achieve a truce in a relationship that was intricate and intimate, surely these stubborn Calvinists and the impetuous young King could reach a simple accommodation. What shocked Henry was that the situation had deteriorated so rapidly in the weeks since he had left Paris. His basic sympathies lay with the Crown, of course, but at the same time it grieved him to see all his father had worked to accomplish being placed in jeopardy.

The basic fault was that of the Huguenots, who were guilty of open rebellion by refusing the King's order to pay the Church tax. Several of his colleagues at the Louvre had made it very clear in their discussions on the subject that nothing in the Edict of Nantes prevented the collection of such a tax from the Protestants.

Yet, at the same time, he was dismayed by the fury of King Louis' reaction. If the truce of twenty-three years' standing was broken by an assault on Montauban, it would be impossible to predict the consequence, other than that France herself would suffer. There was little doubt in Henry's mind that the Huguenot rebellion would be smashed by regiments that, ironically, had been trained in the iron-disciplined tradition of Montmorency. But national unity would be destroyed, and England, that nation of apostates, would gain. So would the fierce young Protestant champion of the north, Gustavus II Adolphus of Sweden, who had sworn to bring every Catholic nation within reach of his armies to its knees.

As Henry paced up and down his draughty bedchamber it occurred to him that his own perspectives had changed somewhat since he had come to Montauban. He was willing to concede, for all the good it would do him as a hostage, that perhaps his father had been right in wanting him to come here. When a man stayed too long at the Louvre, he became short-sighted. One thing was certain in his mind: Vatican Hill could not have approved Louis' venture, and the King had been listening to the Bertram family rather than the infinitely more patient and far-seeing Richelieu.

Henry debated whether to awaken his mother, but finally decided to let her enjoy a night's sleep before breaking the grim news to her. It would be time enough in the morning to tell her she could neither bury his father as she wished, nor herself enjoy any longer the comforting belief that Philippe de Montauban had helped bring lasting religious peace to France.

The rest of the night was a torture of doubts and futile rage, and it was almost dawn before Henry drifted off to sleep. Less than an hour later he was awakened by the blare of trumpets and the rattle of drums.

General Leon de Bertram had fooled the Huguenots by arriving at the gates of Montauban sooner than they had anticipated. Henry peered out of his window across the Tarn, and saw the clustered banners of two cavalry regiments and one of light infantry, Bertram's vanguard. What startled him even more was a glimpse, in the early morning haze, of three artillery batteries, two of cannon and one of catapult, an ugly contraption of wood, with a leather sling, that looked like a scaffold.

Men were shouting and racing through the corridors of the castle as Henry quickly dressed and hurried out into the hallway, intending to go to his mother's suite. He was instantly made to realize his own status when two burly peasants, each armed with a heavy pistol and a knife, fell in on either side of him.

He was relieved when they told him they would wait outside his mother's sitting room.

Louise was already dressed, and Henry rapidly told her all he knew. She listened in silence, and when he finished speaking she patted his arm in a maternal gesture which, under the circumstances, seemed incongruous. Then, before Henry could halt her, she stepped out into the corridor. "Who is in charge of your forces?" she asked one of the guards.

"Mayor de Mercé, milady."

"Where is he?"

"On the battlements, ma'm. He——"

"Take me to him!"

The man opened his mouth to protest, closed it again and silently led the way to a narrow, winding flight of stairs. Henry followed with his white-faced mother, but when he tried to help as she mounted the stairs, she shook him off impatiently, and the guard who brought up the rear stifled a smile.

Fifteen or twenty men, a few in modern helmets and corselets, the rest wearing cumbersome chainmail that must have belonged to their great-grandfathers, were clustered inside a dark, gloomy turret room, peering out of slits in the masonry and talking to each other in low, intense voices.

"Antoine!" There was a ring of authority in Louise's voice.

The men turned simultaneously, and de Mercé stepped forward. He reached for his hat, belatedly remembered he was wearing a helmet and saluted awkwardly as he bowed.

"Frenchmen," she said, "do not make war against Frenchmen in quarrels over Our Lord."

"Milady, our quarrel is with misguided men over a question of money." The mayor was distressed. "I—I can't tell you how sorry I am that you are being caused inconvenience. I'll send a courier to the enemy under a flag of truce, and I'm certain you will be granted the right to leave the town at once."

She pushed past him to the slits, Henry still close beside her, and looked out at the troops gathered on the plain. Horsemen and infantry were spreading out, and men were working to pull the cannon and catapult into place. Directing the operations were five or six handsomely attired men on horseback, above whose heads several banners had been raised. The highest was the lily ensign of France, and only a shade lower was the yellow and green ensign of the Bertram family.

Louise turned and surveyed the men who were staring at her. "Antoine," she said, "you and Leon de Bertram will find some way to reconcile your differences peacefully."

He tried to say something.

She silenced him with an imperious gesture. "Send your courier. Leon has been a guest at my Paris table many times. He knows me, my views—and my husband's views. Send someone to him—at once—and tell him this must stop."

De Mercé wanted to argue, but through her he could hear Philippe speaking, and he wilted. He spoke briefly to one of the men near him, who hurriedly left the turret.

"I want Leon to know there's no trickery being planned. Where can I be seen?" Louise demanded.

The mayor was so flustered he stammered. "The parapet that hangs over the river would be the best place, milady, but——"

"Take me to it!"

De Mercé sighed and led the way through a maze of narrow, stone-lined corridors. Louise followed with Henry, the two ever-present guards and at least half of the men who had been assembled in the turret room. They came at last to a stone door so heavy that three men had to use all their force to push it ajar, and the party emerged into the April sunlight.

As they came into the open a group of three mounted men, bearing a white flag, rode down the cobbled road to the main gate. A huge bar was removed, one side of the gate creaked partly open, and they moved off toward the river bank. The water was high, swollen by the rains of spring, so they were forced to swim their mounts to the far side, where a detachment of royal cavalry rode to meet them.

"Give me your arm, Henry." Louise seemed almost impervious to the activity so plainly visible below.

They began to stroll up and down the parapet behind a waist-high wall, and Louise appeared as unperturbed as she would have been taking an airing in the royal gardens of the Louvre. "Mother," Henry said anxiously, "this isn't wise."

"It's far more intelligent than watching Frenchmen murder one another. Leon will be reasonable, I'm sure. Your father and I had many interesting chats with him about the delicacy of relations between Catholics and Hugenots."

"But how on earth do you suppose a compromise satisfactory to both sides can be worked out?"

"I have no idea. I'm not a man, and I know nothing of political matters. I can only repeat what your father always said. When the security of France is at stake, men of every faith must learn to work together." Suddenly she halted and gasped.

"What's wrong?"

"How very tactless of Leon. Isn't that his brother with him?"

Henry stared across the river and saw the emissaries from Montauban being led to a man in a helmet and corselet of gold, obviously General de Bertram. Mounted on a gelding beside him was a figure previously hidden in the throng surrounding the general. His cloak was a shade of red used exclusively by cardinals, and a closer examination revealed that he was also wearing a Catholic prelate's distinctive red biretta.

Antoine de Mercé and the other leaders of the defending force were peering at him, too, and muttering to each other. Although neither Henry nor his mother could hear what they were saying, it was clear from their tones that they were angry.

"If Cardinal de Bertram wanted an airing," Henry said, "he could have worn less conspicuous clothing."

His mother was even more irritated. "My uncle always said it was a mistake to make Gaston a cardinal. He has so little common sense. Just look at Antoine and his friends. They're furious!"

Henry didn't want to add more fuel to the fire of her discouragement by saying that the cardinal's appearance with the royal regiments made the possibility of any compromise even more remote.

The conference on the far side of the river was very brief. General de Bertram turned away, and the three townsmen rode back to the river, still holding high their flag of truce.

Tension on the parapet mounted, and Henry saw that the gun crews of the two cannon and the catapult were still hard at work. He felt certain his mother's attempt to act as a mediator had failed, and his next task was to get her safely out of Montauban before the actual siege began. "Have your maids pack only as much as you'll need to take you back to Paris," he said. "Three or four of your leather trunk-boxes should be enough."

She gave no indication that she had heard him.

The gate was re-opened as the emissaries reached the near side of the river, and the men on the parapet fell silent. Louise continued to walk up and down slowly, her hand still grasping Henry's arm. The royalist cavalrymen who had escorted the couriers to the river bank were no more than a stone's throw away, and looked up at her curiously. It was impossible to tell whether they recognized her or were merely impressed by the majestic bearing of the lady in widow's black.

After a wait of a few minutes that seemed interminable, the messenger de Mercé had dispatched emerged onto the parapet. Instead of reporting to the mayor he went straight to Louise and, following the old custom still common in rural areas, dropped to one knee. "Madame," he said hoarsely, "General de Bertram sends you his felicitations. But he says your request is too late."

As he spoke there was a flash on the far side of the river, a puff of gray smoke appeared and a cannon roared. Before anyone on the parapet could react, a cannon ball whined, struck the lip of the waist-high wall and then bounced harmlessly to the opposite side of the ledge.

At the same instant Louise slumped, and Henry caught her just before she reached the floor. For an instant he thought she had fainted, but a smear of blood at her left temple indicated that something had struck her.

Antoine de Mercé, unable to speak, pointed in horror at a jagged chip of granite, about four inches long, that lay on the parapet a few feet from her. Obviously the cannon ball had knocked it loose, and it had hit her with a stunning impact.

Henry saw that his mother was smiling, and for some moments it did not dawn on him that her wide-open eyes were vacant. Even when someone behind him murmured, "My God, she's dead," he found it impossible to accept the awful fact. He fell to his knees beside her and raised his hands to his face for an instant, but knew his tears would have to wait.

Straightening, he closed his mother's eyes, and started to cross himself, but could not. Neither could he utter the prayer he had been taught in his adolescence by his confessor.

He stood and turned to the men who, grouped behind him, were staring down at the lifeless body of their countess. "Bury her beside my father in Huguenot ground," he said very softly. Then, suddenly, his voice had a metallic ring. "De Mercé!"

"Sir?"

"This is my castle and my town. Henry de Montauban has come home, and will take command of our defenses against our common foes!"

Cannon balls screamed overhead, there was a steady rattle of arquebus fire from the defenders in the castle, and from the far side of the river came the heavier, deeper sound of muskets being discharged by the better armed royal troops. Henry stood dry-eyed above the graves of his parents, as he did each morning, and then slowly mounted the steep steps of the castle keep. It was the twenty-ninth day of the siege, and in twenty-nine days his world had changed beyond recognition.

In the eyes of the Crown, and of Leon de Bertram across the Tarn, he was traitor and outlaw, leader of a band of heretical insurrectionists who were defying the might and majesty of France itself. To the beleaguered forces of Montauban, and the eight thousand women, old men and children who were being forced to endure the hardships of the siege, he knew he was an inspiration, the son of Philippe who had proved worthy of his heritage.

And in his own eyes? Henry returned the salute of a sentry stationed at the entrance to the corridor that led to the towers above, and smiled wryly. He no longer knew himself, and had no idea what he had become. His grief for his mother was unassuaged, and he knew his cold rage would never be appeased. Perhaps he was incapable of any other feeling. It was the only explanation he could find for his aversion to the faith in which he had been reared. Suddenly, at the moment of his mother's death, he had lost every conviction to which he had clung since childhood, and it was strange that he knew neither remorse nor regret.

Even stranger was the knowledge that he had not replaced one set of beliefs with another. Technically, he supposed, he was considered a Huguenot now, and had picked up a smattering of Calvinism from his fellow defenders. But he no longer had a positive approach to God. His one aim in life was to destroy, and it actually amused him to think that, given the opportunity, he could strangle Gaston, Cardinal de Bertram with his hands. The very idea gave him a sense of pleasure.

Two squads of men were at work in the "artillery hall," a vast towel room in which two iron cannon were emplaced. The possibility that the guns might explode was ever-present, but the crews had become inured to danger, and were laughing heartily at their own coarse jokes when Henry joined them. They greeted him with easy familiarity, and he was equally at home with them. No one was conscious of the invisible wall that ordinarily separated nobleman and commoner. They were sharing the hazards of fighting, learning the art of war together, and their bond of kinship was greater than any that Henry had known or would have believed attainable a month previous.

"Any luck against Zeus yet, lads?" he asked, walking to the apertures used when the cannon were fired. He peered out across the river, spat on the floor and wiped his mouth with the back of his hand, a gesture he once would have considered vulgar. "Zeus" was the royalist catapult, which each day sent bolts of Greek fire, a concentrated, fiercely burning pitch, into the town. And Zeus still stood intact deep behind the enemy breastworks, a cumbersome, menacing engine of destruction.

"We've only fired one round with each gun so far," said the sergeant who was directing the swabbing of the grimy barrels. "We're still too short."

"Can't you get a higher trajectory?"

"Not in here." The man's gesture indicated that the openings were too narrow.

"We've got to knock it out," Henry said. "I suppose you heard that the house of Ventilio the Spaniard was burned to cinders earlier this morning."

The men looked at one another glumly. Ventilio cured and sold wineskins, and was recognized as an artist at his craft. A youth of eighteen, who wore only breeches and shoes, wiped his hands on his seat. "How many?"

"I've just paid them a visit. The younger daughter was killed, and Ventilio's wife was badly burned. They've wrapped her in an oiled blanket, but it's too early to tell whether she'll live." Death and suffering had become so commonplace that Henry spoke without emotion.

"Maybe," the sergeant said in the same matter-of-fact tone, "I can coax a little higher trajectory on the next round."

110

"Try," Henry replied. "If you still can't get the range, we'll have to move the guns onto a parapet, in the open."

Everyone understood the risks involved in such a transfer. The crews would become the targets of the royalist musketeers, and enemy cannon would concentrate on trying to destroy their guns. But no one protested. A battle fought against such heavy odds made a man almost recklessly indifferent to his own fate.

Henry, however, felt the weight of his ultimate responsibility. "We might increase the powder charge again."

The sergeant shook his head. "Every ounce of powder we add to the load makes it all the more likely we'll be blown to pieces. We'd rather take our chances on the parapet, lord Count." Like everyone else in Montauban, he now automatically and unthinkingly addressed Henry by his title.

"We won't make a final decision before nightfall. They'll only fire Zeus twice more today, at the most." Henry left the artillery hall and made his way to his tower command post, where de Mercé and two younger men were awaiting him. The walls in this section of the castle were so thick that it was safe for him to remove his unadorned steel helmet, and he massaged the back of his neck as he joined them.

"They've started digging a new line of breastworks about twenty yards closer to the river," de Mercé said, "and they must have worked all night on it. They completed a section long enough to accommodate two companies of infantry."

The enemy move had been expected, and Henry nodded calmly. "We may not be able to stop them, but after sundown this evening we'll station fifty archers on the river overhang. They can fire flares to guide them, and I estimate each archer can get rid of at least two arrows before a flare dies out. That should slow even the most efficient diggers. Anything else to report?"

Francis, Viscount de Cassaude, who had sneaked through the royalist lines to join the defenders two days after the battle began, was in charge of all scouting operations. An energetic young man with the red hair and freckled skin of the Gascons, he was always cheerful, even when the news was unpleasant. "The vanguard of two new infantry regiments arrived to reinforce Bertram within the hour. The rest should be here by tomorrow, I imagine."

"There's no indication where they intend to set up their lines?"

"None as yet, Henry." De Cassaude was the only member of the defending force to call Henry by his Christian name. "But they're sure to be assigned posts on this side of the river. Bertram must have been wild when he realized how much food reached us in the convoy that came through two nights ago."

"Will these new regiments hamper you, Francis?"

"Oh, I'll manage. Create a diversion for me on Thursday night, when the next shipment of grain is due, and I'll bring in seventy-five wagon-loads before the Papists realize what's happening."

De Mercé's imagination was limited. "It isn't easy to create a diversion after dark, milord."

Henry laughed harshly, without pleasure. "There's nothing simpler, Antoine. I'm rather in need of exercise, so I'll lead a cavalry sortie against the breastworks they've set up on the near side of the Tarn in the past week. That should keep them occupied for an hour or two."

"No, milord Count!" De Mercé was alarmed. "I—I forbid it."

Henry laughed again.

De Cassaude felt he had to intervene. "Antoine is right, Henry. Have you stopped to think of the consequences if Bertram should capture you?"

"Does it matter much what becomes of me?" Henry countered.

The younger nobleman jumped to his feet. "I can think of nothing more important to every Protestant in Europe! They'd parade you in chains on the portico of every cathedral in France. I'm sure they'd even revive the Inquisition to supervise your trial. You've become a symbol to every Huguenot in the country, to every Lutheran in the German States fighting for the right to worship as he wishes, to every Hussite who must pray in the secrecy of his Prague home. Under no circumstances can we run the risk of allowing you to fall into Bertram's hands!"

Henry felt completely frustrated, but realized they were right. No matter how much he yearned for a direct, personal confrontation with his mother's murderers, he couldn't seek only the satisfaction of his own desires. "I suppose it's flattering," he said, "that the Papists think so highly of me." Suddenly it occurred to him that his transformation had become total. For the first time he had used a Huguenot term of contempt for Roman Catholics, and meant it.

The château on the bluff overlooking the Loire River resembled the country house of any great French noble. Part castle, part palace, it was a handsome building of gray fieldstone that boasted many chimneys, large windows and handsomely landscaped grounds. But there were differences that made a visitor realize this was the Queen Mother's residence. Pikemen of her own household regiment, wearing uniforms in the green, yellow and white of the de Medicis patrolled the property in pairs, as did custodians in livery of the same colors, who were accompanied by leashed shepherd dogs of a particularly fierce breed that were raised in Burgundy. Virtually every royal household in Europe had its Burgundian shepherd dogs, and even the English had bought a dozen of them.

There were more than fifty of the dogs at the Château, which wasn't surprising. Marie de Medicis had never been popular with the French, and in recent years her unsuccessful efforts to rule the country through her son had won her the hatred of Louis XIII's subjects. Now, as she strolled through an apple orchard, conversing earnestly with her principal adviser, she was preceded and followed by servants leading pairs of the ferocious animals.

Charles de Montauban tried in vain to curb his impatience as he watched the two black-clad figures. Although he knew they had been notified he was waiting, they seemed unaware of his presence on the terrace. He studied them as closely as he could from a distance, hoping to see some sign that their conference would soon end. The Queen Mother had gained weight in recent years, but Charles, who hadn't seen her since he had been a child, would have known her instantly. He remembered that his father once had said she was the homeliest woman in France and that she wore her widow's weeds in order to make herself inconspicuous.

Charles smiled painfully at the memory. It was difficult to let himself think of his father—or his mother.

The Queen Mother's companion certainly looked neither intimidating nor sinister, contrary to the many rumors that sifted back to Paris. Bishop Armand de Richelieu looked insignificantly slender and small in his black cassock, and his lined face, weary mouth and drooping shoulders made him appear far older than a man in his mid-thirties.

At last, to Charles' relief, Queen Marie went off alone through the orchard, and the Bishop came toward the terrace. His pace quickening, he seemed to straighten, and when he came closer Charles was struck by the unexpected strength and shrewdness in the eyes that were studying him so carefully. Perhaps it was true, as some professors of law at the Sorbonne were saying privately, that Pope Gregory was promoting Richelieu to the rank of cardinal for his own sake, and not because of his fidelity to the Queen Mother.

Charles kissed the Bishop's ring, and murmured, "Your Grace."

Richelieu wasted no time. "You've been given something to eat and drink? Good. We'll sit over here in the shade." He led the way toward a bench under a beech tree at the far side of the terrace. "Accept my condolences on the death of your mother."

"Thank you, Your Grace." Charles swallowed painfully. "That's why——"

"I know why you've come to me," Richelieu said briskly, waving his guest to a seat on the bench. "The siege at Montauban is mad."

Charles blinked. "I—I can't believe the reports I've heard."

"They're true. The King has ordered the town reduced, and your brother has taken charge of the defenses."

With an effort Charles refrained from covering his face with his hands. "But Henry has always been a good Catholic, Your Grace. I can't understand——"

"There is no such thing as a 'good' or 'bad' Catholic—or a 'good' or 'bad' Huguenot." The Bishop's tone and expression remained unchanged. "In this world there are only human beings whose love of God is shallow, and who are therefore unable to accept or return His perfect love. But you haven't come to discuss theology."

"No, Your Grace. I spent three days at the Louvre, trying to see King Louis, but he wouldn't grant me an audience. You're my last hope. This insane siege must be called off."

A flicker of pity appeared in Richelieu's eyes.

Charles responded to the sympathy. "It's a nightmare worse than any I suffered as a child. My mother dead, my brother leading insurgents against the State, while the Crown calls him a traitor—it's too much."

Richelieu reached down to pluck a blade of grass, which he held between his fingers. "Conflicting ideas regarding the nature of God and of the proper ways to worship Him have no part in the drama taking place at Montauban, Lord Charles. I've kept myself fully informed on the situation there. Your mother's death was a brutal, senseless accident that could have been avoided. General de Bertram has never been noted for his good sense, and it's obvious that your brother's grief has warped his mind. I can understand how he feels, and almost condone what he's doing."

Charles was stunned. "You can't mean that."

"The rebellion at Montauban is civil, not religious. King Louis issued a decree, and some thousands of his subjects have chosen to defy him. And so he feels he must assert his authority over them."

Charles' sense of confusion increased. The man didn't even sound like a priest.

"Unfortunately," Richelieu continued quietly, "both King Louis and your brother have shown the lack of judgment characteristic of young hotheads. They're both completely in the wrong."

"Then stop the slaughter; can't you?"

"What can I do?" Richelieu held out his hands.

"You're going to Rome soon for your consecration as cardinal, so surely——"

"At the moment the King has no particular confidence in me, and your brother certainly wouldn't listen to me, nor would the Huguenots of Montauban. Put yourself in their position, Lord Charles. To them I'd be an arch-enemy."

"But Henry is destroying himself, and Louis is devastating our county seat!"

"I'll grant you they're both behaving like savages, but the drama must play itself out. I urge you to read Aristotle's *Aesthetics* on the inevitability of tragedy."

Charles became frantic.

Bishop Richelieu put a hand on his shoulder. "There's nothing you or anyone else can do to stop barbarians from slaughtering one another."

"How can you be so calm about it?" Charles demanded bitterly.

"I urge you to make a closer study of history. Human nature requires the catharsis of a blood-bath before order can be restored out of chaos. Your mother's death was a frightful accident, but there are always innocents who are hurt when young animals fight. Aside from her death, France will benefit from this stupidity."

Charles wondered if the Bishop had lost his senses, too.

"The feeling of revulsion grows stronger everywhere in France each day. The people—Catholics and Huguenots alike—are offended and ashamed. No matter how the siege of Montauban ends, there will be a demand for the restoration of public order and dignity." Richelieu folded his hands in his lap. "No people can be led unless they're willing to accept responsible leadership. Then, when they've been harnessed, they'll go wherever they're driven. It's quite simple."

The sun filtering through the branches of the beech tree was warm, but Charles shivered as Bishop Richelieu continued.

"In time, the incident at Montauban can be of great benefit to the entire country. King Louis obviously doesn't inherit his father's instinct for leadership, and Queen Marie's intricately Italian approach is resented by a nation that prefers more direct methods. The siege is preparing the soil of France for new leadership."

Charles thought he detected a hint of smug complacency in the Bishop's voice. "Then you won't help, Your Grace?"

Again Richelieu spread his hands, but the gesture was empty. No man had ever looked less helpless.

A cloud of black, acrid smoke hung in the still, early morning air above the eastern end of Montauban, where four houses had been demolished late the previous afternoon by Greek fire. No one stirred in these final hours before dawn, but few of the town's citizens were asleep. Behind the barred doors of their tiny houses they lay in their beds waiting for another day of fire and sudden death.

The tension was so thick they could feel it. This was to be the first day of food rationing, under strict orders of the Count. Every civilian inhabitant would receive one cup of wheat flour and six ounces of meat each day; every fighting man would be given one and one-half cups of flour or barley and nine ounces of meat. Sentries armed with muskets stolen from the enemy by Francis de Cassaude were stationed at all entrances to the warehouses, and according to the latest in an unending series of rumors, there was enough food in Montauban only for another week or two. The enemy had sealed off the town from the outside world, and thirteen full regiments of royalist troops were waiting outside the gates for the capitulation that even the most optimistic of the defenders now considered almost inevitable.

The siege was in its fifty-fourth day.

The castle was as busy as the rest of Montauban was still. Infantrymen cleaned their firearms and made bullets for themselves, first melting the pewter cups, copper jugs and other metal objects contributed by the townspeople, and then pressing the half-cooled substance into small molds. Archers repaired their bows and whittled new arrows, and only the small company of pikemen, who had nothing to occupy them until the royalists attempted to scale the walls of the castle, were allowed to sleep.

The most active part of the castle was the parapet overhanging the river. There fifty men labored in their stocking feet, hauling the two cannon of Montauban into place as close to the forward wall as they could emplace them. Barrels and carriages were swathed in blankets of heavy wool, and the men who carried cannon balls to the overhang kept each of the heavy iron spheres carefully swaddled.

Henry supervised the operation, but did not hesitate to give the men a hand whenever anyone stumbled or sagged. Like all the rest he was exhausted, desperate and ready for any venture, no matter how mad it might appear, that would destroy the royalist catapult that continued to wreak havoc in Montauban each day.

Zeus, the superstitious defenders believed, led a charmed life, and Henry was half-inclined to agree with his men. He had moved his brace of guns to three different positions on the top of the walls, all of them exposed, and in spite of suffering heavy casualties, had not been able to score a direct hit on the weapon that had made life in the town so wretched.

If they failed today, Henry didn't know what to do, so he warned himself that they could not fail. The cannon were being put into position at the most forward point in his defense line, and because of its vulnerability the operation was being conducted silently, at night. Very soon now he would test his scheme, and he realized that if he did not succeed, he would pay a heavy price. There was no doubt in his mind that the stronger, more modern enemy cannon could destroy his guns, the only long-range weapons he possessed.

The new royalist breastwork line was no more than fifty yards from the overhang, and the men assigned to the project were aware that any sound could alert infantrymen capable of shooting them down with powerful muskets. No one spoke, and the gun carriages were carefully unlimbered. Then the barrels were hoisted into place, and the cannon balls were brought forward one at a time.

Everything seemed to be moving ahead according to schedule, but suddenly Henry remembered something. He placed his lips close to the ear of the sergeant in charge of the crew and whispered, "Powder."

They went together into the arsenal, hoisted bags of coarse-grained gunpowder onto their shoulders and carried them into the open. The two cannon were primed and loaded, and then Henry gave a signal to a waiting Antoine de Mercé. One hundred of the best marksmen in Montauban crept across the roof and took their places directly behind the forward wall, some of them only a few feet from the protruding muzzles of the guns. It would be their task to immobilize the enemy infantrymen behind the earthworks long enough for the artillerymen to accomplish their vital task.

At last all was in readiness. Antoine de Mercé took his place beside one gun, Henry went to the other, and each was joined by a fusilier who carried a tinderbox and flint. Now there was nothing to do but wait.

The first streaks of a dirty, gray dawn appeared in the sky, and Henry looked down the long barrel of his gun. "Elevate!" he whispered to the members of his crew. "An inch or two more. That's it. Don't change the trajectory. Now a bit to the left." He consulted a carefully drawn chart that had taken three days to prepare; in an effort of this importance, nothing could be left to chance. "A trifle more."

At last the gun was in position, and Henry peered through the gloom at Antoine de Mercé, who was readying the second cannon. Antoine was satisfied, too, and signaled accordingly. It was becoming a little lighter now, and soon Henry was able to make out the bulk of the catapult on the fire side of the river, about four hundred and fifty yards from the castle. The time had come to test his theory that the cannon should be used as long-range muskets to attain their maximum efficiency. If he was mistaken, the harassed defenders of Montauban would be badly crippled.

Henry checked his cannon for the last time, and nodded. The two fusiliers, using their flints and tinderboxes, lighted short lengths of loosely woven, fast-burning rope and at almost the same instant plunged them into holes at the base of the guns. Then everyone moved away from the weapons and, crouching low, placed his hands over his ears. Henry, however, retreated only a few steps and continued to stand erect. He was defying a basic principle of safety observed by all artillerymen, but it was more important that he note the precise range of the shots than worry about being injured or killed if the guns exploded.

De Mercé's cannon was the first to fire, and its roar broke the early morning stillness. Before the echo rolled across the valley, Henry's gun spoke, too, and clouds of pungent smoke swirled across the parapet.

Coughing and brushing tears from his eyes, Henry saw that de Mercé's shot had been short of its mark by no more than ten or fifteen yards, a deficiency that could be corrected by a very slight change in trajectory. His own weapon had missed the target by a far greater margin, and required a much more complicated adjustment. Therefore he concentrated his full attention on the mayor's cannon. Meanwhile the two crews rushed forward and, working under the sergeant's direction, swabbed out the guns with lengths of unbleached wool attached to long poles.

The royalist camp came to life quickly, and before the artillerymen had the cannon prepared for another round, musketeers in the closest siege line started to pepper their position, hampering the operation. The defenders behind the parapet wall came to life, too, and keeping themselves concealed as best they could, directed their own musket and arquebus shot at anyone who showed his head above the breastworks of earth and rubble.

Henry shut out the sounds of the infantry marksmen's duel, oblivious to the bullets that cut through the air close to his head. Time was his most precious commodity; he knew he had only two more opportunities, at most, to find his target before the more accurate royalist artillery opened fire on his guns.

One of the crewmen was killed and another gravely injured before the cannon were cleaned, primed and loaded again. Then Henry took charge of de Mercé's gun, changing its elevation and ordered the fusilier to fire before he readied the second.

The shot smashed through the upper part of the catapult, and the men on the parapet cheered loudly. Several of the infantrymen so completely forgot to take precautions that marksmen in the royalist siege lines shot them down, and three wounded were dragged away while Henry went to work on his second cannon. He realized that, by accident, he had worked out a time-saving system: while one cannon was being aimed and fired, the other could be cleaned and made operable again.

He curbed his sense of elation, refusing to let himself think about his partial triumph. He could not pause to assess the damage to the catapult, either, and urged the feverish crewmen to work more rapidly. The barrel of the gun was tilted higher, and the muzzle aimed more to the right. Henry was not quite satisfied, however, and both the sergeant and de Mercé came over to consult with him.

They were so intent on what they were doing that only belatedly did they realize that an enemy cannon ball had just passed dangerously close overhead. It would not take long for the royalist artillerymen to find their target.

The second cannon was fired, and a moment later bedlam broke loose on the parapet. The shot crashed through the catapult, ripping away the better part of the wheel-springs that provided its thrust. It had been rendered impotent, and for the first time since the beginning of the siege the people of Montauban had nothing to fear from the ravages of Greek fire.

Men jumped up and down, shouting and hugging each other, and their joy was so great that they neither heard nor heeded Henry's plea to take cover. But the celebration was short-lived. A tremendous explosion shook the parapet, and its impact was so great that some moments passed before Henry realized what had happened. He had been knocked to the stone floor, and only when he sat up, shaking his head in a vain attempt to clear it, did he see that an enemy cannon ball had landed on a bag of gunpowder, which was still burning. De Mercé's gun was a twisted mass of useless metal, and the sergeant was sprawled across it, his head almost completely severed from his body.

Henry painfully hauled himself to his feet. "The Papist bastards have found the range, lads," he shouted. "Take the dead and wounded below, and clear the parapet."

The men needed no further urging, and those able to move hurried to obey.

Henry, scarcely aware of what he was doing, began to tug at the carriage of the one remaining cannon. Others saw what he was doing, joined him, and in a moment thirty strong though still dazed men struggled to push the heavy weapon into the vaulted chamber that was safe from enemy fire.

Someone grasped Henry from behind and propelled him through the tower entrance. He turned and scarcely recognized de Mercé, whose face was blackened and blistered.

"Do you want to kill yourself?" the mayor demanded fiercely. "You're too valuable for donkey work!"

His last words were lost in a roar of approval as the cannon finally slid past the entrance. The heavy door was shut, and exhausted, perspiration-soaked men dropped to the floor, indifferent now to the cannon balls landing outside on the parapet.

Henry staggered to the window slit that gave him the best view of the enemy, and began to laugh in hysterical relief. Only one shoulder of the catapult was still upright, and the rest of the huge machine was worthless kindling wood, battered metal and shredded leather. He had won his most important victory of the siege.

Francis de Cassaude slumped wearily against the inside wall of the command tower, slowly munching a chunk of coarse bread. He savored each mouthful, allowing it to dissolve before taking the next, and when he swallowed he flinched, behaving as though his throat hurt. "There, gentlemen," he said as the last of the bread vanished, "is my breakfast, dinner and supper for today."

Antoine de Mercé, his clothes hanging loosely on his rugged frame, made no comment as he poured wine from a jug into three earthenware cups.

Henry accepted one and sipped with relish. "We can be grateful," he said, "that my ancestors put in such extensive wine cellars. Even if we run out of food, which we'll do in another two weeks—or less, we'll still have all we want to drink."

It was the seventy-fifth day of the siege.

A messenger came into the chamber, without ceremony. "Sally!" he panted. "They're attacking the town wall near the old Toulouse gate!"

"How many of them?" Henry wanted to know.

"A company of assault infantry, lord Count."

Francis roused himself. "We have enough men stationed in that sector to beat off two or three companies."

Henry thanked and dismissed the messenger, then exchanged glances with his comrades. "Why the Toulouse gate, I wonder. They know we're strong there."

De Mercé shrugged, and Francis studied his dirty fingernails.

Henry reached for his helmet. "It must be a diversion for a stronger sortie somewhere else." He rubbed his haggard face before donning the helmet. "We'll soon find out. He uses the same stale trick again and again."

"Thank God his imagination is so limited," de Mercé said fervently.

"Thank God," Henry echoed, and realized he was being completely sincere. "Coming, Francis? Antoine, you need sleep. The night watch makes a man feel as tired as an old monk on a penitential retreat." He laughed without humor, buckled on his sword and went out onto the ramparts.

Francis de Cassaude followed, and they stood together, watching a warm breeze ripple the banners of the royalist regiments. As far as they could see in any direction there were breastworks, and a dozen or more cooking fires were still burning far behind the lines. The town was completely surrounded, cut off by the largest force the Crown

120

had put into the field since the defeat of the Spaniards at Amiens. In fact Bertram had built up such a powerful army that the defenders had been forced to abandon hope that a relief column from other Huguenot strongholds might fight its way through to them.

"I wish," Francis said, "that we knew what's happening out in the world. How the rest of France feels. Whether other towns are in rebellion."

"This sounds foolish," Henry replied wryly, "but I know too little about the Huguenot mind to guess whether the rest of the inner citadel has mobilized. As for the Catholic approach, my thoughts swing like a pendulum. One day I'm convinced they're outraged. The next I'm certain they prefer prosperity and peace. I regret that we'll never know. It's odd to realize we have no future."

"And no choice. I always thought that fighting to the last man was a quaint idea that had been abandoned early in the Dark Ages. Yet here we are. I—" Francis broke off sharply. "Here they come, at least a full regiment of them!"

Three hundred or more enemy infantrymen carrying muskets, axes, ropes and scaling ladders were racing toward a point about one hundred and fifty feet to their left. The Huguenots manning the defense post at that position opened a scattered, feeble arquebus fire that did nothing to slow the advance, and Henry cupped his hands as he ran. "Sound the alert!" he called to a sentry.

The order was repeated, echoing through the corridors of the castle, and finally, after the wave of royalist troops had already reached the base of the castle wall, a horn wailed. Men raced from their posts throughout the fortress to the danger point, and while Henry arranged them in some semblance of military formation behind a shoulder-high wall, Francis took charge of a company that had been given the task of boiling tar for such emergencies.

The sortie was similar to others that had preceded it, but never had the royalists assaulted the castle in such strength, and it was apparent that this was a serious attempt to force an entry into the town. The few defenders armed with captured muskets formed in a thin line at the parapet, bolstered by troops with the most ancient and cumbersome of firearms, the flare-muzzled arquebus. Behind them, on a platform, stood the archers, who fired their arrows straight down into the milling mass of light infantry troops struggling to put their scaling ladders in place.

Musketeer marksmen had taken places about twenty yards from the walls, and were trying to pick off the defenders while their comrades tried to make the ladders secure. The men behind the ramparts were tempted to concentrate their fire on the musketeers, but experience had taught Henry that such tactics could cause disaster. Repeatedly he urged, commanded and begged his men to forget

121

the musketeers and direct their full attention to the assault troops. By then it was too late, and steel-helmeted infantrymen were swarming up the ladders.

Francis' pitchmen raced forward from their fires still blazing on an interior portion of the ramparts. Working in groups of three, they ignored the musketeers determined to annihilate them; mounting the ramparts, they poured cauldrons of boiling tar down onto the troops climbing the ladders.

Screams of terror and agony sounded above the rattle of firearms, and the assault was checked. But Francis de Cassaude had too few men and too little tar to accomplish his end, and although the ground around the ladders was littered with the bodies of the dead, the dying and the scalded, some of whom had dropped forty feet or more, other royalist soldiers took their places and swarmed up the ladders.

A young ensign leading his platoon was the first to leap onto the ramparts, but Henry was waiting for him and dispatched him with a single stroke of his sword. Francis had no time to boil more tar, so he improvised, and his pitchmen thrust burning brands at the ladders, trying to burn them. One caught fire, then another, driving the climbers back to the ground, but the company was decimated by steady, methodical musketeer fire by the time all the ladders were rendered inoperable.

By then a full battalion of royalist light infantry had reached the roof. Aware that their line of retreat was cut off, they fought viciously in an attempt to establish a permanant foothold on the ramparts. The defenders fought courageously, too, as individual, hand-to-hand encounters erupted all over the ramparts, but amateurs were no match for trained fighting men, and gradually the royalists gained an advantage. Henry, slashing and cutting with a skill born of desperation, tried repeatedly to rally his men, and finally had to send for more reinforcements. At least the musketeer fire had stopped, as the men outside the walls could not risk hitting their comrades.

A captain in a gold-trimmed uniform of powder-blue and a burnished helmet came at Henry, who recognized him as a member of the Mercoeur family, a man he had known the better part of his life. But in war an enemy was nameless and faceless: the captain feinted, then lunged, and his blade slid along the upper portion of Henry's corselet less than an inch from his exposed neck.

Two royal infantrymen were trying to circle around Henry to attack him from the rear, and he tried to think of the skills he had been taught in the fencing lessons he had found so boring as a boy. The captain lunged again, and this time Henry was ready for him, parrying, feinting and, leaping forward, putting the point of his blade through his opponent's throat. Never, he thought, would he forget the expression of pain and astonishment in the eyes of his dying foe.

His own danger was not over, however, and he whirled on the two soldiers, who were using their muskets as clubs. They were trying to maneuver him into a position between them, but he avoided the trap and concentrated on the smaller of the pair, and after a brief duel in which the sword was almost knocked out his hand, he managed to inflict a shoulder wound which immobilized the man, and the other soldier retreated.

The arrival of newcomers from other parts of the castle restored the balance, and although the defenses were stretched perilously thin elsewhere, Henry could only hope that ignorance would prevent General de Bertram from taking advantage of his weakness. Men had no chance to reload firearms, and resorted to knives, axes and musket butts as the savage struggle continued. A company of pikemen, some of them middle-aged veterans of Huguenot regiments that had fought at Amiens, appeared from another part of the town, and they proved the deciding factor in the combat.

One by one the royalists were eliminated, until their dead littered the ramparts. Finally a lieutenant, the only surviving officer in the attacking force, realized that his cause was hopeless and offered his sword to Henry. But the defenders were so incensed that they continued to fight, and had to be restrained by the pikemen.

The royalists, a pitifully small group, were marched off as prisoners, and Henry took the precaution of assigning a particularly strong detachment of guards to prevent the townspeople from clawing and stoning them. Finally, after order had been restored, Henry braced himself for the task he found the most disconcerting in war, the inspection of his own dead and wounded.

He started to move slowly up and down the lines of bodies stretched out on the rampart, but halted when Antoine de Mercé materialized at his side, touched him on the shoulder and silently pointed to a still figure in the shadow of a buttress. Henry went to it, looked down and caught his breath.

Francis de Cassaude stared with sightless eyes at the sky, a bullet hole between his eyes and another at the side of his neck. The day's victory had been decisive, but Pyrrhic.

A scorching sun burned in a pale sky, and a hot wind blew northward from the Pyrenees, a wind that, according to peasant legend, could drive a man mad if he should be exposed to it too long. In the camp of the royalist army, no one stirred except the sentries. Troops were stationed behind the line of breastworks that surrounded Montauban, but they lolled at their ease on the ground, ostensibly paying no attention to the beleaguered town. No cavalry patrols were abroad, and cannon crews sat beside their weapons but gave no indication they intended to man them.

Inside Montauban, everyone suspected a new trick. A full alert was sounded, and even those men who had been on night watch were recalled to their posts. Firearms were loaded, the little that was left of the supply of tar was boiled, and the gaunt civilians gathered in small groups at street corners and in front of their houses to speculate on what might happen now.

It was the eighty-fourth day of the siege.

At ten o'clock in the morning a colonel of a royalist regiment of infantry rode toward the Tarn River, two aides flanking him and a standard bearer carrying a white flag of truce preceding him. The defenders were surprised but Count Henry de Montauban responded in kind, and the colonel informed his emissary that General Leon de Bertram requested the honor of a conference with the garrison commander for the purpose of arranging terms that would conclude the hostilities. The astonished Henry immediately accepted.

Two men volunteered to polish his stained armor, and a cobbler did everything possible to restore some luster to his shabby boots. The shirt he wore beneath his steel corselet was frayed, but he consoled himself with the thought that the enemy wouldn't realize it.

Promptly at high noon Henry rode out of the Toulouse gate, three standard bearers carrying, respectively, the French lily ensign, the pennant with a red cross on a field of white that the Swedes used as a Protestant banner, and a cloth of truce. Antoine de Mercé rode a half-pace behind him, and his escort consisted of six mounted men armed with captured muskets.

General de Bertram approached from the opposite direction, and Henry felt a sudden surge of hatred when he saw that Cardinal de Bertram was a member of his party. Perhaps it was illogical to think of the cardinal as his mother's murderer; still, he had to control himself in order not to lose his temper or behave rashly.

The General's escort halted, and Bertram came forward alone. Henry ordered his men to halt, too, and went on to meet his arch-foe. They reined in their mounts only a few paces from each other and, their faces drained of all expression, exchanged stiff salutes.

Bertram broke the silence. "On behalf of His Majesty, Louis, the thirteenth King of France of that name, I am authorized to offer terms of peace that His Majesty makes out of consideration for his loyal subjects."

"On behalf of his loyal subjects of Montauban," Henry replied, "I am prepared to hear His Majesty's terms."

"The siege is ended, and the troops are being withdrawn today." General de Bertram flicked a smudge from his gold corselet.

Henry was too tired to be elated; the only sensation he felt was one of dull wonder, tinged with incredulity. "On what terms, General?"

"A full pardon has been granted to all who took part in the rebellion." Bertram took a parchment from a silken pouch and handed it to Henry.

The document bore the signature and seal of King Louis, and a quick glance through it indicated that the defenders would be safe from future retribution. What puzzled Henry was the reason behind the unexpected royal capitulation. He assumed that other nations had brought pressure to bear on the Louvre, and it was possible that Vatican Hill had intervened, too. He was reluctant to reveal his ignorance, but decided it was wiser to gain a thorough understanding of the situation before accepting the offer. It was possible he might be stepping into a trap.

"Montauban cannot agree to these terms if your troops are going to be used against other towns of the area," he said boldly.

A hint of a sardonic smile appeared in Bertram's gray eyes. "One forgets you've been out of touch with events elsewhere for some weeks, lord Count. His Majesty has terminated the siege because he wants no uprisings elsewhere. The imaginations of the poor and ignorant are always inflamed by acts of stupidity they interpret as heroism, and the Crown is anxious to restore peace to prevent other Huguenot communities from following the example of Montauban."

Henry made no attempt to conceal a broad grin. What the General had really told him was that the Calvinists of France were prepared to launch a full-scale civil war, and that the Louvre had called off the investment because a loss of face was preferable to a major internal conflagration that would weaken the country and tempt the Spaniards to seize the territory they had lost under the Treaty of Amiens.

"There are other matters to be settled," he said.

"Indeed." It was the General's turn to smile.

"My people will be allowed to keep their weapons, I presume?"

"Of course. You'll find that His Majesty has covered the point in the proclamation I've just given you. And no punitive measures will be taken against the town or the county."

Henry studied the parchment more closely. "I see no mention of the subject that was responsible for the unfortunate events of the past three months. I hope the King realizes Montauban will not, under any circumstances, pay the Church tax the Ministry of Finance tried to impose on her." Henry spoke loudly, for the benefit of Cardinal de Bertram, and for the first time allowed himself to look at the prelate. He had no idea his naked hatred showed so plainly, and felt a twisted sense of pleasure when the Cardinal averted his eyes.

The General found it difficult to admit defeat, and spoke in a toneless voice. "The ukase ordering Huguenot communities to pay a tithe to the Roman Catholic Church was rescinded ten days ago."

Antoine de Mercé and the men of Henry's escort could remain silent no longer, and started to cheer.

Henry half-turned in his saddle and silenced them with a glance. They would have ample opportunity to celebrate later, and it was unseemly to demonstrate their feelings so blatantly in the presence of their foes.

"The Crown," General de Bertram said, changing the subject with obvious relief, "attaches several conditions to the withdrawal of His Majesty's forces."

Henry stiffened.

"First, normal commerce must be resumed as soon as possible, and produce barges must be allowed to travel freely on the Tarn River."

"Agreed," Henry replied. "Our farmers have spent far too many weeks away from their fields."

"Second, Viscount Francis de Cassaude must agree to retire from public life and not present himself in Paris or at any other place where His Majesty's court may sit. After five years His Majesty will review the situation and, at his pleasure, may alter the terms."

"Tell Louis he needn't bother," Henry said, feeling a stab of deep pain. "Francis de Cassaude is dead."

Bertram was surprised, but reacted swiftly. A gentleman as well as a soldier, he raised his gloved hand to his gold helmet in salute. "I'm sorry to hear it. His talent for convoying food into the town during the early weeks of the siege was extraordinary. Under happier circumstances I would have applauded his ingenuity."

Henry returned the compliment with a bow, thinking that the exchange had no significance. Francis had given his life for a cause that had meant more to him than life, and empty praise wouldn't revive him. "Are there any more conditions, General?"

"There is one." The General looked a trifle embarrassed. "Henry de Montauban is banished from the land, and is forbidden to set foot on French soil again for the rest of his natural life. He is given seven days from this date to comply with the order. Should he be found within the borders of France after that time, he will be treated as a common criminal and subjected to His Majesty's justice."

Henry was stunned.

The General interpreted his silence as a reluctance to accept. "As an alternative," he said, still speaking in the third person, "Henry de Montauban will be permitted to submit his person to an ecclesiastical court on charges of apostasy."

Henry remembered the blood-chilling stories of the Inquisition that one of his Jesuit tutors had told him in his youth. "I'll go into exile," he said quietly.

Antoine de Mercé started to protest.

126

Henry silenced him with a sharp gesture. "I have no reason to remain in France. I have accomplished all I can do here."

"Then the matter is settled, and our business is concluded." Bertram cleared his throat. "Permit me a personal word, lord Count, and accept my condolences on the death of your mother. The murderers responsible for the tragedy acted contrary to my orders, and were executed the same day."

Henry ignored his outstretched hand, wheeled around and started toward the battered walls of Montauban. He would not miss Paris, life at the court or his former position at the Louvre, but it was a wrench to realize that this little place was the only real home he had ever known, and that he was being forced to leave it for all time.

Uppsala was a town that defied reason. In order to reach it a traveler had to ride more than forty miles north from Stockholm on rutted roads that seemed hemmed in by the deep pines and hemlocks of the Swedish countryside. Then, very suddenly, the forest vanished, and the visitor was dazzled by the copper-sheathed spires of its cathedral, the most splendid of Protestant houses of worship in Europe. Even the English ambassador had been heard to concede that it was a more impressive edifice than Westminster Abbey.

The town itself was a solid mass of stone buildings, most of them dormitories, eating halls and lecture auditoriums of the University, whose students were allegedly the most independent and hard-headed on the Continent. They had been known to stone professors they disliked, and on one occasion had set fire to the house of a dean who had dared expel a group of upperclassmen for drinking and rioting. The students of Uppsala paid no attention to the traditions of scholars elsewhere, and not only refused to wear academic gowns, but carried short swords and knives with ornamental handles which protruded from their boot-tops. They did wear mortar boards on their heads for purposes of identification, however, and tassels of different colors indicated their seniority.

On a cliff overlooking the town stood a small castle, difficult at best to approach in peacetime and virtually impossible for an invader to attack. Unlike castles in other lands, it was kept in a state of perfect repair at all times, and a permanent staff of masons replaced worn, chipped or loose blocks of granite.

The castle's armaments were formidable, and strangers who might have formed the impression they were ornaments soon learned better. The guns were tested every morning at sunrise, and farmers who lived many miles from Uppsala heard their roar. The cannon included three demi-culverin capable of firing more than one thousand yards

127

and two long-barreled culverin with ranges of almost twenty-five hundred yards. The pride of the artillery master were his three mammoth sakers, each of them weighing more than three and one-half tons. Their shot could not be fired a great distance, but each had the power to halt a whole regiment of infantry. Unlike the iron sakers of other nations, they were made of brass in accordance with a secret formula developed at the University. The ambassador of James I of England had offered to pay any sum for either a pair of the huge guns or the formula, but had been turned down. The secret was not for sale.

Life at the castle was simple, quiet and disciplined. Members of the household subsisted on a diet of roasted meat, black bread and a mead so bitter that foreigners who ate there wondered if the bees of Sweden were incapable of producing a sweet-tasting honey. The gentlemen who dined at long benches maintained a strict silence at meals, and social conversation was reserved for evening hours, when they gathered in the great hall to discuss philosophy and literature. Their mornings were devoted to fencing bouts, foot races and physical exercises intended to strengthen the muscles of their shoulders, arms and legs. In the afternoons they listened to lectures delivered by the highest-ranking generals in the Swedish army.

Visitors were immediately made aware of the total absence of women at the castle. Queen Maria Eleonora, a gentle princess whose brother was Elector of Brandenburg, preferred the relative comforts of Stockholm, and lived there with her ladies. It was rumored that she had twice asked to visit Uppsala, and had twice been refused. Even the cooks and other servants at the castle were men, and they were required to participate in daily physical exercises, too. The purpose of life at Uppsala was work, everyone was expected to keep fit, and there were no distractions.

Henry de Montauban spent three days and nights at the castle without catching a single glimpse of the man he had traveled from France to see. King Gustavus II Adolphus slept, ate and worked in a private tower suite. There he conferred at length with his First Minister and close friend, Axel Oxenstjerna, and other members of the government, received members of the diplomatic corps who had been forced to follow him from Stockholm, and heard daily reports from the commanders of his four army corps. Courteous staff officers told Henry that the King also fenced every day with two colonels who were reputedly the best swordsmen in his realm, and was receiving instructions in the art of fighting with his bare hands. His tutor was a burly sergeant who had been known to break a man's jaw with a single punch.

On the fourth morning of Henry's stay at Uppsala, when he was beginning to wonder whether his long journey had been in vain, he was summoned to the tower suite. No sentries stood on duty at the entrance, and the man who welcomed the Frenchman was young, only four years his senior, with a high forehead, a clean-shaven face, and eyes as glacially blue as the waters of icy Swedish lakes. He was dressed in rough breeches and a shirt of wool so plain that Henry knew him only because his likeness on the coins of the realm so closely resembled him.

"Your Majesty," Henry said in French.

Gustavus Adolphus shook his hand, and replied in German. "Welcome to Uppsala, lord Count." He paused, then switched to English. "You prefer this tongue?"

"Infinitely, Your Majesty."

"Then we'll speak in it. And don't be so formal."

"As you wish, sir."

The King led him down a corridor to a room lined with thousands of leather-bound books. Other books spilled onto chairs and tables, and Gustavus Adolphus moved a pile to give his guest a place to sit. "Reading," he said, "is my only relaxation."

Henry glanced at the books in the nearest cases, and was awed. He recognized titles in English, Spanish, Latin, Dutch and Italian as well as Swedish. He also saw a number that, he guessed, were written in Russian and Polish.

"My father," the King said with an infectious smile, "insisted I be given a thorough education. I've neglected the language of France, but in view of recent events there, I'll have no need to know it. I'll go there only as a conqueror, after I've finished business elsewhere, and her defeated rulers will have to oblige me by communicating in a tongue I already know."

Henry was surprised to see that he was in earnest.

A servant entered, unbidden, with two very large mugs of the inevitable bitter mead.

"Henry de Montauban," Gustavus Adolphus said, and surveyed his visitor critically. "You've made quite a name for yourself. I've made it my concern to find out all I could about you, and I gather you withstood the siege very handily. You could have forced back the investment lines with cavalry sorties, though."

"I had no cavalry at Montauban, sir."

"Ah, that explains it." The King was silent for a moment. "My agents have kept protective watch over you on your journey here, after you left Basel and Stuttgart. You were foolhardy to have spent two days in Mainz. The Papist bishop there is a zealous man, and had he known you were coming here—which should have been obvious to him—he would have detained you."

Henry smiled.

Gustavus Adolphus eyed him coldly. "My officers are required to make long-range plans to meet every situation. I tolerate no haphazard operations."

"I understand, sir."

"You don't, but you shall. De Montauban, I've heard several accounts of your rather dramatic break with Catholicism, and I'd like to hear your own."

Henry told him, as briefly as he could, the story of what had happened to his mother.

The King sipped his mead. "Your apostasy is emotional. But I assume you're still a Catholic intellectually."

"I've given up the Faith," Henry said, hoping the finality of his tone would end the subject.

Gustavus Adolphus persisted. "Do you miss your inability to take communion?"

"No, sir!"

"Or the fact that you live in a state of sin because you're refused the right of confession?"

"I don't consider myself a sinner. Nor does God, I'm sure."

"Are you? I hope so. Have you embraced Calvinism?"

"No, sir, nor Lutheranism. My relationship with the Almighty has become purely personal. I need neither Catholic priest nor Protestant minister as an intermediary." Until now Henry had discussed his feelings with no one, but realized the king of the Swedes demanded candor. "My theological education has been limited, sir. My tutors were priests. I've never studied the teachings of Calvin or Luther or Jan Huss. I'm not sure what I am, or how I'd be classified, and I don't much care. I can only tell you what I'm not: a Roman Catholic or an agnostic."

Gustavus Adolphus' laugh was a deep-throated roar. "Well said. Although I'm a soldier, not a clergyman, it seems to me that you stand with Servetius, but that's irrelevant to my purposes. Just before his recent death, Pope Paul V did me the honor of calling me Lucifer's deputy."

Henry, like every other literate man in Europe, knew of the Pope's remarks. He wanted to laugh, but saw that Gustavus Adolphus had become sober-faced again.

"I never cease to marvel at the gall of the Roman Church. They think themselves exclusively privileged to engage in missionary proselytization. I think they invented the Holy Spirit for the purpose. I've read every edition of the New Testament in print, both in Greek and Hebrew, and can find no explicit reference to the Holy Spirit in the teachings of Jesus Christ, much less authorization for the Church of Rome to trample on those who refuse their domination. But you'll have to forgive me, de Montauban, I digress.

"I have one ultimate aim. The reforms and church of Martin

Luther must not be allowed to perish. Pope Gregory is continuing the policies of Pope Paul. The issues will be decided in the German states. Don't you agree?"

Henry felt out of his depth. "I—I don't know, sir."

"The question was rhetorical. I'm aware of your ignorance, and have already assigned you a tutor. Gregory is concentrating on the reconversion of Germans to Catholicism. It's a very shrewd concept. If he succeeds, he can apply pressure on the Protestant lands that surround Germany. We'll be in danger, as will the English and the Swiss. Your French Huguenots will either conform or be exterminated. It's a damnably clever scheme, and I must admire Vatican Hill for conceiving it."

Henry had never thought in terms of the strategies employed by the opponents in Europe's great religious struggle, and began, dimly, to understand what they were.

"I must fight fire with my own brand of fire. I've dedicated my life to the preservation of Lutheranism in Germany. Will you stand with me?"

Henry knew only one answer. "I will, sir."

"Very well. One doesn't attack the enemy's center until his flanks are secure. I've already taught the Russians—in several campaigns—to leave Sweden alone when I'm occupied elsewhere, and now I'm ready to move against the Roman Catholics. Some of my staff have revealed my plans to you?"

"All I've gleaned is that you're preparing a campaign, sir. They've been very discreet."

"Good for them. I'll hang any man who talks out of turn." Gustavus Adolphus lost interest in his mead as he unrolled a map of central Europe. "Before I can attack the Papist states in Germany, I must crush Poland. I'm prepared to do it by the end of this year, and I offer you a place in my ranks."

Henry eagerly started to accept.

"Hear me out before you agree, de Montauban. "You did well—against a second-rate general. You were hailed in Hamburg as a hero, but you're not yet a real soldier. I must have commanders who devote their entire lives to the study and practice of war."

Henry was startled, having expected at least a measure of the lavish praise that had been heaped on him in Protestant nations and cities on his journey from France. Gustavus Adolphus' cold appraisal made him feel his victory at Montauban had been in vain.

"Few Catholics have guessed my purpose," the King continued. "When they realize I won't rest until the German states are free to worship as Lutherans if they wish, Vatican Hill will proclaim a holy war against me. I'm preparing for that day, which isn't far off. Officers of many nations are already being trained in my methods of waging war. I invite you to join them, provided you'll accept my conditions."

More cautious now, Henry waited to hear them.

"As my aims become better known, I expect to be joined by volunteers from every part of Europe. It's useful that you speak both French and English, but the core of my army is Swedish, so you will be required to learn my native tongue. In the heat of battle, my generals and I give orders in only one language, our own."

The demand sounded reasonable, and Henry nodded his assent.

"You'll be tutored in battle tactics and campaign strategy, and I'll expect you to become expert in the use of firearms as well as the traditional weapons of nobility. Your exploits this summer deserve recognition, so I'll give you the rank and pay of a captain. Your own talents will determine whether you'll serve with infantry, cavalry, artillery or engineers. And you'll have to earn your promotions in the field. If you demonstrate merit, there's no limit to the rank you can achieve in a growing army. If you fail, you'll be expected to resign your commission and leave my service. I fight for the glory of God, and have as little place in my regiments for amateurs as I have for false sentiment."

Had Henry still believed in miracles, he would have told himself that Divine Providence had led him to a man whose goal and will were as inflexible as his own. But he was not interested in the urges and feelings that had brought him to Sweden. It was enough that he was there. "I accept, sir, unconditionally," he said, and with those words became a mercenary soldier.

People who knew Axel Oxenstjerna only superficially, and he held virtually everyone at a distance, couldn't understand why the brilliant Gustavus Adolphus relied so heavily on him. An insignificant appearance, a portly build and a manner so discreet he sometimes seemed unable to communicate with others combined to create an impression of a nonentity. In the presence of his monarch, however, Oxenstjerna became transformed. His mild blue eyes became alert, his air of modesty vanished and he spoke with the authority of a man who knew his counsel was appreciated.

"Sometimes," he said incisively, "you fool yourself."

"Help yourself to some mead," Gustavus Adolphus told his first lieutenant. "I'm in no mood for a lecture."

"As you wish. But it would be unwise to leave Sweden before we define our objectives in the German states."

Gustavus Adolphus sighed, lowered himself into a chair and nodded. He had always found it useful to analyze the goals of a campaign before waging a new war, and Axel, the only one of his subjects who was his intellectual peer, had been enormously helpful to him in the past. However, he didn't feel like talking now. "Tomorrow, Axel. I'm going out for a canter in the forest tonight."

"Alone?"

"Yes."

Oxenstjerna seemed to read his mind. "Just as I thought. Your meeting with the young Frenchman disturbed you."

"Nonsense. I spent no more than a quarter of an hour with him."

"All the same, you saw a reflection of yourself in him."

Gustavus Adolphus stood, walked to his tower windows and then returned to his chair. "He—and so many like him—think of what's ahead as a holy Protestant crusade, Axel."

"And you don't?" Oxenstjerna, the King's conscience, sat very still, prodding him.

"It's never that simple for a man in my position, and you know it!" Gustavus Adolphus sounded accusing.

Other men shrank when the great warrior raised his voice in anger, but Oxenstjerna shrugged. "Do you find your position so unusual?"

"Damn you, I don't want to be catechized tonight!"

"I wonder," Oxenstjerna said blandly, "whether you remember our meeting with Tsar Michael of Russia at Duelino three years ago."

"How could I forget it? I forced him to cede me half the province of Finland."

"On our last night at Duelino, after everyone had been drinking too much of Michael's vodka, you told him you bore him no grudge because he was the head of the Orthodox Church. You told him your real reason for fighting Russia had been to expand the borders of Sweden."

"I exaggerated." Gustavus Adolphus turned up the fur collar of his hunting jacket to shut out the sound of his friend's voice.

"In spite of exaggerating, you'll admit there was a core of truth in what you said."

"You know as well as I that we wanted Finland!"

"Precisely. So what bothers you now is the thought that you're deluding and cheating the Protestants of Europe. Men like Henry de Montauban offer you their services in a war to the death against the Pope, and your conscience hurts when you accept, because you're fighting for the advancement of Sweden."

"Axel, you have habit of twisting facts. It's a king's duty to further the aims of his own country and people. Philip of Spain was Vatican Hill's strongest supporter, but the cause of Castile and Aragon didn't suffer in his wars. He saw to that. Henry of France made peace with Rome because he needed time to consolidate his country. The Eng-

133

lish are in a position to pursue an independent policy because they have a national church and are responsible to no one but themselves. Even the Portuguese——"

"I was speaking," Oxenstjerna interrupted, "of Sweden."

"Now you're being obstinate," Gustavus Adolphus roared. "My father knew it would take at least two generations to lead this country out of the Dark Ages, and I was trained for my destiny from birth!"

"Would you call it a coincidence that Sweden's rise as a great power is taking place simultaneously with your attacks on the Catholic states?"

"It's astonishing how stupid you can be when you close your mind. The Church of Rome was directly responsible for the Dark Ages. The Church—" Gustavus Adolphus broke off abruptly. "Very well, Axel, I'll stop making speeches and talk sense. Our own Nordic sloth made us backward. Does that satisfy you? That Italian astronomer, Galileo, was denounced by Vatican Hill seven years ago for supporting the theories of Copernicus because some very ignorant men who wore cardinals' hats were unable to distinguish theology from scientific theory. Does that satisfy you?"

"A distinct improvement," Oxenstjerna murmured. "Go on."

"Like it or not," Gustavus Adolphus said vigorously, "we live in a time when religious and national considerations can't be separated. The wealthiest and most powerful nations, which want to preserve present borders, are Catholic, and naturally have the full support of the Pope. Sweden can expand only at the expense of those nations. So the cause of religious freedom for Protestants and the future of Sweden are inseparable."

Oxenstjerna grinned broadly. "You've finally defined our objectives in the coming campaign. I think I'll have a cup of that mead now."

Gustavus Adolphus smiled, too, as he filled two cups. "If you were a Papist, you'd be an archbishop, at the very least. You're a remarkably devious man, Axel."

His friend accepted a cup and raised it in a silent toast. "And you're sometimes too sensitive for your own good. You're always restless before the start of a new campaign, and that's when you worry too much about others."

"I suppose you're right." Gustavus Adolphus drank the better part of his mead, belched and patted his stomach. "Henry de Montauban and all the others like him must recognize themselves as adventurers. My fellow adventurers. You know, Axel, I imagine the Catholic generals feel as we do, and enjoy fighting as much for its own sake as for principle. The Papists have had hundreds of years to reconcile and blend man's love of war with his need for ideals. We've put ourselves in a difficult position. We must match them overnight, so to speak, or

134

perish. It makes me very uncomfortable to realize they'll be praying to the same God before a battle."

It was Oxenstjerna's turn to become disturbed. "Are you growing cynical?"

"Certainly not. I sleep at night for two reasons: We have the better army, and I'm sure in my own mind that we have God's support—because He must know our cause is just."

1632-1633

The sweet, faintly heavy scent of almond blossoms drifted up through the open windows of the master bedchamber on the second floor of the Paris townhouse and seeped through the curtains of light silk that closed off the fourposter bed. Charles de Montauban felt the warm, supple body of the girl beside him and, still half-asleep, pulled her to him. She was barely conscious, too, and offered no resistance as he kissed her and ran his hands up and down her body.

Their desire mounted, slowly at first, then very swiftly. Charles' demands became more urgent, the girl responded with a desire that matched his, and he took her. Only then, after she dropped off to sleep again, did he become sufficiently wide awake to realize all that had happened in the past twelve hours.

He climbed out of bed, hurried into his adjoining dressing chamber and rang for the servants. Plunging his face into a bowl of cold water helped to clear his head, and although he usually ate sparingly in the morning, he devoured a fish poached in white wine, a cold roasted chicken and a slab of thick bread soaked in beef juice. Then, sipping a glass of spiced wine as he dressed, he considered his situation.

It had been a crass, stupid mistake to bring Eloise de Vendôme home with him last night. That much was obvious. On the other hand, after she had made it so patently evident that she had been willing, even eager, to have an affair with him, there had been no other place to take her. They might have sneaked into her apartment at the Vendôme palace, but the very idea shocked him. He could not forget, even though it might be a matter of indifference to her, that she was the adopted daughter of Caesar de Vendôme, son of King Henry IV and Gabrielle d'Estrées. No man in his right mind ravished the daughter of a duke in her father's house.

Of course Charles could have rejected her bold offer of a liaison,

135

and avoided complications, but the thought hadn't crossed his mind, and he smiled wryly. When a man was still a bachelor at the age of thirty, he took love—or substitutes for love—where he could find them. And Eloise was the most alluring young woman at the court of her uncle, Louis XIII. Every man who ever attended a levee at the Louvre was aware of the magnetism of her wide-set, green eyes, the fascination of her wheat-colored hair and the power of the voluptuous figure she rarely bothered to conceal beneath low-cut gowns of thin silk.

She wasn't a princess, of course, as Caesar de Vendôme had been excluded from the right of succession to the throne, and that was a blessing. A man could be hanged for trifling with the affections of royalty, and Cardinal Richelieu, the King's First Minister, was capable of inflicting severe punishment for such an offense. There were other aspects of the situation to be weighed, too. As Eloise had demonstrated so convincingly last night and again this morning, she was no stranger to love. So at least some of the stories whispered about her at the Louvre were undoubtedly true.

Nevertheless, others who had enjoyed her favors hadn't been foolish enough to advertise their indiscretion by taking her to their own homes. And he doubted whether any of them held posts as prominent as his in the government. Richelieu expected his deputies to avoid scandal and keep out of trouble. Charles shuddered, sighed and drained his glass.

"How inhospitable you are! I'm parched and starved, but I haven't been offered a drop to drink or a crust of stale bread!"

Charles turned to see Eloise de Vendôme in the entrance to the dressing room. Her uncombed hair tumbled about her bare shoulders, below which she clutched a robe of thin silk. Although it was far too large for her, she nevertheless contrived to let it fall partly open. He was startled, which pleased her, and she enjoyed his subsequent rush of embarrassment.

"Put on your clothes," he said, "and I'll have you served a banquet."

Eloise sank into a chair and crossed her long, bare legs. "I refuse to move," she announced, "until I've had breakfast."

Charles looked at her for a moment, saw she meant to keep her word, and with great reluctance pulled the bell-rope. The sight of a woman in his private quarters would be no novelty to his staff, but never had they seen anyone of Eloise's stature here. He took care to meet his major-domo at the door, partly blocking the man's view of the lovely Marquise de Vendôme.

Eloise poured herself some wine from the pitcher on the table beside her, and tossed back her uncombed curls. "I had no idea your house could be so charming. You're such an austere man, or least you gave the impression of it until last night," she added with a mischievous, throaty laugh. "I assumed you slept in a hair shirt—on boards."

She was mocking him and he didn't know how to strike back. "The house is as it was in my parents' time. I've changed nothing."

"That, my darling, is obvious." Eloise's eyes narrowed as she looked around the room, absorbing every detail. "This would be far more suitable as a woman's dressing room."

"It was my father's." He felt a little resentful. "My mother used the room on the other side of the bedchamber."

"In your mother's day," she replied lightly, "women used fewer cosmetics and had to be less careful of their appearance. It's impossible to have too much light when putting antimony on one's eyelids, you know—or you wouldn't, really—and this room has a south light. Yes, it's infinitely preferable."

Her breakfast arrived, the tray carried by a maidservant who eyed the visitor surreptitiously, to Charles' increased mortification. Before evening the members of every noble household in Paris would know where the Marquise de Vendôme had spent the night.

Eloise seemed unconcerned about her reputation as she attacked her poached fish. "What a bachelor's life you lead here. Look at all this food! I rarely touch anything but a few slices of dry toast and a hard-boiled egg or two that's been soaked in herbs and brandywine. It's supposed to be good for the skin. I shall have to give your chef the recipe."

"I have no interest in improving my complexion," Charles said.

She smiled, but said nothing.

A clock chimed in the bedchamber, and he took a short dress sword and belt from a cupboard drawer. "I hope you won't think me too lacking in gallantry, but His Eminence is expecting me for a conference this morning."

"How do you plan to send me home?"

Charles was surprised. "In my carriage, of course. I'll ride one of the horses from my stable to the Cardinal's house."

Eloise shook her head. "You escorted me here. I have the right to insist that you escort me home."

He was dismayed. "It isn't yet eight o'clock in the morning!" If anyone saw them riding together so early in the day, the girl's reputation would be compromised for all time. What was more, the old-fashioned carriage was too wide to be driven down most streets, which meant that the coachman would be forced to use the main thoroughfares that led to the Vendôme palace. "Perhaps you've forgotten that Richelieu insists all public officials must be at their desks by half-past eight. We'd be seen by scores of people who know you!"

Another throaty laugh exploded as Eloise toyed demurely with her

137

poached fish. "Are you ashamed to be seen in public with me, Charles?"

"You know I'm not. We left the King's reception together last night. And that's the problem. A great many people will put one and one together."

"My father," she replied, still looking down at her food, "says it was a waste of time to have me tutored. But I do remember that one and one make two."

Charles felt trapped, and wasn't sure he disliked the sensation. He had always told himself he intended to marry when he found the right woman, but in the past year or two he had doubted he would ever meet her. He couldn't pretend to himself that he loved Eloise, but had to admit she was enormously exciting. He could do far worse than marry the adopted grand-daughter of Henry of Navarre, who also happened to be the most ravishing young lady at court.

He realized, to be sure, that Eloise was deliberately maneuvering him into a corner from which there was no escape. But he couldn't decide whether he sought escape. Viewing the matter dispassionately, from its legal and moral aspects, he was forced to admit that, in sobriety and full consciousness of what he'd been doing, he had brought her here and seduced her. And the fact that the experience had not been her first was irrelevant, inasmuch he hadn't known it at the time. Besides, he very much doubted that there were many virgins at court. Richelieu cared nothing about questions of morality, and made no attempt to curb the appetites of the King. Everyone said that, if Louis lived long enough, he'd have more official mistresses than the fifty-six his father had boasted.

"Well?" Eloise demanded, a hint of sharpness in her voice. "Will you or will you not oblige me?"

Charles could temporize no longer. "You'll have to dress quickly," he said. "I can't keep Richelieu waiting."

From the upper stories of his palace, Armand Jean du Plessis, Cardinal Richelieu, could look down and see the equestrian statue of Henry IV that he had erected on a small hill overlooking the River Seine. On the day of its dedication he had gracefully and untruthfully announced that he had made the gift as gesture to King Louis and the Queen Mother. Anyone acquainted with Richelieu knew better. He himself often peered down at the figure on horseback, and drew both inspiration and strength from it. The task begun by Henry to make France the most powerful nation in Europe, Richelieu intended to complete.

A short, dark man with a high forehead, deep-set eyes and a pointed beard that resembled drawings of Satan in the Abbey of St. Martin, where he had passed his novitiate, he liked to give outsiders the impression that he lived frugally. The few nobles privileged to visit his palace instead of his office at the Louvre knew that his appetite for luxury was insatiable.

The palace, five stories high, filled a square city block, and its scores of rooms were crammed with paintings, statues and bric-a-brac, superb tapestries and rich rugs, treasures acquired in every far corner of the known world. Charles de Montauban argued that the Cardinal's attitude was not really a pose. He spent vast fortunes for works of art because he enjoyed beauty for its own sake. Certainly he made no attempt to awe others with his riches.

And certainly he had no need to overwhelm anyone. As the only man who had ever succeeded in halting the interminable quarrels between Marie de Medicis, her son, and the young Queen, Anne of Austria, Richelieu was the absolute master of France.

Charles, bowing at the entrance to the Cardinal's crowded study, felt uneasy as he caught his first glimpse of Richelieu in several weeks. When not in his presence one was inclined to forget that he was so pale and thin; without his billowing red robes he would be as puny as an undernourished street urchin. But one quickly disabused himself of the idea that the man was sickly. His manner was august and somewhat imperious as he beckoned with a thin forefinger, and his intense, almost hypnotic eyes seemed permanently fixed on a visitor's face.

"You do me great honor, Your Eminence," Charles said politely.

Richelieu never wasted time on the amenities. "Sit down, Charles. You'll be interested in fresh news of your brother."

"We don't correspond."

"Yes, I know. I've been informed he fought superbly in the Swedes' campaign to relieve the siege of Magdeburg, and routed the best horsemen in the Holy Roman Empire. Gustavus Adolphus has rewarded him with another promotion, this time to acting commander of the cavalry brigade."

Charles' emotions were so mixed when he thought of his brother that he became upset. Although he knew Richelieu never chatted idly or gossiped, he could think of no adequate reply.

"A pity he serves Sweden, not France. We could make good use of a soldier with his talents." The Cardinal picked up an alabaster statuette of a dog from his desk, a work by the Florentine, Benvenuto Cellini, that he had purchased from the Duke of Tuscany, and stroked it lovingly. "In a sense, he serves France indirectly. Charles, what would you, as my legal adviser, say if I told you I've made a secret compact with the Swedes?"

Charles wondered if the Cardinal was exercising his exquisitely subtle sense of humor, but Richelieu's eyes were solemn. "It would be unusual," he replied bluntly, "for someone of your calling and rank to make a treaty with Lucifer."

"You confirm my faith in you, Charles. Yoo have the finest of all attributes for a man in your profession. You see the world in pure blacks and solid whites, you weigh every concept literally, and you have no imagination whatever. It's quite simple, you see. Who is Gustavus Adolphus' most powerful enemy? Ferdinand of Austria. And who is Ferdinand? A Hapsburg, cousin of the King of Spain. Now, then, I ask you. Who gains if the Swedes are defeated?"

"Austria, the Holy Roman Empire—and Christendom, Your Eminence." Charles was growing more confused.

"Wrong, my dear fellow. The House of Hapsburg. Austria and Spain form a new alliance, a family alliance, and wait for the opportunity to crush France. Therefore Ferdinand must be defeated. Gustavus Adolphus' purse is none too full, after all his years of supporting an army, so I've granted him unlimited credit. In a private arrangement that must be made known to no one, of course."

Charles wondered if the Cardinal had gone mad. "You're giving gold to the anti-Christ, Your Eminence?"

"For the present. Until England becomes more powerful. If King Charles and his Parliament stop feuding, you know, the English represent a very serious threat to our security."

Charles could not think beyond the incredible fact that a cardinal of the Church was supplying the money that paid the wages and brought armaments, food and uniforms for Rome's deadliest enemy. "Does—His Holiness know of your agreement?"

"Certainly not!" Stupidity annoyed Richelieu. "Pope Urban is a pious man who should devote himself to saving souls instead of meddling in international affairs—about which he knows nothing. You were kind enough to make me an analysis of his proposal for a holy war against the Ottomans, so you know he's an impractical idealist. Let him concern himself with the problems of Christianity, which will make it far easier for me to concentrate on the advancement of France."

Perhaps it was true, as so many claimed, that the Cardinal had not celebrated Mass in fifteen years.

Richelieu saw the stunned expression in Charles' eyes, and sighed gently. "I'm astonished that you, the son of a son who must have understood the basic truths of humanity's needs, should be so blind. Your father served Henry the Fourth, the Huguenot champion of champions, who became a nominal Catholic so that all Frenchmen could live together in friendship and work side by side in making this nation great. Is it so strange that I, who was ordained a priest and spent eight years as the spiritual shepherd of a parish, should have found what I believe to be a more urgent need?"

Charles watched the sunlight play on the Cardinal's ecclesiastical ring.

"This nation can lead all mankind into a Promised Land. Sixteen centuries ago the Lord Jesus showed us the road to civilization and peace, but we're still barbarians who make war—in His name. My goals are the same as Pope Urban's—and even those of Gustavus Adolphus. I want peace between men and nations. Let the followers of Calvin and Knox and Luther and the other so-called apostates believe what they wish and worship as they please. May God help me, I must move slowly to prevent too violent a reaction after I'm gone, but I'd grant freedom of worship to Jews. And to Moslems. The Pope's idea of a holy war makes no sense. He should rejoice that the Turks worship God."

The doctrine was too radical for Charles to grasp.

"Never mind," Richelieu said. "Be glad I don't often preach these sermons. I've wanted to see you this morning on a personal matter that isn't irrelevant to what I've been saying."

Charles felt as he often did when he sat in this room. The Cardinal moved so quickly from one subject to the next that it was impossible to follow him.

"Since your brother's banishment, you've been administering the affairs of Montauban. In effect you've been a count, without the title or final authority, and that isn't good. I can achieve a greater administrative efficiency only by insisting that the nobles accept responsibility for their fiefs." Richelieu put aside the alabaster dog, and picked up a seal on which his crest was carved in jade.

"Montauban has demonstrated its loyalty to the Crown ever since the siege, Your Eminence." Charles was disturbed. "If you have cause for complaint against my people, I——"

"I have none." Richelieu tossed aside the jade seal. "What bothers me is a question of finances. You've put aside the greater part of the county's revenues each year."

"Of course. I'm keeping those funds in trust for my brother, and for his son, who will inherit the title."

"You assume Henry will marry. Meanwhile you've accumulated and are still accumulating one of the largest private fortunes in France."

Charles suddenly knew the reason for the meeting. The funds he saved for Henry and Henry's heirs could not be taxed by the Ministry of Finance. Not even Richelieu, whose hunger for gold was insatiable, could rescind the law regarding the handling of trusts without destroying the foundations of the system on which the nobility—and the Crown itself—gained their revenues.

"Now that you're contemplating marriage," the Cardinal continued, "we should review the whole situation in Montauban."

Charles wondered if the man was a sorcerer. A score of people could have reported to Richelieu that he had been attentive to Eloise de Vendôme in recent weeks and that they had left the reception at the Louvre together. But he himself had not contemplated marriage until this very morning, when Eloise had so forcibly raised the issue.

The younger man appeared so bewildered that Richelieu allowed himself the luxury of a half-smile. "I know something about human nature," he said, and refrained from adding that he also understood Caesar de Vendôme's daughter.

"If I could, Your Eminence, I'd release my brother's funds. But I cannot be disloyal to my parents, who would have wanted me to act as I'm doing." Charles' conviction was so strong that he felt no fear of the all-powerful man who sat across the desk from him. "I've never heard from my brother, and he probably doesn't even know I'm saving his revenues for him. But some day his exile will end——"

"It will not, I assure you. Louis has inherited no Bourbon traits except stubborn pride and a long memory. He'll never forgive Henry de Montauban."

Charles could be stubborn, too. "My hands are tied, Your Eminence."

Richelieu removed the stopper from a jeweled perfume container and sniffed the contents appreciatively. "Your lady has expensive tastes."

"Then she'll have to curb them. I live within my income."

The Cardinal stood, indicating that the interview was at an end. "I think it wrong for any man to defy his own conscience. In time, perhaps, you'll change your mind."

Both of them knew what he really meant was that Eloise might try to change it for him.

The Swedes' cannon stood in two long rows almost at right angles to each other, some emplaced on the banks of the Wertach River, the rest on the shores of the River Lech. All were trained on the walled Bavarian city of Augsburg which stood almost fifteen hundred feet above them on a plateau, and they thundered from daybreak until sunset. Heavy clouds of smoke curled up from the older portion of the town, where the Austrian garrison was entrenched in strength, and the attackers could only hope that the commander of the Catholic forces had kept his word and permitted the civilians, most of them Lutherans, to take refuge in the newer portion of the city, which was untouched.

Gustavus Adolphus hated sieges, which were long and dull, and this operation was particularly repugnant to him. "Augsburg must be relieved," he had said to his senior commanders when they had first invested the city. "More than two-thirds of her people are Protestants. They're the Pope's hostages, and I want to spare them suffering, if we can. But, no matter what the cost, the walls must come down."

Swedish infantry, supported by battalions of volunteers from Brandenburg and other Lutheran strongholds in Germany, completely surrounded Augsburg, and each day pushed their lines a little closer to the high walls. "When I take the field," Gustavus Adolphus had once said, "I never rest, and neither do my men. We have no need for rest." The foot soldiers and engineers, who spent their days behind earthworks and their nights digging new trenches, agreed with the first part of his statement.

So did the gunners, who were forced to pour buckets of water from the rivers on their cannon to prevent the frequently overheated weapons from exploding. The siege masters, bringing up fresh supplies of food and filling never-ending requests for munitions and gunpowder, were exhausted, too. But the cavalry claimed they worked harder than all the rest.

They said that Brigadier Henry de Montauban, their commander, ate all his meals in the saddle and never slept, which was a slight exaggeration. They also said he insisted they match his efforts, which was the literal truth. Troops of cavalry were active day and night, driving off relief columns that tried to reach the beleaguered Austrians, preventing the defenders from making sorties that would disrupt the digging of siege lines, and, by their show of determination, convincing the commander of the garrison and his deputies that they would be wise to give in to Gustavus Adolphus' demands for unconditional surrender.

Newcomers to the brigade assumed that Henry was Swedish, which he took as a compliment. The sun had burned his skin a dark brown, and had bleached his eyebrows. The lines in his face were deep, permanently etched after more than a decade of unceasing warfare, and he carried himself, whether mounted or on foot, with an air of self-disciplined authority similar to that of Gustavus Adolphus himself.

"Keep out of musket range," Henry told his horsemen. "When you can, avoid risks. But when you must, be daring. Above all, let no man enter or leave Augsburg, or I'll have your heads for it."

Recruits who had joined the brigade just prior to the laying of the siege discovered he was not using a mere figure of speech. Late one afternoon, during the second week of the siege, a mounted courier galloped out of Augsburg and escaped from a three-man cavalry patrol. At dawn the following morning Henry hanged all three of the negligent troopers in the presence of the entire brigade.

Thereafter, the few sorties attempted by the Austrians collapsed, and no one left the city.

By the time the siege entered its second, dreary month, however, Gustavus Adolphus was becoming impatient. "De Montauban," he told Henry at a staff meeting, "capture some prisoners and learn all you can about conditions in the city. The Austrians know that when Augsburg falls we intend to invest Ulm, and the longer we're forced to cool our heels here, the more time we give them to prepare their defenses at Ulm. I can't wait forever. Find out whether their food supplies will last, or whether people are being rationed. I want to know whether the garrison is still in control, or whether the Lutherans are waiting for a chance to revolt. I don't care how you do it, de Montauban, but capture some prisoners who can tell us what's happening behind those confounded walls!"

Henry set a trap, then baited it. He decreased the size of his patrols operating on the plateau outside the city, in order to encourage the Austrians to send more couriers to Munich, the headquarters of the Hapsburg high command. But he took no chances, and stationed strong forces on the wooded slopes leading up to the plateau from the banks of the two rivers. Sooner or later, he hoped, the defenders would be fooled by his ruse.

The Austrians proved cautious, and King Gustavus Adolphus' demand for prisoners was so insistent that Henry further loosened the web of his net. He completely removed his patrols from the plateau after sundown, but doubled the strength of his units on watch in the wooded hills below. The defenders suspected a trick, and for several nights made no move, but finally the lure proved irresistible, and the commander tried to communicate with his superiors in the outside world by sending three messengers in a desperate attempt to make their way through the Swedish lines.

The night was dark, and a light drizzle fell just before the trio slipped out of the city, but several squadrons of cavalry were waiting, and while one troop of horsemen cantered ahead to cut off the fugitives, scores of mounted men closed in on the trio.

Henry was eating a late supper of boiled beef and black bread in his tent on the bank of the Wertach when the sound of pistol shots sent him hurrying into the open. Members of his staff were running to their houses, too, but before they could mount, an aide appeared from the woods and announced, "We caught three of them, sir!"

"At last." Henry removed his helmet, which gave him blinding headaches when he wore it too long at a time. "Bring them to me."

The junior officer hesitated. "The leader put up a fight to give the others a chance to get away. I—I'm afraid he was killed, sir."

"By whom?" Henry was furious, having stressed repeatedly that anyone trying to flee Augsburg was to be captured, not killed.

"The third troop of the Brandenburg Hussars, Brigadier de Montauban. They——"

"Never mind. I'll deal with them later. Go through the pockets of the dead man for any information that might be useful, and bring the prisoners to me." Henry returned to his tent, where the better part of his meal was still spread on the table, and he began to eat again by the light of a small oil lamp. Through the years he had learned that a casual approach was sometimes the most effective when questioning prisoners.

A broad-shouldered Viking pushed his way into the tent. "I've heard," he said, and helped himself to a mug of dark ale, which he poured from a pitcher. Colonel Erik Lang was a knight, heir to a Swedish barony and, as deputy commander of cavalry, was on terms of easy familiarity with his superior. "Have you sent word to the King?"

"Not yet. I don't want to raise his hopes until I find out how much the prisoners know. Have some beef."

"I've just finished my supper, thanks. You've heard about the Brandenburg Hussars' mistake?"

"Yes, and I'll have their hides for it later." Henry raised his head, then frowned when a junior officer appeared, followed by two soldiers guarding a single prisoner. "Where's the other one?"

The young lieutenant took a deep breath. "He—put a knife into himself as we were bringing him here, sir."

Erik Lang put a huge hand on Henry's shoulder to prevent too violent an explosion, but the gesture was wasted.

"Where in God's name did he get a knife?"

"It was his own, sir. The men who captured him hadn't searched him thoroughly, and——"

"Get out," Henry said, and everyone in the tent knew he would require a heavy penalty for the error.

A moment later he and Lang were alone with the remaining prisoner, a pale-faced man in his mid-thirties who stood patiently, his hands tied behind his back.

"Search him, will you, Erik?" Henry forced himself to simulate calm and speared a chunk of beef on his knife.

Lang started to make a thorough examination of the prisoner, but halted when, throwing open the man's cloak, he saw a silver Crucifix suspended from a delicately wrought chain.

"Who are you?" Henry demanded, addressing the prisoner in German.

"The Reverend Pieter Stein."

"You're a priest?"

"Yes. I have the honor to serve as chancellor of the episcopal see of Augsburg."

Henry exchanged a quick glance with Erik. The first assistant to the Roman Catholic Bishop of Augsburg would be able to provide them with a great deal of information. "Are there so few men in the Austrian garrison that a priest must do a courier's work, Father?"

"My bishop hoped to send me to Rome on a mission no layman could perform."

Erik Lang completed his examination and, satisfied that the prisoner carried no weapons, returned to his mug of ale.

"What was your mission, Father?" Henry still spoke calmly, almost cordially.

The priest answered in the same tone. "It was a private communication, intended only for the ears of the Holy Father."

"But now you'll tell it to me." Henry's smile indicated that his good humor was dissipating.

The priest remained silent.

Henry stood, went to him and slapped him so hard across the face that his head wobbled for a moment. "You elected to defy the siege proclaimed and enforced by His Swedish Majesty, Father. You're our prisoner, and you'll tell us everything we want to know. You could have stayed in Augsburg and starved with the rest, but you tried to leave. Your purpose, by your own admission, was that of carrying a message to the enemy."

"His Holiness," Father Stein said very softly, "is no man's enemy."

Henry ignored the interruption. "In this life," he said, "a man must pay penalties for his failures. In time of war those penalties are particularly high. I have no wish to harm you, but I am determined to find out what we need to know. Will you tell me your message to Pope Urban?"

The priest compressed his lips.

Henry sighed, took a single step backward and looked his victim up and down.

"Let me take care of the rest," Colonel Lang said. "You've had a long day."

Henry shook his head. "Untie his hands, Erik. It still makes me ill to strike a man who can't defend himself."

Lang cut the prisoner's bonds with the knife that had been standing in the slab of boiled beef.

Suddenly, without warning, Henry lashed out with his fist and landed a vicious blow on the priest's cheekbone.

The man dropped to one knee.

Henry hauled him to his feet, smashed another right into his face and followed it with a short but equally hard punch on the side of his head.

Stein toppled to the ground and lay still.

"Is he still conscious?" Lang asked.

"I think so." Henry nudged him with his boot, then kicked him below the ribs.

The priest moaned.

"He's awake." Henry bent over him. "Now, Father, what was your message to the Pope?"

Father Stein's mouth was bleeding, his lips were puffed and it was difficult for him to speak. "His Grace of Augsburg," he muttered, "wanted me to beg His Holiness to send us every Christian soldier in Europe."

"Why?"

"So we won't be murdered by the butchers from the North."

Henry lifted him to his feet, and the priest stood, swaying dizzily.

"Feed him some ale, Erik. So Augsburg is desperate, Father? The bishop—and perhaps the Austrians—think the garrison can't hold out much longer?"

Stein's eyes were glazed, but he refused the ale and again clamped his jaws.

"Papists," Henry said to his subordinate, "sometimes think their faith will sustain them in a time of trial. Amazing, isn't it? Priests are more inclined than laymen to make the mistake." His voice became harsh. "If you must be a martyr, Father, I'll have to give you your chance, but I'd prefer a voluntary statement from you. Tell us everything you know of conditions in the city, and I give you my word that you'll be given a meal, a bed—and an escort to the main gate tomorrow morning."

Blood trickled down the priest's face, but he made no attempt to speak.

Henry was exasperated, and pummeled him hard, raining blows on him so furiously that Lang finally felt compelled to intervene.

"We don't want him to die before he tells us what the King wants to know."

Henry hoisted the sagging, battered priest onto a barrel he had been using as a chair. "Father," he said, speaking slowly and distinctly, "I'll keep this up until you give us the information we seek."

The clergyman could tolerate no more. In a low mumble he explained that food supplies in the city were so short they would be exhausted in another week, that the garrison was rapidly losing control of the Lutherans in the community, and that the Catholics were in an ugly, insurrectionist mood, too. He spoke with great effort, and when he finished his recital he was scarcely able to whisper, "I forgive you."

Henry caught him as he slumped, and Lang summoned the guard.

Henry stared at the still body on the ground.

Lang bent over the priest. "He's dead."

Henry felt irritated, but his mood quickly changed. "It doesn't matter. He told us everything he knew." He beckoned to the soldiers who were waiting at the entrance. "At daybreak," he directed, "take this man's body to the city gates under a flag of truce. Leave it outside the walls, and don't interfere when the enemy collects it. The effect on the garrison will be very unsettling." He kicked a little dirt over the still damp spots of blood on the ground after the guards removed the priest's body.

"Gustavus Adolphus will be pleased," Lang said.

"He should be." Henry took a basin of water from an orderly, and scooped some soft, yellow soap from a jar. "Come with me when I report to him, Erik," he added, washing the stains from his hands. "We'll have a real celebration tonight. I think all of us are tired of Augsburg." He dried his hands and bellowed for the orderly. "Clean up this tent, and get rid of that meat. If there's one dish I can't tolerate cold, it's boiled beef."

An early autumn rain drenched the French countryside, but it was dry and warm in the stone cottage located deep in the woods on Caesar de Vendôme's estate near Saint-Denis, a few miles from Paris. A small fire of aromatic pines burned in the hearth, and Eloise de Montauban sighed happily as she began to unpack a hamper filled with roasted meats, game and loaves of bread. "This is so heavy!" she said as she turned a small stone crock in her hands.

Charles, removing the wax seal from a jar of wine, looked at his wife appreciatively. Her gown of delicate pink set off her skin to perfection, and she had never looked lovelier. It didn't matter in the least that she was impractical, and he laughed as he rescued the crock, which she had placed on the floor near the hearth. "This is butter, so I suggest we keep it closer to the windows, unless you like it melted."

She giggled helplessly. "Oh, dear. Being the grand-daughter of King Henry has its disadvantages. I've never done anything without servants to look after me. Isn't that dreadful?"

She was adorable. He took her in his arms and kissed her.

She clung to him for a few moments, then pushed him away. "The servants are still out there in the carriage, and won't drive back to the château until the rain stops. What will they think if they see us?"

"That we love each other, of course."

She shook her head, and her curls bobbed. "No. They already believe I'm an abandoned woman—an opinion shared by everyone else."

"Except your husband, who knows better." Charles poured a little wine into two cut-glass goblets, and handed her one.

"To my husband," she said, "the only person on earth who has ever loved me for myself." Then, after a pause, she asked, appropos of nothing, "Have you ever been locked away in a dark old castle?"

Charles raised his hands in a gesture of surrender. "I know very little about castles. No one has built them for at least two hundred years."

"The old parts in the castle of Lille are at least five hundred years old. Some rooms are always draughty, and in other places there's no ventilation. It belongs to my aunt, you know. I was hidden away there until I was five, and I still shudder when I think of it. Not that I blame my father. He was trying to prevent a scandal."

Charles opened his mouth to say something, but thought better of it. Perhaps her remarks weren't as irrelevant as he had thought.

"He really is my father, you see. He went through the formality of adopting me to avoid talk. No one knew about my mother except Marie de Medicis, and she hated the idea of my father having had an affair with a serving maid. She must have held a private celebration when my mother died in childbirth." Eloise held out her empty goblet, and he poured more wine into it.

"I'm very pleased that we're leaving France for a time. The only thing I'll miss is this playhouse. That's why I wanted you to see it before we go. I was eight or nine when my father had it built for me."

He looked around at the snugly furnished room. "It suits you."

"I know. I hate the Vendôme palace, and the Louvre is even colder. Poor Cousin Louis. He'll have to live there for the rest of his life, and the worst of it is that he really enjoys it."

"Which is fortunate for France."

A slight lift of rounded shoulders summed up her concern for the future of France. "It would be wonderful to spend the rest of our lives traveling."

Charles looked at her fondly, but decided it would be best not to commit himself too firmly to an unrealistic notion. "I must go where I'm sent."

"Oh, I know, darling! I don't care where we are, really. Besides, Marie de Medicis—my aunt—can't live forever."

Eloise began to wander around the room, picking up trinkets and objects of bric-a-brac, handling them lovingly and putting them down again. "I wonder if you remember going to Mass that first Sunday after we were married."

Even her walk was effortlessly beautiful, and there were few pastimes he enjoyed more than watching her. "Only that we went to Notre-Dame."

"Charles, your memory is frightful. You had to haul me out of bed because I'd never been that serious about going to Mass, and I'd always thought Monsignor de Malerbe was an old bore. So I was sulky, and I pouted all the way there."

"You never sulk, and your pout is the sweetest——"

"Stop flattering me, or I'll take advantage of it!" She kissed him lightly, then escaped before he could catch hold of her. "I've heard you say that you think Monsignor de Malerbe is a bore. Admit it! And if you keep interrupting me, I'll never finish what I've been trying to say."

He clamped both hands over his mouth. "Better?"

"Much. That Sunday the Monsignor used a citation from the Book of Hosea as the text for his sermon. Don't ask me to tell you the exact quotation——"

"I won't." He felt sorry for men who married women with hard, incisive minds. The wonder of Eloise was her ever-present charm.

"It was something about bands of love. That was the morning everything began to feel different."

He realized that she was completely serious.

"I thought of you and me, naturally."

Charles failed to see the connection.

"Cardinal Richelieu says you're brilliant, darling, but he doesn't know you as I do." She sighed in mock exasperation. "The bands of your love have been supporting me. That's why Eloise de Montauban and Eloise de Vendôme are different people."

"I have a high regard for both of them."

"If you had ever done anything that had made you feel untrue to yourself, you'd know what I mean."

"I assure you I'm not a candidate for sainthood."

"So I discovered the first time we slept together." A suggestion of amusement appeared briefly in Eloise's voice, then vanished. "I'm talking about a deep shame that goes all the way down inside you."

Women, Charles supposed, enjoyed dramatizing themselves and their lives. It was an innocent pastime, and he saw no harm in humoring her. Besides, her solemnity was delicious. "I've done my share of squirming in the confessional, but if you insist your wickedness was more sinful than mine, I won't try to compete with you."

The rain continued to drum on the cottage roof, and she watched it flowing in ripples down the leaded windows. "I can imagine how your brother must feel."

Charles reacted as though she had struck him, hard, across the face.

"The longer a person hides in a dark castle," she said, "the more difficult it becomes to go out into the sunlight again. I know."

"Perhaps," Charles said stiffly, "we should eat."

"It's far too early. You might pour me a little more wine, though."

"Of course." He started to fill her glass.

"That's too much."

"Drink what you wish." He splashed wine into his own goblet, and was surprised to discover that his hands were shaking.

Eloise's voice became high-pitched, almost child-like. "I was always glad that my father and I were royal bastards. After two generations of being illegitimate, it meant I'd be free to marry for love. Cousin Louis and Queen Anne are scarcely on speaking terms. All she cares about is clothes—and the gossip from Vienna. One night a few months ago, when Louis had been drinking too much Norman *calvados*, he told me that he doesn't even feel married."

"I've tried to hate my brother, but I can't. I feel desperately sorry for him. Does that satisfy your curiosity?" Charles was digging his nails into the palms of his hands.

"You still hope, Charles. That's why you've put his income from Montauban in trust and refuse to take his title. I sat next to Cardinal Richelieu at the Beaufort dinner last week. He'd like me to—well, help persuade you to change your mind. But I won't."

Charles inclined his head in an awkward gesture of thanks. Eloise began to remove linen cloths that covered the platters of food. "We have some of those pheasants stuffed with olives and almonds that you enjoy so much."

"My brother is damned," he said.

She continued to arrange the food on a table, built for Henry IV at great expense, that resembled a cobbler's bench. "Because he's an apostate?"

Charles hesitated. "You know I don't believe that. My father was a devout Huguenot, and I can't believe he's been condemned to spend all eternity in hell." Charles went to the hearth, where he aimlessly broke up small pieces of kindling. "He and my mother must be together, and I can't imagine them anywhere other than in heaven. Monsignor de Malerbe says that if they are, she won him a place there. But he's hopelessly old-fashioned. I agree with Cardinal von Brückner of Vienna that an individual is capable of achieving everlasting grace even though he's not a Catholic. He interprets a passage of Aquinas——"

"I'm no theologian!" She felt compelled to halt him before he lost her in a maze of religious abstractions.

"I'll put it this way." Charles hurled a handful of kindling into the fire, where it flared high. "It's God's heaven, and it existed long before Christ founded the Christian Church."

"Don't build too big a fire. The chimney will smoke."

"But my brother Henry hasn't a chance. My God, I can't understand him. He's changed so much since we were boys!"

"Everyone changes," she said, and felt inadequate to cope with his distress.

Charles didn't hear her. "He was going to become a great man. Everyone thought so, even King Henry. You won't believe this—I can scarcely believe it myself—but when he was thirteen or fourteen, he wanted to take orders. My grand-uncle was a cardinal, you know, and Henry wanted to be one, too. Cardinal Henry de Montauban. It's ridiculous, isn't it?"

"Perhaps," she suggested, "his religion didn't mean as much to him as you thought at the time."

"But it did! I know it did! I went to Mass because my mother insisted. But Henry tried to live his Catholicism. Every single morning—for years—he delivered sermons telling me what was wrong with me. And then, the moment tragedy struck, he gave up his faith. How could someone who believed so strongly turn away from God?"

"You were only a child yourself. His faith couldn't have been as strong as you imagined."

"All these years he's been fighting a personal war against the Church. It's insane. Once, when he was sixteen, he offended old Montmorency, my father's closest friend, by calling him a murderer."

He paused. "I suppose I'll have to tell you. I don't want you to hear it from someone else. Richelieu has shown me a letter from Cardinal di Oscala of the Holy Office. The Church has been conducting a private investigation of Henry. The Holy Office has proved that he murdered a priest with his bare hands at the siege of Augsburg. But that's impossible!" he shouted. "I know my brother!" The instant he spoke the words he realized their absurdity. It was evident that he didn't know his brother. "If Henry is ever captured in battle by the troops of a Catholic army," he said in a very low voice, "he won't be granted honorable parole as a prisoner of war. He'll be sent to Rome and tried by the Holy Office on charges of murder."

Only a few drops of rain were falling on the roof now, and Eloise seemed to be completely absorbed as she listened to the sound.

"A long time ago—I'm sure Henry remembers the day as well as I do—my father and old Cardinal de Bourbon agreed that the real argument between Catholics and Huguenots was their approach to the same God. We believe the Church mediates, and the Protestants think they need no mediator. What's important is that all of us worship Him. How could Henry have forgotten it? Now he worships revenge and lust."

Eloise put a hand on Charles' arm and drew him to her, offering him solace in the only way she knew.

"He has no faith. He's godless," Charles said as she pulled his head to her breast.

On November 6, 1632, after winning Augsburg and Ulm, the army of Gustavus Adolphus launched a surprise attack on the combined forces of his foes on the approaches to Leipzig. The battle was fought under the worst conditions for both sides: a heavy autumn fog rolled in across the field, and it became difficult to distinguish ally from foe. Nevertheless the disciplined Swedes and their German auxiliaries scored the most brilliant victory of the war, and by nightfall had routed the enemy.

But they paid dearly for their victory. The King was thrown from his horse and, before he could recover, an Austrian cavalryman appeared out of the gloom and killed him with a single stroke of a double-edged sword.

The news stunned Europe. The Catholics, unable to put a new army into the field, had little cause for elation, but in Rome Pope Urban could not resist the temptation to quote St. Matthew: "They that take the sword shall perish with the sword."

Axel Oxenstjerna, Gustavus Adolphus' deputy, had the final word. "The greatest of warriors achieved his goal," he said in an order of the day to troops being released from active service. "Thanks to his intrepidity, the Lutherans of the German states may worship God in the way it most pleases them to worship."

Some senior officers remained in the field with the smaller army the Swedes now maintained, and Oxenstjerna, acting as regent for Gustavus Adolphus' little daughter, Queen Christina, gave a variety of new assignments to others, among them Henry de Montauban. "Baron Muehlmann, our ambassador in London, needs help," the regent said. "There's a great danger that England may swing into the Papist camp, and he writes that King Charles won't listen to his warnings."

"I'm no diplomat," Henry protested.

"Muehlmann wants a soldier, not a diplomat," Oxenstjerna replied. "He says the only language the English understand is the threat of force."

Henry set sail in a Swedish sloop-of-war from Goteborg, the port town founded by Gustavus Adolphus to give his nation a naval base on her western coast. The weather was miserable, the tiny ship was buffeted by high winds and raging seas, and Henry, who had never suffered worse than minor injuries in more than a decade of military service, disgraced himself by spending the better part of the voyage in his hammock. He recovered neither his equilibrium nor his spirits until the sloop reached the more placid waters of the Thames River and sailed slowly upstream to London.

Even in winter the fields of southern England were a deep, lush green, richer by far than land Henry had seen anywhere else in his travels. But if the countryside was attractive, London was the most disappointing town in all Europe. It lacked the charm of Paris, the rugged strength of Stockholm and the dedicated sense of self-discipline found in almost every German city.

"All I can say for the place," Henry told Baron Muehlmann when they sat down together at dinner in the ambassador's house on the Strand, "is that it seems lively. I've never seen so many people in a hurry. The nobles canter through the streets, and the commoners apparently prefer a trot to a walk. And their voices! Why do they shout? Does everyone in London suffer from defective hearing?"

Muehlmann's red face and portly physique indicated that England's food and alcoholic spirits agreed with him. "London is an acquired taste, my dear Count."

"I prefer to be called by my military title."

"I beg your pardon. Brigadier. You'll find they're an odd people. Their principles mean more to them than their comforts, and a man who cheats at cards or seduces another's wife—harmless enough pastimes everywhere else—is either killed in a duel or knifed to death by hired ruffians. They criticize their king scandalously, but let an outsider say one derogatory word, and they turn on him like a pack of wolves from the Uppsala forests. King Charles suspended his Parliament almost five years ago, and has ruled alone. Yet everyone, including members of both the Lords and Commons, insists that England is governed by representatives of the people. They're rude, contradictory and for no reason like to think of themselves as the most important and powerful of nations. Also, their nobles take daily baths, even in this weather." The Baron shivered.

Henry cut the crust of a steaming mutton and kidney pie, sniffed suspiciously and finally forced himself to fish out a small piece of mutton with his knife. As a soldier he had learned to eat any food, but knew that English dishes would not be among his favorites.

Muehlmann saw him hesitate, and smiled apologetically. "I had to hire a native cook. One becomes accustomed to their strange recipes."

Henry had no intention of waiting until the end of the meal to discuss the reasons for his presence in England. Diplomats could dawdle if they pleased, but a military man wanted to know where he stood. "Why did you send for me, milord Baron?"

Muehlmann would have preferred to concentrate on his mutton and kidney pie, and sighed. "The situation is very complicated," he said vaguely.

Civilian amenities annoyed Henry. "In what way?"

The Baron was glad they hadn't been served his favorite dish, boiled tripe, which he liked to savor slowly. "I've been told on the best of authority, although I can't prove it, that King Charles has signed a secret treaty with the Spaniards. England and Spain have agreed to make war together against the Dutch."

"The Protestants of Holland must be protected, milord Baron!"

"You haven't heard the worst. After the Netherlands has been smashed, the treaty provides that the country will be partitioned. The portion England takes will guarantee the rights of Catholics. The part that goes to Spain will become completely Catholic, and Protestantism will be abolished."

"How can a Protestant nation like England agree to such terms?" Henry was incensed.

Muehlmann obviously thought him naïve. "You know very little of developments in this country, it appears."

154

"I've been fighting in far-off places where we heard nothing about secret treaties or diplomatic agreements," Henry said stiffly.

"No offense meant, Brigadier. To answer your question, there's a strong and unfortunate possibility that England may swing into the Catholic camp."

Henry dropped his knife onto the table, where it scarred the brightly polished surface. "I don't believe it."

"Two personal agents sent by Pope Urban are currently in residence here. One of them, a man named Panzini, sees King Charles every day, and they spend at least an hour or two together. A great many English lords share our sense of dismay, I can tell you."

"Panzini. An Italian, of course. Is he a priest?"

"There are rumors, but I'm unable to verify them."

"This is outrageous!"

"Pope Urban has also sent an agent to Queen Henrietta Maria, an Englishman named George Conn who has so ingratiated himself that he's been given quarters at Whitehall and goes everywhere with her."

"Perhaps he's also a priest?"

The ambassador shrugged. "There are rumors and denials. I don't know. But there are rather strong signs that both King Charles and Queen Henrietta Maria are leaning strongly toward Catholicism. For the first time since the reign of Queen Mary, Catholics worship openly, without fear of being imprisoned or fined."

"The King has lost his senses."

"But a sober and industrious Protestant sect, a group calling themselves Puritans, is being persecuted by the Crown. It's quite disturbing."

"It's worse than that." Henry had eaten all his meals in the field for so many years that he completely forgot his manners and smashed his fist on the table, upsetting a glass of wine. "Take me to Whitehall, milord Baron, and I'll tell King Charles in so many words that the armies of Sweden and her German allies haven't spent ten years at war only to watch Protestantism disappear from Europe. We won't tolerate——"

"You'll do no such thing, Brigadier." The Baron spoke quietly but firmly. "No matter how just our cause, no man can threaten the ruler of England and Scotland in his own palace. Not even the most anti-Papist of his nobles would tolerate such an insult. England would declare war on Sweden immediately!"

Henry flushed beneath his tan. "Sorry. But this drift into Catholicism by an established Protestant nation can't be permitted."

"Brigadier, you aren't leading a cavalry charge now. At the appropriate time, you'll accompany me to Whitehall, and before then we'll—ah—rehearse your remarks to the King. We'll work very closely with the French, who share our concern, but for their own reasons. By the way, their new ambassador is a namesake of yours."

Henry felt as though he had been plunged in icy water. "I beg your pardon?"

"I assume," Muehlmann said, again devoting his attention to the meal, "that de Montauban is a fairly common name in France."

"No," Henry said hoarsely. "It isn't."

They faced each other in the principal sitting room of the French embassy, a house on the embankment overlooking the Thames. Neither knew what to say, and Henry finally broke the stalemate. It was his duty, as the elder, to make the first move, he thought, so he advanced toward his brother, and they embraced.

"By right," he said huskily, "I shouldn't meet you here. I'm forbidden to set foot on French soil."

Charles' laugh was forced.

They stood back and stared at each other again. "The fault is mine. I promised myself a thousand times that I'd write to you. But I didn't know what to say."

"I'll share the blame with you. I wanted to write, and then it became easier to remain silent." Charles tugged at his lace cuffs. "There was always one thing I desperately wanted to know. The truth about mother's death. There were so many rumors, so many different stories——"

"Later. Not now," Henry said harshly.

Again they stared at each other, until Charles suddenly remembered his manners. "Come into the library for something to eat and drink. Eloise will be joining us shortly."

"Eloise?"

"My wife."

"You're fortunate, Charles. You have children, I presume."

A hint of anticipatory pleasure appeared in Charles' eyes. "Not yet. You've never married?"

"I've had nothing to offer a woman except the prospect of widowhood." Henry followed his brother into the embassy library, a room lined from floor to ceiling with leather-bound books. "Do you own any of these?"

"All of them."

"I've read nothing but military treatises since I left France." Henry sat opposite his brother. "You've changed very little," he said with a sudden smile. "You're heavier, and you dress more elegantly——"

"Cardinal Richelieu insists an ambassador must maintain the dignity of France."

"An interesting man, your cardinal."

Charles heard the bitterness in his brother's voice, and hastily changed the subject. "I'm not sure I'd have known you, Henry."

"Life in the field ages a man." Henry rubbed a long scar that extended from his hairline to his chin on the left side of his face. "Gustavus Adolphus kept us busy, I can tell you."

"Do you always wear a steel corselet—and that heavy helmet you left in the entrance hall?"

"Always, and I carry this." Henry patted the scabbard of his long sword. "They're the badges of my trade."

"I've heard of your exploits. You've done well."

Henry shrugged. "If a soldier has the wits to stay alive, he wins promotions. It's very simple."

"You're too modest."

"No." Henry loathed delicacy. "To win a post like yours takes real talent, particularly when a man is handicapped by having a traitor for a brother."

"I've never regarded you as a traitor. I've often wondered whether I might not have done the same thing, had I been in Montauban with you. Should you want to marry——"

"Charles, a soldier doesn't lead a very civilized existence. I've gone to bed with more harlots that I can remember, but only with harlots. I've forgotten how to behave in the presence of ladies."

"Let me finish. Montauban is still your inheritance. I've acted in your stead as trustee of your estate, and I've put aside a rather large sum for you."

Henry laughed in astonishment. "Hellfire, brimstone and eternal damnation, boy! What would I do with money? Keep it!"

Charles was a little offended. "I live nicely, thank you. And I have no intention of upsetting the basic laws of primogeniture." He heard a stir in the anteroom beyond the library, and as Eloise came into the room he realized she had been listening to the conversation, waiting for a dramatically appropriate moment to enter.

She was dressed in a semi-transparent gown of thin silk, cut in a style recently introduced by Anne of Austria, and a black velvet beauty patch strategically pasted in the cleavage between her breasts emphasized the daring cut of the dress. "Milord Count," she murmured, and sank to the floor in a deep curtsy.

Henry leaped to his feet in embarrassment. "Milady," he muttered, and gave her his hand to help her rise.

"Please," Charles said heartily, "let's have no formality."

Henry scarcely heard him. He was conscious only of Eloise, and of his sudden envy of his brother's good fortune.

Eloise seated herself between the two men. 'I hope I haven't interrupted at the worst possible time."

"Not at all, my dear," Charles said.

Henry said nothing. His smile was forced and enigmatic.

"Don't let me stop your conversation." She tugged hard at a bell-rope, and when a servant appeared, gave orders in a loud whisper for the provision of refreshments.

Henry turned back to his brother. "Your generosity is the most unselfish gesture I've ever know, Charles, but I can't accept it. Actually, you know, I'm surprised the title hasn't been taken from me and given to you."

"Cardinal Richelieu," Eloise said, giving her husband no chance to speak, "has offered it to him many times, but he refuses it."

"Charles," Henry said, "you live in France. I think it improbable that I'll ever see Paris or Montauban again. If you want the title, take it. If you have any need for the funds you've been saving for me, use them. If not, I'll make out a will, and whatever money is accumulated will go to your first-born son."

Whitehall was the dreariest royal palace in Europe, and Englishmen who remembered the brillant court of Elizabeth I felt ashamed of the impression created by the Crown. Even those who had complained about the garish opulence of James I admitted that he had lived like a king, and said that his taste, although bad, had been better than no taste at all.

The Duke of Buckingham, the most influential of ministers at the court of Charles I, had spent money freely when his friend had ascended the throne. But Buckingham was dead and one by one the trappings of grandeur vanished. The regiment of Household Guards, magnificent in uniforms of scarlet and white, no longer marched on the parade ground each day, and in their places, pairs of somberly clad sentries patrolled the palace grounds and corridors.

Tapestries and paintings depicting the past glory of England had disappeared from their accustomed places on the walls of public rooms and halls, and only grimy smudge marks, which the servants couldn't wash away, were reminders of what had been one of the finest art collections in western Europe. Even the private apartment of the Queen had been stripped of its heirlooms, and meals were served on ordinary wooden or pewter trenchers. The golden goblets and silver knives that had been used at every banquet were locked away in vaults or, perhaps, had been sold. And no banquets were held at the palace.

King Charles I made no secret of his predicament. He, like the royal treasury, was badly in need of funds, and every scheme he devised to raise money was a miserable failure. But only his closest advisers and the relatives of the royal family whose income depended on the King's bounty felt sympathy for the monarch. Buckingham, just prior to his assassination, had summed up the nation's feelings. "King James," he said, "was called the wisest fool in Christendom, and so he was, because he knew his limitations. Charles is far wiser than his father, and therefore doubly foolish, because he thinks himself capable of performing any task, and has never doubted his own talents. He's a Stuart, so he can't help being stubborn, over-proud and ever-conscious of his belief that he rules as the anointed viceroy of Almighty God. But his short-sightedness is his own fault."

The report of Charles de Montauban to Cardinal Richelieu on the same subject was more objective and infinitely less personal. "His Majesty," the new French ambassador wrote, "still tries to rule alone, without Parliament, but new taxes cannot be imposed or funds raised except on the initiative of the Parliament. Therefore the Crown is in dire financial need. I hear that representatives for Vatican Hill now in London have offered the King a fortune, and only his fear that his subjects might learn of an arrangement repugnant to them has prevented him from taking the Pope's gold."

Henry de Montauban was familiar with both impressions, but after his many years of close association with Gustavus Adolphus he was both startled and amused when he finally went to Whitehall with Baron Meuhlmann. By the standards of Sweden's warrior-king, Charles I lived lavishly.

Thick rugs were spread on the floors of the monarch's private audience chamber, and pure white furs covered most of the chairs. King Charles was wearing a magnificent suit that would have cost a brigadier in the Swedish army six months' wages, and his collar was fashioned of rich, brown beaver, a rare fur being imported in very small quantities from England's newly-established, struggling colonies in North America. A huge emerald ring and another of sapphire flashed on the King's left hand, and on his right he wore three diamonds. Henry did note, however, that the room was bitterly cold, with only a small fire laid in the hearth. That, perhaps, wasn't the result of a royal attempt to economize. All Englishmen lived in damp, chilly houses and refused to use enough fuel for their own or anyone else's comfort.

As a man King Charles was unprepossesing. He was cursed with the prominent Stuart chin, small mouth and elongated face. His eyes reflected a quick intelligence, but he was heavy-lidded, which often gave visitors the false idea that he was falling asleep. He was two years younger than Henry, but too little exercise and too much heavy food had given him a paunch, and his movements were those of a middle-aged man.

Henry and Muehlmann were waved to chairs, but the King continued to stand, and Henry was relieved that the Swedish ambassador had warned him of King Charles' quirk. It was shocking to sit in the presence of royalty while a monarch remained standing, and in France or Sweden a man might be expelled from court for committing such a blunder. But the English fooled themselves, and thought the practice demonstrated an easy, informal relationship between a ruler and his inferiors.

The King filled a pipe, then offered bowls to his guests. "My father," he said, "despised tobacco, and I couldn't smoke the stuff until he died. I have reason to hope the growing of the weed will provide me with a source of revenue from my New World colonies."

"Smoking is unknown in Sweden," Meuhlmann said, taking care to sound duly regretful.

The King turned to Henry. "I'm told you're a great hero of the Polish and German campaigns, Brigadier."

"I served with Gustavus Adolphus, Your Majesty."

"And now you've come to London, where there are no Papist regiments to fight." King Charles' smile was sardonic. "I suppose they've sent you here to warn me of the frightful consequences if I join the Spaniards in their war against the Dutch."

Henry was surprised, but did not lose his poise. "Only a stupid man would threaten Your Majesty."

"Then you know our English soldiers, Brigadier?"

"Several squadrons of them served under me. They fought bravely and well, Your Majesty."

King Charles laughed, and pointed a finger at the ambassador. "Muehlmann, you amuse me, and so do the French, the Spaniards and all the rest. Every few months a new rumor sweeps through the foreign ministries of Europe, and secretaries write frightened reports. 'Charles of England,' they say, 'is being converted to Catholicism. The balance of power is going to be upset.'

"So there's a fresh furor, and everyone comes to me with gifts, hoping to save or damn me. The Spaniards offer me territory—that will have to be conquered first. The Pope promises me gold, and knows so little about England that he doesn't realize he might set off the very revolt of my people he hopes to prevent. His none too loyal Cardinal, Richelieu, will bribe me if I refuse Vatican Hill. And you Swedes are too poor to offer me gold, having kept an expensive army in the field for years, so you send me an honest soldier in the belief that you can intimidate me."

The ambassador tried to protest, but King Charles silenced him with an imperious gesture.

Henry smiled behind his hand and abandoned the thought of making the speech he had rehearsed so carefully under Muehlmann's supervision. Others might think King Charles devious, treacherous and erratic, but he liked the man.

"Tell your Regent," the King continued, "to concern himself with his own conscience, and I'll worry about mine. And you might remind him that until the day I openly embrace another faith, I remain the head of the Church of England."

The Baron showed no emotion. "I'll give Regent Oxenstjerna Your Majesty's message."

The fire in the King's pipe had gone out, so he lighted it again with a spill that he first held in the hearth, a complicated business that took a long time. Finally, his head wreathed in a cloud of smoke, he said more calmly, "You and I should discuss matters of religion some time, Brigadier de Montauban. I've heard you're a Catholic apostate, so you should be something of an expert."

"Like Your Majesty," Henry said quietly, "I hold that questions about my conscience are my own business."

The rebuff was so direct and sharp that the ambassador gasped.

But King Charles laughed. "Well said, Brigadier! I like a man of courage. Dine with me, and tell me how you beat the Austrians. That will provide me with a diversion, and I assure you I need one. It will be a joy to listen to someone who isn't trying to use me—or England—for his own ends."

The street noises in the Strand were even more deafening than usual as Londoners by the thousands marched toward Whitehall to protest the Crown's latest money-raising scheme, an ill-advised "levy" of one farthing on every pint of ale or beer sold in the city. The English were exceptionally sensitive to new taxes, no matter what they might be called, and would have resisted paying the "penalty," as they called it, even if Parliament had authorized the new excise measure.

Inasmuch as the King had simply issued a decree ordering the tax, they had a legitimate reason to demonstrate. Members of the diplomatic corps already knew that the King had failed again. He had admitted to the Portuguese ambassador that public disapproval was forcing him to rescind the new decree, and word to that effect had been passed from legation to legation.

So the Swedish and French ambassadors paid no attention to the hubbub as they sat in Baron Muehlmann's study on the ground floor of his embassy. But Henry de Montauban had to speak above the steady roar of the throng so his brother and the representative of the Swedish Crown could hear him. "I've told you every word we exchanged at dinner," he said wearily, "and for the fourth time, I can only add my conviction that the King is an honest man. Baron, you know I'd be concerned if I thought he plans to re-establish Catholicism as the official religion of England."

"Cite one specific statement he made that I can send to Regent Oxenstjerna," Muehlmann said.

"I can't. He hints, he smiles, he nods, and he creates an impression." Henry glanced briefly at his brother. "If the King is intending to become a Catholic convert—or has already become one—he certainly kept quiet while listening to the stories I was telling him about our battles with Catholic troops. Maybe I missed a great many nuances, gentlemen, but I'm not a diplomat." He drained his cup of mead.

Charles drummed on the arm of his chair. "What did he mean when he told you the Church of Scotland needs to be administered with stronger discipline?"

It irritated Henry to repeat himself endlessly. "I have no idea. I'm not a theologian, and I know nothing about the Church of Scotland. It just seems to me that he's not going to outlaw the teachings of Knox."

"Perhaps," Muehlmann said thoughtfully, "there will be no fundamental change in the English position."

Charles continued to tap on the arm of his chair. "I'm inclined to suspect that this may be the one nation in Europe that isn't disturbed—at the moment—by differences of religion. I'm afraid, milord Baron, that you and I must wait and guess. The King will continue to play off one power against another, and take gold from all of them." He sighed and stood. "A packet boat is waiting for my report, so I'll have to write it before sundown."

Meuhlmann was concerned. "I can't offer you an escort, so I'd advise you to wait until these crowds are gone. The English can be treacherous in their dealings with foreigners when they're in an ugly mood."

"It's only a short walk to my house."

"Take one of my horses."

Henry forced himself to intervene. "No civilian can ride through that mob, and he'd only make himself more conspicuous." He rose, buckled on his long sword and clamped his helmet onto his head. "I'll escort you to your embassy, Charles."

His brother smiled. "I'll be delighted to have your company. We've seen nothing whatever of each other since I came back here from Calais on Wednesday. But I certainly don't need protection.'

Henry made no reply, but checked his pistols to make sure they were loaded and primed.

A few moments later the two brothers left the Swedish embassy and moved out into the Strand, where the shouting, angry throng still flowed toward Whitehall.

"Walk on my left," Henry directed, "so I'll be able to draw my sword if I must. And stay close to the buildings. If we get out into the

162

center of the road, we'll be swept all the way to the palace. Do as I tell you."

Conversation was impossible as they walked down the Strand. Here and there men stared at them with bloodshot eyes and started toward them, but changed their minds when the tall soldier in the steel corselet and helmet coolly drew his blade part-way from its scabbard. Charles hated to admit he had been wrong, but knew that without Henry's presence he might have been mauled by the crowd.

At last they turned off the Strand and moved down a narrow street toward the Thames. It was quiet here, and Charles made no secret of his relief. "I'm grateful to you."

"Nonsense." Henry continued to look straight ahead. "I wanted a private word with you, and a chance to say good-by. I've already written my resignation from the Swedish army, and I'm giving it to Baron Meuhlmann before I leave tonight."

Charles was startled. "What——"

"For all the good it did, I carried out my assignment, and saw the King at Whitehall. And the Swedes no longer need me in the German states, so I'm free to go elsewhere."

"Isn't this a very sudden decision?"

Henry didn't reply directly. "I've held several conferences with the Dutch ambassador, and he'll swear me in as a major general before I sail for Holland tonight. The Prince of Orange is barely holding his own against a large and well-equipped Spanish army, so I feel I'm needed. I—belong in the field."

Charles was bewildered by the bitterness he heard in his brother's voice. "You'll do what you feel right, of course, but I can't understand why you're in such a rush."

"I've wasted enough time." They reached the front gate of the French embassy, and Henry halted. "I knew I'd see you today, so I've prepared something for you." He took a folded parchment from the worn leather purse he carried at his waist. "It's my will, Charles. I don't think I've left any bastards in Poland and the German states, but I can't swear to it. This document makes you my official heir. I've also authorized you to take both the Montauban title and trust funds whenever you see fit."

"You already know," Charles replied firmly, "that I'll do no such thing as long as you live. And if you're sailing for Holland tonight, the very least you can do is come in for dinner with me now."

"I can't. I'll be busy the rest of the day."

"Eloise will be hurt if you go without seeing her again."

"I'll rely on you to say my farewells for me."

The finality in his voice made Charles realize that persuasion would be wasted. "When shall we meet again?"

Henry shrugged. "I'm no seer, so I can't predict whether our paths will cross again in this world. But I'm positive they won't in the next. You've already made a place for yourself there, and so, I'm afraid, have I."

The usually placid Maas River had become a churning, racing torrent after eight days and nights of rain, and the downpour continued to fall. Dutch sentries, soaked to the skin, shivered as they patrolled the ramparts of the fortress in the border town of Maastricht and kept watch on the Spaniards whose camp stretched out in the distance beyond the little town of Wijk, on the right bank of the river, which was still in Dutch hands.

Each day the population of Maastricht grew larger as refugees from Spanish-occupied territory made their way through the underground tunnels of the Pietersberg sandstone quarries to the safety of the Dutch lines. Peasants came with their wives and children, sometimes carrying the personal belongings they had been able to salvage, sometimes driving their cattle before them. Word had spread through the surrounding countryside, and everyone in the area knew that Major General Henry de Montauban was keeping his word. All who wanted a haven from Spanish tyranny were welcome.

The ground was so wet that military operations had been suspended, and Henry, eager to learn all he could about the enemy, interviewed each of the peasants himself. All told the same story. The Spanish commander was a warrior-priest of royal blood, Cardinal Prince Ferdinand, who was re-establishing the Inquisition in all territories his armies controlled. Members of the Dutch Free Church were taken from their homes at night by masked men, and were never seen again. Anyone suspected of harboring Protestants was stripped of his land and property, and Catholics whose devotion to their Church was deemed feeble by the Cardinal and his subordinates were flogged in public ceremonies.

"Our capture of Maastricht," Henry wrote to Frederick, Prince of Orange, the Dutch ruler, "is the major turning point in the war. Not only have we deprived the enemy of his key base of operations in the border region, but we have opened the door to all who want escape from Catholic terror.

"Much as I sympathize with the victims of Ferdinand's oppression, I rejoice, too. His night riders and torturers are converting more Catholics to Protestantism than could all the preachers in Holland. You warned me at our last meeting that the Flemish Catholics were a stubborn race, but the fanaticism of the Spaniard brings them into our camp and our churches by the scores and hundreds.

"Two days ago, on the Sabbath, every one of Maastricht's four churches were so crowded with worshippers that the preachers held as

164

many as five or six services. Ferdinand and his zealots are the Pope's worst foes, and long may they flourish! It is with a sense of regret that, when the weather clears and the ground dries, I must drive him from the field for all time. I harbor one secret hope, that I capture the Cardinal. How I would relish marching him through the streets of Amsterdam, naked and in chains, while the victims of his cruelty scourge him, not for the good of his soul, which is past redemption, but for the sheer pleasure of their own revenge."

By the time the rains stopped, the Spaniards had gone into their winter camp in the city of Liege, a two-day march from the Dutch lines at Maastricht. Cold winds blowing in from the North Sea carried with them a promise that winter was at hand, but Henry was too impatient to wait until spring for a resumption of hostilities. He had told the Prince of Orange he wanted to break the power of the Spaniards, and was so anxious to keep his word that he decided to gamble.

The ground had frozen, making it possible for him to move his artillery forward, and his principal problem was that of finding adequate housing in the field for a corps of almost twenty thousand men. He put the issue to his troops. "If you wish," he told them in an order of the day read by company commanders, "you can live snugly until April. But beware the Spaniards, for they, too, will have rested, and by then their ranks will be swollen with levies furnished them by Madrid. If, instead, you would crush the arch-priest and arch-devil, Ferdinand, march with me now and destroy his host."

The troops voted overwhelmingly to suffer the discomforts of a winter campaign, and an urgent request was sent to Amsterdam for extra blankets and all available tents. Henry was afraid the enemy would learn his intentions, however, and began his march before the supplies arrived.

He moved cautiously, his cavalry in the van screening his advance, and his artillery bringing up the rear. He himself rode in the center of the long column, with the infantry and pikemen. Although his order of march was orthodox, his plans were radical. "When we're five miles from Liege," he told his senior subordinates and staff members at a council of war, "we'll feint in the direction of Brussels. It's too rich a town for Ferdinand to leave unguarded, and I think he'll follow us from Liege."

"Suppose he doesn't?" asked Anton van der Graf, the Dutch General of Cavalry.

"Then," Henry replied grimly, "we'll have to lay siege to Liege—and pray that the winter will be mild."

For five days the Dutch army crept toward the southeast, but Ferdinand refused to be lured into the open. Some of the more conservative Hollanders urged Henry to abandon the campaign and return to Maastricht, but he refused. "If we must, we'll take Brussels," he said.

A colonel of infantry protested. "We can't hold it!"

"Then we'll raze every Catholic church in the town, help ourselves to plunder and retire. If we retreat now, Ferdinand will think we're cowards, and our task in April will be doubly hard."

On the sixth day van der Graf, who was riding with his scouts, sent Henry a brief message. "The Spaniards," he said, "are marching out of Liege."

The gamble had succeeded, and Henry, afraid that Ferdinand would scurry back to the safety of the walled town if the Dutch moved too soon, waited for the enemy in the hills of the Spanish Netherlands. He established his own headquarters in the town of Louvain, east of Brussels, where the Flemish Protestants gave him a warm welcome, and anchored his artillery on the heights outside the town. He deployed his infantry on the slopes of pine-studded hills, and sent his cavalry off on the Liege road to lure the Spaniards into the trap he had set for them.

Cardinal Prince Ferdinand was a proud man, and if it occurred to him that he had been wrong to leave the secure bastion of Liege, he hoped to beat the Dutch at their own game. His corps, more than fifteen thousand strong, was almost as large as his foes' army, and his artillery batteries were the best in western Europe. His cannon were of recent design, and his gunners were experts who had worked together for years.

Henry was exhilarated by the impending duel of wits and strength. "We must strike at precisely the right moment," he said at a last council of war before the battle. "Our cavalry and infantry will operate together to prevent the Spaniards from establishing permanent lines, and our artillery will concentrate on their rear so they can't move their own cannon into position. These are the tactics that won Gustavus Adolphus fifty victories, gentlemen, and we'll triumph, too. From this moment, let every member of the corps stand ready to fight!"

The Spaniards tried in vain to penetrate Anton van der Graf's cavalry outposts in order to determine the Dutch order of battle. But Ferdinand had already committed himself to act, and knowing withdrawal would be a form of suicide, pressed toward Louvain.

Henry was ready for him, and on the morning of November 13, 1633, a year and a week after the death of Gustavus Adolphus, he made final preparations for the largest battle ever fought under his own command. He ate breakfast alone in the mayor's office at the Louvain town hall, confident that Ferdinand would move within range of his artillery before noon. He consumed his meal slowly, with relish, and smiled when he thought of the recruits who had no appetites this morning. Professional fighting men ate heartily whenever they could, and were particularly careful to put away a large meal before a battle, knowing they couldn't be sure when they would have the chance to eat again.

Henry finished his cold beef, helped himself to more of the smoked herring that his quartermaster bought for him at a seacoast town and filled a large mug with ale. Sipping it, he closed his eyes and tried to rehearse the events of the next few hours. It was always helpful to review a battle in advance, as Gustavus Adolphus had done.

There would be carnage, of course, and he made an attempt to shut the pictures of the dead and wounded from his mind. Human suffering was inevitable when armies clashed, and a commander had to harden himself to tragedy.

Suddenly, inexplicably, Henry saw himself standing in a billowing tent, his hands blood-stained, an inert body at his feet. He recognized the battered features of the priest—his name was Stein—whom he had killed at Augsburg.

Leaping to his feet, Henry looked around wildly, and although he realized he was really in the mayor's office of the Louvain town hall, he could not rid himself of the fear and oppressive sense of doom that overwhelmed him. He gulped the rest of his ale, then laughed aloud to reassure himself. But the sound of the hoarse cackle that echoed in his ears made him feel worse.

Why should the memory of an insignificant priest haunt him at a time such as this, when he had truly important matters on his mind? It was absurd.

Scarcely aware of what he was doing, he poured himself a cup of brandywine, and just as he was raising it to his lips remembered that it was dangerous to drink strong spirits before a battle. "Damn you, Stein!" he muttered, and threw the cup into the fire. He had often spoken of damnation, but until this moment it had not crossed his mind that the word might be more than a figure of speech. He, not the murdered priest, was damned.

The very thought of murder made him shiver, and he realized a trickle of cold perspiration was running down his back. He caught a glimpse of his reflection in a square of burnished steel that he used as a shaving mirror, and was disgusted by the panic he saw in his own eyes. He was behaving like a recruit going into battle for the first time, and in a sudden rage he snatched the square of metal from the shelf on which it was propped and threw it across the room.

A tap sounded at the door, and an aide came into the chamber, stopping short when he saw his commander's feverish face.

"What do you want?" Henry's voice was so strained he hardly recognized it as his own.

The aide recovered. "Sir," he said, "General van der Graf has established firm contact with the enemy advance guard."

Henry pulled on a shirt of thin chain-mail, donned his steel corselet and buckled on his sword. Then, as he reached for his helmet, the picture in his mind became stronger. Father Stein's face was no longer bloated, and a faint smile creased his pale, waxen face. He seemed to be beckoning, and Henry needed all his strength, all his will power to refrain from running to his horse and riding off somewhere, alone, far from the scene of the impending battle.

Cardinal Prince Ferdinand was a shrewd, seasoned leader, and his Castilians were veterans of many campaigns, men who knew their own worth and did not panic when a battle turned against them. But neither the skill of the Spanish general nor the courage of his troops could save the day. Major General Henry de Montauban conclusively demonstrated to his Dutch subordinates why Gustavus Adolphus had never lost a decisive engagement.

The tactics Henry had devised for the battle were invincible, and he himself was everywhere on the field, insuring that nothing marred their execution. He deliberately drew the Spaniards into his net, boldly committed the bulk of his cavalry and infantry to action, and at the same time ordered his artillery to open fire. He joined the vanguard, rearranging van der Graf's squadrons to hold the enemy at bay, and after retiring for what his exhausted aides mistakenly hoped would be a short respite, moved forward again with the infantry, exhorting the Dutch foot soldiers to advance.

When his artillery fire became careless, giving the Spaniards an opportunity to emplace their own guns, he rode at a full gallop to the heights above Louvain and personally reset the range of each of his twenty-four cannon. Spanish cavalry broke through to his artillery position, but he was oblivious to personal danger, and was content to let his cavalry and pikemen beat off the counter-attack while he continued to supervise the all-important artillery fire.

By mid-afternoon the outcome of the battle was no longer in doubt. The heavy Spanish infantry was retiring on the Liege road, and the light infantry, unsupported, necessarily followed. Henry seemed to sense the enemy withdrawal, and managed to send his reserves into the fray before van der Graf could send him definite word of the retreat. "General de Montauban," said Captain Plaetzer, one of his personal aides, "is either inspired by God or possessed by demons."

The entire Dutch corps was ordered to attack in full strength, but

Henry was dissatisfied with the progress of his regiments, and for the third time went toward the most advanced command post to learn the cause of the difficulty and eliminate it. After a hard ride through the ranks of his infantry, and apparently indifferent to the cheers of the soldiers who recognized and hailed him, he found his cavalry commander at the crest of a small hill.

Ahead, at the base of the hill and in a small valley beyond it, he could see squadrons of Dutch and Spanish horsemen engaging in what looked like a caricature of close combat. The Dutch line inched forward, and the Spaniards retreated at a snail's pace.

"Van der Graf!" Henry roared, half-standing in his saddle. "What's wrong with your men?"

The Dutch cavalry had behaved superbly all day, and General van der Graf felt miffed. "The enemy are professional fighting men, sir," he said. "They yield ground grudgingly."

Henry spat and wiped his mouth with the soft leather palm of his mailed glove. "Right now," he said, "is the time to smash their lines. Scatter them, and they'll never recover! How many of your squadrons are uncommitted at the moment?"

"I've pulled back the First and Fifth Dragoons for a rest, and I've withdrawn all three squadrons of the House of Orange Hussars because——"

"Orange Hussars! Dragoons!" Henry shouted, standing in his stirrups and drawing his sword. "To me! To me!"

His standard bearer knew what was expected of him, and blew furiously on his trumpet.

More than five hundred horsemen converged on the crest, thundering toward it from every direction.

Van der Graf was aghast. It was an inviolable rule of warfare that the commander-in-chief of an army should not risk his own life unnecessarily. "General de Montauban!" he shouted, trying to make himself heard above the beat of pounding hoofs. "Don't do this, sir! I—I beg you to reconsider!"

Henry laughed loudly, wildly. "To me, lads! To me!"

The instant he saw the pennants of all five squadrons, he started down the hill, first at a walk, then a canter, and finally a mad gallop. The astonished cavalrymen spurred forward, forming a double line on either side of Henry as they caught up with him.

The Dutch horsemen already in contact with the enemy could only stare at the saber-wielding troopers charging at breakneck speed toward them. The Spaniards were aware of their new danger, too, and stiffened as their officers called sharp orders. But nothing could stop the impetus of Henry's advance. He and his comrades rode through the Dutch lines and into the ranks of the Spaniards in the valley, their speed unchecked.

Henry slashed left and right with his long sword, wounding a Spanish lieutenant and killing a trooper in his first direct contact with the foe. Inevitably, however, he drew the attention of the enemy, and as he pressed deeper into the Spanish lines, becoming momentarily separated from some of his own men, the Castilians took out the frustration of their humiliating defeat on him. Two cavalrymen engaged him in a duel, another fired a pistol at him from a distance of less than ten feet, and a wounded lieutenant colonel gained enough strength to rally and lead a squad in a wild assault on the general who had shamed them.

Henry went down under a hail of flashing swords.

The Dutch saw him fall, and scores of men pressed toward the spot. Among them was General van der Graf, who had followed his superior, and the cavalry leader rallied his men so swiftly that the Spaniards were forced to flee.

Van der Graf leaped to the ground and knelt beside Henry, who stared at him with glazed eyes. "How badly are you hurt, sir?"

"The enemy." Henry spoke with great effort. "What's happening to the enemy?"

"They've been scattered. The whole field will soon be ours."

"Good." Henry's voice sank. "Maybe I'll be remembered as the man who beat Ferdinand. I'd like that."

Van der Graf had to bend close in order to hear him.

"My brother."

"Sir?"

"Give a message—to my brother," Henry whispered, and a twisted smile appeared on his blood-stained lips. "Count Charles de Montauban. Tell him—my last thoughts—were of him."

BOOK THREE

BOOK THREE

There goes my diet," Charles de Montauban said, beaming as he tasted the delicacy on his plate.

"The true secret of quenelles," his cousin replied, "is that the pike must be very fresh. If possible, the fish should be cooked the same day they're taken from the river."

"Putting the meat through a very fine strainer is equally important," the Bishop added, "and so is the poaching. You use the old family recipe, Philippe."

"Courtesy of Louis the Fourteenth." The Count looked at his guest warily.

"I know what you're thinking. If it hadn't been for King Louis, ecumenism might have been attainable two hundred and fifty years ago."

"That's something of an exaggeration. Neither Protestants nor Catholics were really ready to break bread together."

"I wonder if you knew that the Church itself was opposed to Louis' stand on religious issues."

The Count raised an eyebrow.

"You said something earlier this evening about the outsider viewing the Church as a solid, monolithic block of stone, but rarely in its history has it been united within. Certainly at the turn of the eighteenth century——"

"I'm familiar with our family history, too."

"Forgive me, Philippe. But it does raise a question I

think we should settle. There has been a tendency, particularly in the press of France and the United States, to view the activities of the Second Vatican Council as a battle between liberals and conservatives. They put labels on men. Cardinal Suenans of Belgium is a leader of the liberals. The forces of reaction are led by conspiratorial villains in the Curia. That's a dangerous over-simplification. Everyone at the Council dedicated himself to the task of establishing our own inner position so that we'd be better able to enter into a dialogue with the Protestants."

"Come, now. There are members of the Curia—and a great many others—who are opposed to any dialogue."

"This sauce is exquisite." Charles de Montauban turned to the Count. "Are all Protestant ministers eager to establish a new relationship with Rome?"

"Certainly the majority——"

"All?"

"No, of course not. If every Protestant clergyman of every denomination wanted a reconciliation with Rome, that would be a true miracle, far surpassing the appearance of the stigmata on a statue of Christ in some remote, rural church."

"If you're unable to achieve unanimity, Philippe, why criticize us because a small minority of the Council Fathers opposed ecumenism? I beg you to remember that in October, 1962, when Pope John convened the Council, he stressed that its principal duty was the defense and advancement of truth."

"You place me in the position of Pontius Pilate, Charles. What is truth?"

"I thought you'd ask that. Let me answer in the words of Pope John: 'the Divine Word, made visible at Bethlehem.'" The Bishop pondered for a moment, trying to recall the precise quotation. "'Why is it called truth? Because it is a communication of God; and between man and truth there is no merely accidental relationship, but one which is necessary and of his essence.'"

"No Christian would disagree," Philippe said. "But we part company in our interpretations of that truth. Every denomination, and I'm not accusing Catholicism alone, is convinced that it alone interprets truth accurately."

The Bishop ate the last of his quenelles. "The joint burden we share is our mutual need to speak the same language. Christianity has never been able to afford the luxury of Babel, and today it is urgent that we learn to communicate with each other."

"Or we'll perish," Philippe added.

The Bishop are the last of his question." The joint
language. Christianity has never been able to afford the
communicate with each other.
Or we'll perish," Philippe added.

book three

I am the state.
—LOUIS XIV

1684–1685

"Charles and Eloise de Montauban, my grandparents, were very
handsome, as you can see from their portraits. My own parents were
painted by an inferior artist, and it was their misfortune to die of the
Burgundian plague at an early age. As you can see, they looked like
little more than children, although my mother bore four children.
My sister died of the plague, too, and it was their tragedy, I think,
that turned me toward the Church." Bishop Michel de Montauban
led his guest to the window seats at the far side of the townhouse
library. "And that brings us more or less up to the present, Your
Eminence."

Vittorio Cardinal de Orsini, the Special Papal Legate to France,
sat down and accepted a small glass of a pale pink wine.

"My younger brother, Paul, grows the grapes in our family vineyards at Montauban."

"There are three of you, Your Grace?" the Cardinal asked.

"Yes. Philippe was still a boy in school when he inherited the title,
and I had just entered the seminary," Michel de Montauban said.
"Had my parents lived, I suspect that Paul would have gone into the
army. But he had so little supervision that he did what he pleased.
I'm not quite sure how or when he conceived the idea of making
Montauban a prosperous county again, but he was certainly succeeded. The town is thriving, and so are the outlying farms. Paul spends
at least half of each year in the south."

Cardinal de Orsini looked mildly surprised. "I thought that attendance on His Majesty at Versailles was obligatory for all members of
the nobility."

The Bishop made a wry face. "Between us, as clergymen, Louis the
Fourteenth sometimes confuses himself with Almighty God, and he
likes to keep a fatherly eye on his flock. Fortunately, that gaudy
palace he's been building for years isn't yet completed, so at present
there literally isn't space to house all of the nobility. Philippe, as the
family title-holder, rarely escapes. Technically this house is his, but I
doubt if he sleeps here more than a score of nights in each year. Paul
has more freedom to do what he wishes—so far."

"Will he follow the Montauban tradition of apostasy?" The Cardinal smiled.

Michel was amused, and laughed aloud. "He has his own mind,

176

Your Eminence, and few gentlemen in France enjoy even a token independence under Louis. But Paul is no apostate." He paused, and grew somber. "My own situation is rather delicate right at this moment, you know. It would have been natural for you to seek out Cardinal de Harlay when you arrived in the city this morning, and the King couldn't have made more than a token protest. If a Papal Legate chooses to pay his respects to the Archbishop of Paris, not even Louis can object. Instead you sent a courier ahead asking me to leave Versailles and meet you here. I'm prepared for one of the King's icy receptions. I'm accustomed to them. But don't be surprised if he's impossibly cold with you, too."

"I'm following the personal instructions of the Holy Father," the Cardinal replied, his manner suddenly austere. "I was told to confer with you before seeing anyone else, and to meet you at a safe place in Paris rather than at a palace where the walls have ears."

Michel inclined his head, which was tonsured like that of a monk. "His Holiness may rely on my loyalty and discretion."

"So we hoped, but couldn't be certain. In view of Louis' many arguments with Pope Innocent in the past five years, we were afraid the first loyalty of the King's confessor would be to the King."

Bishop de Montauban drained his glass and stood. "The character of King Louis and the burdens he places on those who serve him can't be explained in a moment. Shall we dine before I try to explain these royal mysteries?"

"I've come a long distance, Your Grace. Dinner can wait."

"Of course. I'll try to be brief. If I were servile, neither Louis nor Madame de Maintenon would want me as his confessor. It's because I refuse to accept a servant's treatment that he respects me."

"It's true, then, that you stood with the Church two years ago in our dispute with France?"

"Naturally. To my mind it's wrong for the King to appoint new bishops when dioceses fall vacant. As Frenchmen we are Louis' subjects, and are responsible to him in temporal matters. As priests we must obey the authority of St. Peter's successor. The lines of demarcation are clear."

De Orsini was studying him closely. "I inquired about your family because His Holiness told me the Montauban clan has had an unusual record of integrity. It's true. Now, Your Grace, explain one thing more to me, and I'll be ready for that dinner the cooks are struggling so hard to keep from spoiling. Precisely what is the difference between the Maintenon woman and the King's earlier mistresses—Marquise de Montespan, Louise de la Vallière and the rest? The reports that have reached Vatican Hill are confusing."

"Françoise d'Aubignè de Maintenon," Michel said dryly, "is a good woman."

"Not by the standards of His Holiness," the Cardinal replied, his rebuke gentle.

"The Marquise de Maintenon can't be judged by the usual standards." The Bishop groped for an explanation. "The whole tone of the King's court has changed under her influence. When the nobles have affairs, they've got to be quiet about it. The ladies dress decorously. When the King's brother and his friends wear women's clothes, they must do it behind the locked doors of private apartments in one of the wings of Versailles. And Louis no longer plays twenty-one or his other favorite card games. There has been no gambling at the palace for the past eighteen months."

"Commendable, I'm sure." Cardinal de Orsini remained unyielding. "The Marquise is still the mistress of King Louis."

Michel de Montauban sighed. "I've barely scratched the surface, Your Eminence. Françoise was responsible for Louis' reconciliation with the Queen—who actually died in the arms of the Marquise last year. I was there, and saw the spectacle with my own eyes."

"Nevertheless——"

"Permit me to finish. It's a more technicality that she's the King's mistress. The situation will be altered shortly. She's been taking such good care of his children, both legitimate and illegitimate, that she's intimidated him. I make you the flat prediction—privately, of course—that they'll be married within six months, a year at the latest."

Cardinal de Orsini tugged so hard at the slender chain from which the Crucifix around his neck was suspended that the strand of silver snapped. "But she was the widow of a poet, a commoner! How can he reconcile his ideas of grandeur with such a woman as his queen?"

"You know the rules governing the confessional as well as I, Your Eminence. Let me just say that she won't become Queen of France. It will be a morganatic marriage."

"Astonishing!"

"Françoise is an astonishing woman."

The Cardinal, recovering slowly from his surprise, became more cheerful. "Then there's real hope of achieving better relations between Vatican Hill and France."

Michel shrugged. "Let me discuss that with you over the roast."

"You don't agree?"

"I find it impossible to predict what the King will do under her influence. She's the first good woman he's ever known since the death of his mother, and from what I've heard, she was none too virtuous. Françoise has her own ideas of right and wrong, and everyone—including Cardinal de Harlay—is afraid to tell her that occasionally she may be mistaken."

"But if she's a devout Catholic——"

"She considers herself devout, yes. But she's had three confessors in the past year, and only now, in Father la Chaise, has she found a milksop she can intimidate. You'll understand her better when you meet her, Your Eminence. She's the sort of woman who would not only tell Pope Innocent to rearrange the furnishings of his private apartments in Vatican Hill—to eliminate influences she believed harmful to his soul—but she'd nag and push until he did precisely what she had told him."

The Special Papal Legate laughed hollowly.

But there was no humor in Michel's dark eyes. "Françoise de Maintenon's virtue is her greatest vice. Poor Scarron's poetry suffered when she was married to him, and she drove him to his grave. Montespan felt sorry for her, and hired her as a governess. Now Maintenon rules at Versailles, and Montespan has retired to the Convent of St. Joseph, where her tears keep the abbess awake every night. I know this to be true, because the abbess sends petitions through me begging for the transfer of her distinguished guest to another convent. Next Maintenon will marry Louis, and then may the Lord in His infinite mercy take pity on France."

The anteroom with the handsome oval windows overlooking the gardens of the palace was crowded, the air was stifling, and the greatest nobles of France, waiting patiently in single file outside the royal bedchamber, reeked of perfume, perspiration and breakfast wine. King Louis was awake, and the tedious morning ritual had begun.

The first to enter were two dukes, both marshals of France, who drew back the curtains of the fourposter and wished His Majesty a good morning. Two other dukes removed the royal nightshirt, which was replaced by smallclothes borne by a prince, a duke, a marquis and a count. Even the perfumed water that Louis dabbed on his eyes was presented to him by a marquis whose ancestors had been prominent members of the nobility for more than five hundred years.

Count Philippe de Montauban stood far down the line, holding a gold-buckled shoe under one arm as he yawned and summoned a page, who brought him a cup of watered wine. For three years he had been a member of the privileged inner circle who helped the King prepare for the day, and the absurd spectacle no longer irritated him. It was an inevitable part of daily living, something that had to be accepted with resignation if not good grace.

Life at Versailles was intolerable only to those who refused to accommodate themselves to the King's routines. Philippe had grown accustomed to the tiny, draughty room in which he slept, and had stopped longing for the comforts of his townhouse in Paris. It was far

179

better to suffer a few minor personal inconveniences than to lose Louis' favor. Those who complained were forbidden to visit Versailles, and soon found themselves hounded by royal tax collectors, deputy crown chancellors who questioned their property rights and bureaucratic inspectors who filed mysterious reports with unidentified government offices.

There had been a time when Philippe had envied his brothers, who were free to come and go as they please, eat elsewhere than at the King's overburdened table, and enjoy frequent baths, a luxury almost unknown at the cramped palace. Michel spent no more than an hour each day with the King, and could always plead Church business in order to escape. Paul was even more fortunate, in part because he was considered a minor member of the nobility whose presence at Versailles was not obligatory, in part because his rehabilitation of Montauban was providing the Crown with a steady source of tax revenue. Louis never interfered with the activities of anyone whose earnings improved the state of the Finance Minister's treasury.

Gentlemen of the bedchamber whose duties for the morning had been completed were beginning to leave now, and Philippe glanced at them as he idly reached up under his ornate wig to scratch his head. The Marquis de Moraine, who helped Louis don his breeches, walked with right thumb and forefinger pointing downward from the hilt of his dress sword, a signal to those still in line that His Majesty was in a foul mood. Moraine's signs usually had little significance, however, as the King ordinarily put on his breeches before eating the hot bread and honey, washed down with a sparkling red wine, that comprised his breakfast.

It was far more serious when the Duke d'Anvers, who was the custodian of the royal wig, also gave the thumb and forefinger sign. The King's mood was indeed bad, and Philippe braced himself, walked past the rigid sentries stationed at the door and entered the royal presence. The drapes had been drawn, letting in sunlight, but the air was still stale, and although the weather outdoors was pleasant, no one had the courage to suggest that a window be opened.

Louis XIV, who insisted that posterity would regard him as the Sun King, was a man who refused to await the judgment of later generations, and his likeness, in bronze, appeared in every town and village square in France. He favored equestrian statues, even though he was actually an inferior horseman, because his short stature was less evident when he was mounted. For the same reason he favored wigs that gave him added height, but he was careful not to wear shoes with heels more than an inch high. Courtiers sometimes whispered that he wanted no one to think him in any way like his effeminate brother.

At forty-six the King looked at least sixty. His face was permanently creased and bloated, there were deep puffs of dissipation beneath his eyes, and whenever his cloth-of-gold cloak fell open, it was obvious that he had a prominent paunch and flabby body. Only his eyes, alert and hard, were reminders that he was the grandson of Henry IV.

Philippe bowed at the entrance, crossed the chamber and bowed again before dropping to one knee.

King Louis seemed unaware of his subject's presence as he allowed Philippe to place the shoe on his right foot. But, just as the Count was about to rise, the King spoke in the petulant lisp that grew pronounced when he was irritated. "We wish to speak with you, de Montauban."

"I'm honored, sire." Philippe remained on one knee.

"Privately," the King declared, and a marquis, who carried his other shoe, backed out of the chamber.

Six other gentlemen also departed, leaving only the sentries, officer of the guard, master of the bedchamber and the four or five high-ranking nobles privileged to hear anything said in this room.

"Why was your brother dining in Paris last night?" Louis demanded.

"I didn't know he was in the city, sire," Philippe replied honestly.

"You own the Hôtel de Montauban." The royal statement sounded like an accusation.

"I do, Your Majesty, but both of my brothers are free to use its facilities." Philippe refrained from adding that there was little enough for a full staff of servants to do while he himself lived as a virtual prisoner at Versailles.

"His Grace didn't tell you his business?"

"The Bishop," Philippe said, slightly emphasizing his brother's title, "doesn't take me into his confidence."

In spite of his annoyance, Louis smiled. Philippe de Montauban was faithful, a trifle dull and totally lacking in imagination. It was not his fault that the other members of his family were sharper and wittier. "You don't know why he chose to entertain the Cardinal at your house?"

"Cardinal de Harlay, sire?"

Louis lost patience. "No, imbecile, the Apostolic Legate who hasn't yet had the courtesy to present his credentials to us in person." Forgetting he was wearing only one shoe, the King started to tramp across the room. Quickly discovering his error, he sent the master of the bedchamber for the missing shoe, a gesture that would convince its bearer that he was out of favor.

Philippe hadn't been granted permission to rise, but his knee ached, so he rose. The worst that might be in store would be a few harsh words on the etiquette required of subjects in the presence of their monarch, but he dared take the chance because it seemed obvious that the King's mind was on other matters.

"I don't even know the Legate, sire," he said.

"They talked from six o'clock in the evening, when Cardinal de Orsini arrived at your house, until sometime after two this morning. Bishop de Montauban then retired to the third floor——"

"His own room is up there, Your Majesty, the room that's been his since he was a child."

"——and the Legate slept in the master suite on the second floor."

A cold feeling crept up Philippe's spine. The deadly efficiency of the King's secret police was frightening, and it hadn't occurred to him until now that any members of his household staff might be in Louis' pay. At his first opportunity he would have to warn Michel to be careful. A duke had gone into exile after the "King's watchdogs" had found evidence against him, never made public, that had distressed Louis, and a marquis, subjected to similar treatment, had vanished, only to reappear the better part of a year later as a much-subdued monk in a remote monastery in the Maritime Alps. Inasmuch as the marquis had been as fond of the ladies as the King himself, and had never been known for his religious devotion, it was difficult to believe that he had voluntarily chosen a life of poverty, chastity and obedience. What was more, he now walked with a pronounced limp, but no one had been courageous enough to ask him whether he had been subjected to physical torture.

As yet no priests had disappeared, and certainly a man who held the exalted rank of a bishop seemed safe from persecution, but it was best to take no risks. The secret police were ruthless, responsible to no one but the King himself, and the mere fact that Michel had been under observation made his future precarious.

Louis drained his wine goblet, handed it to one of his gentlemen to be refilled and then drank far too rapidly, which was a sign to everyone in the room that he intended to pay a visit to the apartment of his mistress. "We hold you responsible for anything that takes place under your roof, de Montauban," he said. "Take heed."

Philippe felt slightly ill.

The King took a staff topped with a knob of pure gold from a rack in a corner of the chamber that he permitted no one else to touch, and swept out of the room, followed by his retinue. The gentlemen gathered in the anteroom bowed low, and in the broad corridor ladies sank to the floor in deep curtsies, but Louis seemed unaware of their presence. He walked quickly toward the new wing, halting only once, to inspect a room filled with marble and alabaster busts of his likeness. The statues were dusted several times each day, and had been ever since the unhappy occasion when he had discovered dirt on one of them. His humor seemed a trifle improved when he emerged, but he was still lost in thought, and conversed with no one.

The members of his entourage fell back when he approached the entrance to Madame de Maintenon's suite, and Louis walked in alone, not bothering to knock. It was obvious that word had been sent ahead of his approach. A half-dozen modestly dressed young ladies-in-waiting curtsied and fled, and he made his way through a series of anterooms to a modestly furnished sitting room. The furniture, unlike that found elsewhere in the palace, was severe, functional and uncomfortable; the drapes at the sides of the windows were made of inexpensive silk, and the rug that covered the floor, although less than two years old, already looked threadbare. One wall was dominated by a huge painting of Christ on the Cross, done by Claude Lorrain in a far more somber mood than most of his work. There were no other decorations, and even wallpaper, used almost everywhere at Versailles, was missing.

Seated in a straight-backed chair near an open window was a woman in a high-necked, long-sleeved gown of black bombazine, a mixture of silk and wool, who looked older than her fifty years. Françoise, Marquise de Maintenon, scorned the use of her wig, and wore her own gray hair in a neat bun at the crown of her head. Perhaps there was a hint of rouge on her lips, but she wore no other cosmetics, and her perfume, made to her order at a convent near Lyon, was inoffensively mild, almost scentless.

She was reading a medieval prayer book that she held in her lap, and did not look up. "You're late," she said.

Louis was prepared for the accusation, and defended himself vigorously. "You know I can't change my routines after all these years. The court expects me to conduct myself with dignity, and I'd lose the respect of everyone. No matter how much I rush the ceremonials, I need more than an hour to dress and eat breakfast."

The lines at the corners of her mouth and eyes seemed to grow more pronounced. "Father la Chaise and I waited for you in my chapel, but I finally told him to say Mass when it became all too clear you weren't coming."

"I'll go to Mass later in the morning." Louis became sulky whenever she aroused his conscience.

Suddenly Françoise raised her head, studied him for a moment and then became maternal. "Sit down. You look as though you had a bad night's sleep."

"It wasn't very restful." He sighed and lowered himself into the one padded chair that was kept in the chamber for his exclusive use.

"Your brother and his friends didn't keep you awake?"

"I didn't hear them. Were they unruly?"

"They held another of their disgusting supper parties, and as usual it turned into an orgy. There were twenty of them, ten dressed as ladies. I have the full list for you."

"I don't want it. I——"

"Your brother is old enough to stop his masquerades."

"He's too old to change," the King said wearily.

"Then punish him!"

"Françoise, we've discussed the problem far too often. If I punish a prince of royal blood, the Crown itself suffers. I wish you'd forget a little company of perverts who do no harm, and listen to some important problems."

Madame de Maintenon bristled. "No harm? I'll have you know that a lieutenant colonel in your household brigade of musketeers was seduced! They draped him in a gown and wig that had been made just for the occasion—secretly, so you and I wouldn't learn of it—and the report I received early this morning says he looked so ravishing that three of them made love to him."

Louis knew she wouldn't drop the subject until he showed concern. "Who is he?"

"Montmorency's youngest son."

The King made the mistake of laughing. "How a warrior breed degenerates."

"I scarcely need to remind you that your brother is the grandson of King Henry!"

Louis hated hints that his grandfather might have been a greater monarch. "I forbid you to say anything more on the matter."

Françoise knew better than to push him too far. She pulled a bell-rope, and one of her ladies, who apparently had been waiting for the signal in an adjoining room, entered with a tray.

The King brightened. "Ah, plovers' eggs, olives stuffed with minced breast of pheasant and a bottle of wine that looks as though it may come from Chaumont." He sniffed appreciatively. "It does."

Madame de Maintenon pretended not to watch him as he ate and drank greedily. "What was the problem that troubled you last night, my dear?" she asked solicitously.

"I thought the Apostolic Legate had been delayed on the road. He wasn't. He spent the whole evening in Paris with Bishop de Montauban, and still hasn't come out here this morning."

"I'm sure there's a logical explanation."

"He has no right to see one of my bishops before he tells me what brings him to France. Pope Innocent doesn't seem to understand that only one man rules France. But if he doesn't know it, de Montauban does."

Françoise became apprehensive. "I hope you aren't going to start another feud with His Holiness."

"I have no intention of fighting with anyone—provided he knows I won't permit my authority to be circumvented or ignored!"

"Patience, my dear. You've never had reason to doubt Bishop de Montauban's loyalty."

"You seem to forget that his position on the appointment of new

184

bishops was questionable. He never said in so many words that he agreed with Vatican Hill, but he didn't give me the support I wanted, either."

"If you don't trust him," Madame de Maintenon said reasonably, "appoint another confessor. I've found Father la Chaise very pleasant. But do nothing until you learn the Pope's reaction to your request that the Church apply stricter regulations to the dealings of Catholics with Protestants."

She had struck a sensitively responsive chord, as she had known she would. "I can't tolerate the independent attitude of the Huguenots much longer. I'd much prefer that Innocent issue new decrees. I was plain enough in my letter to him, when I explained that we can win England back into the Catholic camp if we tread carefully. But I won't and can't wait indefinitely. The Huguenots flout my sovereignty, and if Vatican Hill won't act, I will!"

Paul de Montauban towered over the party walking through the vineyards. Heavily suntanned, with his brown hair streaked a lighter shade, he looked at first glance like one of the peasants employed on his family's estates. A closer inspection revealed that his dusty boots were hand-sewn and made of supple leather, and that his open-throated shirt was of the finest lawn. But his behavior in no way resembled that of a sedate noble. He hailed field workers in a loud, friendly voice, leaped over fences and walked so rapidly that his visitors found it difficult to maintain his pace.

Lord Willoughby, the chairman of the British commission, was panting for breath by the time Paul halted in the shade of a cool arbor, and gratefully mopped his face with a large square of silk.

"These," Paul said proudly, holding up a thick cluster of grapes on a lattice-work wall, "are the best we've ever grown. I'll give you a sample of last year's crop when we reach the wine vaults, and I can guarantee you that this year's pressings will be even better."

Lord Willoughby exchanged quick glances with the other two Englishmen. "If the wine we drank this noon is typical, milord, we're already convinced. The question in our minds is whether you can provide us with enough to make an arrangement worth our while."

Paul had learned that the direct approach was the most effective in dealing with the English. "What's the capacity of your brig, milord?"

"Four hundred and fifty casks."

"And your brigantine?"

"Another one hundred and twenty."

"Very well, milord," Paul said crisply. "I'm prepared to give you a promise, in writing and notarized by the principal royal justice of the county, that I'll deliver five hundred and seventy casks of the first quality Montauban wine to you at the Bordeaux wharves on the first day of October. Our prices," he added casually, "are a trifle higher than those of our competitors because our product is superior. I trust you understand."

"What are you charging, milord?" Willoughby's thin mouth looked pinched.

Paul's large, blue-green eyes opened wide, giving him an ingenuous appearance. "Two of the newly-minted gold francs for each cask."

"Is there a discount because we'd be buying in bulk?"

"I've already taken that into consideration," Paul said, not caring in the least whether the Englishmen rejected his price.

He gathered from the awkward silence that the Englishmen wanted to talk privately, so he nodded to them and wandered off to climb a small hill behind the arbor. From its crest he could see more than two hundred peasants working in the vineyards and, beyond them, many more in the orchards and wheat fields. Soon the harvest would end; he would conclude his negotiations to dispose of the season's yield and would have to return to Paris.

He thought of Philippe, living a lackey's life at Versailles. And he thought of Michel whose lot was slightly better, but only because of the force of his own character. Paul grinned. "You're the last priest in France the King should have chosen as his confessor," he had told his brother. "Louis wants painless absolution granted him while he's being shaved every morning. But one of these days you'll tell him to spend an hour on his knees praying for the Lord's forgiveness. The words will no sooner be out of your mouth than you'll be banished from court."

Michel would enjoy Montauban, and Paul hoped his brother would come here for a visit some day. Even though the townspeople and peasants of the county were Huguenots, they believed a man's religion was his own business, and they carried no grudges against the family of their Count for practising Catholicism. In fact, they showed Paul actual respect when, visiting the graves of his great-grandparents in the courtyard of the castle, he knelt to pray, an act contrary to the basic tenets of their faith. Michel would be the first to agree, he felt certain, that many of them were better Christians than the sycophants at King Louis' court.

Paul was still amazed by Michel's close resemblance to "the warrior of Montauban," their great-uncle Henry, whose equestrian statue stood in the main square of the town, and he hoped that on his next journey to the south he could persuade his brother to come with him. Many of the townspeople said he looked like Henry de Montauban, too, but he couldn't see the similarity, even though he felt flattered.

The Englishmen appeared to have ended their conference, so Paul sauntered down the hill toward them. He whistled under his breath, pleased that it didn't matter whether they accepted his terms. Others were eager to buy his wine, and while Frenchmen wouldn't pay the prices he demanded from foreigners, he would still show a handsome profit.

"Before we strike a bargain," Lord Willoughby said, "I wonder if you'd be good enough to settle some matters that puzzle us, milord."

"If I can." Paul bowed slightly, and wanted to laugh at the incongruity of his gesture when he was in shirtsleeves.

"It's no secret that King Louis thinks only of the grandeur and glory of France, and we've heard he reserves for his own use the finest products of the land. My daughter happens to be a friend of Princess Mary, King James' elder daughter, and I wanted to buy a tapestry for her at Lyons similar to one that Mary owns. But they aren't available. King Louis buys every last tapestry for his own use. Why doesn't he take your supply of wine?"

"There's no accounting for royal tastes," Paul said, and smiled. "His Majesty happens to prefer the wines of the north."

"Yet he allows you to export what you please?"

"His tax collectors take twenty-five centimes out of each franc I earn."

Willoughby was shocked. "A frightful tax, milord."

"It costs a great deal of money to support His Majesty's entourage at Versailles. You visited there, I believe before you came to this part of France."

The Englishmen nodded, and the junior member of the party murmured in his own tongue, "An incredible spectacle. I wouldn't have believed such magnificence could be achieved if I hadn't seen it myself."

Paul replied in English. "The glory of France is our greatest national asset."

The commissioners, surprised he spoke their language, were unable to judge from either his expression or tone whether he was being serious. Willoughby was quick to take advantage of the comment, however. "You can't expect us to pay for your pomp."

Paul refused to be maneuvered. "I expect nothing, milord. The wines of Montauban are for sale. Buy them, if you wish, and you can earn yourself a profit of more than one hundred percent in London after you've paid your shipping charges. If another wine suits your fancy, you are under no obligation to me."

The Englishman was impressed. "You know the London market, milord."

"I try to keep myself informed."

Willoughby turned to his companions. "We've been fooling ourselves all these years, gentlemen. Our nobles aren't alone in their knowledge of trade."

Paul owed them no explanation, but saw no reason to stand aloof. "The younger brother of a count finds very little to occupy him."

Lord Willoughby liked his candor, and impulsively extended a hand. "I hope you'll visit me in London some day, milord. It might be to our mutual benefit. For the present, we'll accept your terms, and if you can spare an additional fifty casks, we'll take them, too, even if we have to lash them to the decks."

Paul shook his hand, carefully concealing his elation. His own share of the profits would amount to more than three hundred of the new francs, the largest sum he had ever earned. And if Michel was right, those francs would double in value when Finance Minister Colbert realized there was too much gold in them and recalled them to the treasury within the next few months.

So many people had warned Bishop Michel de Montauban he was in trouble that he changed into his robes of office as soon as he reached Versailles. Then, clad in his tall miter and ermine-trimmed cassock, and carrying his staff, he made his way to the throne room. Although it was not yet noon, hundreds of smokeless tapers were burning, their brilliance magnified by the mirrors lining the great hall.

Scores of ladies and gentlemen were milling about, as they did for hours each day, hoping that some gesture might call them to the attention of King Louis, who sat impassively on a throne of gold and purple velvet at the far end of the chamber. Michel nodded pleasantly to acquaintances as he made his way down the hall, but conversation stopped as the courtiers became aware of his presence, and by the time he reached the base of the dais there was a tense, heavy silence in the room.

Michel mounted thie dais slowly, then dutifully dropped to one knee and kissed the languid hand the King held out to him. Before Louis could speak, however, Michel stood erect and extended his own hand.

The King blinked.

"It's customary, sire, for a Catholic to kiss the ring of his bishop."

Some of the nobles were unable to conceal their admiration for Michel's courage, while others plainly thought him a fool. The vast majority wanted no part in the contest, however, and edged away from the dais.

"You ask us to honor you, de Montauban?"

"I hope, sire, that as Almighty God's servant, you will pay homage to Him." Michel's arm ached, but his hand remained steady.

Grudgingly the King leaned forward and kissed Bishop de Montauban's ring.

Out of the corner of his eye Michel could see Madame de Maintenon, seated on a divan in the corner of the hall, nodding approvingly. He had won a tactical victory, but it was short-lived.

"Now that we've observed the amenities, de Montauban," the

King said, speaking with a pronounced lisp, "you owe us an explanation. What was your business last night and this morning with the Apostolic Legate?"

"When I left our visitor at breakfast," Michel said, "he was planning to call on Cardinal de Harlay at Notre-Dame. I'm sure the Cardinal will escort him here to pay his respects to Your Majesty and bring you the greetings of Pope Innocent before the day ends."

Louis pounded the arm of his throne only when he was exasperated. "You haven't answered us!"

"We spoke of many ecclesiastical matters, sire," Michel replied quietly. "His Holiness has confiscated eighteen theses prepared by the Jesuits in recent months, and the Society of Jesus is in disfavor. One of these documents questioned the Augustinian doctrine of faith by saying——"

"Enough! What did you talk about?"

Madame de Maintenon was laughing silently at Louis' discomfort, and Michel felt increasingly certain he was on safe ground. "There have been some changes in the secretariat of The Holy See, particularly in the office of the Congregation of Extraordinary Affairs." He spoke earnestly, gathering momentum. Monsignor Rochas has gone on a long retreat, and will probably be assigned to a Tuscan diocese when it ends, even though he has never been on friendly terms with the Tuscan hierarchy. His place has been taken by Monsignor di Gracchi, who was once Pope Innocent's private secretary. The Legate believes he'll be the first to get a cardinal's hat at the next Consistory." Michel paused for breath.

Someone, perhaps the King's brother or one of his effeminate friends, was unable to restrain a high-pitched giggle.

Color suffused Louis' face. "The audience," he said loudly, "is at an end."

High-ranking generals, who were required to act as major-domos at the court, began to shepherd the ladies and gentlemen toward the exits. Everyone respectfully backed away from the King, who was offended if the rules of royal etiquette were broken, and, inevitably, there were collisions between people unable to see behind them. But these minor accidents neither halted nor slowed the steady movement toward the doors. The courtiers were relieved to escape, and no one wanted to be the last to go.

Michel started to back down the steps of the dais, but Louis held up a jewel-adorned hand. "Wait," he said, and glared at Madame de Maintenon, who continued to make herself comfortable on the divan.

She refused to be intimidated, and smiled blandly.

In a few moments the great hall was cleared, and the captain of the guard moved his sentries out of earshot.

"Why didn't you tell me that you and de Orsini were exchanging Church gossip?" Louis demanded, sounding doleful.

"I did, Your Majesty," Michel replied, "the very moment I had the opportunity to speak."

He found an unexpected ally in Françoise de Maintenon. "The King's humors have been strained lately," she said. "He's been struggling with some serious problems of state."

Michel hoped he looked sympathetic. "You need a holiday, Your Majesty."

Louis raised his arms, then let them drop wearily to the arms of his throne. "Who would be responsible for the welfare of France?"

His refusal to delegate authority to any but a handful of obedient subordinates, like Colbert, made it impossible for him to rest, but Michel had no intention of lecturing his monarch on the requirements of statecraft. "There is one thing I learned from the Papal Legate, but it would have been inappropriate for me to mention it in the presence of the whole court."

"I knew it!" Louis glanced smugly at his mistress, and leaned forward.

Michel had no desire to indicate the candor and range of his conversation with Cardinal de Orsini. "You wrote a private letter to Pope Innocent, Your Majesty, and he's sent an emissary to discuss it with you."

Again the King looked at Madame de Maintenon. "I told you I'd stir up Vatican Hill," he said to her. "Popes are like other men. They hate to lose the initiative, and Innocent has been wondering what I meant when I wrote him that I intend to strike a blow for Christianity." Suddenly he turned back to Michel, frowning. "The Apostolic Legate should have paid his respects to me the moment he arrived last night. His conduct has been inexcusable."

"He's an old man, Your Majesty, and he was very tired after his long journey." Michel and the Cardinal had planned an unassailable reply to the criticism. "As I'm sure you'll appreciate, he wants to be at his strongest and most alert when you receive him."

"There, you see!" Madame de Maintenon exclaimed. "He's paying you a compliment."

The King considered the matter for a moment, and then subsided. For the immediate present, subject to a change in his mood, a crisis had been averted.

Under the happiest of circumstances a meal in the private apartments of the King was an ordeal, and when serious questions were being discussed, the tension was almost unbearable. Bishop Michel de Montauban, seated at the foot of the table, was unable to appreciate the lavish dishes set before him. He scarcely touched the cold, creamed filet of sole, served with a hot oyster sauce, and was unable to do justice to the "soup of kings," a triple-strength chicken broth, in which tiny, whole vegetables and squares, crescents and oblongs of chicken breast were floating. The fresh-water lobster, one of his favorites, was ruined by a rich and heavy sauce, and the roasted beef had an alien taste because it had been threaded with so many strips of wine-soaked lard.

Even the main dish was unappealing. Squabs had been baked for hours inside the hollowed cavities of wild geese, which had then been discarded, leaving only the squabs, which had cooked in the juices. The extravagant recipe had been the envy of every royal court in Europe, but Louis, who had his own ideas regarding food, had improved on his chef's concoction by himself inventing a gravy of olives, almond paste, spices and lemon juice. Michel knew from experience that the gravy would give him a severe attack of indigestion.

After the serving of three desserts, a brandywine soufflé, a cake of chocolate coated with glazed, candied orange rinds, and a baked cheese dish, the party settled down to a serious discussion. Cardinal de Orsini, seated on the King's right, was unaccustomed to so much rich food, and looked uncomfortable, but had managed to maintain his equilibrium. The Archbishop of Paris, François, Cardinal de Harlay de Champvallon, had exercised less caution, however, and, as always, had made a glutton of himself. Somewhat dazed, he sat back in his chair and napped, although one or another of the five servants standing behind him stepped forward from time to time and tried to nudge him unobtrusively.

A lacquer screen cut off the far side of the ornately furnished dining chamber, and occasionally Michel glanced toward it, but could neither hear nor otherwise detect the presence of anyone on the far side. He suspected, but couldn't prove, that Madame de Maintenon had slipped into the room and was concealed behind the screen so she could listen to the talk. According to palace gossip, it was a practice in which she frequently indulged.

Louis, affable after drinking prodigious quantities of wine, belched politely and turned to the guest of honor. "Well, milord Cardinal, what word do you bring me from Rome?"

Cardinal de Orsini pushed aside his liquor goblet and folded his hands on the edge of the table. "His Holiness sends you no specific message, Your Majesty. He prefers to learn your thoughts."

Louis' chuckle was indulgent. "So Innocent is learning to appreciate the preeminence of France in the affairs of the world. We make progress. I trust he still bears me no ill over the matter of the appointment of bishops?"

De Orsini's faint smile vanished. "The Holy See," he said, "cannot accept the principle that anyone other than the Pope appoint bishops."

"Nonsense!" Louis retorted. "The Spaniards have been doing it for centuries."

"Without the approval of The Holy See. Our relations with Spain have been less than perfect for a long time, and we regret the decision of France to create new complications in relations that are already clouded."

"The Pope must realize that France is sovereign in all things that affect her destiny." There was a hard ring in Louis' voice. "Accept reality, milord Cardinal, and we'll be the best of friends."

De Orsini was equally unyielding. "Temporal monarchs must accept the spiritual guidance of the Holy Roman Church. Even kings who are Catholics have no choice."

"I take second place to no man in my love for Christianity." The King was still pleasant, but his voice rose slightly, and he began to lisp. "But I permit no organization and no man to interfere in matters that concern France. You say there is no choice, but I beg to differ with you, milord Cardinal. I've taken a different path, and if the Pope chooses to defy my authority in my own realm, it's his prerogative to excommunicate me."

Cardinal de Orsini was shocked. "His Holiness has no intention of taking such drastic measures."

Michel wished there were some way he could indicate to the Legate that Louis was merely threatening in order to improve his bargaining position. But it was impossible to attract the Cardinal's attention without the King's knowledge. Besides, Michel wan't yet certain he knew what Louis wanted.

The King twisted his golden goblet in his hand and watched the lights of the tapers in the crystal candelabrum overhead playing on the gleaming surface. "It's natural that every pope should be anxious to establish his own reputation. I've dealt with four of them through the years, and each one has tried to elevate the papacy at the expense of Catholic nations. Innocent has been the most persistent of them, but I trust that by now he realizes the importance of France."

"His Holiness is well aware of your prestige," the Cardinal replied.

If Louis recognized the barb, he chose to overlook it. "He should be grateful to me. As I pointed out in my letter—rather forcefully, I thought—the national interests of Fance coincide with those of the Church. By strengthening my own position, I improve that of Vatican Hill, too."

"We've come to the heart of the question, Your Majesty. You've been rather mysterious in your references to your plans."

The King smiled. "Quite true. Even Bishop de Montauban knows nothing on the subject. I've confided in no one but Cardinal de Harlay."

The Archbishop of Paris snored gently.

The Papal Legate laughed, and Michel couldn't help smiling.

"Now that James of England openly admits his conversion, the next step is vital." Louis lowered his voice, but the liveried servants standing behind each chair could, nevertheless, hear every word.

It was small wonder, Michel thought, that there were virtually no secrets at Versailles.

"If the Church demonstrates her firmness," Louis continued, "the time is ripe for a return of England to the fold."

Cardinal de Orsini coughed lightly behind his hand. "King James is like so many converts. He's inclined to be a trifle too zealous in his missionary work."

"Are you saying that Vatican Hill is afraid to take a bold stand?"

"His Holiness hasn't forgotten the lessons—or the wars—of the Reformation. The office of the Propagation of the Faith has made a careful study of the situation in England, and the Duke of Norfolk, the first Catholic peer of the land, was kind enough to spend two weeks at Vatican Hill during his recent travels on the Continent." The Legate looked first at the King, then at Michel. "No one, including His Holiness, sees any positive indication that the people of England are ready to follow King James into the Church."

"I disagree," Louis said irritably. "This opportunity can't be lost."

De Orsini was puzzled, and turned to the Bishop for clarification.

"The French navy," Michel said, "is only half the size of England's. No matter how rapidly we expand, they stay ahead of us. Our trade suffers, and our attempts to build a stronger empire are often frustrated."

"My confessor," the King said, "has been an apt pupil. I am a missionary, milord Cardinal, because a Catholic England will be my ally, while a Protestant England remains my most dangerous potential enemy. There's no mystery involved. The whole question is almost ridiculously simple."

"It's too simple, Your Majesty." Cardinal de Orsini sounded sternly remote. "Pope Innocent has established a firm policy of not interfering in the disputes of temporal powers."

"Then Pope Innocent is a fool."

De Orsini was shocked, and Michel stiffened.

The King laughed sardonically. "Have I committed blasphemy, milord Cardinal? milord Bishop? What a pity. Tell the Pope what I've said. He'll lose his influence everywhere unless he inaugurates a new crusade."

The Legate recovered swiftly. "His realm is spiritual, Your Majesty. He doesn't concern himself with trade, or navies, or colonies."

"I hope he's enough of a realist to grasp the fact that if we lose our chance now, we might not have another for generations. Both of James' daughters are heretic Protestants. And there isn't a man alive who doesn't know that Princess Mary's husband, William of Orange, has been my sworn enemy for the past twelve years. He owes his reputation to the good luck he enjoyed against a corps I sent into the field against him."

Michel knew now that, whatever Louis had in mind, he would not yield. If his long-range plan included the destruction of the courageous William, whom many Frenchmen secretly admired, nothing would deter him.

"Do you realize what will happen if Mary reaches the throne of England? Her husband will declare a religious war against me!"

"Surely you exaggerate, Your Majesty," de Orsini murmured.

"Do I? Two years ago he formed an alliance with Sweden and the Lutheran states of Germany!"

"The Holy See has reason to believe that the alliances being made by the Dutch are for purposes of defense, not aggression."

"Then The Holy See is incredibly naïve!" Louis retorted. "England can be won over if we act quickly and firmly. James is married to a young wife, and there's no reason he can't rear a new family, a Catholic family, that will insure a Christian succession in England."

In spite of Michel's warnings that Louis was an extraordinary man, the Legate was astonished. Never had he known anyone to engage in such complicated planning. "Does King James know what you have in mind for him?"

Louis was aware of the sarcasm, but it only made him more regal. "Of course. Vatican Hill must know that I've been supporting him for years. It's common knowledge that he takes my advice as well as my gold."

Michel risked a rebuke by intervening, but felt he had to keep the record straight. "The people of England don't know it, Your Majesty, and neither do your own subjects."

"You speak of people as an entity, de Montauban. They're a shapeless, unthinking mass, who do what they're told and follow where they're led. Why are men of supposed intelligence so obtuse? You sit there shaking your head, milord Cardinal, and your face is so long it droops to the floor, de Montauban. Let the English people know they have a master! Promise them absolution if they'll return to the Church, and threaten to destroy them if they refuse! That, in brief, is my grand design."

There was such a long silence at the table that Cardinal de Harlay sat upright and muttered to himself as he reached for a glass of wine.

"I trust you're aware of the risks, Your Majesty," de Orsini said, speaking very quietly.

"The risks are far greater if I do nothing. Either the Pope will act, or I'll have to set an example for the English myself. I can't allow the only chance of our century to be lost. Tell Innocent I'm determined, no matter what the cost, to advance the twin causes of France and Christianity."

Michel knew Louis would not admit to himself that the interests of France and the Church might not be identical. In spite of his long and intimate association with the King, it hadn't occurred to him until now that the man was a fanatic.

"I'm prepared to be reasonable," the King continued. "Tell Innocent I'll wait six months. I don't intend to suggest how he might convince the English that the patience of the Church is exhausted. I no more want to dictate to him than I'll permit him to give me orders." His expression suggested that he believed himself reasonable in his attitude and approach to the problem he had raised.

"I'll give His Holiness a word-for-word account of what you've said," Cardinal de Orsini replied. "But I hope you realize, Your Majesty, that he'll make his own decisions, and that—above all—he will not allow himself to be intimidated, even by a Catholic sovereign."

"Of course! We're saying the same thing." Louis drained his liquor, and a servant instantly poured more into his goblet. "I issue no ultimatum, and I want to cooperate with him to the fullest possible extent. If he has done nothing at the end of six months, I'll send Bishop de Montauban to Rome as my emissary, and he'll lay my own plans before the Pope. Surely no monarch could be more honorable in treating with an equal."

Paul de Montauban forced himself to stand still and appear relaxed, but his self-discipline failed. He had no idea why he had been summoned to the private apartment of Madame de Maintenon only twenty-four hours after his return to Paris from the south, and although he tried to reassure himself, he could not forget Michel's warning: "She is the most powerful woman in the country. Whatever she may want, don't oppose her. She's utterly ruthless, and she's been known to destroy men far more important than the younger brother of a count, with no title or following of his own."

The sitting room was so bleak that it reminded Paul of the parlor of a convent, and he found the huge oil painting of Christ on the Cross singularly out of place in the suite of a woman who, in spite of her rumored forthcoming marriage to the King, was still no more than his mistress.

Someone entered the chamber, and Paul turned quickly, but his tension lessened when he saw a pretty young woman, modestly attired in a gown of heavy silk that covered her from throat to slippers.

"Madame has been detained," the girl said, "but has asked me to tell you she'll join you shortly."

Paul bowed, studying the young woman carefully. She was even more attractive than she had seemed at first glance.

She was conscious of his scrutiny, and blushed.

The atmosphere at Versailles had become even more like that of a religious house than he had realized. He could remember the time, only a few years earlier, when ladies-in-waiting had been fair game. In fact, it hadn't been unusual for them to take the lead in flirtations and, when it pleased them, to arrange assignations. This girl looked as though she would flee if he winked at her.

"May I bring you some wine while you're waiting?" she asked demurely.

"I'd enjoy it, if you'll have a glass with me."

"Oh, no." She took a step backward, shaking her head. "I thank you, but it isn't possible."

"Do you find me so offensive?" Paul smiled at her.

"I—that's irrelevant, monsieur. The ladies of Madame's entourage don't entertain guests who visit this apartment. The rules are very strict."

The resemblance to a convent was becoming still more marked. "Perhaps," he suggested, "we could share a bottle some other time, either here or in Paris."

The girl made no reply. Walking to a sideboard, she poured some wine from a silver decanter into a matching cup, and offered it to Paul.

He saw that her hand was shaking and, as he took the cup, his fingers touched hers.

She snatched her hand away, gathered her skirts and hurried to the door. There she turned for an instant, smiled timidly and then disappeared.

The atmosphere was incredible. Never had Paul seen such obvious fear in a young woman, and what astonished him was that he had given her no cause to be afraid. His suggestion had been honorable, made without subterfuge, and it was absurd that a young lady couldn't allow herself to accept an innocent invitation from an eligible bachelor. He sipped the mild, almost tasteless wine, his sense of gloom becoming more pronounced.

A woman in rustling black silk swept into the room. "Accept my apologies, monsieur, but I was busy on an errand for the King."

Paul bowed low, and felt confused. He had expected Madame de Maintenon to be a harridan, but in spite of the severity of her dress and hair arrangement, she displayed a charm and graciousness that were the last qualities he had expected to find in her. By no stretch of the imagination was she beautiful, nor had she been when younger, but he realized why the King was drawn to her. She was surprisingly warm, in spite of her obvious strength, and he guessed that Louis had found the combination irresistible.

"I'm at your service, madame," he murmured.

She suggested that they sit, but carefully steered him away from the King's chair. "You're very kind to come here," she said. "I'm sure I've interrupted your appointments in Paris."

Paul started to protest, politely.

Madame de Maintenon shook her head. "Each day your casks of new wine remain unsold, you must pay storage fees on them."

Michel had warned him not to let anything surprise him, but Paul was amazed to discover how much she knew of his affairs. The secret police were even more efficient than his brother had led him to believe.

"You don't care for Versailles, Monsieur de Montauban?"

"I can't permit myself the luxury of coming here often, madame. My brothers need a great deal of money to live as they must." He refrained from adding that Philippe's wife was an empty-headed spendthrift who recklessly spent her husband's profits from his share of the Montauban revenues.

"You sacrifice yourself for the comfort of your brothers?" She looked amused.

"I do not, madame! I have something of a flair for commerce, and although some of my friends laugh at me and call me a merchant, I'm frank to admit I enjoy driving a bargain. I contribute to France in my own way. Philippe attends the King, and Michel serves the Church. I make my contribution to Colbert's gold vaults. If France were attacked, I'd join one of His Majesty's regiments immediately, but if there is no other use for me, I do what I can in my own way."

His earnestness and candor made an impression on Françoise de Maintenon. "I suppose you know it's unusual to find a nobleman of ambition these days."

Paul had discussed the very subject with Michel, and they had come to the joint conclusion that the King himself stifled ambition by forcing so many of his nobles to wait on him at Versailles. It would not be wise, however, to speak too freely to Louis' mistress. "It's enough that my conscience prods me, madame. I can't tell others what to do."

"I'm very pleased that you accepted my invitation, Monsieur de Montauban. You can be of far greater help to His Majesty than you realize."

"Madame?"

"You have a mind and will of your own, and you spend much of your time in the south. A perfect combination, and a far more reliable witness than those who serve the Crown only for money. I'll be grateful for your honest and confidential impressions on a subject of great importance. What do you think of the southern Huguenots?"

The unexpected question so surprised Paul that he didn't know what to say.

Madame de Maintenon revealed the iron behind her charming smile. "There are only Huguenots in the county of Montauban. You spend the better part of each year living with them, working with them, directing their labors. Surely you must know them, monsieur!"

Her flash of temper made Paul uncomfortable, but he tried to reply fairly. "They're amiable, madame, and they respond to orders. They're less venal than the Parisians, and require fewer amusements. I find them far more quiet, too."

She became still more impatient. "Really, monsieur. I want to know what they think of the King!"

"I've heard no disloyalty."

"I've had many reports that indicate the opposite. I'm told the Huguenots of the southern counties complain day and night about the extravagance of the court."

Paul was relieved, and laughed. "Those who have reported to you don't understand the minds of the peasants, madame. It's true they grumble, but they mean no harm. They'd rally to His Majesty if he called on them, and I'm sure they mean no disrespect. Their grumbling is a part of their way of living. I'm willing to wager that their ancestors muttered against all of the great kings of France, even Saint Louis and Henry of Navarre."

"Not Henry," she replied scathingly.

Paul looked at her blankly.

"After all, he was a fellow Huguenot."

Paul was convinced she was mistaken, but worded his rebuttal with care. "I know very little of their religion, madame, but they don't allow it to interfere with their patriotism. They try to live decent lives, and occasionally I've heard them citing the Ten Commandments—as we do. But they no longer keep alive the old feuds of the Huguenots with the Church."

"They're heretics!" Her voice was harsh, grating. "They're living symbols of the anti-Christ, and although I've yet to obtain proof, I'm positive they worship Satan at Black Masses."

Her unreasoning hatred was as startling as her ignorance, and Paul felt compelled to protest. "If they were as vicious as you indicate, madame, I'd have heard something of their attitudes in the past five and a half years. But I'll stake my own soul on their sincerity. Working with them, I've forgotten that they and we are different."

Madame de Maintenon's mouth was compressed into a straight, thin line. "Perhaps there are no differences."

Paul didn't understand.

"Perhaps you've become one of them, monsieur."

"No, my faith is what it has always been, and they've made no attempt to win me away from the Church."

Françoise de Maintenon stood. "Thank you for coming here, monsieur. I'm forced to trust your discretion, and hope you'll say nothing to your friends in the south of my interest in their affairs."

"You may rely on me." Paul had been dismissed, and bowed low. He could feel her watching him as he left her apartment, and when he reached the corridor he breathed a deep sigh of relief.

Several courtiers were standing in the outer hall, apparently waiting for appointments with the King's mistress, but Paul paid no attention to them. He made his way to the older portion of the palace, and after a brief search found Michel in one of the anterooms near the King's great hall. He started to speak, but the Bishop pressed his arm in warning, then led him outdoors.

A stiff breeze sent showers of dead leaves from the pruned beeches, chestnut and walnut trees swirling through the gardens, but Paul was impervious to the cold. Michel made an attempt to pull his biretta lower on his head, trying in vain to coax a little extra warmth from it, and buttoned his cloak. "I'm sorry to bring you out here," he said, shivering. "We may catch the ague, but it's better than being overheard."

Paul's boots thudded on the gravel path, spewing small sprays of stones behind him.

"The Duke of Burgundy," Michel said quietly, "was so angry after a talk with Madame de Maintenon that he rode off to his estates and absented himself from the court for almost a year. He didn't return until Louis sent a messenger to fetch him."

"I feel ill." Paul repeated his conversation, and was seething by the time he finished. "I thought France had become a civilized nation. How much longer will these stupid religious hatreds exist?" He stopped beside a stately oak and absently ripped off a chunk of fungus-infected bark. "Even the gardeners here aren't efficient," he muttered.

Michel put a hand on his brother's brawny shoulder. "Patience, lad. There are diseases that can't be cured in a day."

"There's poison in that woman. Something must be done to silence her!"

"Who will do it?"

Paul halted and jabbed a forefinger at the cross embroidered in gold on his brother's cloak.

Michel shrugged.

"You must, before she influences the King. If he believes the superstitious drivel she spews——"

"Louis is too intelligent a man."

Paul looked skeptical.

"Unfortunately, he has a great many swords of his own to sharpen. There are international political considerations I'm not free to discuss. The Huguenots are a natural scapegoat for him, and I'm afraid he's always disliked them because his control over them isn't absolute. Now that he's appointing his own Catholic bishops, he'll eventually gain total mastery of the Catholic faithful. But he can't bring the Huguenot clergy to heel. There have been developments since you last came to Paris that make me uneasy."

"I would have laughed at you an hour ago." They had reached the end of the path, and Paul halted. "You're his confessor, and you don't owe your miter to him. Can't you convince him that the efforts of almost one hundred years will be wasted if he allows that woman to spread her lies?"

Michel took a pipe from the pocket of his cloak, spent a long time stuffing it with tobacco, and then stood with his back to the wind while he manipulated a tinderbox and flint. "We've come full circle, you know, yet everything is changed. In our great-grandfather's day, every priest in France was opposed to the Huguenots. Today the clergy wants only peace."

"We've never known such prosperity, but the country will be driven into bankruptcy if the Huguenots are molested."

"The Church will do all it can to preserve order."

"If you're strong enough."

"The French hierarchy has its allies, you know."

"I hope they're powerful."

"They are," Michel said, and studied the glowing bowl of his pipe. "I find it odd that the newcomers to the Church are the least willing to forget the old enmities. There aren't many who know that Madame de Maintenon's grandfather was Agrippa d'Aubigné, one of King Henry's generals, and that her father was an active Huguenot."

"Was she herself——"

"Her background explains her excessive devotion. She's trying to purge herself, as it were. She was baptized a Catholic, reared as a Huguenot and then brought back into the faith as a young woman."

"Then she knows there's no truth in that rubbish about Protestants worshipping Satan at Black Masses!"

"She knows only what she allows herself to believe, Paul. What I dread is the harm that she—and thousands like her—can do if Louis, for his own reasons, gives them free rein. Hatreds in one land breed counter-hatreds in another. That defensive alliance Prince William of Holland has formed is unstable, but it will become solid overnight if Louis raises a hand against the Huguenots. And then may the Lord have mercy on Catholics in the German states and Holland."

Paul bent down, picked up a stone the size of a small egg and sent it sailing through the air. "You're even more concerned than I am, Michel."

"I don't know that it can be measured."

"Is there anything I can do?"

"Yes, for your own sake, stay out of trouble. I doubt if Madame de Maintenon really thinks you've become a Huguenot. She's usually suspicious of everyone, and she'll be inclined to forget her meeting with you today, provided you do nothing to call yourself to her attention again."

"I'll be very pleased if I never see the woman from now until I die! As soon as I sell our wine, I'm going back to Montauban. I can breathe there."

"I wish I could go with you."

"Why don't you? You've never looked so drawn, and you need a holiday."

"No," Michel said. "I can best serve God—and France—by seeing this new madness through to the end." He glanced at the watery sun, and spoke with forced cheerfulness. "Come along. Philippe and his wife will have their carriage waiting. We'll drive into Paris, dine at the house—and pretend we don't have a care in the world."

1685—1686

Cardinals and lesser members of Vatican Hill's staff, visiting clergymen, and the Roman nobles whose privileges were being sharply curtailed regarded Pope Innocent XI with varying degrees of awe and fear. "His Holiness is so pure in thought and deed," said Bishop Ernst von Grube of Bavaria in a remark that was to establish his reputation as a wit, "that there is no need for him to dress in white."

The Roman aristocracy put it another way. The Pope closed their gaming houses and bordellos, forced ladies to cover their heads and arms in public, and forbade the awarding of offices and sinecures to his own relatives or those of his cardinals, bishops and monsignors. "His Holiness," said Prince Andrea della Sargossino, "isn't satisfied with the purity of his own reflection in his shaving mirror. He must also bleed us white."

Bishop Michel de Montauban had expected to meet a frail, saintly figure, and was surprised to find that the Pope had the robust physique and high coloring of the peasants in his native Lombardy. In spite of his advanced years he was so vigorous he went for a ten-mile canter before breakfast every morning, and after spending long hours at his desk he relieved his fatigue by fencing with one of the young gentlemen of his personal household.

But his asceticism manifested itself when Michel sat down with him to dine. There were no other guests, and only two servants were in attendance, far fewer than graced the table of the most insignificant French nobles. The Pope spent ten minutes in prayer before allowing any food to be placed on the table, and the meal itself was comparable to that served by Italian peasants. There were stewed Tiber River eels, served with squares of toasted bread soaked with garlic and cooking juices, and ample but ungarnished portions of an inferior cut of roasted veal. The only beverage was a cheap, raw white wine made from grapes grown on one of the papal estates outside Rome.

Innocent ate quickly, methodically, and evidently neither enjoyed nor disliked the plain fare. Food, like sleep and exercise, were necessary to sustain life, but were a boring waste of time. When he was done he wiped his mouth with a coarse linen serviette, sat back in his chair and waited none too patiently for his visitor to finish.

Michel ate a few more mouthfuls, but found it impossible to linger over his meal under the Pope's brooding, hazel-eyed scrutiny.

Innocent signaled the servants, who removed the plates and left the oak-paneled room. "I can't say I'm glad to see you, Bishop," he said, speaking unaccented French. "Whenever Louis of France sends me an emissary, there's fresh trouble."

Michel's smile was wan.

"Cardinal de Orsini tells me The Holy See may depend on your loyalty."

"You may rely on my devotion, Your Holiness."

"To me or to the Church?"

The question was surprising. "I haven't made a distinction," Michel replied, "and I can't imagine a situation that would force me to choose. Assuming your question is hypothetical and based on principle, I serve God through His Church, and I willingly obey you, Christ's Vicar."

"Theologians have given me far more complicated answers. A Bohemian bishop who fancies himself as a protector of the Jesuits once became so abstruse I had no idea what he was talking about, and he spread the word to the Bohemian hierarchy that I'm an ignoramus." The Pope's smile put his visitor off guard. "Does King Louis know your feelings?"

"I've had no cause to discuss them with him, Your Holiness."

"Let me ask you in another way. Would you serve the Church at the expense of France?"

Michel felt increasingly uncomfortable. "God wouldn't create such a dilemma for me."

"No, but Louis might." Innocent absently tapped his Fisherman's ring on the edge of the unpolished table. "He's still determined to force England back into the Church fold?"

"To the best of my knowledge he hasn't changed, Your Holiness. I've tried to make him see the dangers, but he won't listen to me."

"Well, I've written him three long letters in the past six months, but he's acknowledged none of them. I don't even know if he's read them."

"He has." Michel hesitated.

"You were going to say he swore that Innocent, damn him, has no understanding of the real world."

"His language was somewhat less temperate."

"How fortunate that Louis sits on his own throne rather than mine. It isn't enough that France has prostrated herself before him. He wants obeisances from every other nation, and he'll only succeed in alienating the English more strongly. He refuses to recognize the conversion of James as personal rather than national, and it would be too much to expect him to share my doubt that it was sincere. I've been tempted to excommunicate James. I can't believe his conscience prompted him to become a Catholic. He's so profligate he needs Louis' money for his household treasury. But I musn't impose my burdens on you, Bishop. I've braced myself, so give me your message from the King of France."

Michel reached beneath his vestments, and handed the Pope a square of heavy, folded parchment.

Innocent was surprised, and turned the document over in his hands. "Well, he's actually committed himself on paper, and has used three royal seals. Do you know the contents?"

"No, Your Holiness. Louis was unusually secretive, and would only tell me I'm well qualified to present his arguments."

The Pope broke the seals with a small table knife and unfolded the parchment. His face remained unchanged as he read, but the color faded slowly from his face.

Michel dug his nails into the palms of his hands and waited anxiously.

"The crucified Christ is testing me," Innocent murmured. "King Louis is revoking the Edict of Nantes."

Michel felt dizzy and ill.

"He says it here in so many words. He's weighed the consequences, and he scorns the reaction of the Protestant nations. He's convinced that every Catholic monarch will approve, and he even has the temerity to say he's certain that, after I've weighed the matter, I'll give him my blessing."

"He can't be permitted to do it!"

"Who will stop him, Bishop? All I can do is try to prevent the spread of this madness."

Michel forgot he was in the presence of the Pope, and buried his face in his hands. "Louis is repudiating the heritage of his grandfather, the integrity of France—and the Sermon on the Mount." He straightened, his eyes bleak. "Holy Father, help our people."

Innocent's anguish was concealed beneath a surface tranquility that no human tragedy could pierce. "You find this move unexpected."

"I've been afraid he'd do something to curb the Huguenots. But I never dreamed he'd go this far."

"Will they revolt?"

"Impossible. Louis' army is the best ever trained and assembled anywhere in Europe. Our generals are the finest professional soldiers on earth. Our engineers are superbly qualified. Our artillery specialists and cavalrymen are magnificent."

"Will the generals accept the new decree?"

"They're not Huguenots, Your Holiness. And they think only in military terms. For years Louis has pruned and weeded his high command. The generals will do what they're told."

"And the Huguenot troops?"

"They have no generals or colonels. Their common soldiers have been scattered, a few to a battalion. They're powerless to oppose the King."

The Pope's twisted smile revealed his deep pain. "Here is your opportunity, Bishop. I asked if you would serve God or France."

"I must serve both. If I were to raise my voice against Louis, either from the pulpit or in the streets, he'd send me off to one of his monastery-prisons, and I'd vanish for life, as so many others have done. I must work as best I can to correct this wrong."

The Pope stood and touched his shoulder. "We'll be more comfortable in my study."

They walked slowly down a corridor lined with works of art, but Michel saw neither the paintings nor the statues. He was ashamed of his sudden weakness, but needed Innocent's hand on his arm to keep him from stumbling. They went into a small room, its walls lined with leather-bound books, and Michel sank gratefully into the armchair that was offered to him.

The Pope stood beneath the chamber's only work of art, Michelangelo's painting, *Resurrection*. "Apparently," he said, "you've been too close to King Louis to recognize the inevitability of what has now happened. I saw it two years ago, and have been preparing for this catastrophe ever since. Three of the French cardinals will remain faithful to their vows, and only Harlay will follow the King—when he's sober enough. I'm convinced that only five of the bishops are unreliable, but even they may be reluctant to disobey my direct orders. As to the lower clergy, I don't know where they stand. Undoubtedly there are the venal, corrupt and ambitious among them, as there are in any calling."

"Why must the weak, who have done no wrong, be made to suffer?"

"Why are the faithful put to the test, Bishop?"

Michel bowed his head and wept.

"The French cardinals already have sealed instructions, written in my own hand. They will summon a congregation of the religious. Every bishop, every parish priest, every abbot and every abbess will be directed to help those in need, regardless of their faith. Every house of worship, monastery and convent will be told to give refuge to those who require it."

The Pope's daring was breathtaking. "Louis won't tolerate such interference, Your Holiness."

"I think you're mistaken, Bishop. If he defies me, he reveals himself to the world as a cynical adventurer, and defeats the very cause he's hoping to aid."

"He may not act directly. But he'll apply subtle pressures. He'll hold back the wages of priests——"

"They've grown fat in France. A diet less rich will restore their humility."

"And I know he'll refuse to pay The Holy See a share of the tithes he collects."

"The Church has other sources of income, and Louis won't be the first temporal monarch who has tried in vain to starve her into submission."

"Will you tell the world where the Church stands in this affair?"

"I've prepared letters to the Protestant kings and their parliaments."

Michel was dazed. Never in the history of the Roman Catholic Church had a pontiff communicated with sovereigns who were regarded by the faithful as heretics.

"If Louis persists, I want no holy war waged for or against the Church. The little I can do is passive, but at least I can demonstrate to the world that Louis of France stands alone in his folly. If other nations unite against him, as they must, I will offer prayers for those who will die needlessly. But who am I to say that a greater good may not emerge from this horror? I can only repeat, after Christ, our Lord, *Our Father which art in heaven, Hallowed be Thy name. Thy kingdom come. Thy will be done in earth, as it is in heaven.*"

The greater part of the old castle had been closed and sealed off, but could be opened again if Philippe and his family should find it possible, some day, to pay an extended visit to Montauban. Until then, the small apartment Paul was using proved more than adequate for his purposes. His bedchamber had two windows, one facing south that picked up the gentle breezes from the Mediterranean, and the other on the north, which enabled him to enjoy the mistral, cold, sometimes violent winds that swept down from the north. No matter how hot and humid Montauban became, he was always cool at night.

His dining room, although inadequate for truly elaborate entertaining, was large enough to accommodate about thirty guests without unduly straining the four servants who looked after him; his drawing room, although furnished with old-fashioned benches and cross-backed chairs, met the needs of a young bachelor who enjoyed simple living. Paris seemed far away as Paul sat there, on a warm spring evening, with his seven field supervisors. The season's planting was done, the new May wine had been pressed, and an impromptu celebration had developed.

The supervisors had asked Paul to join them in eating a quartered ox and roasted pig, and after feasting in the open, he had impulsively invited them to share a cask of new wine. The men of Montauban never allowed themselves to forget that Paul was the brother of their count, yet they paid him the compliment of relaxing completely in his presence, speaking without reservation or fear. He, too, had rolled up his shirtsleeves. His boots were muddy, and his breeches, like theirs, were grass-stained. There were no tasks they performed that he was unwilling or unable to perform himself, and only his speech and polished manners set him apart from them.

He laughed as heartily as everyone else at one man's ribald account of his pregnant sister-in-law acting as midwife at the birth of a calf. And could speak as earthily as any one of them whenever he joined in the talk. Montauban had become his home, and he was content here. He supposed that some day, when he married, his wife would insist that he choose his social companions with greater care, but he had yet to meet a girl who awakened his abiding interest, so marriage was somewhere in the distant future.

Until then, he would continue to live, profitably, as he pleased. Soon Michel would return to Paris from his visit to Rome, if he had not already arrived, and Paul intended to write him a pressing letter, urging that he come to Montauban for the holiday that would be of such benefit to him. Perhaps one of the reasons Michel procrastinated was because of a fear that Huguenots would be reserved in their reception of a Catholic bishop. Such fear was baseless; the Protestants of the south, unlike Madame de Maintenon, had put aside their old hatreds.

Paul joined in teasing one of the supervisors, who was planning to be married shortly, but the conversation was interrupted by the unexpected blaring of trumpets and the roll of drums. Everyone hurried to the windows, and was astonished to see the cavalry vanguard of a royal military force, preceded by a trumpet and drum corps, marching through the town gates.

The supervisors looked at Paul, expecting that the lord of the manor would be certain to know what was happening. But his shrug indicated that he, too, was uninformed, and he went down to the castle courtyard with them. The troops were marching past the great complex of stone buildings, however, and when one of the men saw citizens by the hundreds making their way to the main square of the town, the group left the castle grounds to be swallowed up in the throng.

Row after row of infantrymen swept past the crowds, their ranks straight, their pale blue uniforms immaculate and their muskets polished. Two companies formed a cordon in the square, and into it rode an officer, followed by his staff. Paul saw the gold epaulet on the man's shoulder, realized he was a brigadier, and wondered whether war had been declared against Spain. He could imagine no other reason for the dispatch of approximately twelve hundred men to remote Montauban.

The trumpeters blew an insistent fanfare, and the brigadier held up his hand for silence, then began to read from a parchment scroll in a loud, harsh voice.

"By order of His Christian Majesty, Louis, the fourteenth of that name. Be it known to all our subjects that France will fulfill her destiny and achieve the greatness that lies within her grasp only if all Frenchmen swear fealty exclusively to us and our successors on the throne of France.

"In order to achieve this end we do hereby revoke, annul and declare void all provisions of the decree promulgated eighty-eight years ago by our grandfather, Henry, the fourth of that name, said decree bearing the popular name of the Edict of Nantes.

"As of this day, Huguenot worship, whether in churches, private homes or elsewhere, is forbidden on the soil of France.

"As of this day, all Huguenot clergymen are ordered to leave France forthwith, for ever, and must quit the soil of France within a fortnight. Those who do disobey, for any reason, and remain, will automatically become traitors to the Crown, and will be prosecuted accordingly.

"As of this day, all companies of Huguenot troops are disbanded.

"As of this day, all Huguenots are dismissed from our armies, our navies, our ministries, our bureaus, and all other branches of our government.

"As of this day, all Huguenot churches and other properties owned in common by this heretic sect pass into possession of the Crown, and henceforth will be the property of the Crown.

"As of this day, all meetings and other gatherings of Huguenots, for religious and all other purposes, are forbidden.

"As of this day, all Huguenot courts in the realm are disbanded. Henceforth our Huguenot subjects will receive justice from the courts we established for the welfare and equity of all our subjects.

"As of this day, all special prerogatives granted to Huguenot members of our nobility are nullified and made void.

"As of this day, all grants, special rights and purlieus granted to members of the Huguenot sect by us or any of our predecessors on the throne of France are revoked, nullified and made void.

"Signed at Versailles, this twenty-ninth day of April, in the Year of Our Lord One Thousand Six Hundred Eighty and Five.

"Louis, by the Grace of God, King."

There was a stillness in the stunned, bewildered crowd.

Then an officer gave an order, and soldiers nailed copies of the royal decree at the entrance to the cathedral and on the main door of the town hall.

Another order was shouted, and infantrymen, holding their muskets ready for instant use, took possession of both buildings. Meanwhile other companies began to fan out through the town for some unknown purpose.

The crowd recovered, and men raced off to their homes, not knowing what to expect.

Paul saw that his supervisors, who had clustered around him, had vanished, too. As angry as he was dismayed, he pushed forward toward the center of the square, where the brigadier was conferring with several other officers.

"Here, you! Get back!" A burly young infantryman shoved Paul in the chest and pointed a musket at him.

Too late Paul realized that his rough clothes gave him the appearance of a commoner. "Tell the brigadier that Lord Paul de Montauban wants an urgent word with him."

"Stand back, by God, or I'll fire. I have my orders." The soldier appeared more frightened than annoyed.

A young lieutenant heard the shouting, and came to investigate. Paul quietly repeated his request, and the officer studied him briefly, then went toward the group in the square. After a brief consultation a colonel rode toward the cordon.

"You're Lord de Montauban?"

"I am, Colonel." Paul rigidly returned the officer's stare.

"Your dress appears otherwise."

"I wasn't expecting guests."

"According to our information, a Lord de Montauban is in residence here, and is believed to be a loyal Catholic."

"I am he, and I'm a member of the Roman Church. My brother, Bishop de Montauban, is His Majesty's confessor."

The colonel showed less antagonism. "Pass him through the line."

The soldier stood aside, and Paul walked across the square, the colonel riding close beside him, with one hand on the butt of his pistol. It was obvious that the military were taking no chances.

Somewhere in the distance a volley of musket fire rattled, and flames leaped toward the sky.

"Ah," the colonel said, "they're starting to burn the churches. Good."

Paul warned himself that he had to control his temper. There was nothing he or anyone else in Montauban could do to halt the brutal business, and he felt certain that similar columns of troops were making simultaneous appearances in other Huguenot strongholds.

"Lord de Montauban!" The officer in command dismounted.

Paul recognized Brigadier de Maynard, an acquaintance of Philippe's, whom he hadn't known from a distance in his burnished helmet.

De Maynard held out his hand.

After an instant's hesitation, Paul reluctantly went through the formality of shaking hands. It wasn't the officer's fault that the conciliatory efforts of almost a century had been undone. As a royal servant, a soldier merely obeyed orders.

"I hope we haven't disturbed you, but you understand, I'm sure, why we could give no advance notice of our arrival here." Brigadier de Maynard smiled pleasantly, ignoring another sheet of flame leaping high in the air.

"Is it necessary to destroy property?" Paul had to speak up for the people who he had worked with for years.

"The burning of their churches will convince them the Crown is in earnest."

"Some of the buildings in the older parts of town may catch fire," Paul said.

"If they're that flimsy, there will be no great loss." Brigadier de Maynard sounded unconcerned. "Besides, I'm planning to billet my troops only in the more substantial houses."

209

His callous indifference to the rights of French citizens was as shocking as the royal decree, but Paul realized that one was the direct consequence of the other.

"But never fear. We have accurate maps of the whole county that the corps of sappers prepared for us, and the Montauban estates will be protected."

"You intend to post guards at the castle, too, I suppose?" The huge stone complex of buildings would be safe even if a fire gutted the rest of the town, so Paul couldn't resist making the subtle thrust.

Brigadier de Maynard didn't hear the sarcasm in his voice. "There will be no danger. The company commanders will see my flag hoisted from the ramparts, and will leave the place unmolested."

Paul knew that what he was about to do was petty, mean and insignificant. He could neither help the Huguenots of Montauban nor prevent the royal brigade from committing outrageous acts of destruction. But, perhaps, a gesture would indicate to his friends where he himself stood. "I'm afraid," he said calmly, "that I can't offer you hospitality at the castle."

Brigadier de Maynard was startled. "I assumed that my staff and I——"

"My brother is the Count of Montauban. I could not invite guests to live under his roof without his permission."

De Maynard was uncertain whether he was being subjected to a snub, and nodded stiffly.

"Of course," Paul said with mock innocence, "you could requisition the castle, and then use it as you pleased, I dare say."

"No, that would be impossible." The officer was horrified. "I have no authority to impose on honorable Frenchmen. The rights of His Majesty's subjects are sacred."

Apparently Huguenots were no longer considered Frenchmen, and Paul felt still more ill. "You're busy," he said abruptly, "so I'll bid you goodnight." He walked across the square, passed through the cordon and made his way to the castle, the story of Henry de Montauban's stand against Louis XIII fresh in his mind.

He guessed that the harried people of the town were waiting for him to make a move, and he felt certain they would rally to him if he tried to defy the power of the King. But resistance would be futile, and scores of lives, perhaps hundreds, would be lost. Louis XIV was far shrewder than his father; with royal troops already holding the town, it would be impossible for the castle to withstand a long siege.

Four fires were raging by the time Paul reached the castle, and as he stared at them helplessly from the ramparts, occasional bursts of musket fire erupted in the town. It was plain that the army had been ordered to crush any show of resistance with a heavy hand, and Paul's impotent rage became more intense. He had to make some gesture on behalf of the people of Montauban, but as custodian of Philippe's property could do nothing that might invite armed reprisals.

Finally, long after midnight, he went up to the highest of the towers and hoisted the family flag. In the morning it would be seen by the townspeople and farmers of the area alike. Then, returning to his own quarters, he summoned his four servants, all of them wide awake and as angry as they were miserable.

"If I stay on here," Paul said to them, "I'll be tempted to run a sword through an officer, but that would be folly, and I can't see martyrdom serving any really useful purpose. King Louis is too good a card player, and he holds a winning hand. I know I'll do something rash if I don't leave, so I'm returning to Paris now, tonight. Come with me if you wish, or stay behind with your families and friends, if you prefer."

All four of the servants, local Huguenots, elected to remain behind.

Paul paid each a year's wages, and then, with their help, locked all the doors and closed the shutters of the small suite he and they had been using. He gathered enough of his belongings to pack away in two small saddlebags and, while the servants saddled his horse and took what food remained in the kitchen, he went to the garden. There, in the flickering glare of the burning churches, he dropped to his knees and prayed at the grave of the first Philippe de Montauban.

The servants were waiting for him, and all five men raised the drawbridge. In the morning the people would see the symbol, along with the flag fluttering from the tower, and would know that one member of the Montauban family sympathized with their plight. Paul shook hands with the servants, mounted his horse, and watched as the men climbed down one bank of the dry moat and up the other. Life in Montauban had been so peaceful that there had been no water in the moat for at least twenty years.

Paul felt like a coward as he rode across the moat and left the town to its fate. Common sense told him he could do nothing for the Huguenots, but if he were more courageous, he told himself, he would not listen to the voice of reason. What shamed him more than anything else was the realization that, although he felt a deep sympathy for the Protestants, he couldn't in good conscience make their cause his own. He believed in the teachings of the Holy Roman Church, and no matter how great his anguish, couldn't take up cudgels on behalf of the members of another faith, no matter how badly they were being mistreated.

Louis had won, he thought, because other Catholics, nobles and commoners alike, lacked the conviction to help the persecuted. The cause of bigotry had triumphed because men of good will, who had been preaching brotherhood, were unwilling to fight for their beliefs. Paul bowed his head and was unable to turn for a last look at the castle and town of his ancestors. In a moment of supreme trial, he was unworthy of the Montauban name.

The journey to Paris was a nightmare. At Limoges and Gueret the Huguenots had been turned out of their homes, which mobs had then ransacked, and the dazed Protestants were beginning a long journey on foot to the distant asylums of Geneva and Savoy. In Châteauroux the leading Huguenots, a judge and a banker, were hanged in front of the town hall, and their bodies were left dangling from the gibbet.

In Bourges a young priest led the crowd that set fire to the one Huguenot church, while the bishop, who was known to be on friendly personal terms with several Protestants, was forced to flee from the diocese and put himself under the protection of a major general. In Blois the two Huguenot families of the town were murdered after a mob broke the hastily erected barricades at their doors, and the local courts refused to prosecute, insisting that the identity of the killers could not be established. Only Chartres, a city from which Huguenots had been excluded under the terms of the arrangements that had followed the promulgation of the Edict of Nantes, was at peace. There people seemed untouched by King Louis' revocation of the edict, and a stranger who had not witnessed the upheavals elsewhere would not have guessed that France was in turmoil.

Strong detachments of royal troops were everywhere, and a heartsick Paul de Montauban guessed that virtually the entire army was on duty in the emergency situation. They were zealous in preventing Huguenot gatherings of any kind; blind to the outrages committed by vast throngs against the Protestant minority. A new concept of the King's justice had swept the land, and men in uniform were its executors.

Paul still had no clear idea of what he himself would do. One moment he regretted his hasty flight from Montauban, but in the next breath he knew he had been wise. When so many innocents were being hounded and bullied, a rash sympathizer's attempts to assist them would have gone unnoticed. Paul's one thought was to reach the capital, where he could seek advice from Michel. The tragedy confused him, as he felt sure it did many others, but Michel, who was wise and patient, would tell him what to do.

The instant Paul rode through the unguarded south gates of Paris he knew the situation in the city was even more explosive than in the provincial towns. The windows of a house down the street on the left had been smashed, and a smaller building several yards away on the right had been burned and gutted. Three young men armed with clubs formed a loose guard across the cobbled street, and when one of them shouted, "There's one," more than a dozen others appeared from narrow side lanes.

All were armed with knives or clubs, and as they raced toward Paul, he was tempted to draw his horse and spur forward. But he had done nothing to incur the wrath of the mob, and refused to dignify—or openly recognize—their attempt to frighten him. They surrounded him, and only when one unshaven, ragged young man tugged at his left boot did he put his hand on the hilt of his sword.

"Christian or heretic?" the self-appointed leader of the mob shouted.

The others were raising their voices, too, and Paul had difficulty making himself heard. "I am a Roman Catholic," he declared.

The leader folded his arms. "Prove it! Recite the Creed!"

The demand was humiliating, but Paul had no choice. "*Credo in unum Deum, Patrem omnipotentem, factorem caeli at terrae, visibilium omnium, et invisibilium. Et in unum Dominum Jesum Christum, Filium Dei unigenitum. Et ex Patre natum——*"

"That's enough," the leader said. "Let him pass, lads." He peered up at the dusty traveler. "You haven't been in Paris of late, eh?"

"No." Paul was suffused with shame, and answered curtly.

"Then take a friendly word, and stay off the streets. Some of the lads aren't being as generous as us, and they're attacking without waiting to find out whether a man is a heretic."

"Or you could join in the fun," one of the others added.

The leader was examining Paul's attire with interest. Although travel-stained, it was obviously expensive. "Seeing we've been so generous, to you, maybe you'd like to show us how much you appreciate it. You know, friendliness on the one hand deserves a little friendliness in return."

A few coppers would have scattered the men, but Paul had been subjected to enough humiliation. Swiftly, in a single motion, he drew his sword and held it ready for instant use. "I'll give you exactly the kind of friendly treatment you've given me. Stand back!"

He spurred forward, and the combination of his unexpected firmness and sharp command unsettled the group. Several jumped aside, and he was able to drive his gelding forward through the opening they created.

The leader shouted something, and a loose cobblestone flew through the air, landing with a crash on the street, ahead of Paul and to his left.

Unwilling to let the rabble know he was afraid, he increased his mount's pace gradually, and soon left the mob behind. The experience shook him, and he had no idea he still held his blade in his hand.

Traffic became heavier as he drew nearer the center of the city, and he saw that the advice of the mob leader had not been inaccurate. Other groups of men were wandering about, and gentlemen of substance were riding in carriages or on horseback with armed escorts. One noble, whose carriage bore a familiar-looking crest, was surrounded by mounted pikemen, and a younger member of the gentry, perhaps one of his relatives, was acting as an outrider on the open box of the coach. The youth held a loaded, cocked pistol in each hand, and appeared ready to discharge the weapons at the first sign of trouble.

A lady who was being carried in a sedan chair by four liveried servants had taken even greater precautions. A lieutenant of royal musketeers preceded her, his drawn sword in his hand, while a half-platoon of his troops marching in pairs formed a tight square around the sedan chair. Obviously she was a personage of consequence, since members of the King's brigade of household guards rarely offered personal protection to anyone other than one of Louis' relatives or closest associates.

It was equally apparent that Paris was being subjected to chaotic terror unknown in the memory of living men. Paul was reminded of accounts he had read of the St. Bartholomew's Day Massacre, and the last shreds of his pride as a Frenchman vanished. The nation was no more civilized now, in a supposedly advanced era, than it had been in his great-grandfather's youth.

Directly ahead, in the shadows of the Pont Neuf, there seemed to be a commotion of sorts, and both riders and pedestrians were hurrying away from the entrance to a narrow alleyway. Paul was determined not to be intimidated by another band of ruffians, and staying on his course, soon heard a woman's muffled screams. He spurred forward for the last fifty yards, then slowed his pace to peer down the dark, twisting alley.

Several men were clubbing and kicking a crumpled figure on the cobblestones, and when he caught a glimpse of white hair, Paul realized the victim was an old man. Three other members of the mob were tussling with a woman near the entrance to a building opening onto the lane. Two of them were holding her, in spite of her frantic efforts to escape, while the third seemed to be trying to disrobe her.

The humiliating frustration that had been mounting in Paul since he had first heard the royal proclamation read in the Montauban square suddenly exploded. No longer caring what happened to him, he charged down the alleyway, half-standing in his saddle. He vaguely realized he was shouting, but not until much later did he recall that he was cursing the tormentors of the old man and the woman. When he drew closer he lashed at the men with his sword, using it like a riding crop as he brought it down first to the right, then to the left.

The fury of the mounted man's unexpected assault caused the ruffians to panic. Several took to their heels immediately, and Paul concentrated on those who dared to stay behind. He maneuvered one burly figure toward the stone wall of the building on one side of the alleyway, beating at the others as he used his horse to press the villain against the wall. The man struggled in vain, and when he went down, Paul purposely rode his gelding back and forth across his body.

One member of the band hurled a knife as Paul bore down on him, but the man's throw was hurried, and he missed his target. Paul's sword was more accurate, and opened a gash in the side of the knife-thrower's neck that spilled him to the ground and sent his life-blood gushing from his body.

All at once it was very quiet in the alleyway, and Paul realized he had routed the mob. The old man lay very still on the cobblestones, sightless eyes staring from his battered face. Three of the villains were either dead or badly injured, but the woman appeared to have suffered no serious harm. She stood, dazed and gasping, her long brown hair streaming down over her face and shoulders as she tried to rearrange her torn woolen dress. "They killed him," she said in a dry voice. "My grandfather. They would have killed me, too, after they raped me."

When she brushed her hair away from her eyes, Paul was surprised to see she was very young, no more than sixteen or seventeen.

"You had better go," she begged. "They'll come back. They'll kill you, too, for helping Huguenots."

On impulse he reached down and lifted her up into the saddle. "Come along." He turned his horse with some difficulty, and quickly rode out of the alleyway into the heavier traffic of the streets leading to the Pont Neuf.

"They'll find you, after what you've done. Every marauder in Paris will be looking for you."

Paul laughed harshly. "Let them look," he said, and headed toward the Montauban townhouse.

Few people paid any attention to him or to the girl in disarray who sat in front of him on the saddle. Paris had become accustomed to many strange sights in recent days, and her citizens were bent on minding their own business. Paul frequently glanced back over his shoulder, and to the best of his knowledge was not being followed, but he wanted to take no unnecessary chances. Night was falling, so he stayed on the main thoroughfares in the vicinity of his family's house, and when he estimated that the shadows of twilight had become deep enough, he swiftly turned into the street that led to the stable at the rear of the house.

The members of Philippe's household staff were eating their evening meal in the servants' dining room, and the stable was empty. Paul left his horse there, not taking time to unsaddle the animal or take his belongings. It had occurred to him that, in a time when all France appeared to have gone mad, he couldn't be certain that all of the servants were trustworthy. So, if possible, he wanted to keep the girl's presence a secret. Before the nightmare had started he would have deemed it inconceivable that any member of the staff might be guilty of disloyalty to the family, but now he knew anything was possible in a world where reason had been discarded.

He warned the frightened, still numbed girl to be silent, led her across the dark courtyard to a side entrance, and took her upstairs to his own small apartment. There he handed her a shirt and a pair of breeches from his wardrobe to replace her badly ripped dress, and directed her to wait quietly in his dressing-room.

Returning to the sleeping chamber, he pulled a bell-rope, and soon a breathless servant appeared.

"We didn't know you were home, milord!" the man exclaimed.

"Obviously, I am. Bring me a platter of meat and bread—and anything else at hand. I'll need some buckets of water, and have one of the grooms look after my gelding in the stable. Oh, yes," he added casually, "send Jean to me." Jean, the major-domo for more than thirty years, was one man who could be trusted.

The servant left, and the house quickly came to life, as it always did when a member of the family was in residence. Jean appeared, and Paul closed the door of the bedchamber before greeting him. They somberly embraced and the major-domo made no secret of his relief.

"We were afraid for you in the south, milord," he said. "Count Philippe will be pleased to know you're safe."

"He's at Versailles?"

"As always, milord."

"And the Bishop?"

"He's there, too, milord, since he returned from Rome three weeks ago."

Paul was torn. He needed Michel's help and advice as quickly as possible. Not only was he himself now a refugee whom the street gangs would be hunting, but he was hiding a Huguenot girl under the Montauban roof. The hazards were enormous. He might be wise to wait until morning before sending a message to Michel, but there was no way of estimating how many fresh complications might develop between now and then. In three hours, four at most, Michel could reach the city. Dinner was rarely served at Versailles until late in the evening, so no one might think it strange that he was being called to

Paris after sundown by the family major-domo. The risk was worth taking.

"Jean," Paul said, "go to Versailles, find the Bishop and tell him I'm here, but say nothing to anyone else, not even Count Philippe. Ask the Bishop if he can meet me here, tonight, without calling attention to himself."

The major-domo started to question the order, but saw the expression in Paul's eyes and left. As he departed, other members of the staff arrived with the water, and although one or two of the manservants usually helped Paul bathe, they did not think it unusual when he took the buckets from them at the outer door of the suite. As everyone on the staff knew, he was the least predictable member of the family.

He took the water to the tired girl hiding in the dressing-room. "Help yourself," he said. "I'll use what you don't want."

A few minutes later the food he had ordered arrived, and after leaving word he didn't want to be disturbed, he locked the outer door. The girl had used only a little of the water, and Paul told her to eat whatever she wanted in the bedchamber while he bathed. A quarter of an hour later he rejoined her, and was surprised to see the food untouched. "Why haven't you eaten?" he demanded.

"I'm not hungry, thank you," she said dispiritedly.

Paul guessed that, wearing the right clothes and cosmetics, she might be fairly attractive. "You'll feel better after you've taken something." He splashed some brandywine into a glass for her, and put some cold, larded beef and pickled mutton on a plate for her.

"I'd rather you take me to bed and have done with it," she said.

Paul stared at her.

"That's what you want, isn't it? I should have guessed when you helped me, and I knew when I listened at the door and heard that you're a nobleman who is friendly with a bishop."

He felt sorry for her, but couldn't help laughing. "You're quite safe, I assure you. I don't attack children."

The girl was miffed. "Then why did you bring me here?"

"My family," he said, "makes it a habit to help ladies in distress." He was relieved when she smiled and began to eat. "Now," he continued, heaping food on his own plate, "who are you, and why was there so much violence this afternoon?"

Her name, she told him, was Simone Duelle, and the old man who had been killed had been her grandfather, a prosperous Huguenot merchant who had been her only relative. When the Edict of Nantes had been revoked they had locked themselves in their home, not daring to stir for days, but finally the old man had become worried about his bolts of cloth and other property stored in a warehouse on the alleyway. In spite of Simone's protests he had insisted on inspecting his property, and she had gone with him. A band of ruffians had been lying in wait for him, apparently realizing that sooner or later he would appear.

"You know the rest," she said, and took a small, tentative sip of brandywine. "I can't even give him an honorable burial. Huguenot funerals have been forbidden, so the night watch will throw his body into a common grave in a field outside the city."

Paul found a choice slice of beef, and put it on her plate. "How old are you?"

"I was sixteen on the day the edict was revoked."

She was going to prove even more of a burden than he had feared. "Have you any friends who could help you reach Geneva?"

Simone shook her head. "They're either dead or have been scattered."

Her situation appeared hopeless.

"And now you're in trouble because of me," she said.

"If it hadn't been you it would have been someone else. You'll have to stay here until we can decide what to do about you."

"I don't care what becomes of me."

"You will.'" He refilled his own glass, but refrained from pouring more for her.

When they finished their meal Paul sent her back to the dressing-room while he summoned the servants to remove the buckets and what was left of the food. Then he bolted the outer door again and, returning to the dressing-room, discovered that Simone had fallen asleep in the chamber's one comfortable chair. He left her there, and settled down in the bedchamber to wait for Michel.

Time dragged, but it was only a little after ten o'clock when a soft tap sounded at the outer door. "It's Michel."

Paul admitted his brother, and they embraced. Each told the other he looked haggard, and Michel asked, "Why the secrecy?"

The younger man told him the story of what had happened late that afternoon.

"I should have known it was you. The death of two street fighters has already been reported, and Louis himself has called them heroes. A reward of one hundred francs in gold has been offered for the capture of their murderer."

"Nothing surprises me any more."

"You're fortunate you became involved, Paul. You were already in enough trouble, and might have been arrested had you gone to Versailles. Brigadier de Maynard sent a letter to the King complaining that you were inhospitable to him at Montauban, and I'm sorry to say Madame de Maintenon remembered you. She's convinced you're a Huguenot who won't admit his heresy."

"I'd become one, but I can't give up my own faith!"

"I thank God for that much. The girl you helped is here, in this house, now?"

Paul jerked a thumb in the direction of the dressing-room. "She's sleeping."

"She can't stay here, of course. It's unfair to Philippe to jeopardize his position at court."

"Philippe doesn't resent all this madness?"

Michel shrugged. "I wasn't followed, and the two servants I suspect of being informers have no reason to keep watch on me tonight. Apparently you have no romantic interest in this girl——"

"None!"

"Then I'll take her with me at once."

"Where?"

"You're too curious. If you must know, Mother Augustine at the Convent of the Sacred Heart has been magnificent in these past few weeks. I'm reluctant to add to her burdens, but as this girl could masquerade as a novice, it shouldn't prove too difficult. I'll take her there tonight."

Paul was astonished. "The Convent of the Sacred Heart right here in Paris?"

Michel's smile was weary and cynical. "There's no better place to hide these days. The excesses being committed in the provinces convince me we're a nation of barbarians, not Christians."

"I've just come up through the provinces from Montauban."

"I know, and we'll have to do something to safeguard you, too. I'll see what can be done before morning."

"Is my situation that bad, Michel?"

"No one knows any more. Only the day before yesterday a band of men broke into the house of Sully's great-nephew and stabbed him to death in his bed. His wife and three children have disappeared, and the King refuses to have them traced."

Paul saw that his brother's hands were trembling. "Are you safe?"

"I wear the ring and miter of my holy office. If I'm in danger, the little that's left of our civilization will perish." Michel stood and put a hand on his brother's shoulder. "You're in far greater jeopardy than you know. If you're caught, they'll torture you until you confess you've become a heretic, and then they'll have the excuse that they want to have you put to death."

"I'm no longer afraid of death. I've discovered the importance of principles."

"They would be fine, Paul, if your death served a purpose. But a sacrifice hidden from the world is a waste."

"It wouldn't be completely hidden. God would know."

"I can't believe," Michel said firmly, "that God is asking His children—of whatever faith—to become martyrs. There's no conflict here between one type of Christianity and another. I can only repeat to you what Pope Innocent said to me just before I left Rome. You must live so you can carry on God's fight for justice and righteousness on earth."

"How can I fight if I'm hidden away in a monastery?"

"You won't be. You'll have to leave France. I'll attend to the details as best I can." Michel clasped and unclasped his hands, then tugged at the sash of his cassock. "To the best of my knowledge, the unreliable members of the household staff don't know you're out of favor at Versailles. There's no reason for them to have been told. But word travels swiftly these days, so you'd best be prepared to flee if any body of armed men, soldiers or civilians, comes to the house before I return."

Paul's sense of being trapped in a nightmare became worse.

"Now bring me the girl."

Paul tapped on the dressing-room door, and Simone Duelle sat up with a start, her hand covering her mouth. He smiled at her reassuringly. "You'll be safe now," he told her. "Everything is arranged."

She followed him into the other room, then stepped backward in horror when she saw the man in a priest's robes.

"How far have we fallen?" Michel asked. "I wouldn't have thought it possible that a Crucifix could cause terror in France."

"This is my brother," Paul explained to the frightened girl, and quickly outlined Michel's plan to save her.

She stood for a moment, undecided, then let her hands fall to her sides. "I have no choice, really. I'll go."

"You won't regret it," Michel assured her.

Paul brought her a long cloak from his chest of drawers and draped it over her shoulders. "Good luck to you," he said, "and remember that some day this insanity will pass."

"What will become of you?"

Paul glanced over her shoulder at Michel, and smiled. "I'll manage," he said.

Dawn came, and Paul remained alert and restless. Sleep had been impossible, but he had eaten another meal that Jean had brought him, and he felt no need to rest. The early morning light spread slowly over the tiled roofs of the city, and another gray, humid day began. A few energetic housewives swept their stoops with straw brooms, weary members of the night watch trudged homeward with their heavy pikes under their arms, and the city's earliest risers, the bakers, began to tend their ovens.

Paul stared down from his third story bedchamber window into the still-deserted street in front of the Montauban townhouse, and thought it strange that, although he was familiar with every detail of the scene below, he felt like a prisoner. Nothing prevented him from leaving, of course, but he realized that his chances of escaping unaided from the city were slim. Constables of the watch, off-duty soldiers and the unruly Paris mobs would be searching today for a man who matched his description, their appetites whetted by the reward in gold that had been promised for his capture.

In spite of his predicament, however, he could not regret the chain of events that had caused it. Faced with the same choice again, he would unhesitatingly go to the aid of Simone Duelle and her grandfather. He had discovered that a man's ability to remain passive was limited when the principles in which he believed were being violated. The lesson was the most important he had ever learned.

A slight tap sounded at the door, and he went to it at once. "Who is it?" he whispered.

"Michel."

Paul opened the door to admit his brother, who carried something bulky under his cloak. "I didn't see you come down the street."

"I used the stable side," the Bishop said, and sat down on the foot of the bed to stretch his tired legs.

"Did all go well with the girl?"

"Mother Augustine took her in, as I knew she would. There is now a new novice at the Convent of the Sacred Heart."

"How long will they let her stay there?"

"Patience, lad. She's safe from harm for the present, which is more than can be said for you. Have you given any thought to your future?"

"I've thought of little else all night," Paul said. "If I can get there, I'd like to go to England."

Michel showed surprise.

"I know their language, and when Lord Willoughby bought our Montauban wine, he indicated he'd like to do more business with me. He might be less anxious to deal with a penniless refugee who can't even claim the distinction of being a Huguenot, though."

Michel handed him a heavy purse. "Not quite penniless, and when you need more, my friends there have means of writing to me in care of Cardinal de Bercy of Rouen. I'll see to it that you don't starve, and Philippe, for all his indecision, will help, too."

"I can't ask it of you."

"False pride is less satisfying than bread," Michel said tartly. "You'll have to avoid the Channel ports. Louis allowed several waves of Huguenots to cross over to England, as part of his policy of letting the English know that France has a firm master. But he doesn't want England overrun, for fear there will be too much sympathy shown for the refugees. So there are troops stationed at the Channel towns now, and only those who carry passports for government business are being allowed to sail."

"Perhaps I can find a fisherman willing to take a risk." Paul jangled the coins in the purse.

"No doubt you can, but the navy has established a patrol in the Channel. You don't want the imprisonment of a fishing master on your conscience."

"What do you suggest?"

"The road to Reims is the best in France," Michel said. "Take it, and cross over into Luxembourg. William of Holland moved into the duchy when he learned that Louis revoked the edict. You'll be safe in Holland, and you can cross the Channel from there without difficulty." He glanced out of the window. "It's growing late, and the streets will soon be filled."

Paul strapped on his sword-belt and took a loaded pistol from the top of his chest of drawers. "I'm ready."

Michel managed a smile in spite of his exhaustion. "Not quite. You look a trifle too belligerent to travel more than a few hundred feet. This should help."

Paul opened the bundle, and found it consisted of a priest's robe, a Crucifix on a chain and the broad-brimmed hat worn by provincial Catholic clergymen. "I can't take these! It would be a sin to pretend I've been ordained——"

"I'll absolve you, and I'm sure our Lord won't take offense."

Paul reluctantly donned the disguise.

"That's better. There's a mule waiting for you in the courtyard. I rode it here."

"A mule?" Paul was dismayed. "It will take me a week to reach the Luxembourg frontier by mule!"

"A poor country priest couldn't afford to own that gelding you ride. He must have cost you twenty gold francs."

"Twenty-five." Paul laughed ruefully. "I see what you mean, Michel. What will you do now?"

"While you leave by the side stairs, I'll go down to the great hall and make something of a scene. I'll say I've come to join you for breakfast, and I'll be very annoyed because you aren't here. Then I'll decide you've left for Versailles, and before I go back there myself—using your gelding, so the staff can't piece together any discrepancies—I'll have them serve me breakfast. There's one advantage I enjoy as a perennial bachelor, you know. Everyone expects me to be ill-tempered, and I promise you I'll have everyone in the house running and fetching and cooking for me before I'm satisfied this morning."

Paul forced a stiff smile.

Michel's smile was pained, too.

"When will we meet again, do you suppose?"

"When God wills it."

"Give me your blessing." Paul dropped to his knees.

"May the blessing of Almighty God, the Father, the Son and the Holy Spirit, descend upon you and remain with you forever."

The road seemed endless, the dust was thick and the sun that beat down from a cloudless sky seemed far more cruel than it had ever been in the fields of Montauban. Paul was so dispirited and tired that it was easy for him to simulate the role of a travel-weary priest. He slumped on the back of the sturdy mule and made no attempt to brush away the dirt that accumulated on his robe. The vineyards that stretched out toward the horizon on both sides of the road made him yearn for the estate in the south he loved so much, but he tried not to think of his past.

His future was hazy, and his present, such as it was, he found distasteful. Never had it occurred to him that a priest might be held in so much contempt by his fellow-citizens in a land that professed to be ardently Roman Catholic. Nobles clattered past him in their carriages, indifferent to the suffocating clouds of dust raised by their vehicles, and army officers were actively rude, frequently forcing him to the side of the road as they marched their squadrons of cavalry and battalions of infantry across the land. Only the poor showed him the respect due a member of the clergy, and he was moved by the willingness of the country peasants and the unskilled laborers in the towns and villages to share their food and homes with him. Paul's conscience nagged at him each time he complied with a request to give his blessing, and on one occasion, when asked to administer last rites to a dying woman, he had been forced to refuse, insisting that the woman's family call in their own parish priest or his curate. His disguise had limits he was unwilling to exceed.

Late on the fifth day of his journey, after traveling almost one hundred miles from Paris, he came to Reims, the "holy city" of France, where most of the nation's kings had been crowned in the great Cathedral of Notre-Dame. He wanted to pray at the magnificent church, both for his own safety and the troubled land he was leaving, but he knew the risk was too great. A visiting priest would be expected to pay his respects to Archbishop de Saliéré, but Paul had no idea where the Archbishop stood in the matter of the new persecution of Huguenots. And it seemed unlikely to him that, in any event, de Saliéré would welcome an impostor.

So he rode through the city without pausing, and headed almost due east toward the fortress town of Metz, capital of the duchy of

Lorraine. Two days later he caught sight of it in the distance, the narrow spires of its cathedral rising high above the crests of surrounding hills. Not until he drew closer, however, did he fully appreciate the power of Louis XIV. A new series of walls and fortifications had been built a few years earlier by the King's gifted military engineer, Vauban, who had made the place virtually impregnable to attack from either the Germans or the Dutch.

Too late Paul realized that every road in the area led to one of the town's ten gates, and that it was impossible for someone on muleback to travel across the rough, wooded terrain between these roads. Therefore he had to ride through the town in order to continue his journey eastward. The many pennants flying from the battlements told him there were a large number of regiments, artillery batteries and cavalry squadrons stationed in the garrison, and he knew from the presence of the cathedral that Metz was the diocesan seat of a bishop. He would need luck as well as skill to see him through the place.

An arrogant but efficient artillery captain was in charge of the guard at the western gate, and Paul immediately found himself in trouble. "Please show me your passport, Father," the officer demanded.

Paul feigned indignation. "I'm a clergyman!"

"To be sure, but you're traveling in a frontier military district where no outsiders are permitted unless they have Crown approval."

There was only one way to avoid being turned back. "I'm here on ecclesiastical business."

The captain raised an eyebrow. "You priests think you're above the King's law. You've come to see Bishop von Haefner?"

The name meant nothing to Paul. "Yes," he said.

"Sergeant, take him to the Bishop!"

The noncommissioned officer of the guard and three soldiers surrounded Paul and escorted him down a broad but twisting street. There appeared to be no way to avoid a confrontation with a senior Churchman.

The twin-spired cathedral was located in the center of the town, and adjoining it stood a substantial three-story building of rugged Lorraine stone. Paul made a desperate attempt to think of some logical reason he could give the Bishop for his need to continue his journey eastward, but his mind was still a blank when the guards left him with a tonsured monk who, it appeared, acted as the doorkeeper at the diocesan headquarters.

"His Grace," the monk prompted, "will want to know who is calling on him."

"My name is de Montauban." The words slipped out before Paul could halt himself, and it was too late to undo the damage.

The monk led him up a flight of stairs and asked him to wait in an anteroom. There Paul made a still more frantic effort to compose himself. As he carried no letters of introduction, no orders from any high-ranking cleric or any identification, the only excuse he would be able to offer was that he was traveling on personal business to a place near the border. The alleged reason was as flimsy as it was feeble, but he could muster nothing more convincing.

Amadeus von Haefner, Bishop of Metz, appeared in the door to an inner chamber, and Paul's first thought was that he was a frail, elderly ascetic. His hair and eyebrows were white, his face was lined and the hand he extended was as fragile and slender as that of a girl.

Paul couldn't remember whether priests greeted their superiors as civilians did, so he had no choice but to genuflect as he kissed the Bishop's ring.

"Come in, Father." Von Haefner's voice was surprisingly deep and robust. "Are you by any chance related to Bishop de Montauban?"

Paul winced. "Distantly, Your Grace." In an attempt to gather his wits he looked around the chamber, but was not reassured. It was so sparsely furnished it looked more like a military headquarters than the office of a bishop.

"You've come from Paris?"

It was best not to be caught in too many lies. "'I have, Your Grace."

"Are conditions as bad there as I've heard?"

"They're—difficult." Paul tugged hard to lower the hem of his robe so von Haefner wouldn't notice his layman's boots.

The Bishop sat back in his chair. "I've been so busy this morning I've managed to spend only a few moments in my chapel. I wonder if you'd care to say Mass with me."

Paul struggled to overcome a sense of panic. "I've already celebrated it, Your Grace."

"Oh?" Von Haefner sounded casual. "Do you carry hosts and wine on your travels?"

Paul found himself slipping deeper into deceit. "No, I stopped at a small village church earlier this morning."

The Bishop's face remained expressionless. "I understand you have business with me."

"Not really, Your Grace. I merely want your permission to visit a place in your diocese—near the frontier—on a matter of personal concern."

There was an uncomfortable silence. "You're a Huguenot refugee, of course," von Haefner said calmly, "and, it appears, a very clever one."

"No, Your Grace!" Paul realized his reply was too loud and emphatic.

"It's customary for members of the clergy to address superiors of my rank as 'Your Excellency.' Laymen call a bishop, 'Your Grace,' and so do archbishops and cardinals, if they choose." Von Haefner enumerated his points on the tips of his delicate fingers. "There is no church in any town or village close enough to Metz for a man traveling on muleback to have celebrated Mass there earlier this morning. I wouldn't have paid attention to your boots if you hadn't glanced down at them as you tried to hide them."

Paul jumped to his feet.

"Sit down, please," the Bishop said soothingly. "I don't know who you are, and I don't care to know. I'm merely telling you your errors for your own future welfare."

Paul thought he was being deliberately tormented, but obeyed the order to sit.

"A number of Huguenots have come this way recently," von Haefner continued. "Most of them were turned back by the garrison, since this is a military district forbidden to civilians. A few were rather ingenious, and I was able to help them." Suddenly he smiled. "In spite of your mistakes, you're the most clever of them all, and I'd be lacking in appreciation if I didn't do what I could for you."

Paul dared to hope again.

"You're making a pilgrimage to the shrine of St. Anselm of Lorraine." The Bishop dipped a quill pen into a jar of ink, and began to write rapidly on a sheet of parchment. It stands next to the church at Thionville, less than a day's journey from here, and only a one-hour ride on muleback from the Luxembourg border." He signed his name with a flourish, sealed the document with wax on which he made an imprint with his ring and then sanded the document. Smiling broadly, he began to dust the sand into a small, embossed silver dish.

"I am grateful to you, Your Grace."

"Your accent and manners," the Bishop said, studying him curiously, "indicate you're a man who has received more than a commoner's education. That will be helpful in the role I'm required to ask you to play between now and tomorrow morning. It's too late in the day for you to leave now for Thionville. The military would become suspicious, and General de Veauvaunt, the commandant, might want to make his own investigation of you, which could prove awkward."

"Very." Paul saw no reason to speak less than frankly now.

"On the other hand, not all members of my own staff feel as I do, and you'll still be here when we celebrate Mass early tomorrow morning. It would be embarrassing, to say the least, if a supposed priest didn't know what to do."

"Obviously a layman can't say Mass, Your Grace, but I'd like, more than I can tell you, to receive Communion."

226

The Bishop stared harder at him. "It's true, then, that you aren't a Huguenot?"

"I was baptized a Catholic as an infant, Your Grace, and I've never wavered in my faith."

A hint of doubt appeared in von Haefner's eyes. "If you're telling me the truth, you must be the first Catholic who is leaving France in the present situation." He sat back in his chair again. "Now you place me in a delicate position. It may be that you're an espionage agent for the Dutch, although I've yet to hear a Hollander speak French without a gutteral accent."

"I believe I can establish my nationality, Your Grace." Speaking rapidly, Paul described both the palace at Versailles and the Louvre, outlined the undergraduate lecture curriculum at the University of Paris, and then, with a slight laugh, talked in detail about several of the Montauban family's favorite dishes.

Bishop von Haefner held up a hand. "Enough. You're a Frenchman." He picked up the quill again, and it snapped between his fingers. "'And you aren't unique. I'm sure that others who are patriots and loyal Catholics will be leaving the country in protest against this tyranny that denies the Crucifixion itself.'"

Michel looked at the King, who was smiling complacently, then at Cardinal de Harlay, who seemed vaguely troubled. It was Louis' attitude rather than the Cardinal's mildly perturbed state that warned him to be on his guard: the King's smugness, when he believed he had won a difficult and delicate maneuver, was insufferable.

"We've been talking about you, de Montauban." Louis' voice sounded positively oily.

Michel didn't dare sit down in the sovereign's private drawing room without being asked, but felt he had to indicate in some way that he considered the occasion informal. After a moment's hesitation he leaned against a leather-inlaid lectern that the King used to rehearse his supposedly impromptu speeches.

"You've been paid a great honor," Louis continued, still smiling. "Harlay was just telling me about it."

The Cardinal looked embarrassed as he cleared his throat. "I'd like to invite you to deliver the sermon at Notre-Dame at the High Mass this Sunday, Your Grace."

"A High Mass, Your Eminence?" Michel asked politely. "It must be a special occasion." He knew it was neither a Church holiday nor a saint's day.

"We're inaugurating a campaign this week to rally the faithful to

His Majesty's new policies." Cardinal de Harley glanced at Michel for an instant, then looked past him into space.

Michel remained polite. "Thank you for your kindness, Your Eminence, but I've already agreed to celebrate Mass at Orléans this Sunday." He hadn't made any such arrangements, but a hastily scribbled note to the monsignor at the church of St. Aignan would take care of the matter. He and the monsignor had been seminary classmates, and held similar views on the current situation.

"Change your plans, de Montauban," Louis said sharply.

"I'm afraid that won't be possible, Your Majesty." Returning the King's angry stare, Michel remained bland.

"Leave us, Harlay," Louis ordered. "I want to discuss this matter with Bishop de Montauban in private."

The Cardinal accepted his dismissal with the meekness of an insignificant courtier. He gathered his robes around him and, aware that the King was waiting impatiently, stumbled in his anxiety to leave the chamber quickly.

Louis did not speak until the door closed. "You're defying me, de Montauban."

"If you choose to interpret my personal disapproval of the Huguenot persecutions as defiance, Your Majesty, I suppose you're right. Let me remind you that I've never made any secret of my feelings in our private conversations, but as your confessor I haven't spoken out in public."

"You're following Pope Innocent! You've stood with him in this business ever since you came back from Rome."

"I happen to agree with his opinions." Michel had hoped he could remain at Versailles as a moderating influence, but he was being forced to declare himself.

"I demand obedience to my orders."

"I must first obey my own conscience, Your Majesty."

"I'm not the only one who has been aware of your betrayal!"

"To me it isn't a betrayal, Your Majesty. And I've made no attempt to hide my convictions from Madame de Maintenon."

The thrust made Louis flush. "Any man who opposes me in one thing is my enemy in all things!"

"I'm sure," Michel said quietly, "that Father la Chaise has long been prepared to succeed me as your confessor."

"No one resigns from my service! I discharge you!"

"As you please, Your Majesty." Michel's temples were pounding, but he remained outwardly calm.

Louis turned a heavy gold and ruby ring on the forefinger of his left hand. "I dislike scandal when it touches my own household, Montauban. This isn't the first time I've changed confessors, and it may not be the last. But I urge you, in the name of our past friendship, not to flout me by refusing to deliver the sermon at Notre-Dame."

Michel well knew that the King was indifferent to gossip about his personal life or staff. What he feared was the open opposition of prominent Churchmen to his Huguenot policy, and if the bishop who had acted as his intermediary with The Holy See spoke out in his favor at Notre-Dame, it would be far easier for him to force other clergymen to accept his position. Conscious of his strength, Michel merely shook his head.

"You refuse?"

"I can't disappoint the congregation at Orléans."

Louis ripped the ring from his finger and threw it to the floor. "Then you compel me to take disciplinary action against you, Montauban. This is your last warning."

"Allow me to warn you, Your Majesty, that you're meddling in matters beyond your authority. His Holiness has taken no step beyond that of letting the Christian world know he opposes your revocation of the Edict of Nantes, and the excesses you've permitted. If you place me under arrest or harm me in any way, you'll force him to excommunicate you, and your entire pose as a Christian sovereign will be undermined."

"You're mistaken!" Louis' lisp was pronounced now. "Cardinal de Harlay is your superior in the Church. You disobey him when you refuse to speak at Notre-Dame, and he therefore requests me, as your temporal liege lord, to administer discipline."

"Your knowledge of ecclesiastical authority is faulty, Your Majesty." Michel was encouraged because he knew he was in the right, and therefore spoke firmly. "Harlay cannot command me, nor can any other cardinal or archbishop. As a bishop, I stand in the place of Christ's Apostles, and am responsible only to His Vicar, the Pope!"

Louis had been checked, and was shrewd enough to realize the consequences might be calamitous for him if he forced a fight with the Church. His manner changed abruptly, and his anger seemed to disappear. "I dislike threats and counter-threats between men who have been friends."

"So do I, Your Majesty."

"Then let's discuss this situation reasonably. It would be difficult for both of us if I were to keep you here as my confessor——"

"I quite agree," Michel interrupted.

"That leaves you without a place of your own. But I'm prepared to appoint you to the first major diocese that falls open."

The offer was even more cunning than it appeared at first glance. Inasmuch as Michel was already a bishop, Louis would not antagonize Vatican Hill by appointing him to a diocese. Under other conditions Michel would have welcomed the opportunity, and knew that Pope Innocent would have been pleased, too. It was a diplomatic move that, on the surface, if not beneath it, would have healed The Holy See's breach with France. On the other hand, no matter how subtle the King's gesture, it was still a bribe, and had to be treated accordingly.

"I'm sure I'll keep occupied, Your Majesty," Michel said.

"Without income?"

"I have private means."

"What will you do?"

Michel took a deep breath and threw down the gauntlet in what Louis could not fail to regard as a challenge. "I'm sure, Your Majesty, that many pulpits in France will be open to me, even though I won't be asked to speak at Notre-Dame again."

The Dutch lieutenant of infantry saluted his superior, and then placed a sword and a loaded pistol on the table. "The prisoner was carrying these, sir, and under his priest's robe he's wearing boots and breeches and a lawn shirt. Good boots they are, too, sir, worth at least three gulden if you had them duplicated by an Antwerp cobbler."

"Leave the prisoner with me." Colonel Arnold van den Huert puffed on his *segaro*. "Don't worry about me, Lieutenant. I've tamed bigger and stronger."

The younger officer saluted again, and withdrew, taking the three sentries with him, and Paul de Montauban was alone with his principal captor.

"Now," the Colonel said briskly, "who are you?"

"The same man I've always been," Paul replied irritably, "and no matter how long you keep me chained in that dungeon, I won't change. If I'd known the kind of welcome I'd be offered, I certainly wouldn't have come to Holland."

"You're stubborn, and consistent. I'll say that much for you."

"If your executioner beats me again, I'll probably change my name and make up a story about my background to suit you. But you'll have to tell me what you want me to say. Then you'll have what you want, I'll be granted a little peace, and everyone will be more or less satisfied. But if this is your idea of hospitality, spare me your kindness. Put me on board the next ship sailing to London, and have done with it."

"Sit down, please." Van den Huert poured some colorless liquid into a glass and pushed it across the unpainted pine table.

Paul wanted to spite him by continuing to stand, but was too weary. He sank into the chair and accepted the drink. Its odor was

230

pungent but unfamiliar, and one swallow seemed to set his insides on fire.

The Colonel chuckled. "Your first taste of our gin, eh?"

"This," Paul replied hoarsely, "is a slightly more refined type of torture than what I've gone through since yesterday."

Van den Huert looked mildly sympathetic. "If your story is genuine, I can only offer you my apologies. But I must ask you, in fairness, to place yourself in my shoes. Either the Prince of Orange will declare war on France at any moment, or King Louis will issue a declaration first. We've been giving asylum to Huguenot refugees, but suddenly a man appears who isn't a Huguenot, he says, and isn't a Papist priest, although he's disguised as one. What's more, he's carrying a substantial sum of money in francs." He slid Paul's money pouch across the table.

"Does this mean I'm free to go?"

"No, it's merely a token of my good faith, nothing more. You seem too inept to be a French spy, although I still wouldn't take an oath on your innocence. I've been discussing the problem with several of our generals, and they agree that the Prince of Orange will want to see you himself. He'll decide whether we set you free or hang you as a spy."

Paul ran a finger inside the collar of his soiled, blood-stained shirt.

"Whatever he does," the Colonel added cheerfully, "he can't blame me for making a mistake."

Paul downed more of the gin. "I look forward to an audience with His Highness."

"Don't call him that! He hates formalities."

"Thank you. Will I have a chance to make myself a little more presentable?"

"My own barber will shave you. I'd rather not trust you with a razor, you understand. Nothing personal. And we'll find you a clean shirt and some breeches."

The gin was relaxing Paul, and in spite of his fears and concerns he grinned.

"Don't expect cordiality," van den Huert warned. "The Prince dislikes most foreigners, and he positively despises all Frenchmen, even the best of you."

The quills scratched on the parchment as Prince William of Orange dictated first to one secretary, then the other. A broad-shouldered man in a dark gray suit, he moved restlessly up and down the chamber that served as his workroom in the modest house known to residents of The Hague as "the summer palace." Whenever one or the other of the younger men hesitated or made an error, he frowned, snapped his fingers and ran his fingers through his short, gray hair. Twice, as he roamed, he brushed against his ornately curled wig, which was hanging on a wall peg, but was unaware of it. As all his subordinates knew only too well, he had the ability to shut everything from his mind but the immediate business at hand.

"I'm delighted," he said, still dictating rapidly, "that the *Riksdag* has agreed to raise taxes in order to provide Your Majesty with the additional troops and ships that Sweden must have in order to wage a major war. Make no mistake, France will fight us to the death, and if one member of the alliance demonstrates weakness, our cause will be lost.

"My general staff awaits final word from your high command, and three divisions of our best infantry will meet your legions at the border. But hurry. The Danes are too weak to prevent you from marching through the duchy of Holstein, so I see no reason to fear adverse consequences."

An aide came into the room, carrying a sheaf of papers.

William snatched them from him, and pointed an accusing finger at the younger officer. "Did you know the Duke of Holstein-Gottorp is the uncle of Charles of Sweden?"

"I—I suppose I have heard of the relationship, sir." Members of the Prince's staff never quite knew what to expect from him.

"Then why must I write to Charles every other day, urging him to send his army across Holstein? The French aren't going to wait until it's convenient for us to strike. Look at this—a report that Louis is moving still more artillery up to the border. It will soon be too late to catch him off balance." William signed each document after scanning it, and simultaneously resumed his dictation. Then, abruptly, he broke off. "Make a final copy of the letter to King Charles before you do anything else. And show the Princess my suggested letter to her father. She knows James better than any of us, and may find a more diplomatic way to tell him we don't want anyone to mediate our quarrel with France. Now, go."

The secretaries hastily gathered their papers, quills and ink jars, and left the chamber.

"I'll see the leaders of the States-General at one. No, at two, so I can give them dinner. When a man wants more money from his parliament, it's always best to make the request after a good meal. Tell the Princess we're having guests." William wrote his bold signature on the last of the documents before him. "Is that young Frenchman waiting?"

"Yes, sir," the aide said. "He's been here all morning."

"I'll see him now." William reached for a set of figures for a proposed new tax schedule, and sat down to study it.

A few moments later Paul de Montauban came into the room. After his first meeting with the Prince, three weeks earlier, he had often despaired of being granted another audience, but this morning, while eating breakfast at the military headquarters in The Hague where he had been quartered as a "guest," he had suddenly been summoned to the palace, only to be left in an anteroom for several hours.

William didn't look up, so Paul continued to stand, waiting to be recognized. The hawk-nosed Prince, who dressed like a merchant and conducted his business with the informality of a commoner, was unlike any member of royalty Paul had ever known, and therefore made him uncomfortable. It seemed very strange not to kneel before him or kiss his hand.

"Sit down," William said abruptly, not looking up from his paper. Paul took the nearest hardwood chair.

Again there was a brief silence. "Have my people been treating you well?" William made a notation beside a column of figures.

Paul had gained weight on a diet of heavy, plain Dutch food, but had no intention of showing a Frenchman's contempt for another nation's diet. "Very well, sir."

"Good. There was a delay in checking the story of your identity because Baron Churchill, who looks after matters of a confidential nature for me in England, was absent from London, and just returned last week." William finally looked up from the paper. "'He informs me that Lord Willoughby confirms everything you claimed about yourself." He spoke in a brisk, matter-of-fact tone, even though he undoubtedly realized he was granting another man complete exoneration from suspicions that otherwise would have led to his execution.

"I'm very grateful, sir." Paul saw no need for tact now. "I assume I'm free to go where I please?"

"If that's what you wish, but I wouldn't have told you the news myself unless I had a purpose in mind." William continued to show no emotion. "Am I right in believing that a refugee from the court of a tyrant is anxious to see morality and honor restored in his land?"

"Of course, sir." Paul hesitated for no more than an instant. "I'd have been blind, living at a Dutch army headquarters in these past weeks, not to have learned that a major campaign is being planned against France. I hope you won't misunderstand me, Prince William, but in spite of the outrages being committed in France, I can't take up arms against my own countrymen."

For the first time the Prince showed feeling, a distinct sense of annoyance. "I hope I'll never be so bankrupt that I'll have to enlist French mercenaries."

Even a sovereign who believed in dispensing with the trappings of his high office wasn't above making unnecessarily rude remarks, but Paul bit back his retort. William was the most powerful Protestant leader in Europe, and he couldn't allow himself to forget it.

"Lord Churchill tells me you could perform a very valuable service for us, if you're willing."

"That would depend on the nature of the service, sir," Paul replied carefully. "It's clear I'm no espionage agent——"

"Very clear!"

"And I wouldn't want to do anything that might be harmful to the French people."

"I've been a student of the Protestant and Catholic consciences for years, and I've finally come to the conclusion they're identical. We've been taught from early childhood, all of us, that we can find happiness only if we're honest and open in all our dealings. I'm afraid I'm like you, de Montauban, even though a close examination of history proves that the most successful kings, the wealthiest bankers and the victorious generals resort to any means to achieve their ends."

It dawned on Paul that the Prince thought his heavy, sardonic observations were witty. Apparently he was making an effort to be pleasant.

"We shall ask you to do nothing that might compromise your integrity or injure France. I wonder if you're familiar with the status of England at present?"

Paul reminded himself that James II was William's father-in-law. "Only in general terms, sir."

"The King," William said tersely, "has openly embraced Catholicism. The great majority of his subjects belong to the Church of England, the Church of Scotland, and the Church of Ireland—all of them Protestant. But there's a strong Catholic minority in England, a considerably smaller one in Scotland, and a majority in Ireland."

He sounded, Paul thought, like a lecturer at the Sorbonne, and his manner was professorially impersonal too. It was difficult, at this moment, to think of him as the hereditary ruler of the Dutch and, through his wife when she succeeded her father, the master of England.

"Louis of France is trying to form a hard and fast alliance with James," the Prince continued. "If he does, he'll try to force the English to resume her formal relations with Rome. James has already made several attempts to strengthen the Catholic Church, but so far each of his plans has been blocked. Louis confuses the temper of his own subjects with that of the British, and doesn't realize that his Huguenot persecutions have made James' Protestant subjects more determined than ever to stop the spread of Catholicism.

"What I'm trying to prevent is another civil war in England. She hasn't yet recovered from the blood-letting of forty years ago. And prevent it I shall!" William had the knack of expressing conviction without raising his voice. "What we ask of you is quite simple. Lord Churchill believes you can help us learn the depth and extent of James' understanding with France."

"I've had no experience in diplomacy, sir——"

"So much the better. Churchill will tell you what he has in mind, and you're under no obligation to accept. I'm sending a schooner to London from Rotterdam tonight, and offer you passage—without charge."

Paul concealed a smile. The Dutch officers with whom he had spent the past weeks never tired of joking about William's miserliness, and had even suggested that the Prince might charge the "guest" for his meals. Suddenly the idea wasn't as ludicrous as it had seemed. "I'll be happy to sail tonight on your schooner, sir," Paul said.

Every pew in the great Norman cathedral was filled, and Michel stood quietly at the canopied pulpit, waiting for the rustle of the crowd to subside. The revocation of the Edict of Nantes had dealt a severe blow to the city of Rouen, which had suffered greater hardships than any other major community in France. It was small wonder that the men looked weary and that only a few of the ladies were wearing new fur-trimmed gowns and hats.

Scores of weathly Huguenot merchants, shipowners, grain dealers and silk manufacturers had lost their businesses, and then had been forced to leave the city by a militant group of Catholics. Now those zealots were paying for their intolerant enthusiasm. Men who had been eager to seize the property of the departing Huguenots had little knowledge of the various businesses they were now expected to manage, and all Normandy was feeling the worst financial pinch the province had known in two hundred years. Warehouses were empty, ships rotted at their moorings in the tidal waters of the Seine, and the wheat and oats and barley, the apples and pears, the sleek cattle and plump chickens that had made Normandy the most prosperous district in Europe remained unsold.

Every class was hurt. The nobles were turning large portions of their estates into pasture lands, the shops of the middle class had few customers and there was little call for the services of the artisans. The poor, as usual, absorbed the heaviest punishment and went hungry.

Michel glanced at Cardinal de Guernoy, Archbishop of Rouen, who was seated imperturbably on his throne. They had been discussing Normandy's plight since the previous day, and the Cardinal had urged Michel to speak his mind freely. "I've scolded them so often they won't listen to me any longer," he had said. "Perhaps you can stir their souls."

"In the Epistle of Paul, the Apostle, to the Galatians," Michel said, his voice carrying to the farthest reaches of the huge, domed cathedral, "we read: *'Be not deceived; God is not mocked: for whatsoever a man soweth, that shall he also reap. For he that soweth to his flesh shall of the flesh reap corruption; but he that soweth to the Spirit shall of the Spirit reap life everlasting.'*

"Two years have passed since I last visited Rouen. Then the docks on the River Seine were busy, and ships flying the same proud banner that William the Conqueror carried with him to England sailed to many lands with the sweet produce of this most blessed of provinces. Today there is no breath of life at those same docks. Then the shops were filled to overflowing with the good things of this earthly life, silks and bolts of the purest wool, cups of gold and silver wrought by master craftsmen. Today the shelves of those same shops are bare, and their doors boarded. Then the grain of Normandy stretched swayed in the breeze, and grapes grew heavy on their vines. Today the grain and the grape wither and die.

"Why does this land, once so fair, now lie barren, like a skeleton whose bones have been plucked clean by vultures? Have you brought this devastation and ruin on your own heads, my children? Have you offended our Lord by disobeying His Commandments and closing your ears to His teachings?

"Some among you were greedy. When your neighbors suffered evil days, you coveted their land, their ships, their farms, all their property. You stole it from them, and gave them nothing in return.

"Some among you were without pity. When those who were in need wanted your help, your understanding, your sympathy, you reviled them. Instead of opening your doors and hearts to them, you drove them from your midst.

"Some among you were without conscience. When you saw others whipping and cursing those whose only crime was that of worshipping Almighty God in their own way, you closed your eyes, your ears, your minds. You neither stayed the hands of the oppressors nor raised your voices in protest.

"Some among you are worse than thieves. You are murderers. You beat life from the bodies of men and of women and even of little children. You reveled in orgies of bestial brutality.

"And all of you are guilty of a crime worse than any of these. You have shown no remorse. You have not begged our Lord to forgive your sins. You have placed your immortal souls in jeopardy.

"Heed the words of St. Paul. *Be not deceived,* he tells us. *God is not mocked.* Are these mere words? Look at your docks, your shops, your fields! You have not deceived God. You have mocked Him in vain! Now, my children, now, before it is too late, pray to Him for the compassion, the humanity, the gentleness of spirit, the humility that Christ showed when he was made flesh and dwelt among us.

236

"Now, before it is too late, heed the warning of the Lord, as he spoke it through his Prophet, Isaiah: *'Therefore will I number you to the sword, and ye shall all bow down to the slaughter: because when I called, ye did not answer; when I spake, ye did not hear; but did evil before mine eyes, and did choose that wherein I delight not. Therefore thus saith the Lord God, Behold, my servants shall eat, but ye shall be hungry: behold, my servants shall drink, but ye shall be thirsty: behold, my servants shall rejoice, but ye shall be ashamed.*"

1686–1687

John Churchill, Baron, Lord of Eyemouth and Major General, acting commander-in-the-field of the Royal Army, puzzled his friends, irritated his enemies and was the darling of England's commoners, who believed he could do no wrong. Even men who were close to him admitted that he himself shared that conviction.

He had a round face with a pugnacious jaw and eyes that could be merry one moment, stormy the next. His moods were violent and unpredictable, but everyone who had ever been associated with him knew he talked incessantly and insisted on holding the center of the stage at any gathering. Even his foes reluctantly conceded that he was a many-sided genius. He had repeatedly demonstrated his extraordinary skill as a soldier and had mastered the principles of naval warfare. He had proven himself an able administrator, and was by far the most energetic member of the Privy Council of King James II. His letters were hailed as literary masterpieces and he sometimes painted diverting landscapes as a hobby. At private parties given by Princess Anne, James' younger daughter, he sang in a pleasing baritone, sometimes with his wife, and also played the spinet.

The envious questioned his judgments, the Catholics were afraid he was opposed, at any cost, to the official recognition of their Church, and his fellow members in the Church of England, including the Archbishop of Canterbury, were convinced that his familiar, sometimes jocular references to the Almighty were blasphemous. But no one doubted his ardent, eloquent patriotism or his unflagging belief in the destiny of England as a great nation. He ate heartily, drank prodigiously and, to the despair of the many ladies who found him enormously attractive, was completely devoted to his wife.

A large portrait of his late father, Winston Churchill, dominated the cramped, book-strewn library of his London house, and the family resemblance was so strong that Paul de Montauban at first thought the painting was a recent one of Lord Churchill himself. But the son was taller, and although he gave the impression of being overweight, was actually trim and in the best of physical condition.

Churchill's charm was dazzling, as he well knew, and he used it to put his visitor at ease. "I owe you an apology," he said in execrable French, which he nevertheless used recklessly. "I've kept you waiting a half-year for this meeting."

Paul elected to reply in fluent English. "I can hardly blame you, General. You spent the better part of last year in the field."

Churchill beamed. "Hunting down rebels isn't my idea of a military campaign, but my troops did win a place for themselves in history. And I understand from Lord Willoughby that you haven't been wasting your own time."

Paul could afford to be a trifle smug, too. "Lord Willoughby and his partners were good enough to find a position in their company for me, and I've been fortunate. My journeys to Portugal and Denmark for them in the past six months have both proved profitable."

"Yes, Willoughby tells me you're being granted a partnership. Splendid! And now," Churchill added with a candor that many who dealt with him found disconcerting, "you have an opportunity to repay your obligation to England."

Paul was conscious of the attempt to maneuver him, and his only reply was a guarded smile.

"King James now goes to Mass openly, and makes no secret of keeping a private confessor at his court. Each day he moves closer to the position of Vatican Hill and Versailles."

Like so many Protestants, Paul thought, Churchill falsely assumed that all Catholic nations automatically adopted the attitudes and policies of The Holy See. "The ideas of Pope Innocent and King Louis are very different."

Churchill's mind was closed on the subject, which he dismissed with a firm wave of his hand. "They're too close for the tastes of Englishmen. Louis' persecution of his Huguenots is making it inevitable that we'll join the Dutch and their allies in their war against him. Unless he changes, which isn't likely. When an absolute monarch has committed himself to a course, he can't alter it without losing stature. He's accused of defeat."

Paul was positive, too, that the lot of France's dwindling Huguenot population would not improve. A note of despair had been evident in the letters from Michel that had been waiting for him when he had returned, three days earlier, from his foreign journeys.

"James uses Louis as his model. He'd like to rule as an absolute monarch, too, but he has neither the ability nor the strength. He shares the usual Stuart belief in the divine rights of kings, and he's endowed with all his family's other failings, but none of their virtues.

We—some friends and I—are afraid that one of these days he intends to prorogue Parliament and rule alone, which would lose him his head as surely as his father was executed by Oliver Cromwell. We—men who love England and will do anything in our power to prevent another civil war—are desperately anxious to learn how far advanced his thinking may be."

"I'm a stranger to King James," Paul said firmly. "I can't imagine him confiding in me."

"You're wrong!" There was a ring of ultimate authority in Churchill's booming voice. "He won't speak the truth to any of us who have been close to him in the past. He dissembles. He tells us what he thinks we want to hear. He'd be more inclined to be frank with you."

Paul remained unconvinced. "Why?"

"For one thing, you're a fellow Papist. I mean nothing offensive by calling you that, to be sure. The Duke of Norfolk and a number of other Papists are very dear to me."

"Then why can't the Duke of Norfolk sound him out?"

"Because Norfolk and the others love England too much—and the King knows it! But you're French, a subject of his idol, Louis."

"I'm also a refugee from French justice," Paul said dryly. "There's a price on my head."

"Ah, but James doesn't know it!" Churchill winked, and a deep chuckle rumbled up within him.

"Surely the French ambassador would tell him my background."

"I intend to present you privately to James, without the French envoy's knowledge. I may not have James' real trust these days, but he hasn't dared to dismiss me from my military command. Or it may be he's trying to outwit me." Frowning, Churchill paused for a moment to consider the point. Then, with a faint but self-assured shrug, he resumed his argument. "Whatever his reasons, I still have enough influence at Whitehall to guarantee you a totally private audience."

Paul remained unconvinced. "If he really hopes to emulate King Louis, he might discuss matters with the French ambassador. Or with the French priest who has become his confessor——"

"I'm sure he does. But we have access to neither of them, you see."

"All the same——"

"Your credentials are impeccable!" Churchill roared, losing patience. "You're French. You're a damned Papist!" He seemed unaware of his slip, or perhaps he literally didn't care. "You belong to the nobility, and your family's title is an old one. I know, because I've taken the trouble to look into your whole background. Why, even your brother is a damned bishop!"

In his self-confidence Churchill was so insultingly undiplomatic that Paul couldn't help laughing aloud.

"You'll do it, then?"

Paul capitulated. "I have no faith in your idea, but it can do me no harm. And I'm curious about your King James. I can't see how a man can be as incompetent as he's pictured, and yet be so feared."

"When you've met him, you'll understand. His grandfather, James I, was known as the wisest fool in Christendom, which means he knew his limitations. The trouble with his namesake is that he confuses himself with God Almighty and thinks he's omnipotent. That's why he's so bloody damned dangerous."

The city of Lille, said Parisian wits, didn't know its own identity, and there was enough truth in the jest to make her citizens wince. High above her Citadel, the mighty fortress that guarded the gateway to Holland, the Spanish Netherlands and the German states, flew the lily ensign of Louis XIV, but older residents remembered that only twenty-nine years earlier the place had been Spanish. In her seven-hundred-year history, Lille had known many masters, some Austrian, some Flemish, some Burgundian, and even now, after almost three decades of French rule, her people thought of themselves as a breed apart.

Lille reflected her heritage by speaking a French dialect that men born more than fifty miles from the Citadel's ramparts found difficult to understand. The sausages made by the farmers of her hinterland resembled those of the Dutch, and it was customary for the students at the Institute, her school of higher learning, to riot in the streets when Spanish saffron wasn't cooked with their stews. Her taverns served no wine other than heavy Burgundy, and visitors to Paris from Vienna had been known to travel an extra one hundred and fifty miles for her Austrian honeycakes, which were sprinkled with caraway seeds.

The city was so important as a military and communications center that her many masters had been careful to safeguard the personal freedom of her citizens, who had long enjoyed privileges denied the people of larger and supposedly more sophisticated communities. The Jews of Lille always had lived where they pleased, and had not been confined to a ghetto, or walled district of their own. And her influential Flemish minority, who had been Protestants since the early days of the Reformation, a century and a half earlier, had been active in business and trade, farming and the pursuit of intellect at the Institute.

When King Louis captured Lille he promised to respect her heritage, but practical considerations made it virtually impossible for him to keep his pledge. The garrison at the Citadel, the largest in France, was made up of men from every part of the country, and it proved unrealistic to expect them to obey one set of laws while the civilians were governed by another. Decrees applied elsewhere were now enforced in Lille, too. And only one year after Louis revoked the Edict of Nantes, the character of the city had changed.

Bishop Michel de Montauban, accompanied by the two young priests who had become permanent members of his traveling entourage, was prepared for a new atmosphere. He knew that the Protestants of Lille, who had scoffed at danger, were scattered, while the Jews, the first to sense coming waves of religious persecution, had quietly fled to Holland.

The usual, strong military guard was stationed at the ornamental South Gate that Louis had built to commemorate his capture of the city. As always, the troops were courteous and respectful. Neither the two officers on duty nor their men indicated by word or gesture that they had heard Michel branded as a trouble-maker, and he was admitted to the city immediately after identifying himself.

He and his companions, all mounted, started up the broad new Avenue of Louis XIV toward the cathedral located in the center of the city, directly below the towering cliff on which the Citadel was built. Approximately one house in three stood vacant, which was not out of the ordinary anywhere in France, but Michel saw no other horsemen and no pedestrians, which struck him as strange. The city appeared to be deserted.

Then, very gradually, he became aware of singing from the direction of the side streets on both sides of the Avenue. The tune was vaguely familiar, but he couldn't make out the words, and glanced at the young priests.

"It's an old Burgundian hymn, Your Excellency, *Christ Have Mercy*."

"Oh, yes. They always sing it here on holy days." Michel drew in his breath. "Have we been derelict and forgotten a holy day?"

"No, Your Excellency."

All at once people began streaming out of the side streets behind leaders carrying lighted torches of woven reeds. It was evident at once that this was no impromptu march, but had been organized and rehearsed. Many of the marchers, men and women alike, were barefooted, all were hatless and most had rubbed ashes into their hair. Some carried cumbersome, homemade crosses made of two pieces of raw lumber lashed together, and Michel saw many rosaries in the throng.

The crowd fell in behind Michel and his companions, their hymn gaining in volume as hundreds of additional marchers joined the procession. Here and there were ladies in fine silks, mincing painfully on bare, tender feet, and Michel was astonished when he recognized Baron de Polignac, the hereditary lord of Lille, who was wearing no wig and had poured ashes onto his head. For whatever the reason, both rich and poor were taking part.

No explanation was offered, so Michel decided to ride on. The singers were devout, and he felt deeply touched. Suddenly he saw one of the young priests staring up at the great fortress on the heights above, and felt a chill. Whatever the aim of the marchers, the military did not sympathize with them; at least ten of the shining brass cannon were trained on the crowd that now filled the Avenue of Louis XIV.

Michel resisted the urge to increase his pace, and held his horse at the same slow walk. The single spire of the ancient cathedral was directly ahead on his left, a distance of three or four city squares. He was relieved to see it so close, knowing he would feel better when Bishop Pierre Rambeau explained the purpose of the solemn penitential procession. As he approached the cathedral, however, another shock awaited him. A company of infantry was waiting on the steps of the building, bayonets affixed to their muskets, and other companies lined Cathedral Square.

Several officers in the light blue and gold uniforms of the high command were seated on horseback at the base of the steps, and one of them moved forward when he saw Michel approaching. A single glance identified the dashing François de Neufville, who had succeeded the previous year to the duchy of Villeroi. Michel immediately dismounted, and the Duke did the same.

They walked toward each other, and Michel became aware of the tense silence; the hymn singing had stopped. He was deeply embarrassed, and could see that Villeroi, who was wearing the gold epaulets of a full general on his shoulders, was equally ill at ease. They were approximately the same age, had known each other well since they had been small boys and had been close friends until Villeroi had left Paris for a military career.

The Duke made the first gesture, genuflecting and kissing the Bishop's ring. Then they shook hands and embraced. "I knew you were coming here today, Michel," Villeroi said, "and I've never in my life been less pleased to see anyone."

Michel took a step backward and saw that his friend was close to tears. "You have a duty to perform, François?" he asked gently.

Villeroi nodded, then rested his left hand on the hilt of his saber and addressed the crowd in a loud voice. "Acting in the King's name in my capacity as deputy commander of the Northern Department and commandant of the Lille garrison, I have closed the cathedral. It will reopen when Bishop de Montauban, who is not welcome in the city, has departed. I will myself escort him to the gate and see him on his journey."

No one spoke or moved.

"I'm sorry, Michel," the Duke murmured. "The King wrote me his instructions in his own hand."

"What have you done with Bishop Rambeau?"

"He was escorted to a monastery in the hills this morning, and he'll be returned after you've gone. He's a harmless old man."

"But I'm not." Michel's face hardened. "What will you do if I celebrate Mass right here in the square?"

"Don't, I beg you. My instructions are firm. I've been directed to fire into the crowd if the people refuse to disperse, and some will be hurt."

"I want no killing on my conscience. There has been enough blood spilled in France." Michel turned to face the throng. "My children, go to your homes." Making the Sign of the Cross, he bowed his head in prayer.

The huge crowd obediently started to break up.

Villeroi removed his helmet and wiped a film of perspiration from his forehead. "Thank you, Michel."

"I did it for them, not for you, François, although I bear you no ill will, and certainly not for your master."

"He's your master, too, Michel."

"No, I serve only one." Smiling in spite of the deep sorrow he felt, Michel walked back to his horse.

Villeroi mounted, too, and they started down the Avenue of Louis XIV toward the South Gate. "You're forcing the King to curb you, Michel. Each month more bishops and priests are joining you, and he can't permit this unpatriotic movement to keep spreading. Why must you challenge him when what he does strengthens the Church?"

"It doesn't. It denies the essence of Christianity."

It was apparent from the Duke's expression that he had no understanding of the issues at stake. "You know Louis even better than I do. Surely you realize he won't allow any group, not even Churchmen, to defy him."

"Louis' power is limited," Michel said with a weary smile as he watched the people of Lille streaming toward their homes. "But the Lord God Almighty is omnipotent, and no man may flout His holy commands. We're directed to love one another."

Villeroi was silent. "I spent a few days at Versailles last week. I've never seen Louis so angry, and Madame de Maintenon goads him constantly. It's been rumored they're married, you know."

"So I've heard."

"Michel, I don't know what you hope to gain by disobeying him. Believe me, the troops of every regiment stand behind him."

"You saw the people of Lille just now."

"If I had given the order to fire, they'd have dispersed fast enough. I can't believe that the people of France are willing to sacrifice their lives for Huguenots!"

"You're probably right, François, and I hope they'll never be put to the test. But they're beginning to think and wonder. They're no longer following the King blindly. They're listening to their own consciences."

"And to you."

"It's the duty of priests to awaken the consciences of the faithful."

Villeroi moved closer, so that neither the members of his own staff or the Bishop's companions could hear him. "Listen to an old friend who wants to help you. If you persist, Louis will silence you for all time."

"He knows Pope Innocent supports me. He doesn't want an open fight with the Church."

"You priests are so infernally naïve! You're dealing with the most ruthless man in Europe! While there's still time, go off to a monastery for a year or two. Give this situation time to become calmer. It's your only hope!"

The tiny anteroom at Whitehall was dark, stuffy and, although there were only a few heavy pieces of furniture in the chamber, very cramped. It seemed inconceivable to Paul that the private apartment of a reigning monarch could be so badly in need of repairs, but the plaster on the ceiling was chipped, the damask wallpaper was grubby and there were two threadbare spots on the rug beneath his feet. Under no circumstances could he imagine a king of France allowing his palace to deteriorate, but evidently James II of England had no pride in such things.

Paul was sorry he hadn't refused Lord Churchill, and wished himself elsewhere, but it was too late. Churchill had made the necessary arrangements for the private audience, as he had said he would do, and promptly at nine o'clock in the morning Paul had presented himself to a royal equerry. He had been guided to this hot, gloomy little room, and left to his own devices. It was now eleven, and had he been waiting to see anyone but a king, he would have walked out. No matter how important the information he had been sent to obtain might be to the Prince of Orange and the British nobles who were worried about James' plans, his own time was too valuable to be totally wasted.

For another quarter of an hour Paul paced up and down slowly, trying in vain to curb his impatience, but at last a double door opened, and a valet in livery appeared. "His Majesty will see you now," the man said.

Paul followed him into a large chamber lighted by two smoking oil lamps that cast a feeble glow. Heavy drapes were drawn over the windows, and only a crack between them let in a little sun. The curtains of a fourposter bed had been drawn, and a middle-aged man in a silk nightshirt was sitting on the edge of the bed, eating a breakfast of cold meat and ale from a rickety table. He was barefooted, and his thinning hair was tousled.

Paul moved closer, and comparing King James to his likeness on a newly-minted shilling piece, bowed low. The monarch's resemblance to the heroic profile on the coin was slight. There were deep pouches beneath his eyes, his face was lined and his skin was the color of chalk. Continuing to eat, he waved the valet out of the room.

Waiting for the King to address him, Paul tried not to study him too closely. The air was almost unbearably musty, and the strong scent of an unpleasant perfume made him feel slightly ill. The indentations in the bedclothes revealed that James had not slept alone and, combined with the pungent scent, indicated that the rumors circulating so freely in London might be true: it was said that the King slept with a different trollop every night of the week.

"Sit down!" James commanded suddenly in a rasping voice. "What little appetite I have is ruined when I see someone fidgeting. No, over there, and while you're about it, you might pour me an ounce or two of whiskey from that decanter."

Paul did as he was bidden, and handed the King a cup.

James downed the liquor quickly, shuddered and sipped a little of his ale. Then, after a brief silence, he brightened. "That's better. I have no business drinking after midnight, but sometimes it's unavoidable. Help yourself to a drink, and give me your message from King Louis."

"Perhaps Lord Churchill made a mistake, Your Majesty," Paul said diplomatically. "I'm afraid I bring you no specific message——"

"Oh, yes. Now I remember. You have a brother who is a marquis, and another is a cardinal."

"The eldest of us is a count, Your Majesty, and the other is a bishop."

"Well, the details don't matter. How are conditions in France?"

Paul took a chair near the bed. "When I left the country, they were rather chaotic."

"So everyone tells me." James sounded peevish. "Are the Huguenots resisting Louis?"

"No, Your Majesty. But there are Catholic elements in the country that are none too happy about his policies. They've sympathized with the Huguenots."

"I told Louis I thought he was going too far, but he's positive he knows his people. Mine wouldn't tolerate new restrictions, I can tell you. Unless they were directed against the Catholics, and even then there would be an uproar."

245

Here was news, perhaps. If James' words were to be taken at face value, he was at least hinting that he didn't intend to hamper the freedoms of the British people in any way.

James ate the last of his meat and gazed steadily at his guest.

Paul realized he was expected to reply. "I think Your Majesty is wise."

James nodded complacently. "Foreigners always grasp the principles of what I'm trying to accomplish. My own subjects are so convinced I'm plotting against them they refuse to understand that I want to extend and enlarge the rights of our Catholics, not hamper the prerogatives of our Church of England majority."

If true, James' ideas made a great deal of sense. "France," Paul said, "is very much interested in Your Majesty's plans."

The King veered away from the subject. "Tell me more about the Huguenot struggle."

"There's little new, Your Majesty. Most of them have left France, and a great many are grateful to you for granting them asylum here."

James showed annoyance. "They needn't thank me! We have enough frictions without adding new ones, but even the Privy Council insisted, and I didn't think the matter important enough to make a major issue of it. What galls me is that they wouldn't show the same sympathy for Catholics!"

He was probably right, but Paul didn't want to become involved in a discussion of English affairs. "I know very little about your country, Your Majesty."

James tugged at a bell-rope. "How is Louis handling the rebellion of his clergy? Or are the stories I hear exaggerated? I find it difficult to believe that three cardinals and most of your bishops are opposed to the regulations against the Huguenots."

"The stories aren't exaggerated," Paul said, "and there's considerable friction." He remembered what Michel had said in his last, brief letter after being expelled from Lille, and echoed his brother. "I don't know where it will all end."

"Surely Vatican Hill will take disciplinary action against clergymen who defy the authority of their king! I'm told on excellent authority that Pope Innocent is weighing various measures against them."

Apparently James was being given false information by the French priest who had become his confessor, and Paul made a mental note to make certain he remembered the point when he reported to Lord Churchill. "I'm afraid," he said, trying to make his evasiveness sound apologetic, "that I know nothing about the plans of the Church."

James waved a bony, accusing finger under his nose. "Your brother is a bishop!"

Paul inclined his head.

"Where does he stand?"

The door opened, and a barber came into the bedchamber, carrying a tray laden with razors, jars of tonic and bowls of scented water.

The King submitted to the barber's ministrations, and Paul felt infinitely relieved that the interruption had saved him an embarrassment. "The French clerical hierarchy is split on the issue, Your Majesty, so I believe King Louis will win."

The barber was massaging James' face, making it difficult for him to speak, so he pushed the man away. "He's already won! The Huguenots are gone, and their property has been confiscated. The priests who have opposed Louis will be put in their place, and so will anyone else who defies him!"

Paul was afraid he was right.

"He acts as a king should, as he must." James leaned back and, as he closed his eyes, handed Paul his cup. "I'll have another drop."

Paul poured more whiskey into the cup and gave it to him.

"I've yet to meet a French nobleman who disagrees with me. Visit me again before you leave England." James gulped his whiskey and allowed the barber to lather his face.

Paul had been dismissed. "Thank you, Your Majesty," he said, and backed out of the room.

He left Whitehall by the same small, private entrance he had used on his arrival, and as he walked rapidly toward the Strand, he tried to recapitulate what had been said to him. But the longer he pondered, the more confused he became. In one breath King James sounded like a champion of religious tolerance, while in the next he heartily endorsed the authoritarian attitudes and acts of Louis. It was small wonder that the English nobles didn't know what would happen next, for James himself was muddled. Only one clear fact emerged from the interview: James' confessor, and anyone else close to him, were purposely misleading him. His belief that Vatican Hill supported the French position was dangerous, and might push him in the direction of rash behavior.

At any rate, the audience hadn't been wasted. Paul headed toward Lord Churchill's house, where several English leaders were waiting for him. He had no idea what they could do to counteract the malevolent influences being exerted on James, but he was certain that, with an unstable monarch on her throne, there were unstable days ahead for England.

"No one knows why the people of Britanny are more independent and less willing to submit to authority than the citizens of any other province," said Bishop Jean de Laval of Rennes, sipping a coarse local wine with his guest. "All I can tell you is that we Bretons glory in our heritage."

Bishop Michel de Montauban glanced out of the windows of his living room in the Abbey of St. Melaine, and thought that no city in France had ever looked more tranquil. Hundreds of citizens were filing out of the adjoining cathedral after Mass, and no one shouted, quarreled with his wife or hurried off to a tavern. It was difficult to believe that these quiet men and women were perennial rebels, the "thorns in my crown," as Louis had called them eleven years earlier, when he had been forced to send four regiments to Rennes to collect the new taxes that the city had stubbornly refused to pay.

"Perhaps I shouldn't have come here, Jean," Michel said. "You've had more than your share of woes."

"I welcome you, and does every pastor in the diocese. It was just six months ago that our parishioners paid the final installment of King Louis' punitive tax. Even though we've had no Huguenots in Rennes, we know what it means to be an oppressed minority."

Michel found the wine too strong, but didn't want to offend his host. Bishop de Laval, like every other citizen of Rennes, had been forced to live for years on a tiny fraction of his income, and apparently had not been able to afford better wines. "When were the last troops withdrawn, Jean?"

"One week after we paid the last of the tax. It's hard for outsiders to realize that we lived for ten years as a conquered people. When our young men were taken into military service, they were sent to garrisons far from Britanny. Every time the provost of our university applied for Crown funds to buy new books, he was refused. And twice the King tried to close my monasteries, including this one, but I wouldn't admit his troops. I thank God that French soldiers still respect a bishop, even though their king doesn't."

Michel smiled painfully.

"Louis thought he'd break our spirit, but he was wrong. If he had punished us and forgotten the matter, it would have been different. But ten years of watching his regiments swagger through our streets gave the people a new kind of courage. They're waiting for a chance to thumb their noses at him again. I can promise you they'll be receptive to your sermons on the Huguenots."

"The more I hear, the more I think I shouldn't have come here," Michel said. "I must be fair to you, Jean, and tell you that for the past three days I've been followed by the Crown's agents."

"In uniform?"

"The secret police uniform," Michel replied, and both laughed wryly.

"We've had our fill of them, too. Hulking fellows who dress in

248

black, trample pedestrians in the street and push everyone else aside at Mass so they can be the first to kneel at the communion rail."

"I've been harassed in many ways during these past months, but this is the first time Louis' secret police have trailed me. It couldn't be accidental, Jean. The King knows there's a potentially explosive situation here. I don't want the people of Rennes to suffer because of me. They've had more than enough trouble."

"We'd be mortally insulted if you left! Our pastors have already been promising their parishioners that you'll spend several weeks with us delivering sermons, and the whole diocese will be grievously disappointed if you don't speak." The cathedral carillon began to chime, and he glanced out of the window at the gathering dusk, then stood. "Come with me to Vespers, and later I'll present some of the monsignors of my staff to you. You'll change your mind fast enough when you see how eager they've been to meet you."

Michel still had reservations, but this was not the moment to make a decision. He stood, too, and reached for his biretta.

"Wear your cloak," Laval advised. "We'll cut across the lawn, and it's chilly tonight. Two of the seminarians are waiting at the cathedral with vestments for you."

They walked together down the stone corridor of the abbey, opened a heavy door of oak and stepped out into the night. There was a suggestion of winter in the air, and Michel, who loved the cold, breathed deeply.

Suddenly several dark shapes loomed in the twilight. "This is the one!" a man with a husky voice called, and grasped Michel's arm, spinning him around.

Before he could cry out, he saw the dull gleam of a knife, and felt its excruciating pain as it was plunged into his side.

A second man came up behind Bishop de Laval and clamped a hand over his mouth to silence him, while the third joined in the attack on Michel. Again and again the knives cut into his body, and the assault was so swift that he was unable to protect himself. He felt as though he had been immersed in flames as he crumpled onto the stone path.

"Death to traitors!" the man standing above him said in a distinct voice.

Michel thought he could make out the sound of running footsteps, but his agony was so great that everything else was blurred. Then, as though from a great distance, he heard Jean de Laval praying, in Latin. The sound grew steadily fainter, and finally faded away.

Sleet rattled against the expensive new panes of glass in the windows, but Lord Churchill was not the type of man who was concerned over the premature arrival of winter. He greeted Paul de Montauban with a quick handshake, and didn't bother with the amenities of apologizing for summoning him on such a dreary day. "I want to return a favor," the Englishman said, "and I hope you'll pardon my brusqueness, but I'm pressed for time."

Paul knew that he wasn't expected to reply.

"We're being forced to act."

There was no need for Paul to ask what he meant. The recent birth of a son to King James' second wife had made it imperative that the question of the succession to the throne be settled. And there had been rumors for days that Churchill had been holding long meetings with Lords Danby, Halifax and Shrewsbury, all of them powerful members of the Church of England.

"The French ambassador is being taken into custody for his own protection, and is being escorted to a Channel port. Father Petre, the King's confessor, is already on his way out of the country."

Paul was startled by the English nobleman's ruthless calm.

"For your own good," Churchill told him, "I urge you to go to your living quarters and stay there for a day or two."

"I have a small suite at the Thistle——"

"A splendid inn, and so much the better. Eat all your meals there, too. French isn't a popular language in London at the moment, and French Catholics will be deported. Some may be handled a bit roughly. I've prepared a special passport you can show in case of trouble, but you'll be wise to avoid public appearances. Our people are well-mannered as a rule, but they can become as ugly as mobs anywhere else."

Paul took a document bearing Churchill's bold signature and seal. "Thank you. May I ask what——"

"Everyone in England will know in a few hours. King James is with one of my divisions of Salisbury, and will have been told within the hour—if all has gone as it should. Princess Anne has gone off to a safe place with my wife to avoid possible unpleasantness with any of James' more enthusiastic followers—assuming he has some." Churchill escorted his visitor to the door. "I'm leaving immediately for a meeting with William of Orange and Princess Mary, who are landing on English soil tonight."

The implications were staggering, and Paul felt overwhelmed as he made his way back to his office. Driving sleet soaked his cloak, the cobblestones underfoot were slippery and he was forced to avert his face from the wind, but he was too intent on analyzing the significance of what he had just heard to feel uncomfortable. Of primary importance was Churchill's casual statement that he was meeting William and Mary. Only one interpretation was possible: England's senior military officer would promise the full support of the army to the Protestant heir to the throne and her ambitious husband. James, meanwhile, was being immobilized by a division of Churchill's troops, and would be taken into custody or sent into exile. In either event, he would be compelled to abdicate.

Louis of France had lost his gamble, and England would remain, more securely than ever, in the Protestant fold. It seemed inevitable, too, that with William of Orange directing her affairs, England soon would join the Dutch, Germans and Swedes in their war with France. The prospect of further bloodshed, both for his own country and for the land that had given him refuge, gave Paul a feeling of hopeless despair, but he realized there was nothing he could do to stem the tide. Each side was claiming God's protection and was determined to prove itself His champion.

The offices maintained by Lord Willoughby and his associates were directly ahead, and Paul slowly climbed the stairs to his own private chamber. He would heed Churchill's advice, of course, and decided to leave for his quarters at the Thistle as soon as he gathered together some documents to read during the next few days. It was a small consolation that he would have the time to work out the intricate details of an arrangement in which he and his partners were acting as middlemen between the East India Company and the leading import-export company in Berlin.

A cloaked woman, her hood thrown back, was standing before the hearth in Paul's office, and turned as he came in. It took him a moment to recognize Simone Duelle, who had matured since the night Michel had spirited her away to a convent.

"I've been waiting for you, milord," she said, curtsying.

Paul was still too dumfounded to reply, but bowed.

"I just arrived in London today," she said, "and came straight to Lord Willoughby. My grandfather did business with him for years, and I knew you were here, too."

Paul found his voice. "You look well, mademoiselle. You—fled from France?"

Simone nodded. "The abbess decided I was no longer safe after your brother—" She broke off sharply. "You know?"

"The Bishop of Rennes smuggled out a letter to me two weeks ago."

"He was wonderful," she said, and choked.

"Michel died for his beliefs." Paul knew that in the months and years, he, too, would have to take a stand for his convictions in a world at war. But there were more immediate problems to be settled, and it occurred to him that he and the girl had been speaking in French. "Do you know English?" he asked.

"Only a few words." Simone was startled by his abrupt change of subject.

251

"Where do you intend to live?"

She was embarrassed, and gazed down at the floor. "Lord Willoughby is away from London. I had hoped . . ." Her voice dwindled and became inaudible.

"He's in Plymouth arranging for some shipping, and won't be back until next week." Paul realized that, aside from Willoughby, he himself was probably the only person in England the girl knew. He assumed she was virtually penniless, but hesitated for only an instant before accepting both responsibility and its possible consequences. "You can't be allowed to wander around London for the next few days. You won't be safe."

Simone's eyes grew larger.

He busied himself at his desk, stuffing papers into a pouch. "There's no time to explain now. You'll have to come back to my inn with me. If I can engage a room for you. I will. If not, I'll have to give you a part of my suite. You'll come to no harm there."

For the first time she smiled. "If there's one person in this world I can trust, I know who he is."

Paul opened the door and let her precede him into the corridor. It was remarkable, he thought, that a frightened adolescent waif could have blossomed into such a handsome young woman. "I'm afraid," he said as they reached the street, "that there will be no public carriages for hire in this weather. It isn't too far, but we'll have to walk."

Simone took his arm as they went out into the storm. "I don't mind," she said.

Paul discovered that he didn't care, either. Perhaps the future wasn't as bleak as he had thought.

BOOK FOUR

BOOK FOUR

prologue—four

"O ne of the basic flaws in the achievements of the Vatican Council," Philippe de Montauban said, putting a slice of artichoke bottom on his fork and eating it with his beef, "was its failure to reach hard enough or far enough toward the Jews."

The Bishop, who had been cutting his tournedos, halted in surprise. "Surely you aren't serious."

"I've never been more in earnest. I realize you took a position, finally, and that it was unfortunate that the stand on relieving Jews of the responsibility for Christ's death was weakened somewhat by the—ah—you refuse to call them conservatives."

"Surely the Church's official position, in its final form, was strong enough to make amends to them." The Bishop was concerned.

"To those who felt the need for such amends, Charles, and were mollified by them. But to other Jews, the mere issuance of a declaration was an offense, an act of condescension."

"We were trapped by the anti-Semitism of the ages, Philippe. We were damned if we ignored the matter, and damned if we brought it into the open. I believe we took the best possible action on a delicate matter in an imperfect world, even though there were some at the Council who felt that too strong a declaration would offend the Arab nations."

"I'm concerned with more basic issues. I hope you'll

255

admit that the position taken by Catholicism through the ages contributed to anti-Semitism."

"Have the teachings of the Protestants fostered a love for the Jews, Philippe?"

"No, but you haven't answered my question."

"Catholicism is always a convenient whipping-boy. Of course we've been responsible for our share, but anti-Semitism is too complex a phenomenon to attribute all the guilt to one source."

"It seems to me that, aside from the one declaration, the Jews were ignored by the Council."

"You've been ill-informed."

"Pope John, and Pope Paul after him, stressed the reconciliation of Christians. Doesn't that leave the Jews out in the cold again?"

"You exasperate me, Philippe. At times you deliberately try to manufacture flaws in the work of the Council. We hope there will be dialogues with the Jews that will lead to a greater mutual understanding and mutual tolerance. But Christianity must set its own house in order. We must build bridges across the chasm that separates the Catholic and the Protestant."

"Before reaching an understanding with the Jews?"

"Yes. First things must come first." Charles de Montauban sighed. "The Council was merely a beginning, remember, and we—Catholics, Protestants and Jews —can't overcome the prejudices and misunderstandings of centuries overnight. Pope John often emphasized the principle of the fundamental equality of all peoples in the exercise of rights and duties within the entire family of nations. It is on that premise that our dialogues begin."

book four

If God did not exist, it would be
necessary to invent him.
—VOLTAIRE

1739–1740

Simone de Montauban smiled at her grandson, then at her husband. Their remarkable physical resemblance had been a family joke for years, although Paul, even in his prime, had never been as tall as Maurice. A lifetime of travel on the Continent, Paul liked to say, had stunted him, and Clarissa, Maurice's English mother, was fond of adding that not even foul London weather had prevented her son from achieving his full height. No one quite knew how Maurice had grown to an astonishing six feet, four inches; his late father, Paul the younger, had been no giant, and Clarissa was tiny, at least by Montauban standards.

It was a terrible wrench to realize that in less than twenty-four hours Maurice would be leaving, and even though Simone had promised not to make a scene, tears came to her eyes. It was her privilege to feel exceptionally close to her only grandchild, and it didn't matter in the least if Paul and Clarissa scolded her. Unlike Paul, she had never become Anglicized in her attitudes. She was still French, in spite of having lived all these years in this alien land, and was incapable of hiding her emotions.

"Your mother will come to dine with us?" she asked, sniffing loudly.

"Yes, ma'am," Maurice replied in his booming voice. "She knows you don't want her to be alone after I've gone." It was Simone, of course, who would need comforting, but the young man carefully maintained the fiction that it would be his grandmother who would be offering consolation.

Paul reached out to pat his wife's hand, then sat back in his chair and tugged at his velvet waistcoat. "I think it unlikely," he said to his grandson in an English almost completely devoid of a French accent, "that King George will be able to offer you any real help. But I'm charging him no interest on that forty-five thousand pound personal loan, so he's indebted to me. He has even less influence at the French court than he has at his own, and I understand there's a great contempt at Versailles for our Hanoverian monarchy. But it can do you no harm to be carrying a letter from your own king. Louis XV must be least pretend to respect it, no matter what his private opinion."

"I understand, sir." Maurice's gesture of straightening his own waistcoat was an unconscious imitation of his grandfather's habit. "You still think I'm wasting my time going to France, all the same."

"No, that's too strong. You have everything to gain and nothing to lose, so your gamble is sound. The odds against your father and me were much worse when we made the transaction with the Turks twelve years ago that still pays Montauban and Company a handsome annual dividend. But a commercial arrangement isn't the same as claiming a title from a petty tyrant. When my brother Philippe's line died out two years ago, the Montauban estates reverted to the French Crown, and I've yet to hear of any king voluntarily giving up property."

"But I don't see how King Louis can refuse a valid claim." Maurice spoke with the firm, almost brash confidence of a young man in his mid-twenties. "You've renounced your rights of succession to the title and estates in my favor, and since I'm a Catholic, the French can't exclude me on religious grounds."

"A king may do what he pleases, and even the flimsiest of excuses would be enough, since he's accountable to no one but himself." Paul glanced at Simone, aware that any mention of their son might upset her. "I'll be surprised if he doesn't reject your claim because we've never been able to prove that your father died."

Maurice was conscious of his grandmother's sensitivity, too. "The proof was good enough to convince the lord chief justice."

"Yes, but he isn't king of France. And although your grandmother taught you to speak reasonably good French, there are strong traces of English in your accent. You know how people here feel because King George can't speak pure English. You'll be battling the same prejudices at Versailles. I'm not trying to discourage you, Maurice. I'm merely urging you to look after our business interests in Vienna and Berlin, and think of your visit to France as something of a holiday. I don't want you to be too badly disappointed."

Maurice was careful to let no note of disrespect creep into his voice. "I hope you'll forgive me for saying this, sir, but times are changing rapidly. Kings aren't absolute monarchs any more. They're responsible to their ministers and parliaments—and, eventually, to their subjects. What's more, there's a genuine respect everywhere for law."

Even Simone smiled at his ingenuousness.

Paul, however, knew better than to lecture his grandson. Maurice had shown great promise in learning the intricacies of the family business, which outsiders sometimes found mysterious. In essence, the operations of the company were relatively simple. In England, as in Prussia, Austria and various other countries on the Continent, there were hundreds of small firms that made various consumer products, from leather belts to silk stockings, and that lacked the funds to export their manufactures. Paul found markets for these goods in other lands, simultanously creating similar markets in England for imports. By financing the entire exchange, he was in a position to act not only as a banker, but to control a considerable quantity of international trade.

And it pleased him to know that Maurice had mastered the subtleties of the business far more quickly than anyone had expected. If he was ingenuous in his beliefs that kings were no longer masters in their own houses and that people were learning greater respect for law and order, he would learn otherwise, in time.

"I believe, at least I hope," Paul said gently, "that you'll find life as an English merchant and banker preferable to existence as a French nobleman. No one who breathes the free air of Great Britain quite realizes how viciously intolerant the rest of the world can be."

The more charitably inclined of King George II's ministers ignored him when possible, placated him with small talk when seeking favors and found it convenient most of the time not to understand his heavily accented English. Frederick, Prince of Wales, set the tone for the court's attitude when he remarked, "My father is a far better Englishman than my grandfather was. My grandfather spoke no language but German, while my father merely thinks in it."

King George's private audience chamber, study and parlor in St. James's Palace had been draped in black for the better part of a year, and it was said that the King had been inconsolable since the death of Queen Caroline. In fact, his few friends loyally insisted his feelings on the matter were so delicate that he refused all of his many mistresses permission to set foot in the suite his late wife had occupied.

Maurice de Montauban wished he had worn heavier clothing for his meeting with the King, as the room was bitterly cold. A small fire of inexpensive peat burned in a grate, and occasionally George himself grudgingly threw another small piece of the inferior fuel onto the blaze. Perhaps, Maurice thought, his own fat kept him warm; certainly his suit of a conservative, dark gray wool, which a senior clerk at Montauban and Company would have been ashamed to wear, was inadequate protection against the chill.

But King George apparently suffered no discomfort as he sat in a padded chair covered with wine stains, and absently counted a pile of one shilling silver coins bearing his own likeness. "I would like, Mr. de Montauban, to have one thing clear," he said, speaking in an accent so thick that his visitor was forced to concentrate on every word. "Why do you wish to claim the French title of your ancestors?"

Maurice was prepared for the question. "I have several reasons,

Your Majesty," he said, and immediately advanced one that was certain to appeal to a man who had gained an international reputation as a miser. "The Montauban estates are enormous, from what my grandfather tells me. Their income is substantial. For years it supported my grandfather and his brothers in style, and I'm told that my uncle—the son of Count Philippe de Montauban, whom I never met —lived quite handsomely before he was killed in a duel over his wife's honor."

"It is good for a man to have a large income." The King's manner was sententious.

Maurice waited for the usual proverb, and was not disappointed.

"A penny in the purse more better is than a friend at court." George looked like a pudgy owl.

"I'll remember that, Your Majesty. Thank you." Maurice hoped they could drop the subject of his motives.

"But you have reasons more than money, I think? You are ambitious."

In spite of his many absurd personal habits, the King was anything but stupid, and Maurice thought it wise not to evade or sidestep. "It's true, Your Majesty, I'd like the title."

King George sighed. "Twice my father to your grandfather offered an English title, and twice I have done the same. Always he refused. He was born a Frenchman and wishes to die a Frenchman. I am thinking, myself, this foolish. I was not in England born, but now I am English." He shrugged, indicating that lesser men were shortsighted. Then, in a sudden change of attitude that his ministers and courtiers found so infuriating, he blithely reversed himself. "But you are English, Mr. de Montauban. You were in England born. You are the only heir to your grandfather's business. You should be more patient. A virtue, the English say, is patience. Some day I might to you offer a title, or after me my son would give you one."

Maurice hoped he looked grateful. It would be inappropriate to suggest that he had no desire to use his grandfather's wealth to buy an English title.

George let his spectacles slide down his nose and peered over them. "It might be you would stay in France if Louis makes you a count?"

The question was dangerous, particularly when dealing with a man whose father had not hesitated to change his nationality in order to gain a crown. "It would be very tempting to stay in France, Your Majesty." Maurice was reluctant to reveal that there were others in Montauban and Company who could supervise affairs in London after his grandfather's retirement, and that, provided his quest was successful and he liked France, he envisaged opening an office in Paris and expanding the business. Ever since joining the company after his graduation from Oxford he had thought Paris would be preferable to London as a center for Montauban operations on the Continent.

However, Maurice reminded himself, certain amenities had to be observed when dealing with royalty. "I'm Your Majesty's subject, and have no intention of becoming anything else."

No one who knew George II gave him credit for a sense of humor, but he laughed until tears fogged his spectacles. "Every minister we have sent to France tells us the same. Louis plays at being King. He is not like his grandfather. Louis the Fourteenth was—how do you say?—from his birth a king. Not so this Louis. He is French, he is a Papist, he is weak, but he enjoys his throne. If he is not mad, he will not give titles to foreigners."

Maurice knew he would labor under severe handicaps when he went to Versailles, but was not prepared to tell George of England that, like the Hanoverians, he was prepared to transfer his allegiance if the rewards proved sufficiently great.

Suddenly George sobered. "You also are a Papist, no?"

Maurice had never concerned himself with questions of religion. His parents had reared him as a Catholic as a gesture of respect to his grandfather, but like so many members of his generation at Oxford, which he had attended without admitting his Catholicism openly, he had preferred the study of logic to theology. Yet, somewhat to his surprise, the suggestion in the King's patronizing tone caused him to bristle. "I was baptized a Catholic, Your Majesty," he said, controlling his irritation, and saw no reason to add that he seldom found it convenient to attend Mass.

George reached for a pile of sixpenny coins, and began to count them. "The French bishops will think of your grandfather's good English gold, and will tell Louis to give you the title. If he agrees, we have troubles. My ministers would not sleep nights if they thought the gold of Paul de Montauban would flow into the strong-boxes of Vatican Hill and Louis the Fifteenth. But I sleep well." He stopped stacking coins long enough to hand Maurice a folded letter already bearing his seal. "Here. This presents you to Louis. If you stay with him in France, we make a new law to keep English gold in England."

Maurice saw that the King was devoting his full attention to the sixpenny coins, and realized he had been dismissed.

"Only in their fickleness are human beings consistent, and we French have been civilized for so long that we lack even the sincerity of more primitive people. What I enjoyed most during my years of exile in England was your honesty. You build your trade, your North American colonies, your empire. You're truthful because it isn't yet profitable for you to lie. Only we who are in a state of decay find it convenient to rationalize our failures. Go back to London, Montauban. If you stay here, you'll either have to apologize for your natural cupidity or pretend you aren't a gentleman."

Maurice laughed, but suspected that his host, in spite of his witticisms, was being serious. François Marie Arouet, who called himself Voltaire, had achieved international renown as an iconoclast, and it was difficult to determine when he wanted to be taken literally.

The small, dark-haired man in his mid-forties frowned and stopped twirling his glass of cognac. "You are amused, de Montauban? I'm not. Look around you. A year—no, eighteen months—ago this coffee house did not exist. Today there are scores like it in Paris, and the affluent pay thousands of francs daily for the privilege of sitting in them. They pay good money for bad spirits, impossible service and unpotable cups of that noxious Turkish brew, coffee. Those who would like to be considered affluent do the same. The poor, who need real nourishment, come in the hope of being noticed by the wealthy. Even I come. Why? Because there's no other place to find one's friends, now that the ladies have closed their salons. Paris is a city of whims. We have had coffee houses inflicted on us because we've opened trade relations with the Ottomans, and we import so much coffee that no one would have known what to do with the foul drink had it not become fashionable." Either he shuddered, or else his narrow shoulders were quivering indignantly.

Maurice enjoyed the company of the man his grandfather had befriended in London, but hoped the torrent of words would stop long enough for him to gain some practical help.

"Look around you, my young friend. Observe. Do you see that man at the far corner table, scribbling? He is my colleague, an author, but his plays are inferior to mine, his verses have an odor more offensive than the courtiers at Versailles before they anoint themselves with perfume, and he knows nothing—nothing, mind you—of philosophy. The old man to our right, the one sitting with that very young woman who will catch a rheum in the chest if she continues to expose her bosom to the night air so carelessly—is a professor of physics at the Sorbonne. He is an idiot, and can't make out a word of my books on natural order."

A clergyman entered the coffee house, the ermine collar on his black cloak marking him as a personage of importance. Several young priests followed him, deferentially remaining a few paces behind him. He halted, glanced around the restaurant, and nodded rather severely when he saw Voltaire.

The author jumped to his feet, and his bow was so low it became a caricature. "Ah, Your Grace. The very man I want to see."

"Oh?" The bishop was wary.

262

"Only you can tell me what I want to know. Is the Almighty enjoying good health?"

Several patrons smiled, and the underdressed young woman with the elderly professor emitted a high-pitched giggle, but the bishop's expression did not change. "His Eminence tells me it may be necessary to ban the presentation of your new play, Voltaire."

"What a pity."

"It's more than that. When a man of your age and supposed standing writes drivel, it's a shame."

"I find it a shame, Your Grace, that Paris' loss will be London's gain. And Brussels'. And Amsterdam's. There's so little of lasting value being presented on the Paris stage these days that His Eminence should subsidize my plays, not ban them."

The bishop did not deign to answer, and swept through the room, his entourage at his heels.

"There goes an ass," Voltaire said to Maurice, not bothering to lower his voice. "Much as it pains me to say it, the auxiliary bishop of Paris is the second most stupid member of the Church hierarchy in the archdiocese. Only the cardinal is more of an ignoramus, which is why he wears a red hat. The dunce's cap went out of style several hundred years ago."

Maurice saw that two high-ranking army officers in gold-braided uniforms were glaring at them, and that an inconspicuous friar sitting nearby was taking down every word Voltaire said. Maurice wondered whether he had come to the wrong man for assistance.

"I see I embarrass you, my young friend. Or could it be you're losing faith in humanity because you've seen so many fools and knaves since you arrived in France? Take heart, de Montauban. The poor are decent and honest and good because neither the Church nor the State have taught them to read. So they remain free of the corrupting influences of the written word." He summoned a waiter with a lordly gesture. "Charge my bill to the account of the Marquise du Châtelet. Don't look so shocked, de Montauban. She's my mistress, so I faithfully pay all her bills on the first day of each month. The Church may close the theaters that present my plays, but my books of history, philosophy and natural science are already classics, so I'm solvent. In fact, I'm probably the only author in the history of French literature who has ever subsidized himself."

Maurice was relieved when they left the coffee house and strolled out into the Paris night.

Voltaire took the younger man's arm. "Forgive my monopoly of the conversation in there," he said, his strident voice becoming quiet, "but I didn't want your problems to become a matter of public record. Brother Alessandro is a Milanese, so his French is inadequate,

263

and he misquotes rather shockingly. Captain de Laussaup is almost as bad."

"There were two men transcribing your comments?"

Voltaire nodded cheerfully. "Often there are three."

Maurice was confused. "But you said some outrageously provocative things!"

"Of course. It's expected of me. But you might recall I said nothing against the Crown, which is the most inept of our institutions. King Louis confuses himself with his grandfather, which is ridiculous, but he secretly fears he'll wake up some morning to find himself stripped of his glory. I'm trying to persuade him to let me write his biography, which will not only make him immortal but will give me a share of the money he squanders, and I want nothing to spoil our precarious relationship of the moment. Now, what brings you to this decadent city?"

Maurice thought Paris was beautiful, and said so before explaining his reasons for coming to France.

"Surely you wouldn't give up your English citizenship to become a member of our flabby nobility. I long ago lost my faith in humanity, but there are a few intelligent men on this earth, and I can't believe the grandson of Paul de Montauban would sell his birthright for a useless title. There's a chamberlain at Versailles who sells titles—giving the Crown the usual seventy-five percent, of course—so I can arrange to buy you one if you really have your heart set on it."

"I want Montauban," Maurice said, and glanced around cautiously before continuing. "My grandfather said you can be trusted, so I'm willing to take you into my confidence. We had a discreet survey made after my uncle died. The county of Montauban is worth an income of forty thousand gold francs per year."

Voltaire whistled softly under his breath. "I should have been a landlord instead of a poet."

"The production of wine for export fell off badly after my grandfather went into exile. By producing it again, I can earn an additional twenty thousand. And it would give me a solid base for our Paris operations."

Voltaire steered him toward the middle of the cobbled street so they wouldn't soil their shoes on the garbage that littered the gutter. "I apologize, my young friend. You have the mind of a de Montauban. Now, tell me precisely what happened when you presented your letter of introduction from King George."

"I was passed from one nobleman to another. They were very courteous—and very curious. But I told none of them why I wanted an audience with King Louis."

"It wasn't necessary. They knew, and so did Louis. I'm sure he suffers acute pains in the purse when he contemplates giving up an income of forty thousand a year."

"You may be right," Maurice said. "I wouldn't know from a personal encounter with him. He sent one of his gentlemen to me with his regrets. His Majesty was very much occupied, and so forth. I was given a bumper glass of champagne——"

"The best of champagne, no doubt."

"It was excellent. And then I was provided with a military escort back to Paris."

"To make certain you didn't loiter at Versailles."

"That was late this afternoon, and I came straight to you after finding lodgings."

"Do you have other business here?" Voltaire asked.

"None."

"Then save your money. You look and sound like an Englishman, you know, so I'm sure your innkeeper is charging you at least twice what your quarters are worth. Spend a day or two seeing the city, if that sort of thing amuses you, and then leave France. I'd urge you to stay for the opening of my new play—if it opens—but it will be done in London within the year."

Maurice stopped abruptly. "Are you telling me, sir, that I'm wasting my time in Paris?"

"In a manner of speaking." Voltaire urged him to start walking again.

Maurice was annoyed. "You speak plainly when it suits you. I'll appreciate candor now."

"You've chosen an inappropriate time for your mission. I regard money with a fondness and awe as great as that of any de Montauban, I assure you, but I wouldn't think of pressing King Louis for the dubious pleasure of writing a spurious biography on the subject of his non-existent glory at the moment. In six months, perhaps, the climate will change. It may take as long as a year." Voltaire fell silent as they walked past several officers in the broad-brimmed, plumed hats of royal musketeers.

Maurice started to speak, but the older man's fingers on his arm warned him to say nothing.

"That's better," Voltaire said as they moved out of earshot. "A man is safe in France these days provided he keeps quiet in two places, the confessional and in the presence of army officers. I protect myself as best I can. I haven't confessed my sins to a priest in years, and my mistress is the wife of a lieutenant-general. I've learned so much about him—and his colleagues—that I can always threaten to write what I know about them if they make life uncomfortable for me."

Maurice was too immersed in his own problems to laugh.

"Unfortunately for you, my young friend, King Louis is in the process of changing mistresses. When you and I give up a woman and take another, we do it simply. We give the departing wench a small gift, and greet the new one with another. If we're lucky, and the woman who is being jilted refuses the gift, we give it to the new one instead, and save money.

"But it would offend Louis' sense of dignity to behave like an ordinary mortal man. He's having a palace built for the departing lady, and I'm told on excellent authority, that of a jeweler from whom I occasionally buy a second-hand bauble, that he's having a set of necklaces and earrings made for her. They won't be too ostentatious, as she has only been in favor for two or three years. I imagine he's buying gems abroad for the new mistress-to-be. Everyone at court is trying—very discreetly, as you can imagine—to guess her identity."

"There are subtleties in all this that escape me," Maurice said, "and I don't really see the connection between royal mistresses and the Montauban title."

"That, my young friend, is because you're an Englishman. You haven't been corrupted by idleness and luxury. Listen, and you'll understand how France has fallen from the real glory she knew in the time of Henry the Fourth. King Louis is passionately fond of beautiful women, a weakness he shares with all other males. But he has a conscience so tender he can't bear to let a former mistress face the world alone. When he gets rid of one, he first builds her a magnificent house and presents her with gifts of great value. Then he finds her a husband, any member of the nobility who takes her fancy, and if he happens to be married, his cardinals persuade Vatican Hill to annul the man's marriage. The former mistress becomes secure and respectable, and Louis goes on to the next mistress. I keep hoping that some year we'll have a new pope in Rome who stands up to him, and spoils his little game, but it hasn't happened yet."

"And in the meantime," Maurice said, "the changing of mistresses is an expensive business."

"So expensive that he has no funds for any other purpose. The best time to present your claim," Voltaire said, "will be a few months after a new mistress moves into Versailles. He'll complain about her extravagance, but it will be the usual alarm of a man who can't understand why he must pay a heavy price for the privilege of bedding a wench who has refused payment for the same prerogative from the less wealthy. The pinch of losing forty thousand a year won't hurt him as much, and he'll be able to devote the resources of his mind, such as they are, to the possible advantages of bringing new de Montauban blood and an impressive de Montauban fortune into his hierarchy."

"You make the procedure sound thoroughly unattractive," Maurice said.

"One needs a strong stomach to be a patriotic Frenchman these days," Voltaire replied. "I've always enjoyed the avocational pastime of ogling a shapely woman's bosom. But, as a moralist, I deplore a sport that interferes with the making of national policies. And, as a historian, I am appalled by the influence of bosoms on our political and cultural heritage. If you have business elsewhere, attend to it, and wait until Louis' passion is surfeited before you approach him again."

Dresden, the capital of the ancient German Kingdom of Saxony, was justifiably proud of her beauty. Her royal palace, the Georgenschloss, sat astride the busiest thoroughfare in the Old City, and the carriages of wealthy nobles, the carts laden with the produce of peasants, and the horses of cavalry troops actually rumbled down the broad, cobbled street directly beneath the private apartments of the Elector Augustus II. The tower of the Georgenschloss was the highest in Europe, and Augustus, an enthusiastic amateur architect, was erecting an even taller one on the Town Hall in the New City, near his recently completed Japanese Palace, where he and his family spent their summers.

For more than five hundred years Dresdeners had been conscious of their city's grace, and their cumulative efforts to make her even more attractive were everywhere apparent. Roofs of green copper or tile blended into a harmonious whole; the libraries, museums and government buildings that lined the banks of the Elbe River showed a gradual, gentle transition from the styles of the Middle Ages to those of the Renaissance, and even the military barracks sat in the center of informal gardens as pleasant as the city's many parks.

Only in the Jewish ghetto of the New City, actually the older part of the town, were there no public buildings, open spaces or avenues. The six thousand Jews of Dresden were crowded into an ancient quarter surrounded by a twenty-foot-high stone wall. Its two gates were opened at sunrise, when the inhabitants were permitted to leave and other Dresdeners allowed to enter. The firing of a cannon at sunset signaled the closing of the gates, and any Jew caught outside the ghetto was whipped in a public ceremony, stripped of his possessions and sent into exile.

"We've become acclimated to a way of life," Aaron Goldschmidt said. "It isn't as rigorous as it sounds, or as unpleasant."

Maurice de Montauban sat in the parlor of the Goldschmidt house, simultaneously feeling alien and at ease. Never had he been subjected to so many contrasts, and they bewildered him. The building was very old, and although the quarters occupied by Goldschmidt, his wife and their two children were cramped, they were comfortably furnished. Jews were not permitted to engage servants, but dinner, which had been prepared by Frau Goldschmidt and her daughter, Rosa, had been delicious. The dumplings of a special meal in the soup had been unique, the roasted, stuffed duckling had been a delight, and the dessert, a concoction of thin pastry and honey, had been extraordinary.

Goldschmidt touched his full beard. "I'm told that in other countries the Gentiles often wear beards. Here they're the obligatory mark of a Jew. Our neighbors and friends wear them. My son, at sixteen, is already growing one so he'll never know the feeling of being clean-shaven. To the Gentiles, our beards set us apart. But we've become so accustomed to them that we pay no attention to them. We've discovered that a man's attitude is what matters. We accept the inevitable, and learn to live with it."

Maurice wondered how the Jewish banker could speak so calmly. "I'd think you'd want to revolt."

Goldschmidt's smile was weary. "There are fifteen hundred of us in the ghetto capable of bearing arms. The Elector keeps a garrison of eight thousand Saxons stationed in the city, and in the past few months, since relations between Maria Theresa of Austria and Frederick of Prussia have deteriorated, he's brought in four additional regiments of Polish cavalry. The Poles, in particular, are savage brutes who find genuine pleasure in cracking heads. We prefer to obey the law, mind our own business—and survive."

Maurice marveled at the man's patience. What puzzled him was that Goldschmidt, aside from his beard and gentle dignity, seemed very much like the bankers he had met in other German states. "If you'll forgive an impertinence, why should Jews be set apart and restricted in so many lands?"

"Only an Englishman could ask that question. Human memory is short, and people forget that once there were ghettos in England." Goldschmidt seemed amused. "Why were your Huguenot ancestors persecuted? Why were Catholics driven from Sweden? For that matter, why did the Roman pantheists persecute the Christians? I've always found it fascinating that when the Emperor Constantine made Rome Christian by signing a decree, and the tables were turned overnight, it was the pagans who were persecuted. If you'll study the history of so-called civilization, you'll find that religious minority groups have always been harassed. We Jews have been in the minority for most of our five thousand years, so we know it better than anyone."

Maurice smiled painfully. "You make me feel very foolish, Herr Goldschmidt. In England there's been no persecution of the Catholic minority."

"There has been religious peace in England for almost a half-century—because the Catholics there have had the good sense not to flaunt their faith."

"But the Jews of Dresden don't live ostentatiously. Why should you be persecuted?"

"I contradict myself, don't I?" The Jewish banker sighed. "I'm afraid I can't answer your question. I've asked it myself too often, and I don't know. They shackle us and think they rob us of our freedom, but they're mistaken. They can't take away the essence of our real liberty, our worship of God as we believe he should be worshipped." Goldschmidt stood, crossed the small parlor and offered his guest a glass jar of stuffed, glazed fruits. "Enough of problems you and I can't solve. You travel next to Berlin?"

"Yes, I intended to go there earlier, but had to change my plans when the old king died. And I'm glad I waited. Everywhere I've gone I've been told that young King Frederick is lowering tariff barriers and encouraging trade."

"It's true," Goldschmidt said. "My reserves are very small, a drop of water in the sea. But I've been following the example of the Fuggers and the other Christian bankers. All of us are supporting him."

"You feel there's the capital in Berlin for an expansion of trade?"

"I'm sure of it. No matter how much business Montauban and Company did with the old regime, you should quadruple the volume. There's a new spirit in Prussia, and I envy you your journey."

"Come with me," Maurice said, and realized when he saw the expression on the Jew's face that he had blundered.

"I've applied for a special permit, and if it should be granted, I'll take my family to Berlin." There was a note of wonder in Goldschmidt's voice as he added, "Frederick has abolished ghettos in Prussia."

They were interrupted by the arrival of the banker's children, who stood quietly in the parlor entrance until they were noticed. Rosa, who had red hair and green eyes, was in her late teens, but seemed younger, perhaps because her entire life had been restricted to such a small area. Saul, her brother, was dark and slender, and in spite of his youth there was already a hint of gentle wisdom in his eyes.

"It will soon be evening, Papa," the boy said when his father glanced at him.

Goldschmidt looked out of the window at the sky and nodded. "Wait below so you can escort our guest to the North Gate before they close it. I'm sorry," he said, turning back to Maurice, "that our visit has been so unsatisfactory, although I've enjoyed our talk. I did business with your grandfather and your late father for many years, but Saxony is a sick land. The Elector thinks only of his title as king of Poland. Not only did he become a Catholic in order to hold it, which is madness in a Lutheran state, but he's either sold or pawned most of Saxony to pay for his wars with Sweden and Russia. Even if Augustus' subjects assassinate him, which they may, this has become a nation of paupers. Take your trade offers elsewhere, and I hope to join you in a happier place."

The banker's wife came in to say her farewells, and Goldschmidt walked with his guest down three flights of narrow stairs to the street.

"There's no need for your children to escort me to the gate." Maurice was embarrassed, and vaguely realized how a Jew in Dresden felt. The very thought of being locked behind high walls at sundown was unbearable. "I came to your house alone, and I'll find my way back to gate without help."

"You're not only a Gentile but an Englishman. How could you understand? If Rosa and Saul go with you to the gate, they can help you answer the guards' questions. How those guards can shame visitors! First they accuse you of shaving off your beard so you can escape. Then they force you to prove you haven't been circumcised. Then—no, enough. The children will walk with you."

They shook hands when they reached the street. There were some strangers not far away and Maurice lowered his voice when he expressed the hope that they would some day meet in Berlin.

Rosa and Saul fell in on either side of Maurice as they guided him down the twisting street. "Is it true," the girl asked, "that in London and Paris Jews may live where they please?"

Maurice nodded.

"They go to theaters and inns?" Rosa demanded eagerly. "They walk in the avenues, and no one stops them?"

Maurice said, "Yes."

"Where are there fewer restrictions on us, in England or France?" she wanted to know.

"I've spent only a few days in France as a visitor. I don't really know the country. But in England Jews are free." That wasn't the whole truth, Maurice thought. He had never seen a Jew in the taverns where his grandfather and other merchants dined, nor did Jews own homes in the more fashionable districts of London. But, to the best of his knowledge, there were relatively few laws that discriminated against them. He wasn't certain, of course, never having really thought about the matter.

"Then I'm going to live in England some day," Rosa said.

"I'm not," Saul declared, a surprising ferocity in his voice. "I'd have to learn English, and I'd speak it with an accent. Everyone would know I was a foreigner. I want to be a Prussian. Isaiah Blumenthal went to Berlin, and he's accepted there as the equal of the Gentiles!"

Maurice had always thought that Jews flocked together by choice, but now he was becoming confused. The enforced segregation of ghetto life compelled them to stand together, but, if he interpreted the boy correctly, Saul intended to escape from his Jewish past. "Suppose the arrangements can be made and you go to Berlin some day. Will you become a Lutheran convert?"

Rosa giggled in astonishment.

Saul blinked, but spoke with great composure. "I am a Jew, my dear sir. And I won't deny my heritage."

Maurice had thought his question logical, but apparently he had completely misunderstood the approach of these people.

"Any of us," Rosa explained, "could leave the ghetto today if we were willing to become converts to Christianity. A few have done it, and have hidden behind the mask of Catholicism or Lutheranism. But they've turned their backs on God, and they must be miserable. I feel sorry for them. You Christians see those walls holding us in. We don't feel that way. To us, the walls keep the impure out."

"But your brother doesn't agree with you."

Saul's smile indicated a weariness and wisdom far beyond his years. "I despise the physical restrictions of the Dresden ghetto. They're degrading. It's an insult to man—and far worse, a blasphemy against God—to station armed men at gates to restrict the movements of people who have as much right as any others to worship as they believe God should be worshipped. But there's no real difference between Rosa's position and mine, and by real, I mean spiritual."

"You speak in riddles."

The boy and girl exchanged glances, and neither was amused. "Rabbi Schneller tells us we're an enigma to the Gentiles," Saul said. "I haven't known many, but I can see what he means. It doesn't matter whether we're confined in the Dresden ghetto or free in Berlin. We're still Jews. We believe in one God, and His ethical standards have become our standards. We're dedicated to justice and mercy in this world. We don't necessarily deny there's a life after death, but we don't affirm it, either. We try to follow His law here——"

"So do we!"

"——for its own sake, without seeking a reward in the next. Virtue is absolute, not relative, because it God's virtue. You Christians hate us because you say we reject Jesus, but you over-simplify. The question of Jesus' divinity has no meaning to us. His teachings are those of Isaiah and David, who preached the doctrine of loving one another, so we find nothing new in Christian theology. Jesus, a Jew, upheld the basic tenets of our faith, so you and we seek the same goals. We say, as you do, that man must live a good life on this earth in order to please God. When he succeeds, he pleases his fellow man and himself. When he fails, he creates his own hell, right here."

"My brother," Rosa said proudly, "has been studying to become a rabbi."

"In Berlin," Saul added. "Here, where our choice is so limited, it isn't difficult to be a practicing Jew."

Maurice thought he was beginning to understand. There was a basic, perhaps primitive, need for God in everyone, and ghetto life actually helped Jews to remain steadfast because they had so few distractions.

Saul confirmed his analysis. "In the outer world we're restricted only by our own consciences, so our faith must be stronger." He made a sweeping gesture.

Maurice noticed, for the first time, that two fingers were missing from the boy's left hand. Before he could stop himself he asked, "Were you in an accident?"

Saul stiffened, and made no reply as he walked a little more rapidly toward the gate.

Rosa hesitated, and then said reluctantly, under her breath, "It was the Poles."

Maurice had no idea what she meant.

In spite of her brother's attempt to silence her, she felt she should explain. "The Elector's cavalry." Clearly she had no desire to dwell on the subject, much less emphasize it. "When the Elector can't pay their wages, they become restless, and they need to think about something else."

Maurice still appeared not to fully understand.

Saul lost patience with him. "Haven't you ever heard of pogroms? They ride through the ghetto with drawn swords, and slash at anyone who gets in their way."

"He was much younger." Rosa sounded almost apologetic. "So he couldn't run very fast."

Embarrassment suffused Maurice. "But—why?" he asked feebly.

"Because we're Jews," Rosa said, her tone indicating that, in a world of hate, no further explanation was necessary.

Berlin was proud of her Protestant heritage. Dutch refugees from Spanish tyranny had been responsible, late in the seventeenth century, for her initial growth from a sleepy country town in the principality of Brandenburg; an influx of French Huguenots in the last decade of the century had completed her transformation. Now, the capital of the kingdom of Prussia, she was expanding at a dazzling pace, and her population had increased in less than a half-century from a paltry eight thousand to more than one hundred thousand.

Her proud citizens gave credit to young King Frederick, as they did in all things. A dozen new buildings were being added to the Acad-

272

emy of Science founded by his grandfather, he was constructing the most ornate opera house in the world, and a simple royal decree, augmented by stiff taxes, had created the Tiergarten, Europe's largest public park.

Recruits, enlisted in the army under a new policy of universal conscription, paraded down broad avenues, past newly planted linden trees, slept in the most modern barracks and obtained their arms from arsenals so new that in some the whitewash on the walls was still damp. The people listened to concerts by superbly drilled military bands, watched maneuvers of cavalry regiments, and attended performances of classical plays in theaters built by King Frederick in feverish haste.

The new royal prison was probably the most efficient on the Continent. Armed sentries from the most trusted battalions patrolled a high stone wall in pairs, and other guards, accompanied by trained shepherd dogs, wandered through the grounds day and night, varying their schedules according to a meticulous, prearranged plan. Heavy oak doors, reinforced with iron, shut off each unit of cells, and every individual cell was sealed by a similar door. Prisoners were held in solitary confinement, and could be observed through tiny windows set in the doors.

King Frederick's much-publicized love of humanity did not extend to the prisoners incarcerated in his new penitentiary, however. Although he spent money lavishly on the publishing of new books of poetry and the production of dramas by Sophocles and Shakespeare, his involuntary guests in the royal prison ate two meals a day of thin soup and stale bread, went naked when their clothes wore out and were allowed no recreation facilities, no visitors and no relief from their solitude.

Maurice de Montauban felt certain, after spending nine weeks in confinement, that he would soon go mad. He had been placed under arrest on the day of his arrival in Berlin, and although subjected to frequent, long interrogations by his captors since that time, still had no clear idea what he had done to incur the wrath of the authorities. He had been questioned repeatedly about his nationality, his travels, his religious beliefs and his views on many subjects, but his captors, some of them civilians and some military officers in gold-braided uniforms with insignia of rank he had been unable to identify, had calmly ignored his own requests for information on the charges against him. The experience, following so closely on the heels of the grisly tragedy he had witnessed in Dresden, had been shattering.

Then, without warning, his status changed. He was transferred to a hunting lodge in a forest outside Berlin, and although sentries saw to it that he did not leave the extensive grounds, he was treated as a pampered guest rather than a prisoner. Substantial, well-cooked meals

273

helped him regain the weight he had lost, his featherbed in a huge private sleeping chamber was luxurious, and he was encouraged to chop trees and engage in other forms of physical exercise with the officers of the guard. His hosts supplied him with ample reading matter, including several volumes by Voltaire, as well as copies of a partly-completed history of Brandenburg and a number of vaguely worded, almost incomprehensible poems, penned in French, by King Frederick.

He was supplied with a handsome new wardrobe, carefully tailored to his measurements, and two evenings each week he found an amenable but uncommunicative young woman waiting for him in his bedchamber when he retired. He was not permitted to send or receive letters, however, and the men who watched over him made it plain they were not permitted to discuss the reasons for his strange imprisonment.

One day, after Maurice had spent a month at the hunting lodge, there was an abrupt change in the routines his captors had established. He spent part of the morning chopping firewood, then went for a swim in a small lake on the property, and, after dressing, wandered out into the garden behind the lodge to read for a time before the serving of his main meal of the day. Another man was relaxing in the sun, reading a play by Voltaire, and Maurice assumed he was a fellow prisoner.

The newcomer was in his late twenties, and his smile of greeting revealed his warmth and charm. He was quietly dressed in a conservatively cut suit of wool, but Maurice noted that the fabric was expensive, as were his dark silk stockings and his gold-buckled shoes. He shunned a wig, and his own light brown hair was cut short and uncurled. His only jewelry was a signet ring on the middle finger of his right hand, and, as he twirled a pair of spectacles, he looked like an alert and intelligent student for a higher degree at Berlin's Academy of Science.

Surprisingly, he addressed Maurice in French as he made a few banal remarks about the weather, but did not introduce himself.

Maurice sat, too, and was equally cautious. "Do you enjoy the work of Voltaire?"

"I think he's the most accomplished and profound of living authors. I trust you agree, sir?"

"His studies of physics and natural law are beyond my grasp," Maurice replied. "And I must admit his theology is disturbing. It seems to me he goes out of his way to mock the Church."

"He has no love for Protestantism, either."

"True, but he heaps most of his ridicule on Rome."

"In my opinion," the young man said calmly, "he doesn't go far enough. Within the past two years I've completed repudiated Christianity."

A few months earlier Maurice would have been shocked. "I must admit," he said, "that few people I've seen follow the teachings of Jesus."

"Ah, that's another matter entirely." The young man's smile was bright. "I accept the bulk of his philosophy, although I can't and don't believe that the meek will inherit the earth. This world belongs to the strong, provided they use their strengths wisely. What I deny is the divinity of Jesus."

"You are a Jew, sir?"

"A former Lutheran who dabbled in Catholicism. I'm inclined to question the existence of God, too, although I refuse to call myself an atheist."

"Then you're quibbling. Anyone who denies God——"

"I question, sir. I haven't gone to the ultimate conclusion of denial. Have you ever seen God? Has anyone of your acquaintance seen Him? Can any clergyman prove His existence to you? Can the theologians? Augustine—and Aquinas after him—base their reasoning on the assumption of faith by revelation, but if we deny blind faith, we cannot demonstrate the reality of God. Luther and Calvin are more logical, and strip their arguments of dogma that makes little sense, but they're equally vague, you know. Man uses his own reason to achieve happiness and create good in this world. I'm convinced of it."

"I can agree with you," Maurice said slowly, "to the extent that I can't understand why Catholics and Protestants persecute one another—and why both bedevil the Jews. I can't believe that an omnipotent God would permit such incessant testing of man's faith. But in the last extreme I can only fall back on the belief that I'm incapable of understanding His ways and His motives. Call my logic weak, if you will, because it leaves me with no support except my faith."

"Is your faith that strong?"

"Apparently. I've been undergoing a strange experience for many weeks, and I've had nothing to rely on except my faith. I find it has been sustaining me." Maurice was wary, and preferred not to talk about himself. It was possible that the stranger was an interrogator, and he didn't want to say something, inadvertently, that would cause him to be returned to the royal prison. It was far safer to speak in generalities. "My faith or lack of it is unimportant. I don't believe that man can make a truly objective study of God's nature until all faiths are allowed to live together in peace."

"You'd turn a whole society into a theological seminary?" The young man was amused. "I hadn't thought of it in that light, but Prussia has become a model state, according to your definition."

"I know nothing about Prussia." If the man was an informer, Maurice thought, he would get little satisfaction.

"You will, and so will the rest of the world. King Frederick believes that persecutions weaken a nation. Prussia is predominantly a Lutheran state, but Catholics have been granted the right to hold public worship services, and I understand on good authority that Frederick is negotiating with Vatican Hill. I believe it will soon be announced that Berlin will become a diocesan seat."

"Won't the Lutherans be upset?"

"They'll soon learn that Frederick places no restrictions on any religious group. Some of his subjects weren't happy when he abolished the ghettos, but the Jews are proving their value. They're even allowed to own property now, and are forbidden only to hold commissions in the army and seats in the judiciary. Not even you English have an arrangement more liberal. In the next few years, Prussia will astonish the world." The boast was so quiet, so lacking in bombast, that it was impressive. "I see you're reading Frederick's *Anti-Macchievel*. What's your opinion of it?"

Maurice didn't want to be trapped into saying something derogatory about the new Prussian monarch, nor was he willing to admit that he was reading the book only because he had gone through the rest of the small library that had been made available to him, and consequently had nothing else to read. But there was no reason to hide his already-revealed English citizenship. "I haven't read *The Prince* since I was an undergraduate at Oxford, but I've never held a very high regard for Machievelli."

"May I know why?" There was real interest in the young man's eyes.

"My view is completely English. We don't believe the state is more important than its people, or that their primary purpose is the glorification of their ruler."

"Precisely the point that Frederick makes!" the young man said triumphantly. He leaned forward in his chair, took the leather-bound volume from Maurice and quickly riffled through its pages. "Listen to this. 'The prince is not the absolute master, but only the first servant of his subjects.' The English," he added, demonstrating a faint touch of arrogant pride, "have no monopoly on enlightenment, just as the French aren't alone in cultivating the arts." He lowered his voice confidentially. "Your royal Hanoverians have never read Newton, your greatest philosopher of the past century, and wouldn't recognize, much less appreciate, a truffle-and-cream sauce. Louis of France is a gentleman, but he's allowed his country to become morally and ethically decadent. A nation becomes great and remains great only when her people are guided by rulers who understand the essence of liberty."

An army officer appeared at the far end of the garden, but made no attempt to call attention to himself.

The young man saw him at once, however, and stood. "I'm expected at a meeting," he said, "and I believe punctuality is a primary social obligation. Join me at my lodge on the opposite side of the lake in an hour. I want to continue our talk, and I believe my cook prepares a more delicate dinner than the meals you've been given here." He walked away rapidly, falling in beside the officer, and disappeared into the woods.

It was obvious to Maurice that he was someone of stature, in addition to being personable and well-informed. And, at the very least, the invitation to dine held out the hope that Maurice's strange position as a gentleman-prisoner might be changed.

A lean, distinguished Prussian army officer who introduced himself as Colonel von Graebner presented himself as Maurice's escort, and the crests stitched in gold on the saddle-blankets of both horses caused Maurice to suspect the identity of the amiable young man who had chatted with him. The guess was strengthened by the presence of smartly-uniformed armed sentries at the gates of the estate, and the lodge itself was so large that Maurice was virtually certain he was right.

A number of gentlemen, some in uniform and some in casually elegant civilian boots, breeches and open-necked shirts, were chatting in the huge, informal drawing room of the lodge. A few glanced at Maurice, and it suddenly occurred to him that all were conversing in French, which seemed odd. Clustered together at one side of the chamber were several willowy, languid young ladies in figure-revealing gowns who stopped chattering and eyed the tall Englishman with frank interest as Colonel von Graebner led him through the room and down a corridor.

The Colonel tapped on a door, opened it and stood aside to let Maurice enter. Two walls were lined with books from floor to ceiling, and a number of musical instruments, most of them flutes, rested on shelves against the third wall. The amiable young man was seated at a table, signing papers, and looked up with pleasure when he saw his guest.

Maurice bowed low. "Your Majesty," he said.

Frederick looked disappointed. "You recognized me during our little talk?"

"No, Your Majesty. Not until Colonel von Graebner came for me did I begin to realize who you were."

"Then my little deception was successful. I'm delighted." Frederick rubbed his hands together and beamed as he walked to a tray on which stood a decanter and several glasses of French crystal. "Let me give you an aperitif. I also owe you an apology for the unhappiness and inconvenience I've caused you—and an explanation."

Maurice raised his glass. "To Your Majesty's health."

"To yours, Monsieur de Montauban. It's important to me, I assure you. I've been searching for someone like you for a long time, and thanks to Voltaire I found you." He waved his guest to a Louis XIV chair.

Maurice sat, although King Frederick remained standing.

"Voltaire and I correspond at length, frequently. I haven't yet been able to persuade him to visit me, and I frankly envy you, Monsieur de Montauban. You know him, and I don't. What's more, you made a strong impression on him. If I showed you his letter describing your virtues, it might turn your head."

Maurice was pleased, but the mysteries of recent months still rankled.

"First, accept my word that your family knows you're well and safe. The chargé d'affaires of my legation in London has paid several calls on your grandfather."

"You seem to have been taking a great deal of trouble on my behalf, Your Majesty."

"I've been testing you, Monsieur de Montauban. The spirits of many men have been broken in the royal prison, but you remained strong—and discreet. And your conduct has been exemplary since you were moved to my private lodge. You've remained alert, too. I like that."

Maurice was nettled, in spite of the compliments, but tried not to show it. A monarch who, regardless of his professed love of liberty, was capable of having someone imprisoned because of a whim, as yet undisclosed, was a man to be treated with great caution.

"Your family background is French—and distinguished. I have faith in the French aristocracy." Frederick began to tick off points on his fingers. "You're British born and educated. My schools will soon rival Oxford, but I confess, a bit reluctantly, that there is none better than Oxford. England isn't involved in the current disputes over territory on the Continent, which is so much the better. You're considered neutral in our arguments. You speak an excellent French and a passable German. To be multilingual has great advantage. Best of all, you represent a distinguished merchant and banking house that wins you acceptance everywhere. No borders are closed to you, and you're received on the highest level."

"Not in France, Your Majesty. King Louis refused to grant me an audience."

Frederick smiled. "So Voltaire wrote me. If I were in Louis' place, I might be a trifle shy, too. However, that's irrelevant. I have no need of your services in France."

Maurice was becoming impatient. "Just what is it you want of me, Your Majesty?"

The King's smile was placating. "In return for the inconveniences you've suffered, Monsieur de Montauban, I've already instructed my Ministry of the Treasury to channel all trade with Great Britain through Montauban and Company. That should make you feel a little happier."

"It certainly does!" The arrangement would be worth a fortune each year.

"I have no intention of rescinding the order to my Treasury, even if you should find the idea of helping me distasteful," Frederick said. "I stress this, because I don't want to insult a man of means by trying to buy him."

His approach, Maurice thought, was as clever as it was smooth.

"On the other hand, I hope that as a humanitarian you'll see fit to work for a cause in which we both believe."

Maurice inclined his head, but said nothing.

King Frederick knew better than to expect a reply. "You're planning a visit to Vienna on behalf of your mercantile interests, I believe."

"I'm prepared to leave for Austria as soon as your Ministry of the Treasury and I can work out the details of our agreement, Your Majesty."

"I wish you good fortune in Vienna. The death of the Emperor Charles has left affairs there in something of a turmoil, and the accession of a woman to the throne hasn't improved matters, I'm sure. I'm told Maria Theresa has wit and beauty, but women are notoriously unstable rulers, and I've never held too high an opinion of the Hapsburgs, male or female."

"I'm not competent to judge them," Maurice said politely. "I only know that relations between England and Austria have been friendly since their alliance of thirty to forty years ago, and my grandfather and I are interested in the possibility of expanding our trade with them."

Frederick seemed to be brooding. "As partners in trade they might be reliable enough. But they still live in the Dark Ages, I'm afraid. Their Catholicism is more than a State religion—it's a crusade. Is it true, as Voltaire writes me," he asked abruptly, "that you believe Pope Benedict is right in his attempts to reconcile the Church with the Protestant powers?"

"Anything less is a mockery of Christianity, Your Majesty. Without religious peace there can be no lasting temporal peace."

Again Frederick indulged in his habit of rubbing his hands together. "I've found the perfect man for my mission! A Catholic—and the Austrians will accept no one but a Papist—who believes in the enlightened humanitarianism of our time! I'm more fortunate than I knew."

"As a British subject," Maurice said, "I couldn't accept a formal appointment as your representative, Your Majesty, no matter what the purpose."

"I need no reminders of the basic rules of diplomacy." For the first time Frederick sounded waspish, but immediately became blandly charming again. "What I need is far simpler. My father and the Emperor Charles quarreled for years over the rights to three Silesian duchies. The issue must be settled. Maria Theresa is determined to annex them, and make them Catholic, even though most of the people there are Protestants. I say they must be free to choose their own faiths, which they can do only as Prussians."

"You plan to annex the duchies?"

"Of course. When a prince believes in a righteous principle, he must be willing to fight for it. And I shall fight for Silesia. If the Austrians refuse to cede it to me, let Maria Theresa fight me, and I'll show her generals what a modern army can do. I grow impatient when I hear monarchs basing their claims to territory on past conquests. It's what our regiments do today that shapes the borders of a nation, and if you'll study a map, you'll see that Silesia is a natural geographical extension of Prussia. I want those duchies—and I shall have them."

Maurice had been wondering whether Frederick actually believed in the principles he had been expounding, whether he had been rationalizing or had merely been seeking a convenient excuse to expand his rule. Now he had made himself clear. In spite of his many subtle complexities as a human being, he was first and foremost a king, and therefore differed from other men. He wanted territory, and was making it very plain that, come what may, he would take it.

Maurice hastily revised some of his views on the waning power of princes and the universal respect for law.

"If Maria Theresa will cede me Silesia," Frederick said, "I've offered her a generous cash settlement, plus the right to take any part of Catholic Bavaria she wants to round out her borders. I couldn't be more cooperative! But she won't give me a direct answer, and I don't know why she's procrastinating. I must find out."

Maurice realized he had to brave the possible wrath of a monarch who had already proved he could be ruthless. "I couldn't serve you as an espionage agent, Your Majesty."

Frederick laughed as he refilled their glasses. "I have all the men, trained men, I require for that purpose. I know as much about the disposal of Maria Theresa's divisions as the Austrian general staff, and I feel sure she knows mine, too. These are technical details. What concerns me are her real motives, and no espionage agent could ferret them out for me. Too many wars have been fought because of technical miscalculations based on evidence supplied by

280

spies, who by the nature of their calling are men of an inferior breed."

His reasoning, Maurice thought, made sense.

"What I require is information on the real thinking of Maria Theresa and her ministers. Voltaire says we live in the first rational century since the dawn of civilization, and we must be worthy of our time. I'll go to war only if compromise fails. But I must base my decision on the judgment of a man whose intellect I trust, someone whom the Austrians will accept, not as my envoy, but as a welcome, disinterested neutral. That, Monsieur de Montauban, is the task I very much want you to perform for me."

Maurice sipped his aperitif.

"Don't make a hasty decision," Frederick said. "If you decline, you're under no obligation to me. If you accept, you won't find me ungrateful. We must nurture our idealists if there is to be genuine progress in this world. The question is so important to me that I beg you to think carefully before you give me a final answer."

Maurice had been doing a considerable amount of thinking ever since he had witnessed the plight of the Jews in Dresden. And although he still resented the way the Prussians had treated him, he had to admit that they had been clever. Certainly he would have rejected Frederick's proposal had it been made without the weeks of imprisonment that had preceded it.

"I accept Your Majesty's offer," he said.

The delighted Frederick embraced him. "You won't regret it, Monsieur de Montauban! Come along to dinner, and we'll celebrate."

The other guests were already gathered in the dining room, waiting, and Maurice was presented to a distinguished company that included three Prussian generals, two French poets, a noted Milanese composer who wrote songs for Frederick to play on his flute, and several philosophers. The attractive young ladies had vanished, and only men sat down at the table together.

The conversation, which ranged from the arts to theology to political affairs, was lively, candid and uninhibited. To Maurice's surprise, no one was in awe of Frederick, and his guests felt free to argue with him vehemently, as his equal. When he became insulting in several heated exchanges they taunted him by calling him Frederick the Great, a name which Prussian newspapers were using with increasing frequency. He accepted the teasing, laughing at himself, and Maurice gradually became convinced that here was a monarch unlike any other on earth. Only the memory of recent months spoiled his sense of pleasure.

The meal itself was a banquet. French dishes were served, all of them superbly prepared, and Maurice had never eaten a better prepared dinner. A number of French wines were poured, all of them excellent, and although King Frederick drank sparingly, he constantly urged the others to refill their cups. He was the perfect host, and Maurice understood why philosophers, poets and musicians were happy to spend months under his roof.

The talk continued to flow as the party adjourned to the drawing room, and soon thereafter the young women reappeared. One of them flirted boldly with Frederick, and he beckoned to her, hauling her onto his lap as he argued with one of the philosophers on the essence of human nature. For a time he fondled the girl absently, but gradually his caresses became more intimate, and finally he kissed the girl, unmindful of the company's presence.

Suddenly he stood, almost tumbling her to the floor, and slid an arm around her waist. "Continue your talk, my friends," he said, "and ring for more wine when you want it. I'll rejoin you shortly."

No one seemed in the least embarrassed when he and the young woman left the room.

Another of the girls, a full-lipped blonde, was fluttering her antimony-blackened lashes at Maurice, and he returned her gaze with interest.

But Colonel von Graebner, who had been present at the party from the start, tapped Maurice on the shoulder. "A word with you in private," he muttered.

They strolled out onto a terrace overlooking the woods, and Maurice thought the Colonel intended to tell him that no one but the King was permitted to make love to the girls.

"This is an unusual place," von Graebner said stiffly.

"It is," Maurice agreed, certain that no other monarch was capable of demonstrating such informality.

The Colonel stared at him. "I'm not sure you understand. What do you think of the women here?"

"They're very pretty."

"It's as I believed. You don't know." Von Graebner's voice became contemptuous as he added, "They aren't women."

For a moment his meaning wasn't clear, and Maurice turned to look at the blonde and two of "her" companions, who were still in the drawing room. Never had he seen such completely feminine creatures.

"If you share Frederick's tastes," the Colonel said, "they're yours for the taking. If not, beware."

Maurice didn't know what to say, but felt his skin crawl.

"In the old regime, one of my captains was a drunkard. Always he tried to persuade others to drink too much." Von Graebner paused. "So it is with Frederick. If he thinks you might be tempted, his harem will try to seduce you. If he thinks you are repelled, he'll try to trick you into making love to them."

282

"They're not for me."

"Then you'll be wise to ignore them."

Maurice thanked him, and when they returned to the drawing room, he refused to look in the direction of the "girl." Gradually, as he recovered from his initial shock and disgust, he realized his advantage in having learned of Frederick's weakness. Maurice no longer felt hobbled by a feeling of inferiority to someone of approximately his own age who had appeared to be so much wiser, stronger and more steadfast.

Suddenly, Maurice realized that although Montauban and Company would benefit from his present situation, his energies were being diverted to an irrelevant cause, the quarrel between two alien powers over several obscure central European duchies. He had agreed to help Frederick because the issues between peace and war, religious liberty and persecution had seemed to be clearly marked, and he had thought he would be serving his own ideals.

Yet a monarch who had thrown a British subject into prison simply because it had suited his own purposes was just as much a tyrant as a man devoted to freedom. Maurice had made an agreement from which it would be impossible to withdraw without arousing Frederick's anger. The privileges so casually granted to Montauban and Company could be as casually withdrawn. And the word of a king was elastic. He was bound by no code of honor other than that which he elected to interpret for himself.

1741

"We Austrians," said Stephanie von Starhemberg, "are the most complacent people in Europe. Perhaps you remember how bewildered I was when I visited London with Anton and Maria five years ago. That was because we, and I certainly include myself, refuse to accept any standards except our own."

Maurice looked across the drawing room in the Garden Palace of Anton Wenzel, Prince von Kaunitz-Rietberg, and his quick flush indicated he recalled every detail of his meetings in London with the Prince's lovely young sister-in-law. He had developed a strong interest in her at that time, but had subsequently tried to put her out of his mind, assuming she would marry an Austrian nobleman. However, she was still single, miraculously, and had become even more attractive, if possible.

No young man could fail to be affected by her thick masses of blonde hair, eyes that seemingly changed from blue to green according to her mood, and the exquisite, slender figure of a patrician who spent hours each day riding a horse. He had found it difficult to concentrate on anyone or anything but Stephanie since his arrival in Vienna, and considered himself fortunate beyond measure because she showed such an obviously strong interest in him, too. In fact, he sometimes wondered how they found so much to discuss when they spent most of their waking hours together.

"I'm afraid," he said, more interested in the girl than in her opinions, "that I don't quite know what you mean by complacent."

Stephanie's laugh was infectious. "You're like everyone else. You know nothing about us. There are more Hungarians, Bohemians, Slavs and other foreigners in our empire than Austrians. The influence of the Turkish invaders is still so strong here that women have fewer rights than in any other civilized country, yet we're ruled by an Empress only two years older than I am. And I assure you, Maria Theresa may be only a woman and only twenty-four, but her husband is no more than her consort."

"We've had women rulers in England, too. Queen Anne——"

"It's not the same." A ruby ring on Stephanie's hand caught the light as she gestured. "This house is smaller and less ornate than your grandfather's, but we call it a palace. You don't even call yourself Lord de Montauban——"

"I have no rank in the English nobility."

"——but here everyone has a grand, impressive title. They're so common no one is impressed. Let me think for a moment. Oh, yes. Except for Jews in the ghettos, poor things, we have only one faith, so we take our Catholicism for granted. The Jesuits are dedicated men, but the rest of us are sybaritic barbarians."

As nearly as Maurice could judge, she was serious in her criticism of her nation's faults. It was astonishing to find a feminine and attractive young woman so concerned and well informed.

"I can cite you still another example of our inconsistencies. Nobles are expected to live on their inherited incomes, but if their families are poor, they must starve gracefully, as Maria and I did. Anton's father was a count who lost his estates at the gaming tables, and you'd think Anton would be admired for doing such brilliant work as managing director of the City Bank of Vienna. The Empress was so impressed she rewarded him by making him a prince, but we're so stubbornly provincial that nearly everyone at court snubs him."

A deep male voice joined in the conversation from the entrance. "The worst of our faults," Anton von Kaunitz said with a broad smile, "has been that of allowing the Jesuits to educate young ladies. These women know all our weaknesses, and parade them before us. I must apologize for Stephanie."

284

The girl became scarlet.

Maurice tried to defend her as, grinning, he exchanged bows with his host. "I've enjoyed myself."

"Of course." Kaunitz, obviously fond of his sister-in-law, looked at her with mock severity. "The Jesuits gave her a sharp tongue, but she honey-coats it with her beauty. If she were plain, she wouldn't dare talk so freely."

Stephanie rose and shook out the full skirt of her pale yellow silk gown. "I can tell you a great deal more, Maurice."

"I'd like nothing more than to hear it," he replied, a ring of sincerity in his voice indicating he was being more than gallant.

Her poise vanished, and she became flustered.

Kaunitz delicately raised an eyebrow. "You shall have your opportunity at dinner, and I believe Maria has engaged a box for four at the opera this evening."

Stephanie made no attempt to conceal her pleasure as she curtsied and left the room.

Maurice watched her until she disappeared.

Kaunitz coughed diplomatically. "I was going to apologize for keeping you waiting, but that would be superfluous, I gather." He offered a *segaro* to his guest, then took one himself. "I was delayed at the court. Our real problem—and I sound like Stephanie—is that only the Empress makes decisions of consequence. It seems very natural to you and to me that there should be an agreement between Montauban and the new Kaunitz trading company at Ostend, but I've had to submit the decision to Maria Theresa. She reserves her approval until she learns more about you, which means she'll rely on her woman's intuition when you're presented to her."

Several Austrians had told Maurice that the Empress rarely granted audiences to foreigners, and he was delighted.

Kaunitz cautioned him with a frown. "You may be forced to stay in Vienna longer than you'd planned. Maria Theresa's appointments are scheduled weeks ahead." He took his guest's arm. "Let's walk in the rose garden. My wife can't tolerate the odors of tobacco."

They walked out through a pair of high French doors into an inner courtyard where, even now, in the early spring, roses of five or six shades were blooming.

"This house was given its name because of these flowers," Kaunitz said dryly. "I know nothing about roses, but Garden Palace sounds so grand that I cultivate them."

It appeared that the man shared his sister-in-law's self-mocking cynicism, and Maurice wondered whether all Austrian aristocrats believed in such deprecation. Certainly Kaunitz had every reason to be proud of his achievements. Although physically short, dark and deceptively unprepossessing, his bank had become one of the most powerful international forces in Europe, his new trading venture promised to be equally successful, and he was so active in his nation's affairs that, at the age of thirty-one, he had already become one of the young Empress' most influential advisors.

"You've just come from Berlin," Kaunitz said abruptly, "and we've been told you've met Frederick the Great. Our proposed partnership will prosper if you can give me some idea of his present thinking."

It appeared that the Austrians kept themselves well informed, and Maurice smiled. "His Majesty asked me to find out the intentions of your Empress."

Kaunitz' laugh was strained. "He doesn't trust normal diplomatic channels, either. Everyone will suffer if there's a war, and I'm afraid we'll have one soon. Our claim to the Silesian duchies is the most valid, but everyone clamors for them. Frederick insists they're his, the Spaniards want them, and even France is entering a demand, although her grounds are legally absurd."

"Everyone but the Silesians themselves will decide the issue." International diplomacy, Maurice thought, was irrational.

Kaunitz did not smile. "Silesia is merely the excuse, as usual. Vatican Hill is to blame for the present tensions."

Maurice was startled.

"Pope Benedict is too conscientious a Christian for the world's good." Kaunitz' dark eyes reflected his sardonic attitude. "Instead of rallying the Catholic nations, he preaches the doctrine of loving one's neighbor. He's so pious he actually believes that everyone else worries as he does about human souls. He's so naïve he doesn't realize that the rulers of Europe are wild animals with insatiable appetites for land and glory. You know Frederick, so you understand me."

"I've met few kings, so I'm not in a position to compare them," Maurice said tactfully.

Kaunitz puffed hard on his *segaro*. "Frederick knows the world is amused by his personal tastes, so he insists on proving his valor. Louis of France is a man of little talent who is furious because he hasn't acquired his grandfather's reputation. Philip of Spain is humiliated because Frenchmen hold all the posts of real power in his country, and he considers himself virtually their prisoner—which he is. And our Empress must stand up to these men. If she doesn't prove she's their equal in ruthless resolve, they'll devour her. And when war comes, England won't be able to afford the luxury of neutrality. She'd lose her commercial standing on the Continent."

"You're simplifying complex issues, Anton."

"No, I'm merely stripping them to their essentials. The nations of Europe are like swordsmen. Each stands alone, uncertain of his friends and even less sure of his foes. Soon the comedy will end, however, and when the inevitable alliances are formed, the blood will flow."

286

"I can't accept the inevitability of such alliances," Maurice said. "The English have no desire to become involved in the quarrels of others, I know, and I believe Frederick wants an honorable accommodation with Austria."

"He considers only his own terms honorable." Kaunitz flicked a long *segaro* ash onto the gravel path. "But neither he nor any of the other swordsmen recognize the real issues at stake. The one man who knows them is Pope Benedict, and he elects to close his eyes to them. Ever since Martin Luther began corrupting the souls of the faithful, there has been only one real cause of conflicts between nations, as we proved when we fought the Turks. All wars are holy wars."

"You exaggerate!" Maurice was scornful.

"I make you a flat prediction. Frederick resembles the Jesuits. He makes obeisances to the philosophical gibberish of our time and pretends he seeks a greater freedom for all faiths. I shock you, I see——"

"I don't regard such attitudes as gibberish."

"Then I feel sorry for you, because you'll discover that the Protestant majority in England have little sympathy for Catholics when they're at war with Catholic powers. Prussia and England are natural allies, and the Dutch will join them, as they have in the past. The anti-Christ always has its advocates. France and Spain have little in common with us except faith, but that faith will suffice. Their regiments will support Austria's. War could be avoided if Pope Benedict issued an appeal to all Catholic nations to join together. The forces of the anti-Christ would be afraid to take the field against such a powerful foe. But he's been fooled into believing that this is a rational age and that men can be taught to bury their differences. His weakness encourages pagon zealots like Frederick."

Maurice was aghast. If a man of Kaunitz' stature actually saw the nations of Europe divided on a basis of religion, the so-called enlightened approach of the period was a myth cultivated by a handful of myopic optimists. "I hope," he said, trying to find common ground, "that your new holy war won't destroy the trade relations you and I are trying to build."

"Our commerce will be interrupted," Kaunitz said cynically, "but it will recover. People develop a liking for other nations' merchandise, and no one asks whether a leather purse or an iron skillet has been made by Christians or infidels. Two hundred years ago we burned heretics at the stake, and the only advantage I see in our approach today is that you and I recognize the hypocrisy of the world for what it is—and happily pocket our share of the profits."

"If you're right," Maurice said, sudden anger disrupting the calm of their discussion, "there's no hope that different nations and religions will achieve an understanding."

"In my view, there's none, and I thank God I'm not alone in seeing the dangers, or innocents like Benedict and the Jesuits will open the doors to heretics. Frederick of Prussia would destroy us by destroying our faith, and we can survive only by standing firm against his kind."

Maurice knew Frederick's response to such an attitude would be swift and violent, and he could only hope that Maria Theresa proved more malleable than her counselor.

Stephanie von Starhemberg rode her mare with the easy grace of a young cavalry officer, galloping at such breakneck speed on the path deep in the Vienna Woods that Maurice was hard pressed to keep pace with her. For a while he had been alarmed for her safety, but when he saw she was completely at home in the saddle he concentrated on trying to win their race. Only at the last moment, when he saw the shore of a little lake directly ahead, did he deliberately fall back a pace and allow her the triumph of victory.

Stephanie dismounted, and turned breathlessly to Maurice as he joined her. "You purposely let me win!" she said accusingly.

"No," he lied, "I tried my best."

"I've ridden Rudi too often not to know his gait. You reined him in at the end."

"Then I must apologize."

She relented. "I hate to be granted favors simply because I'm a woman."

"It's difficult to avoid granting them to you." He took a bottle of Hungarian *tokaj* wine from his saddlebag, tied it to a length of cord and immersed it in the lake to cool it. "Are you always so wilfully independent?"

The girl considered the question for a moment. "Almost always," she admitted. "But I find it difficult being a lady in Austria. Men defer to us and pamper us, but they always think of us as their inferiors. It was easy for Maria. She was never taught to use her mind, and she accepts whatever Anton says to her. I've found it's best to keep quiet when I hear his bigoted ideas, and I suppose it's good training. My husband will think as he does, I'm sure."

"Are you betrothed?" Maurice asked in surprise, helping her spread a blanket on the carpet of pine needles.

Stephanie shook her head. "No, but nearly everyone in Austria shares his opinions. The few who were taught by the Jesuits before they were forced to close their schools are afraid to speak out. The bishops are very firm, and everyone is expected to agree with them."

"Pope Benedict doesn't agree, and neither do I."

She removed a band from her hair and shook it loose. "Then I'm right about you. I've noticed that you say very little when Anton speaks on important matters, but you look disapproving."

"He isn't the sort who can be persuaded to change his mind. I doubt if he's amenable to reason."

Stephanie laughed. "Father Radetsky will think I've been influencing you." She saw Maurice's blank look, and hastened to explain. "I've asked him to share our cold chicken and wine. Although I'm allowed more freedom than most, it isn't considered proper for an unmarried woman to spend an afternoon alone with a man in the Vienna Woods. I hope you don't mind."

"Of course not," Maurice said gallantly.

"Thank you. There are many reasons I want you to meet him." She sat on the blanket, and motioned him to a place beside her. "Father Radetsky was the headmaster of my school and my own principal tutor. Now he is nothing. He is a member of a noble family, but they think his ideas are radical, and will not make him welcome in their homes. It's sad, and frightening, too."

"He's a Jesuit, of course."

The girl nodded.

"And it isn't accidental that you've chosen the woods for a meeting of your own with him. Prince von Kaunitz wouldn't want him as a guest."

Stephanie glanced at him for an instant, then looked away.

"I won't give you away." Maurice reached out to touch her.

She made no attempt to withdraw her hand, and remained silent, staring out at the pines on the far side of the lake, then suddenly said, "I feel sorry for Maria Theresa."

Her remark was so unexpected that Maurice didn't know what to reply.

"Lottie von Mauchenheim, who is one of her maids-in-waiting, was my schoolmate. She says the Empress wants friendship with every country so she can do more for her own subjects. But everyone at court, even her husband, believes Frederick of Prussia is Satan come to earth."

"He's a damnably clever man who wants a great many things in this world. But I believe he's devoted to the cause of reason."

"Then there's nothing to fear from him, is there?"

"I'm not sure. He and your Empress might not think the same things reasonable." Maurice found it difficult to help someone else when his own thinking had become so muddled, but the last thing he wanted to discuss with this lovely and desirable girl was the dispute between Prussia and Austria. "How much do you know of my background?" he demanded.

The sudden change of subject did not appear to surprise her. "I've met your grandfather, remember, and I've heard him speak of dreadful things in France years ago. I agree with him, but I'm sure Anton would think Louis the Fourteenth was right."

"I've been trying to regain the Montauban title. It's partly a matter of good business, partly pride in my ancestry, but I've had no success. I, and my descendants after me, may spend our days as commoners in England."

"I don't think very highly of titles."

It was then that he kissed her; lightly. And for a minute afterward they stopped talking.

It required only another half hour (fortunately Father Radetsky's arrival had been delayed) for them to decide they were in love. They kissed again, and then Maurice proposed marriage. They kissed a third time, and sank onto the blanket.

"I believe I've appeared at just the right moment."

The couple struggled to a sitting position, and Maurice saw a tall, gray-haired priest in unadorned black.

Color rose in Stephanie's face as her companion struggled to his feet, but she retained her poise. "Father Radetsky, she said, "permit me to present my future husband, Monsieur de Montauban."

It occurred to the embarrassed Maurice as he shook the priest's hand that his earnest proposal of marriage had not been formally accepted.

"Accept my congratulations, sir," Father Radetsky said, and turned to the girl. "You mentioned nothing of a betrothal in the note I received from you this morning. Do your sister and brother-in-law know of it?"

"Everything was just decided in the past few minutes." She was still blushing.

"Anton may have other ideas."

"I think not," she said firmly. "He and Maurice have business plans that will earn Anton a large income. He may not approve of Englishmen, or of anyone who doesn't agree with him in all things, but he allows nothing to interfere with his profits."

"You have a Catholic heritage, sir, which should stand in your favor with Prince von Kaunitz," the Jesuit said. "I wish you well, but don't think you can tame Stephanie. She'd fight the battles of my Order with the Austrian hierarchy if I didn't restrain her. It will be something of a relief to be rid of her," he added with a grin. "I live in constant dread that she'll make my situation worse than it is by pleading my cause with Cardinal von Hecker."

"I know nothing of your situation, Father," Maurice said, "but I'm not sure I can promise I can control her."

"No man can do that," Father Radetsky said.

"Sit down, both of you," Stephanie commanded, pleased that they seemed to like each other. "I've been planning this meeting for days, and there's so much I want to discuss."

"She is a martinet," the priest said with an exaggerated sigh as he obeyed.

Maurice took the bottle of *tokaj* from the lake and cut the heavy wax seal from the top with the small knife he carried in his waistcoat pocket. His own happiness was so intense it was difficult for him to think of anything else.

"It is better for Stephanie if she does not advertise her friendship with members of my Order," the priest said.

"I don't care who knows my feelings," the girl replied while removing food from a wicker hamper.

"I do," Father Radetsky said soberly, "and if this young man intends to marry you, so does he. Stephanie," he explained to Maurice, "is being reckless in support of a cause that's lost. She can do herself great harm."

Maurice poured wine into three glasses of exquisite, rainbow-hued crystal as Father Radetsky continued.

"The Society of Jesus recognizes no earthly authority except that of the Pope himself. That's part of the problem. Cardinals and bishops can't force us to accept their policies, nor can kings and queens. We're devoted to the cause of truth as we see it. We try to think in terms of decades, so it's inevitable that the short-sighted should disagree with us."

Stephanie was placing chicken cutlets, a cold purée of lettuce and peas, tiny loaves of bread filled with chopped nuts and mounds of ginger-flavored pancakes on gold-rimmed plates. "If Maria Theresa could do as she please, there would be no problem."

"I'm not prepared to say who is responsible for her decisions," the priest said. "Only Catholics are allowed to worship in Austria," he told Maurice, "except that no one cares what the Jews do behind the walls of their ghettos, of course. The Society of Jesus believes these restrictions will lead to rebellions, perhaps full-scale civil wars. There are a quarter of a million Hussites in Bohemia, and almost as many Lutherans in the South German duchies. No one has ever taken a census of the Moslems in the sections of the Empire we conquered from the Turks, but there are a great many of them. Regardless of whether we agree with their beliefs, we're convinced they should be granted the unlimited right to worship as they please. Repression always leads to violence, as you undoubtedly know, sir."

"You stand with Pope Benedict," Maurice said.

"Yes, His Holiness and Frederick of Prussia, who has offered us sanctuary. I have no way of gauging the sincerity of Frederick's principles, but I'm inclined to suspect he's happy to stir up fresh troubles in Austria."

"I wouldn't put it past him," Maurice said.

"Now you know our situation, sir. His Holiness refuses to interfere in what he considers national political matters, so he won't help us. The Society of Jesus stands alone, not for the first time. Stephanie, how much longer must we stare politely at this food? We're starved!"

The girl handed them linen serviettes and cutlery of solid silver. "Some of the Viennese Jesuits have accepted the invitation of King Frederick and have gone to Berlin," she said. "I've been trying to persuade Father Radetsky to leave, too, but he won't listen to me. I've been hoping that you might help me, Maurice. Perhaps you can convince him that Frederick isn't the Devil's deputy on earth."

"In the first place," Maurice said, "I'm not certain he isn't. And what's more, I can't presume to advise someone else about a situation he understands intimately and I don't know at all."

Stephanie sighed in exasperation.

"Thank you, sir," the priest said. "What this child fails to realize is that I am an Austrian. A patriot doesn't run off to exile when his country needs him."

The man's attitude was similar to that of Maurice's martyred great-uncle. The true heroes of Christianity were those who fought their hopeless battles quietly.

"You don't know what will happen to you if you stay here," Stephanie cried. "If you heard Anton making dark predictions every day, but refusing to explain his threats, you wouldn't be so complacent."

"I'm far from complacent, I assure you," the Jesuit said soberly. "I fear for Austria, and I weep for her. As for me, it doesn't matter. The worst they can do to me is expel me from the land."

Stephanie turned to Maurice in mute appeal.

He shook his head. "I can't come between any man and his conscience."

She was on the verge of tears. "What will you do, Father?"

"There's only one thing I can do. I pray that God will grant Maria Theresa the wisdom and strength to avoid catastrophes that would weaken this nation for all time."

Maria Theresa, Archduchess of Austria, Queen of Hungary, Queen of Bohemia, Duchess of Styria, Carniola and Carinthia, Lady Margrave of Moravia, and Countess of Tyrol was called the Empress because it was a foregone conclusion that her husband, Francis of Lorraine, Grand Duke of Tuscany, would be elected Holy Roman Emperor by the cardinals and temporal monarchs of the German-speaking states. Until his election, however, Francis remained in the background as a silent consort, and the Empress reigned alone in her vast domain.

Members of the diplomatic community claimed that the young woman with blue eyes, exceptionally long lashes and delicate mouth, who had been spared the angular features of male Hapsburgs, used her overpowering femininity as her primary weapon in conducting affairs of state with members of the opposite sex. They were correct. She used antimony to darken her lashes, wore rouge on her lips and dressed in seemingly modest gowns that, nevertheless, subtly called attention to her charms. She also had the disconcerting habit of smiling steadily into a man's eyes when he addressed her.

August, Cardinal von Hecker, primate of Austria, found it difficult to organize his thoughts. "The Jesuits," he said, "are playing into the hands of that damnable Prussian tyrant. In my opinion they're traitors." He failed to realize that this was the third time he had made the assertion.

Prince Anton von Kaunitz came to the clergyman's assistance. "His Eminence is right, madame. We should make two moves simultaneously. It has already pleased Your Imperial Majesty to agree that the Prussian demands for the Silesian duchies must be rejected. You have also agreed that the power of the Jesuits must be broken. We must take action that the whole world understands!"

Maria Theresa sat back in her throne-chair, taking care that the strands of hair in her high, powdered wig did not snag on her initials, embroidered in gold thread above her head. Her slender fingers brushed gently against the fringe of purple velvet on the arms of her chair, and she looked like a hurt and bewildered little girl. "Pope Benedict will be very annoyed and hurt if I send his Jesuits to prison——"

"Benedict spends all his time reading sacred literature," Cardinal von Hecker interrupted, tugging at his gray-flecked beard. "In the year he's held the highest office in Christendom he's done nothing to curb the spread of heresy, and he never will. What's more, madame, he isn't courageous enough to rebuke anyone."

"I'd be mortified if I were the first," she replied in her sweet, soft voice.

"I offer you my protection!" the Cardinal thundered.

Maria Theresa's blue eyes widened. "Are you telling me, Your Eminence, that you're more powerful than His Holiness?"

Von Hecker was embarrassed by her gentle thrust, but again Kaunitz came to his rescue. "He is, madame. Pope Benedict has abdicated his place in the world. But Cardinal von Hecker fights for God's justice on earth."

The Empress regarded him thoughtfully. "Does it really matter so much if I leave the Jesuits untouched? Surely it's enough to send them into exile."

"You'll encourage every rebel in the Empire unless you treat them firmly." Kaunitz wished she would stop staring at him. "Let the younger priests go, and good riddance to them. But send the real troublemakers to prison for the rest of their days, and hang the ringleaders like Radetsky. If you don't, there will be revolutions in Prague and Budapest and Graz—and a score of lesser cities."

"There are heretics in all of them," the Cardinal added pompously, "just waiting for a signal."

"How could it be," Maria Theresa asked ingenuously, "that members of the Society of Jesus are leaders of a revolt of heretics? Aren't they devoted priests who take their vows seriously?"

"They're power hungry," Cardinal von Hecker said.

"They're misguided," Kaunitz added. "They should be concerning themselves with administering the sacraments, as other priests do. Instead they dabble in political matters beyond their understanding."

"Even though they attend special schools for thirteen years before they're ordained as priests?" The Empress sounded bewildered.

"They're taught," Kaunitz said patiently, "by other Jesuits. The ignorant teach the ignorant, the blind lead the blind."

She dropped the subject for the moment, and there was a new note of firmness in her voice as she said, "I cannot and will not declare war against Prussia."

The two men looked at her in dismay.

"It's bad enough when kings are aggressors. But people are always eager to think the worst of a woman. Irene of Byzantium was maligned, and so was Margaret of the Netherlands. If I declare war, I'll be called greedy, and all Europe will sympathize with Frederick. But if he makes the first move, everyone will feel sorry for a helpless girl."

For an instant Kaunitz seriously considered the possibility that she might flutter her lashes, but she spared him that.

"I still hope," she said, "that Frederick can be persuaded to negotiate with me."

"Your troops," Kaunitz said, "should be prepared for any emergency."

"They are," she replied crisply, but immediately softened again. "I've thought of suggesting a personal meeting with King Frederick to resolve our differences, but I'm afraid it wouldn't accomplish much. His dislike of women would prejudice him against me. Still, I hope we can arrange a peaceful compromise that will hurt no one's dignity, and I feel we must make the effort. Anton, you've mentioned your new English partner who is joining your family. You've told me he's an unofficial envoy of Frederick's, is that correct?"

"Not precisely, madame. He's been given no power to negotiate."

"Bring him to me tomorrow morning, and tell the chamberlain to rearrange my appointments."

Kaunitz bowed his head.

Cardinal von Hecker was unhappy. "Too many compromises will cost Your Imperial Majesty the throne."

Maria Theresa stroked the velvet arms of her chair.

"If you don't show strength and courage, the kings will think you're a weak, foolish young woman. They'll band together and tear apart the carcass of Austria." The Cardinal's voice became louder and more authoritative. "Deal with Prussia as you will. I'm no expert in temporal matters. But I beg you, madame, don't permit the Jesuits to defy you. Crush them, and you'll find Frederick more amenable."

The Empress' lack of experience made her uncertain, and she glanced at Kaunitz for confirmation.

"There's no other way, madame."

The fluttering of her hands was a genuine expression of her sense of inadequacy. "Do what you think best," she murmured. "Tell the chancellor to draw up the necessary decrees."

The solid Gothic bulk of the Cathedral of St. Stephen seemed to dominate the Hofburg, but the royal palace, a collection of oddly matched buildings constructed over a period of more than five hundred years, comprised a world of its own. Everywhere the wealth and pomp that had so long been trademarks of the house of Hapsburg were evident. Hussars, wearing boots that covered their kneecaps, tight breeches, and gold-encrusted capelets thrown over one shoulder, stood on sentry duty with drawn sabers held a fraction of an inch from the visors of their plumed, silver helmets. The floors of priceless mosaic tiles were covered with even more precious rugs captured from the Ottomans in many wars, the drapes at the sides of the high windows had been made by a staff of weavers hired for that purpose alone, and the crystal chandeliers in every room, even the antechambers, were so valuable that an assistant chamberlain had no duties other than to act as their custodian.

But, in spite of the splendor, there were innumerable small touches that made the home of the Hapsburgs unlike any other royal court in Europe. Nestled in corridor niches near statues and paintings executed by artists of a dozen nations were bowls of candied fruits and other sweetmeats that courtiers, officers and guests were expected to nibble if they felt hungry. Three fountains strategically placed near the throne room, the imperial council chamber and the private apartments of Maria Theresa and her consort splashed new May wine day and night—Sundays and holy days excluded—and goblets of cut glass lined nearby racks. No one at the Hofburg ever went thirsty.

Sausages, cheeses, pickled vegetables and an assortment of breads were always available in a dining chamber for those who found waiting for an appointment with the ruler or members of her staff tedious. And Maria Theresa had added a typical touch of her own: mirror-lined rooms near every hall in the palace, where ladies could inspect themselves before appearing in public.

The Empress' private audience chamber was elegantly modest. A small room, it had been painted a pale shade of gold, and the chairs, tables and bric-a-brac were done in various shades of gold, too. Frilly curtains of light yellow covered the windows, and in one corner, instead of a desk, stood a sewing table onto which an unfinished royal seal in cloth-of-silver embroidery had been thrown. The overall effect was that of a boudoir rather than a reigning monarch's workroom.

Maurice de Montauban felt uncomfortable when he was admitted, alone, to the chamber, but Maria Theresa quickly put him at his ease. She congratulated him on his betrothal, complimenting him on his taste as well as his good fortune. She flattered him by offering him a dish of English rock candy, which he hadn't eaten since leaving London, and she surprised him by demonstrating a considerable knowledge of his personal problems.

"I was sorry to hear of your failure at Versailles," she said. "I can't pretend to know why King Louis found it inconvenient to receive you, but it's my opinion he would have strengthened his nobility by granting your request."

It was difficult for Maurice to realize that this charming young woman was the almost absolute ruler of more than ten million people who spoke more than thirty tongues. He inclined his head to show his gratitude.

"Anton von Kaunitz has told me something of your joint commercial plans. I know nothing of finances," she lied, "but he sounded very optimistic."

"If there is no war, Your Imperial Majesty, we should do well."

"That brings us to the reason for this meeting," she said with a smile. "What's your impression of King Frederick?"

Maurice couldn't bring himself to tell her he thought she and the Prussian ruler exuded the same kind of near-hypnotic charm. "He's a man of intellect, wit and stubborn convictions."

"But he thinks me stubborn because I won't cede my rights to Silesia."

"He's determined to win those duchies, madame."

Maria Theresa looked wistful and helpless. "I'm just as determined to keep them," she said.

Maurice was not fooled. "I'm no diplomat, madame. I can only repeat what King Frederick told me. He's willing to offer you a number of concessions if you'll give up your claims to Silesia. I'm not familiar with the details——"

"I am, and his offer doesn't interest me."

Maurice found the unwavering intensity of her blue eyes unnerving. "King Frederick asked me to stop in Berlin on my journey west. What shall I tell him?"

"I can only hope you've formed a favorable impression of me."

He realized she was deliberately making his task as complicated as she could. "I'd be impertinent if I expressed my opinion too candidly, madame. But I'm afraid King Frederick has no interest in my personal views. He doesn't trust ambassadors and ministers——"

"He trusts no one!"

"——so he asked me for an informal report that might reflect the present situation more accurately. Do you wish me to inform him that you won't change your stand on the Silesian duchies?"

"If he tries to take them by force, he'll be damned on two counts. I can promise him that the whole world will condemn him for attacking a woman. And I shall rally every Catholic nation to a sacred cause."

"Madame, a holy war would be as harmful to Catholics as it would to Protestants."

The Empress' manner changed instantly. "The audience is at an end. You have leave to retire."

Clouds of blue tobacco smoke drifted upward through the rambler rose vines in the enclosed, open square of the Garden Palace as Maurice and Anton von Kaunitz paced up and down the gravel walk.

"I suppose it's just as well to humor Stephanie and come back next year for a big wedding," Maurice said. "I was disappointed when she insisted there wasn't time to be married and come with me now, but with war almost certain to break out, you and I will have to review our situation in another six to twelve months."

"I'm wondering how we can maintain trade relations if we should be on opposite sides," Kaunitz said, chewing on his cigar. "It will be inconvenient."

"If the Protestant and Catholic nations should take up arms against each other, I'm afraid I'd have to suspend our operations until the end of the war."

The Austrian raised an eyebrow. "I hope you aren't forgetting you're a Catholic."

"I hope you aren't forgetting I'm a British subject, Anton. And I'm totally opposed to war on religious grounds."

"We intend to win by any means available. When do you plan to leave?"

"In two days, if that's convenient."

"I suggest you go tomorrow instead. I'm neither being inhospitable nor trying to separate you and Stephanie, but I must tell you something in strict confidence. The borders are being closed at midnight on the day after tomorrow. Don't go due north by way of Moravia and Bohemia, because the imperial regiments there won't let you pass. If you leave early tomorrow, you can cross into Bavaria by the following evening, provided you don't loiter on the road. I must apologize for the inconvenience, but the orders are very strict, and no permits are being granted to anyone after the frontier has been sealed."

As a general rule, borders were closed for only one reason. "Is Austria that close to a declaration of war?"

Kaunitz shook his head. "It's war of a different kind. A band of traitors was given a chance to leave the country, but now it will be too late. Their leaders will hang, and the rest will go to prison. Once we've proved to the world that our patience is limited, the Prussians may be less eager to attack us."

His reasoning was specious, but Maurice knew it would be a waste of effort to argue that Frederick wouldn't be deterred by Austrian demonstrations of firmness in their internal affairs. Besides, the information Kaunitz had just revealed was of far greater immediate importance. Maurice tried to sound casual as he said, "If I'm going to change my plans, I should tell Stephanie at once."

Kaunitz' amused, slightly patronizing smile was the kind so frequently bestowed on young lovers. "Of course. Our business talks are finished for the present, so I urge you to devote the rest of your stay to her."

They went inside, and a servant was sent upstairs for Stephanie, who had not expected to see Maurice so early in the day, and took her time completing her toilet. Both men were waiting for her when she finally came down to her brother-in-law's study.

"I'm anxious to spend the morning with you," Maurice said.

"I'm so sorry. I promised Maria I'd help her shop for some watered silk she wants for a new gown." Something in his expression warned her this was no ordinary request. "But I'm sure she wouldn't mind going alone or waiting until another day."

"Good. Change into your riding habit so we can dine at the tavern in Klosterneuburg you mentioned to me the other day." He strolled with her into the corridor, beyond the hearing of Kaunitz, who was beaming at them. "While you're changing," he murmured, "write a note to Father Radetsky, asking him to meet us in the Vienna Woods as quickly as he can ride out there. But don't give the letter to one of the Kaunitz servants to deliver. We'll get someone outside to do it."

"At the least, Father, you'll be imprisoned," Maurice said, "but I suspect the regime intends to hang you."

"I'm sure of it." Stephanie was in tears. "Everyone knows that you and Father Braun and Father von Weisel are the leaders of the Jesuits in Austria.

The priest looked up at the top branches of a spreading white pine. "I'm grateful for your warning. With God's help the members of the Order can scatter in time to avoid arrest, and perhaps some will cross the border safely."

"What will you do?" she asked.

The Jesuit shrugged. "I've never thought of myself as a candidate for martyrdom, but it would be cowardly to run away."

"Your execution would help no one," Maurice said. "Go, while you still have the chance."

"It may be too late for me now," Father Radetsky replied wearily. "I was followed when I started out to meet you, and it wasn't easy to lose the man. Those agents for the Ministry of the Interior are leeches."

"All the more reason for you to go!" Stephanie exclaimed.

Maurice had been undergoing an inner struggle, and reached a decision. "Come with me, Father. You'll have to disguise yourself, of course, so I'll gladly give you some of my clothes to wear. You're not quite as tall as I am, but they should fit you reasonably well."

"No!" Stephanie clutched his arm. "Tomorrow may be too late. If others of the Order are seen leaving Vienna, the government will know they've been warned. And Father Radetsky will be taken into custody earlier than they had planned. They'll do anything to make an example of him and Father Braun."

"She's probably right," the Jesuit said. "One can try to remake the world, but sometimes it is impossible to escape one's own destiny."

Stephanie refused to accept defeat. "You'll have to leave today," she told Maurice.

"Anton would think it very strange," he said.

She tapped her foot as she puzzled over the problem, and then smiled. "It's quite simple, really. I'll come with you, too."

Both men stared at her.

"I'll leave a note for Maria and Anton, saying we've eloped. And so we shall. Nothing could be more natural or plausible, and they'll accept the story without question. What they won't know is that Father Radetsky will travel with us."

The priest chuckled wryly. "I had no idea when I taught Stephanie logic that she'd find a practical application for abstract principles."

Maurice considered her plan. "It might be very difficult for us to leave Vienna. If the Ministry of the Interior is keeping watch over Father Radetsky, they'll assign still more men to follow him after losing him once today."

"Then he can't go back to the city," Stephanie said.

"I must," the priest replied, a note of finality in his voice. "I can't save myself at the expense of the others. I can make no attempt to leave until I've warned them."

Maurice respected his decision. "Then we'll find a way." He kicked absently at a small mound of pine needles. "Could you meet us later this afternoon at the Danube waterfront, Father?"

The priest nodded. "You've learned much about Vienna in your short visit here. Men from the Ministry of the Interior aren't popular in the artisans' districts, and the people who live there are devout."

"Frankly," Maurice said, "I knew nothing of those advantages. It occurred to me that a barge belonging to Anton von Kaunitz' trading company tied up at the Emperor Charles wharf last week, and is scheduled to leave again fairly soon with a load of cargo for Regensburg and Ulm. The last place anyone would look for you—or us—would be one of Anton's own barges."

Stephanie was so excited she hugged him. "That will be perfect!"

Maurice put his hands on her shoulders and held her at arm's length. "This will be no holiday, you know. If anything goes wrong and we're caught, you and I will be punished for helping a supposed traitor escape. I'm not certain I can allow you to take the risk."

"I much prefer that Stephanie remain behind," Father Radetsky said.

"I refuse," the girl declared flatly. "If you go without me, a whole regiment of imperial Hussars will be searching for you by sundown."

The men looked at each other, and Maurice was torn by his love for Stephanie and his desire to save the Jesuit from certain death.

"You have no choice," Stephanie told them. "The decision is made."

For the first time Father Radetsky lost his composure. "Then may God keep watch over us and protect us from harm."

The barge was a cumbersome, ungainly craft with a deck of rough planks, a crowded cabin containing four narrow bunks and a stove used for both cooking and heat, two old sails of limp canvas, and a crude shelter similar to a sentry's box to protect the man who sat at the tiller in the stern. The crew consisted of the barge's owner, Max Grüning, a taciturn man in his fifties, and his equally uncommunicative son, Adolf.

About an hour before sundown the three fugitives went on board, Father Radetsky wearing one of Maurice's long capes to conceal his somber clerical garb. Stephanie, on her own initiative, had dressed in an inconspicuous gown of plum-colored silk, with a matching cloak and a broad-brimmed bonnet to hide her blonde hair. Maurice deposited their leather traveling boxes on the deck and led them to the cabin, where the proprietor and his son were eating a meal of sausage and bread.

Grüning wiped his mouth on the back of his dirty sleeve and stood.

"I happen to know," Maurice said, "that you carry cargo for Prince von Kaunitz, and that you're sailing tomorrow for Bavaria. We'll make it worth your while if you'll leave right now."

"I still have some cargo to take on board in the morning," Grüning replied, apparently neither disturbed nor surprised by the unusual request.

Maurice pressed two newly-minted gold thalers that bore Maria Theresa's likeness into his hand.

"Of course," the man said, "I could always take on some bales of wool at Linz."

Maurice gave him two more thalers.

"His Highness won't like it, but there's nothing in our agreement that says I can't buy and sell my own goods."

Maurice silently handed him a fifth thaler. The man had now earned more than he could make in several journeys up and down the Danube River.

Grüning turned to his son, who was stolidly eating his garlic-flavored sausage. "Hoist the sails and weigh anchor, Adolf," he directed. When the young man was gone, he turned back to the anxious trio with a toothless grin as he fingered the gold coins. "I would have been honored," he said, "to take you with me at no cost to you. Father Radetsky's sermons make more sense than the frothing of von Hecker's footmen."

Stephanie looked stunned, and Maurice tried to deny the identity of his silent male companion, but the Jesuit put a restraining hand on his arm. "Do you know me, then?"

Grüning became belligerent. "I've never seen you in my life, Fath—Sir."

The priest started to bow, changed his mind and slapped him on the back.

The barge owner rewarded him with another broad grin. "The Jesuits," he said, "fought for us when the Emperor Charles refused to let the sons of commoners inherit the property of their fathers. This barge isn't much of anything, but it's all I own, and some day it will belong to Adolf, thanks to Father Braun and Father Radetsky. I got drunk the day the old Emperor tore up that stupid decree, glory be to God. And when Count von Schlemmer and his hirelings at the Royal Treasury tried to tax the poor for the Empress' coronation, may their souls rot in purgatory, it was the lightning and thunder of Father Braun and Father Radetsky from the pulpit that saved us the few pennies we've scraped together for the day when we're old and sick."

The Jesuits of Austria were not friendless, Maurice thought, and a sense of relief flooded him.

"Never you fear, sir," Grüning continued. "I've never seen you, and I ask no questions."

Father Radetsky was deeply moved. "If I should be caught," he said, "don't let yourself be frightened into changing your story. I don't want your punishment on my conscience."

The barge owner squared his heavy shoulders. "How often can a nobody help the like of you?" he asked quietly. Not waiting for a reply, he stared out in the direction of the wharf. "Did anyone see you come aboard?"

"I'm sure," Maurice said, "that we weren't followed."

Grüning seemed satisfied. "All right," he replied, his manner suddenly brusque. "Don't leave the cabin until we reach the open countryside after dark. I'll tell you when it's safe to come out. Right now I'll cover your clothing boxes with a canvas, and then I'll take the tiller from Adolf. There are as many boats in this river at Vienna as there are carriages in the Käntnerstrasse these days. It's terrible, terrible." He walked out, closing the door behind him.

Maurice tried in vain to peer out through the oiled paper that served as a substitute for glass to cover the window. Then, very cautiously, he opened the door a fraction of an inch and looked out. "The old man is at the tiller now," he said, "and the young one is letting out sail. It doesn't appear that they're going to report us."

Father Radetsky stood in the center of the little cabin, gazing at the double tier of bunks against the starboard bulkhead, then at the same arrangement on the port side. "There are five people on board this raft," he said, "and only four beds. For your sake, Stephanie, I hope you had marriage in mind when you planned this elopement."

"Of course, Father!"

"Do you want to marry her, Montauban?"

"Certainly!"

"Then hand me the ring you're wearing on the little finger of your left hand, and stand together." His anxiety seemed to lessen as he added, "Perhaps a runaway priest can serve at least one useful advantage. Kneel before me, please."

They were startled by the abruptness of his request, but obeyed.

Father Radetsky clasped his hands. "*Our help,*" he intoned, "*is in the name of the Lord.*"

"*Who made heaven and earth,*" Maurice and Stephanie replied in unison. She had wanted a formal wedding in the Cathedral of St. Stephen, and he had been willing to wait a year in order to indulge her wish. Instead they were being married in a tiny barge cabin that smelled of garlic and fish and musty blankets. But neither felt regrets.

"*O Lord, hear my prayer.*"

"*And let my prayer be heard.*"

"*The Lord be with you.*"

"*And with your spirit.*"

"*Let us pray. O Lord, let our actions be prompted by your inspira-*

tion and accompanied by your help, so that every prayer and work of ours may begin from you, and through you be completed. Through Christ our Lord."

As the barge inched out into the busy waters of the Danube, Stephanie von Starhemberg became the wife of Maurice de Montauban, unsuccessful claimant to an ancient French title, English merchant and fugitive from imperial Austrian justice.

The voyage up the Danube was quiet, serene and agonizingly slow. Rain had been heavy in recent weeks, and the great river, fed by hundreds of lesser streams, flowed at a speed with which the barge was scarcely able to cope. After the first twenty-four hours the travelers abandoned their faint hope of reaching the border before it was closed, and when the craft inched through narrowing waters in the foothills of the Austrian Alps, Father Radetsky said, "We ourselves can do nothing."

Maurice and Stephanie slept in the same narrow bunk, but the proximity of others was an inhibiting influence, and their marriage remained unconsummated. But their desire remained unabated, sharpened by intimacy and an ever-present feeling of apprehension.

Thirty-six hours after the sealing of the frontier the barge docked at the mountain town of Linz, and when Grüning went ashore with his son to buy provisions and wool he could resell in Bavaria, the young couple and Father Radetsky stayed behind in the cabin, taking care not to let themselves be seen by dock workers, soldiers from the small local garrison and the waterfront prostitutes. Through the day Adolf Grüning returned to the barge several times, carrying bales of wool which he dumped on the deck and covered with canvas, but his father remained ashore until long after sundown.

Finally he came on board, told his son to cast off and, his breath reeking of cheap *schnapps* from a nearby tavern, joined his passengers in the cabin. "I've heard there's a great manhunt all through the Empire for Jesuits," he told them. "They say here that at least twenty who were trying to leave the country have been captured."

"Did you learn any names?" Father Radetsky asked, his voice tight.

"Yes, yours," Grüning replied with a sour laugh. "They swore that Hussars caught you and stoned you to death in the Vienna Woods. After that I didn't listen."

West of Linz the river cut through steep mountain gorges, its current swift, but a breeze blowing from the east filled the barge's sails, and although she still crept onward, her progress was steady.

Maurice repeatedly raised the question of avoiding the frontier patrols, but the barge owner made it clear he considered himself the master of his ship. "When the time comes," he said, "and we see how many sentries are stationed on the Austrian side of the border, we'll decide what to do."

It was clear that he considered himself responsible for the safety of his passengers, and spent most of his waking hours on deck, staring up at the cliffs on both sides of the Danube. "If I wanted to keep watch for people who are running away," he explained, "I would do it here. At the border the ground is not so high, life is dull at the garrison, and the troops there amuse themselves by visiting the young women at Passau, across the border. They're homely, those German girls in Passau, but after a man has been stationed for a long time at the frontier, they look pretty, I guess."

He said they would cross the border early in the afternoon, and late in the morning Stephanie went out onto the deck to take a change of clothing from her leather box. She had worn only one dress on the entire journey, and became so engrossed in examining her belongings that she failed to see a uniformed Austrian cavalryman on the heights to the north until she heard him shout to a companion and point in astonishment.

Aware that it would be an indication of guilt to flee into the cabin, she forced herself to remain in the open, taking a change of clothing from the box. She stayed there until the soldiers rode off.

Maurice and Father Radetsky were dismayed when she told them what had happened, but Max Grüning remained calm. "Now," he said, "we know what to do." Unexpectedly he reached out, felt the thin silk of the gown that Stephanie carried over her arm, and grunted in approval. But he offered no explanation of what he had in mind.

Less than an hour later, after Stephanie had changed, the spires of Passau's many churches became visible, and gradually the group on the barge could see the main outlines of the town, which was situated on a rocky peninsula between the Danube and its tributary, the Inn. Two connecting fortresses, the Niederhaus and the Oberhaus, faced the Austrian shores, but relations between the two nations were friendly at the moment, and the gun ports of the forts remained closed.

On the Austrian side was a smaller fort, located about a quarter of a mile from the bank of the Danube. There were no troops in sight, but Maurice studied the gray stone building uneasily. "With the border closed," he said, "they're certain to halt us for an inspection, particularly as Stephanie was seen."

Even as he spoke a small cutter put out from the shore and headed downstream toward them. At its masthead flew the Austrian ensign, and two men, an officer and a soldier, were on board.

Grüning took charge. "Father," he said, "you and the Englishman will hide yourselves under the canvas. The lady will stay in the cabin."

Maurice protested. "There's no reason I should hide," he said. "My place is with my wife!"

The barge owner was polite, but had no intention of discussing the matter at length. "You're gentry," he said, "and a foreigner. They wouldn't believe any reason that the like of you would make a journey with your wife on my barge. They'd ask questions and take you to their colonel. He wouldn't know what to do, and he'd send to Vienna for instructions. There would be slips, bad slips."

Maurice had to agree that the man's thinking was sound.

"It's much better," Grüning went on, "that the frontier guards think the lady is my—ah—friend."

Stephanie's bright smile indicated that she looked forward to play-acting.

Maurice felt misgivings, but the cutter was drawing closer, so he and Father Radetsky started to climb under the canvas that covered the cargo near the stern. Before he could conceal himself, however, he felt a tap on the shoulder, and Adolf Grüning, who had scarcely spoken to him on the voyage, handed him a long, double-edged knife with a bone handle. He accepted it gratefully and, grasping it in one hand, joined the priest beneath the tarpaulin.

Stephanie hurried into the cabin to complete her transformation into her version of a bargeman's doxie. She applied a thick coating of rouge to her lips, added some to her cheeks, and after darkening her lids with antimony, put a conspicuous beauty spot directly above the dimple on the left side of her face. Pleased with the gaudy results, she hauled down the sleeves of her gown to bare her shoulders and emphasize her cleavage. Then, imitating the trollops she had sometimes seen in the Kärntnerstrasse and other streets near the Cathedral of St. Stephen, she went out onto the deck, hips rolling in an exaggerated fashion as she took short, mincing steps.

The frontier guards had tied their cutter to the barge and were just climbing aboard as she appeared. The officer was a lieutenant in his early twenties, a wiry man with a thin, hawk-like face who stared at Stephanie with a frank, lewd interest she had never before encountered. The other soldier, a burly sergeant, was somewhat older, and regarded the girl sleepily, but his desire was equally evident.

Max Grüning's idea was proving a little too successful, and he concealed his alarm. "Come into the cabin," he said quickly, "and I'll show you my identification, ship's papers and manifest."

The lieutenant followed him, but continued to gape at the girl. "Save her for me, Schultz," he called.

"Don't worry, sir. There's enough here for both of us." Before

Stephanie could retreat, the sergeant's brawny arm encircled her waist and pulled her close. "What are you doing on this garbage scow?" he demanded.

She felt a surge of panic, but knew it would be unwise to struggle too hard. "It's not so bad. They're good to me."

"One is too old and the other is too young. You need a real man." He hauled her still closer. "Come ashore with me. There's a little house near the barracks you can use, and you'll have no competition. The whole garrison will go mad over you. But just remember, I come first."

She gasped as he plunged a hand inside her gown, and before she could resist, he was kissing her. She began to struggle in earnest, but was incapable of coping with his strength. His grip tightened, hurting her breast, and his kiss was so ardent she was unable to breathe.

Maurice, peering out from beneath the tarpaulin, was unable to restrain himself. A wild fury shook him, and indifferent to the consequences, he climbed out onto the open deck and threw himself at the sergeant from behind, one hand catching him around the neck.

The attack was totally unexpected, but the man responded to it instantly, releasing Stephanie and twisting around to meet his assailant.

Maurice was still in a rage, and his only desire was that of obtaining revenge against the man who had tried to soil his wife. Scarcely aware of what he was doing, he raised the knife and plunged it into his opponent's body. The sergeant was jarred, but continued to fight, and Maurice stabbed him a second time, then a third.

The soldier slumped to the deck, moaning, and then lay still in a messy pool of his own blood.

The Austrian lieutenant rushed out of the cabin, his sword in hand, and Maurice's temper abated as he realized the gravity of his situation. His own sword was locked away with his belongings, he had no pistol, and would have to defend himself with no weapon except the knife.

The lieutenant took in the situation at a glance, saw his dead subordinate on the deck and started toward Maurice, sword poised.

Max Grüning seemed stunned, his son sat motionless at the tiller as the barge continued to drift slowly toward the Bavarian border, and Stephanie stood with her hands covering her mouth, her eyes bright with terror.

Maurice backed onto the canvas tarpaulin, climbing and stumbling over the cargo stowed beneath it. The officer followed, waiting for the opportune moment to strike, and Maurice tried to remember all he had been taught in the years he had taken fencing lessons. He realized the odds against him were great, and knew that, at best, he would have only one chance to save himself. A combination of luck and perfect timing might enable him to defend himself against the far longer reach of the lieutenant's sword.

The officer lunged, and his blade cut through Maurice's frock coat, waistcoat and shirt, grazing his ribs. Had the strike been an inch closer, it would have incapacitated and perhaps killed him. He knew he could not afford to wait, and still backing away, moved toward the soft bales of wool that had been taken on at Linz. They had been stowed carelessly, and were piled high beneath the canvas, so he used them as a shield, half-standing and half-crouching behind the mound.

The lieutenant, impatient to end the unequal duel, came after him. But the footing on the bales of wool was soft, and gave way as he moved. He stumbled, dropping to one knee for an instant.

This was the moment for which Maurice had been waiting. He sprang at the Austrian, the knife held high above his head, and brought it down with all his might. He felt it dig into flesh, but the momentum of his jump had carried him forward, and he was unable to extricate himself. He and the officer rolled over and over on the tarpaulin, stopping no more than a foot or two from the edge of the deck.

Only then did he realize that the lieutenant was dead. Within a span of a few minutes he had murdered two men.

Stephanie was weeping in silent hysteria, her tears streaking the rouge and antimony on her face.

Maurice found Father Radetsky standing beside him, and heard the priest say, "We've crossed the frontier." Trying to focus, Maurice saw it was true. The little Austrian garrison was behind them, and the barge was sailing beneath the shadows of the twin forts on the Bavarian side.

Stephanie, racked by sobs, gasped that she was to blame.

The Grünings were still too dazed to react sensibly.

Father Radetsky took charge. "Keep sailing until we've left Passau behind," he directed. "It is essential that no one knows what has happened."

The barge bobbed up and down as the swirling waters of the Inn River emptied into the Danube.

The Jesuit was practical and calm. "Fortunately for all of us," he said, "no one in the Austrian garrison saw what happened. No one else was on duty at the border. Now, when we reach open country again, we'll transfer the bodies to the cutter. And we'll lower the Austrian flag. Then I'll transfer to the boat, sail up the Inn River and find a place to bury these poor souls in dignity, with a prayer."

"Suppose you should be seen before you bury them, Father," Maurice protested. "It's too great a risk for you."

"No, you must let me look after myself now. You've done enough for me, and all of us must part company here. Grüning must be allowed to continue his voyage to Regensburg. Maurice, you'll be wise to hire or buy horses and a pack mule or two in Passau, and ride north through the Bohemian Forest into Saxony. You should have no difficulty reaching Prussia."

"What will you do, Father?"

"First, I must make certain Grüning won't suffer for the spilling of blood. He must be allowed to return safely to Austria. Then," the priest added, "I have God's work to do. I've been spared for His sake, not my own, and must devote myself to His service."

Voltaire seemed to be the master of King Frederick's hunting lodge at Potsdam, near Berlin, rather than a guest. The largest and most handsomely furnished suite had been placed at his disposal, a staff of servants had been assigned to take care of his needs, and Frederick's guests accommodated themselves to his erratic schedule, dining at odd hours after he finished his day's writing.

He received Maurice and Stephanie in an old silk dressing gown spattered with ink stains, and insisted they eat some cold meats, plovers' eggs and cheese, even though they had been asked to dine an hour or two later at Frederick's table. "If I had my life to live again," he told the young couple, "I believe I'd like to live it as a king. I love the luxuries that royalty takes for granted. Try that cold salmon mousse. It was made up for me from a recipe that dates back to the reign of James I of England. I was curious to discover the taste, and two chefs labored for a whole day to make it for me. That's what I mean by luxury.

"There are only two drawbacks to being a king. It's always possible you'll lose your throne, and if your subjects have taken a really active dislike to you, they may take your head, too. What would be worse is that I'd have so little time for my writing. On second thought, I prefer my own work. I'm free to travel, you see. A little too free."

Stephanie didn't know what to make of Europe's most renowned author, and Voltaire grinned at her.

"You're disinclined to believe me, my dear? I've just spent several months in Brussels, which is a manner of wearing a hair shirt in atonement for one's sins. Brussels was hospitable, however, which is more than I can say for Paris these days. Some verses I wrote for my own amusement were published without my knowledge, and I'm relieved to say that King Louis and his bishops are so dull-witted they thought them irreverent. What they failed to realize is that they're also treasonable—and positively scurrilous."

A manservant interrupted the monologue, tapping at the door and announcing, apologetically, that the King wanted a private word with Maurice.

"I'll entertain your lady," Voltaire said. "She'll gain a better understanding of France after I've told her of the trial performances of my new play, *Mahomet*, in Lille. The audiences cheered for fifteen minutes, but an archbishop, a bishop and eleven monsignors walked out, just because I insisted that we and the Moslems worship the same God. And I've been forbidden to present the play in Paris. I'm beginning to think the real purpose of the Trinity is to give Catholics, Protestants and Moslems different facets of the Godhead to worship. The Jews are excluded, which is unfair, because they were the first to discover the Lord."

He was still talking at a rapid clip when Maurice left the room and made his way down the corridor.

King Frederick, who received his guest in his workroom, looked tired and irritable.

"I made it plain to the Empress," Maurice told him, "that I was representing you unofficially, and I told her in so many words that you were prepared to be generous if she would cede the Silesian duchies to you."

"But she rejects reason." Frederick fingered a tinderbox fashioned in the shape of a tiny cannon.

"She'll fight rather than give them up."

The monarch who was busy creating the most powerful army in Europe looked gloomy. "Then the blame isn't mine for what will happen. No civilized man could do more to keep the peace."

"Maria Theresa plans to wage a holy war, Your Majesty."

"Cardinal von Hecker has persuaded her that God will give her military as well as spiritual support, but I've always believed that the walls of Jericho tumbled because Joshua's sappers dug tunnels under them. And these days, when it's so easy to influence clergymen, even a devout woman should know better than to put her faith in any force other than her infantry, artillery and cavalry. Besides," Frederick added with an indulgent smile, "the Lord may be planning to chastise her because of her persecution of the Jesuits. How she can support the Church with one hand and chop down its most resilient branch with the other is the ultimate in feminine inconsistency."

Maurice was still waiting for some word of Father Radetsky's fate, and often dreamed of the two Austrian border guards he had killed. "I know very little of her campaign against the Jesuits, Your Majesty," he said cautiously.

"More than eight hundred were expelled from the Austrian Empire," Frederick said crisply, "fifty were imprisoned, and four have been hanged, including a remarkable fellow named Braun. His mistake was preaching brotherly love, which is as revolutionary a doctrine today as it was eighteen centuries ago."

"I wonder if you know what may have happened to another Jesuit named Radetsky."

Frederick eyed his guest shrewdly. "He's disappeared, and some rather strange stories are being told about his escape."

Maurice stared out of the window at a clump of silver birch trees.

"I'll read your written report," Frederick said, tactfully changing the subject, "and if I have anything further to discuss with you, we can talk again after dinner. When do you leave for England?"

"As soon as Your Majesty is satisfied with the information I've brought. But I'm not going direct to London. I'm hoping my marriage will help convince the French they were wrong not to consider my claim to the Montauban title, so I'm planning to go by way of Versailles."

"You've served me well, and the least I can in return is repay you with more than a commercial agreement." Frederick paused. "For your wife's sake as well as your own, avoid France as you would the pox." He spoke with deliberate solemnity, but offered no further explanation.

1742

The ritual of being shaved twice daily was an agony for a man with an exceptionally sensitive skin, a dread of being nicked with a razor, and a wiry beard. But Louis XV of France endured the ordeal because he loathed beards, and some of his courtiers suggested that his hatred for his father-in-law, the exiled king of Poland, to whom he had given an estate in Lorraine, had made him unreasonable on the subject. Only the most favored members of the court were permitted to witness Louis' torture, and no more than fifty to seventy-five gentlemen and ladies were in attendance when he submitted himself to the ministrations of his barber, among tham dukes and duchesses, cardinals, heads of government ministries, the highest-ranking generals and, of course, the current mistresses and lovers of the elite.

The routine was the same morning and evening. The company convened in the barbering room at Versailles to sip chilled wine and converse in low tones. Everyone knew His Christian Majesty could scarcely tolerate the necessary evil, so no one laughed and only the most beautiful and self-assured of the ladies dared to smile. Then male members of the royal family and marshals of France entered in single file, carrying the barber's tools, and behind them came Louis, a plump man who tried to conceal his excess weight beneath skillfully tailored silks which, unfortunately, were so dazzling they actually called attention to his pudginess. He also tried to overcome his short stature by wearing sandals with heels two to three inches high, but again his vanity overcame his judgment, and the heels, done in gold, silver or scarlet, were unavoidably conspicuous.

Only princes or dukes were permitted to remove his ermine-trimmed cloak, and a silence descended on the assemblage when he sat in the padded chair of royal purple that was used for no other purpose. He suffered himself to be kissed by his mistress of the moment and several other attractive ladies, including Queen Maria, if she happened to be at Versailles rather than visiting her father's miniature court in Lorraine. Sheets of silk were draped around the King's body, and then someone summoned the barber, who slipped unobtrusively into the chamber, carrying a pile of hot towels which he used to cover Louis' face.

It was an unwritten law that no one could speak unless addressed by the King, and His Christian Majesty was so morose during the quarter-hour operation that he seldom uttered a word. So it was customary for the barber to work in sepulchral quiet.

One afternoon early in January, 1742, while the court was still recovering from a five-day celebration of the new year, Louis was no sooner seated in the barber's chair than he broke with tradition. "Leave us," he ordered.

The guests were personages of such prestige that each assumed he meant the others, and no one moved.

"Clear the room," the King said impatiently, and several generals hastened to obey him.

As the ladies and gentlemen departed they noticed that one man remained behind, and the cardinals and bishops were particularly interested in the priest who wore unrelieved black. But he seemed unaware of the stir he created, and stared over the tops of the towering wigs worn by the ladies.

"You may begin," Louis told the barber when the doors were closed, and winced as the steaming towels touched his skin. "I could give you no other time today," he said to the priest, "but I find your mission so unusual that I wanted to hear more about it. Once again, your name?"

His voice was muffled by the towels, and the priest had to strain in order to understand him. "Pierre de Cheney, Your Majesty."

"You're French, of course, and therefore one of my subjects."

The priest had no intention of reopening an old and bitter argument. "I serve God in the Society of Jesus, Your Majesty, and for many years I've lived in Rome."

Louis' face was invisible beneath the towels, but he sounded annoyed. "How does it happen that you were chosen to deliver a letter to me from Pope Benedict?"

"I don't question the commands of the Holy Father, Your Majesty."

"You Jesuits are disliked by everyone," Louis said acidly, "because you're incapable of giving direct answers to questions! You're familiar with the contents of the letter?"

"I am." Father de Cheney realized he was being challenged to prove it. "His Holiness has requested you, in confidence, to give favorable consideration to the petition of a successful young banker of French extraction, Maurice de Montauban, to the title and estates of his late cousin."

Louis startled the barber by pulling off the towel and sitting upright. "What I want to know is why Benedict should concern himself with a temporal matter of a purely domestic nature!"

"If you'd care to glance at His Holiness' letter again," de Cheney said soothingly, "you'll note he says in so many words that Your Majesty has complete jurisdiction in the case, and that he's writing to you in a personal rather than an official capacity."

The barber watched in dismay as his towels cooled.

"A number of people seem to be advocating de Montauban's cause," Louis said petulantly. "The very week that I became the ally of Prussia in the war against Austria, King Frederick sent me a letter on de Montauban's behalf. Of course, Voltaire has been paying frequent visits to Potsdam, so I simply assumed this was another of his jokes."

"I assure you, Your Majesty," the Jesuit said in righteous horror, "Rome has nothing to do with Voltaire."

Louis glowered, waving away the barber, who approached him with the last warm towel. "It can't have escaped Pope Benedict's attention," he said, biting off his words, "that France has gone to war with Austria. I wonder if the Pope knows that de Montauban's wife is not only Austrian, but is related to Prince von Kaunitz, who has just been made Maria Theresa's First Minister. He also happens to be de Montauban's business partner."

"King Frederick has also become a business associate of the man, and he's Your Majesty's ally."

"Ah, then you do know something about the case!" Louis did not enjoy his little triumph. "Even a holy man who seals himself at Vatican Hill and ignores the world's affairs must realize my association with Prussia is only temporary. I don't trust Frederick any more than he likes me. Now, de Cheney, tell me more about this Montauban matter."

"The only other information at my disposal," the Jesuit said, "is that de Montauban and his wife have been waiting in Brussels for permission to enter France."

"The British legation in Brussels," Louis said testily, "has been told the right won't be granted."

"Surely you know he and his wife faithfully practice Catholicism, Your Majesty. The Church would be disturbed if they were being excluded because of heresy in his ancestry. There are few houses in France that don't bear such a taint."

If Louis recognized the none too subtle allusion to his own descent from Henry IV, he did not indicate it. "Vatican Hill may find this difficult to understand," he said caustically, "but decisions of State are sometimes based on considerations other than those of religious faith." He turned to the waiting barber. "Must I sit here all night?"

The man began to apply a scented lather to the royal jowls.

Father de Cheney stood patiently, saying no more until the stubble on the King's face had been removed. "May I ask Your Majesty's reasons for excluding a wealthy man who will become still wealthier when his grandfather dies?"

Louis winced as the barber applied the first of several lotions to his face. "Find a scent that doesn't sting!" He turned to the priest with a haughty smile. "Vatican Hill, I suppose, shares the common opinion that I'm a fool."

"I've never heard anyone express such a view, Your Majesty."

"Then the last three of my ministers to The Holy See have been unmitigated liars. I'm holding de Montauban at arm's length for the same reason he wants his cousin's title. It's purely a question of money. The taxes he'd be required to pay if he were a French subject would be large, but the income I enjoy from the Montauban estates is larger. You may tell Pope Benedict I'm capable of adding and subtracting simple sums, particularly when they're in gold francs. The war with Austria promises to be expensive, unless Frederick wins some quick victories, in which case Prussia will take the lion's share of the spoils. I can't afford the luxury of recognizing claims to valuable properties. And if Vatican Hill is so interested in France, I wish Benedict would start paying the wages of my bishops. There was a time when the Church rewarded the Crown for its privileges, but these days the bishops cost me a fortune every year. I sometimes wonder whether a State religion is worth the expense."

"At the age of sixty-six I find it very difficult to start answering to a new name," the old man said, staring out of the British legation windows at the rain that was cleaning the cobbled streets of Brussels. "When I'm called Sir Robert I know someone is speaking to me, and when they refer to me as Walpole I know they're talking about me. I should be very pleased with my title, I suppose, but I take no satisfaction in being Earl of Orford."

It was difficult for Maurice to believe that the frail, bitter man who sat opposite him had been the most powerful of Englishmen for more than three decades. Recently dismissed as Prime Minister, he had previously held every post of importance in the British government. It was an honor to have been summoned to meet him at the legation, even though he had lost his post as head of the Whig party.

"We're a strange breed, we Englishmen," Walpole continued. "Our lives are built on the substance of what we create, but we seek the shadow of glory. You may take my word for it, that shadow is a travesty. I'd much prefer to be holding the reins of government in London at this moment than hearing myself addressed as 'milord Earl.' My only real joy these days is knowing that both houses of Parliament are in an uproar because I've come to the Continent. They suspect me of dire plots against the new government's policies, and they're positive I intend to connive with the Continental powers. For thirty-four years they've praised me as the most honest man of my generation. But they refuse to believe the simple truth, that my physician wants me to try the waters at Leuven for my gout." He stared reproachfully at his swollen left foot, which was propped on a hassock and swathed in bandages.

"I'm grateful to you for this meeting, Sir Robert." Maurice deliberately refrained from calling the old man by his new title. "It's very good of you to bring my grandfather's greeting to me."

"Paul de Montauban is still a Frenchman in many ways, but he's sensible. He decided many years ago that England was his permanent home. You ought to do the same, instead of wasting your time trying to win a worthless foreign title."

"I haven't been wasting my time, as my grandfather well knows. I've been establishing an office at Ostend to work with Prince von Kaunitz' new trading company. And the French title isn't worthless. The estates in southern France are worth a great fortune."

"You don't need the money," Walpole said dryly, and laughed. "Help England stand apart from these damned civil and religious wars on the Continent. Do you know why I was dismissed from office?"

"I've heard several stories, but it's my guess that none of them are accurate."

"I insisted that England remain neutral in this new war between Austria and Prussia. I was certain France would join the Austrians, but she's gone in on the other side, which means that Catholics and Protestants have banded together to fight Catholics. The situation is so confused we should stay apart and let them weaken each other."

"England is going to enter the war, Sir Robert?" Maurice tried to speak calmly.

"I'm afraid so."

"On which side?"

"Ah, there's the great question! The war party was convinced the Austrians were spearheading a Papist plot to dominate Europe, but when France, Catholic France, leaped in against Maria Theresa, their neat theories were blasted. Now they don't know which way to turn, but war fever is in their blood."

"It makes no sense, Sir Robert."

"When you've lived to be my age and seen as many wars as I've fought, you'll know none of them make sense. Forgive me for my rudeness, but I'm afraid I can't walk you to the door."

Maurice shook hands with the greatest English statesman of the age, and took his leave. The rain was coming down still harder, and although he had only a short distance to ride, he was soaked by the time he handed the reins of his horse to a groom at the house he had rented.

Stephanie was waiting for him, and after taking his cloak, insisted he stand before a coal fire in the drawing-room grate. She listened as he told her of his conversation with Walpole, and when he was done, she asked, "What will you do?"

"It's plain I'm not wanted in France, and it isn't accidental that Sir Robert delivered a little homily on the worthlessness of titles so soon after being given an earldom. My grandfather was responsible for that, you can be sure."

"I won't know what to say when I meet your grandfather."

Maurice smiled at her. "You and he will take to each other."

"We're going to England?"

"We have no choice."

Stephanie looked at him, and took his hand. "You aren't happy over the decision."

"I should be satisfied. We'll soon rival the East India Company, and I have a lovely wife. Some men have the knack for earning money, and I seem to be one of them. But I wanted something else in life."

"Then the Montauban title means more to you than the property that's involved."

"Yes, although being a count for its own sake is an empty honor." Maurice turned to her. "For one hundred and fifty years my family has been fighting against persecution. I wanted to do my share, in France, where my ancestors died for their beliefs. But apparently it isn't to be. You and I know there's still bigotry in the world. We've seen it. Yet whom do we attack? The good and the evil fight shoulder to shoulder against foes no better and no worse, and even in the evil there's good. How shall I know my enemy until I've seen his face?"

Priceless sculptures and paintings executed over a period of more than five hundred years had been removed from the papal sitting room, and the only decoration on the wall was a Crucifix, less than twelve inches high, that had been carved in marble by Leonardo da Vinci. Cushions had been removed from the chairs of polished cherry wood, and there was no design on the rug of dark wool that covered the floor. The smoking of pipes and *segaros* was strictly forbidden, and members of the diplomatic corps accredited to Vatican Hill knew they would never be served any beverage stronger than the mildest wine.

"This is the Lord's house," Pope Benedict XIV had said on the day of his coronation, "and it is fitting that we remember it, always."

People presented to the Pope for the first time expected to meet a frail ascetic, and were astonished to find him a rugged, red-faced man in his middle years. "The Lambertinis of Bologna," he sometimes told visitors, "would be stonemasons if the Holy Spirit hadn't descended on us and given us the light to use our intellects."

The staff at Vatican Hill, accustomed for three centuries to sophisticated pontiffs and the aristocratic protocol of popes who came from the ruling families of the Italian states, were bewildered by Benedict. He appointed commissions to modernize canonical law and prepare accurate histories of the Church; he considered it more important to establish new bishoprics in America, Africa and eastern Europe than to engage in political struggles with temporal rulers; and his interest in archeology was so great that the harried members of his staff learned to search for him at the Coliseum and other Roman ruins whenever he was missing from his office.

Perhaps his most annoying habit was his eagerness to meet ordinary people. Papal chamberlains frostily recalled that his three immediate predecessors had rarely granted audiences to clergymen below the rank of archbishop and laymen who came from other than princely families. But men from every walk of life were welcome in the papal apartment now, among them professors and students, minor officials of various European governments and, from time to time, pilgrims who, when visiting St. Peter's, were dumfounded to be greeted by the Pope himself.

Therefore no one thought it strange that the refugee Austrian Jesuit, Father Radetsky, had access to Benedict, and sometimes was closeted with him for several hours. Cardinals who were members of the Curia assumed that the priest was being groomed for high office, but the Vicar General of the Jesuits, who apparently knew something of the conversations, smilingly shook his head.

One night in the early spring of 1742, lamps burned late at Vatican Hill after the Pope received a courier who arrived with a sealed leather bag, and early the following morning, to the surprise of no one, Father Radetsky presented himself for a private audience. Benedict received him in the sitting room, and the Jesuit kissed his ring.

"The pot boils so furiously," the Pope said, "that the stew has become too thick to ladle. Maria Theresa is paying a heavy price for her expulsion of the Jesuits. Bavaria and Saxony will join the war against her this week, and both Spain and Sardinia are expected to take up arms against her in the immediate future, too."

Father Radetsky paled. "Poor Austria," he murmured.

A smile softened Benedict's craggy face. "Not many would show your compassion."

"Few countries have ever been so bedeviled and confused. She lives and worships in the past."

"Tradition is important in prayer," Benedict said. "It gives man a sense of religious continuity, and what he learned as a child comforts him as an adult. But, if I could, I'd change all prayers and ceremonies except the Sacraments. However, I hesitate to make too many radical changes, even though I'm convinced a prayer from the heart has far more piety than a 'Hail Mary' said by rote. I'm afraid, though, that in a time of change, like ours, too many laymen—and too many priests, if you will—would become confused. But we digress, Father, as you and I so often do. I want your opinion."

The Jesuit waited until Benedict seated himself before taking a chair. He knew now why he had been summoned to Vatican Hill, and tried to summarize a complex situation for a man so concerned with spiritual matters that he found it difficult to grasp worldly problems. "An attack by so many enemies will unite the Austrians. Even the people who have been shocked by the treatment of my Order will support Maria Theresa."

"Will she be strong enough to hold off all her enemies?"

"No nation is that strong," Father Radetsky said. "But the coalition is so powerful that neutral nations can't afford to let France and Prussia dominate Europe. The Dutch must be particularly fearful. If Frederick and Louis win too decisive a victory, they'll partition her between them." He smiled wryly. "I'm reasonably certain we're about to see the spectacle of Holland, the Protestant champion, joining forces with Austria, which likes to think of herself as the rock of Catholicism."

"Isn't she too small to be of much help to Austria?"

"She can muster only a few regiments, but France and Prussia will be forced to divert some of their troops to the west. And the Dutch navy is the second most powerful on earth. She can establish a blockade that will hurt Frederick and Louis."

"You corroborate what I've heard elsewhere. I suppose the strongest navy belongs to the English?"

"It does, Your Holiness."

"If they hadn't made common cause with Austria only a generation ago, I'd say it would be inconceivable that the English would join Maria Theresa. But I wonder if that's what they'll do."

"The Anglo-Saxon mind is unfathomable," Father Radetsky said.

"The English like to believe they fight only for principle, and they rationalize. Walpole lost his place as Prime Minister because he saw nothing to be gained by fighting the French, and King George is reluctant to go to war against Frederick."

The Pope nodded. "So I've heard. I'm told the British and Prussians have a great feeling of kinship for one another."

"You're exceptionally well-informed, Your Holiness. The Jesuits have made the same analysis."

"I find Voltaire's attitudes illuminating in most matters."

Father Radetsky was startled. "You've had a letter from Voltaire, Your Holiness? The French bishops force him to spend about six months out of every twelve in exile."

"The French bishops still believe they can use terror to command unquestioning faith, which is absurd. I try to help them by corresponding regularly with skeptics like Voltaire and heretics like Frederick of Prussia."

The Jesuit was too astonished to reply.

"I want to know why these men of intellectual integrity feel contempt for our teachings. It isn't enough that we believe our doctrine is the truth. Ordinary citizens everywhere are learning to read and write—and think. People are no longer accepting the word of the parish priest as final. I'm accused of being indifferent to what men do on earth, I know, but mine is the ultimate concern. If we don't provide answers to the legitimate questions of the faithful— honest, searching answers that prove the validity of our doctrine—the Church will collapse."

"That's what the Society of Jesus was trying to do in Austria, Your Holiness, but the bishops fought us, the priests resisted us, and so did their parishioners."

"You'll recall," Benedict said, "that St. Paul met constant opposition when he tried to preach the truth, too. I'm afraid, Father, that self-complacency may be our undoing. Cardinals and bishops speak in clichés when I try to discuss theology with them. Only the Voltaires and the Fredericks think independently and speak out courageously. We must prove ourselves capable of meeting them on their own terms, and defeating them. Perhaps you think I'm digressing from the subject of this ghastly war?"

The Jesuit didn't know what to think.

"I'm not," Benedict said. "The issues have become blurred, and will become meaningless if the Dutch and, perhaps, the English become the allies of Austria. Then Catholics and Protestants will be fighting on both sides, and neither will be able to wage a holy war. Both will pray to God, of course, asking for His help, and the victors will be sure He heeded their pleas."

"If both Holland and England go in with the Austrians," the Jesuit said, "the match will be fairly even. I doubt if either side will be strong enough to win a conclusive victory."

"So much the better. Then men of good will, like your friend, de Montauban, whom I was unable to help, will be in a better position to make their influence felt."

"You have a greater faith in mankind than I do, Your Holiness."

"I have none in man, only in God. What makes the schism between Catholic and Protestant so insanely frustrating is that both ask favors from the same God, but refuse to obey Him. After this war, or some day perhaps, they will finally do what He told them through Isaiah: 'beat their swords into plowshares.' "

Four huge ships-of-the line rode at anchor in the harbor at Dover. Each was armed with seventy-four cannon, and sailors were practicing lowering the gun ports and running the huge artillery pieces into place. At least a score of other Royal Navy vessels dotted the harbor, too. There were swift frigates, only a shade less powerful than the great men-of-war, trim sloops capable of outmaneuvering any other ships that sailed the high seas, and squat, ugly ketches carrying bombs strong enough to demolish any fortress.

On the heights behind the harbor, far above the gray-white chalk cliffs facing the sea, a regiment of foot soldiers in brilliant scarlet tunics marched on the parade ground, bayonets attached to muskets. Cavalry squadrons in scarlet and white thundered up to the ramparts of Dover Castle, leaving clouds of dust behind them, then rode down through the sifting dirt to practice the maneuver again. Meanwhile, at the waterfront, supplies from warehouses of wood and stone were being loaded onto unprepossessing merchant ships that had been purchased by the government for use as military transports.

Stephanie de Montauban clutched her husband's arm as they stood together on the deck of the square-rigged brig that slowly nosed toward her berth in the teeming harbor. "The war," she said, addressing him in German, "has come here, too."

Several passengers who heard her use a foreign tongue stared at her suspiciously.

Maurice knew this was not the moment to tell her that any alien language made the people of the British Isles uneasy. "There has been no successful invasion in almost seven hundred years," he told her, taking care to reply in English. "But Sir Robert was right. Either we've entered the war or we're about to go in."

They watched crewmen carrying their leather traveling boxes onto the deck, and when the brig was tied securely to a long wharf, they were the first passengers to go ashore. They made their way down the quay, and entered a small, ramshackle building where an unshaven customs officer wearing a sash of scarlet and green across his chest was waiting to examine their passports.

"Have we gone to war?" Maurice asked him.

"That we have, sir," the man replied, "and we'll bring the bastards to their knees in a hurry, you can bet!"

Maurice hesitated for an instant, then asked, "Which side are we taking?"

The man stared at him. "We're fighting the bloody Papists, of course!"

War was no laughing matter, but Maurice had to curb an impulse to smile. He would have to wait, he thought, and obtain specific information elsewhere.

But the customs official unknowingly told him what he wanted to learn. "This here lady," he said, jerking a grimy thum in the direction of Stephanie, "was our ally before she married you, sir!" He handed the passports to Maurice with a flourish.

England had gone to the aid of Maria Theresa, and Frederick's Lutheran Prussia as well as the France of Louis XV had become the enemy. Maurice didn't have the heart to ask the customs officer if he knew that Austria was a Catholic nation. The man simply wouldn't believe him, and would remain convinced that England was fighting on the side of Protestant allies against a coalition of Catholic enemies.

Stephanie thought her command of English had been inadequate, and was puzzled.

Maurice guided her past a waterfront tavern, where a number of sailors lounging near the entrance gaped at her, and waved aside several beggars as he led her to the coach that would carry them to London. "People are incapable of going to war," he said, "without enlisting under the Lord's banner. You'd find that most Englishmen would cheer Maria Theresa's persecution of the Jesuits, if they knew of it, and they'd swear that anyone who has acted as she has couldn't possibly be a Catholic."

"Surely the Catholics here would know better?"

"Some of them may have heard that Austria is a Catholic state, but they'd insist that the actions against the Jesuits are lies invented by Papist France to confound them."

Paul de Montauban looked very frail and old as, propped on pillows and covered with a spread of white silk, he received his grandson in his bedchamber. "You did well on your journey," he said, speaking his native French.

Maurice sat down beside the fourposter and replied in the same tongue, realizing that the old man's illness might be more severe than anyone had known. "Austria's supply lines have undoubtedly been cut, so I don't imagine we can do more than a token trade with Kaunitz' company in Ostend. And I'm certain the privileges King Frederick granted us will be suspended until the end of the war. If you haven't seen this morning's *Post*, there's an article on a bill pending in the House of Commons prohibiting all traffic with the enemy."

"I was speaking of your good fortune in finding the right wife." Paul managed a feeble smile. "A wife who will give you sons is worth far more than trade agreements. Your mother and grandmother approve of her, and I'm delighted."

Maurice patted the thin hand that rested on the coverlet. "Stephanie says you spoil her."

"Why shouldn't I? Through her the Montauban line will live."

Whether a merchant family survived was purely a matter of personal pride, Maurice told himself, but didn't want to upset his grandfather by voicing his thoughts. The opportunity to live up to the Montauban traditions had been lost.

Paul was watching him. "While Louis remains on the throne of France, give up your dream," he said gently. "I knew the reception you'd be given in France, but I had to let you find out for yourself that Louis would refuse you. And one thing more, Maurice. Let the future take care of itself."

Maurice wanted to retort that the world would drift unless men of conscience took positive action. He had seen Jews persecuted for no reason, Jesuits hounded and God denied. In spite of the old man's illness he could not remain silent. "Must I stand aside and see the world crumble into barbarism?"

"Can you prevent it? England gave us a home. Be grateful for it, and serve her well. Bring up your sons as you were reared, to honor the Lord and obey His rule that we love one another. It may be that the Montauban destiny lies elsewhere than in France. I know only that if God has need of you or of your sons, He will call on you. Wait patiently, and your chance will come." Paul closed his eyes, and drifted into a deep sleep.

The Crown and Sceptre, in spite of its name, was a haven for members of the House of Commons, in part because of its physical proximity to Parliament, in part because of its informal atmosphere. It had become something of a headquarters for the younger members who had broken Walpole's power, among them Foreign Secretary Carteret and the group scornfully known as Cobham's Boy Patriots. Maurice preferred the quiet dignity of the Fleet Street taverns that catered to bankers and merchants, and ignored the hubbub as he made his way through the crowded taproom to the curtained booth

321

that stood last in the row on the left side of the chamber. It gave him no sense of satisfaction to be recognized as one of London's most influential men of trade, and he had far too much on his mind to appreciate the stares of politicians and their followers.

A tall man with a long face, prominent nose and thin mouth who would have been homely had it not been for his exceptionally alert eyes stood and extended his hand as Maurice entered the booth. "Your servant, Mr. de Montauban. I'm very pleased you could take the time to meet me."

"Your servant, Mr. Pitt," Maurice said, shaking hands and shedding his cloak. He had been irritated when a note from William Pitt inviting him to dinner for a discussion of a "matter of urgent mutual interest" had been delivered to him at his office, but he had come to the Crown and Sceptre because of a reluctance to offend the man. Pitt, the acknowledged leader of Cobham's Boy Patriots, had been so brash that he had offended the new Prime Minister, Henry Pelham, and as a consequence held no office in the government. It was generally regarded as inevitable, however, that he would some day rise to a post of great power, and Maurice had considered it wise to accept the invitation.

"Since both of us are busy," Pitt said in a deep, liquid voice, as pleasing as that of the young actor, David Garrick, "I've taken the liberty of ordering. I always have oysters, and then a kidney and beefsteak pie. I trust you won't mind."

Maurice loathed oysters, and shared his grandmother's conviction that kidney and beefsteak pie was an English abomination. "That suits me fine," he said, and sat down.

"Accept my condolences on your grandfather's death," Pitt said. "He was a credit to England, and we shall miss him."

Maurice picked up the glass of sack at his elbow. He had no desire to talk about his grandfather with a stranger.

William Pitt showed a rare sensitivity, immediately understanding his feeling. "Mr. de Montauban," he said crisply, changing the subject, "you and I share similar ambitions."

"We do, sir?" Maurice was polite, but waited to be convinced.

"Our generation will make England the greatest nation on earth, or see her decline into the insular provincialism she knew two hundred and fifty years ago under Henry the Sixth. We must either push toward the one goal or fall back to the other extreme. Your interests are mercantile, mine are in statecraft. They go hand in hand."

Maurice nodded, wondering what the politician wanted.

"At present we're saddled with a government of gibbering maniacs who will destroy our wealth with senseless war. I am not," Pitt added with a laugh, "trying to solicit your opinion of either Pelham or Carteret."

Maurice waited until the barmaid placed platters of oysters before them and retreated from the booth. "I must agree," he said cautiously, "that the war is not to our advantage."

Pitt was an ungainly man, but showed surprising dexterity as he opened an oyster shell with a thin-bladed knife. "I refer specifically to you and to me, Mr. de Montauban. The French occupation of Austrian owned Belgium makes your agreement with Prince von Kaunitz worthless, and you can't enjoy your trading monopoly with King Frederick while we're still at war with Prussia."

"You know a great deal about my affairs, Mr. Pitt."

"That, sir, is the necessary business of a statesman. My own problem is equally delicate. I stand outside the government and must watch us squander our national strength."

Maurice struggled with an oyster, nicked his thumb with his knife, but finally managed to pry open the shell.

Pitt was concentrating, and didn't notice. "I believe you and I can be of assistance to one another."

Maurice sprinkled powdered East Indian pepper on the raw oyster and ate it very quickly.

"First, if I may, a question. I know of your attempt to obtain recognition of your family title from King Louis. Are your leanings French?"

It was less difficult for Maurice to smile than he would have imagined a year earlier. "My reasons were purely personal," he said, "and I've made a final choice. I was born an Englishman, and I shall die one."

"Very good." Pitt was emphatic, and his rolling voice rose above the clatter of dishes and the hum of conversation in the main taproom. "In my opinion, England has only one real enemy: France. Our national ambitions clash in the one place where the real power and wealth of the future lie, the New World. There isn't room in North America for both of us."

"I do only a modest trade with our American colonies."

"You'll do more," Pitt assured him. "You know something of France, so I'm sure you'll agree with me. No two nations could stand at farther poles. Here, the people elect the men who govern for them. There, one incompetent autocrat rules. Here, every man may worship as he pleases, criticize Crown and Commons in print or in a speech as he sees fit, and gather for any purpose except that of stirring up a rebellion. I'm sure I needn't tell you that in France there are no liberties worthy of the name."

"Perhaps you can understand, Mr. Pitt, why I wanted a voice in France."

"A commendable ambition, but short-sighted. No one man, no small group of men can recast a nation's attitude. Probably you were

323

taught, as I was, that France began to deteriorate after the reign of Henry the Fourth. Our philosophers and historians are wrong. Henry broke with an otherwise solid tradition, and even he used authoritarian methods to achieve relatively liberal results."

"I suppose he did," Maurice said, but nevertheless felt a sudden surge of pride in the first Philippe de Montauban.

"Our rivalry with France is more than political and commercial." Pitt's manner was overwhelmingly persuasive, a combination of brusque, self-confident realism and unassailable optimism. "There's no room in Europe for both their way of life and ours. The pox and the black ague cross borders, and so do ideas. One system or the other must be destroyed. They're strong and wealthy, and so are we. It may be a long struggle, and I have no false hopes. It may take a generation. But we can't let their backward philosophy win."

Maurice felt a glimmer of hope. It might be possible, after all, to help France achieve the ends for which his ancestors had fought, even though he might make his contribution in a way that had never occurred to him. "How do I fit into your scheme, Mr. Pitt?"

"Pelham and Carteret refuse to take any initiatives to alter the present alignment of European powers, but they can be forced to act if others take the initiative. We have an ally in King George, who is frightened almost to death that Prussia is going to invade and annex his Electorate of Hanover. Most members of the Commons are unhappy, too. They have no quarrel with Prussia, Spain, Saxony or Sardinia. I believe I can guarantee their support for a new approach after I've conducted a brief instructional campaign. The task I have in mind for you is somewhat more delicate."

They waited while the barmaid placed their kidney and beefsteak pies before them. Maurice broke the crust of his serving with his knife, and then sat back to avoid smelling the steam that curled up toward the blackened beams of the ceiling.

"Prussia has occupied the Silesian duchies, and has no real reason to remain at war with Austria. She also has no cause to be fighting us. The Austrians could be offered compensations if they're willing to withdraw from the war, too. You know Frederick, and you know Maria Theresa. I propose you visit them as an unofficial envoy. If you succeed, you'll be doing more than performing a patriotic duty. Your own profits will rise overnight."

Maurice scarcely knew Maria Theresa, but reminded himself that Kaunitz had become her First Minister.

"Pelham's government doesn't think highly of me, but I still have enough influence to send you to Prussia in a Navy sloop-of-war and provide you with a Royal Marine detachment as an escort on the whole journey."

Maurice realized that he was being offered the opportunity to serve

England and at the same time do something that could be of ultimate benefit to France. "I'll do it," he said, and even the kidney and beefsteak pie was more savory than he had thought it would be.

The headquarters established by Frederick of Prussia in his father's grim Berlin castle were cold, functional and without ornamentation. The stone floors were bare, only military maps covered the walls and the chairs lacked cushions. Sentries in dusty gray field uniforms stood on guard duty at every turn in the labyrinth of corridors, and an adjutant armed with two loaded pistols was stationed at the main entrance, where he signed permits allowing those on strictly official business to enter the ancient fortress.

King Frederick had changed, too. He wore a plain infantry officer's uniform of gray wool, his boots showed signs of hard wear and there were several bullet creases in his steel helmet that hung on a wall peg beside his stained cloak. Only the narrow green ribbon he wore across his chest distinguished him from the lowest-ranking officer in his forces, but a flute and a pile of sheet music on a small table behind his desk were reminders that his tastes had not completely changed.

"I'm willing to hear any reasonable offer of an honorable compromise, de Montauban," he said stiffly, "although I consider it strange that you carry no credentials from Prime Minister Pelham."

"I've given you King George's private letter," Maurice replied in the same tone, "and you'll either have to accept or reject my assurances that Mr. Pitt has mustered enough votes in the Commons to insure the British government's approval of a cease-fire on the right terms."

"What are those terms?"

"You've beaten the Austrians in two campaigns, Your Majesty, you've won great personal glory in several battles and you've occupied Silesia. Unless you've changed, you've accomplished the goals you set out to achieve."

"I'd be satisfied," Frederick replied after a pause, "but the Austrians refuse to concede me Silesia."

"If I can persuade them to accept the loss of the duchies, would you sign a peace treaty with them?"

"Certainly, but it's plain you expect something from me in return. How expensive is it?"

"It will cost you nothing in either territory or prestige. Withdraw your support of the French in the Lowlands, and they'll be forced to return Belgium to the Austrians. Louis isn't strong enough to fight a long campaign against a combined English-Dutch force there, particularly with his seacoast blockaded."

Frederick suddenly looked less austere. "My compliments to your

Mr. Pitt. A very ingenious scheme."

"Those are our suggestions, Your Majesty. It wouldn't be accurate to call them conditions. Agree to them, and we're prepared to resume trade relations at once, even before a formal armistice is arranged."

Frederick drummed his desk. "The English and Dutch will demand at least a token of victory. I'm opposed to the currying of public opinion, but it's important in both your country and Holland. What little triumph can Pitt give them?"

"We intend to insist that Austria grant freedom of worship to the Belgians."

Frederick stared at him incredulously. "I wish you luck," he said, "and the unstinting help of your God."

It was unnerving to discuss affairs of state in a completely feminine parlor in the Hofburg while the Archduke Joseph, heir to the throne of Austria, drooled on the boots of the First Minister and crawled around the room on all fours. But Maria Theresa apparently took comfort in the presence of her baby, and Anton von Kaunitz had necessarily become accustomed to finding the diaper-clad child underfoot.

Maurice had no idea where he stood. Two days earlier, immediately after his arrival in Vienna, he had presented the entire British plan in detail to Anton, who had made no comment, and had gone off at once to confer with the Empress. They had held almost continuous meetings ever since, but neither Maria Theresa nor her First Minister was indicating either relief or displeasure.

"Her Imperial Majesty," Kaunitz said, moving a polished shoe out of Archduke Joseph's reach, "is grieved by the loss of Silesia. It has been her unalterable purpose to recover territory that rightfully belongs to Austria, but I hope I've persuaded her to accept its loss. We can't win back the duchies by force of arms, and she is anxious to devote herself to the prosperity and welfare of her subjects, so it may be she can be persuaded to seek a non-military solution."

Maurice silently applauded his performance. Anton was his business associate and relative by marriage, but these ties carried no weight when more important considerations were at stake. There could be no question that he and the Empress had worked out every nuance of Austria's bargaining position, but his seeming ignorance was a masterpiece of play-acting.

Maria Theresa was even more accomplished. Blithely ignoring the pressing problems of peace and war, national prestige and power, she changed the subject. "I'm so sorry you didn't bring Stephanie with you," she said.

"I'm sorry it wasn't possible, madame," Maurice replied, using her

326

own phrase and tone, "but our physician advised her not to travel at present. We expect a child within a few months."

The Empress forgot she was the ruler of ten million people, and clapped her hands together. "How wonderful!" She beamed, then gazed fondly at her own son, who was now chewing on the ribbons of the gown he wore over his diapers. "You have no idea how much joy a child can bring to a family." She took a deep breath preparatory to launching into an anecdote on her favorite subject.

Kaunitz was familiar with the signs. "Nothing," he said quickly, "can repay Austria for the permanent loss of Silesia, and we want our allies to understand that Her Imperial Majesty will carry the scars of her tragedy for the rest of her days."

"All England sympathizes with her distress," Maurice replied, aware that he was speaking only for Pitt and himself. "King George, who is a father to all his subjects as well as his own family, is very upset." He hoped the Austrians hadn't heard that the British monarch was engaged in bitter, never-ending disputes with his own children.

Kaunitz' solemn bow expressed Austria's official appreciation of His Britannic Majesty's concern.

Maria Theresa's mask dropped. "I want all of Belgium restored to me," she said, "including the areas the Dutch conveniently forgot to return under the Treaty of Utrecht in 1713."

The Dutch, Maurice hastened to assure her, were willing to make the sacrifice. He saw no point in adding that they had been forced to keep troops in the territory in order to maintain order, and would be delighted to be rid of their responsibilities.

"Also," the Empress said, "I have no intention of giving up the Spanish possessions in Italy that Austria acquired at Utrecht. My cousins in Madrid are greedy, and need to be taught a lesson."

The Spaniards were too weak to press their claims without help from other nations, and Maurice nodded agreeably. London and Amsterdam had nothing to lose by accepting conditions that cost them neither territory nor money.

Having achieved what she wanted, Maria Theresa became feminine again. "I hope you and Stephanie will have your son's portrait painted twice each year. We treasure the miniatures of Joseph made six months ago."

Before Maurice could make a polite reply, Kaunitz intervened. "Bavaria and Sardinia won't make peace with us unless we reward them."

"Mr. Pitt discussed that problem with me. The promise of minor territorial concessions should satisfy them. He asked me to stress to you and Her Imperial Majesty that the demands of small powers often remain unsatisfied." Maurice realized he was saying, in effect, that Austria need not feel bound to honor any agreement made with her two minor foes. But he had become sufficiently cynical to feel that a stable peace in central Europe was far more important than the expansionist aims of two insignificant, opportunist states.

"That seems to settle virtually everything," Kaunitz said, his manner indicating the contrary.

Again Maria Theresa took charge. "I was prepared for any demand from Frederick. After all, he's an atheist. But I was astonished and sickened when Prince von Kaunitz told me that my allies, people in whom I've placed my trust, demand freedom of worship for the Belgians."

"England and Holland haven't treated their responsibilities lightly, madame," Maurice said, unaware that his own tone had become firmer. "They require something in return for the lives they've lost and the money they've spent."

"The Church," Maria Theresa retorted, "won't tolerate the practice of heresies in Austrian territory."

"By the Church," Maurice countered, "you mean the Austrian hierarchy, madame?"

"Of course. I held a long meeting with two of my cardinals yesterday afternoon, and they're adamant!" When she bared her teeth her feminine charm vanished.

"If it should be necessary," Maurice said, "England and Holland are prepared to obtain a public declaration from Pope Benedict to the effect that he supports the principle."

"But you're heretics!" Her wail was as disbelieving as it was angry.

Maurice knew it would be a waste of breath to tell her that he himself was a Catholic. Her attitudes were too rigid to admit the existence of his kind of more liberal Catholicism. "His Holiness," he said, "believes Catholicism will become stronger there in an atmosphere of freedom. Centuries of Spanish rule, combined with the methods of the Inquisition, have created a religious apathy in the Belgians. If the Church doesn't show a sympathetic concern for their problems, they'll join the Dutch Protestants. That's been happening in some of the Flemish districts, and the movement will spread. Within a few years the Belgians will revolt, and I'm afraid Austria can expect no help from either England or Holland under such conditions."

Maria Theresa had scarcely bothered to listen. "I can't believe Pope Benedict would tell heretics his views."

Kaunitz' eyes narrowed. "Has His Holiness actually been in direct correspondence with someone of standing in England?"

"He and Mr. Pitt have exchanged letters on the subject of the Belgians." Maurice carefully refrained from adding that he himself had been responsible, with the help of Father Radetsky. The mere mention of the Jesuit's name would cause an explosion.

Maria Theresa's mouth was set, and when her jaw jutted forward she looked like her Hapsburg ancestors.

Thanks to Father Radetsky's foresight, Maurice was ready to cope with the ticklish situation. "Madame," he said, "the Apostolic Delegate to Vienna, Bishop de Ciardi, is prepared to corroborate what I've just told you. He's familiar with Pope Benedict's views."

Maurice had seen enough bigotry to know he should be able to accept her blind hostility calmly. Nevertheless it disturbed him that Maria Theresa, a ruler who took such fierce pride in her supposed devotion to Catholicism, should shun Pope Benedict's opinions because they were more advanced than her own. The moment had come for him to show her that he was negotiating from a position of strength.

"If you refuse to grant freedom of worship to the Belgians, madame," he said, "you face two alternatives, neither of them pleasant. Perhaps the war will continue on its present basis, but you can't depend on it. England and Holland may make a separate peace with Prussia and the smaller nations in order to concentrate on their struggle with France."

"The British legation," Kaunitz said sharply, "had given us no indication that Prime Minister Pelham's government is even considering a separate peace."

"I thought you realized, Anton, that I've come to Vienna, as I went to Berlin, in a strictly unofficial capacity, representing a group in Parliament and certain commercial interests, among them the East India Company and my own. I'm making my headquarters at the legation only because I was provided with a formal escort of Royal Marines. I speak for His Majesty, not His Majesty's government," he added with a grin.

Kaunitz scowled, and Maria Theresa used one of her more potent weapons, an expression of crushed bewilderment.

"If the war goes on," Maurice said, "I can promise you that William Pitt will actively oppose Prime Minister Pelham on the issue of making a treaty with Prussia. He's rallying support for a peace party, and so is King George. Pitt feels confident he can muster enough votes in the Commons to bring down the government."

Maria Theresa fell back on the last gun in her arsenal, tears.

She wept for the sake of maintaining bigotry in the Lowlands, Maurice thought, and was unmoved.

Kaunitz handed the Empress a handkerchief, and she pressed it to her face, but was careful not to smear the antimony on her eyelids.

Archduke Joseph began to wail, too, and his mother picked him up, cradling him in her arms.

Maurice waited with as much patience as he could muster, feeling a trifle sorry for the diplomats who were required to visit the Empress' court regularly. It would be impertinent of him to point out the advantages of accepting the scheme he had outlined, and he might actually damage its cause if he pressed too hard. So it was better to remain silent and wait for Maria Theresa's hysteria to pass. Then, perhaps, she would tell him her decision.

Anton von Kaunitz unexpectedly came to his assistance. "The war with Prussia is exhausting us," he said. "We must make peace."

Maria Theresa peered at him over the top of his handkerchief, sniffling.

"The Church hierarchy," the First Minister said, "may be unhappy with the granting of freedom of worship to the Belgians, but the hierarchy isn't paying the costs of the war."

The Empress refused to admit complete defeat too quickly. "Frederick is the anti-Christ!"

"All I know," Kaunitz replied, showing irritation with her for the first time, "is that one of his divisions can beat two of ours. We have fourteen in the field right now, at a monthly cost of one hundred and seventy thousand thalers for each division. At this rate the Imperial Treasury will be empty by Christmas."

"It's the Pope's fault," Maria Theresa insisted. "If he'd support us, we could do what our own cardinals think right in Belgium."

Neither of the men replied.

She wearily hoisted her baby to her shoulder, supporting his head, and stood. "Do as you please, Anton," she said, suddenly vexed with him. Nodding distantly to Maurice, she swept from the room.

Kaunitz immediately relaxed, his attitude that of a man dealing with a business associate and relative. "Austria," he said with a slow smile, "accepts your proposals."

A sudden wave of exhilaration swept over Maurice. Just as his grandfather had predicted, he had found an unexpected way to fight bigotry, and had won a major battle. Ironically, he had also helped set the stage for a major Anglo-Dutch assault on the great stronghold of religious intolerance, France, and by playing a role in the confrontation had cut himself off forever from the land of his ancestors.

BOOK FIVE

BOOK FIVE

W e've managed to reduce our definition to these terms,"
Philippe de Montauban said. "The majority imposes—
or tries to force—its will on the minority, regardless of
whether that minority is religious, ethnic or what will
you."

"Therefore," Bishop de Montauban said, "you find a
persecution of Catholics in Protestant lands, and vice
versa."

"And a persecution of Jews everywhere."

"The best expositions I've ever read on the rights and
obligations of minorities are in Pope John's Pacem in
Terris."

"The Encyclical Letter, Peace on Earth, destined to
become the single most widely quoted document of
time, if it isn't already. If you'll serve the salad, I'll get
my copy from the library."

"You have it?"

"Even a heathen may have the perspicacity to appreciate Pope John's mind."

The Bishop took crisp, green salad from the bowl and
put it on their plates.

Philippe returned with a paper-bound pamphlet.
"There's so much here," he said, sitting and opening
the booklet. " 'The right to worship God according to
one's conscience. This too must be listed among the
rights of a human being, to honor God according to the
sincere dictates of his own conscience, and therefore

the right to practice his religion privately and publicly.' "

"I was thinking specifically of clauses ninety-four to ninety-six," the Bishop said, reaching for the pamphlet. "He's speaking of the striving of people of the same ethnic group to become independent and to form one nation." Clearing his throat, he began to read.

" 'Since this cannot always be accomplished for various reasons, the result is that minorities often dwell within the territory of a people of another ethnic group, and this is the source of a serious problem.

" 'In the first place, it must be made clear that justice is seriously violated by whatever is done to limit the strength and numerical increase of these lesser peoples; the injustice is even more serious if vicious attempts of this kind are aimed at the very extinction of these groups.

" 'It is especially in keeping with the principles of justice that effective measures be taken by the civil authorities to improve the lot of the citizens of an ethnic minority, particularly when that betterment concerns their language, the development of their natural gifts, their ancestral customs, and their accomplishments and endeavors in the economic order.' "

"It takes a Protestant to realize that the next clause balances Pope John's thoughts on the subject." Philippe took the pamphlet from his cousin, and read. " 'It should be noted, however, that these minority groups, either because of their present situation which they are forced to endure, or because of past experiences, are often inclined to exalt beyond due measure anything proper to their own people, and to such a degree as to look down on things common to all mankind as if the welfare of the human family must yield to the good of their own ethnic group. Reason rather demands that these very people recognize also the advantages that accrue to them from their peculiar circumstances; for instance, no small contribution is made toward the development of their particular talents and spirit by their daily dealings with people who have grown up in a different culture since from this association they can gradually make their own the excellence which belongs to the other ethnic group. But this will happen only if the minorities through association with the people who live around them make an effort to share in their cus-

toms and institutions. Such, however, will not be the
case if they sow discord which causes great damage and
hinders progress.' "

"Amen," Charles de Montauban said.

tons and institutions. Such, however, will not be the
hinders discord which cause great damage and
hinders progress.

bias nedtan bad............said.

book five

*You profess the Holy Scriptures: but what
do you witness and experience? What
interest have you in them? Can you set
to your seal that they are true by the
work of the same spirit in you that gave
them forth in the holy ancients?*

—WILLIAM PENN

1770

"Tar and feather the son of a bitch!"

It was quiet in the taproom of the Boar's Head, the most popular
tavern in the western frontier town of Springfield, and although
rough talk was common in the British New World colony of Massachusetts Bay, several of the men gathered at the long table of scarred
pine looked uneasily at the speaker.

"Not so damn loud, Tom," one of them said, and jerked his head
in the direction of a pair of militia officers who were starting to eat
their dinner at the opposite end of the long, starkly furnished room.

The man called Tom shrugged, gulped down his drink of spiced
rum and signaled to the barmaid for another. "If they wasn't on duty,
they'd join us."

Several of his companions agreed.

But the spokesman for the minority held his ground. "Hell, they're
on duty! They've took an oath to protect everybody, even that scum.
I agree with you, tar and feather the bastard, but we don't have to
print an advance notice of it in one of the Boston newspapers."

Tom wiped his mouth on the sleeve of his greasy buckskin shirt.
"Them two will look the other way. I happen to know they feel like
we do."

"All the same, let's not start a riot the militia will have to put
down. My brother is on duty this month, and he takes his military
service seriously. The rest of the year he's as quick as anybody else to
judge right from wrong, and if he wasn't on the palisades this very
minute, he'd be as anxious as you and me to rid this town of the dirty
hog. But not this month. No, sir. If his lieutenant gave him the order,
he'd put a rifle shot through me, his own brother."

Tom accepted his fresh drink, then ordered another round for
everyone else. "Sometimes you don't think good, Eddie," he said
earnestly. "Ever since the Algonkin scare two weeks ago, the whole
blame half-battalion has been up on the palisades. Right?"

His friends nodded. Only a fortnight earlier a party of warriors from the northern Algonkin tribe had been seen only a few miles above Springfield on the Connecticut River, but had escaped overland before they could be taken and questioned. The town, long accustomed to raids by hostile savages, had taken the necessary precautions, and both companies of militia on duty at present had been stationed in the blockhouses located at intervals on the wall of point-topped logs that surrounded the wilderness community.

"Like you say, Eddie," Tom continued, "it's their duty to protect everybody, even curs that stink worse than the garbage before it gets collected every Friday. But there ain't more than one or two, maybe, in the half-battalion, who would stand up for the bastard if they wasn't on duty. The rest of them agree with us, right down the line. Am I right?"

"I guess so," Eddie conceded.

"Suppose our platoon was on duty. Which would be more important to us—keeping watch for the Algonkin or going off to stop our friends from making Springfield a proper place for God-fearing Christians to live in again? You know damn well that every last man in our platoon would stay at his post up there on the palisades, that's what. We wouldn't cheer or whoop it up if Major White was around, but we'd be hoping the boys would pour that tar nice and hot, and spread on the feathers thick. Right?"

"Right." Eddie spread his thick woodsman's hands in a gesture of defeat. "Let's get started, huh? My jaw is tired from all this talking, and it'll be night in a few more hours. The whole town has been waiting, so they got the right to celebrate in daylight."

A new sense of purpose came over the entire group. No one spoke again, drinks were drained, and coppers were thrown into a mug at the center of the table. Each man scrupulously remembered how many cups of rum he had ordered, and each took care to leave a ha'penny for the barmaid, too. Honor was all-important in wilderness towns, and it did not occur to anyone to cheat either the proprietor of the Boar's Head or the woman who had served the party.

The men filed out quietly and, blinking in the early spring sunshine, moved off down Pynchon Street. Farmers who had brought their wares to market, trappers who were idling away the afternoon, and townsmen who had nothing better to occupy them looked at the group with curiosity, asked a brief question or two, and then fell in behind them.

The word spread swiftly: "They're going after Dale."

A tanner, a greengrocer and a gunsmith locked up their shops and joined the group. So did two carpenters at work on a house they were building for one of the newly-rich merchants in the expanding town. Not wanting to miss the occasion, they left their tools on the open platform that, when completed, would become the second floor of the building. It did not occur to either of them, or to anyone else, that their saws and hammers might be stolen; men were still hanged, without recourse to law, for committing such offenses in a frontier town.

By the time the group turned in at Queen's Lane it comprised at least fifty determined citizens. At the back of Martin's stable two drums of tar were rolled toward a fire someone started, and the black mass was poured into cauldrons. Other men went to work stripping a pine log that had not yet been cut into lumber, and four or five volunteers went off to Gibson's little featherbedding factory to obtain feathers. They planned to pay for what they needed, but Jeremiah Gibson was pleased to make them a gift of all they wanted.

"It's high time we did something," he told them. "I can't come with you because my bad back is acting up, but at least I can give you the feathers. Plaster him good with them, boys. It'll be great to breathe clean air again after today."

By four o'clock in the afternoon, the crowd was ready.

Most of the houses on Essex Street, fronting on the Connecticut River, dated back to the middle of the seventeenth century, and had been erected soon after Springfield had been established. Residents of the town had good reasons for considering them undesirable. Located close together, they were cramped log cabins with open spaces filled with clay. Since they were only a few feet from the river, they lacked the protection of the palisade that was built in a three-quarter circle around the rest of the community. Nothing but their own vigilance protected those who lived in these miserable dwellings from uninvited visits made by trappers, hunters, fishermen and even an occasional, stray Indian who happened to approach Springfield by boat. Only families who could afford no better housing lived on Essex Street.

The cabin at the north end of the row was different because William Dale had cut a door into the wall that looked out onto Kent Street, at the rear of the house, and had made a stone-lined cooking pit on the Essex Street side. It was a feeble attempt to insure greater privacy, but it was better than no effort, and when Annie Dale cooked dinner and supper for her husband and their little daughter, she wasn't forced to converse with all the other women, whose pits were located on the Kent Street side.

Annie listlessly stirred the contents of the blackened pot with a ladle her husband had carved for her from the branch of an oak, and although the scent of the cooking food was savory, it gave her no pleasure. A tired woman in her late twenties, she looked many years older; her blonde hair was faded and wispy, she was almost painfully thin, and her stooped shoulders accurately reflected her admission that she felt a sense of permanent, bitter defeat.

The stew was nourishing, she had to admit, but she was heartily sick of venison, wild parsnips and herbs. Granted that William brought home the food from the forest, so it cost them literally nothing to eat, but a steady diet of wilderness meals over the past two years had ruined her appetite. There had been a time when she had dreamed of the meat pies, eggs and fruit trifles she had taken for granted in her parents' home, but she no longer thought of such things. Food was nothing more than a necessity. Sighing, she wiped perspiration from her forehead and cleaned off her hand on her threadbare apron.

William Dale appeared in the cabin entrance, and stood for a moment, watching her. A lean man many years her elder, with the mark of the wilderness indelibly stamped in his impassive face, permanently tanned skin and hooded blue eyes, he moved with a quiet that had become second nature to him when he finally joined her at the pit.

"Will supper be ready soon?"

Annie gasped. "You startle a body when you sneak up behind me, William!"

"Sorry. I keep forgetting. Do you want me to wake up the baby for supper?"

"Not yet. Venison takes cooking to make it tender."

He nodded and sniffed. "Smells good."

Annie wanted to scream. Apparently he was satisfied with venison twice daily, every day of the year, and she could manage only one reply. "I hope you like it."

"I will." Suddenly he put a sinewy hand on her shoulders. "One of these days things will get better, I reckon. You'll see."

"Of course they will," she replied mechanically.

"You knew when you married me that we'd never be rich like John Hancock——"

"I hate even hearing his name!" Her lethargy gave way to sudden passion.

There was a flicker of expression in Dale's eyes before they became guarded again. "There's no need to take on like that," he said mildly.

"You talk about him all the time. I keep wishing you hadn't spent that year working for him."

"I never saw really rich people until I met him. I never knew people lived like he does. And you can't blame a man for wishing, sometimes, that he could buy a heap of nice things for his wife and daughter, and have servants to wait on them, and carriages for them to ride in——"

"William Dale, you ought to be ashamed of yourself!"

There was no apology in his slow grin.

Annie made an effort to return his smile, but she felt certain he knew her reaction was forced. "There are so many things more important than money."

He nodded, stroking his long jaw.

She became contrite. "I didn't mean to preach a sermon at you, William."

"It makes no mind." He hesitated for an instant. "I've been doing some wondering. I can't help thinking we'd be a heap better off living somewheres else. A place where I'm not known."

Annie turned her rigid back to him and stirred the contents of the pot furiously.

"I'm thinking of you and the baby, not me."

"I have a right good idea of what's going through your head, William Dale. I'm telling you plain—for the last time, ever—that if I'd wanted to spend my life hiding and sniffling in Philadelphia, that's what I'd have done. But I'm here, in Springfield, with you."

Again he reached out to pat her shoulder.

Only Annie knew that in spite of his great physical strength and coordination, he was a shy man. As her father had warned her before she had married, one who had spent so much of his life alone in the wilderness was difficult to understand, and the woman who became his wife would seldom know what he was thinking. But she could take consolation in the realization that his love for her was strong and undeviating.

"It's when they act mean to you in the streets that I start getting churned inside," he said.

"We knew it would happen."

"That doesn't make it easier to bear." Dale hitched up his trousers of faded buckskin. "Sooner or later," he said, "life here has got to change for the better." The refrain was so old that he was unable to make it sound convincing.

Annie was too tired to keep up the pretense. "Supper is ready," she announced abruptly.

"I'll go wake up the baby."

"Let her sleep a spell longer. You and I can eat now. Her share will keep warm. So just carry the kettle inside for me."

With the skill of long practice he slid a pole made from a sapling beneath the handle of the pot and, balancing the heavy container with ease, carried it into the cabin. As always, it was dark inside, no matter how bright the sunshine, for thick, oiled paper covered the windows, and just enough light filtered through to make it unnecessary to light a cheap candle.

The most that could be said for the one-room dwelling was that it was clean. The bare earth floor had been swept so vigorously that the

340

marks of the straw broom had left an imprint in the hard-packed soil. The old patchwork quilt that covered the sagging bedstead was spotless, and so was the softer blanket that covered the small child who was asleep in a crudely-made crib in the far corner. The single chest of drawers in which the family's possessions were stored had been scrubbed, and so had the plain pine table and the tree stumps that were the only chairs in the house.

Annie, watching her husband drop the kettle onto a hook at the side of the hearth, loathed the cabin with all her being, but took care not to let her husband see how she felt. She had learned that a man who had spent countless years sleeping in the open regarded any roof over his head as a luxury. Certainly it had not crossed William's mind that their house was a dismal, forbidding place, and that, if she could, she would exchange it for any other dwelling on earth.

The problem was that she couldn't leave. William insisted they remain in Springfield, and either would not or could not admit to himself that they had no hope of making a happy life for themselves in western Massachusetts Bay. There were times when she admired his stubborn resistance to pressure that would force other men to buckle, but in this instance, she was convinced, he was going too far. Had they moved into Springfield as total strangers their lot might have been different, but everyone in town knew William—and remembered. Annie shuddered.

She ladled venison and parsnip stew into two bowls, which she placed on the table, and they sat down on tree stumps to eat in silence. If she indicated as much as a hint of her own bleak despair to him, she thought, they would be on the Chicopee trail to Worcester and, perhaps, Boston, within twenty-four hours. But the price would be too great to bear. William would be destroyed. He had elected to make his stand in Springfield, and it was her duty as his wife to remain uncomplainingly at his side.

The noise, at first, sounded like water tumbling over rocks somewhere in the distance. Then, as it grew louder, the couple at the table realized that men were either shouting or chanting, but it was impossible to make out the sense of their words. Annie frowned and stopped eating, her spoon suspended in air, but William continued to concentrate on his venison stew. He seemed indifferent to the commotion until the mob reached Kent Street.

Then, very casually, he stood. "I reckon I'd better see what's happening," he said, and went to the door that opened onto the Kent Street side.

A crowd of jostling, gesticulating men was surging down the street toward his house, and a single glance was enough to tell him their mood. He stepped inside again, bolted the door and hurried to the Essex Street door in order to make it secure, too.

Annie's nervousness gave way to raw fear. She clutched her husband's arm and looked up at him, hoping he would dispel her fright with a word.

But the situation was too grave for him to dissemble, and he told her, wordlessly, that her nightmare was being realized.

She burst into tears and clung to him.

"Dale, you bastard, we know you're in there!" a man shouted.

"Come out, or we'll come in after you!"

William Dale stood very still in the center of the cabin until a rock thudded against the wall. Then, moving very quickly, he took his skinning knife from his belt and slashed at the oiled paper over the front window.

The mob, startled by his unexpected gesture, fell silent for a moment when they saw him framed in the open window.

Dale looked out, his face betraying no emotion, and knew the leaders. Suddenly he pointed a bony forefinger at the square-jawed man who stood in front of the others on his small patch of yard. "You, Tom!" he called. "Are you attacking women and babies these days? Don't you have anything better to do?"

The bewilderment in the faces of Tom and those clustered close behind him indicated they had forgotten, in their zeal, that Dale had a family.

Dale was unyielding. "Well?"

"You know damn well we don't mean no harm to your wife and son."

"Daughter," Dale corrected.

"Whatever. We'll leave them be."

"Do you expect me to trust you?"

"No more than we'll trust you, you bastard." Tom turned to confer with several of his lieutenants.

The mob became restless, and its deep, ugly rumble was menacing.

Tom raised a hand for silence. "Dale," he called, "send out your wife and daughter. Jimmy Harkins left for Worcester with a fur convoy about an hour ago, and we'll give your family an escort until they catch up with him. They'll be safe, I give you my word of honor."

In spite of her near-hysteria, Annie became caustic. "Word of honor!"

"He means it," her husband assured her.

"How about it?" Tom demanded.

"Hold on. Let me talk to my wife."

"No tricks!"

"I'm not in a position to play tricks, am I?" Dale asked.

A score of men replied with loud, mocking jeers.

"You'd better go, Annie," Dale said quietly.

"No, William. I—I can't leave you. They're going to kill you, and——"

"Go," Dale said, lifting the sleeping child from her crib and, wrapping her more securely in her blanket, handing her to his wife.

Annie's tears rendered her speechless.

Dale kissed her, then brushed the sleeping baby's face with his lips. "Don't you fret about me," he said. "I'll meet you in Worcester. I can take care of myself just fine."

She made a desperate attempt to recover, not wanting the mob to see her weep.

Another rock smashed against the log wall.

Dale glanced out of the window, saw that the crowd was holding firm, and estimated his chances. Until they actually broke toward the cabin, there was an outside possibility he might get away.

Sliding back the bolt, he grinned at Annie. "I want you to do just one thing," he said. "Take your time out there. Stand outside the door as long as you dare. Then walk slow as you go toward them. As slow as the baby crawls when she's half-asleep. Now, Annie, before their blood boils up too high."

He half-opened the door, pushed her into the clear, then slammed and bolted it again. Under the unvarying code of the wilderness, violence was never committed in the presence of women, so the mob wouldn't rush him until Annie and the baby were removed from the scene. With luck, that would give him one to two minutes to get away.

He raced to the rear door, moved the bolt silently and opened the door a crack. The fire in pit was still smoldering, but no one was in sight. It had not yet occurred to the mob to surround the cabin.

Dale made a wild dash toward Essex Street, then ran down it at full speed toward the wharves two squares away. A dozen householders and pedestrians saw him, but that couldn't be helped. Until he reached the protecting shield of the forest he would need speed and skill as well as luck.

Someone gave the alarm, and the mob charged after him, its rage all the worse because it might be denied its sport.

Two young, husky men in buckskins blocked Dale's path to the Essex Street wharves, but he made a quick loop around them before they realized what was happening. Then, hearing the roar of the crowd and seeing the sprinting men in the van, they asked no questions. They gave chase, too, and one drew a pistol.

There was a crack, and Dale heard a bullet whine close overhead. He was too breathless to offer a prayer of thanks.

Several boats were tied to the dock, but he was no river man, and knew his pursuers could catch him if he tried to maneuver an ungainly craft. At the far end of the wharf, however, he saw a frail canoe of birchbark and fir that belonged to an Essex Street neighbor, a half-breed who earned a precarious living as a fisherman. He climbed into it, cutting the line free with a single slash, and discovered that his hands were trembling as he picked up the paddle.

The spring current was swift, and a canoe was one vessel with which Dale was thoroughly familiar. Manipulating deftly, he nosed out into the stream, and not until he began to move swiftly did he realize that men were firing pistols and rifles from the shore. He crouched low and, heading in the direction of the far shore, paddled on an erratic, zigzag course.

Sweat poured into his eyes, half-blinding him, and he sucked precious air into his lungs, but could not get enough. Twisting his head for an instant, he saw that several boats had put out after him, and he knew his pursuers would not give up the chase until they caught him.

But he had an opportunity to think more clearly now, to plan rather than improvise. He was already out of firing range of the men on shore, and had enough of a start that the men in the boats would need to exert great efforts to overtake him. All the same, they would follow him, so he needed the knowledge of the New World wilderness acquired over a lifetime to save himself.

It was growing dark now, and that was his greatest single advantage. The moon wouldn't rise for an hour or two and, assuming the men in the boats could be left behind, he might outwit them. How? Paddling swiftly, with long, sweeping strokes, he pondered his terrible dilemma.

If he were Tom or one of the other leaders of the mob, he would assume that a refugee from their wrath would try to head westward, deep into the wilderness of the Berkshire Mountains. In fact, that was where he found himself heading. So his first, obvious move should be to return to the eastern shore of the Connecticut River and start in the direction of the seacoast. There were deep forests on that side, too, and Dale felt certain he could take care of himself in the woods.

Slowly, a little at a time, in order not to lose the full advantage of the current, he edged back toward the eastern bank of the river. When he went ashore, he decided, he would smash the canoe and scatter its parts so he would leave no traces. Thereafter it would be simple to make his way through the forest without leaving tracks. He had done it scores of times, and now he had more than ever at stake.

Inching toward the eastern bank, he smiled painfully. He had told Annie he would meet her and the baby in Worcester, and he intended to keep his word.

The men from Springfield were clever. Although they had probably guessed that Dale was heading toward the high Berkshires, they took no chances, and thirty or more armed men spread out inland on the eastern side of the Connecticut River, too. The task had not been entrusted to ordinary shopkeepers and artisans, either. These men were trained woodsmen, wilderness guides and hunters as familiar with the forest as Dale, as adept at traveling swiftly, at searching for some tiny clue, left in a single moment of carelessness, that would lead them to their quarry.

William Dale realized he had miscalculated the cunning and determination of his foes. For six days and nights he had been making his way eastward on a solitary march that seemed endless. For each mile he actually advanced in the direction of Worcester, he was forced to go three miles north or four south in a never-ending battle of wits. He had to avoid the Chicopee trail and the other major routes, knowing that all of them would be watched, and twice he had bone-chilling escapes when he heard his enemies only a short distance away. The first time he plunged deep into a thicket of briars to elude them, cutting his face and ripping his shirt; the second was even more harrowing, and he spent hours hiding under a dead, decayed oak while ants and other insects crawled over him.

There were rivers, creeks and small lakes everywhere, so he was able to satisfy his thirst. But a lack of food was driving him out of his mind. He had no firearms, and would not have dared to use a pistol or rifle had he carried one. He was adept at setting traps, but the knowledge was useless. For one thing, a man in flight had no time to wait until an animal fell into a trap. For another, he wouldn't have been able to light a fire to cook meat.

One night, on the thickly wooded shore of a tiny lake, he fashioned himself a spear with his skinning knife, caught a fish and then ate it, raw, after scaling and gutting it. That had been his only real meal. Berries weren't yet ripe, so he was forced to live on wild parsnips and other roots, but it took so long to hide the signs of digging that, more often than not, he decided the effort was not worth the bother and time it consumed.

All the same, by the afternoon of the sixth day he realized his strength was ebbing. He needed solid food, a place to rest, and enough time to discourage his foes.

Dale had no idea what made him think of Ossie Jones. Only a truly desperate man would turn to Ossie for assistance, but someone in dire need had no choice. And Ossie offered a perfect refuge. A former trapper, he lived in a cave in the hills above the little Ware River, about half-way between Springfield and Worcester, and no one ever made a deliberate visit to him. Folks from civilized places said that Ossie was mad, but wilderness dwellers had a simpler explanation.

He was forest fey, they said, which meant he had spent so many years in the wilderness alone that he was a trifle daft, but harmless enough. Nevertheless, even those who had met other forest feys avoided Ossie because his high-pitched laugh made them uneasy. And the Indians, who were afraid of madness, never stole from Ossie, so he lived peacefully in his isolated cave. He liked it that way, and apparently was never bothered by a lack of company.

After Dale made up his mind to seek Ossie's help, he had to march an extra day and a half to reach the cave, and wondered if he could survive long enough to get there. He had worn through his moccasins, and his feet were swollen. Occasionally, he discovered, his mind wandered, and that frightened him. He had no time to lose.

Ossie Jones sat cross-legged before a small wood fire outside the entrance to his cave, an old man with a wizened, leathery face and a matted, white beard and hair. His spidery body, encased in ragged buckskins, looked frail, but like so many who were demented, Ossie possessed surprising physical strength.

His piercing cackle greeted Dale, who struggled slowly up the slope toward him. "I see ye coming," the old man said. "I seen ye down yonder in the valley, and I wagered me an extra drink o' acorn whisky ye'd drop dead afore ye got here. I lose."

Dale was so completely out of breath he couldn't speak, and although he felt like crawling on his hands and knees, pride kept him upright.

"First off, ye need a drop o' soup. I been brewin' it for ye, and I'm right glad ye didn't die. I don't like the taste o' soup, but God punishes them who waste."

Dale's hand trembled violently as he accepted a steaming gourd. The broth was rich, with a meat flavor, and he drank it gratefully.

"Not too fast, mind ye!" Ossie ordered. "Ye been a wilderness man long enough t' know ye'll start retchin' if ye down take it slow, Dale."

The mention of his name was a shock, and Dale peered inside the cave.

"There ain't nobody here, and ain't been since the geese went south!"

It was astonishing, after all these years, that Ossie had remembered his name. The old man might be a forest fey, but there was nothing wrong with his memory.

"Ye'll take kindly t' a few strips o' this here jerked venison and a mite o' parched corn."

Dale took the food from a hand so thin it resembled a filthy claw.

"Slow. That's it. And wash it down with a drop o' acorn whisky."

The fermented brew was so bitter it brought tears to Dale's eyes, but he did not dare offend his host by refusing it. "Ossie, you've saved my life."

"I reckon," the old man said comfortably. "This time."

346

Dale glanced at him.

Ossie did not stir. "Eat, young 'un. Then ye'll need sleep. We got time a-plenty t' talk."

William Dale struggled to consciousness through deep layers of sleep. He thought he heard a wolf howling, and that a full moon was shining, but when he opened his eyes he discovered the light was coming from a bright fire at the entrance to the cave. Then he remembered and, orienting himself, knew that he had been asleep on a bed of pine boughs in the inner recesses of the cave.

The howling noise disturbed him, however, so he reached for his skinning knife and crept quietly toward the mouth of the cave. Then he halted, abruptly, and felt sickened. Ossie Jones was sitting cross-legged on the far side of the fire, both scrawny arms extended toward the sky as he bayed at the stars. Dale couldn't be certain, but thought he saw froth on the old man's lips.

Ossie seemed to become aware of his presence without looking at him. "So ye be awake? Dale, I been readin' the stars, and ye won't like what I feel bound in honor t' tell ye. This past week ye've been saved from a horrible death, but the next time ye can't escape."

Dale passed a hand across his face, wondering if he was dreaming. "It's writ right up there." Ossie jabbed a scrawny finger in the direction of the stars.

The old man was raving mad, Dale thought.

Ossie's wild laugh filled the cave, its echo bouncing from wall to wall.

Dale had always relied on his ability to face life on his own terms, but now a numbing chill crept up his spine.

Worcester had a reputation as the "bad luck" town of Massachusetts Bay, a name which its fifteen hundred inhabitants stolidly ignored. It had a promising future, they insisted, and explained its prospects to any visitor who would listen to them. They were located only forty miles west of Boston in fertile farm country, water power supplied by the Blackstone River was excellent, as their three mills demonstrated, and the town's position in the center of New England meant that, as the area's population grew, it would be the hub of all trade routes.

Few were impressed by the arguments. Originally established in 1657, it was twice abandoned in the next half-century and burned to the ground by Indians. Even now, although situated far behind the wilderness frontier, it was still surrounded by a high palisade, and a platoon of volunteer militiamen stood duty on its ramparts. There had been no Indian raids in more than a quarter of a century, but Worcester was taking no chances.

A wit from New Haven had remarked that no one objected to the abominable roads because no one rode on them, that it didn't matter if the food in the two inns was inedible because no one ever dined there, and that the chief purpose of Worcester's existence was to prove there was a Purgatory. The few wealthy families quietly agreed, and went to Boston for most of their purchases and entertainment. The two local general stores sold only essentials: salt and cooking utensils, bolts of thick cloth and farm tools.

But the majority of the town's citizens were content with their lot, confident that in time Worcester's merits would be recognized. Farmers sent their sons to be educated at Harvard College in Cambridge, and the crude frontier attitudes of such communities as Springfield were held in universal contempt.

Annie Dale and her baby were welcomed by the entire town, and even though the young woman was penniless, living quarters were found for her at the King William, a crumbling, decrepit inn, and she was told not to worry about the cost. The beef served in the dingy tavern on the inn's ground floor was tough and the cod was so salty it gave her a great thirst, but she found any food preferable to the steady diet of venison stew she had endured for so long.

What she enjoyed most was Worcester's ability to mind its own business. No crown warrant had been issued in Boston for her husband's arrest, and she was promised that, if and when William arrived, he would be safe from Springfield's wrath. And if people wondered about the attempt on his life, they had the tact to ask no questions. When put to the test, Worcester amply demonstrated its sophistication.

On the afternoon of the eleventh day of Annie's stay in the town, William staggered through the gates of the palisade. His shirt and trousers were in shreds; he was barefooted and so thin that his wife wanted to weep for him. But he managed to climb without assistance to her tiny attic room on the third floor of the inn, and in his eyes she saw his sense of triumph.

"I told you I could look after myself just fine," he said, and collapsed in her arms.

William Dale's recuperative powers were astonishing. Abel Ross, the rotund owner of the inn, told the customers who came to his general store, where he earned his real living, that he had never seen such a swift and dramatic recovery. "The day that fellow came weaving and tottering in from the forest," he said, "I was sorry we used up those coffins I had sent in from Boston last winter. But in just four days he's as hale as ever I've seen a man."

The men clustered around the salt and sugar barrels communicated with each other silently. Finally one of them said, "When we thought he'd left a widow and orphan, everybody agreed to pass the hat for their keep. But if he's strong enough to work, that makes things a mite different."

Ross laughed heartily. "That family won't cost us a farthing, boys! Dale insisted on going to work for me as a handyman this morning, and he swears he'll stay until he's paid off the whole debt. He was hammering away at dawn, fixing that place at the west end of the roof that's been leaking the last two-three years, and when I left to come over here he was putting a new door on the taproom. Not only that, but his wife was scrubbing the pantry."

Several of the men nodded and thought that, in time, the inn might be worth an occasional visit.

"He's no sluggard, believe me," Ross continued. "The very day after he got here, he sent off a letter to somebody in Boston, even though he was so weak he could scarce sit up in bed. And from what I—ah—just happened to hear him saying to his wife, I think he expects to be getting work at good pay off in Boston."

It was Ross' luck, the men's covert glances said, that the visit of the Dale family might prove financially profitable for him.

"Why do you suppose the folks in Springfield were after his hide?" one of the group asked. "He doesn't look like a murderer to me, but you just can't tell about somebody who has lived in the forests for a long time."

There was a silence, and Ross shrugged.

Three parties had enjoyed their noon dinner at the King William, and everyone praised Annie Dale's cooking. The taproom was clean for the first time in years, the new door opened and closed with ease and the rotting beams that had threatened the collapse of the end of the room near the hearth had been replaced. Abel Ross had found a couple worth far more than their lodging and board.

Now, with the customers gone, William and Annie Dale sat at a table near the pantry exit, eating their own dinner. As always, they were silent, the man absorbed in his own thoughts, the woman resigned to her husband's ways. Each had a small pie of veal, ham and hard-boiled eggs; Dale was drinking a modest cup of ale, while his wife preferred her own brew of sassafras tea.

Ross, approaching the table, told himself he was fortunate that their appetites were small. "The post has just arrived from Boston," he said. "There's a letter for you."

Dale accepted it with a nod of thanks, and when he broke the seal Ross saw several one-pound notes folded inside.

The communication itself was brief and crisp:

My dear Dale:

I reply to yours of the 5th Inst., and learn of your recent
Experiences with regret, but am not surprised by these
Difficulties. No man can with Impunity defy the will of the
People.

I am prepared to offer you a Position in my Employ on a
temporary status, and I feel reasonably Assured it will be
possible for me to place you in a more permanent Position
where your qualities of Workmanship can be effectively
utilized.

I enclose for your immediate Needs the sum of three
pounds, which I advance to you against your future Earnings, and on which I shall charge you no Interest.

I am, sir,

Yr. Obdt. &c. Svt.,
John Hancock

Dale passed the letter to his wife without comment.

Ross, who had received a communication from Hancock some
years earlier, recognized the bold signature of Massachusetts Bay's
most prominent merchant. The refugee from Springfield, it appeared,
had friends in high places.

"Mr. Ross," Dale said, "we'll be sorry to leave you, but we're going
on to Boston tomorrow. I can pay you in cash now for whatever we
still owe you for our keep."

"You owe me nothing," the proprietor said. "But I wish you'd
reconsider. I can make it worth your while to stay on here."

"Thank you, but I can't accept the offer," Dale said. "It isn't
fitting that my wife work, not when I'm able to make a living and we
have a child who needs her. I'll hire us post horses after dinner."

Ross accepted the loss with good grace, but his curiosity finally
overcame him. "It's none of my business, but would you mind telling
me why the folks out Springfield way were after your scalp?"

Dale looked up at him with eyes drained of all expression. "We're
Friends."

The innkeeper was puzzled.

"Out yonder," Dale said, "jerking his thumb over his shoulder in
the direction of the frontier, "they don't like Quakers."

1771

"My dilemma is both personal and absurd, which makes it no less
difficult to resolve." Dr. Benjamin Franklin, the most renowned of

American colonials living in England, removed his spectacles and absently cleaned them with the ruffle of his lawn shirtfront. Philosopher and scientist, author and publisher and diplomat, he was Deputy Postmaster General for Britain's North American colonies, as well as his compatriots' unofficial but exceptionally articulate spokesman in London. "The repeal of the Townshend Acts taxing virtually everything the colonies import from England did not include tea. Therefore Americans are continuing their embargo on tea, naturally. I am an American. I am offered tea. Do I or do I not drink it?"

Maurice de Montauban glanced across the drawing room of his London house and exchanged an embarrassed smile with his son, Bernard.

The younger de Montauban, as tall and sedate as his father, but a trifle more urbane, was equal to the occasion. "I suggest a practical solution, Dr. Franklin," he said in the same light, half-mocking tone. "My father will be delighted to have the butler remove the tea tray and bring you coffee or a glass of port instead."

Franklin, who loathed powdered wigs, passed a hand over his balding head. "I'm partial to port, of course, or to any other form of alcoholic spirits. Coffee, I'm sorry to say, gives me violent indigestion. It's the penalty I pay for eating too much rich food."

Maurice reached for a bell-rope.

"One moment," Franklin commanded. "Young man, your proposal merely evades the issue, which is no answer to the problem. Since I live here, I face the dilemma frequently. Now, on the one hand, a refusal to drink tea seems ridiculous. There's no embargo in England, and the East India Company won't be in any worse financial condition than it has been for the past year if I refrain. On the other hand, am I being disloyal to my fellow Americans if I reject this fragrant brew?" He sniffed appreciatively. "Calcutta long-leaf with a pinch of something more exotic, I believe."

Bernard realized that Franklin expected him to reply, and his father was deliberately remaining silent. "If I were you, I'd refuse—as a matter of principle."

"The young," Franklin said to Maurice, "are very firm believers in principle. They can enjoy so many of the world's delights they can afford to take lofty attitudes. At my age, unfortunately, the taste of food and drink affords a man his only sensual pleasures."

Bernard was uncertain whether the famous colonial was serious, and wished he hadn't asked for a meeting to obtain Franklin's advice. In spite of his own sophisticated background and years of travel abroad prior to his marriage, he felt himself incapable of coping with one of the age's most subtle, deft minds.

"I suppose, Bernard," Franklin said with a faint smile, "that as a Catholic you'd ask God to help you make certain your choice is the right one. Imagine how impossible it is for me. I don't suppose you've read Tindal's *Christianity?*"

"I had no interest in Deism at Oxford, Dr. Franklin."

"So you close your mind to it. To me, young man, the Almighty is not personal. He created and ordered the world, and He maintains its equilibrium, but in a completely abstract way. He has no interest in me, or in what I drink. So I'm forced to cope with a moral problem of my own making, if you'll pardon the redundancy. By definition, all moral questions are self-made." Franklin's manner became more sympathetic. "I'm neither trying to make a fool of you nor upset you, Bernard. There's a reason for this cross-examination."

"So I assumed, Dr. Franklin."

"Your father tells me you're thinking of migrating to the colonies. We Americans are absorbed in moral evaluations. We make a fetish of them. Don't go unless you're prepared to search your soul regularly." Franklin reached for the teapot and poured himself a large cup of the brew, which he sipped with obvious enjoyment. "My own conscience is both pragmatic and eclectic."

Bernard looked inquiringly at his father. "How much of my situation have you told him?"

"Only the outlines," Maurice said.

The younger de Montauban turned back to his father's guest. "The world appears to be changing very quickly these days. Our family business, like the East India Company and everyone else engaged in international trade, has suffered a serious decline."

"We expanded too rapidly," Maurice added.

The encyclopaedic Franklin often confessed that he knew very little about finances other than his own, and nodded vaguely.

"The Montauban profits," Bernard said, "will support my parents in the way they've been accustomed to living. But there simply isn't enough for Felicity and me, particularly since our second child was born. We've acted as agents for Thomas Hancock and Company of Boston from time to time, and I can't help wondering whether I might be able to earn a better living in the colonies than I can here."

Franklin drained his tea, took two tiny pinches of snuff from a worn mother-of-pearl box and sneezed. "John Hancock of Boston would be better able to advise you."

"I've been in correspondence with him for some time." Bernard hesitated.

His father glanced at him and frowned. "My son isn't telling you the whole story, Ben. He and Felicity want to leave England for reasons that aren't completely economic."

Franklin folded his hands across his paunch. "Don't tell me more than you want me to hear."

"I really can't ask for your help unless you know the truth."

Bernard spoke reluctantly, but his voice gradually became more firm. "You know we're Catholics, and you've spent enough time in England yourself to be aware of religious discrimination here. But, as a Protestant, perhaps you're not too conscious of it."

Franklin looked like a cherubic, slightly wizened owl. "The one disadvantage of being a publicly acknowledged Deist is that—no matter where I go—someone is always trying to convert me to a less rational form of Christianity. I was writing treatises on religious persecution long before you were born."

Bernard flushed. "I beg your pardon. All the same, people of your reputation are always treated gently. You aren't an almost unknown merchant-banker with a wife and two small children. Oh, I'll grant you that England is allegedly free of feelings against any faith. In theory, even an agnostic may hold public office. But the barriers are there, even though they're invisible. There are thousands of them. When I applied for membership in a club, I was told there were no openings. A few years ago, soon after Catherine was born, Felicity found a house she wanted near Birdcage Walk, on James Street. She fell in love with the place, as only a woman can. I made inquiries, and when I learned it was available, I opened negotiations. But within twenty-four hours of the time the owner discovered we were Catholics, he suddenly announced he had changed his mind and wasn't selling the place."

Franklin's jowls quivered when he sighed.

"Naïveté is a privilege of the young," Maurice said.

His son glanced at him sullenly, and it was apparent their differences of opinion were not new. "You and mother don't mind, but you belong to a different generation."

Maurice smiled apologetically at his guest. "Stephanie and I saw the persecution of the Jesuits in Catholic Austria when we were even younger than Bernard is now, and it made realists of us. We expect to be snubbed by the bigoted, the ignorant and the stupid, and we don't take offense."

"I want to call out anyone who regards my wife and children as inferior," Bernard said angrily.

Franklin helped himself to another cup of tea. "If you do, you'll have to give up merchant-banking and become a professional swordsman."

Maurice chuckled.

But his son failed to appreciate the colonial's renowned wit, and remained glum.

"You want me to tell you," Franklin said, "whether you'll be free of persecution in the American colonies. That's like asking whether your ship will sink in the Atlantic. It depends on the captain, the weather and the ship itself."

"I'm afraid you're being too cryptic for me, Dr. Franklin."

"Sorry. I find it difficult to resist making pseudo-literary allusions when I speak. It's a lifelong vice I haven't been able to curb. What part of the colonies do you have in mind?"

"I'm not sure. New England, I suppose. For business reasons."

"Massachusetts Bay and Connecticut are basically Congregational, which means they've inherited the worst of the Roundhead traditions of the Puritans. Rhode Island is the one colony that, theoretically, welcomes people of any faith, even Jews."

"We're not Jewish."

"And I've never lived there, so I can't vouch for the climate of tolerance." Franklin tempered the sharpness of his words and tone with a quiet smile. "No two colonies are alike. Even within colonies there are differences. Philadelphia, where I make my home, is influenced considerably by the Society of Friends, but the German Lutherans who have settled in other parts of Pennsylvania have created a far different atmosphere. New York Town is predominantly Dutch Reformed, but elsewhere in New York you'll find a great many Anglicans. Virginia is rather aggressively Anglican. If you want a basically Catholic society, you might think in terms of Maryland or South Carolina, but there are Anglicans in Maryland, too, and the descendants of French Huguenot refugees in South Carolina."

"I was reared on the concept that a completely Catholic nation can be as narrow-minded as one that actively persecutes its minorities." Bernard glanced in his father's direction. "My parents never allowed me to forget what happened to the Jesuits in Vienna."

"Jesuits are unpopular everywhere." Franklin waved a pudgy hand. "As a Freemason I was opposed to them myself—until I met some in France and the German states. They're so superbly educated that the ignorant are afraid of them, and all of us attack what we fear." He leaned forward in his chair. "I wish I could give you specific advice, Bernard, but you put me in an awkward position. Your ideas of religious liberty and mine might not be the same, for emotional reasons, even though we might meet on common intellectual ground."

"Our family has known for many generations," Maurice interjected, "that feeling in religious matters muddles principles."

Franklin slowly buttoned his waistcoat, a sure sign he was about to take his departure. "Even the Spanish Inquisitors thought that they were purifying Christianity, endowing it with greater liberty." He stood, tugging at his watch fob. "We're far more concerned about issues of political freedom in America these days, and that's a subject I really know. If you'd like to discuss it, have dinner with me at the Gamecock any evening you're free."

A few moments later father and son were alone. "He spoke in

generalities, as I knew he would," Maurice said. "You expected too much."

"Thank you for asking him here."

"It's always a pleasure to entertain Dr. Franklin. Bernard, why are you so determined to emigrate to the New World? Surely you aren't so thin-skinned that an occasional snub makes you miserable."

"I was ridiculed every day of the three years I spent at Oxford because of my French name and my religion! I see no reason why Joseph should be subjected to that kind of bullying."

"Joseph is an infant, and there's no way of telling what kind of world he'll live in as an adult. Teach him good from evil, and he'll find his own way."

"As I'm trying to find mine. I appreciate your concern for me, Papa, and I'm grateful for all you've done for me. But I've got to live according to my ideas of right and wrong, not yours."

"There's no need for you to raise your voice to me."

"Then don't nag at me!" Bernard knew he was shouting now but he continued, "We're not going to the ends of the earth, and we're not depriving you and Mama of your grandchildren for all time."

"I've been hoping that after you saw Dr. Franklin you'd rescind your resignation from the company."

"My decision is final!" Bernard turned away quickly, so Maurice wouldn't see he was on the verge of tears.

Boston was an astonishing, lusty and self-contradictory city. With a permanent population of more than twenty thousand and half again as many farmers, travelers from other colonies and visitors from the interior of Massachusetts Bay crowding her inns and rooming houses, she boasted that she was the largest English-speaking metropolis in North America. But her citizens spoke with a nasal twang that sounded like a foreign tongue to people newly arrived from England.

Nowhere were the contrasts between rich and poor so sharp. A gentleman's person and wallet weren't safe at the seamen's taverns on the sprawling waterfront, a shabby area dominated by huge, one-story warehouses of whitewashed wood, at least half of them owned by the ubiquitous Thomas Hancock and Company. In the harbor two sleek British frigates-of-war rode at anchor, and a number of merchantmen, particularly those that flew the Hancock flag, were substantial and trim. Other merchant ships, most of them flying no banners what-ever, were raffishly frail, and looked as though they would break up in a heavy sea.

Most of the people lived in cramped houses that London slum-dwellers would have scorned, yet seemed strangely content. The majority of men dressed in drab, dark gray suits of a locally made material known as linsey-woolsey, and the gowns of the women were shapeless, totally lacking in style. Ninety-five percent of the people of both sexes went wigless, and the men, including the students from Harvard College, located across the Charles River in Cambridge, tied their hair at the napes of their necks with eelskins.

Nevertheless, as Felicity de Montauban pointed out to her husband, there was none of the gauntness so common in the faces of the English poor. Food was absurdly cheap, and street vendors sold ears of roasted corn for a farthing, meat pies for a ha'penny and foaming mugs of a strong, colonial-made ale for a penny. Not only was everyone well fed, but even the lowliest dockhands and artisans carried firearms. Never had Bernard and Felicity seen so many pistols, muskets and elongated muskets called rifles.

Shaggy-haired visitors from the interior wandered around the city in faded, greasy buckskins, and betrayed self-consciousness only when someone stared at them. These men, wilderness dwellers, were quick-tempered, and twice Bernard narrowly avoided fist fights after gaping at them. He soon learned discretion, however, and was equally careful when he looked at the similarly clad Indians, proud, copper-skinned men who casually slept in doorways or in dirt roads, but carefully avoided the few cobbled streets.

Bostonians and their visitors subsisted on hearty but plain fare, and apparently no one in the colonies understood the art of good cooking. Even at the best inn, the Bunch o' Grapes, where the de Montaubans had engaged a suite, menus were bewildering. Bernard and Felicity quickly learned it was best to eat the native dishes. Roasted venison, boiled lobster and bear bacon were served daily, as were corn and a delicious vegetable called ascutasquash, but imitations of English dishes, notably beef and kidney pie, were so heavily seasoned with strange and pungent American herbs they were scarcely edible.

The mutton was tough, and chicken, which everyone in England boiled, was invariably fried by the colonials. But the oysters, which were large and plentiful, were exquisite, and so were clams, a shellfish unique to North America, that were sometimes served in a thick soup. Portions were gargantuan, and the de Montaubans could eat only a small amount of the food placed before them, which so perturbed the barmaid who served them that she was certain they were ill.

Bernard thought it amusing that cattle and sheep should be grazing on the Common, a large green, only a few yards from the Governor's official headquarters, the King's Mansion. It was sobering, however, to see awkward men in homespun learning the rudiments of military drill in parts of the Common, and to note that soldiers of Royal Army regiments never wandered around the city alone, but always went in pairs.

Boston was crowded with shops, and there were scores of them on the main thoroughfare, Treamount Street, but the wares they offered held no interest to new arrivals from England. Colonials, Felicity said, seemed interested only in buying kettles, frying pans and cooking utensils, steel needles and bolts of cloth. What they did with the cloth was a mystery, however, as none of it seemed to have been made into clothing.

The homes of the wealthy, some lining the Common, others rising on Beacon Hill beyond it, were "wooden palaces," as Felicity put it. The largest of them, at the crest of the hill, had been built by the late Thomas Hancock and enlarged by his nephew and heir, John, the present occupant. Riding toward it in the Hancock carriage, which had called for the de Montaubans at the Bunch o' Grapes, Bernard murmured that it appeared only a shade smaller than the huge palace erected by the first Duke of Somerset on the Strand.

It was evident, too, that Hancock lived in a style seldom seen in England, and, Bernard guessed, rarely in the colonies. A coachman and footman in royal purple livery sat on the carriage box, and two grooms in the same uniforms were waiting at the main entrance to the mansion. A butler conducted the guests through a series of anterooms, then a maidservant in a dress of white with purple trimming and a sash of purple took Felicity's cloak.

Two hostesses greeted the de Montaubans in a large drawing room crammed with bric-a-brac from a dozen lands. Thomas Hancock's widow, Lydia, was the type who awed strangers. Exceptionally tall, she was badly overweight, but moved with surprising grace for one of her advanced years and size. Her gown, which had been done in the latest French fashion, had a skirt with many folds and a bustle, but she handled it as though she had worn nothing less complicated in her life.

The younger woman at her side was Dorothy Quincy, who was betrothed to John Hancock, and Felicity saw at once that the air of pretty charm she radiated was balanced by sharp eyes that missed no detail when she studied the guests. It was Dorothy who took charge. Giving no explanation for the host's absence, she rang for servants who marched through the chamber in an almost endless procession, bearing platters of oysters, smoked deermeat sausages, another cold delicacy that Felicity thought delicious until she discovered it was thinly sliced elks' tongues, and tiny ears of corn, no larger than a child's finger, that had been soaked in a tart wine.

The hostesses ate heartily, so Bernard and Felicity did the same, thinking they were being served a buffet meal. Then, suddenly, the door at the far end of the drawing room opened, and John Hancock came in from his library, apologizing for his tardiness. Bernard, who had held two meetings with him in his office, was prepared for him, but Felicity found his personality overpowering.

An exceptionally tall, rawboned man, he spoke and acted with the assurance of one who had not only been accustomed to great wealth all his life but had multiplied his fortune. Even his appearance was stunning. His powdered wig was the most expensive the guests had ever seen, and his tailcoat of pale blue velvet, waistcoat of a darker blue, and white satin breeches were dazzling. There were large buckles of gleaming gold on his shoes, and rows of gold buttons on his tailcoat that would have been vulgar in London, but were not out of place in the overwhelming atmosphere of his own home.

He gave the ladies small glasses of wine, to which he carefully added water, then poured tumblers of an exceptionally dry, white rum for Bernard and himself, proudly explaining that liquor rum was unique, that it was produced in very small quantities and required more than ten years of aging.

Bernard found it so potent that he sipped it very cautiously, knowing he would become intoxicated if he finished it. But Hancock casually drank two tumblers, then poured himself a third as he ushered everyone into the dining room. Completely sober, he dominated the conversation as course after course was brought to the table. After an appetizer of cold salmon from the Maine District of Massachusetts Bay, the party had a choice of clam chowder or a lentil, onion and sausage soup. Lydia Hancock was unable to decide between them, and ate a large bowl of each. There were enormous portions of Connecticut River shad, followed by venison that had been marinated in wine before being roasted. Then came a beef stew, seasoned with herbs, and the main course, a mammoth roasted turkey, which Hancock carved at the table. The stuffing of cornbread, oysters and walnuts, seasoned with sage, was unlike anything Bernard and Felicity had ever tasted.

The principal dessert was a large tart of blueberries, a native American fruit, which Lydia Hancock cut and served at the table. Then came a variety of sharp cheeses, and at the conclusion of the meal everyone received a silver bowl overflowing with hot, roasted chestnuts. The men drank ale, and there were wines with every course, too. When the dishes were cleared away, a pot of tea was placed on the table, and Hancock was careful to announce that it was green tea imported from Holland.

Bernard and Felicity tried to sample a little of each dish, but were floundering by the end of the meal. What impressed them most was that all three colonials not only ate everything placed before them, but seemed to accept such a banquet as commonplace.

Hancock delivered a monologue on the history of Boston and of Massachusetts Bay during the meal, and there was only one embarrassing flurry. "We have seventeen churches in the city," he said. "Think of it! Have you visited any of them?"

"We've searched for a Roman Catholic church," Felicity replied, "but we haven't been able to find one."

There was a brief pause, but Hancock was not the sort who would allow table talk to lag. "Most of them are Congregational," he replied briskly in his booming voice, "and three or four are Church of England. The Anabaptists have a little place of their own, and so do the Calvinists, most of them French Huguenots. I believe the Quakers have a meeting house somewhere or other, although I've never been there."

Felicity avoided her husband's warning glance. "How does it happen there are no Catholic churches, Mr. Hancock?"

John Hancock looked puzzled for an instant, but his ordered mind rejected confusion. "I reckon," he said, "it's because Boston doesn't take kindly to Papists."

His aunt and Dorothy Quincy attempted to change the subject.

Hancock was slightly annoyed. "I know these people are Papists," he said, "but I'll be damned if I'll pussyfoot. An honest question deserves a straight answer. I have nothing against Catholics myself. I've never really known any of them too well, but once, when I was down in Providence on business, there was a priest who ate dinner with some friends of mine and me, and he seemed human enough. Live and let live is what I say."

What was extraordinary about his attitude Bernard thought, was that Hancock was actually free of religious prejudice. He decided to test his conclusion. "Would you object if there were enough Catholics in Boston to build a church of their own?"

"Why in thunderation would I object?" Hancock was wide-eyed. "They've got as much right as anybody else to put up a prayer house. It just happens there aren't any Papists living in this part of the colony. Let me tell you plain, I'd fight anybody who'd try to stop them from building a church. Matter of fact, I own a choice parcel of land on a good site that I'd sell them cheap, and a construction company I own could do the job for them better and faster—and for less money—than anyone else in the business." Having disposed of the subject to his own satisfaction, he helped himself to more turkey, stuffing and ascutasquash cooked with mild green peppers.

After the meal, the two men adjourned to the library, where Hancock was careful to point out that he owned more books than anyone else in the colony, several clergymen excepted. He insisted that his guest accept a dark West Indian *segaro*, lighted one himself with a taper he plunged into a hearth of glowing hickory logs and pungent cedar, and then, abruptly, seated himself behind a desk with an ornate top of ingrained, gold-embossed leather.

"I've been studying your plans, de Montauban," he said, "and I like them. I'm prepared to invest ten thousand pounds in your enterprise, provided your trade with France reaches an annual volume of thirty thousand pounds. You'll act as your own managing director, to be sure, but I want fifty-five percent of your shares."

Bernard puffed on his *segaro*, and found it fresher and milder than any he had tasted in England. "It wouldn't be worth my while to go into business," he said, "unless I keep control of my company. I'll give you a forty-five percent interest."

Hancock appeared indifferent. "Without my ten thousand pounds, you'll find it hard to buy furs, lumber and tobacco—the goods Europe wants."

Bernard spoke almost without inflection. "You could fill your warehouses with prime beaver, fox and sable, if you wished—although I've heard the demand for sable is limited. The English market is uncertain for political reasons, the Spaniards are tardy paying their debts and the Dutch prefer to deal through their own companies. If you want trade with France, you need me. Paris doesn't like dealing with someone who has been channeling his products through London."

John Hancock enjoyed dueling with an equal. "Fair enough, but there are import and export duties collected on trade outside the British Empire. Your profit margin will vanish by the time you've paid duties to the Royal Customs Office."

"If I use Boston as my base, yes. There's a full staff of collectors here. That's why I went off on a little journey last week. Newport, Rhode Island, appears to be ideally suited for my purposes. It's a port with a small volume of tonnage going through, so there are only three customs officials stationed there: a deputy collector and his two assistants. All of them are American colonials hired by the Crown, and they're none too fond of King George's policies these days, so they can be persuaded to look the other way and forget most of the duty taxes."

Hancock feigned astonishment.

"I refused to take their unsupported word, naturally," Bernard said with a laugh, "so they showed me their private records. I accuse no one of smuggling, to be sure, but Thomas Hancock and Company has been slipping at least one privateer in and out of Newport every month for the past fifteen years."

Hancock grinned. "As much as I hate not to have the voice of ultimate authority in any of my interests, I'll accept forty-five percent of your shares."

Bernard sat down opposite the desk, not indicating elation over his victory. "It will be helpful to both of us if my merchandise buyer is a man who knows American products. Perhaps you can recommend someone to me."

"Of course. I just hope you won't find life in a small colonial town a strain. I spent the better part of a year in London, and the difference is quite marked." Business concluded, Hancock was the perfect host.

"Thanks for your concern, but I'm sure we'll be happy in Newport." Bernard saw no reason to add that the atmosphere of religious tolerance in Rhode Island was exactly what he and Felicity had been seeking.

"There are too many Quakers in Rhode Island, but every man to his own taste. I'll have to get you together with Sam Adams before you move there. He'll arrange to have you meet some of his friends on the Rhode Island Committee of Correspondence."

Since arriving in the New World Bernard had gleaned that each of the thirteen British colonies boasted such a committee, and that these organizations worked together to oppose the activities of Lord North's government which they disapproved. "I'm grateful to you, but I have no wish to become involved in your quarrel with the Crown."

"In the first place it isn't my quarrel, and in the second it's impossible to stand aside when you live here, as you'll find out. Anyway, Sam is anxious to meet you."

Bernard couldn't imagine what he might have in common with the pamphleteer and editor who seemed to be devoting his life to creating friction between the colonies and the government of King George III.

Hancock answered the unspoken question. "He didn't tell me why, but I reckon you'll find out fast enough. Sam isn't one to keep his reasons for anything a secret."

Bernard had spent only two hours in the quarters of the Caucus Club, a second-floor suite of rooms located over an inn frequented by artisans, a greengrocer's shop, and a dressmaker's establishment. But he felt as though he had been held there as a prisoner for weeks. The shabby, sparsely furnished rooms formed a world of their own, the odors of cheap ale and strong pipe tobacco stung his nostrils, and the shouts of men who seemed to enjoy haranguing each other made it difficult to carry on a normal conversation. Most of all he was exhausted by the interminable questioning to which Sam Adams was subjecting him.

Adams was determined to unearth every conceivable scrap of information about the reactions of people in England to the colonies' growing dispute with the mother country, and because Bernard had been associated with his father's banking-trading company, refused to believe the young Englishman knew virtually nothing on the subject. Bernard had told him repeatedly that most people in London, including members of the banking community, were too occupied with their own concerns to care what people were thinking or doing in a remote portion of the Empire three thousand miles from home.

This attitude was inconceivable to Adams. The colonies were the center of his universe, and he hammered at his theme with a concentrated fury that would have made Bernard suspect he was a lunatic were he not so lucid in his approach. A short, homely man with long, dirty hair, grease-stained clothes and scuffed boots, he looked more like an unemployed printer than the publisher and editor of the most widely circulated weekly newspaper in the colonies.

Suddenly, unable to get what he wanted, Adams changed his tactics. He rubbed his bloodshot eyes, sent a boy to the tavern below for another pitcher of ale and, leaning his elbows on a rickety table, smiled at his guest.

The smile transformed him, and neither his grubby appearance nor the smell of the ale on his breath were offensive. Bernard was beginning to understand why the man had a magnetic effect on the poor of Massachusetts Bay, who followed his lead in all things and accepted his word as Gospel.

"So you're becoming one of us," he said, and stuffed a pipe, brushing crumbs of tobacco onto his waistcoat. "Either you'll become an American within a year or you'll go back to England."

"Is there that much difference between Englishmen and colonists?"

"Americans are a breed apart." Adams spoke with such conviction that he seemed to believe his own words. "Let me show you what I mean. Johnny tells me you're a Papist——"

"I prefer to be called a Catholic!" Bernard wouldn't have lashed out had he been less tired.

"No offense meant." Adams reached out and patted the younger man's shoulder with ink-stained fingers. "I don't care what a man believes, just so he stands with this land of ours. Me, now, I go to church Sundays because my wife makes life miserable for me if I don't. It's Socrates and Xantippe all over again. Poor Socrates. If he went to Hades after he drank that hemlock, I'll sure as hell meet him there. Church-going is a waste of effort for a reprobate like me. Now then, Bernard, where was I?"

Bernard winced slightly, unaccustomed to being called by his Christian name when addressed by a casual acquaintance.

"You show good horse sense, going off to Rhode Island. The preachers who founded this place and kept it alive during its first fifty years or so didn't take kindly to Pap—to Catholics. And some of their feelings have been handed down from generation to generation. But here's my point, and don't miss it. No matter how narrow and bigoted some people might be, they'd accept you one hundred percent—once you showed them you believed as they do in other things."

"Are you telling me I've got to take the American side in the argument with the Crown or face religious discrimination?"

The boy returned with a dripping pitcher of ale, and Adams filled two battered pewter mugs. "We're not a very sophisticated or learned people, Bernard. If you understand French, and maybe you do, with your name, we fit a description by Montesquieu. *'Ce qui m'a toujours nui, c'est que j'ai toujours méprisé ceux que je n'estimais pas.'* I have always done myself much harm by despising those people for whom I have no respect."

"You sound learned and sophisticated to me."

Adams reddened, indicating an unsuspected shyness. "Hell, I just have a good memory. Drink up."

Not wanting to be impolite, Bernard sipped a little of the bitter ale.

"As I was saying. Some of the Quakers here in town haven't had an easy time because they're fence straddlers, which seems to come natural to them. But those who side with us are as good as anybody else. Now then, down in Philadelphia, where there are Quakers by the thousand and not many Congregationalists, it's the other way 'round. Those Quakers are every last bit as patriotic as we are, you see. But God help the Congregationalists who side with the Crown. Quakers don't believe in violence, but as sure as we're sitting here drinking third-rate ale—which is the best I can afford to buy—they'd ride those bastards out of Philadelphia on a rail!"

Bernard forced a smile. "I gather that colonists are passionate in their convictions."

"We'd rather be called Americans. We have our own sensitivities. Anyway, Rhode Island is the place for you. We prattle about freedom of worship, but they really practice it. And once you're feeling cozy and at home, you might want to get in touch with me, and I'll direct you to the Committee of Correspondence people in Providence and Newport. We have a real army of volunteers there, but we can always use active help." His rheumy eyes became shrewd. "What's more, a lad who was once a banker in London and still has ties there might prove particularly useful to us."

Although Sam Adams was not the sort of person with whom Bernard could have formed a friendship, the man's single-minded devotion to the cause in which he believed was impressive. Under no circumstances, however, would Bernard reveal any details of confidential correspondence he might receive from his father, but he felt under no obligation to spell out his loyalties to a stranger. It was simpler to smile and let the New Englander assume what he pleased.

Adams instantly recognized his basic attitude. "Ever since I was a boy I've seen fortune-seekers come here from England. They hope to become wealthy and then go back home again. But it doesn't work out that way. America is like a wife, not a mistress. If you want more than token pleasures from her, you've got to give her genuine, consistent devotion, and you've got to be honest with her. I'm not preaching a sermon. This is just a helpful word of advice. Ever since the first settlers came to Jamestown more than one hundred and sixty years ago, Englishmen have expected to find gold nuggets on our beaches and diamonds in our forests. Well, I've yet to hear of anyone finding either. America will repay you well if you're loyal to her. If you aren't, may God be merciful to you. Keep it in mind."

Life in the colonies was proving far more complicated than Bernard had imagined. It was already apparent that the colonists demanded unswerving devotion to their own ideals, but he couldn't help wondering whether they were as firm and united in their beliefs as their articulate spokesmen indicated.

Newport, Rhode Island, was a small city, with a population of about one-third of Boston's, yet she had a distinct cosmopolitanism of her own. She boasted two theaters, a concert hall and a lecture hall, as well as a park where puppet shows and other entertainments were held for children in warm weather. Scores of schooners, brigs and sloops, most of them ships of Dutch, French or unidentified nationality were tied up at her twelve wharves. The largest, Long Wharf, was claimed by her citizens to be the busiest in the colonies.

Most of the vessels were engaged in the West Indian trade, and there were many taverns and inns on the main waterfront thoroughfare, Thames Street, to accommodate visiting seamen. But, unlike similar establishments in Boston and London, these eating and drinking places were relatively sedate, and were kept that way by volunteer constables, all of them merchants, ship owners, artisans and even cargo handlers, who were determined to maintain the decorum for which the town was noted throughout the New World. There were few trollops on Thames Street, and they, helping to maintain the town's traditions, were exceptionally discreet.

Newport had a passion for learning which was symbolized by the location of the Academy, a school for older boys and girls. Aside from the courthouse, it was the only occupant of the community's principal square, where Queen Street and Ann Street came together to form two long arms of a triangle. A strictly observed municipal law, unique in the colonies, required all children to attend school until the age of sixteen. Newport's love of learning was reflected in her three libraries, one of which, the Redwoods, was reputedly the largest in New England, competing with that of Harvard College for the honor.

Fanning out from the square on Griffin Street, Farwell Street, Spring Street and Bull Street were the town's houses of worship, most of which were located within a short distance of each other. The Second Baptist Meeting House, the Third Sabbatarian Baptist Meeting House and the Jews' Synagogue stood side by side, and the Second Congregational Meeting House was only a two-minute walk away. In all, there were two Congregational churches and four Baptist, one Church of England house of worship and one Roman Catholic, the Synagogue, an independent church with Deist leaning that preached rational Christianity and called itself the United Brothers Meeting House, and a small Friends Meeting House, that stood separate from the rest in a field behind Farwell Street.

There were contradictions in the attitudes of Newport, however, as Bernard and Felicity soon discovered, that were at odds with the town's seeming preoccupation with religion. Soon after renting a house on Upper Banister Street, not far from the Redwoods Library, which had been established by a wealthy Quaker, they were guests of honor at an outdoor barbecue roast given by their neighbors, and learned that Newport was more unusual than they had imagined. The men consumed prodigious quantities of rum, and were surprised that Bernard drank cautiously.

One of the hosts unhesitatingly and loudly informed the newcomers that he was in the smuggling business, which he had inherited from his father, and was proud of the fact that his income was greater than that of his many competitors in town. "I make more," he said, "because my privateers take more chances. Some of the boys try to sneak their ships into port past the garrison on Goat Island late at night, which is just asking for trouble. Not me! There are only fifty Redcoats stationed at Fort George there, and they're stupid, like all professional soldiers. Naturally they're going to be suspicious if they see a sloop creeping into port at midnight. My ships come in as bold as you please, in broad daylight. My captains carry a half-dozen flags, and they fly whatever suits their fancy. Sometimes they're Dutch, or French, or Swedish. If they've met a Royal Navy squadron at sea, they fly the British Union Jack. All it takes to make a living in my work is a little ingenuity, courage and common sense."

Bernard also learned that in Newport, as in other parts of Rhode Island, counterfeiting was an avocational pastime practiced by many men. Respectable citizens were reluctant to admit they made imitation British bank notes on wooden presses or fashioned coins with molds, but everyone, it seemed, knew someone else who augmented his income by these activities, which were considered serious criminal offenses in England.

Virtually every family living within a radius of three town squares, Bernard and Felicity found, was on close terms with all of its neighbors. The women exchanged recipes and gave samples of new dishes to their friends, the men drank together and the children became inseparable. Basic friendships depended on one's neighborhood rather than a family's church or business affiliations, a concept that seemed strange to newcomers from England.

But it was heartening to find that, as Dr. Franklin had predicted, no religious intolerance was evident in Newport. One other Catholic family, that of a physician, Michael Allen, lived on Upper Banister

Street, as did that of a Jewish drygoods store owner, David Grune. Both were on intimate terms with the Congregationalists, Baptists and Church of England members who were their neighbors. One of the leaders of the group was Isaiah Winters, a ship owner who was an elder of the United Brothers, and everyone liked the bachelor, Eduard Beachamp, a Huguenot from South Carolina who had settled permanently in Newport instead of following the practice of many others from Charleston, who had summer homes in Newport.

Bernard opened the subject with Dr. Allen when they were strolling homeward from Mass one Sunday morning, their wives walking several paces ahead of them. "I couldn't believe we'd find this atmosphere anywhere on earth," he said. "Nobody is interested in anyone else's faith."

"Why should we be?" Allen a scholarly man, adjusted his velvet bicorn more firmly on his head as a stiff breeze blew in from the harbor. "If I bleed you or Grune or Winters, your blood will look the same."

"I know, but most people don't. In the three weeks we've been here, I've been astonished. Does this attitude apply in everything?"

The physician considered the question. "Well, the Protestants intermarry freely, of course. Dave Grune's son married a Jewish girl, though, and my daughter is betrothed to a Catholic lad. The barriers have been lowered most of the way, but they haven't completely disappeared. The Protestants may belong to several sects, but together they do form a majority. So we and the Jews have to be a trifle more careful. Does that answer your question?"

Bernard nodded. "Just last night Felicity and I were marveling at the reception we've been given. At the oxen and venison roast on Thursday night in the Bartons' field, we saw people of every denomination except the Friends."

Allen looked at him obliquely for an instant. "That's right," he said, his voice curiously flat.

Bernard was unaware of his change in tone. "I suppose that's because there are none living in our immediate area."

"Correct, sir. There are no Quakers in our neighborhood."

Bernard blinked, gazed at his companion and saw that Michael Allen was staring straight ahead, one hand clamping his bicorn.

The incident made no lasting impression, but another followed only forty-eight hours later. Bernard had arranged to buy merchandise from Beauchamp, who maintained ties with fur trappers in Canada, and to send his cargoes to France on Winters' ships. His plans were rounding into shape rapidly, and his next step was to rent a small warehouse and office. He found what he wanted, at a reasonable fee, on Frank Lane, but both Winters and Beauchamp protested, and insisted there was better space available, just as close to the waterfront, in the adjoining square, on Mill Street.

They accompanied him on a tour of inspection, and showed him the property. "This warehouse," he told them, "is somewhat bigger than I'll need for the next few years. And there seems to be more of an air seepage through the chinks in the wall."

"So much the better," the burly Winters replied. "Fur bales can catch fire, and so can the lumber and tobacco you'll send off to France. The danger of fire is reduced if you have more air circulating in your storehouse."

"Oh, I'm satisfied that the fire hazard at the Frank Place warehouse is minor," Bernard said. "Besides, I can rent it for three pounds per month less than this place would cost me."

The others said nothing as they headed back toward the main entrance, which stood ajar. Suddenly Beauchamp, a man of considerable charm in his mid-thirties, put his hand on Bernard's arm. "As one Frenchie to another," he said, "take my advice. Lease this place. It's well worth the slight difference in cost."

Bernard looked at him, then at Winters in the light that slanted in through the open door. The faces of both his new friends were stony, their eyes veiled.

"The warehouse on Frank Place has been vacant for about five years," Isaiah Winters said, hooking his thumbs in his waistcoat pockets, "even though Newport's shipping has been growing so blamed fast that we haven't storage room to handle merchandise moving in and out of the port. Ed and I happen to have learned this place is empty, but if you don't want it, someone else will snap it up mighty fast."

"We're trying to do you a favor, de Montauban," Beauchamp added. "Take my word for it plain, we aren't trying to line our own pockets. We won't get a ha'penny for ourselves from the rental of this place, and the old widow who owns it will have a dozen people clamoring for it once the word is out that it's available. Now, what I've got in mind is that one of these days you may want to buy, and she'll be willing to listen to a reasonable offer from somebody who is already doing business with her."

"Thanks for your interest," Bernard said, "but I've got to plant some roots before I can start thinking of buying property. I've got to move carefully."

"All the more reason not to take the Frank Place warehouse," Winters said.

"What's wrong with it?"

The two men exchanged swift, covert glances. "It's owned," Winters said, "by Quakers." He made the word sound like a curse.

John Hancock's letter was terse. "After conducting a thorough search," he wrote, "I have at last found a man whose Talents are suitable for his employment in our joint Enterprise. He has himself been a hunter of Game, and hence knows well both Furs and Lumber. He is modest, and professes to have only a passing Knowledge of Tobacco, but I have found him equal in his judgments to the Tobacco Buyers on whose Skill depends the profits shown by Thomas Hancock and Company. I commend his diligence to you.

"You will, I trust, sir, forgive this long Delay in obtaining the Services of one worthy of your Employ, but the growth of Commerce makes it Difficult, indeed, to find experienced buyers of Merchandise. I can but pray he will not prove a Handicap to your Efforts."

The final sentence of the communication made no sense to Bernard, who found the usually blunt Hancock's delicate reticence odd. He was pleased, however, with the appearance of the man who came to see him at the warehouse and office he had rented on Frank Place.

"I trapped beaver before the French-and-Indian War," William Dale said, "and I know fox, otter and sable, too. Nobody will sell me dried pelts for prime, Mr. de Montauban, and you can stake your life on it. I was a lumber buyer for a spell in Portsmouth, up New Hampshire way, and when I was a youngster I worked in the Connecticut tobacco fields, so I know the difference between bright-leaf and burley."

"I'm delighted to have you," Bernard said, and they quickly settled details of Dale's wages. "I can't afford to pay you more than thirty pounds a month in Rhode Island currency at the start, but I hope to earn profits that will let me give you sixty after the first year."

"I can support a wife and daughter fine on thirty pounds a month, Mr. de Montauban," Dale said.

Bernard privately admired his thrift. He and Felicity were finding it difficult to support two children on fifty pounds per month, and since Dr. Allen had confirmed their belief that another baby was coming, their expenses would mount still higher. "Now that you're hired, Mr. Dale, I wonder if you'd satisfy my curiosity. That suit you're wearing cost as much as mine, and you're wearing expensive shoes. How can you live so frugally?"

Dale regarded him somberly. "I reckon it's because we don't drink hard spirits or squander our money. But don't credit me. It was Annie who taught me to find other satisfactions in the world."

"Annie is your wife?" Bernard knew it was impolite to pry, but was interested.

"She sure is. When I married her I was a bloodthirsty woodsman sick of killing and of myself. I don't reckon you ever scalped anybody, Mr. de Montauban——"

"Certainly not!"

"Well, I carried twenty scalps on my belt, but after I went to a

368

couple of the Society meetings with Annie, I threw them away. That's all it took."

"The Society?"

"Of Friends."

"I see."

"I assumed you knew I'm what folks call a Quaker. I told Mr. Hancock right off when I saw him, and I figured he'd write it to you."

Bernard shook his head; Hancock's vaguely worded warning beginning to make sense. He wanted to make his own position clear, and said hastily, "I neither knew nor cared what your faith might be. It hadn't crossed my mind."

"Thanks kindly. I'd leave if it bothered you."

"Why should it?"

"Well, we're none too popular hereabouts."

"Let's understand each other, Dale. I'm a Roman Catholic, and we weren't any too popular in England. We're a minority here, too, I might remind you."

Dale's smile, which Bernard was not capable of identifying, was that of the wilderness frontiersman, slow and quiet. "I'm not trying to compete with you, Mr. de Montauban, but I honestly believe Newport thinks less of us than of you Catholics. So we win, hands down in any free-for-all."

Bernard, who was becoming accustomed to New World humor, laughed aloud.

Dale quickly sobered. "There are two reasons I accepted your offer. Annie has relatives here, and the Friends in Newport need support, so we were glad of the chance to come. The other was—you."

Bernard was surprised.

"Word gets around, Mr. de Montauban. We heard how you rented this warehouse when you could have had another over on Mill Street."

"There was a matter of principle at stake." Bernard was embarrassed.

"We're saying the same thing. I didn't think it was because you have any great love for Friends."

"I have no feeling one way or the other. I know nothing of your theology or creed."

"We have no creed."

For a moment Bernard thought he was joking. "But you call yourselves Christians?"

"We are Christians. Maybe this is too much to swallow in one gulp, but we have no sacraments in the usual sense, no liturgy, and we're the first church in all history that makes women the equal of men. Year before last the head of our Society in Providence was a woman."

Never had Bernard heard anything so extraordinary.

"We have no priesthood, either."

Apparently the man was making the formal distinction between a priest, in the Catholic or Anglican sense, and a minister, in the usual Protestant sense. "Surely you have clergymen!"

"No, sir, we don't."

"Then who——"

"We have meetings, and any member of the Society who feels moved to speak is free to say what's on his mind."

The sect's unorthodox approach to religion was bewildering.

"The same Holy Spirit that caused men to put the Bible on paper enables men today to interpret Scripture. There's nothing mysterious about the way we worship."

"Then you do believe in the Father, the Son and the Holy Spirit."

"We don't define the Trinity as you do, just as we have no outward rituals of Baptism and the Eucharist. But we're no band of lunatics, Mr. de Montauban. I think William Penn and his followers have managed to prove in Pennsylvania—and in New Jersey, too—that we're sensible as well as God-fearing people."

Bernard tried to remember the precise objections of Isaiah Winters and Eduard Beauchamp to the Quakers. "This is hearsay, you understand, but I've been told you refuse to support the colonies' opposition to the Crown policies of taxation."

"That depends on what you call opposition, Mr. de Montauban. When the Committees of Correspondence declared an embargo on all goods the Commons was taxing, we did our share. You won't find a colony with a better non-importation record than Pennsylvania. But Friends don't go out into the streets to taunt Redcoats, the way those lads did up in Boston. We don't hold with physical violence, and we won't bear arms."

Bernard had been approached by Beauchamp and David Grune, who had offered him a commission in the Newport battalion of Rhode Island militia, and therefore was conscious of the role being played in the colonies by volunteer, part-time soldiers. "Quakers don't serve in the militia?"

"No, sir."

"In Pennsylvania?"

"There are no exceptions. Members of the Society won't go to war." Again a slow smile creased Dale's face. "I fought for three years against the French and their Ottowa allies. When New Hampshire and Massachusetts Bay had themselves an upset over their border line, I fought for a spell on one side, and then I changed because the other paid me more. I've fought the Seneca for pleasure, and the Algonkin because I had a feud with them. You might say I've had my belly full, and I thank God I'll never carry a rifle again."

The man's vehemence was ample testimony of his sincerity, and Bernard felt himself warming to this believer in a strange faith. "The way you explain it, your religion makes sense."

"For the past eighteen hundred years, nearly, Christians have been killing pagans and each other. We Friends believe in turning Christianity into the religion of Christ—who preached peace, and went to His own death rather than start the war that would have broken out if He had given the word."

For the first time in his life Bernard wished he had a greater understanding of theology so he could debate intelligently with this man whose formal education was obviously inferior to his own. At the moment he could only say, lamely, "I'll defend your right to believe as you please."

"That's a big commitment, Mr. de Montauban, and I won't hold you to it."

Bernard saw that Dale was grimly serious.

"You're going pretty blamed far by hiring me, you know. There are folks hereabouts who won't like it."

"I'll hire any man I deem competent," Bernard said gruffly. "I'm taking John Hancock's word that you are, and unless you prove otherwise, you'll keep working for me. We have a tradition in my family. We tend to our own business, and we expect others to do the same."

Dale stood, looked over the crude partition of boards that separated the office from the warehouse proper, and suddenly grinned. "Annie and little Annie wanted to come down to Newport with me, but I told them to stay in Boston until I'd seen you. I'll send for them now. I'm going to like it here." He inhaled deeply, loudly. "There's nothing like free air in a man's lungs to make him feel at home."

In the scant two years the Reverend Samuel Hopkins had spent in Newport as pastor of the First Congregational Meeting House, the fifty-year-old clergyman had already lived up to his reputation for unorthodoxy. A former student of the equally radical Jonathan Edwards, his views had led to his dismissal from two posts in Massachusetts Bay, but he had received an enthusiastic welcome in Rhode Island, which was proud of its long traditions of freedom of worship and speech for all, as well as its opposition to central authority. Every town in the colony made its own self-governing laws, quietly defying the Crown, and every member of the clergy interpreted those laws for the benefit of his flock as he saw fit.

But even Newport didn't quite know what to make of the Reverend Mr. Hopkins. Virtue, he had declared in his first sermon, was the demonstrated love of good for all mankind, even if its achievement placed an individual's immortal soul in jeopardy. Thereafter he had immediately started proving his theories to his own satisfaction and the approval of his admiring colleagues.

Slavery, he declared, was a violation of God's natural law and a contradiction of the spirit of Holy Writ. His vigorous campaign had resulted in the freeing of every slave in Newport. Now he had extended his fight to all of Rhode Island, insisting that colonists had no right to demand, from the Crown, greater freedom for themselves while holding other human beings in bondage. His success in liberating both slaves and indentured servants who had committed themselves to periods ranging from seven to fifteen years of servitude was so great that the economy of the colony was threatened. Conservative men of wealth in Newport, Providence and the smaller towns predicted total financial ruin for everyone, but the Reverend Mr. Hopkins was not impressed. Christ, he roared from his pulpit, had driven the money-changers from the temple, and the Almighty was supremely indifferent to pounds, shillings and pence.

Some of Newport's more substantial citizens, many of them members of his own congregation, became alarmed when he launched new, vehement attacks against smuggling and counterfeiting. They controlled a majority of the seats on his own church's board of trustees, and tried to silence him by cutting off his own wages. The spidery little clergyman promptly countered their move by delivering one of his most stirring sermons. Using as his text the passage from the Gospel of St. Luke that the laborer is worthy of his hire, he denounced his would-be censors by name, and then asked for a special collection to support himself and his family. His detractors were shamed, and the campaign against him came to an abrupt halt.

In a community the size of Newport everyone of standing knew everyone else, and Bernard de Montauban had met the Congregational minister on several social occasions. He was totally unprepared, however, for a note, delivered to his warehouse-office one day late in 1771, inviting him to call at the Hopkins' parish house whenever he found it convenient.

Intrigued, even though he suspected the clergyman might try to convert him from Catholicism, he paid his visit that same day. Hopkins greeted him at the front door, and led him to the most disordered room Bernard had ever seen. Oiled paper had been tacked over a broken window, making the chamber so dark that, even in mid-afternoon, it was necessary to burn two oil lamps that smoked slightly and emitted unpleasant odors. A pair of ragged rugs covered only a part of the scuffed hardwood floor, and books were piled everywhere, making it necessary for the clergyman to dump several stacks on the floor so he could ask his guest to sit in a sagging chair.

"Would you like a cup of sweetened cranberry juice, Mr. de Montauban? The cranberries come from my brother's bogs in Plymouth, up in Massachusetts Bay. If you prefer, I was given a box of tea by one of my parishioners last week. Although he insists it came from the Dutch East Indies, I suspect its origins may be English, so I won't touch it myself. But you're welcome to it."

Bernard surprised himself by the firmness of his own immediate response. "I prefer not to take the chance, Mr. Hopkins." Apparently his attitude was becoming more like that of the American colonists than he had realized.

"Let me see. We have coffee, but my wife brews it abominably."

"I really need no refreshments."

"Ah, but they're a symbol of the offering of a host's hospitality and a guest's acceptance of it, aren't they?"

Bernard could be gracious, too. "I'll take whatever you're having, sir."

"Splendid!" The Reverend Mr. Hopkins beamed, and after rummaging on a table, found two dusty glasses, which he casually wiped with a handkerchief he took from his sleeve. Into them he poured a liquid from a large, dark green bottle. "I keep no alcoholic spirits in the house, and I tell myself it's a matter of principle, but that's nonsense. Our Lord not only changed water into wine, but probably drank wine every day of his life. To be truthful, spirits don't agree with me, and give me the colic. This herb tonic is sent to me by a former parishioner in Housatonick, in Massachusetts Bay. He makes it from a recipe he learned from one of the Iroquois tribes out there on the frontier—frankly, I can never remember which. It does wonders in cleansing and healing one's system."

Bernard almost gagged on the bitter brew.

The clergyman, however, drank his glass with great relish. "Your pastor and I were having a chat about you a few days ago. Father Curtis tells me you're making a success of your business."

"It shows promise, Mr. Hopkins," Bernard said, always conservatively cautious in financial matters. "If I'm paid what's owed me in Europe, I'll be able to take out enough to pay my family's living expenses, and I can't ask for more in only a few months of active operations."

"You smuggle, of course." The statement was matter-of-fact.

Bernard knew of the clergyman's attitude on the subject, and became slightly flustered.

"Why should you be the exception? I'm thinking of changing my stand on smuggling, you know. A member of the Ellery family is active in the Rhode Island Committee of Correspondence, and he's more or less convinced me that we hurt no one but the British who are trying to curtail our liberties. I'm still wrestling with my conscience, but I have an idea smuggling will win. I'm finding it difficult to believe the Lord frowns on that pastime. If he does, Rhode Island will become a latter-day Sodom, which is too distressing a thought to contemplate."

Bernard felt a sense of relief, but nevertheless took care not to admit that he avoided the payment of customs duties. The conscience of the clergyman might prove less elastic than his own.

The Reverend Mr. Hopkins stared at him for a moment or two, then suddenly asked, "If you were the Lord God Almighty, what would be your first rule in governing the universe?"

Bernard was too startled to reply.

"I'm not trying to trick you, Mr. de Montauban, nor is this the opening wedge in an attempt to persuade you to leave your faith for mine. If this will be of any help to you, Father Curtis knows I planned to have this chat with you, and gave me his approval."

It was impossible to guess the reason behind the question, so Bernard decided to move one short step at a time. "I can't imagine myself in God's place, Mr. Hopkins. I wouldn't presume to try."

The clergyman nodded, then laced his hands behind his head. "Wouldn't you say it was His aim to produce the highest degree of happiness for the universe as a whole? That's my theory."

Bernard mulled the question. "I can't necessarily agree with you. God's realm is already perfect, by definition."

"Ah, you speak now of the hereafter. For the moment let's concern ourselves only with this world. It, too, is His realm."

"Well, yes."

"His sovereignty is absolute. Although we belong to different churches, neither of us questions His omnipotence."

Bernard inclined his head in agreement.

"It's my belief that, since He is all-powerful, we can commit sin only with His permission. This doesn't in any way relieve us of the choice to select good or evil, and it doesn't make the commission of sin any less degrading. Nevertheless, God's ultimate purpose in granting us the freedom of selection—and allowing us to commit sins— must be to nudge us closer to the perfection of His universe. Do you follow me?"

"I do, sir, but I think you'd find it much more pleasurable and profitable to discuss your theology with Father Curtis." Bernard felt lost.

"I'm not dealing in abstract philosophy or doctrine for its own sake. I'm sure we agree there is no heaven on earth, but Newport comes closer to it, in some ways, than any other community I've ever known. We have a gratifying breadth of tolerance here that is unique, to the best of my knowledge. There's no discrimination against you Catholics, nor is there any feeling against the Jews. We

374

don't happen to have any Moslems in town, but, if we did, I'm sure they'd be free to build a mosque and pray in it. Our only citizens who create frictions are the Quakers."

Bernard's temper flared. "If you wanted to discuss my merchandise buyer, I wish you'd said so. William Dale is not only a valuable employee—worth several times the wages I can afford to pay him—but I enjoy his company. And my wife and I have become fond of his family."

The Reverend Mr. Hopkins raised a hand. "There's no need for belligerence. It's true that I'd like to have a few words with you about him, but I thought we should examine the question in its overall context."

"I hope," Bernard said, still seething, "that you don't consider it a sin for me to employ him or to see him socially. I respect your profession, sir, and I've never yet told an ordained clergyman to go to the devil."

The minister chuckled. "If I'd obeyed every such order, I'd have been boiled long ago. No, Mr. de Montauban, I don't stand in judgment, nor do I consider it sinful for you to have hired him. The sinners are those who criticize for what you've done."

Somewhat mollified, Bernard sat back in his rickety chair.

"I've created storms far more often than I've poured balm to calm them," the Reverend Mr. Hopkins said. "But at the same time, I can't help wondering—even though you're totally blameless and your attitude is in many ways admirable—whether you might be doing a genuine service to the Quakers as well as everyone else in Newport if you took a less militant stand."

Bernard saw a sheepish humiliation in the clergyman's eyes, which did nothing, however, to relieve his own sense of outrage. "Are you suggesting, sir, that I discharge a competent employee because there are people in town who disapprove of his church?"

"No," the minister said hastily. "Of course not. The record of Rhode Island, and of Newport in particular, is extraordinary. I'm merely seeking some way to help the community grow more tolerant."

"The Quakers," Bernard said, "have contributed a great deal to the welfare of this city. You speak of records, Mr. Hopkins. I've looked into the background of the Quaker history in Newport ever since some of my neighbors have made disparaging remarks about them, and they've done more for the town than your parishioners or the members of my own church."

"There's no doubt of it. The feeling against them began to ferment when the colonies started taking active measures to oppose the economic and political policies of King George and his government. Militiamen have been drilling in every town and village green in the colonies—except Philadelphia. As Sam Adams wrote in a far-sighted editorial in his Boston *Advertiser* just two or three weeks ago, nothing will convince the Crown we mean what we say except the threat of force. The Quakers have strong scruples against either the use or the threat of force——"

"I've become well aware of their position."

"——so their stand is bound to be misinterpreted and misunderstood by men whose religious tenets are more primitive."

"It seems to me that the Quaker beliefs are basic Christianity. I'm sorry that all I was taught as a child won't allow me to subscribe to them. But my views are no one's concern. They're strictly my own business and that of my priest, who is my intermediary with God." Bernard's voice became cold. "I presume you have some ideas to suggest?"

The Reverend Mr. Hopkins' manner changed. His apologetic air vanished, and he became more dignified. "I've spent my life fighting for the right of all Americans to worship as their consciences dictate. I believe my good will to men of every faith is well known, so there's no reason for me to feel guilty simply because I advocate moderation. There are sensible men in England, just as there are here, so our disputes are certain to be solved amicably. When that happens, the irritation with the Quakers so many of our people feel will die away, too. My chief aim now is to prevent relations between the Quakers and the rest of the community from becoming too ugly. It will be far easier to resume normal living with fellow Americans if the schism isn't allowed to become too profound."

"I'm quite certain that when I came to the colonies earlier this year, I'd have agreed with you, Mr. Hopkins. Perhaps I was naïve, but it's more likely I was over-civilized. I've learned since I've been here that the feelings of New World men lie close to surface, which is why it becomes so much simpler here to recognize and grasp fundamental issues."

"You aren't the first to make that discovery." The minister thought it a distinct improvement that they were able to converse quietly, like gentlemen. "The wilderness has bred a strain of violence in us. When we can't settle our problems quickly, we use our fists—or our rifles. I'm trying to think of Newport's future after all the hard feelings and suspicions are gone. Rhode Island must set the example for the other colonies, as she's done since the time of Roger Williams one hundred and thirty-five years ago. If we can't demonstrate that men of all faiths can live together in friendship, freedom of worship in America will become the futile dream of oppressed minorities."

"I'm sure you're right, but you still haven't told me how I can help to achieve the goal of liberty in my treatment of William Dale."

The clergyman carefully poured himself another glass of herb tonic, and seemed disappointed when he saw that his guest had scarcely touched his drink. He took several swallows of the brew, wiped his mouth with a cloth he used to clean his quill pens and stood. "For the sake of long-term peace and amity, short-range sacrifices should be made," he said.

Bernard bit back a protest until he learned the details.

"Dale has become something of a symbol, and should be sent away until men here regain their sanity. Give him work to do elsewhere."

"My operation is a very small one, Mr. Hopkins. Aside from his usefulness to me here, I have no need for his services anywhere."

"I'm sure I could help find him and his family a temporary home in some other town."

"That won't be necessary, Mr. Hopkins." Bernard was surprised to find himself speaking without anger. "I'm positive that on my recommendation a place could be found or made for him in John Hancock's company, either in Boston or in one of the branch offices, perhaps as an agent in Philadelphia."

"Philadelphia would be perfect."

"But I won't do it!"

The minister opened his mouth to speak, then closed it again.

"If I give in now to the pressures and hatreds of bigots, there will be no religious liberty in Newport by the time friendly relations with England are restored. I know very little of theology, Mr. Hopkins, and I'm not capable of weighing my creed and proving it more or less valid than yours. But my family has known bigotry for generations, and I was taught as a small boy to loathe it. There soon would be no freedom of worship in Newport if I surrendered to the men who are opposed to Dale. After the Quakers it would become the turn of the Jews, and then of the Catholics. I don't know whether you Congregationalists outnumber the Baptists here, but eventually one or the other would be squeezed out."

The Reverend Mr. Hopkins saw his whole plan to restore religious peace to the community being destroyed. "You exaggerate, Mr. de Montauban."

"Americans refuse to compromise with principle. We say we're practical idealists." Bernard failed to realize he was speaking of himself as an American. "The House of Commons repealed its taxes on all of our imports from England except tea. That tax has been kept because His Majesty and Lord North want to prove to us that the Crown is still our master. If we refused to make an issue, the tax on tea would be removed in a year or two. I don't know what the King feels, but I'm certain, as is every intelligent man, that Lord North would be relieved to be rid of an embarrassing situation.

"But British tea is rotting in shops and warehouses in all thirteen colonies. Those who don't care or want a compromise are persuaded to buy no tea. Those who put their loyalty to the Crown first are frightened into staying at home. The result is that we buy no British tea, any of us. Why? Because there's a principle at stake! And surely, Mr. Hopkins, you—of all men—must agree that our right to worship freely is at least as important as our right to gain a voice in our own taxation." Bernard forgot to be polite and thumped the minister's cluttered desk. "Now, sir, you know why I won't yield on the question of Dale. I'll fight for this principle, and be damned to the bigots!"

1772

Joseph Maurice de Montauban was baptized on January 20, 1772, at St. Mary's Church in Newport, with the Reverend Francis Curtis officiating. Dr. Michael Allen was the infant's godfather and Isaiah Winters' wife, Helen, the godmother. After the ceremony the whole party, which included the many neighbors and friends of Bernard and Felicity, adjourned to the house on Upper Banister Street. A coating of snow lay on the ground, and a stiff, cold breeze blew in from the harbor, but most of guests, long acclimated to New England winters, chose to walk from the church.

Bernard went ahead with his wife, their three children and Father Curtis in a hired carriage, and the moment they reached home the host and hostess made a last-minute inspection of the preparations for their first large party in the New World. There were hot rum and whisky toddies to drink, as well as claret, port, sack and a pipe of a vintage, unidentifiable Spanish wine that had found its way to Newport by means that no one questioned. The manservant hired for the occasion also presided over two kegs of ale and one of porter, and there was a non-alcoholic fruit punch for the ladies who disliked spirits. Tea was notably absent.

A hot venison stew and platters of cold turkey, mutton and beef were the main dishes gracing the sideboard in the dining room. There was also steaming swordfish, caught the previous day in Rhode Island Sound near Block Island, and simmered in wine, then garnished with butter and onions. Felicity also served roasted oysters and two favorites that were considered essential to any social gathering in Newport: clam cakes and thin strips of codfish which had been fried in a batter of cornmeal. On arrival each guest was handed a large bowl of corn and clam chowder to ward off the chill, but this appetizer was believed necessary for reasons of health, and was not, strictly speaking, part of the festive meal.

New Englanders ordinarily refused dishes with which they were unfamiliar, so Felicity had baked only a few of the cakes made with cherry and peach brandywine from her mother-in-law's recipes. Most of the desserts were conventional American pies of mincemeat, ascutasquash and pumpkin flavored with ground currants.

Few Old World amenities were observed. The guests greeted their host and hostess, the infant's godparents and Father Curtis, and then headed straight for the dining room and library, which was being used as an auxiliary serving room, to gorge on food and drink. As always, the success of a party was judged by the quantity as well as the quality of what the older generation called "grog and grub," and there were no complaints. Bernard, circulating constantly, went again and again to his tired wife and whispered to her that, in her first effort, she had met Newport's most exacting standards.

After eating, the men congregated in the parlor and enclosed sun-porch beyond it to discuss politics, while the ladies discreetly retired to Felicity's second-floor sitting room to learn her recipes and peer into the nursery for another look at the sleeping Joseph Maurice.

Some of the guests left for their own homes soon after eating, and Bernard was able to relax with the men who had become his closest friends and associates in this land so far from England. He had become a respected and substantial member of the community, and only in the colonies, he thought, could he have achieved business security in such a short time. Not only was he solvent, but, as he had written to his father, only an unexpected catastrophe could prevent him from showing a monthly profit as great as his income had been in London. He had achieved his own basic vocational goal and, knowing his parents had not been forced to trim their own standard of living, he was content.

"Bernard," David Grune said, "Colonel Talbot asked me to inquire whether you've decided to take the militia commission he's offered you."

"As a matter of fact," Bernard replied, "I wrote the Colonel a formal letter just yesterday, accepting the First Lieutenancy."

Everyone shook his hand, and Grune said with a smile, "This is the best news I've had in a long time. I've grown too old for military service, and I'm going to train you to succeed me as battalion adjutant."

"Thanks, but I have no head for paper work," Bernard said quickly.

His friends, who were aware of his business success, laughed at him as they toasted him.

"Now you're really one of us," Isaiah Winters said, "and you can help us find some way to persuade Talbot he ought to retire. We're tired of his stories of fighting the French, and no one can convince him that if we ever get into a fight with the British, it will be a different sort of war."

"I can't imagine a war with England," Bernard said flatly.

Dr. Allen, who was a member of the Committee of Correspondence, raised an eyebrow. "I can."

The thought made everyone uncomfortable, and there was a moment's silence. "Suppose they increased the garrison on Goat Island," Grune said. "Even if two or three thousand Redcoats were stationed there, we could still raise a militia force several times larger. I don't see how they could beat us."

Bernard remembered what his father had told him about the defeat of untrained Huguenot hordes in southern France by relatively small units of professional soldiers. "If you'll study history," he said, "you'll find that freedom can be suppressed by a minority. The achievement of liberty—and I mean every kind of personal liberty—requires the combined, active cooperation of all the people in a community. Or in a province, for that matter, or a nation."

Grune and Dr. Allen, representatives of religious groups that depended on the good will of the majority, seemed to understand what he meant more readily than did the others.

"We'd push the Redcoats into the sea, and London knows it," Winters said.

Eduard Beauchamp thought he was being too optimistic. "You're assuming we'd have the full support of all the people. I know a number of prominent men, more of them in Providence than here, who would remain loyal to the Crown. And I'm sure there are militiamen who'd hesitate before going into the field against British troops."

"I'm one of them," Bernard said. "To my mind militia duty is a civic responsibility, but it must stop short of treason and open insurrection."

"You're still new to America," Beauchamp replied. "You'll probably change, as others have, when you've been here longer. But let me finish answering Isaiah. Aside from individuals who would stand with England, there are whole groups that wouldn't make a move to help us in a war. They might not oppose us openly, but they'd be a drag, like an anchor tugging at a skiff in a boat race."

"You're thinking of the Quakers, of course," Winters said.

Beauchamp nodded.

"Aren't you being unfair?" Bernard demanded. "There are more ways of fighting than going into battle with muskets. The Newport Quakers have been as careful as everyone else not to buy tea from the East India Company."

"They know we'd tar and feather them if they broke the embargo," Winters said harshly.

Dr. Allen cleared his throat. "Bernard, I saw that fellow who works for you, Dale, at the church today with his wife. Why should people who deny God attend a Baptism? Quakers like to pretend they're meek, but they have real gall."

"Bill and Annie believe in God as strongly as any of us. What's more, they went to St. Mary's today because Felicity and I asked them to be there." Bernard realized that his friends, who stood in a semi-circle around him, were regarding him with a coldness that verged on hostility. He bridled, and added, "We also invited them here, and we're disappointed that they didn't come."

"At least they had that much good sense," Winters said, and his tone made it unnecessary for him to add, "even if you didn't."

Bernard tried to stare him down, and they glowered at each other.

David Grune stepped in as a peace maker, and put a hand on Bernard's shoulder. "You just don't understand."

"We disagree." Bernard knew it was futile to argue, as well as rude to snap at guests, but could not let the narrow-minded attitude remain unchallenged.

Grune refused to take offense. "Were you friendly with many Quakers in England?" he asked, carefully feeling his way.

"Bill Dale is the first I've ever met."

The others exchanged significant glances, and Beauchamp tried to speak gently, not realizing he sounded patronizing. "We've had experience with them all our lives. Trust our judgment."

"Do you think Dale is going to contaminate me? Or my wife and children? He's efficient in his work, which you know, Ed. And so do you, Isaiah. He's sober, he hurts no one, and he lives with his own kind on Quaker Hill. What possible harm can he do any of us? Your opposition to him isn't reasonable or rational."

"It's his attitude that's dangerous," Dr. Allen said.

Bernard looked slowly around the semi-circle. "After I won my degree at Oxford, I was sent on a year's tour of Europe. It's something of a tradition in my family, and so is visiting certain places. I spent a week in the ghetto at Dresden, because my parents believed it important to my education. Have you ever been in a ghetto, David?"

"No, thank God." Grune flinched.

"The Jews of Dresden live apart from other Saxons, as though they had the pox. Their only crime is being Jews. Michael, I don't suppose you know Sweden."

"I went to medical school in Edinburgh," Dr. Allen said gruffly, "and then I came straight back to Rhode Island. I couldn't afford to gallivant around the Continent."

Bernard ignored the slur. "There are no Catholics in Sweden. The Lutherans drove them out long ago. I was the first that many people had met, and I honestly think they were surprised that I didn't have horns and a tail. At first I was angry, and then I felt pity for them.

Don't you see? The appeal of America is the right to pray as we please."

"We're not stopping the Quakers. If they want to think the Holy Spirit perches on the shoulder of someone who suddenly pops up at one of their infernal meetings and starts interpreting Scriptures like a preacher, let them do it. But they have their own colony, and we don't need them here. Let them go off to Pennsylvania, where they belong."

Bernard's self-control began to slip. "I thought all you were proud of Rhode Island's tolerance!"

"He just doesn't understand about Quakers," Winters said heavily.

As always, the breakfast table atmosphere was serene. The de Montauban maid-of-all-work removed the plate with the remains of Bernard's broiled whitefish, and put a platter of steak, fried eggs and rice seasoned with herbs before him. Felicity diluted her husband's wine with water, poured herself a cup of strong West Indian coffee and, as soon as they were alone, sat back for the morning chat that meant so much to her.

First, however, there were housekeeping details to settle. "Will you be home for dinner this noon, dear?"

"I think it unlikely. One of Isaiah Winters' brigs, the *Gugono*, is sailing on the early afternoon tide, and I want to see her off. Every last ounce of cargo she's carrying is mine. So you might send someone to the warehouse with a little cold meat and bread for me late in the morning."

Felicity sipped her coffee, then rubbed her arms. "Is the ship a privateer?"

Bernard, engrossed in his breakfast, nodded absently.

"She's sailing straight to France?"

"Of course."

"And you're avoiding the payment of export duties?"

"Naturally. The Crown has no right to impose taxes that rob a man of almost all his profits. They'll be real profits on this voyage, too. We'll have enough to keep us comfortable if the Royal Navy should step in and cut off our foreign trade for six months or a year."

"I'm worried," Felicity said.

He looked up from his plate. "If your conscience is bothering you again, forget it. I'm no worse than anyone else in Newport. Or in Boston or New Haven or New York Town or Philadelphia, for that matter. Or Charleston. There isn't one merchant in America who is willingly paying the Crown's export-import taxes."

"Philadelphia, you said. Are some of the merchants there Friends?"

Bernard grinned. "Of course. They have a living to earn, like everyone else. Don't let the prejudices of our friends warp your perspectives."

Felicity tactfully shifted ground. "What really worries me is that the garrison has a new commandant."

"Forget him, too. Sir Thomas Martin is like all the other senior officers in the Royal Army. He thinks New World duty is a bore, and he wants to serve his time here quietly, without complications, so he can go back to England with a clean record. He's also very fond of the ladies, which is an expensive pastime."

"Oh, dear. You bribe him."

"Felicity, a wife shouldn't pry into her husband's business. I'm not responsible for the system of handling trade in the New World. I've merely accepted a method of accommodation that has been used for many years. When the King and his ministers realize that Americans are free men who deserve a voice in their own affairs, I'm sure the Commons will pass new laws that are equitable. Until then, we have our own way of dealing with the situation."

He had said nothing she hadn't heard previously, and Felicity sighed.

"You're taking Catherine to little Annie Dale's birthday party this afternoon?"

"I think not. She's still sniffling. Spring in Newport isn't any warmer than spring in England. There's still a bite in the wind."

"But Dr. Allen said she's completely recovered from the ague."

"I prefer not to take chances."

"Catherine has been looking forward to the party," Bernard said.

Felicity looked away. "I'll make it up to her. I'll invite some children to play with her here next week."

He finished his meal and pushed away his plate. "Are you quite certain," he asked, "it's the ague that will prevent you from taking Catherine to the party?"

"I've already told you my reason!"

"Yes, I heard you. I'm also aware that your friends disapprove of Bill Dale's child."

"They're your friends, too."

"They are, but I pay no attention to their opinions of Quakers. In fact, I don't give a damn what they think."

"Well, I do. Snide remarks and sharp little looks make me uncomfortable."

"Then you admit you're keeping Catherine away from the birthday party because of comments that have been made by women who ought to be minding their own affairs."

"I'm not on trial, Bernard!" she flared. "And you're not a Crown prosecutor trying to trap me into admitting something in the witness box."

He reached across the table for her hand. "Forgive me for using the wrong word. We want the same things for ourselves and our children, so we have no quarrel. Bill Dale is valuable to me at the warehouse, and he's my friend."

She knew what was coming, and tried to ward it off. "I'm fond of Bill and Annie, too. But I'm sure they'll understand——"

"What you mean is that they'll accept a snub silently. They'll be graceful about it because they have no choice. But they'll be hurt if you don't take Catherine over there today."

"I'm sending the child her birthday gift."

"To hell with a gift. She's expecting Catherine. How can her parents explain to a little girl that our daughter isn't being allowed to go to her birthday party? Do you suppose they'll explain that some people in Newport consider her religion a curse somewhat worse than leprosy?"

"I—I don't know." Felicity was troubled. "I want to be fair, and I have no reason to harm people I like. But I wish Annie Dale had been more considerate. She's having the children of other Quakers at the party, so she needn't have asked Catherine."

Her logic was so faulty that Bernard wanted to smile, but felt too pained. "She wanted Catherine there because——"

"I know, dear. I understand her motives, and I appreciate them. But I wish she'd stopped to think of our position."

"When the parents of a little girl extend birthday party invitations, I assume they're thinking only of the children involved."

Bernard's irony was lost on Felicity. "Catherine and Caroline Gibson have been inseparable. It's only natural, I suppose, with the Gibsons living next door, but the girls really do enjoy each other, and Catherine would be crushed if she couldn't see Caroline again."

Bernard pushed back his chair and looked out of the leaded windows of the dining room toward the Gibson house, a handsome structure of red brick with a white portico, done in the neo-classical style popular in England for a decade and now being copied in the colonies. "I can imagine no reason," he said evenly, "why Catherine couldn't play with a child who lives only a stone's throw away."

"Then you've never heard Daphne Gibson expressing her opinion of Quakers."

"I had no idea she was a theologian."

Felicity was in no mood for what she interpreted as humor. "James isn't much better. They have closed minds."

"The next time I need the services of an attorney, I'll go to someone other than James Gibson."

"That won't help Catherine, either. And it won't make us any more popular."

"Do you mean to tell me that our social standing, and that of our children, depends on our willingness to give up relations with a couple who belong to a sect Newport dislikes?"

"Daphne Gibson is too much of a lady to threaten, but she made her intent clear."

"It wouldn't bother me in the least if we never set eyes on Daphne and James Gibson again."

"I wouldn't care, either, but Catherine and Caroline are the same age, and in two more years they'll be going through the same school as classmates."

Bernard's patience was exhausted. He stood, throwing his serviette on the table, and stalked toward the door. "The Gibsons and all the other bigots in this town may go to blazes," he shouted.

Not until a quarter of an hour later, as Bernard approached his warehouse after a brisk walk through the city's streets, did it occur to him that his show of temper had accomplished nothing. Perhaps he had been afraid to insist that his daughter attend the Dale child's birthday party. In any event, the issue remained unresolved, thanks to his own failure to take a firm position. So, he knew, Felicity would keep Catherine at home.

It would be best, he decided, not to mention the matter to Bill Dale, who would know nothing of Catherine's absence until evening. It might be cowardice to remain silent, Bernard told himself, but he saw nothing to be gained by bringing up the subject. Dale would be hurt soon enough, and it would be pointless to cause him additional pain and humiliation.

Newport was crowded, in the summer of 1772, with seasonal visitors from Charleston, Georgetown and other South Carolina cities escaping the heat of their own lowlands. Relations between Great Britain and her colonies had improved, with everyone taking England's tax on tea and the consequent American embargo for granted, and the possibility of war receded. It was no longer fashionable for gentlemen to parade with the militia on Saturday afternoons, and enrollment in the local battalion declined drastically.

In fine weather the ladies, wearing tight new corsets beneath their gowns, strolled up and down Broad Street, carrying parasols, which had become an overnight rage, and were so popular that men used a somewhat larger version to protect them from the elements on rainy days. Every afternoon except on Sundays there was horse racing in the Meadow, a flatland beyond the town limits, that was particularly enjoyed by the South Carolinians. And cockfighting, although banned by both Newport and Rhode Island laws, was also common, with matches held in the barns of farmers pleased to augment their income with ten percent of the sums that changed hands in wagers.

Two theatrical companies enjoyed great popularity, one devoting itself to the plays of Shakespeare and other classics. The second, which alternated light operas with concerts and chamber music, achieved its greatest triumph with John Gay's *Beggar's Opera* and its sequel, *Polly*, which the elders of several churches considered salacious.

The business community was thriving as never before in Newport's history. The harbor was crowded with brigs, sloops and ketches, the largest of them more than four hundred tons and the smaller thirty tons or less. Some engaged in European and West Indian commerce, others were busy in coastal trade, and virtually all were smugglers. Early in July a squadron of Royal Navy ships commanded by Commodore Sir Robin Rich put into port for a week's visit, and just before their arrival the privateers quietly and conveniently vanished. The alarm had been given by the master of a fishing boat who, having seen the squadron off Point Judith, in Block Island Sound, had returned to Newport under full sail to spread the word.

Bernard de Montauban's import-export business was flourishing, and he was able to repay John Hancock's initial investment only fourteen months after beginning his operations. The French continued to buy all the goods he sent them, paying him higher prices than he could have commanded in England for the same wares. In return they sent him silks, wines, perfumes, and several consignments of the finest dueling pistols made. The demand for the French merchandise was great, and he disposed of it with ease, much of it being taken by Hancock, who stored it in barns and sheds outside Boston, in areas never visited by the Royal Collector of the Port.

By August, Bernard was ready to take a step symbolic of his desire to make a permanent home for himself and his family in the New World. After several long discussions with Felicity, he approached Eduard Beauchamp, who acted as agent for the absentee owners of the property he rented. "I want to buy the house we're living in," he said, "and I'm prepared to pay the full price in sterling."

Beauchamp would earn a juicy commission, and was pleased. "Good," he said, "but there's a complication. Your house is part of a larger property that includes the place the Gibsons are renting and the vacant house behind you, on Upper Church Street. Old Mrs. Carey wants to sell all three together."

"I don't have that much in silver, Ed."

"You won't need it. Pay for your own house in cash, and I'll guarantee that she'll grant you comfortable credit terms on the rest. What's more, you can pay her off without effort. The Gibsons will be just as happy to rent from you as from Mrs. Carey, and you can rent or sell the Church Street property without any difficulty. The demand for houses is so great these days that a half-dozen people have come to me with offers in recent weeks, but they were just interested in the one parcel. Once you own it, you can do with it as you please."

The idea seemed sound to Bernard, and twenty-four hours later he accepted the deal. James Gibson acted as his attorney, jocularly refusing to charge his new landlord a fee, and the necessary papers were signed and filed at the office of the Newport town clerk. A Crown tax of two shillings and thruppence was required to make the transaction legal, and although the fiery Beauchamp said it was an outrage for King George to demand a penny when the land wasn't his, Bernard paid the token without protest.

He returned at once to his warehouse, where a new consignment of trimmed cedar for France had arrived that morning, and was mildly surprised to see the usually solemn William Dale wreathed in smiles. "You've found some otter pelts," Bernard said. Otter was unusually scarce, and the French demand for it was insatiable.

"For your sake, I wish I had," Dale replied. "I've just learned some personal good news. I'm going to be a pa again."

Bernard shook his hand and wished him well.

"I'm blamed if I know why I'm so happy, though. There's hardly enough space to turn around in up in that little place we rent from Annie's folks."

Quaker Hill was crowded and, as Bernard knew, members of the Society of Friends had difficulty finding adequate housing elsewhere in the city.

"But I'm not complaining, mind you." Dale's grin seemed ineradicable. "If anyone had told me ten years ago that an old leatherskin like me would be a respectable married man with a family and a good, steady income, I wouldn't have believed it."

"Look here," Bernard said. "You know where I've been just now, don't you?"

"Sure, at the town clerk's office, buying—Hold on!"

"You listen to me, Bill. I've just become the owner of a two-story clapboard house on Upper Church Street that's standing vacant. What could fit more neatly? The very day I get a place, you find you need one. It's a happy coincidence."

Dale's manner had changed. "I know the house. Leastwise, I've seen it from the outside, and it's big. It's also located in an expensive neighborhood. So it's too dear for my purse."

Bernard had already given him two justly earned increases in wages, but he deserved another. "An extra ten pounds a month ought to help. Besides, I'd be paying it to myself, really. Rent from me, and you'll be handing the money back to me as fast as I pay it to you."

Dale's lips were compressed. "Thank you kindly, but I don't aim to rent. When Annie and I move, we want a place of our own."

"Then I'll sell it to you," Bernard said.

His merchandise buyer stared at him. "You couldn't possibly mean that."

"Why not? I'd rather sell to you than——"

"It wouldn't work out," Dale said.

Bernard felt his face growing warm.

"I don't believe," Dale said carefully, "that your wife would appreciate having us as neighbors."

"Felicity thinks as highly of you as I do!"

Dale inclined his head awkwardly in what was intended as a gesture of thanks. "Maybe so, but there are plenty of folks in this town who'd like to hang my scalp from their belts."

"I don't believe you have one personal enemy." Bernard realized his denial sounded feeble.

"I wouldn't want anybody to think that Annie and I are trying to push in where we aren't welcome."

His candor required equal honesty in return, but Bernard didn't know what to say so he remained silent.

"We'll work out something with our own kind. I know New England better than you do, and Newport isn't going to change overnight. I reckon that by the time your children and mine grow up, we'll be accepted here, the same as we are in other places."

Bernard hated to admit defeat when a basic principle was at stake, but unless Dale took a stand with him, there was nothing he could do. "Let me know if you change your mind," he said, starting into the warehouse to inspect the cedar. "And I'll do some thinking, too. I hate giving in to bigotry."

"How can you be so inconsistent?" Felicity demanded, waving her arms. "You claim you love principle, but in your own acts you deny it!"

"Hold still," Bernard grunted, kneeling on the floor of their bed-chamber, "or I can't lace this confounded corset."

"You bribe the commandant of the garrison and the customs officers. You smuggle in cargo from France and you send out one shipload after another of goods without paying taxes. Heaven only knows how many laws you break!"

"Is this good enough?"

"No, tighter. You talk and talk about freedom of worship, but you're dishonest in your dealings with the Crown."

He tugged harder at the laces of the corset that transformed her figure from that of a somewhat plump young matron into one of a smaller-waisted beauty. "There's a principle at stake in business, too. If Lord North and the Commons treated America fairly, we wouldn't have to use bribes and trickery to earn an honest living. The day they stop trying to use taxes on our legitimate trade to support people in England—who pay far lower taxes—every merchant in America will open his books and the holds of his ships to the Crown's tax collectors. But we'll be damned if our hard work is going to benefit them, at our expense."

"Now you're pinching me."

He released the laces a fraction of an inch.

"That's better." Felicity went to a cupboard, took out a gown of pink satin and, after climbing into it, again turned her back so her husband could hook her into it. "I must confess that business is very confusing to me. I'm grateful that we're doing so well, and as so many respectable gentlemen smuggle and give bribes as you do, I suppose I shouldn't try to judge you. But I certainly don't agree with you about freedom of worship!"

"I hadn't realized you'd become an expert on the subject, but I'm sure you'll tell me my errors."

She sat down at a small dressing table, dipped a finger into a pot and began to apply rouge to her face. "No one tries to stop the Quakers from holding worship services—or whatever it is they do when they get together at their meeting house. They're free to go there every day of the week, if that's what they want. And what they say and do there is their own affair. There isn't a single law on the statute books of either Rhode Island or the city of Newport that restricts them in any way."

Bernard knew she disliked the odor of smoke in their bedroom, but he found a *segaro* soothing when he became perturbed, and lighted one. "I have an idea you've been listening to Helen Winters."

Felicity bristled. "Is she wrong?"

"No, I believe there are no colony or city laws that prevent the Society of Friends from holding Divine services in their own meeting house." Bernard sat down on a chair near the dressing table and leaned toward his wife. "But there's more than the law involved in genuine religious liberty. An atmosphere of freedom is necessary, too, if people are to pray as they wish—and live as the equals of their fellow citizens."

She made no reply, but appeared somewhat puzzled as she continued to apply her cosmetics.

"No one actually persecuted us in England, but you must admit we suffered snubs—and didn't like them."

Felicity turned to him, her eyes grave. "I see what you mean, and you're right."

"Think how much worse it is here for the Quakers. They're literally excluded from all social intercourse with outsiders."

"It's so hard to know what's right." She sighed, then turned listlessly back to her mirror.

"No, it's simple to distinguish right from wrong. Doing what's right is difficult."

"Why can't they move to Providence? Everyone says there's no feeling against them there."

"How would we have reacted if people had suggested that we move from London to York because there's a large Catholic population in the Midlands? There's no need to answer a rhetorical question. Both of us would have been furious. Well, the Quakers try to live their religion, just as we try to live ours, but they aren't saints. Some of them are descended from people who settled in Newport three or four generations ago. This is their home, and no one has the right to drive them out. No matter what excuses are made, that's gross religious intolerance."

Felicity picked up her hair brush, then let her arm fall again. "Why must we fight their battles for them, dear? Surely they're capable of standing up for their own rights."

"They are, and they do it well. But ever since the time of Philippe de Montauban, nearly two hundred years ago, my family has believed that bigotry is evil, that the persecution of one minority is the persecution of all minorities. I can't keep silent when I see what's being done to innocent people here."

"You and I are new to the colonies, Bernard. We're just establishing ourselves, and we've been fortunate. But people are always more reserved with comparative strangers than they are with old friends. I'm sure there must be many men who feel as you do. Please be sensible, and don't spoil what we're achieving. Let the others do battle for the Quakers."

"If I could close my eyes and ears, I would. But it seems to me we're being negligent in repaying God's kindness to us if we refuse to hold out our hands to others who need help." He stood and, chewing on the *segaro*, began to pace up and down the room.

Felicity watched him. "You've been brooding for the past few days."

"I didn't realize it, but I suppose I have."

"That's always a sign you're planning something drastic."

Bernard smiled, but remained silent.

"What do you have in mind?"

"I'll do nothing violent, I assure you. Even though I'm assistant adjutant of the militia battalion, I'm not a very belligerent or war-like man."

"All I can do is beg you not to offend our friends or your business associates. We've committed ourselves to a life here, and you've put all our money into this property. Don't do anything rash."

"I believe I've got to make it clear that I fully support an able and loyal employee—who happens to belong to the Society of Friends. I

390

don't want to embarrass Bill Dale—or myself—but I can't live with a troubled conscience."

Felicity began to brush her hair quickly, methodically, shielding her face with her arm so he wouldn't see the tears in her eyes.

The Prince of Wales tavern on Farwell Street was always crowded in the early afternoon, but several booths at the rear of the establishment, where it was quiet, were reserved for gentlemen of standing. At the bar itself farmers who had brought their produce to town were chatting and laughing, and officers from a recently arrived squadron of merchant ships were helping themselves to the sharp cheese and blood sausages that were served free of charge to the patrons. The two groups appeared convivial, and the nephew of the proprietor, who maintained order with the aid of a staff with a sharpened end, was able to relax his vigilance.

The atmosphere was tense, however, in the booth farthest from the door. Eduard Beauchamp was expertly opening oysters with a long-bladed hunting knife and handing them to his companions, but they ate absently, scarcely aware of what they were doing. "I want to make certain I understand the situation," he said, his voice hard. "Dale, the Quaker, has made you an offer to buy the clapboard house on Upper Church Street."

"He has not." Bernard was equally cold and precise. "In fact, ten days ago he refused to make me an offer. But after thinking about the matter, I'm going to sell it to him at a price he can't afford to refuse."

Isaiah Winters gulped down an oyster, drank the liquer from its shell and then dropped it with far more force than was necessary into the pewter bowl. "Why create an issue where there is none?" he demanded. "This fellow Dale is apparently intelligent enough to know his place——"

"Just what is that?" Bernard knew he shouldn't be creating antagonisms, but realized, too, that he had been spoiling for a fight.

"He lives on Quaker Hill, where he belongs. Let him stay there!" Winters raised his voice above the noise at the front of the tavern.

"He has the right to live where he damned well pleases," Bernard said.

Beauchamp raised his head, his knife poised above a closed oyster. "I'd say it pleases him to live with other Quakers."

Bernard saw a chance to clarify the point he was trying to make. "Perhaps he lives where he does because he's had no choice. Perhaps he'd prefer to live elsewhere."

Winters became angry. "Why should you care where he lives? The man just works for you. He isn't related to you by either blood or marriage. It could be you're trying to stir up trouble. Or maybe you and Dale have worked out a plan together. The two of you might have the idea that it will be easier for him to buy the house if he pretends he isn't interested in it."

"Your church preaches universal brotherhood," Bernard said, refusing to dignify the absurd accusation with a denial. "Aren't Quakers your brothers?"

"I don't need them breathing down my neck!"

Again Beauchamp intervened. "I hope you've weighed the consequences of selling the Upper Church Street house to Dale, Bernard. Although I can't speak for the Gibsons, I'm certain they won't want Quakers as neighbors. You'll lose a tenant."

"People are clamoring for houses. I'll find another."

"A Quaker, I suppose," Winters said bitterly. "How they'd love to move into our part of town."

"Not necessarily," Bernard replied, "although those I've met are honest men who pay their debts. I'm sure a Quaker wouldn't default on his rent."

Winters threw another oyster shell onto the pile. "Why are you so fond of them?"

"Why do you hate them?" Bernard countered.

"I didn't meet you here to defend myself." Winters was livid. "If you want your property values to drop, that's your privilege. But I've put a fortune into my house, and I don't intend to lose it. You can do what you want, de Montauban, but I'll tell you one thing, and Ed is my witness. Sell that house to Dale, and you can find somebody else's ships for your cargo. Mine won't be available. I get more requests to carry freight than I can handle, and I don't need your business!"

Beauchamp deftly slit an oyster and handed each of the others a half-shell. "I'm inclined to suspect," he said gently, "that Mrs. Carey will raise the interest rates on the money you owe her when she learns you've sold to a Quaker, Bernard."

"But——"

"Her agreement with you was informal, remember. She agreed to put nothing in writing so that neither party would have to pay a Crown tax. Under the circumstances, there would be nothing illegal in raising the interest rate. I couldn't blame her, really. She'd be careless if she didn't protect herself, and land hereabouts loses its market appeal when Quakers move in."

Bernard was stunned. He had been prepared for vigorous, even violent protests, but it hadn't occurred to him that men he regarded as friends would take deliberate punitive action against him.

Isaiah Winters' tone and manner changed, and he became solicitous. "You're looking poorly," he said. "Have another cup of ale with your oysters. And, Bernard, take it from someone who hopes to be doing business with you for many years, don't make too hasty a decision. Just the other day I was talking about those new florins and half-crowns that have been in circulation lately. At first glance they're very shiny, attractive coins, but you've got to examine them on both sides and see if the edges chip to find out if they're counterfeit."

At first glance Quaker Hill seemed like other parts of Newport. The houses, although small, were constructed of either red brick or clapboard, and the shutters and trim boasted fresh coats of paint. Yards and gardens were tiny, but well-kept, and thrifty housewives grew vegetables and herbs. But the differences between the section and other portions of the city soon became apparent.

The Society of Friends Meeting House, a solid structure of gray Rhode Island stone that only vaguely resembled a church, stood at the crest of the hill and dominated the area. Fanning out from it were four roads, none of them cobbled. There were no carriages and few horses on these dirt roads, as the Quakers were poor, and could afford few luxuries. Pedestrians, even the children, were somberly dressed in gray or black, and the district was very quiet. Youngsters, among them two boys climbing an apple tree, did not shout, and the women sweeping their front stoops with brooms made of stiff rushes, nodded to one another but did not call out.

Bernard, sitting near a grape vine lattice-work wall behind the Dale house, found the silence as oppressive as it was unusual. To an extent his own associates were right: the Quakers were indeed different. Elsewhere children were screaming loudly as they played their games, horsemen clattered homeward on cobbled roads, and ladies hurried back and forth between their main houses and kitchens as they supervised the preparation of the evening meal. Perhaps, Bernard thought, the Quakers ate supper later than did others; he neither saw nor smelled food being prepared. Then, sheepishly, he realized that the kitchens were built into the houses, as they were in the dwellings of the poor everywhere.

If William Dale was aware of his poverty-stricken surroundings, he gave no indication of it, even though he and his guest both sat on crude chairs that he had probably made himself. He straddled his chair, absently rolling a twig from the grape vine between his hands, and stared down at the ground as he spoke.

"Words don't come easy to me, Bernard," he said, "so I hope I don't offend you. If I do, forgive me before I start. First off, I wish you'd keep out of my business. You mean well, but it does nobody any good to rile up men who live up yonder across Broad Street.

"We believe in live and let live, but they haven't learned to turn the other cheek. That's why, in a town like this, Friends take extra care not to show off. You might say modesty is a scruple, and we try

393

to live according to it, but it's a protection, too. If you've ever seen a deer in the forest, you'll know what I mean. The animal's color blends in with the trees, and blamed if you can see the deer from fifteen paces.

"That's the way it is with us. Most members of the Society work as clerks and such-like in shops and shipping companies. They do what's expected of them, and after they've earned their pay, they go home. The less they're noticed, the less fuss there is for all the rest."

It was difficult for Bernard to apologize. "I've been offensive, not you," he said. "I've been so eager to strike a blow for the equality of different faiths that it didn't occur to me I could be doing you more harm than good."

There was no rancor in Dale's slow smile. "You meant well by us, so Annie and I are grateful to you. I tried to tell you I wasn't interested in the house on your property, but I reckon you were excited because you'd bought it the same day, and you weren't listening to me."

The achievement of religious tolerance, Bernard decided, was a goal beyond the grasp of any one man. At the same time he had to curb a sudden feeling of resentment against the man he had tried to help. The Quaker was right, but his bluntness was discomforting.

"I'll take that extra ten pounds a month you mentioned to me the day you first offered me the house. I'm accepting it because I believe I've earned it, not because my family is growing. If I thought you were offering me charity, I'd—well, I wouldn't take it. Now, about the house."

"Obviously, I should rescind my offer, and I do."

"I thank you kindly. You've tried to hand it to me nearly free, and that's one reason I can't accept. If you made me a straight gift of it, I'd be obliged to give it back. I wouldn't feel at home on Upper Banister Street, any more than you'd live easy here on the Hill."

Bernard started to protest.

Dale raised his voice slightly. "We're both Americans. I was born here, and you came over a year and a half ago, but that doesn't matter. I've seen enough of you to know we want the same things. What you've tried to do for me proves it. And we're both proud of being free-born English citizens. In spite of all that, we aren't the same. It isn't that you're rich and I'm poor——"

"I'm hardly wealthy."

"By my standards, you are. And it isn't really the differences in our religion, either."

Bernard was embarrassed by the man's unexpected vehemence. "I've said all along that we worship the same God."

"That isn't what I mean, either. One of the best friends I ever had was a Mohawk warrior who went to meetings of the Iroquois Confederation. We got to know each other at Albany Town, and we went off hunting together for a month or two every year, usually in October. He prayed to a rain god and a sun god and an earth god—and the Lord in His wisdom only knows how many others. He was a pagan and I was a Christian, but that didn't matter to either of us. We had real trust. I could go to sleep at night knowing he wouldn't scalp me and sneak off with my rifle. He could rest easy knowing I wouldn't cheat him." Dale snapped the twig.

Bernard wanted to ask what had happened to the Indian, but something in Dale's expression made him hesitate.

"What separates you and me," the Quaker said, "is Broad Street. There are no portages across it. Some day, maybe, but not yet."

"Perhaps I'd feel as you do if I went down to Pennsylvania. As a Catholic in Philadelphia——"

"I don't think it'd be the same, but I'm prejudiced, remember. Everybody's prejudiced. Every last man I've ever met likes to thump himself on the back and say, 'I've got me the best wife, and the best rifle, and the best religion in the world.'"

"I'm afraid you're right." Bernard rose, feeling as weary as he was frustrated. After this I'll know better than to build bridges for people who want to stay on their own sides of the road."

Dale held out his hand.

Forcing a smile, Bernard grasped it.

"No hard feelings?"

"None."

The subject, Bernard knew, would not be mentioned again. They would see each other daily at the warehouse, and would resume their previous relationship. Yet something had changed, and his inability to define it made him uneasy.

1773

The unspoken truce that had allowed Great Britain and her thirteen American colonies to live in harmony since the repeal of the Townshend Acts was broken in April, 1773. Many Americans held King George III personally responsible for the eruption of the new, unexpected crisis after a provocative comment he had made was repeated in the House of Commons and subsequently printed in every colonial newspaper.

"The Americans," he said, "continue to defy me, making me a

monarch in name only if they continue, indefinitely, to challenge my authority. They force me to test their loyalty."

The actual situation, as Bernard de Montauban learned through correspondence with his father, was far more complicated than it appeared on the surface. An emergency meeting of Newport's merchants, ship owners and traders was called at the Thames Street Market House, outsiders were barred, and Bernard offered a detailed explanation to his colleagues.

"Our boycott of tea has been so effective," he said, "that the warehouses of the East India Company in London are overflowing. And the Company's finances were so bad that it would have been forced into bankruptcy without government help. Parliament has provided that help with a new law called the Tea Act. All taxes on the importation of tea into England and on its reshipment to the New World have been abolished.

"Obviously, this remission cuts the price of tea to the consumer. The domestic purchaser in England—and here—will be able to buy it for a fraction of what would have been paid a few weeks ago."

Someone at the rear of the auction hall, where the meeting was being held, called out, "The transportation tax of twelvepence per pound and the import tax of thruppence per pound have been rescinded, de Montauban?"

"That's right," Bernard said. "But we aren't being allowed to escape taxation completely. The Tea Act requires us to pay a new Crown import tax of a ha'penny per pound."

Isaiah Winters jumped to his feet with such force that his chair toppled over backward with a crash. "Hold on, Bernard. Do I understand that we're the only ones who must pay this new tax?"

"Only Americans."

An angry murmur filled the hall, and when an importer named Sutton declared, "The price is still attractive," the others glared at him.

"That's the idea behind the new scheme," Bernard said. "They're making the price attractive so we'll find it irresistible."

William Ellery, the city's most prosperous merchant and chairman of her Committee of Correspondence, said flatly, "We won't pay it. No matter how small the tax, we'll refuse to pay any duty designed just for us."

Bernard held up his hands for silence. "That's where the Commons and the directors of the East India Company are being clever. We ourselves aren't being asked to pay it. The Company's own agents in our port cities and towns will pay it when the tea is landed, and will simply add a ha'penny per pound to the price they charge our retail merchants."

There was a brief, stunned silence, which Winters broke. "If there aren't any East India Company agents to accept the tea," he said, "they couldn't sell an ounce of it."

A roar of approval echoed through the hall.

Ellery made his way to the auctioneer's podium. "Gentlemen," he said, "the Committee of Correspondence will be busy in the next few months. I have a notion there will be no one to receive the tea and pay the Crown's new tax."

Everywhere in America the new Tea Act met stiff resistance. As Ellery had predicted, the Committees of Correspondence coordinated their efforts, and groups of citizens paid quiet visits to the agents of the East India Company, themselves Americans. Persuasion and the threat of force were effective, and at three of the colonies' four major ports, where the act was to be tested, there were no agents to receive the cargo. Masters of merchantmen who arrived at Philadelphia and New York returned to England with their holds still filled with tea. At Charleston the cargo was landed by troops of a Royal Infantry regiment and held in Crown warehouses, but feeling in South Carolina ran so high that not one merchant attempted to buy any tea, or pay the ha'penny per pound tax.

Only in Boston did it appear that the Americans might suffer a major setback. There the East India Company representatives were nephews of Governor Thomas Hutchinson, and could be neither cajoled nor intimidated. Their uncle publicly promised them the protection of a full battalion of Redcoats, if necessary, and they, in turn, announced they would accept the cargo. Boston was forced to consider other, more drastic means of resistance, and at the Caucus Club, Sam Adams and his associates quietly discussed ways and means of boarding the ships when they reached port, rendering the tea useless and escaping undetected.

Basically the Crown was frustrated in its efforts to compel America to pay the tax that had become a matter of principle for the politicians on both sides of the Atlantic, and the East India Company, with the help of Lord North's government, turned to a slightly different approach. Since their attempts to land the tea had been blocked at the major American ports, where pressures were strong, they began making attempts to recruit agents at some of the smaller cities on the seacoast.

They found men to represent them in Baltimore and in Portsmouth, New Hampshire, moves which caused the Committees of Correspondence in both towns to redouble their vigilance in order to prevent the tea from reaching commercial warehouses. Officials of the East India Company also visited Newport, creating a stir in the business community.

"The problem," Bernard told Felicity at noon dinner on the day the Company officers arrived, "is that people in general really want tea. Once boxes of it have been landed, with the tax paid, and are stored in privately owned warehouses, merchants will start buying it."

"Then it's wrong to stop the landing of tea," she replied. "You're imposing your will on the public."

He shook his head. "Most people don't understand what's at stake. They've done without tea for years, and they're tired of making a sacrifice. All they realize is that tea may soon be available at the lowest price in history, and a ha'penny tax is so small they can see nothing wrong with the idea of paying it."

"It doesn't sound criminal to me."

"If the tax were one-tenth of what Parliament has imposed, it would still be too much."

"It seems to me that you and Isaiah Winters and all the others are just being stubborn."

"We are, but for a reason we understand as well as the Crown. America has taken the position that we won't pay any tax unless we have our own representation in the Commons. We demand the right to express our opinions—and vote on everything that concerns us."

"My knowledge of politics is limited. But if Lord North's government passed the Tea Act by a large majority in the Commons, wouldn't such an act be passed again, even if the colonies were represented?"

"Yes, I think it very probable that there would be no chance of our winning, even if every member of the Opposition voted with us."

"Then you're raising a storm over nothing. I miss tea dreadfully."

"I often want a cup myself. The issue isn't this tax, as such, Felicity. What we're trying to establish is the right of a minority—in this case the two million people of America—to speak their minds in the appropriate legislative forum created for that very purpose. The ultimate stake is the essence of liberty itself."

An hour later the intricate problem was still on his mind as he went down to the waterfront to check the inventory of a cargo he was shipping to France on one of Winters' brigs. The lists balanced, and with the help of Winters, who accompanied him, he found everything in order. The task completed, he was about to depart for his own warehouse when Winters drew him aside.

"Have you heard the latest news from Baltimore? If the directors of the East India Company haven't yet learned their lesson, this will teach them we won't be bullied or foxed. They hired three agents there, but one decided to leave town after the Committee boys talked to him, and the others changed their minds and wouldn't accept the work. It was either that—or tar and feathers."

"The Baltimore Committee was wrong," Bernard said. "Violence or threats, which are the same thing, create more problems than they solve."

"What matters," Winters replied with a grin as he and Bernard parted at the head of the Long Wharf, "is that no Crown-taxed tea is going to be available in Baltimore."

America was still a primitive land, Bernard thought as he made his way down Thames Street. On the surface, cities like Boston and Newport seemed civilized, but people were still influenced by the raw wilderness, and almost automatically tried to solve even the most subtle and complex moral and ethical questions through demonstrations of physical strength. He had acclimated quickly to the New World, and in almost all respects considered himself an American now, but he was still jarred by the casual approach to brute force that everyone else seemed to take for granted.

It was natural for a frontier people to rely on their own efforts and expect no help from anyone else, but tarring and feathering was an evil that denied the very principles the Baltimore Committee had sworn to defend. When justice was mocked, and any man was denied the full protection of society, the fabric of freedom itself was destroyed. America was passionately devoted to the cause of liberty, but had not yet discovered and practiced the self-restraint that enabled all men to live as equals.

Still pondering, Bernard entered his warehouse, went to his desk and opened his ledger. He had been so busy in recent months that he was behind schedule in bringing his accounts up to date, but it was gratifying to know he was enjoying a far greater prosperity than he had imagined possible when he had left England to make a new life for himself in the colonies. If his business continued to expand at the present rate, he would become one of Rhode Island's leading merchant-traders within another year.

"If you're not too busy, I'd like a word with you."

Bernard looked up to see William Dale standing at the entrance to the cubicle. "Take a chair, Bill," he said expansively, plunging his quill pen into a jar of sand.

"If it's all the same to you, I'd rather stand." Dale looked pale beneath his permanent, leathery tan.

No flaw had marred their relationship since they had reached their understanding, and Bernard studied the Quaker surreptitiously. It was evident that the man was tense and ill at ease.

"How long will it take you to find another merchandise buyer?" Dale asked abruptly.

"It hadn't crossed my mind I might need one. Are you unhappy here, Bill?"

"No, sir. You've treated me fair and fine from the very first day I walked in here. That's not all. You've been my friend, and I'm not forgetting it. There isn't much I can do to return the favor, but I'm not leaving until you can find somebody else who'll do my work the way you want it done."

"I'll make inquiries. When do you want to leave, Bill?"

"As soon as you hire the right man."

"If it's that urgent, I wouldn't want to hold you back."

"It wouldn't set right in my own mind if I left you with a need, so I'll have to do this my own way. I've already explained it to the people who are hiring me, and they understand, so it's honest all around."

"You're taking another position?" Bernard wished that Dale would sit.

"I couldn't ask for better from you." Dale groped for the belt into which he could hook his thumbs, but was frustrated by the waistcoat he had been wearing in recent months. "I've got me two youngsters as well as a wife to support, though, and a man has to think of himself."

"Naturally."

"Ever since the new baby came, Annie has been poking at me to move down to Philadelphia. The wages you've been paying me are higher than I deserve, and I couldn't hope for more in this kind of work. Annie has been saying the only place I could make more would be with our own kind down in Pennsylvania."

Bernard nodded, knowing it was true that the opportunities for advancement open to Quakers in Newport were limited.

"Me, I haven't wanted to leave. That would be surrendering when there's still breath and spunk left in me. So I've been holding back, and now I don't have to leave."

"May I ask who has hired you?"

Dale hesitated for no more than an instant. "They want to keep this confidential until I actually join them."

"Of course. You can rely on me to tell no one, and I'm delighted for you, Bill."

"I'm going to work for the East India Company," Dale said. "I'm going to be their Newport agent."

"My God!" Bernard felt ill, and wondered if the man had lost his wits.

"Before you say anything, I've been thinking about this ever since they wrote to me ten days ago. I know why they've hired me, and what they expect of me. They made that mighty clear when we talked this morning."

"Bill, you can't do it!" Bernard was appalled.

"The way I feel, I wouldn't buy one ounce of their tea myself, and I wouldn't drink a cup if you poured it down me. But I'm blamed if I have the right to stop other people from doing what they want.

When I lived out on the frontier, nobody told anybody else what to do. It's the same here. Storekeepers who don't want tea won't have to buy it from me. Anyone who wants it can get as much as he pleases, though."

What Winters had said about the threats of tarring and feathering in Baltimore were still fresh in Bernard's mind. "You're making the biggest mistake of your life, Bill. The Committee of Correspondence won't stand for it."

Dale's slow smile spread across his face. "It takes a heap to scare me."

"They'll do more than scare. But aside from subjecting yourself to personal risk, you're violating a principle that men in every colony have banded together to defend."

Dale's eyes became hard. "Everybody talks about principles, but it's only the principles of the majority that are important. I'm tired of listening to people fool themselves. Parliament was within its rights to pass the Tea Act, and we're within ours not to buy or drink the stuff. Well and good. But I say that if there's just one man in all the thirteen colonies who is willing to pay King George's tax on tea and can drink it with a clear conscience, he has every right on this earth to buy tea! That's my idea of freedom, and I aim to do something to support what I believe!"

He was so emphatic, so adamant that Bernard felt a sense of panic. "You're wrong. If you'll just sit down and let me try to explain what——"

"I thank you kindly, but don't bother. I don't reckon you can tell me anything I haven't already heard from the elders of the Society. They've been hammering and pounding at me ever since Annie went to them a week ago. But they can't make me change, and neither can you."

"I probably shouldn't mention this, but I feel I must." Bernard steeled himself. "You won't be doing a service to your fellow Quakers, you know."

"That's what the elders have been saying. But they don't live with my conscience. I do."

"It would be bad enough if you were an Anglican or a Congregationalist. Or, if you prefer, a Catholic. But in this city, where Quakers are already so unpopular, you'll be hurting all of them."

"I aim to make it clear to everybody in town that I'm the only one responsible for what I do."

"Have you learned so little about bigotry since you became a Quaker? Have you forgotten the storm raised by people who didn't want a Quaker for a neighbor when I planned to sell you a house?"

"No, sir." Dale's voice had become rasping. "I remember it plain."

"Then use your good sense, Bill! You won't be just a dirty traitor. You'll be a dirty Quaker traitor!"

"Do you think that's liberty—in a colony that says everybody has freedom of worship?"

"Certainly not! It's bigotry, and you'll be making it worse!"

"I have to live according to my own ideas of what's right and wrong, not what the majority in Newport think. Just like I've got to support my family. If they were starving, the people who live across Broad Street would let them go hungry. Well, that won't happen. The East India Company takes care of the people it hires. When this business of tea is settled, they're going to give me a still better place at more money. They've put it all in writing, and I've signed my name to the contract."

The man's incredibly naïve attitude was as horrifying as what he was doing.

"So it's all settled," Dale said. "I've made up my mind, and there's no turning back."

With the assistance of Eduard Beauchamp, Bernard hired a new merchandise buyer to supervise the purchasing of furs, timber and tobacco. But he told no one Dale's plans, which, if they materialized, were certain to create a dangerously explosive situation. He spoke privately and at length with Annie Dale, who was afraid her husband would be running grave risks, but who confessed her inability to influence him. Conferences with several senior members of the Society of Friends also proved fruitless. They, too, were unable to persuade Dale to change his mind.

While Bernard waited apprehensively for the crisis to erupt, the East India Company, working closely with Lord North's government in London, made careful plans for the landing of a cargo of tea. The stakes in the venture were enormous, and everyone concerned knew that if the Company succeeded, and tea found its way into the homes of individuals, resistance would crumble overnight in all thirteen colonies.

By October, 1773, the stage was set. Two merchant ships owned by the Company, the *Jay* and the *Frances*, both heavily laden with tea, sailed past the southern tip of Aquidneck Island, on which Newport was located. They had made a rendezvous at sea with a Royal Navy squadron consisting of two frigates and three sloops-of-war, which escorted them; the masters of privateers and fishing vessels hastily weighed anchor when they saw that the fighting ships were stripped for action, with their gunports lowered and the muzzles of cannon protruding from the openings.

The Redcoat garrison stationed on Goat Island had been alerted, and the troops under the command of Colonel Sir Thomas Martin had crossed from Fort George to Newport by the time the ships docked at Long Wharf. Royal Marines unloaded the cargo, while Redcoats with bayonets attached to their rifles stood guard. No civilians were permitted to approach the area, and when the boxes of tea were moved to a warehouse owned by the Crown on Thames Street near the foot of Long Wharf, strong detachments of troops assigned to sentry duty were stationed around the building.

Hundreds of Newport's citizens gathered at a distance to watch the operation. Merchants and artisans, seafaring men, and farmers from the outlying area watched as the Marines carried several thousand pounds of tea into the warehouse. No one made a move or even a token gesture in opposition to the Crown forces, no one shouted, and there was virtually no conversation. Perhaps the most impressive feature of the Rhode Islanders' reaction was their silence. Both Sir Thomas and the commander of the Navy squadron, a Commodore, who stood together at the foot of Long Wharf with their staffs, seemed surprised. They had been prepared for opposition, either physical or verbal, but the colonists were demonstrating extraordinary self-discipline, and the quiet made it difficult to assess their mood accurately.

When the storing of the tea had been completed, an operation that lasted well into the afternoon, a newly appointed Collector of the Port, who had traveled to the New World on board one of the frigates, came ashore and vanished into the warehouse. Tension rose swiftly, and citizens who had vanished through the day suddenly reappeared. Then William Dale, to whom no one had paid particular attention, worked his way forward through the crowd.

Clad in black, his manner solemn, he moved into the open. Sir Thomas signaled, a junior officer called a sharp command and Dale was passed through the sentry lines and admitted to the warehouse.

For a moment the onlookers were stunned, and then an angry, low murmur ran through the crowd.

Bernard, who had been standing alone, beads of perspiration on his forehead even though the day was cool, felt a hand on his shoulder.

"Does this mean what I think it does?" Isaiah Winters was white-faced.

"I'm afraid so." Bernard absently wiped his clammy hands on the sides of his breeches.

"That Quaker left you to become an agent for the East India Company? You're sure?"

Afraid to trust his voice, Bernard nodded. Precisely as he had feared, Winters' first reaction had been that of identifying Dale by his faith.

"Is he a lunatic?"

"I believe not." There was no reason now for Bernard to keep silent about the matter. "He told me he planned to go to work for the East India Company, and although I did everything I could to persuade him he was making a mistake, his arguments were logical enough. I couldn't agree with them, but he knew what he was doing."

Winters, his shoulders hunched, glowered at the closed door of the Crown warehouse. "The man is a dangerous lunatic. He confirms what I've always said. Anybody who believes in that trash the Quakers preach must be insane. My God, the man was born in Massachusetts Bay, out near Springfield when it was real frontier country there, and he's lived in America all his life. Why is he doing something that could destroy us all?"

"According to his thinking, and it's his alone, Isaiah—he believes he's taking a stand for liberty."

"Quaker sophistry!"

"No, it isn't." Bernard spoke very carefully and distinctly. "I've talked to several senior members of the Society of Friends, and they're as completely opposed to Dale taking this post as we are."

Winters ignored the basic point that Bernard was trying to make. "You've known about this for some time."

Bernard was forced into the defensive. "I heard about it, yes."

"Why didn't you tell me? And some of the others?"

"There was nothing you or anyone could have done at that point. Besides, it wasn't really an accomplished fact until just now, when Dale went into the warehouse to pay the tax on the tea."

"I think we could have stopped him." There was an ugly note in Winters' voice.

"As you said yourself just now, he comes from the frontier. He isn't the kind who can be threatened or frightened."

Winters' smile was glacial.

"I hope you understand that he doesn't have the support of the Quaker community," Bernard said. "The people I saw up there are very disturbed about all this."

"Are you thinking of becoming a convert, Bernard?"

"Hardly!"

"Then why try so hard to protect them?"

"Because the fact that Dale is or isn't a Quaker is irrelevant. He's a man who is guilty of muddled thinking, and his religion isn't an issue."

"You're wrong! Only a damned idiot of a Quaker could think he's helping to protect liberty by doing the one thing that can destroy freedom for everyone in America!"

"I'm not trying to defend him, Isaiah. Remember I have as much at stake as you. I can't send off one ounce of cargo to France—in your

404

ships or anybody else's—while the Royal Navy squadron stays in port. And once the principle of paying the tea tax is established, I can be taxed out of business by duties on imports and exports."

"I'm glad you at least realize that your own future isn't very bright—if we let Dale get by with this monstrous scheme of his."

"I'm sure the idea itself wasn't his. The East India Company went to him with it."

"I don't care who started it! The Quaker is an agent for the Company, and I can name you four or five storekeepers in town who will leap at the chance to buy tea from him. Dave Grune knows all of them. Ask him."

"That won't be necessary. I'm sure I could identify two of them myself."

"Unless we move quickly, there will be tea brewing in half the homes of Newport within a fortnight."

For the first time Bernard could see the point that William Dale had made to him. If the shopkeepers of Newport were willing to sell tea, and if the citizens were eager to buy it, perhaps it was a denial of liberty to refuse them the opportunity. On the other hand, the blow struck on behalf of freedom would be no more than temporary. Once the British Parliament had established its right to tax the colonies as it pleased, the Commons majority could impose unlimited restrictions on Americans. The problem appeared insoluble.

Bernard sighed as he looked at the muskets of the Redcoat sentries reflecting the autumn sunlight. "What can we possibly do, Isaiah? What they've done was planned with great care in London. Look at those frigates riding at anchor. Each of them must have thirty or forty guns—"

"Forty-four."

"—and Sir Thomas' troops are ready for any disturbance."

"Do you think the Royal Navy would start shelling Newport? That's absurd!"

"Perhaps," Bernard said, "but I'd hate to take the risk."

"And I suppose," Winters continued, not hearing him, "that the Redcoats will shoot down civilians."

"Well," Bernard said, "as I understand it, that's what they did in Boston."

"That was several years ago, under far different circumstances. They've been under orders not to get involved in fights with Americans. Lord North knows—and so does King George—that any repetition of the Boston Massacre could start a real war. They realize we aren't spineless cowards who are going to tie our hands behind our backs while fellow Americans are murdered."

His belligerence was so great that Bernard realized it would be useless to point out to him that the Redcoats wouldn't be at fault if the colonials were the first to take violent action. "Isaiah," he said, "I'm as unhappy as you about this entire situation. But I don't see what we can do about it."

"Offhand, neither do I. But we've got to do something. If we sit back meekly, that damned Quaker will make us slaves!"

The Unicorn and Sceptre, for more than two generations the most exclusive and expensive of Newport's inns, was no longer open to the public. A solid, two-story structure of gray Rhode Island stone, it was located in one of the oldest parts of the city, at the point where Passage, Shipwright and Triangle Streets converged at Thames Street. Now a private club for gentlemen, it continued to use its old name, but was known to its members as The Patriot. There the local Committee of Correspondence made its headquarters, and the mood of its members was best exemplified by a recent clipping from the Newport *Mercury*, a newspaper published by Benjamin Franklin's nephew, which was tacked to a whitewashed wall at the head of the second-floor landing. The editorial read:

> The challenge is plain and must be met. A resident of this city has elected to accept a position as the principal Rhode Island sub-agent in the employ of the East India Company, and has paid the illegal tax on tea imposed by the English Parliament. This threat to us and to our sister colonies cannot and shall not be ignored.
>
> May Divine guidance prompt the ill-advised sub-agent to retire with grace and seek a position elsewhere. While respecting his motives, we deplore his judgment, and earnestly implore him to reconsider his rash act. The people of Rhode Island, who worship the Lord God Almighty in many forms, from the naves and pews of churches and meeting houses of many denominations, both Christian and Hebrew, join in prayer, hoping that the Holy Spirit will shed Grace upon him and thus enable him to correct the error of his ways.

Someone who apparently doubted the efficacy of prayer had scribbled in the margin of the clipping, "Hang the bastard!"

No one had bothered to obliterate or erase the sentiment.

The so-called reading room of The Patriot, located a few paces down the corridor from the spot where the clipping had been tacked, bore no resemblance to a library. The leather-bound works of John Locke and David Hume occupied places of honor, but most of the space on the dusty shelves that lined two walls of the chamber was occupied by copies of prominent colonial newspapers and stacks of pamphlets on current political questions. Virtually all of these treatises had been written by Sam Adams, but did not bear his signature, and it was an open secret that they had been printed at John Hancock's expense.

No one was admitted to the reading room except men whose devotion to the American cause was unquestioned by the members of The Patriot. There had been a time when only a handful of Newport citizens had been allowed to enter this inner sanctum, but now, on an evening early in November, 1773, so many had crowded into the chamber to hear a report by William Ellery that the air was stifling and the smokeless French tapers in the wall sockets burned low.

The throng was restless as it waited for Ellery, who was dining with friends on the ground floor, and a sustained roar greeted him when he finally made his appearance. Someone gave him a chair, two or three others lifted him onto the seat, and he stood for a few moments, trying in vain to silence the crowd. Not until a trumpeter attached to the local militia battalion blew a few ear-shattering notes did the men finally become quiet.

"I'm not here to make an address," Ellery said. "I just want to tell you, very briefly, about the meeting of the Rhode Island Committee of Correspondence that adjourned late last night. For two days we studied the problem posed by the landing of East India Company tea here and the payment of the Crown tax by the Company's agent. We reached no final conclusions."

A number of men jeered.

Ellery raised a hand for silence. "My good friends, the question is not an easy one to resolve. We explored the possibility of burning the warehouse where the tea is stored——"

"Good!" someone shouted. "Burn it to cinders!"

"——but we voted unanimously against such a blatant display of violence. The Crown authorities are prepared for just such an attack, and Sir Thomas Martin's troops are under orders to shoot any intruders attempting to destroy Crown property."

"We're not afraid of the goddam Redcoats," a man at the rear called.

"Perhaps not, but we feel certain that Lord North would use any act of violence against Crown troops or property to pass new regulations restricting the freedom of the colonies. We want to give him no excuse."

"Then the Quaker must be made to resign," Isaiah Winters declared loudly.

"His religion has no bearing on the situation," Ellery replied sharply.

Bernard, standing beside Winters, felt a wave of relief. The rising tide of bigotry in recent days had become increasingly unbearable, and it was good to know that men of tolerance as well as common sense were in charge of coping with the affair.

"I beg you remember," Ellery continued, "that bias against any faith can be more destructive to our cause than the sale of tea to everyone in Newport. Let me remind you that two prominent members of the Rhode Island Committee are members of the Society of Friends."

"Get rid of them," Isaiah Winters muttered, and several men near him nodded in agreement.

"Not only that," Ellery went on, "but our primary purpose is to work in coordination with the Committees of other colonies. Approximately half the Pennsylvania Committee is made up of Society of Friends members."

"Then Pennsylvania is lost," Eduard Beauchamp said.

Ellery looked hard at him. "If I recall correctly, Beauchamp, you're a Calvinist."

"That's right. We've been Huguenots for almost two hundred years."

"Then how would you feel if the Pennsylvania Committee took action to punish a member of the Huguenot minority in Philadelphia?"

"If he was a traitor," Beauchamp retorted, "I'd say he deserved what was coming to him. America—and the Huguenots—would be well rid of him!"

Some of the men began to cheer.

Ellery waved energetically to silence them. "The Rhode Island Committee of Correspondence," he said, "has been considering the problem created by William Dale, agent of the East India Company, not William Dale, Quaker."

"If he wasn't a Quaker," Dr. Michael Allen said to the group around him, "he wouldn't be working for the East India Company." Those within earshot seemed to find no fault with his logic, and Bernard felt pained.

"When I came home this afternoon," Ellery said, "I paid an official visit to Mr. Dale on behalf of the Rhode Island Committee."

A sudden, tense hush enveloped the throng.

"I asked him, in the Committee's name, for the good of the colony and of all America, to resign from the East India Company. He refused."

Men shuffled their feet and spoke to one another in low, angry tones.

"Are you surprised, gentlemen? I'm not. I've assumed from the start of this unfortunate business that Dale is a man of conviction, and although I found his reasoning specious, I can't deny there's some merit in his arguments."

"Don't go over to the other side, Bill!" someone with a deep voice called.

Ellery controlled his temper, and remained poised. "We're now

408

forced to eliminate Dale from our thinking as we seek a solution of the problem."

"Like hell we are," Isaiah Winters said under his breath.

"We can turn in only one direction, that of the shopkeepers. Dale is offering them tea. So far, because of the ferment in the community, none of them have dared to buy from him. But the Committee can't maintain pressure on our retail merchants indefinitely. Eventually tensions must relax. And when that time comes, some of our shopkeepers almost certainly will give in to temptation and buy tea from him." He looked down at David Grune, who was standing a few feet from his chair. "Am I right, Dave?"

"I'm afraid so. The Patriots won't budge, but not all the storekeepers feel as we do. Some of them are neutral, and think only of their own potential profits. There are a few who sympathize with the Crown, too, and make no secret of their feelings. Both groups are dangerous to us. It's going to be hard for anyone but a really devoted Patriot to resist the profits. Some of the merchants are already saying there are so many people in town anxious to buy tea that we can't brand all of them as traitors to the American cause."

"You can see why the problem is complex, gentlemen," Ellery said. "I'd like any of you who'll volunteer for duty with the Committee to come up to me after the meeting. The Committee can see only one way to handle this matter. We'll call on the storekeepers—not just once, but frequently—and persuade them to stand fast with us."

"May I interrupt, Bill?" Grune asked politely. "Your suggestion is good, but not good enough."

Again the crowd stirred.

"Why not, Dave?"

"The man who buys tea to sell to the public needn't be someone who is already a merchant. When the profits are as big as they are in this situation, what will stop anyone at all from going to Dale, paying him for the tea and then selling it from his own home?" Grune paused for an instant, then answered his own question. "Nothing! Someone loyal to the Crown may even feel he'll be regarded as a hero in England if he becomes a tea seller."

"Mark my words," Winters whispered to Beauchamp and Bernard, "half the people living on Quaker Hill will start clamoring for the exclusive rights to sell tea to the public."

His prejudice had become so intense, Bernard realized, that he had blinded himself to reality.

"So you see," Grune continued, "the problem is even worse than many Patriots have realized. Nearly every householder in Newport is a potential tea seller. If he doesn't have the money to buy the merchandise, I wouldn't be surprised if the East India Company will extend him credit. They'll do anything to put their tea into general circulation. And we can't go from door to door, asking everybody in town not to sell the tea. We'd make more enemies than friends that way."

"What's your answer to that, Bill?" Winters demanded, shaking a fist.

"We can only do our best," Ellery replied calmly. "Dave is right when he says we face the danger of almost anyone in the city becoming a merchant for the purpose of disposing of the tea. And although he wasn't explicit, I'll spell this out. If we start threatening everyone, support for the Patriot cause will vanish. We want people to join us of their own free will, not become secret Crown sympathizers. So we'll follow the plan I've outlined to you. We'll call on every retail merchant, regularly. Beyond that, all I can suggest is that we keep our eyes and ears open; if we discover that someone not already a storekeeper has taken the tea, we'll find out what we can about him and try to persuade him to see things as we do."

There was scattered applause as he climbed down from the chair, and a number of men went forward to offer their services in calling on the merchants.

"I don't like this," Isaiah Winters said. "You don't wear a powdered wig and silk gloves to a fight down at the wharves. You arm everybody on your side with spars and clubs—anything that can be used effectively as a weapon—and then you start cracking heads open." He jabbed a thick forefinger at Bernard, then at Eduard Beauchamp. "I tell you, boys, if the Rhode Island Committee can't do anything about that damned Quaker, we'll have to take care of him ourselves."

It was unusually quiet on Quaker Hill. Most people had retired for the night, few candles and lamps were still burning, and Bernard heard no sound but the beat of his own horse's hooves on the hard-packed dirt road. It was a dark night, with heavy clouds sweeping in across the harbor and obscuring the new moon and stars, and twice he lost his way. The little houses looked remarkably alike, and for him to knock at the wrong door would be disastrous. He was already taking a considerable personal risk.

Finally, however, he felt reasonably certain he had found the right place. He dismounted, looked in vain for a hitching post before remembering there was no need for them on the Hill, and then, still holding his reins, tapped at the door with his free hand.

After a long wait he caught a glimpse of light through the window of the tiny parlor, and a moment later the door opened. William Dale, a small oil lamp in one hand, had donned an old pair of buckskin trousers over his nightshirt, and blinked in sleepy surprise at his visitor.

410

"Forgive me for coming at this hour," Bernard said, "but it's urgent."

"Come in." Dale was polite but unenthusiastic.

"I can speak my mind right here. It won't take long. I don't intend to persuade you to change what you've done. I know I couldn't. You're entitled to your ideas, even if I disagree with them. But I'm worried about your safety."

"I've had notes and threats for quite a spell. If this is another warning, don't waste your breath."

"I'm trying to help you," Bernard said angrily. "There are men in this city who are becoming desperate, and there's no telling what they may do to you."

"Thanks." Dale started to close the door.

"Wait! For your family's sake as well as your own, protect yourself. If you want to work for the East India Company, that's your business. But move to Providence, where there's a bigger community of Quakers and you aren't as well known. You'll be safer there, and you can sell your infernal tea as easily as you could here. In fact, it will be easier. There's a different atmosphere in Providence. They're—more civilized."

"This," Dale said, tapping the wall, "is my home. Nobody is going to make me leave it."

"For God's sake, listen to me! Think of Annie and your children——" The door closed, and Bernard stood alone. A bolt was slammed into place, and he wearily turned away.

Mounting his horse, he peered for some moments at the Dale house. As a man of conscience he had done everything in his power to prevent a shocking personal tragedy, and his own hands were clean. Or were they?

Although he had cast his own lot with the Americans, he was uncertain whether he had been influenced, in the main, by their love of freedom or the economic success he had enjoyed. He was still an Englishman, a subject of King George III, and was obligated to uphold law, decency and order. So it was his duty to go to Colonel Sir Thomas Martin and inform the commandant that the life of the East India Company's newly appointed agent in Newport was in grave peril. Sir Thomas, he felt certain, would respond by providing Dale with a day and night escort of Redcoats, regardless of what the man himself wanted.

On the other hand, such a visit to the garrison commander would result in economic and social disaster. Bernard realized that his associates and friends would shun him as a traitor to American principles, and his wife and three children would be isolated, too. His income would drop overnight, and instead of enjoying comfortable earnings, his business would be destroyed.

It would be impossible to move elsewhere in the colonies. The

Committee of Correspondence would see to that, and he would be branded as an informant as long as he remained in the New World. His alternative would be to return to England, where he would be forced to resume his post in his father's company. In another ten years there wouldn't be enough business to support either of them.

Bernard hadn't been aware of the cold, and shivering, pulled up the beaver collar of his cloak. One thing was certain: if Isaiah Winters, Eduard Beauchamp and the others learned he had visited Dale tonight, they would be unwilling to accept any explanation he might offer.

Wishing he had worn a broad-brimmed hat, he tugged his bicorn lower on his forehead and started off on the dirt road that led past the Society of Friends Meeting House. He encountered no one, and felt relieved when, at last, he emerged on Broad Street. No one who saw him now could guess that he had just paid a visit to Quaker Hill.

He rode slowly, mulling his dilemma, and halted when he reached the Court House. If he turned right onto Queen Street, he would reach Long Wharf in a few minutes. There he could speak a few words to the Redcoat officer of the day in charge of the sentry detail, and would be provided with a gig that would row him out to Fort George on Goat Island. In less than a half hour he could insure the safety of William Dale—at the cost of all he had struggled to achieve in the New World.

He could continue to ride in a straight line down Spring Street, however, and in less than ten minutes would be snug in his own home, where Felicity and the children were sleeping. Was it sophistry, he wondered, to argue that he had already taken more than his share of risks for Dale, and that it was no longer his concern if the man would not heed advice and refused help?

A merchant seaman and one of the town's few trollops strolled past him, their arms around each other's waists as they made their way toward one of the waterfront taverns. They were laughing, and Bernard envied them. No matter what his decision, he would never again be able to laugh so gleefully.

His hands and feet became numb as he continued to sit, and the cold stung his cheeks and ears. He was afraid to pray for guidance, even though he knew it was childish to feel that God would be angry with him if he refused to accept the prompting of Divine Providence.

Abruptly, suddenly, Bernard straightened in the saddle and, his chin thrust forward in an attitude of defiance, headed toward his own house on Upper Banister Street.

On Saturday, November 19th, the Newport battalion of Rhode Island militia, Lieutenant Colonel Isaiah Winters in temporary com-

412

mand, held a review and parade. There were occasional snow flurries that afternoon and the wind was raw, but the entire city, with the exception of the Quakers, turned out to watch the martial display. Parents and children alike were bundled in stocking caps, mufflers and heavy mittens, and only the young ladies who wore throat-baring gowns dared to risk the chance of catching the ague.

Vendors of steaming, mulled cider did a brisk business, and so did the sellers of hot venison pies, roasted oysters that had been sprinkled with a sauce of stomach-warming herbs, and toasted groundnuts. Even the elderly gentlemen afflicted with gout who rarely ate spiced foods found it impossible to resist what was offered.

Members of the Redcoat garrison were distinguished by their absence. Aside from the inevitable sentries surrounding the Crown warehouse where the East India Company's tea was stored, the troops remained in their barracks at Fort George in order to avoid the almost inevitable exchange of insults that might lead to more serious incidents.

Several senior members of the British regiment were on hand, however, led by Colonel Sir Thomas Martin; they watched the parade from the official reviewing stand of rough-cut timber that had been erected on Broad Street. Knowing they were being observed, they exercised great self-control, and not once did any of the professional soldiers smile.

There was much at which they could have laughed. Few of the militiamen wore uniforms, and the majority looked comical in their drab, ill-fitting suits of linsey-woolsey. Only the cockades of red, white and blue in their bicorns identified them as part-time soldiers. But their officers more than made up for their own lack of luster. Nearly all were attired in burnished, plumed helmets, dark-green tunics and matching capes with scarlet linings, white breeches, and knee-high boots. Unfortunately, many were unaccustomed to swords, and spoiled their martial appearance by tripping over their blades as they marched.

The battalion carried a motley collection of firearms. Captain Eduard Beauchamp's company of marksmen, which came first in the line, owned their own long rifles, and it was obvious from the way they handled the weapons that they were familiar with them. Sir Thomas' eyes narrowed, and neither he nor his subordinates felt like laughing as they watched the riflemen, whom they knew to be superior to their own light infantry.

The rest of the battalion, however, presented a somewhat ludicrous appearance. A few carried the long wilderness rifles, which they appeared to fear. Others held ordinary muskets on their shoulders, a bayonet sprouting here and there, while some were armed with old-fashioned fowling pieces. An occasional militiaman struggled with a blunderbuss at least one hundred years old, a weapon that, if fired, would be almost certain to explode in his hands. Significantly, very few of the militiamen wore horns of gunpowder, and Sir Thomas subsequently advised the War Office in London that the Patriots of Newport, like those of other major colonial centers, were suffering from a shortage of gunpowder.

Bernard, wearing the uniform of a Captain, rode beside Major David Grune with the other staff officers at the head of the column, and felt slightly ridiculous. Eventually he overcame his embarrassment, however, and when he saw Felicity standing with their children on Broad Street, he laughed as he returned the frantic waves of Catherine, Joseph and little Roger. The day was a festive occasion, he reminded himself, and although war clouds were gathering in the distance, the threat of open hostilities with England was not yet imminent.

The parade itself lasted for more than two hours as the men marched up and down the main thoroughfares of Newport. Then everyone adjourned to the fields at the north end of the city, past the Burying Ground, and there the militiamen of Beauchamp's company put on an exhibition of marksmanship, shooting with such accuracy and skill at moving targets that Sir Thomas had much to ponder.

Dusk was enveloping the field by the time the exhibition ended. The ladies had long since retired to their homes to feed their hungry children, and when Isaiah Winters finally dismissed the battalion, the militiamen quickly scattered. Most of the officers adjourned to The Patriot, and energetically sought to dispel the chill they had endured. Brandywine, whiskey and hot rum punch redolent of cloves and other spices flowed freely.

The day had been successful, the battalion had accomplished its purpose of reminding the Crown that the colonies were not helpless, and everyone was in good humor. One drink of the steaming rum punch was enough to warm Bernard, and rather than accept another, he joined David Grune at a table heaped high with roasted and boiled meats, shellfish and game birds. Both ate heartily, and were thinking of going off to their respective homes when Winters and Beauchamp joined them.

Isaiah Winters' face was flushed. "Did you boys notice there were no Quakers at the parade?" he demanded. "Not a damned one!"

"That's not surprising," Bernard said.

"Of course not," Grune added. "We all know how they feel about war."

Beauchamp nudged Bernard, and when he spoke his speech was a trifle slurred. "We know what to do with traitors. The damn Quaker."

This was not the appropriate moment for a serious discussion, so Bernard smiled vaguely. "Dave and I were just leaving," he said. "It's getting late."

"Not as late as it's going to be," Winters replied, "and you're not going home. I sent off for our clothes, and we'll change right here."

"Change?" Bernard exchanged an uneasy glance with Grune.

"Tonight's work can't be done in militia uniform," Winters said.

"Sir Thomas would love the chance to break up the battalion," Beauchamp added, "but we won't give it to him." His laugh ended on a high-pitched note.

Winters, however, remained somber. "There will be twenty of us. Boys who know what to do and can keep quiet about it. There will be nobody squeamish going on this party, nobody who talks too much. Maybe Sir Thomas and some of the others will guess, but they won't be able to prove anything."

The hour Bernard dreaded had arrived. "Everyone has had quite a bit to drink," he said. "It might be a good idea to discuss all this tomorrow."

"Our plans are set," Winters replied heavily. "We'll go upstairs two or three at a time to change, and then we'll slip away."

Beauchamp looked at the merrymakers and grinned. "Nobody will miss us, that's sure. They won't even know we've gone."

Bernard turned to Grune and asked in a low tone, "How can we stop them, Dave?"

Winters heard him. "Nobody is stopping us, and you're either with us or against us. You've been splitting your breeches straddling that fence long enough, Bernard, and you'll either join us or we'll know you're our enemy."

Trapped, Bernard made a mute appeal to Grune.

The merchant's weary shrug was compounded of cynicism and a sense of helpless defeat.

Beauchamp's good humor had disappeared. "We leave in a quarter of an hour," he said. "Come upstairs to change."

Following him, Bernard thought there was no escape. He had hoped that by standing aside he could lose himself in anonymity, but he was being made to pay a terrible, lasting price for his vacillation.

Soon men began to leave The Patriot in groups of twos and threes, the wide brims of old-fashioned Cavalier hats shading their faces, their collars raised. The party rode by separate routes through the business district, converging behind the dark Society of Friends Meeting House. There they halted, and in the silence that followed they checked their pistols and swords. The heavy silence was ominous.

Four muffled figures rode off down the hill, one of them leading a riderless horse.

The wait became interminable. Bernard had never felt so miserable and ashamed. He was a coward, he told himself repeatedly, but even if he dared, he could think of nothing to stem or change the swift current of tragedy.

The men behind the Meeting House heard hoofbeats, and several

415

raised their pistols, but relaxed again when they recognized their approaching comrades.

The fifth horse was no longer riderless. Mounted on the gelding's back was William Dale, a gag in his mouth, his hands tied firmly behind his back.

It was a waste of effort to speculate on the method of his capture, Bernard thought. Apparently he had been lured from his house and made captive quietly, so that his wife had not given an alarm.

With Isaiah Winters in the lead and four riders surrounding Dale, the party rode northward down Quaker Hill, carefully avoiding the more heavily populated residential areas. The route had been planned with great cunning, and at no time did the men emerge onto a road. They cut through yards and empty fields, then increased their pace when they came to the Burying Ground. They crossed it and the site of the marksmanship exhibition, and came at last to a heavily wooded area that was a reminder of Newport's proximity to the raw wilderness of the New World.

Evergreens were fragrant, their scent sharp in the autumn air, but Bernard looked up at the leafless branches of oaks and elms and beech, and shuddered. The night was very cold, but his shirt was soaked with perspiration.

Winters drew to a halt in a small clearing deep in the woods, and Bernard involuntarily raised a hand to his mouth when someone produced a long rope, one end of which was fashioned into a noose. The rope was thrown over the thick branch of an oak, and Dale's horse was led forward.

"This what you've wanted, you goddam Quaker," Winters said.

Bernard made a last effort. "No," he shouted. "Thousands of Quakers are good Patriots. So is he, in his own way. His idea of liberty isn't the same as ours, that's all. You can't condemn him because of his faith."

No one bothered to acknowledge much less reply to the anguished protest.

The noose was dropped over Dale's head, and the knot made secure behind his ear.

"Remove the gag," Winters directed. "Well, Quaker, how do you feel now?"

Dale, holding his head high, smiled slowly but did not speak.

"Do you want a blindfold over your eyes?"

"That won't be necessary."

Six men caught hold of the loose end of the rope and made it taut.

"Do you want to say anything?" Winters asked gruffly.

"Yes." Dale turned to Bernard. "I feel sorry for you," he said. "You're the only one here who doesn't have the courage of his convictions."

Winters gave a signal, and two men pulled Dale's horse from under him.

The following minute seemed like an eternity, but at last the figure at the end of the rope stopped kicking.

Dr. Allen rode forward, dismounted and gestured. The rope was lowered, and he examined the inert figure. "The Quaker traitor," he said, "is dead."

BOOK SIX

BOOK SIX

Books and pamphlets were spread in disarray on the table in the stately dining room, and the bowl of fruit was neglected.

"Patience, Charles. Patience," Philippe de Montauban said as he searched through one book, then flipped through the pages of another.

Bishop de Montauban munched on a chunk of buttered bread, on which he had spread a thick coating of Camembert cheese. "I'm being patient," he replied cheerfully. "Take your time."

"Here it is. Thomas Jefferson's 'Statute of Virginia for religious freedom.' It was adopted by the legislature of the state of Virginia in 1786, and is still valid today, if you please."

"Jefferson was a Deist, I believe."

"Yes, and very proud to be one. Read the preamble later, if you wish. To me, right here, is the most succinct guarantee of religious freedom I've ever seen." The Count tapped the open page before he began to read. " 'Be it therefore enacted by the General Assembly, That no man shall be compelled to frequent or support any religious worship, place or ministry whatsoever, nor shall be enforced, restrained, molested or burthened in his body or goods, nor shall otherwise suffer on account of his religious opinions or belief; but that all men shall be free to profess, and by argument to maintain, their opinions in matters of religion, and that the same shall in nowise diminish, enlarge, or affect their civil capacities.

" 'And though we well know this Assembly, elected by the people for the ordinary purposes of legislation only, have no power to restrain the acts of succeeding assemblies, constituted with the powers equal to our own, and that therefore to declare this act irrevocable, would be of no effect in law, yet we are free to declare, and do declare, that the rights hereby asserted are the natural rights of mankind, and that if any act shall be hereafter passed to repeal the present or to narrow its operation, such an act will be an infringement of natural right.' " Philippe looked at his cousin in triumph.

The Bishop continued to eat his bread and cheese.

"Well?" the Count challenged.

"If you expect me to disagree, I'm sorry to disappoint you. As recently as one hundred years ago, I dare say, you'd have found scores of Catholic bishops becoming apoplectic. But the work done by the Vatican Council should prove to you that the Church lives in the present. Don't belabor us today for our attitudes of yesterday. For every Jefferson in the non-Catholic world, there have been one thousand bigots."

"At least."

The Bishop wiped his hands, then began to hunt through the pamphlets. "It's my right to match you, Philippe. I wonder if you're familiar with the letter sent by the Papal Secretary of State on behalf of Pope John to the president of the French Social Week back in 1962."

"Since the copy comes from my library, I assume I've read it, but it made no particular impression on me."

"It should have. Listen to this excerpt. 'The element which constitutes a people, over and above the peculiarities of race, language, culture, tradition and religion which delimit it, is found in its collective will to live, which expresses itself in common ways of thinking, feeling and living. Is this not the case of Europe, whose economic social and political components draw their unifying force from what may be called the European spirit, based upon the perception of common spiritual values?

" 'There exists, in fact, a European patrimony which is humanist and universalist, whose elements appear in each national culture. Bringing it into play should bring more peace and fraternity.

" 'One finds there Greek humanism, with its feeling of balance, of measure and of beauty; the Roman juridicial spirit, giving to each individual his place and his rights in a solidly constructed political community——' "

"I've yet to hear anything about freedom," Philippe said, interrupting.

The Bishop smiled and resumed his reading. " 'But above all, what has shaped the European soul over nearly two millennia is Christianity, which has outlined the traits of the human person, a free being, independent and responsible.' "

book six

Man errs, until his strife is over.
—JOHANN WOLFGANG VON GOETHE

1805

"We rejoice because France and the United States once again enjoy the close friendship established between us during your Revolution." Louis de Feroux, deputy Minister of France to the United States, was a fastidious man, and it was apparent in every move, gesture and expression that he had a low opinion of his nation's legation in Washington City, a hastily constructed wooden edifice in a new town of rutted mud roads and half-completed government buildings. "Our countries and our people have a natural affinity for one another."

Joseph Maurice de Montauban crossed his legs carefully in order to avoid rumpling his one good pair of wool trousers. "You've forgotten our undeclared war of six and seven years ago, Your Excellency." A light of humor showed behind his spectacles.

Feroux dismissed the unpleasantness with a wave of a neatly manicured hand. "A temperamental misunderstanding between young nations. President Adams did not understand us."

Joseph wanted to retort that the President, like the American people, had both understood and resented the unprovoked raids on their shipping by French warships that had stopped only when Britain's Admiral Lord Nelson had destroyed Napoleon Bonaparte's fleet at Alexandria. He still had no idea, however, why he had been invited to Washington City, with the French legation paying his expenses from New York, and it would be foolish to antagonize someone who might provide him with work that would enable him to augment his pitifully small salary as a professor at Columbia College. "I must admit," he said politely, "that France was in the last stages of her own Revolution at the time."

The diplomat was quick to take advantage of the point. "As one who spent his childhood in a land of ferment, you must know that Napoleon had not yet consolidated his hold on France. Many things that happened in those years were deplorable."

Joseph shifted slightly in his chair, and wondered why the legation had gone to the bother of looking into his past. As tall and solidly built as the de Montauban men of previous generations, his scholarly appearance made him seem rather fragile, and he sometimes took refuge behind its façade. Feroux was guilty of over-simplification, but it did no harm to pretend his argument was valid. "During a time of change," he said, speaking a precise but American-accented French, "nations sometimes forget their responsibilities."

"Exactly so!" Feroux beamed, and offered his guest another glass of wine, which was refused. "But the magnificent gesture of the Emperor two years ago, when he was still First Consul, in selling the Louisiana Territory to the United States for mere pennies, restored our old ties."

The reason Bonaparte had sold Louisiana, as Joseph well knew, was that his war with England had forced him to concentrate his full attention and resources on affairs in Europe.

The deputy minister seemed carried away by his own enthusiasm. "The best of all signs for the future is that the Emperor was crowned on December 5th of last year, the same day your President Jefferson was re-elected."

Joseph did not find the coincidence significant, and could not help asking, "Is it true that Napoleon took the crown from the hands of Pope Pius at Notre-Dame and placed it on his own head? The New York *Evening Post* is usually reliable in its accounts, but I found this one a trifle bizarre."

Feroux was embarrassed. "The Emperor is an extraordinary man," he murmured, "as I hope you shall have occasion to discover for yourself."

Joseph immediately became alert, while appearing relaxed. It was a trick he had first learned in his childhood during the British occupation of Newport, and it had served him well during the long, gloomy years of his father's fatal illness.

"France is very fortunate." The diplomat's manner and tone became portentous. "My predecessor in the legation spent a year searching in vain for you, and if you had not married in Martinique last year, we might still be hunting for you."

"My sister has lived in Martinique since her marriage to a former officer who served with Count d'Estaing during our Revolution, and it was during a visit to her last year that I met and married my wife."

"Ah, yes. Adrienne de Saint Ronne. An old and excellent family."

Joseph wanted to smile, but knew Adrienne would be pleased to hear that the regime of the upstart French Emperor approved of her family, which traced its lineage back to the reign of Louis XI.

"We have since learned a great deal about you and your family. Your brother is lay administrator for the bishop of Quebec——"

"Roger is entitled to live and work as he pleases." Joseph had been on distant terms with his brother since their violent arguments on religion.

"——while your sister rears a splendid and noble family of her own in Martinique." Feroux smiled in obvious approval.

"You've gone to considerable trouble to find out what you can about me and my relatives." Joseph's impulsiveness was one of his worst traits, but he had already spent the better part of an hour at the legation, and his patience had worn thin. "Why?"

The diplomat assumed an invisible cloak of great dignity. "If you please, permit me to approach a subject of importance in my own way. If you do not object, I have been instructed to ask you a few questions."

Joseph shrugged. Whether he chose to answer them remained to be seen.

"You teach French history and language at Columbia College."

Joseph nodded. His vocation was a matter of public record.

"Perhaps you would satisfy my own curiosity. I find it odd that the son of a merchant should become a teacher."

A feeling of annoyance welled up in Joseph. He felt certain the legation had learned more about him than the deputy minister was revealing. "My father was forced into bankruptcy by some of his former associates in Newport, and would have been sent to debtors' prison if death hadn't saved him the embarrassment. As for me, a man does what he must."

"Then you have no great love for the teaching profession?"

Joseph remained silent. It was no one's business but his own, and perhaps Adrienne's, that he despised his life of genteel poverty.

Feroux understood more than he indicated. "France," he said, seemingly changing the subject, "finds herself in a strange situation. Thousands of nobles were murdered by the Terror, and those who fled to exile in England hope for the restoration of the Bourbons. Some are loyal to the Emperor, to be sure, but he has already found it necessary to enlarge the peerage."

Joseph laughed to himself at the idea of the opportunist general from Corsica building a new nobility to help him justify the title of Emperor he had given himself.

"There are other, legitimate titles of long standing that he would like to restore to their rightful claimants."

Joseph's amusement vanished, and he became tense.

"As a student of French history, you must know that you have a right to call yourself Count of Montauban."

Pretending indifference, Joseph gestured vaguely. "As I understand it, my grandfather, who died in England some years ago, renounced all claims to the title."

"The claim is valid if you choose to exercise your rights," Feroux declared solemnly.

"What would be required of me?" Joseph became crisp.

"I am informed that the properties at Montauban suffered less damage than most during the Terror. You would be expected to occupy and restore them——"

"I have no funds for the purpose."

426

"I feel certain the Emperor would work out an accommodation with you——"

"Why should he deal generously with an obscure American who has never displayed any talents of note?" Joseph demanded.

Feroux hesitated, decided to be honest, and spoke in a low tone. "The people of France have been very enthusiastic in their support of the Emperor's decision to take the crown. He has restored their sense of national pride. But elsewhere, particularly in England, men who don't know him or his goals laugh. That is dangerous."

"True. It's difficult for a monarch to be taken seriously when he's ridiculed."

"Ah, you grasp the essence of his dilemma! Splendid. I neglected to mention that the fine old de Montauban townhouse in Paris would be restored to you, too. It was last occupied by the uncle of a mistress of Louis XV, a gentleman who lost his life during the worst days of the Terror, and was mourned by no one. As a student of history you might want to collect paintings of the de Montauban family that have been scattered throughout France, and——"

"I hope I'd be given tasks more useful than just serving as a puppet noble!"

Feroux instantly became guarded. "His Imperial Majesty," he said, "makes all decisions regarding the enlistment of people in his service."

"I'd be expected to swear allegiance to France, I presume?" Adrienne would be delighted, Joseph knew.

"Oh, yes. And to His Majesty, personally."

"You realize, I'm sure, that I'd lose my American citizenship."

The deputy minister walked to the windows of the legation parlor and gestured in the direction of the drab new wooden buildings that housed the government of the United States. No other reply, his manner indicated, was necessary.

"How soon do you want a decision?"

"The Emperor has already been notified that the heir to the de Montauban title has been found, so you must make up your mind at once! He permits no delays, no excuses, no rationalizations—in anything."

For three and one-half weeks the Emperor had followed the strict instructions of his physicians and eaten none of the heavily spiced foods he loved. The chronic pains below his ribs had subsided, and he had been so energetic, so exuberant that the members of his harassed, overworked staff were near collapse. And their problems were compounded by physical handicaps that, as they bitterly told one another, could have been avoided.

Eleven large royal residences were available in or near Paris for the

Emperor's use, among them the Louvre and the palace at Versailles, either of which would have been eminently suitable to house and feed the officials who were coming to see him in an unending stream during a period when he was reviewing the past and making plans for the future. He had chosen to make his headquarters for the spring, however, at the little country mansion called Malmaison, which he had presented to the Empress Josephine as a gift during one of his increasingly rare moods of generosity. And he was too obstinate to admit that Malmaison was too small to be used simultaneously as a private dwelling, supreme military command post, government conference center, and the gathering place of lawyers, architects, artists and merchants in whose affairs he was taking interest.

The Empress was in residence, too, for the making of a new spring wardrobe, so one entire wing that otherwise might have been utilized was occupied by her friends, ladies-in-waiting and dressmakers. A battalion of the Guards regiment charged with the protection of the Emperor's person had been forced to pitch its tents and cook its meals on the back lawn, creating an atmosphere that the minister from the Electorate of Saxony had called similar to that of a Corsican gypsy camp. The highest ranking government officials, when required to remain overnight on business, slept in the stables, displacing all the horses except the Emperor's own two favorite mounts. The frenzied chef, unable to keep count of the comings and goings of so many, daily prepared afternoon and evening dinners for seventy-five guests.

But the chef, too, was frustrated. Meetings of one kind or another almost invariably were taking place in the dining room until a few minutes before the serving of a meal, making it impossible to set the tables in a style worthy of the man whose Foreign Minister, Talleyrand, called the busiest monarch in the history of civilization. To make matters worse, the Emperor himself rarely appeared in the dining room, preferring to have meals of cold, unseasoned meat, bread and salad greens served in his study.

The heads of government departments and foreign envoys sometimes had to wait days for an appointment. The Apostolic delegate, Archbishop Cigoni, took umbrage when he was offered a tiny cell in the servants quarters for a night, and indignantly returned to Paris, even though the Emperor's most competent aide, his stepson, Eugene, tried to reassure Cigoni that neither he nor Pope Pius VII was being slighted.

By mid-April the pace increased. Every three hours, day and night, a courier arrived from the headquarters of the Imperial Navy on the Channel to report on the progress of preparations for the invasion of England that was scheduled to be launched later in the spring. The commanders of the three army corps stationed in the Paris area made personal visits to Malmaison for instructions every afternoon, and the generals in the Italian states, the Low Countries and on the German border exchanged long daily letters with their Emperor.

April 16th was a day everyone associated with Napoleon would long remember. It began a few minutes after dawn when the Emperor, as usual, stamped into his office in boots, breeches and the old dressing robe that had been his favorite ever since the Egyptian campaign. Over cups of hot, green tea from Holland he gave detailed orders to his liaison officers for political, economic and social, or cultural, affairs. He had no military liaison officer because, he boasted, he filled that place himself.

While he took a quick bath in a room adjoining his study and, thereafter, his barber shaved him, a secretary read him the latest news and editorials from the newspapers of seven or eight nations. He did not bother to hear accounts from the Paris press, since he himself dictated their policies. Twice he interrupted the reading, once to send off a note to an agricultural expert at the University of Paris, asking for an opinion on a new, supposedly disease-resistant strain of Scottish barley that was being discussed extensively in the British newspapers. The second interruption, somewhat longer, was sparked by an article from a Berlin newspaper on the growth of industry in Leipzig. He sent a detailed letter to his minister in Saxony, requesting replies to more than thirty specific questions he asked.

Over a breakfast of broiled fish, plain rolls and porter, he reviewed the blueprints for the beautification of Paris and approved several recommendations made by the architects who had been waiting four days to see him. By then his secretaries had finished sorting his mail, and he began dictating replies while his valet helped him to change into cream-colored trousers, a conservative tailcoat and matching waistcoat, and a shirt with a modified version of the high, starched collar he refused to wear because it chafed his neck. He deluded himself into believing that no one except the valet knew there were thick soles and two-inch heels on his low boots. His sensitivity on the subject of his short stature was so intense that he had made it a rule to let others sit while he stood, and found it hard to believe that taller men were so in awe of him they rarely were conscious of his lack of height.

He spent an hour studying semi-annual budget plans with three Treasury officials, and received a delegation of silk-makers from Lyons who presented him with samples of their latest manufactures. Absently ordering the cloth sent upstairs to the Empress, he spent the rest of the morning hurrying between a meeting, in the dining room, of distinguished jurists who were revising and modernizing the legal codes that had remained virtually untouched since the reign of Henry IV, and another conference, in the main drawing room, of trade experts who were planning a drastic overhaul of tariffs.

At one o'clock he dined in his office with his generals, who were resigned to his fare of tasteless beef, green salad and a wine so mild it had almost no flavor. Then the Empress joined him in the drawing room for a reception at which newly arrived diplomats presented their credentials, but the Emperor, much to the annoyance of Talleyrand, sneaked back to his study to rearrange the spring schedules of the Paris theater and opera companies.

A grim session followed with the shipbuilders who were trying in vain to create a fleet as large and powerful as that of the British. For the first time that day the Emperor lost his temper, and the aides, hearing him shout, shuddered as they braced for tirades directed at them. They did not have long to wait. The Emperor called in three secretaries to whom he dictated replies to the mail that had arrived since noon. He cursed at them in French, Arabic and Italian because they were too slow, and was not mollified until an artist arrived for a sitting of a new portrait to be used on coins the next year. During the session the Emperor dictated a document he really enjoyed, the establishment of training schedules for four new brigades of cavalry, and his good humor was restored.

His sense of well-being was short-lived, however. The most debauched of his dissolute relatives, his sister, Pauline, arrived from Paris with a plaintive request for five thousand gold napoleons. She had just heard that the Empress, with whom she was not on speaking terms, was having a new wardrobe made, and wanted to match it. The Emperor tried to be evasive, but Pauline was adamant, so he signed an order on the Treasury and gave it to her, preferring the squandering of money to the loss of his precious time that would have resulted had she created a scene.

Wanting to make certain Pauline left Malmaison rather than become embroiled in another squabble with the Empress, he walked with her to the front door and saw her off in her carriage. A dozen or so men who had been waiting in anterooms to see him clamored for a moment of his attention as he made his way past them, but he ruthlessly brushed them aside, and when he sank at last into his own leather chair behind his desk, he felt his first twinge of weariness.

Then the door opened, and the one man in the Empire who needed no appointment to see him came into the room. "What do you want?" Napoleon demanded.

Joseph Fouché was a tall, lugubrious man with a pock-marked face and manner so lacking in ostentation that he was the only important member of the regime who could walk unrecognized through the streets of Paris. He was in his mid-forties, but looked older, and his mild blue eyes and gentle smile were deceptive. He held the twin portfolios of Minister of Police and Minister of the Interior, and it was rumored that ten thousand secret agents scattered throughout the Empire were in his employ. The Emperor believed there were twenty thousand, and only Fouché knew the actual number was closer to thirty.

He lowered himself into a leather chair, unbidden, and reached for a mint from the silver bowl the Emperor kept to dispel sudden discomfort when he ate unwisely.

Napoleon picked up a miniature saber, given to him as a memento by the veterans of his first Italian campaign, that he used to break the seals on confidential letters. He aimed it, and made a swift thrust.

Fouché, anticipating the stroke, withdrew his hand and popped a mint into his mouth. "I've made my contract with Satan," he said.

"Then you have no one to fear except me," Napoleon replied coldly. "I'm very busy today, and my wife is giving a dinner for the Duke of Savoy tonight, so I've got to make a token appearance. Be brief, please."

Neither awed nor impressed, Fouché deliberately took his time as he drew several papers from the inner pocket of his elegantly tailored tailcoat. "Bishop Andrazzi of Turin has seen the light, and has promised to keep me informed of the secret deliberations of the Curia."

Napoleon laughed. "Joseph, you're a fool. Do you suppose I care what Pius and his Curia say in their secret meetings? I drew his sting in the Concordat four years ago. The French state, not The Holy See, appoints our new bishops, and we're completely independent of the papacy. What's more, four of my best regiments are on duty in Rome for Pius'—ah—protection. So he's helpless."

"For the moment. But don't forget, Your Majesty, that there are millions, including people in the newer parts of the Empire, who take his words seriously. There's no doubt he's afraid of you, but you know these Italians. He'll wait for the right moment to undermine you." Fouché handed a paper across the desk.

"I suppose you're right," Napoleon grumbled. "It does no harm to be prepared."

Fouché was always surprised by the Emperor's ability to read and assimilate a document in a single, swift glance.

"You're paying Andrazzi too much. He'd have been happy to accept half."

"You'll note we didn't specify the currency. I intend to pay him in the specie of The Papal States, so he'll get a little less than half of what I'd have had to pay him in napoleons." Fouché's smile was smug.

Napoleon sat back in his chair, running his forefinger around the embossed laurel wreath surrounding the "N" on the jar of sand that held his pens. "You're always complaining you're overworked. Surely you didn't drive out from Paris just to tell me of an agreement you've made with a slightly tainted Italian bishop."

There were times, Fouché thought, when his master knew him too well. He craftily measured the distance to the bowl of mints, then snatched another before the Emperor could stop him. "Well," he said casually, "I've been doing a few other things in the same general sphere. I've been corresponding, through intermediaries—and on the purest level, of course—with the Lutheran bishops in the German states."

Napoleon's dark eyes narrowed, and a vein bulged near his high hairline on his left temple, but he said nothing.

After an association of almost ten years, a relationship that had begun when both had been maneuvering for power, the Minister of Police and the Interior knew the danger signs. "I haven't involved you in any way, Your Majesty, either directly or indirectly."

Napoleon sat very still, and it was astonishing how the atmosphere became ominous when he grew tense.

"We have every reasonable assurance that when—if you decide to protect the German states and add them to the Empire, the Lutheran bishops will cooperate with you. They supervise a disciplined church, so that means the pastors—and ultimately, the parishioners—will accept you."

"What do you know of my plans regarding the German states?" The Emperor spoke so softly his voice was almost inaudible.

Fouché concealed his nervousness by folding his arms across his chest. "It stands to reason that if your invasion of England should fail——"

"It will not fail!" Napoleon roared, and his fist crashed on the desk so hard that a small bust of himself in a military bicorn teetered precariously before righting itself.

The aides in the outer office heard his tone and looked at each other apprehensively.

Fouché began again. "Regardless of the outcome of the attempted invasion, the Austrian problem remains. Austria is the heart of the Continental alliance against you. Neither Russia nor Prussia could stand up to you if the Austrians were crushed. I've heard you say as much yourself. So you've got to wage a land campaign against Austria."

"Have any of the generals been talking out of turn?"

"Not one, Your Majesty, I swear it."

Napoleon remained suspicious, but relaxed.

"It's no secret, Your Majesty. The Austrians know there will be a major confrontation either this year or next."

"Let the military collect their own information in their own way," Napoleon said sharply.

"I do, and I have no intention of interfering." The military could do no wrong, and civilian agents rarely received full credit from the Emperor for their efforts. It was frustrating. "Nevertheless, my people do pick up bits of news here and there that are sometimes useful."

"Don't be so sensitive, Joseph, and stop digressing. Tell me about your understanding with the Lutheran bishops."

Fouché folded his arms more tightly across his chest. "The defeat of Austria is essential to the long-range safety of France, which means you'll have to destroy the old Holy Roman Empire and incorporate the German states into your own."

The man was insolent and couldn't be trusted, but Napoleon admired intellect, and Fouché's strategic analysis was sound. The Emperor favored his minister with a fleeting smile. "Go on."

"It would be impossible to garrison troops everywhere in the German states, as you've done in Rome. You need local support, with my agents warning you if trouble threatens anywhere. So it's plain that the help of the Lutheran hierarchy is essential."

The Emperor felt an unexpected but familiar stab of pain below his ribs. He rose, moved around the desk and stood over his subordinate. "If you've promised them bribes, I'll strip you of every office you hold and send you to prison for the rest of your days. The Germans aren't like the Italians, and the Lutheran bishops aren't like Andrazzi."

"I wish," Fouché said plaintively, "that you'd credit me with a little basic good sense. I'd no more try to bribe a Lutheran than I would a Bavarian Catholic. No matter what their religion, they take matters of honor very seriously."

The Emperor was pleased. "You do know something about them. Honor has been all-important to them for two thousand years."

Fouché had no desire to hear a long diatribe on the lessons taught the ancient tribes of German savages by Julius Caesar, one of the very few men in history whom the Emperor admired. "I've taken care not to offend the honor of the Lutheran bishops. I've simply passed the word to them, in a subtle manner, that if they'll give you their political support, you'll guarantee them unqualified freedom to worship as they wish, and to conduct their church affairs in their own way."

Napoleon was dumfounded. "My God, Joseph! Haven't you learned yet that the granting of absolute religious liberty to all people, French and foreign, is one of my basic principles? Don't you understand that I don't care how they worship—or whether they worship at all—provided they swear political allegiance to me?"

Fouché seldom won a battle of wits with his master, and couldn't squelch a gloating laugh that showed his yellowing teeth. "We're saying the same thing, Your Majesty."

The Emperor frowned, then raised an eyebrow.

"We know you'll issue an edict granting freedom of conscience to every sect in Germany, even the Jews, when you march in. But the

Lutheran bishops don't know it. So I've won their loyalty at a cheap price. I've promised them nothing they wouldn't have been granted in any case. Here are their letters to my intermediaries."

Napoleon chuckled and pinched the lobe of Fouché's ear, a sign he was satisfied. "You're a scoundrel on a grand scale, Joseph."

"I work for you, Your Majesty."

The Emperor nodded as he glanced through the letters. "I particularly like this one. I'll be invited to attend services at the castle church in Wittenberg, where Luther nailed his ninety-five theses. I always thought that church had remained in Catholic hands."

"The Protestants have gained possession of it from time to time. The Lutherans happen to hold it right now."

"Have someone prepare me an outline of the ninety-five theses so I'll know what I'm talking about with their bishops and pastors. There's no hurry, of course." Napoleon had no intention of giving a hint to anyone, even Fouché, regarding his invasion schedule.

The Minister helped himself to one of the Emperor's pens and a sheet of paper, on which he scribbled himself a reminder.

Napoleon made it a rule to praise his followers when they had accomplished something of note. "You said you've made a contract with Satan. He'll be delighted with you."

"I serve him by serving you, Your Majesty." Not even Talleyrand or Eugene dared to speak so impertinently.

Napoleon chuckled, running a hand forward through his thinning hair. "Your quarters in Hades are assured, Joseph."

"We'll meet there, Your Majesty."

Again Napoleon laughed. He was nominally a Catholic, but everyone close to him, with the exception of his devout mother, knew religion meant little to him. "If there really is such a place, I imagine we will. Since no one has ever returned from a reconnaissance there to make a headquarters report, though, I prefer to concern myself with what happens in this life. You've done well with the Lutherans. Use the same tactics with the German Catholics and the Jews—and I'll be hailed as the liberator of the German states. I'd use the same technique in England, if I could, which would guarantee the success of my invasion. Unfortunately, they take freedom of worship for granted, so it's no wonder I'm not popular there."

The old palace built on the Left Bank of the Seine by some forgotten king for a mistress no one remembered was a dark, ramshackle building that the marshals and dukes, admirals and administrators of the new Empire did not want. It was inconveniently located in a district that had never become fashionable, the roof leaked and the sanitary facilities were inadequate. In part because of its isolation, in part because of a contrary streak in his nature, it suited the purpose of Charles Maurice de Talleyrand-Perigord, Minister of Foreign Affairs and Grand Chamberlain of the Empire.

The roof was repaired, plumbers made a number of necessary alterations, and the old palace was refurnished from cellars to attics at great expense, with the bills sent to the Treasury. And there the second most powerful man in France established what Napoleon peevishly called his own kingdom within the Empire, relying on a staff that had been loyal to him for the better part of a decade.

Joseph de Montauban was overwhelmed by the grandeur of the Quai d'Orsay. The main lobby and corridors were tiled, the walls were lined with double-damask silk, and discreet servants in handsome livery were on hand to guide visitors to their appropriate destinations. Everywhere there were busts of the Emperor, some in marble and some in plaster, most showing him with a laurel wreath resting on his balding head. Paintings portraying him in heroic poses, usually on horseback, could be glimpsed through the open doors of officials' private offices, too.

The atmosphere in the suite at the rear of the second floor seemed, at first glance, to be similar, but more opulent than the rest of the building. The rugs were thicker and more expensive, there were flecks of real gold in the double-damask wallpaper, and the drapes that framed the high windows were made of the purest silk. It occurred to Joseph that something was missing, however, and belatedly it dawned on him that there were no busts or portraits of the Emperor in any of the anterooms.

The huge inner chamber was dazzling in its magnificence, and resembled a drawing room rather than an office. There seemed to be no desk, and only a careful scrutiny revealed that a leather-topped table in one corner was used for that purpose, with a sand holder and pens in solid gold half-hidden behind a large vase filled with roses that had been cut that same morning. Opposite the desk, on a delicate little Louis XV table, stood the one concession to the times, a miniature portrait of the Emperor done in subdued colors.

Joseph shifted his weight from one foot to the other, feeling increasingly ill at ease. The splendor of the Quai d'Orsay made a teacher from Columbia College feel very drab and insignificant.

"My dear Count, it's a pleasure to welcome you to France." Talleyrand posed dramatically in the entrance that led to still another private chamber in the suite. There were threads of gold in his slightly old-fashioned suit of ivory silk; he wore gold buckles on his shoes and it was impossible to tell whether his curled and pomaded hair was his own or a wig. His long, thin face was creased in a professional smile that masked his real feelings, and he leaned on a gold-handled walking stick as he limped across the room.

Joseph was unaccustomed to being addressed by a title, and flushed.

Talleyrand extended a hand on which a diamond and emerald ring worth a fortune blazed beneath the crystal chandelier. "I was told you arrived in Paris ten days ago, and I haven't been neglecting you, but the peace negotiations with Austria have been exhausting, and I've been working to finish them before the end of the year—as a Christmas gift to the people of France. And to the Austrians, of course."

It was impossible for Joseph to guess whether the man might be sincere. His charm was as overpowering as his surroundings.

Talleyrand waved his guest to a divan covered in white velvet, a type of furniture the Empress had made popular. "At any rate, you're here, and you couldn't have arrived at a better time. The Emperor was unapproachable after the failure of the English invasion, but his victory at Ulm improved his spirits, and the total defeat of the Austrians at Austerlitz on the first anniversary of his coronation was something of a miracle. He'll be delighted to see you." He rang a tiny gold bell, and a liveried servant came in with a bottle of champagne that had been cooled by immersion in the chilly waters of the Seine.

Joseph, who had studied French history from afar, was tongue-tied in the presence of a man who made it.

"You found your townhouse in order, I hope? And the servants have been satisfactory to you and the Countess?"

"My wife and I," Joseph replied carefully, "have been drowning in luxury."

There was no warmth in Talleyrand's laugh. "You'll soon take the little pleasantries of life for granted."

Joseph's polite but unyielding smile demonstrated unexpected strength.

"You haven't yet visited your holdings in the south."

"They aren't yet mine, and I may not claim them." Joseph seized his opportunity to make the little speech he had been refining and rehearsing for days. "At the moment, Mrs. de Montauban and I are visitors in France, nothing more. We've been grateful for the voyage at the expense of the French government for a journey we ourselves couldn't have afforded. And it's been a privilege to live for a little while under the roof of my ancestors. But I hope your legation in Washington City has made it clear to you that I'm still an American citizen. I've been granted a leave of absence by Columbia College, but I haven't resigned from the faculty there. In brief, Your Excellency, I've burned no bridges behind me until I make certain what's in store for me on this side of the water."

When Talleyrand found it expedient, he could speak bluntly. "What do you want?"

436

"Security for my family, and the right to enjoy the liberties my father's generation established in the United States," Joseph said, finding it easier than he had imagined to express himself unequivocally. "I also want to find out precisely what's expected of me here. I learned as a boy that we pay a price for everything we receive. So I can't accept at face value the explanation of your legation in Washington City that I'm to be made wealthy overnight simply because Napoleon Bonaparte is trying to establish an enduring aristocracy."

"It happens to be true," Talleyrand said blandly.

"All the same," Joseph insisted, "he—you—or someone—wants something more from me."

"Spoken with the cynical reserve of an apostate."

"Not quite. I was baptized a Catholic as an infant, but my parents left the Church when I was very small, and I've never received any of the other Sacraments."

"Once a Catholic, always a Catholic," Talleyrand said lightly.

His tone as well as his words put Joseph on guard. It was common knowledge that Talleyrand himself had been a bishop prior to the French Revolution, and had abandoned the Church in order to save his own life while turning to the political career in which he had shown such talent. It might be possible to glean the information he wanted, Joseph thought, by attacking.

"Do you think of yourself as a Catholic, Your Excellency?"

"I do, but Pope Pius is a prisoner of convention and hasn't seen fit to reverse the stigma of my excommunication. But man is almost always able to make his peace with God." Although he was past fifty, he seemed unworried.

"It's man's relationship with his fellow man that concerns me," Joseph said, hoping he could remember the entire conversation so he could repeat it to Adrienne. "I can't decide whether to accept your government's offer until I know how I'm expected to earn my title and privileges."

Talleyrand picked up an alabaster statue of a peacock with sapphire eyes and a multi-jeweled tail. He held it up to the tapers burning in the chandelier, then lovingly turned it over in his hand. "Our legation in America has sent me three reports on you in the past year," he said, "and none of them do you justice. I'm seeing the Emperor tomorrow morning, and I'll give him a full account of our conversation, as well as my own impressions of you. He'll send for you."

Joseph's hunch had been right. There were reasons he hadn't been told for the French offer of the de Montauban title and properties, but it was apparent that Talleyrand, at least for the present, had no intention of enlightening him. "When——"

"I could tell you the Emperor will see you in a day, or a week, or a month, and when I prove to be a liar, you can berate me. No member of the diplomatic corps here will accept my word any more. The truth of the matter is that the Emperor makes his own rules and follows his own schedules, which are unpredictable. Until he calls you to Malmaison, or Versailles, or, for that matter, a military camp five hundred miles from Paris, enjoy yourself. You and the Countess have been granted unlimited credit in the shops, and we ask only that you make no attempt to get in touch with anyone in England. The Emperor has a very thin skin where the English are concerned."

A wet snow had blanketed Paris during the night, but now a bright, early morning sun was shining through the windows of the master bedchamber on the second floor of the townhouse. Adrienne de Montauban looked very tiny as she sat in the huge fourposter bed, propped up on pillows. Her blonde hair tumbling down over her shoulders and her thin negligee of pink silk, a recent purchase, made her look very fragile, but she was sipping steaming coffee from a large cup with gusto.

Joseph, his own breakfast finished, paced up and down the room. "Coffee," he said testily, addressing her in English, "will make you queasy."

She preferred to reply in her own tongue. "It will not. You forget I grew up in Martinique, and that I can't possibly begin a day without coffee."

He stubbornly continued to speak English. "Tea is far better for you."

"Tea, indeed! Sometimes I wonder why the Americans bothered to fight their Revolution. All your attitudes and habits are English."

Joseph thought it best to ignore the challenge, or an argument would develop. "I'll grant you," he said carefully, "that the British blockade of the Continent is making it difficult for the French to import the better kinds of Indian tea. But that's irrelevant. If these damnable Paris physicians know their trade—a somewhat dubious premise, I'll grant you—coffee is the very worst thing you could drink for breakfast."

Adrienne continued to sip her coffee, looking pleased with herself. "What are you planning to do today, dear?"

"What I've done every day for weeks. Wait."

"Why don't you come shopping with me?"

"In the first place, I despise the haggling that women find so pleasurable in shops. In the second place, I disapprove of spending money that isn't ours. And what's more, I don't think you should leave the house. That snow must be at least three inches deep."

438

"I have no intention of spending the next seven months in bed, dear."

"I'm only asking you to take reasonable precautions, Adrienne."

She giggled, and brushed back a stand of hair. "That's why I want to do as much shopping as possible before my figure changes."

"It won't change that much today or tomorrow." Joseph turned to face her. "I've been thinking, and I've made a basic decision."

Adrienne sobered at once, knowing he would become furious if she failed to match his solemnity.

"I want the baby born at home, and I want to leave before it becomes too risky for you to travel." He braced himself. "I paid a visit to the American legation yesterday, and explained the problem to them. With the British and French blockading each other, there is no such thing as neutral shipping these days. But American merchantmen are safer than most, and a brig out of New Haven is scheduled to put into Brest in about three weeks. The legation will let me know when she arrives, and we'll sail on her. We'll be back in New York before you become too far advanced."

Adrienne looked at her husband, then out of the leaded windows, and when she spoke the disappointment was evident in her voice. "You've given up the idea of accepting the title here?"

Joseph shrugged. "I've neither abandoned nor accepted it. But I can't tolerate being kept in the dark, and now that we know the baby is coming——"

"You've always been impatient, so don't use the baby as an excuse."

"——I'm more anxious than ever to have things settled. I realize that Bonaparte is a busy man, and has more important things to do than grant an audience to an American with a claim to an old French title. But I can't stay on here indefinitely as a guest of the French government. It's immoral to accept hospitality without knowing why it's being offered."

Adrienne stretched her arms high over her head. "I think it's lovely here, and my husband has such an active New England Puritan conscience that I don't believe he's descended from the French nobility. And please don't call the Emperor Bonaparte. I've heard he hates it."

"I was speaking to you, not making a public address. But the way I feel these days, I'd just as soon call him by his family name the next time I see Talleyrand. If I see him again." Joseph stamped out of the room, closing the door behind him, and went down the stairs.

It was wrong of him to take out his frustrations on Adrienne, he knew, but Christmas had come and gone, the New Year was approaching and he still had no idea why he had been invited to

France. Three visits to the Quai d'Orsay had been futile exercises, and the last time he had gone there, two days earlier, had been a particularly irritating experience. Neither Talleyrand nor any members of his immediate staff had been there, and no one else had known anything about the business of the American with the French name.

Wandering from room to room on the ground floor of the old house, Joseph finally found himself in the library, where a portrait of the first Philippe de Montauban was hanging over the hearth. It had been obtained by Talleyrand from an art dealer, and Joseph hoped he could buy it when he and Adrienne sailed for New York. Looking up at the stern figure in early seventeenth-century attire, Joseph saw more than a family resemblance. Without being able to put his reactions into words, much less define them, he felt a strange affinity with his ancestor. If Philippe were alive now, he thought, they would understand one another.

Someone was knocking at the front door. Still unaccustomed to servants, Joseph went off himself to answer the summons, and opened the door. His shock of recognition was so intense that he could only blink at the short man in the cape and bicorn hat.

"It's chilly out here," the Emperor said, enjoying the surprise he had created. "I hope you'll ask me in."

Joseph heard himself stammering something inadequate.

Napoleon turned to the party of horsemen in uniform who had accompanied him. "Take my mount around to the courtyard and wait for me there, Colonel. I assume there is a courtyard?"

"Yes, sir." In his agitation Joseph momentarily forgot the proper way to address a monarch.

"Crowds always gather in the street when I pay a private visit to anyone, and I dislike seeing traffic obstructed." The Emperor closed the door, and indicated, with a gesture, that he wanted his host to lead the way. "I assume you're de Montauban?"

Joseph was beginning to recover his poise. "Yes, Your Majesty." He started toward the library, and joined in Napoleon's laugh when two of the servants hired by the Foreign Ministry looked around a corridor corner, then vanished instantly.

The Emperor moved close to the paneling of the library, inspecting it with care and rubbing it with the palm of his left hand. "This is fine old wood. It's the quality I wanted at Malmaison, but I had to settle for something less."

"Could I offer you some refreshments, Your Majesty?" Joseph was still stunned, but was handling himself with aplomb. The Emperor, he saw, was shorter and smaller-boned than he had thought, but he had been totally unprepared for the magnetic force of the man's personality.

"A mug of tea would be good on a morning like this."

"Of course." Joseph thought of his conversation with Adrienne a few minutes earlier and wanted to laugh. "Perhaps you'd enjoy a little cognac in it?"

"A very little, and I'll pour it myself. I have five physicians, all of them unable to cure a burning in my chest and throat when I drink spirits. They're imbeciles."

A servant responded at once when Joseph pulled the bell-rope.

Napoleon was busying himself examining the books that lined the shelves of the library, pausing occasionally to take down one and leaf through it. "I've never cared for Rousseau. His simplicity was forced. Gibbon. The Romans would have nailed him to a cross for oversimplifying the reasons for the decay of their Empire. Ah, John Locke."

Joseph stood near the hearth, stirring the fire and wondering what one said to the master of France, conqueror of Austria, and overlord of more than half of Europe.

"What's your opinion of Locke?" The question was an explosive challenge.

"The American Revolution—and your own here in France—wouldn't have taken place without his philosophical dedication to freedom," Joseph said, wondering whether he was being tested.

"Revolutions are the response of man to a desire for personal liberty. They don't depend on philosophers." The Emperor closed the book he was holding and slid it back into place on its shelf. "But it was Locke who said, 'All men are liable to error; and most men are, in many points, by passion or interest, under temptation to it.' He was far wiser than Montesquieu, with his bleating about, 'Great lords have their pleasures, but the people have happiness.' Montesquieu was a baron in the Old Regime. What in God's name did he know of the people and their happiness?"

The servant arrived with two mugs of tea and a jar of cognac, which he placed on a table with trembling hands.

The Emperor carefully measured a few drops of cognac into his mug. "How the newspapers of the English would gloat if they learned that I'm fond of one of their writers. But Locke is himself liable to error. Are you familiar with his *Letters of Toleration?*"

"No, sir." Joseph was fascinated by the man. Napoleon, it appeared, was more than the barbaric warrior his enemies in England and critics in the United States made him out to be.

"Like everyone else, his concept of liberty is limited by his own beliefs. In one breath he pleads for a simple, common sense acceptance of the Gospels, whatever that may mean, and he's so naïve he thinks the practice of his doctrine would unite the Protestants. But he won't grant tolerance to atheists, on the specious grounds that they shirk their ethical obligations to God. And he opposes Catholics because they must obey the successor of St. Peter in Rome. Is that liberty?" The Emperor was scornful. "Not by my definition! He's a muddle-headed liberal, and he fails, like all the rest of his breed, because he's willing to grant liberty only to those who think as he does."

Napoleon was warming to his theme, but broke off abruptly when there was a stir at the door.

Adrienne stood in the frame, her face flushed from the exertion of dressing rapidly. She was wearing a new, high-waisted gown of semi-transparent silk that was an echo of the Empress' tastes, her hair had been pulled up to a simple Grecian knot at the crown, and she had found time to daub herself with scent, too.

Joseph had never known her to curtsy, and was surprised when she sank to the floor with flawless grace as she murmured something to the effect that she had never known such an honor.

The Emperor went to her at once, kissed her hand and drew her to her feet. His appreciation of her beauty was so intense that Joseph remembered having heard rumors about Napoleon's fondness for other men's wives.

The Emperor quickly made it clear, however, that he had no intention of trespassing. "My wife knew your family in Martinique," he said, "so I've heard a great deal about your relatives."

Joseph held his breath. His mother-in-law and her sisters, as he had often heard, had considered the former Madame de Beauharnais unworthy of their recognition.

Adrienne was equal to the occasion. "It was the great privilege of my mother and aunts to know Her Majesty, and I regret that I did not share their good fortune."

It was common knowledge that the Emperor and his wife were not on good terms, which may have accounted for the amusement in Napoleon's eyes. "That lack can be remedied after your husband and I strike a bargain."

Adrienne was wide-eyed. "Am I interrupting?"

Joseph had no desire to hurt her feelings, and remained silent.

But the Emperor did not believe in mincing words. "You are," he said, "but the interlude was well worth every moment."

To Joseph's surprise, she showed no resentment as she withdrew.

The two men faced each other again, and the Emperor said, "A lovely young woman, worthy of a coronet."

Joseph decided to reply obliquely. "You've gone into a great deal of bother to look into our backgrounds, Your Majesty."

"Not at all. Strictly routine. But I want to hear your religious beliefs from your own lips. All I know is that your parents had no church affiliation after an unpleasant incident when you were very small, and that you received no religious instruction as a boy."

"That isn't entirely accurate. I had no formal instruction and attended services at no church, but my parents taught me to honor and respect God."

The Emperor tugged thoughtfully at his lower lip. "You've gone to that new little Huguenot church behind the Palais Royale every Sunday since you've been in Paris."

It made Joseph uncomfortable to realize he had been under surveillance. "It was his faith," he said, gesturing in the direction of the portrait over the hearth. "I was curious at first, and I've since found that my views are compatible with those of the Huguenots."

"Splendid!" Making himself completely at home, the Emperor walked to the desk and sat down. "You're aware of my efforts to create a new nobility, but your own reluctance to accept a place in it has been admirable. I want you, de Montauban, because there is a specific task you can perform for me, for France and for the brotherhood of man."

At last, Joseph realized, he would learn why he had been called to Paris.

"The English picture me as a monster, a fiend, and so do the nobles who flee from the lands my armies liberate. I'm trying, in various ways, to destroy that portrait and paint another. In time, if you're interested, you can study the various methods. I'd like to confine this discussion to you. You're an American, and in certain circles—here, elsewhere on the Continent and even in England—there is an admiration for the American attempt to establish a new type of government. It would be impressive if you joined me."

"I was able to piece together that much myself."

The Emperor absently scratched the letter "N" on the desk top with a letter opener, and drew a laurel wreath around it. "You're an intellectual——"

"Hardly, Your Majesty. I'm not a theologian, philosopher or essayist!"

Napoleon disliked being interrupted. "You teach. So you believe the workings of the human mind paramount." He glared at Joseph before continuing. "You were born a Catholic, but now you incline toward the Huguenots. So there's a place you can fill for me, a place that needs filling. There are poets, physicians, lawyers, men of every profession in my employ. The Code Napoleon will be the finest, most thorough body of the law ever assembled and refined. And so forth."

"Just what is it you want me to do?"

"Everywhere I'm opposed by men who don't understand my goals. You would be a living example of those aims. Everywhere I grant total freedom of worship, or even the right to reject God, if that will make a man happy. From time to time I would expect you to confer with non-Catholics who hate me, and convince them they're mistaken. For centuries men have wanted liberty of conscience. I give it to them, and they draw back, just as John Locke did one hundred and sixteen years ago. Astonishing!"

What was even more amazing was the Emperor's encyclopaedic memory. But Joseph was confused. "I'd think you'd want a Huguenot or Lutheran clergyman for the purpose, Your Majesty."

Napoleon often became exasperated when the minds of others proved to be less nimble than his own. "A clergyman would be tempted to proselytize for his own church, and would be suspected of it even if he didn't. No, de Montauban, I need a layman, someone whose family has been devoted to the cause of religious liberty for centuries, and whose exploits are known to the people of France. You."

Joseph hooked his thumbs in his waistcoat pockets. "I know something of what you've done for the cause of freedom of worship, Your Majesty, and I could argue for you with a clear conscience. But I must ask you to remember that I'm an American who has spent his adult life protected by the Bill of Rights under our new Constitution. What of the other freedoms we believe important?"

The Emperor laughed and ran his hand forward through his hair. "Freedom of speech, perhaps? Say what you please—about me or anyone else. Go down to the produce markets near the river and listen to the farmers grumble. There's no power on earth strong enough to prevent a Frenchman from saying whatever comes to his mind."

Joseph was not satisfied. "I've been reading the Paris newspapers ever since I've been here, and they praise everything you say and do."

"They approve of me, then." Napoleon looked contented.

It would be indelicate to assert that the press was supervised by the regime, but Joseph disliked the Emperor's vagueness. "Let's assume a hypothetical situation, Your Majesty. Suppose a newspaper here—or in one of the German states you've just annexed—should attack you. What would you do?"

"I'd feel hurt, but that's beside the point you're trying to establish, isn't it, de Montauban? I'd talk with the editor, and try to make him understand my ideas. To be more specific, he wouldn't be sent to prison or abused, and provided he hadn't preached sedition, his newspaper would be allowed to remain in business. The same is true of free assemblage and all the other freedoms you Americans prize."

Perhaps it was naïve to take him at his word, but Joseph could find no flaw in his reasoning.

"I'm called a tyrant by people who don't share my dream, the dream of Julius Caesar and Alexander of Macedon. I'm trying to create a united, peaceful Europe."

"Under your sovereignty, of course."

"To be sure. Any body politic must have a head, and I'm so completely convinced my dream can be realized that I'm fighting for it. The one thing I can't and won't tolerate is treason, but my attitude isn't unique, is it? Seven and one-half years ago your own Congress passed an act to prevent sedition, and President Adams signed it. No government that permits its citizens to conspire against it can survive."

Again, Joseph thought, he made sense.

The Emperor drained his cup of tea, carefully wiped his mouth with a handkerchief he took from his sleeve and stood. "I need you, de Montauban," he said. "Will you help me?"

There were imperfections in his argument, Joseph knew, even though they weren't readily apparent, but no system was perfect. Adrienne wanted to live in France, their child's future would be assured, and they would never again know financial want or worry. Even more important, he himself would be working for principles in which he believed. "I'll join you, Your Majesty. How do I swear fealty to you?"

Napoleon extended his hand, and grinned when Joseph clasped it. "That's good enough," he said. "I believe in formality and pomp only when the people demand a Roman circus. Then I satisfy them, and they give me their loyalty in return."

1810

Skilled carpenters had lined the walls of the old castle with wood, which eliminated most of the draughts, but on rainy mornings the dampness seeped in through the stones. Joseph shivered as he closed his dressing gown around his throat, sipped his coffee and looked down into the courtyard at the graves of so many of his ancestors. It was strange how his cares dropped away when he returned to Montauban from his travels, how he had learned to regard the old castle and the town itself as home.

He was willing to admit to himself that he was tired, of course, and small wonder. The Emperor had proved to be a demanding taskmaster, and in recent years Joseph had visited every part of the still expanding Empire. It was astonishing how close to realization Napoleon's dream had come, and Joseph never ceased to marvel that the greater part of Europe now acknowledged him as its overlord. Even Austria and Prussia had been forced to become his allies, and the

Turks, who controlled no territory of significance north of the Danube except Wallachia and Moldavia, had reached a tacit understanding with France, each power respecting the other's borders. Only Great Britain, Russia and a few minor allies, Portugal and Sweden and the Grand Duchy of Finland among them, were Napoleon's avowed enemies.

There was dissension within the Empire, to be sure, and Napoleon sometimes was high-handed in his treatment of a conquered nation, giving his foes the opportunity to renew their charges that he was a tyrant. But Joseph had no cause to regret the agreement he had made with the Emperor, although he sometimes wished he could spend more time with his family. Napoleon's guarantees of personal liberty were being upheld almost everywhere, even though such freedom had been unknown in places like the Grand Duchy of Warsaw. And the violations of individual rights committed by the secret police had declined sharply in recent months, ever since Fouché, who now gloried in his title of Duke of Otranto, had fallen out of royal favor and had been sent into semi-exile as governor of Rome.

The door of the tower bedchamber opened, and Adrienne entered, looking daintier and more fragile than ever in a peignoir of pale green silk. "The servants just told me you were home," she said as her husband embraced her.

"I arrived so late last night that I didn't want to disturb you. So I came up here."

"But you hate this room."

"Not really. I'm home." He held her at arm's length. "You look lovely."

"I should," Adrienne said dryly. "I had this peignoir made just before I left Paris. You'll get the bill next month. Was it dreadful in Norway?"

Joseph shrugged.

"You've lost weight, dear."

"The English blockade is hurting the Norwegians badly, and they're short of food. I don't care for fish, so I lost a few pounds, but I'll soon regain them."

"Did your affairs go well?"

He supposed he should be pleased that his wife was interested in his work. "Kristiania is a miserable little town, and Count Wedel-Jarlsberg's castle is the coldest place I've visited. He lives as his Viking ancestors must have done. What's more, he's a patriot. He hates the Danes for forcing Norway into an alliance with us, he despises the Swedes and he loathes the English. I don't think he cares much for France, either, but he was civilized enough not to say so in front of me."

"Oh, dear."

"He called the Lutheran bishops together for a meeting with me, and they drove me mad. As nearly as I could find out, everyone in Norway is a Lutheran. There are no Catholics, Jews, Anglicans or Presbyterians there. The bishops agreed with me, but didn't understand a word I said. Their idea of religious freedom is that every Norwegian is free to embrace Lutheranism."

Adrienne giggled, but immediately apologized. "I didn't mean to laugh."

Joseph smiled wearily. "I sometimes think the world is too backward to accept Napoleon's ideas. How are the children?"

"The baby has had another little cough, but Mathieu is fine. I deliberately didn't tell him you were here, or he'd have come running up before I had a private word with you."

Joseph relaxed for the first time, grinning. "We'll take him to church with us this morning."

"When I heard you had arrived I completely forgot it's Sunday."

"We've got to go," he said. "It's expected of us."

An hour later the Count and Countess, their elder son and heir seated between them, rode in an open carriage to the Huguenot church located behind the Place Nationale. It was a small building, and now that the people of Montauban were free to attend any church they wished, the pastor was forced to conduct three services on Sundays in order to accommodate the throngs of worshippers. The crowds became increasingly dense as the carriage approached the Place Nationale; farmers and their families strolled aimlessly, and there were men in the uniforms of a score of French regiments everywhere.

The coachman slowed the team of bays to a walk, and Joseph went through the ritual of doffing his hat and waving to the citizens who cheered him. "You must wave, too, Mathieu," he whispered to his son. "Always remember you're a de Montauban."

The child obeyed, laughing at the game.

"Look at the cathedral," Adrienne said. "It's absurd!"

Joseph glanced in the direction of the ancient edifice. The main doors were open, and he caught a glimpse of candles burning deep inside. "What's absurd?"

"It's nearly empty! Monsignor Jaquin is lucky if fifty people go to Mass on a Sunday morning. Even fewer go to St. Jacques, but we're filled to overflowing, and some Sundays I can scarcely breathe. Why can't the Huguenots appropriate the cathedral?" She saw her husband's face, and hastily added, "Or buy it. A word from you would be enough."

"That word," Joseph said sternly, still returning the greetings of the pedestrians, "would be enough to undo everything Napoleon is trying to accomplish. The cathedral has changed hands too many times through the centuries. It belongs to the Catholics, and they have as much right to keep it as we have to own our church. What does it matter if one generation lets it sit deserted? The next will fill it! Only one thing is important, that there be churches available for men of every faith who want to offer prayers to God."

Adrienne sat back against the plush upholstery and fell silent. Napoleon had been wiser than even he had realized when he had selected her husband to preach his gospel of tolerance. Joseph's dedication sometimes frightened her, and she was afraid of what might happen if he should ever become disillusioned.

A full brigade of Guards, armed with loaded muskets and bayonets, stood sentry duty at the ancient palace of Fontainebleu, forming a ring around it, while two regiments of Hussars rode back and forth through the Fontainebleu forest to prevent interlopers from approaching the palace. Residents of the little town of Fontainebleu had been accustomed to the presence of royalty in their midst since the time of Louis VII in the twelfth century, and both instinct and tradition prompted them to remain in their homes behind closed doors and pretend that nothing unusual was happening nearby.

Two men walked slowly around the oval formed by the buildings that Francis I had constructed, and anyone seeing them from a distance would have imagined they were friends enjoying a stroll. But no one else was present, and both were very angry.

The Emperor, dressed in his favorite uniform of colonel-in-chief of the Guards, hated to lose his temper, but under the circumstances found it impossible to refrain from shouting. "I insist we speak in French!"

The man in the simple black habit of a priest was exasperated. "I think more clearly in Italian, and to you it's a second language. The very least you could do is oblige me in this one minor matter."

"As you well know, I speak Italian with an accent, which would give you an advantage."

Even the closest associates of Pius VII admitted that he more closely resembled the Benedictine monk he had been than the pope he had become. But there were moments when his simplicity gave him strength. "Since I am your prisoner, Your Majesty, we will speak in French."

The Emperor neither thought nor acted simply in any situation, but he, too, knew the value of dignity. "I prefer to think of you as my guest and my friend, Your Holiness."

The Pope's laugh was brittle. "Your troops forced their way into Vatican Hill, took me captive and then carried me off to Savona

448

before bringing me here. Should I have fought them before qualifying as a prisoner?"

Napoleon's amusement was genuine. "You and I do battle in different ways."

"We do."

The Emperor sobered. "I think of you as my friend because you were kind enough to give a cardinal's hat to my uncle, the old fool."

"It was nothing."

"I agree." There was a rasp in Napoleon's voice, and his smile was forced. "I spent a half-day riding here from Paris, and I hate wasting time. I propose we settle our disputes in a friendly discussion."

Pius fingered the Crucifix suspended from his neck. He said nothing, however, knowing from previous encounters over the period of a decade that the Emperor always took the initiative.

His silence was a warning, and Napoleon became ingratiating. "I can understand your reluctance to join my blockade of England."

"Can you? For three years you've insisted I join you."

"Oh, I still insist," Napoleon replied. "I can sympathize with your desire to keep The Papal States neutral. It's a laudable ambition. But I'm engaged in a war to the death with England. My control of Europe won't be complete while they continue to resist me, so either they or I must perish. I'm forced to use every weapon at my command. The Catholic minority in England will obey you, and so will the Irish. It will give me the crack in England's wall that I need."

"I've given you one answer in all these years," Pius said wearily, "and I give it again. The Church must stand aloof from politics."

The Emperor laughed savagely. "The Church has played the game of politics for more than fifteen hundred years."

"All the more reason she must stand aloof now."

"You yourself were a politician nine years ago, when we signed our Concordat."

The Pope considered the accusation. "In a manner of speaking, that's true. The Church had been barred from France since the Revolution, and could return only if I made an agreement with you. I've never said this to your face, but you tricked me."

"I thought it essential for the French state to control the appointment of bishops. I still think so. You got what you wanted. The churches and cathedrals were reopened, most ecclesiastical property was returned to you——"

"Some, not most."

"I refuse to quibble about real estate," Napoleon thundered.

"I'm your prisoner because of a quibble over property, if that's what you choose to call it."

"A team of horses must pull a cannon—or a carriage—in unison."

Napoleon spoke gently, as though addressing a child, and only the cold anger in his eyes indicated his true feelings. "Europe cannot survive unless her economy and politics are coordinated."

"Europe—or your Empire?"

"They're the same, as you well know," Napoleon snapped, and fought for self-control. "All of Italy was working together, except for The Papal States and Rome. So I had to annex them."

"You had no right to take them."

"You claim Divine rights in the spiritual realm, Your Holiness, and I respect them. Why can't you show me the same courtesies in the temporal?"

"The Papal States and the city of Rome have been an integral part of the Church for centuries."

The Emperor felt the pain in his side beneath his ribs, and pressed his fingers against the spot. "I've kept the map-makers busy for years. Tradition, for its own sake, is meaningless. We've entered a new age, Your Holiness, and if you bury yourself in the past, only Catholicism will suffer. You have a choice between spiritual power and world power. I urge you to take the spiritual, since I have no intention of trying to compete with the Almighty."

"How wise of you."

"And how foolish of you to think you can keep Rome and The Papal States as Church possessions."

"They were taken from us once before—and we recovered them. We will again."

"For the sake of argument, let's assume that through a series of miraculous happenings—and I don't believe in miracles, Your Holiness—England destroys me. My enemies will try to turn back the clock, and the short-sighted will help them."

"What you're saying is that The Papal States and Rome will be returned to the Church."

"For a time. A decade, perhaps several. But the people will have tasted a new kind of freedom, the liberty only I am able to give them. A man who has tasted it never rests until he gets more. He's like a drunkard who must have liquor."

"Are you suggesting that liberty is an evil, Your Majesty?"

"That's sheer sophistry. Perhaps it amuses you, but my sense of humor is lacking. There's a drunkard in my family, and I know how liquor can destroy a man. I've set millions free, and I know what liberty can do to restore the dignity of a man's soul."

"I'll thank you," Pius said, stroking his long chin, "not to preach to me on the subject of the soul."

"Very well, Your Holiness. I defer to you as the expert on the subject. All I ask in return is that you leave worldly matters to me."

"You want me to make you a gift of Rome and The Papal States. I can't do it. I'll grant you that by stealing them from me you've won, for the present——"

"One moment." For the first time since they had started talking, Napoleon's manner became menacing. "I suppose you had to excommunicate me. I wasn't surprised when you did, but you went out of your way to be unpleasant. There was no need to call me 'the robber of the patrimony of Peter.'"

A faint smile touched the corners of the Pope's mouth for an instant, then vanished. "When your step-son was living in Rome—and what a fine young man he is—he told me you're successful because you never hesitate to use every available weapon in a war. I must do the same."

"The war is ended," the Emperor said contemptuously, "and you have no weapons."

The Pope smiled.

"I occupied Rome and The Papal States," Napoleon continued, a note of self-justification creeping into his voice, "because you gave me no choice. If you had cooperated with me, there would have been no need for me to take such drastic action. But I couldn't allow one stubborn man to prevent western civilization from realizing the vision of centuries."

"You have the audacity to call your desire for personal power the universal vision of mankind?"

"I can't discuss reality with someone who won't recognize it. Haven't you ever asked yourself why the Roman Church is losing members everywhere?"

"Because you've destroyed the old disciplines men need."

"How convenient to blame me," Napoleon said. "I wasn't responsible for the betrayal of trusts that led to the French Revolution. I haven't caused the yearnings of the people in the German states for a single national entity. I didn't force the Americans to guarantee free worship for everyone in their Constitution. The whole world is stirring, Your Holiness. There was a spiritual earthquake nineteen hundred years ago, and we're living through the beginnings of another."

"Do you dare to think of yourself as Christ's equal?"

Napoleon raised his hands in despair. "You twist my ideas and put words into my mouth. No, Your Holiness. I am not the Son of God, nor are you."

Pius was uncompromising. "You forget I am His Vicar on earth."

"You don't hold the post permanently. You're mortal, as I am."

"I've been wondering when you'd threaten to have me killed. The English are right when they say you have no conscience."

The Emperor shook his head in wonder. "How little you know me. I've never yet murdered a helpless old man, and I refuse to give you the martyrdom you apparently seek. I have no intention of destroying myself by disposing of you. There are simpler methods of getting what I must have."

The Pope averted his face for a moment so he wouldn't reveal his anxiety.

"I make a final appeal to you. Join my crusade, and England will be forced to surrender in less than six months. Russia will stand alone, and the Tsar, who is a dilettante and a weakling, will seek a new accommodation with me. You claim you want peace. It's yours for the asking, and the lives of thousands of fine young men will be spared, most of them Roman Catholics."

"You offer me Satan's choice."

"If you refuse, you give me no option. I'll hold you here for years, if necessary. I'll issue a new Concordat, and when I publish it, only you and I will know it isn't a legitimate agreement. I'll even bring the College of Cardinals together to depose you and elect someone who'll be more amenable to take your place."

"Do what you will," Pius said. "The world already knows I'm your prisoner, and no one will accept your Concordat unless I embrace it publicly. Call a meeting of the College of Cardinals, and learn a lesson in humility. You'll find they have no authority to depose me, and wouldn't if they could."

Napoleon was pale, and there was a tremor in his voice as he said, "You were right a few moments ago, Your Holiness, and I was wrong. The war between us goes on. And we must fight it on the battlefield of your choice, so you and I will never know, in your lifetime or mine, which of us has won. The issues that separate us may not be decided for many years, but I'm confident that eventually a new relationship will develop between the churches—all churches, not only the Church of Rome—and the State. You won't win, and neither will I. The real victor will be the ordinary man who wants only freedom."

The climate was invigorating and the scenery was magnificent. From the terrace of the chalet situated above the village of Coppet, the Swiss Alps filled the horizon, and a visitor found it difficult to stop looking at the snow-capped peaks.

Joseph found it a relief to stare at the view rather than exchange baleful glares with his hostess, and was strongly inclined to agree with the Emperor that Anne Louise Germaine Necker, Baronne de Staël-Holstein was the most unpleasant woman he had ever encountered. She was also the homeliest. Her kohl-rimmed eyes were her only redeeming feature, but she had apparently convinced herself during the course of her forty-four years that she was a great beauty. Her fleshy cheeks and thin, masculine lips were rouged, a heavy application of rice powder emphasized her already prominent nose, and her hair was so frizzy her Grecian curls looked absurd. She chose to exhibit rather than conceal her plump figure, and he wanted to wince whenever he caught a glimpse of the neckline of her gown that displayed far too much of her ample breasts.

At least she had stopped flirting with him for the moment, so he could breathe a trifle more easily.

"Bonaparte," she said in her strident, deep voice, "is a liar, a cheat and a fraud. He prattles of liberty, but his promises are a sham. He not only grants no freedom, but he doesn't understand the meaning of the word."

"Aren't you being a little harsh, Baroness?" Joseph ardently wished he had been given an assignment, any assignment, other than that of trying to arrange a truce between the Emperor and the most renowned of feminine French novelists and essayists. On second thought, she was infamous rather than renowned. His own knowledge of literature was limited, but he had yet to meet a critic who thought her work better than third-rate. Her talent for creating personal crises and international scandals, however, was limitless, and her feud with the Emperor was hurting France.

"I always tell the truth. Bonaparte knows it. That's why he's afraid of me."

She enjoyed thinking that Napoleon feared her, Joseph realized, and knew it would cause a fresh outburst if he told her the Emperor's real attitude, that he considered her an insufferable gadfly and nuisance.

"I spent more than three years working on my book on Germany." She paused long enough to eat one of the miniature cream tarts that stood in a bowl at her elbow. "I decided to test Bonaparte's sincerity by publishing it in Paris."

Joseph had been briefed on the details before coming to Switzerland. "You knew you could have published it in Geneva or Frankfurt, both cities in the Imperial domain, without any difficulty whatever?"

"I insisted on Paris! He doesn't care what's done at a distance. He worries only about things close to home!"

Her view of Napoleon was so warped it was futile to correct her. Joseph thought of the daily reports from every part of the vast realm that the Emperor studied, and, having read them, filed away the most minute details in his incredibly retentive mind.

"Naturally, I had to submit my manuscript to the censors." Madame de Staël's bright red lips twisted in a grimace of disgust.

"The sole purpose of the board of censorship is to prevent the publication of seditious material harmful to the State," Joseph reminded her.

"There wasn't one sentence, not one phrase in my book that could have hurt the State," she declared vehemently. "I'll gladly show you a copy of the book, Count. Ten thousand copies were printed, and all ten thousand were confiscated. You'll never know how many people I had to cajole and bribe to get my hands on a few paltry copies for my own personal use."

Again she exaggerated, Joseph thought. She had written so many letters to the Emperor that he had finally ordered that she be given several hundred copies of the book in order to obtain a respite.

"If my manuscript wasn't seditious, I demand to know why the book was banned!" She trumpeted her triumph, and capped it by popping another miniature tart into her mouth.

Joseph knew he was treading on sensitive ground. "I believe you sent a letter to the Emperor, daring him to allow the book to be published."

"I certainly did! I wanted every move made by both sides to be a matter of permanent record. Would you care to see a copy of the letter, Count?"

Joseph took a deep breath. "Thank you, Baroness, but I've already read the original."

"Then you know I'm right!"

"Wouldn't you say it was gratuitously insulting?" He thought the question rather mild, having been astonished when he had discovered that Madame de Staël had called Napoleon a pig, a donkey and the son of a street-walker.

"I saw no reason to flatter him!"

He raised his glass of wine to his mouth in order to hide his smile. The Emperor might have ignored some of the epithets, but she had gone too far when she had called his mother a prostitute. If he respected, feared and truly loved any one person in the world, it was his rigidly moral mother.

"Perhaps you failed to realize," Joseph said politely, "that the Emperor can be thin-skinned on occasion."

"Has he been considerate of me?" Madame de Staël demanded. "A few days after my book was confiscated, I was sent back here—into exile." She lowered her voice conspiratorially. "And even here he hounds me. I know that my life is in danger."

Joseph found her distortions too great to accept meekly. "You've been ordered not to go back to Paris," he said, "but you're free to live and travel where you please. I assume you stay in Coppet because you have a home here." Afraid he had aroused her ire, he added placatingly, "An exceptionally attractive home."

Her huge eyes widened, and she began to flirt with him again.

He hastily looked out at the mountains. "The view is extraordinary," he murmured, "and must be an inspiration to an artist."

"It would be heaven on earth," she retorted, "if I weren't as much a prisoner here as Pope Pius is at Fontainebleu!"

They had come at last to the real reason for Joseph's visit to Coppet. "I understand you've been eager to attend a meeting of poets and philosophers in Cologne next month. With all due respect, Baroness, may I urge that you arrange a journey and go? I'm positive no one will interfere!"

Madame de Staël called his attention to her bosom by brushing away a tart crumb from her cleavage. "That's where Bonaparte is so infernally clever. He'd let me go to Cologne, wouldn't he? Then he could pretend to the whole world that I'm free! But I'd still be trapped in his cage, like that sad old priest."

Joseph knew he would never forget the Emperor's words on the subject of Madame de Staël: "I swear to you, de Montauban, I don't care where the woman goes or what she does, if only she'll stop attacking me and pushing her long nose into my business. If I thought she'd accept without making a commotion, I'd gladly give her one hundred thousand napoleons—in gold—to settle in America or the Ottoman Empire. The Americans would laugh at her, which she couldn't tolerate, and the Turks would really silence her, which would drive her mad. Either punishment would be too good for her, but would be worth every sou."

"Count," Madame de Staël said, "I challenge you to tell me you agree that the imprisonment of Pope Pius is right."

"It's my personal opinion that he's making a mistake," Joseph said quietly. "I've told him as much in so many words."

Her luminous eyes became brighter.

"So have Talleyrand and several others," Joseph continued, "but only the Emperor and Pope Pius know what was said at their private meeting, and Napoleon is convinced he has no choice."

Madame de Staël's voice became shrill. "Bonaparte proves what I've said for years! He's a tyrant!"

Joseph stood, hoping that if he spoke slowly and distinctly, she might listen to him. "He's a man who believes in the principles of freedom for the individual citizen. He's done more for the cause of religious liberty than anyone else in history, but it's his misfortune to be caught in a dilemma. In order to advance the cause of tolerance, he must silence Christendom's most important spokesman. He knows the risks he runs, but he believes the ends are worth the harsh methods he's employing. And while I myself think the imprisonment of the Pope is wrong, I'm willing to leave the final judgment to posterity. I've come here for just one reason, Baroness, to ask you to do the same."

Madame de Staël eyed him coldly. "What rot. Anyone who condones a single act of despotism aids the despot. Anyone who blinds himself to evil is himself evil. Persecution is always practiced in the guise of tolerance, and the persecutor pretends he liberates rather than binds. The Pope has no need for my support, and I imagine he'd prefer to reject it. But he has a far more powerful ally than a silly woman's vindictive pen, and the Lord will punish Bonaparte in His own way for this mockery."

The Louvre had been the home of the Bourbons for so long that Napoleon found it impossible to eradicate the innumerable signs of their long family reign. Sculptors, carpenters and painters placed his own crest everywhere: the design of stately bees that had become his informal insignia were to be seen on drapes, bedspreads and even rugs, and the Imperial banner that floated high on a very tall flagstaff built for the purpose could be seen in many sections of Paris on a clear day. Nevertheless Napoleon hated the place.

Circumstances and the size of his own staff forced him to use it as his headquarters in the city, however. Malmaison was close to Paris, but the Empress Josephine had continued to live there after his divorce and remarriage to the Archduchess Marie Louise, and in a sentimental gesture he had later regretted, he had made a gift of the place to his first wife. Versailles was inconvenient, and was crowded with so many of his relatives that he avoided it. And the other palaces in Paris were too small to house the executives, advisers, experts and assistants with whom he conferred at all hours of the day and night.

So he had to make the best of the Louvre, and established his office in what had once been the bedchamber of Henry IV. This was his private workroom, to which only his immediate subordinates were admitted; most visitors were received in an ornately furnished chamber adjoining it. There were no decorations in the office. The walls were bare, there were no drapes at the windows and a plain rug covered the floor. The Emperor's desk and chair were utilitarian, but neither they nor the few visitors' chairs were expensive. Napoleon's sword hung from a wall peg near the entrance, and the atmosphere was reminiscent of a military headquarters in the field, which was precisely the air he tried to create.

As he once told his brilliant cavalry commander and brother-in-law, Murat, whom he had made King of Naples and whose love of luxury was notorious, "I think best under battle conditions."

Others failed to share his Spartan tastes, and it amused him now to watch Talleyrand moving from one chair to another in a vain effort to find a comfortable seat.

The retired Foreign Minister was aware both of his gaze and the reason for it. Talleyrand minced no words. "I really think you can afford a padded leather chair or two. If not, I'll send you a pair as a gift."

"Save your money, Charles. The Treasury will probably have to increase taxes again next year."

Talleyrand groaned.

"Unless you can persuade the Russians not to join in an open alliance with the British. Their friendship pact with me is worthless, and if I'm forced to fight them, it's going to be an expensive campaign."

Talleyrand polished the gold handle of his walking stick with a silk handkerchief.

"You disapprove. I knew you would."

"Your Majesty, you must tighten your internal defenses before you even think of another major war!"

Napoleon grinned. "Are you giving me military advice? Don't tell me your ambitions include a marshal's baton."

"My only ambition is to establish a balance that will give us peace everywhere! I mean it, Your Majesty. You've won the greatest Empire in all history, greater than Caesar's and equal to Alexander's. But it will crumble away overnight unless you take steps to preserve it."

"You haven't come all the way to Paris from your comfortable nest in Touraine to give me vague advice, Charles."

"I resigned as Foreign Minister three years ago, but I've served you faithfully on the Imperial Council, and I've kept my promise to keep watch over our foreign affairs. I see a copy of every important document that goes in or out of the Quai d'Orsay."

Napoleon nodded impatiently, tired of hearing protests of loyalty from virtually everyone who came to see him.

"Your Majesty," Tallyrand said, thumping his walking stick on the floor for emphasis, "set Pope Pius free!"

"You're wasting your breath, Charles."

The older man took a sheaf of notes from the inner pocket of his heavy silk tailcoat. "Two months ago there was a riot in Madrid. You were called the anti-Christ."

"The British hired agitators. It was cleverly done."

"In Naples, the statue of you that Murat put up near that new bridge of his, the Ponte della Sanità, was stoned by a mob that called you the anti-Christ."

"Murat sent me a long report in his own hand. Bourbon agitators were smuggled into Naples from their base in Sicily. The operation was very crudely handled, and wouldn't have happened in the first place if Murat had been alert. He's being careful now, I assure you." Napoleon was unruffled.

Talleyrand remained firm. "Four weeks ago yesterday, a crowd paraded through Warsaw with a dummy of you, which they hanged. They called you the anti-Christ."

"The secret police tell me the Russians were responsible, although it can't be proved."

"Your Majesty, the Poles have loved you ever since you established the Grand Duchy, and they've hated Russia for more than one thousand years. I don't believe the Tsar has enough gold in the vaults of the Kremlin to bribe them."

"That's a matter of opinion." The Emperor shrugged, unimpressed.

"And just last week there was another riot in Brussels. Again you were branded as the anti-Christ." Talleyrand held up a hand as Napoleon started to speak. "And please don't tell me that the British did it. My God, can't you see a pattern in all these demonstrations? I've stayed at home as long as I could, but when I read the account from Brussels, I came here immediately."

The Emperor pulled at his lower lip for a moment. "I can't blame you for your interpretation, but it's false. Of course there's a pattern, an identical pattern. It's so unvarying I'm convinced it's part of an English scheme to discredit me. I'm willing to admit it has been fairly effective, and I don't mind telling you I'm very annoyed with the Russians. The next time I meet the Tsar, I intend to tell him my opinion of his trickery."

"I wish you'd put Fouché in charge of the secret police again. He's no gentleman, but he's always been honest with you, which is more than I can say for those sycophants who tell you only what you want to hear."

Napoleon rose, walked around the desk and gave the older man a pat of reassurance that knocked the breath out of him. "In times of strain, all of us turn to our early loyalties. Even though you left the Church years ago, you can't help thinking as a bishop in this situation."

Talleyrand struggled to regain his breath. "Must I remind you that, like you, I'm outside the Church? I haven't celebrated Mass since the early days of the Revolution."

"All the same——"

"I'm no longer in a priest. I haven't thought or acted like one for years."

"It would be contrary to human nature if you didn't feel some regard for papal authority."

"You have a convenient but imperfect memory, Your Majesty. Apparently you've forgotten it was I who negotiated the Concordat with Pius nine years ago."

The Emperor chuckled. "Yes, and you beat him at every move. It was brilliantly done." His smile faded. "Now that you're older and may be giving more thought to the rewards of the next world, I think it likely that you may feel more tenderness for our friend at Fontainebleu."

"I'm not that old." Talleyrand was still indignant.

The dubious expression in Napoleon's eyes said far more than words.

"Don't you trust anyone, Your Majesty?"

"Of course, my regiments and their commanders."

Talleyrand stood, and spoke with great dignity. "I have served France for many years, and I will serve no one else until I die."

The Emperor unexpectedly covered his face with his hands.

Sitting again, his retired Foreign Minister regarded him uncertainly.

"I was reared as a Catholic, Charles." Napoleon's voice, behind his hands, was muffled. "Not your kind of Catholic. You belonged to the real aristocracy. You took money and station—and your eventual place in Heaven—for granted. We grew up on the fringes of the aristocracy. We never had enough money to buy what we wanted. We had to trim here, sacrifice there. Once we ate stew for a week so my sister, Caroline, could buy a gown my mother wanted her to have. Heaven and Hell and Purgatory were very real to us, and we had little hope of reaching Heaven." Suddenly he straightened, blinking. "My mother has refused to speak to me since I made Pius a prisoner."

"Perhaps you're thinking of the next world, Your Majesty." The unexpected confidences had made Talleyrand uneasy, and he didn't know what else to say.

"Life has made me a realist," the Emperor said harshly. "I live only in this world, and I'll take my chances in another, if one exists. I have no fear for the immortality of my soul. My work here will live after me. That's what I sought, and that's what I've achieved. No, my conscience doesn't bother me when I think of that old man saying Mass and puttering in the garden at Fontainebleu."

In spite of his long experience as a diplomat, Talleyrand was still at a loss for words.

"What sickens me is the damage that's being done all through the Empire." Napoleon looked haggard. "I fool myself by agreeing with the secret police reports of British plots and Russian bribes. But I know as well as you that I've turned people against me by the hundreds of thousands. In Spain, the Italian states, Poland, Bavaria—the list is endless. Only here, in France, where there's never been any real liking for papal authority, are people indifferent. Elsewhere men whom I've given more freedom and greater prosperity than they've ever imagined possible, security beyond their dreams, are calling me anti-Christ and a tyrant."

"If you've recognized the truth, act accordingly," Talleyrand said.

"I can't." The Emperor replied. "It would be useless to set him free without restoring Rome and The Papal States to him. If I do that, I've admitted defeat. I can succeed—and survive—only as long as I'm successful. People believe I'm invincible, but once they discover I'm mortal, there will be rebellions everywhere, and the Empire will collapse."

Talleyrand managed to smile. "You think of yourself as a realist, Your Majesty, but you're incurably romantic."

"My life has been a romance, if that's what you mean."

"I'm speaking of your own attitudes. The British Navy has beaten us in battle after battle, so you can't really claim you're invincible."

"Ah, sea battles. I didn't fight them myself. The regiments pay no attention to what happens at sea. Most of my troops have never heard of Horatio Nelson, but when I ride through a bivouac, they cheer themselves hoarse."

"Do they know how miserable the guerillas in Spain have been making life for some of their comrades?"

"That's a different kind of warfare, too. It isn't a genuine campaign. No, Charles, I know the source of my strength, and I can't allow it to be abused. When Alexander was delirious, his generals hid him from his veterans so they wouldn't realize he was a mere human. When Caesar drank impure river water, he retched in his tent and slept in the midst of the stench so his legions wouldn't know he was subject to the sicknesses that plagued them. I must tolerate the curse of being called anti-Christ, and hope the storm will pass. But I can't release Pope Pius until he surrenders to me—on my terms."

Two strong influences shaped the character of Weimar, the newly designated capital of Saxony, which, with its medieval wall, narrow streets and old buildings with high, slanted roofs, appeared to have retained an aura of the Middle Ages. One was virtually invisible: the French troops stationed there for the protection of the Elector Charles Augustus lived in a bivouac outside the city, and as a concession to the liberal and artistic tendencies of the Saxon ruler, were nominally under his command.

The other influence was all-pervasive. Johann Wolfgang von Goethe, the Elector's Minister of State and universally recognized as the greatest of German poets, had transformed Weimar into one of the most modern cities on earth. The new palace, which had taken fourteen years to construct, had been built under his direct supervision, as had a handsome outdoor theater at the château of Belvedere, a mile or two outside the walls. His own home, a handsome house near the ancient Stadkirche, was a gathering place for philosophers, authors and statesmen of many lands, and work had been started, in the center of the town, on a new theater which he had planned.

A huge park, part-forest, part-garden and part-lawn, had also been fashioned at his direction, and at its edge stood the Garden House, a rough-hewn cottage with a high-pitched, ninth-century roof, where the poet-diplomat spent his summers and weekends. The house was small, but sufficient for Goethe's simple needs. There were two bedrooms, one of which was used by Goethe and his wife, the other by their son. The kitchen was an out-building with a covered passage-way that led to the main house, the dining room was cramped, and only the drawing room was impressive. A vast chamber, lined on every wall with books, served as a library, conference hall and work-room. Papers were piled high on every available inch of space on a desk and a table beside it, but these documents were stacked in rows, each with a neat label identifying it. Charles Augustus had been right when he had said that Goethe's desk was as orderly as his mind.

Count Joseph de Montauban was scarcely aware of his surround-ings, however, and felt overwhelmed by Goethe himself. Most wise men he had met looked like ordinary people, but the sixty-one-year-old poet was the exception. His head was massive, every line in his face reflected his depth of character, and his eyes reflected compassion as well as intellect. He had a knack, too, for making a guest feel at ease, and Joseph was able to relax.

"You're acquainted with the Emperor," Joseph said, "so I needn't tell you he's a very complex man."

"Complex and remarkable," Goethe replied. "We held a long meeting four years ago, and I shall never forget it. Artists are inclined to like people who admire them, but anyone who knows Napoleon must be impressed by his mind. He could have been a scientist or a philosopher if his military talents hadn't been so formidable."

"You understand him better than I do, so perhaps you can help me. From your own writing as well as statements attributed to you in the press you have a sympathy with his goals——"

"He and I have the same goals, the liberation of the human spirit."

"There are so few who can see that he genuinely seeks freedom for mankind," Joseph said.

"People confuse his aims with his methods. The same thing happened to the Jesuits, you know, and led to their downfall. A genius works in ways that are his own, and make lesser people feel inferior. Napoleon is abrupt and dictatorial, and the butchery of these incessant wars has turned the people of many lands against him."

Goethe's summary was so complete that Joseph could only nod.

"There are other factors, of course. As I told him, he's too ambi-tious. The English remember William the Conqueror, and don't want another French ruler. If Napoleon promised to leave Great Britain in peace—and promised her an attractive trade alliance—the

461

war would come to an end very quickly. But he believes it would be a sign of weakness to seek an accommodation, and his pride won't permit it."

"Is it true," Joseph asked, "that he told you he admired America and would like to establish a United States of Europe?"

"He did, but he admitted it would take many years, principally because religious enmities are so strong on the Continent." Goethe smiled. "He has a visionary's dream of forcing the leaders of the principal denominations to work out an agreement to respect one another's faiths. But I can't see the Pope, the Lutheran bishops and the Archbishop of Canterbury sitting down at the same conference table."

The idea was so ludicrous that Joseph laughed. "I didn't know Napoleon had such a plan."

"He thinks of himself as a realist, and he is in military matters, perhaps in politics. But he's fundamentally a romantic who appeals to the imaginations of men by using dramatic techniques. If he learns to use reason rather than emotion, it's quite possible he'll actually achieve most of his ambitions."

"The reason I've come to Weimar," Joseph said, "is because his methods are causing a reaction against him everywhere. Pope Pius——"

"Of course. A frightful error."

"The Emperor insists he must keep the Pope a prisoner, that he has no choice."

"He gives himself no choice," Goethe said.

The poet, Joseph realized, was the true realist.

"If he wished, he could find ways to control Rome and The Papal States without formally incorporating them into his Empire. He could make a token obeisance to Pius, and to the Catholic Church itself, by leaving Vatican Hill with the trappings of power. Unfortunately, a great man who has an insatiable appetite for power must take lands in his own name, in the same way a miser must gather coins and hide them in a strongbox."

"The Emperor," Joseph said, "argues that it would be a sign of weakness if he handed the territory back to Pope Pius. The world would believe he had suffered a defeat, and there would be uprisings against him everywhere. He didn't tell me his attitude himself. He won't discuss the problem with me. But he was candid with Talleyrand."

Goethe twisted a forelock of gray hair. "Once again we find man playing God, eh?"

Joseph didn't understand.

"Only God is invincible in the last analysis, is it not so? Very well. A few exceptionally gifted men in human history have accumulated power. Charlemagne. Napoleon's idols, Alexander and Caesar. Napoleon himself. Eventually, like Alexander, who actually issued a decree conferring divinity on himself, they come to believe themselves omnipotent. In a metaphorical sense, they sell their souls to Satan, who eventually demands payment from them.

"Charlemagne was a genius—but a corrupt genius—with legitimate children by three or four wives, and whole palaces filled with his bastards by a half-dozen mistresses. The last four years of his life were spent in the tortures of several incurable sicknesses, and on his deathbed he begged in vain for release from torment.

"I doubt that Alexander wept because he had no more worlds to conquer. That's a pretty fancy, but a man who had fought so many battles and treated so many subject peoples so cruelly could have had no tears within him to shed. I've often wondered whether he died thinking himself divine, and how disappointed he must have been if he did. It's a fascinating subject.

"Caesar believed in equality, you know—for Romans. And he may have been the first of the great rulers to appreciate the Jews. But he became brutal, too, because power breeds brutality. His death was the ugliest of them all, because he was murdered by Brutus, who may have been his son."

Joseph knew that Goethe was hinting, very strongly, that the Emperor's end would be tragic.

"Napoleon, with all his greatness, with all his glorious visions of the future, has been corrupted, too. His fear is not that others will realize he is weak, but that he himself will come to know that his invincibility exists only in his own mind, and that once he starts to entertain serious doubts, he will crumple like all the others before him. There is little that you can do for him, that anyone can do. I respect him, but I fear for him, because he has created his own destiny, and sooner or later must face it. The ancients understood. There's a line from the Book of Deuteronomy in the Old Testament that Napoleon would have been wise to heed, before it was too late.

"The Lord said to Moses, 'To me belongeth vengeance, and recompense.' And no man, not even Napoleon, can evade God's justice after breaking His laws."

1816

The year 1812 marked the beginning of the end. Napoleon marched into Russia with his Grand Army, more than six hundred thousand strong, and after a series of sharp, costly battles took Moscow. The Russians refused to fight again, their saboteurs burned the city, and the Emperor was forced to make a long retreat, in winter. The Grand Army was destroyed: approximately four hundred thousand troops were killed in battle or died of starvation and exposure. Another one hundred thousand were captured.

Great Britain and Russia and Austria, the four great enemies of France, banded together in a new alliance, and no one but Napoleon could have staved off complete, immediate disaster. He raised a new army, and in October, 1813, met his foes at Leipzig. He fought hard, but ineptly, and again was forced to retreat. France was sick of war, and the following April, immediately after the release of Pope Pius VII from imprisonment, the Emperor abdicated.

The French Revolution, it appeared, had been fought in vain. The Old Regime of the Bourbons was restored to power, and the most reactionary of its survivors took the throne as Louis XVIII. The victors met in Vienna to divide the spoils, but their triumph was short-lived.

Napoleon escaped from the island of Elba, where he had been sent in exile, and landed on French soil on March 1, 1815. His subjects once again flocked to his banner, and for one hundred days he ruled supreme. He, who did not believe in miracles, seemingly had performed one, but his was an exhausted genius, and the combined armies of Great Britain and Prussia inflicted a final defeat on him at the Battle of Waterloo. He himself was sent as a prisoner to the distant South Atlantic island of St. Helena, and for the second time in a year the Bourbons came to power.

France, occupied for months by enemy troops, was too tired to resist the will of her new masters, and the few who mentioned the old Revolutionary goals of liberty, equality and fraternity spoke of them wistfully. "We must learn to live with adversity," Count Joseph de Montauban told his wife and children, expecting that his title and properties soon would be taken from him.

To his surprise he was not molested, and on the surface, life appeared almost unchanged. A new tax collector was appointed by the Crown for the county, but the tax rate remained fixed. Local veterans of Napoleon's Guards regiments were given posts in the constabulary, and two of the Emperor's former generals who bought farms in the county were permitted to live peacefully in retirement there.

There was only one significant change in the life at Montauban. Ever-increasing crowds attended Mass at the cathedral and the church of St. Jacques, and the resurgence of Catholicism was so great that a new bishop was appointed for the once-defunct diocese. Joseph noted with wry amusement, as did others, that Louis XVIII was happy to abide by Napoleon's Concordat of 1801; the King recommended the nominee, and Pope Pius, who had no intention of opening a new dispute with France, promptly confirmed him.

In the spring of 1816 Joseph received a royal command ordering him to appear at Versailles in order to swear a personal oath of allegiance to Louis XVIII. He felt he needed advice before taking such an important step, after having spent too long a time in a country town far from the center of the nation's activities, so he went first to Paris.

There, in an office on the second floor of the Quai d'Orsay, he found a familiar figure. "I spent a few months as Foreign Minister after representing France at the Congress of Vienna," Talleyrand said, "but I found it embarrassing. Too many people stared at me, precisely as you're doing, Joseph. So I've found it more comfortable merely to supervise foreign relations from my new position as High Chamberlain."

"You have as many lives as the proverbial cat, Charles." No matter how great his contempt, Joseph forced himself to remember that it was he who had sought Talleyrand. Hence it was his obligation to observe the amenities of polite intercourse.

"Shall we understand each other?" Talleyrand took a scented handkerchief from his sleeve and sniffed it. "I serve France, which is precisely what I've always done. The peace terms at Vienna would have been much harder on us if I hadn't been there to protect our interests. And our relations with the rest of the world would be in a terrible muddle right now if some Bourbon imbecile who has spent the better part of the past twenty years as a refugee in London were in charge of the Quai d'Orsay."

There was a great deal to what he said, but Joseph couldn't resist asking, "How do you justify Fouché's acceptance of an appointment as ambassador to Dresden?"

"I don't." Talleyrand was curt. "Fouché is an opportunist, and always was. On the other hand, few men actively seek death. I'm told that when the Austrians captured Murat, he hadn't heard what had happened at Waterloo. He shouted, 'Long live the Emperor!' And they shot him. I have no idea whether the story is true, but it does illustrate my point rather neatly."

"There's no doubt that Murat was executed. But the way I heard it, he begged for clemency, and reminded his captors he'd been feuding with the Emperor. Either way, of course, he's dead."

"Spoken like a diplomat. And now you're in Paris. I happen to know you've been called to Versailles, so it isn't very difficult to imagine that you're having prickles of conscience."

"I'm seriously thinking of going back to the United States, Charles."

"You'd give up your castle and lands? And that splendid town-house?"

"If they're to be taken from me, what do I have to lose?"

"Louis may be a stupid, fat old man with gout, but he isn't mad. He's given France a constitution, he's sworn publicly that he'll take no reprisals against any of Napoleon's supporters, and he's trying hard not to alienate anyone, although for my taste he's too friendly with the reactionary royalists who favor the establishment of closer ties with Vatican Hill."

"I didn't know there was such a group."

"Of course. Every irritant causes a counter-irritant. The Bourbon refugees took up the cause of Pope Pius while he was being held prisoner at Fontainebleu, naturally. The more sympathy they created for him, the more it helped their own cause. So they've developed some close relationships in Rome."

Joseph frowned as he tried to weigh the information.

"But the last time I dined with King Louis," Talleyrand said with a smile, "he told me his secret vice. He reads Voltaire for an hour every night before he goes to bed. I can't believe that anyone who enjoys the work of Voltaire would try to destroy the advances toward freedom that France has made during the Revolution and the Empire."

"Well," Joseph said uncertainly, "Adrienne is unhappy at the idea of going back to America. She's always thought of herself as French, and she doesn't have very pleasant memories of the short time we spent in New York. We were poor—and we'd be poorer still, with the children to support."

"How many do you have now?"

"Four. Only Mathieu is old enough to understand anything of the world around him, of course."

"It's a difficult decision."

"The vineyards earn me an excellent income, Charles. Even in the year of the Russian campaign, when it was so hard to find field workers, we showed a good profit. If I felt reasonably certain I could keep my lands, I'd stay. I'd like to be able to give my children some security—and pass the title to Mathieu, of course."

Talleyrand twisted the handkerchief. "I'm not certain I can advise you. I've had invitations to settle in the United States myself, and although I'd suffer the loss of my place in Touraine if I left France, I have enough—ah—investments abroad that I wouldn't be in serious want. But I'm staying. There are rumors of retaliatory acts against the Bonapartists that are being planned by the Bourbons, but even if half the stories are true, life will still be very comfortable for a gentleman of stature. You worked hard for France, and it seems to me you've earned your reward."

466

A few minutes later, as Joseph left the Quai d'Orsay, he was still undecided. But, as he rode along the Seine, Paris seemed to envelop him. He realized that France had become his home, that he had indeed made a place for himself here. He was middle-aged now, and the thought of cutting all his ties, returning to America and starting a new, hard life depressed him. Talleyrand was right, he told himself. He would be running only a small risk by staying.

"You were reared as a Catholic, although I'll grant that you were never very devout." Joseph stood, facing his wife in the great hall of the castle at Montauban. "You became a Huguenot when I did, just to please me."

"You needn't make it sound like an accusation," Adrienne said.

"I'm not. I'm just trying to make you understand why all this means so little to you, but is so important to me." He turned and, raising his voice, called, "Mathieu! Are you ready?"

"Yes, Papa." The boy walked into the room, dressed in somber black, as was his father.

"Must you take him with you?" Adrienne instinctively took a step toward the child.

"I insist. I've been derelict enough in my duty, and in this I have no choice."

Adrienne sighed and let her hands fall to her sides.

"We'll be home in time for Sunday dinner," Joseph said gently. "I won't forget that you like to serve a meal as soon as it's been prepared."

"You're taking the carriage?" Adrienne asked.

"No. We'll walk." Joseph's tone was curt.

Mathieu looked at his parents, aware of a strain and slightly bewildered by it.

"We've been fortunate," Adrienne said.

"I count our blessings. Daily. Come along, son."

The Count and his heir left the castle, walking across the ancient drawbridge that had not been raised for many years. The bells in the cathedral and the church of St. Jacques were pealing, and the streets were filled with townspeople and farmers in their Sunday best. Women curtsied awkwardly and men hauled off their stocking caps when they saw the lord of Montauban, and Joseph replied courteously, gravely, by touching the rim of his old-fashioned, black bicorn.

Mathieu was accustomed to the homage, but something in the faces of the people that he couldn't define made him uneasy. Some peered sharply at his father, studying his face, while others seemed embarrassed and turned away abruptly. It seemed odd to the boy that no one smiled at them, and that his father was so grim, too.

They came to the Place Nationale, and when they made their way past the cathedral, Mathieu glanced inside. His brother, Victor, was insane, wanting to become a Roman Catholic. Those stained glass windows and all those burning candles were so alien. The odors of incense always made him sneeze, too. He preferred their own plain Calvinist church, with its bare pews, unadorned altar and ordinary windows.

It was odd that he and Papa were walking to church today, dressed as though for a funeral, and that Mama had not come with them. They had always gone together, the three of them, riding in the open carriage in fine weather and in the closed coach when it was cold or damp. A boy became confused when he tried to understand the ways of adults.

Familiar sights were reassuring, of course. Everywhere there were veterans of the Emperor's regiments, many still wearing the breeches or tunics, stripped of insignia, that had been part of their uniforms. The usual wine-sellers were on hand, too, selling individual drinks from skins, with the buyers providing their own cups. Virtually all of the men who crowded around them were veterans, and Mathieu remembered what Papa had said a few weeks ago, when Mama had protested that it was wrong for men to be drinking in the Place Nationale on a Sunday morning. Papa had smiled, but hadn't seemed in the least amused as he had muttered, "It's their last illusion." The boy was still wondering what he had meant.

A man named Rodel, the proprietor of the largest inn in town, formerly called the Emperor's Eagles but now simply known as the Montauban, came up to join father and son. He sometimes came to the castle for dinner, and usually was quite jolly, so Mathieu grinned at him.

But Rodel, who was also dressed in black, seemed preoccupied and excited. "Have you heard, milord?" he demanded. "The schoolmasters have been discharged, and the bishop is replacing them with priests."

Joseph nodded. "I know. We're going to send our children to school in Paris this year. The regime can do what it pleases in the provinces, but there would be riots in the city if they tried such tactics. We're selfish, I'm afraid, but better a few lads grow up with open minds than none."

"One by one we took the oath of allegiance to Louis. We were tricked."

Here and there in the throngs Mathieu saw other members of the Huguenot congregation walking toward their own church, and noted that they, too, were dressed in black. Perhaps there was going to be a funeral, after all, and Papa hadn't mentioned it to him. However, he hadn't heard of any friend of the family dying in recent days.

468

"I believe you make a very complicated problem too simple, Rodel," Joseph said. "I've had little else to think about since my trip to Paris, God knows. And from what I saw of the regime, both in the city and at Versailles, there seems to be an awareness that the clock can't be turned back thirty years. Too much has happened in all that time."

"They're trying, though," the innkeeper said bitterly.

"The zealots are the worst offenders, and the bishops who spent years of exile in England haven't yet realized the times have changed. They'll learn."

"Meanwhile it's we who suffer."

"It was inevitable the pendulum should swing in the opposite direction. And I can't deny the obvious, that we're being made to suffer. All the same, I'm convinced that we'll fare better than we did when Louis the Fourteenth revoked the Edict of Nantes. The great irony of our day is that the Emperor's conquerors will protect us."

Rodel stared at Joseph, unable to believe he was speaking in earnest.

"I'm serious, my friend. England has her own church. Prussia is Lutheran, and Russia may be Catholic, in a manner of speaking, but doesn't recognize the authority of Rome. Only Austria will approve of clerical excesses here. The others still supervise everything that happens in France, and they didn't beat us in order to make a gift of the country to Vatican Hill."

"I suppose they might step in, if they weren't so busy with their own affairs that they forget us."

"They won't. Just this past week the *Times* of London published an interview with the Duke of Wellington. He called France a land of revolutionaries and Papists, and he swore that he'd allow neither to prosper."

"By the time he realizes what's happening here, it may be too late."

"We must live from day to day." There was a note of weary resignation in Joseph's voice that his son had never heard.

Mathieu looked up at him curiously, but his attention was diverted by the sight of several soldiers in white tunics, breeches and boots. Even the plumes on their helmets were white, and the child tugged at his father's coat. "Look, Papa!"

"I see them," Joseph said curtly.

"Who are they?"

"King Louis' soldiers. France has a very small army now. They may look like toy soldiers, but their muskets are real."

Mathieu was dazzled by the uniforms, but thought it best to keep his opinions to himself. It was apparent that Papa, for whatever his reasons, didn't have a high regard for the troops.

A crowd was gathering in front of the Huguenot church, and Mathieu realized that most members of the congregation were there, all of them in black. He wondered why they didn't go inside. The door was closed, and six soldiers in white, all of them armed with muskets and bayonets, seemed to be blocking the entrance.

The people moved aside to allow the Count and his son to make their way closer to the door.

An officer in white, whom Mathieu hadn't seen, came forward to greet them. He was wearing a long sword, his uniform was trimmed in gold, and he looked particularly impressive.

"I've been expecting you, sir," he said to Joseph, and saluted.

Mathieu was shocked when his father, who was always polite to everyone, just stared at the officer, neither replying nor doffing his hat.

"I regret this occasion," the officer said.

"Far less than we regret it, Colonel," Joseph said.

The crowd, which had been strangely silent, came to life and murmured its approval.

The officer looked embarrassed. "Our sole purpose is the prevention of bloodshed. The Ministry of the Interior's only motive is to spare Montauban riots."

"Huguenots, Catholics and non-believers have lived side by side here, in peace, for more than a generation," Joseph said, speaking loudly so that all of his fellow parishioners could hear him. "Until today, there has been no bad feeling here. If it exists now, it is not the Huguenots, Catholics or non-believers of Montauban who have created it."

The officer was scarlet. "The Ministry of the Interior has authorized me to give you every assurance that as soon as the danger has passed——"

"Your masters at the ministry answered a call from the bishop, who is an old fool living in the past. France has endured enough violence in the past thirty years, Colonel. The bishop has a surprise in store for him. He's going to discover that most Catholics in the county disapprove of this sort of act. He may even find that there are enlightened men at Vatican Hill who deplore the revival of ancient customs that stir up ancient hatreds." Joseph turned to face his fellow parishioners. "We've served our purpose here. Go to your homes."

The people moved off quietly, some of the women weeping.

Mathieu saw there were tears in his father's eyes.

"Look at our church, son," Joseph said, "and remember this morning. The government of France prevents us from worshipping here, and has stationed her troops outside our door to enforce her order."

Everything fell into place at last, and the stunned Mathieu understood. He tried to swallow, but his throat felt too dry.

"If I hadn't sworn allegiance to King Louis, we'd be on our way to the United States by now," Joseph told him. "But I gave my pledge, and I insist on standing by the people who look to me for leadership. Some day you'll inherit my title—and my responsibility. So don't forget what you're seeing at this moment. Bigotry is the worst enemy of the human race, Mathieu."

The boy watched in crushed silence as his father, shoulders slumping, turned and started toward home, his shuffling walk that of an old, tired man.

1840-1850

The steps of the little Huguenot church in Montauban were cold and very hard.

It felt odd to be pressing his face against them, but small boys sometimes did strange things. Mathieu became confused, however, when he realized he was no longer a child. In fact, he wasn't lying on the steps, but on warm ground, and he could smell the faintly sweet scent of grass. How could he be a boy in Montauban and, simultaneously, a man somewhere else? Nothing made sense any more, perhaps because his head was aching so badly.

There were men in Paris who believed that Pondicherry was a small area of France transplanted in the East, but their claim was arrant nonsense, and anyone who knew India laughed at their ignorance.

Mathieu de Montauban was paying his sixth visit to the tiny capital of the French possessions on the Coromandel, or eastern coast of India, approximately one hundred and twenty-five miles south of Madras, and was just beginning to feel at home here. The casual traveler, of course, could see surface signs of France everywhere on the waterfront, but as Mathieu had learned in twenty years at sea, colonizing Europeans in the East merely succeeded in superimposing a thin layer of their culture on a far older civilization.

Most of the men sitting on the long, open porch of the Hôtel Emperor Napoleon, sipping gin drinks, were French, of course, virtually all of them merchants, ship owners and traders, with a sprinkling of politicians in their midst. A short distance away on the crescent-shaped harbor stood the palace of the governor, with the tricolor flag of the Revolution, restored ten years earlier by King

Louis-Philippe, flying above it. Adjacent to the palace was the largest building in Pondicherry, Government House, where the privy council and general council sat, and where the representatives of the colony in the French Senate and Chamber of Deputies maintained impressive suites of offices.

On the opposite side of the hotel were the small Catholic church and the small Huguenot house of worship, standing as neighbors in apparent amity. The former was a weatherbeaten structure, built in 1683, when the French had founded their colony in Pondicherry, and the Jesuits, rehabilitated as a missionary and teaching order, maintained a seminary on the grounds. The Huguenot church had been built within the last decade, after the Revolution of 1830, a brief, abortive uprising that had driven Charles X, the brother and successor of Louis XVIII, from the throne of France. With few exceptions, the two hundred thousand Indians of the colony were immune to the attractions of both churches.

A small number of natives worked as servants in the spacious homes of the Frenchmen whose houses fanned out behind the waterfront, but most of the natives were scarcely aware of the presence of their supposed masters. Pondicherry occupied only one hundred and fourteen square miles, and there were only a few tea and cotton plantations in the area, all of them in the hands of the descendants of the earliest French settlers. Most Indians lived as their ancestors had, on tiny plots of land and in dire poverty.

The Frenchmen who lived in the colony earned their living in trade, which meant, for all practical purposes, dealing with British India, which surrounded the enclave. The secrets of Pondicherry's prosperity were the agricultural products exported at an incredibly low cost, thanks to the near-starvation wages paid to Indian labor, and to the ships riding at anchor in the harbor.

Mathieu looked at his own multi-sailed clipper, with her long hull, rakish prow and three masts, and wondered why he no longer felt any sense of pride in her. French naval architects and designers had been the first to build the swift clippers, more than sixty years earlier, and he had long felt a sense of satisfaction in knowing he could sail faster than could any of the Baltimore clippers developed in the United States within the past few decades.

The sea had lost its challenge, and life its savor. Mathieu sighed, and belatedly realized he was being subjected to a close scrutiny by his Indian business associate of many years, Krishna Mahishasura. He submitted himself to the chisel-featured Hindu's gaze without rancor, and waited for the inevitable questions that were sure to follow.

Mahishasura did not disappoint him. "You are unhappy, Mathieu," he said in the precise French he had learned in the Jesuit school before returning to his own faith and a life as an international trader.

472

"Isn't everyone?" The day was hot and sultry, and although Mathieu suffered less from the Indian climate than did most of his compatriots, he felt too lazy to become involved in a long argument that led nowhere.

Mahishasura continued to watch him. "Frenchmen are contented in this incarnation only when they have families, or so I have observed. You have been too long at sea, too long a bachelor."

"Perhaps I've spent too long at sea," Mathieu conceded, and tried to remember a few of his many mistresses. "But I've never met the woman I've wanted to marry."

The Indian politely pressed his fingertips together, and their friendship of many years made it possible for him to ask, "If you have no heir, your title goes to another, is it not so?"

Mathieu shrugged. "I have three brothers. One of them works for Louis-Philippe, long may he reign as king of the middle-class, and lives in my Paris house. The other two share my castle and vineyards in Montauban, and fight incessantly. They're welcome to my property, title and the money I've earned." He twisted in his wicker chair and returned the stare of the dark, searching eyes. "You Indians are so damned polite, but you really like to dig into a man's soul, don't you? All right. My father was a failure in life, except for the few years he served the Emperor Napoleon. I had to prove I was the better man. Well, I've proved I can earn a better living than he did, which means nothing to me, and wouldn't have to him."

Mahishasura, obviously uncomfortable in Western dress, smoothed a wrinkle in his fawn-colored trousers. "You make me confused, Mathieu. Once I sailed around the world with you, and twice you have visited my family home, but I do not really know you, nor you me."

"The way I've been feeling these past two or three years, I'm not sure I know myself." Mathieu snapped his fingers, summoning a waiter, and speaking a reasonably good Hindi, ordered more tea and barley cakes.

A French banker and the vice-governor, who were seated at the next table, turned in surprised. No self-respecting Frenchman ever ordered anything but gin. Then they recognized the Count, and paid no more attention to him; at the very least, everyone of substance in Pondicherry thought him odd.

"I'll try to explain, Krishna." For his own sake, as much as his friend's, Mathieu wanted to clarify his thinking, hoping to shake off the depression that had been plaguing him. "Ever since I was ten years old, the French government tried to teach each generation of schoolchildren that the Emperor Napoleon was a wicked despot. But the people refused to be fooled. Just this year, little Louis-Philippe, a whore among kings, if ever there was one, who'll do anything to win

473

greater popularity, had Napoleon's remains returned to France. I happened to be home when they buried his 'sacred ashes' in the Invalides. What a grotesque spectacle!"

"Napoleon was not a good man?" Mahishasura spoke very softly.

"I'm not sure what you mean by good. And don't try to tell me, Krishna. Every time you try to explain your *Smartas* philosophy to me, I become more bewildered."

"That is because we are so new. Sankara Acharya did not found our sect until eleven centuries ago."

The Indian was so sincere that Mathieu smiled briefly. "I must answer you in the only way I know. Napoleon was a great man, a man of vision, whose enemies have benefited from his dreams as much as his followers."

"Then he was truly great." Mahishasura bowed his head.

"It's because of his influence that the Huguenot church over there opened. Yes, and thanks to his ideas of freedom, the Jesuits are able to function again all over the Catholic world, after being barred from many lands. The English, who defeated him and kept him prisoner until his death, have been moving closer to his concept of giving the vote to every man. I don't want to bore you by singing his praises, Krishna. It's enough for me to tell you my father died of a broken spirit because he thought all that Napoleon had accomplished was being destroyed."

Mahishasura was silent while they were served their tea and barley cakes. Then he asked, "What of your spirit, my friend? Why is it broken?"

Mathieu looked at him in surprise.

"On your last visit, I think it was, you told me you are no longer a follower of the faith of Calvin."

Mathieu smiled sourly. "My brother, Victor, would have become a Huguenot minister, I think, if his wife hadn't persuaded him to work for the government—and hope I'd die a bachelor so he could inherit my title and estates. My younger brothers are ardent Catholics, and although they wouldn't admit it to their confessors or themselves, they hope that both Victor and I will die without legitimate issue."

"You are bitter."

"Not at them, really. At everyone. Titles are important, money is important, and churches are filled every Sunday with people who have no piety. That's why I went to sea."

"Perhaps you are closer to the Divine Spirit than you know."

"I have no religion," Mathieu said, hoping to change the subject. In spite of his many visits to the East, he still marveled at the sensitivity of Indians to some subjects, while being callously impervious to the feelings of other people.

Mahishasura broke a small barley cake into quarters, and put two pieces on his companion's plate.

Mathieu recognized the peace offering, and accepted in Indian fashion, by pressing his fingertips together for an instant.

Mahishasura had no intention of turning to other topics, however, until he expressed a thought preying on his mind. "I have known Brahmans who have thought for a time, as you do, that they have rejected the Divine Spirit. It is not so. For two months of each year I go to a place owned by my family for many generations, and there I meditate to achieve a closer union with the gods, and to better understand the eternal mysteries. It is near to the border of Pondicherry and the British district of South Arcot, in the foothills of the Penner Mountains. It is very remote there, very quiet, very primitive. No foreigner has ever been to this place, but I would be honored if you cared to join me there."

"Thank you." Mathieu was touched by the invitation, but preferred not to journey into the crowded interior, where sanitary conditions were shocking.

"I shall go there in a few days, when you and I finish our business, and I shall leave travel instructions for you with my office. Come when you wish, and stay as long as you please. It may be, you will find what you are seeking."

The men of the Montauban family, even Papa, had always prized principle so highly, or thought they had, which was tantamount to the same thing. Papa had gained financially and socially, of course, which had made it more difficult to respect him. If only he hadn't spoken French with a trace of an American accent, it would have been so much easier to think of him as truly French. But, Mathieu realized, he had no right to criticize Papa. He himself wasn't French, either. He was nothing—or was he? It was impossible to think clearly when his head was throbbing.

The summer monsoons began early, sweeping across the lower tip of the Indian sub-continent from the Arabian Sea to the Bay of Bengal, bringing with them the promise that the seasons were about to change and the rains begin. Colonials who have lived for years in Pondicherry were fond of telling new arrivals that the French settlement was uniquely blessed, that the winds sweeping down on them from the Penner Mountains actually brought cool air rather than hot.

Such stories were myths, Mathieu de Montauban thought. Naked to the waist, he stood in his high-ceilinged room at the Hôtel Emperor Napoleon, listening to the howling of the monsoon and the dismal, hollow rattle of his shutters. He poured an inch or two of gin into his glass, wiped the sweat from his face and opened the shutters. It was far better to endure a little sand and dirt, he told himself, than to die of suffocation.

It occurred to him as he gulped the gin that he hadn't really wanted the liquor, and, in fact, had already consumed far too much. But anything that would deaden his mind and dull his senses would be a help. His clipper ship, riding securely at anchor in the harbor with her sails furled, would be secure enough. But he had delayed his departure too long, and would have to wait indefinitely, perhaps as long as four or five weeks now, before sailing. His mate would curse him—privately, of course, behind his back, and his crew would be unhappy. But they would be here, waiting, whenever he called them.

Life in Pondicherry might be miserable, but had its advantages. The masters of ships caught by the monsoon winds in British ports lived in dread, afraid their crews would desert. But French sailors literally had no where to go. British customs officials prevented them from crossing the border, and only madmen went into the interior, so they stayed in the town of Pondicherry, sweltering on half-pay until ordered to sea again.

Mathieu drained his gin, heard a faint sound behind, scarcely audible, and turned. Focusing with difficulty, he saw the girl on the bed, and realized he had forgotten her. Apparently she had awaked from her sleep, and was staring in terror at the open shutters. Until now he hadn't quite realized she was very young. He didn't like to think about her age, having learned that a man's conscience bothered him if he became too inquisitive about prostitutes in the East.

The girl transferred her gaze to Mathieu for a moment, then looked back at the windows again as she reached for her long skirt and blouse, the only clothes she had been wearing. They had been made for her here in Pondicherry, obviously, by someone who had copied Western styles, and Mathieu guessed they were the only wardrobe she owned.

"Here," he called, reaching into a pocket of his trousers and throwing her a silver franc. "Buy yourself some sandals with high heels. Then every sailor in town will come sniffing after you, like dogs after a bitch in heat."

She couldn't understand a word he said, but snatched the coin, her teeth bared like an animal's, as she hauled on her clothes and fled from the room in her bare feet.

The wind swept through the room into the corridor beyond, leaving a spray of dust in its wake. Mathieu hurriedly closed the door and bolted it, then laughed aloud again.

To his own surprise, the laugh choked in his throat, and he poured the last of the gin into his glass. The girl's antics hadn't amused him in the least, and he knew it. In fact, he didn't know why he had picked her up in the saloon bar of the hotel and brought her to his room in the first place. He hadn't wanted a woman in a long time, and the girl had given him no real satisfaction, no pleasure beyond a fleeting, mechanical sense of release.

The gin burned in his throat, and he threw the glass to the floor in sudden self-disgust. He was just sober enough to realize how stupid he had been to drink. He had never been able to handle strong spirits, and for more than a year had tasted nothing alcoholic except beer or an occasional glass of wine. Tomorrow he would pay for his asininity by feeling wretchedly ill all day.

The sensation of sand and dirt stinging his skin became unbearable. Mathieu cursed, made his way to the window with half-closed eyes, and after a long struggle that left him panting for breath managed to close the shutters. Catching a glimpse of himself in the mirror over the bureau, he thought he looked like a chimney-sweep. He had always been fastidious, so he poured some water into the basin from a pitcher, spilling most of it onto the floor, and washed himself vigorously, if inadequately.

Mathieu discovered it was impossible to dry himself adequately. He was bathed in perspiration, blinded by it, and could tolerate the room no longer. Pulling on an open-throated shirt of the sort that was virtually a uniform for Europeans in India, he stuffed the tails inside his trousers and staggered out into the corridor. It was dark, stuffy and so humid he found it difficult to breathe, so he made his way down to the lobby, weaving slightly.

The wind had driven the French residents of the hotel indoors. Some were sitting in the palm-decorated lobby, chatting interminably about the prices of sandalwood and tea. Others filled the saloon bar, where the topics of conversation were the same, but voices louder. Mathieu knew he had already consumed more than enough to drink, and turned away. He caught a quick glimpse of the girl he had taken earlier in the evening, sitting with another potential client, and he tried to remember whether he had felt sorry for her. If so, he had been foolish, for she deserved no pity.

"No pity," he muttered aloud, and drifted toward the double doors that led to the main waterfront thoroughfare, François Martin Boulevard, named after the French founder of the colony. He had no idea where he might be going, and the men sitting in the lobby watched him without trying to call him back. He wasn't the first or the last who had felt suffocated by the monsoon, and they knew from experience that an attempt to stop him would end in a violent argument.

The heat was searing, the wind fierce. Palms, always surprisingly supple, bent almost double in the direction of the harbor, their fronds flapping like the distinguishing pennant of a clipper ship in a gale. The street was deserted, but Mathieu was not seeking the company of others. He began to move up Martin Boulevard, pausing occasionally to brace himself as a particularly strong gust of wind threatened to knock him from his feet.

Soon he found himself in front of the Huguenot church, and, without trying to analyze his motives, decided to go inside. The door was locked, and he rattled the latch angrily, but there appeared to be no caretaker on the premises. He tried to peer in through the nearest window of plain glass, wiping dust from the pane, but in the dark could see only the vague outlines of the severe, unornamented chamber. Withdrawing so quickly that he stumbled and fell to one knee, ripping a hole in his trousers, he continued down the street.

Directly ahead now was the Catholic church, Notre-Dame. He wondered if it, too, was closed, and tried the door. It opened, and he had difficulty in closing it behind him. The glow of a score of candles was reflected in the warm stained-glass windows, and the scent of incense was strong.

Papa had told him not to forget, and Mathieu remembered every detail of the day when royalist troops had closed the Huguenot church in Montauban. He could still see the cathedral, with its many candles burning deep in the interior, and suddenly he gagged. Running unsteadily to the door, he wrenched it open, slammed it behind him and stood on the worn stone steps, panting.

He had only a remote notion of what had impelled him to seek refuge in the place, and all at once knew he should return to his hotel room before he became ill. But it was too late. Retching, he lost his footing. The monsoon seemed to be mocking him, and he crawled on his hands and knees, hoping in desperation that he could make his way to his bed before he lost consciousness.

Mathieu wished he could decide whether he was a child or a man. He really couldn't make up his mind about the first Philippe de Montauban until he knew. As a boy he had been taught to venerate the old Chancellor, which was absurd. The Huguenots in the family had always regarded him as a saint, but Calvinists rejected the very basis of sainthood, which made the de Montaubans inconsistent. Was he himself equally inconsistent? Everyone in the world he had left behind undoubtedly thought so. Perhaps, if the pain weren't spreading into his chest, it might be easier to analyze his dilemma.

The view from the simple pavilion near the Pondicherry border was superb. Below, to the east, lay a tropical forest of hardwoods, bamboo and sandalwood, and at its edge stood a tiny village of clay huts built around a water hole. To the west stood the brown-green peaks of the Penner chain, their crests rounded by the erosion of the ages. The pavilion itself seemed isolated, part of neither, because it stood on a small, shelf-life plateau, with its vegetable gardens on one side and a rice field in a bog-like valley below the cliff.

A stone building that had been constructed to withstand the elements, the pavilion was remarkably cool, perhaps because an outer roof of hardwood had been built above the flat stone roof, with a layer of air between. There was only one room in the interior, simply furnished with several mats, a few utensils for cooking and eating, and a shelf of fine, old books, inscribed by hand on parchment. The monsoon winds had subsided temporarily, the bamboo blinds had been raised, and the gentle breeze that swept down the heights was surprisingly refreshing.

Mathieu and Krishna squatted on the bare floor, eating bowls of rice, mixed with groundnut oil-seeds and tender bamboo shoots that had been boiled together. Neither man spoke until they finished their simple meal.

"You were searching for the Divine Spirit when you went into the Pondicherry churches," Krishna said, "and you were still seeking when you came here."

Mathieu was willing to admit the possibility, but smiled. "If I was searching for God, no one could have strayed farther from Him than I did."

"You denigrate yourself too much. You neither murdered nor assaulted another living creature."

Mathieu waved aside the interruption. "And I've lost my way these past few weeks. Granted that my Hindi is imperfect, but the *Bhagavadgita* and the *Chhandogya Upanishad* make my mind whirl."

Krishna laughed. "Often one who is twice-born will spend all of his lives trying to learn the Truth, while catching no more than glimpses of it."

Mathieu held up a hand. "Wait, and don't confuse me. When you speak of the Divine Spirit, you seem to be saying that Brahmanism is a monotheistic faith."

The Indian nodded.

"Yet for weeks I've been reading of many gods. You worship the elements, living things—everything and anything."

"They are all a part of the universe, is it not so?"

"Of course, but that makes the Hindu faith a polytheistic pantheism, according to what I was taught at the Sorbonne and Lausanne!"

"We quibble now over semantics," Krishna said gently. "Your interpretation differs from mine, and who is to say which of us is right? It is enough that both of us seek the Divine Spirit."

Mathieu admired his friend's tranquility, but deplored his reasoning. "Isn't it true that different local gods are worshipped in every one of India's tens of thousands of towns and villages?"

"To be sure. The people are ignorant, and mix superstition with theology. But they, too, are seeking a greater understanding of the Truth. They do it on a level compatible with their own thinking."

Mathieu began to feel irritated. "Forget the masses for the moment.

Let's confine ourselves to the more intellectual sects of the upper-caste Brahmans. You have three principal gods: Brahmā, creator of the universe; Vishnu, preserver of the universe; Śiva, destroyer of the universe. So how can you claim you're monotheists?"

"They form a trinity, and are parts of the same Divine Spirit. In Christianity, you, too, worship a trinity, yet you claim to be monotheists."

"But each of your divinities have goddesses as wives, and their children form a fantastic order of lesser gods!"

"Yet they all spring from the same trinity, and therefore are a part of it." Krishna pressed his fingertips together.

"Do your lesser trinities, like Agni, the god of fire; Indra, the god of sky; and Sūrya, the god of sun, fall into that category?"

"If you wish to see them in that way. There are some who see in them a reflection of the basic trinity."

"What bothers me," Mathieu said, "is that there are no absolutes in Brahmanism!"

"Who is man to define the absolutes? It is enough that we try to cleanse ourselves, to rid our senses of the worldly, to seek detachment from the earthly so that we may obtain a clearer understanding of the Divine Spirit. There is only one reality, whch is both the cause of *jīva*, living things, and the goal of all souls."

Mathieu raised both hands. "Enough for one day, Krishna."

The Indian nodded politely, but remained firm. "Yesterday you were concerned because Śiva, the destroyer, should be a part of the elemental trinity."

"Yes, it seems to me," Mathieu replied wearily, "that a destroying force is the opposite of God, what we call Satan."

"The Jesuits taught me something about Satan, but our concept is different. Śiva destroys, but death is natural, is it not so? Then Brahmā creates, and we are reincarnated, perhaps rising a trifle higher in the order of living things as our understanding grows."

"What I can't accept is reincarnation, I suppose, and without it Hinduism makes no sense."

"Every faith leads to greater understanding, because the activities of the Divine Spirit never cease. There may be those among us who are Christians or Jews or Buddhists in another incarnation. It doesn't matter."

"Or Moslems, perhaps?"

Krishna hesitated for an instant. "It may be," he said, "that they are followers of the Prophet, Mohammed."

Mathieu stood and stretched. "Congratulate me, Krishna. I did fairly well without a chair today. I'm still playing a mental game of some sort, but I'm certainly feeling better than I have in a long time. This simple life agrees with me."

480

"You become more spiritual as you withdraw from the world. There are those among us who find their salvation in work, or in teaching, perhaps—or as members of the warrior sects, although I myself do not approve of them. It is your pre-ordained fate to seek the Absolute that you must have, and to do it through detachment from the world."

"I'm inclined to doubt it," Mathieu said lightly, "but I do know one thing. We'll go hungry tonight unless we go back to work in the rice field!"

The first great warrior in the family—what had been his name?—had died on the field of battle. Mathieu had always wondered how he had felt in those last moments, and now, perhaps, was learning. But he couldn't be certain. So little was known of the old general. Or had he been a colonel? The family records were so vague. Papa had been told by Grandpa that the old warrior had been a murderer, which everyone in the family thought shocking. Mathieu wanted to laugh, but the pain in his chest had become excruciating. Every man was a murderer, really, but the de Montaubans were too proper, too conventional to realize it.

In his sixty-one years Governor Léon Charbert of Pondicherry had known no employer except the government of France. The winner of a battlefield promotion in one of the regiments in Napoleon's Guards at Wagram, he had later been wounded; his pronounced limp had made him unfit for further military service, so he had been given a post in the Ministry of Colonial Affairs, where he had worked zealously, no matter who sat on the throne. His industry had been rewarded, and he was spending his final years prior to retirement on a pension as the principal representative of the Crown in India.

The finery of his palace was somewhat faded, thanks to the niggardliness of Louis-Philippe in providing his viceroy with an adequate salary or housing allowance. Nevertheless Charbert wore a white uniform, tricolor sash and plumed cockade hat every day of his life, and was ever-conscious of the dignity of his office.

Mathieu de Montauban had always thought him overbearing, and a stickler for the laws governing the export of raw materials from British India by way of Pondicherry. But, until today, he had always wanted something from Charbert, and was enjoying his unique situation. He noted any number of little things that had escaped his attention on previous visits to the Governor's office. The damp collar of Charbert's high-necked tunic had been permanently stained by sweat; the dusty, leather-bound books on the shelves below the portrait of King Louis-Philippe looked as though they had not been touched in years, and the distinct odor of gin leaked from the carafe, ostensibly filled with water, that stood at the Governor's elbow.

Eight years of living near the southern tip of the Indian sub-continent, combined with his relish for gin, had given him a deep complexion, but he was red now beneath his tan. "If you want to send your clipper back to France under the command of your mate, and then make a gift of the ship and her cargo to your brothers, that is your business. As long as your papers are in order——"

"They were drawn up for me by the best lawyer in Pondicherry," Mathieu said.

"Ah, yes. Delacroix. An able legal advocate. So competent, my dear Count, that you will find your gesture cannot be rescinded."

"I have no intention of changing my mind, Your Excellency."

Charbert shook his head, started to reach for the carafe and then withdrew his hand. "I, too, have relatives whom I've supported for many years. It doesn't pay, my dear Count. They're not only ungrateful, but they actually hate you when you stop showering them with gold. As one gentleman to another, I urge you to reconsider."

"The documents are already signed," Mathieu said.

The Governor looked still more doleful. "What's done is done. But the request you make of me is sheer madness."

"All I ask," Mathieu said impatiently, "is that you witness my oath abandoning my title and properties in favor of my legitimate successor, Victor de Montauban."

"You ask too much."

"Delacroix tells me that a title may be renounced only in the presence of the king, in France, or before his personal representative in a teritorial position. You are his viceroy here, Governor Charbert. I don't see why you should care what I do, but it's your official duty to hear my oath and to sign the documents Delacroix has prepared."

Charbert took the papers, shuffled them and slapped them on his desk. "Frenchmen shouldn't go into the hills. The sun is too hot. It twists the mind."

"I'm enjoying better health now than in many years. If you doubt me, I'll gladly submit to a medical examination."

The Governor studied him, and was forced to concede he had never seen the Count look more robust. He had been rather flabby for a tall, big-boned man, but was lean now, with the muscles in his biceps showing beneath the sleeves of his Madras shirt. The pouches that had been more pronounced beneath his eyes each year had vanished, and the whites of his eyes were clear.

"I hope," Charbert said, "you will forgive an impertinence. Not only does my duty require that I make this inquiry, but I have lived long enough in the East to have seen what sometimes happens to younger men. Is it possible that you have developed an appetite for the milk of the unripe poppy?"

Mathieu grinned. "I once experimented with opium in Calcutta, but it was very bitter and made me ill. I am not under the influence of drugs, Your Excellency." A sudden thought struck him and he laughed aloud. "Nor have I been placed under a spell by the Moslems who do tricks in the bazaars."

"I am distressed," Charbert announced unnecessarily as he pushed back his chair and stood. "I wonder if you realize how many men in France would gladly exchange places with you? Why, I myself have worked for almost forty years in the hope that some day I would earn a title. But it was my bad luck to be too young when the Emperor was giving them to his deserving followers. After all these years of loyal service I should be granted a title, but Louis-Philippe keeps the gates of his nobility closed. Not that I'm criticizing the King, you understand. It's just that he was always close-fisted, even when he was Duke of Orléans. Those who have always held grand titles don't know how much other men envy them!"

Mathieu made a futile attempt to interrupt.

The Governor was working himself into a rage. "You're even more guilty than the King. You don't see him abdicating, do you, in spite of all his troubles with the agitators in the working classes? Of course not! But you, who knew from birth that you would some day inherit an old and respected title—and properties worth God knows how many gold francs—you want to abandon your heritage."

"On the contrary," Mathieu said, "I'm hoping to find and nourish my real heritage."

Charbert had no idea what he meant, and glared at him.

Mathieu felt a sudden sympathy for the old man. "In my family, there are principles that have always been more important than position or wealth. We've tried to obey God's Commandments"—

"Go down the Boulevard and talk to the Jesuits!"

"I am not a Catholic, Your Excellency," Mathieu said, and anticipated the next question. "Nor am I a Calvinist, although I grew up in the Huguenot church."

Charbert reddened again. "I'm no clergyman, but I've never yet heard of an atheist who obeys God's Commandments!"

"There are many ways to seek Him, and Christianity doesn't provide the only roads."

The Governor sank into his chair, slumping, lost in thought. "You told me when you first came in that you returned from the hills a few days ago. May I ask where you've been?"

It would be simple enough for him to find out, and Mathieu saw no reason to be evasive. "I spent several weeks with a friend, a business associate."

Only natives owned homes in the hill country, and Charbert raised his head.

"Yes, he's an Indian," Mathieu said. "A Brahman."

"Now I suppose you'll tell me you've become a convert to Hindu rot!"

"No, there are many things in Brahmanism that I can't accept, now or ever," Mathieu said quietly. "But there are others worth exploring and contemplating."

The Governor was horrified. "I thought at first you were planning to stay in Pondicherry because of some woman, which would have been bad enough, but understandable." He groped for words. "This is outrageous!"

Mathieu needed Charbert as his witness, or his renunciation would not be valid. "My title has never meant anything to me," he explained, "so perhaps I'm the wretch you think me. My brothers and their wives have lived for years on the income from my vineyards, which I've preferred to regard as family property."

The Governor was speechless.

"I've spent all of my adult life at sea. I've sailed around the world three times, and I've known every pleasure. I've had more women than I care to remember, and once, in Egypt—" He broke off abruptly, and began again. "I've eaten so many rich foods and drunk so many strong liquors that my sense of taste has been destroyed. I've almost destroyed myself, but it isn't too late for me to make my peace with God."

"You're not yet forty!"

"I've lived a very long time."

"Go back to France and join a monastery. The Huguenots must have them, too."

Mathieu smiled. "They don't, but a monastery life is too ordered for me. I must create my own disciplines."

The Governor looked as uneasy as he felt.

"According to your standards, Your Excellency, it may be that I've lost my reason. If I have, I've begun to find my soul, which is infinitely more important."

Charbert could stand the tension no longer. He poured some gin into a glass, added several drops of an Indian berry elixir and downed the mixture in a single gulp.

"My wants are very simple," Mathieu continued. "I've enough clothes to last until the end of my days——"

"I can't allow a prominent subject of King Louis-Philippe to vanish into the interior of India. I demand to know where you intend to live!"

"I'll provide you with a map showing you the precise location of the pavilion, Your Excellency."

"Pavilion?"

"It belongs to my friend." Mathieu saw the Governor staring at him peculiarly, and added, "No, you attribute the wrong motives to me. He's literally a friend, nothing more, and I'll be alone there for ten months of the year."

"This becomes worse and worse." Charbert unfastened the collar of his tunic and groaned.

"I'll be growing more food than I'll be able to eat, and intend to give what I don't use to the people of a village in the vicinity. So, as you can see, Your Excellency, I'll be in no danger of starvation."

"There are poisonous snakes in the interior, and at least a dozen different kinds of insects and other creatures that can kill men. There's always a chance of sunstroke——"

"Last year," Mathieu interrupted, becoming very firm, "my clipper rode out two Pacific typhoons in less than a week, both of them violent. A few years ago in Constantinople—no, it was Athens—a Greek attacked me with a knife because I was having a drink with his woman." He bared his chest to reveal a long, jagged scar. "The assault was very unexpected, because I didn't know she had a lover. I escaped with only this scratch, which is more than I can say for the Greek."

Charbert used will power to prevent himself from taking another drink. The occasion called for sobriety and an accurate memory, so he could send a full report of this incredible conversation to the Minister of Colonial Affairs in Paris. "For the sake of argument, let's assume you're physically and mentally equipped to take care of yourself and avoid dangers. What if you become ill?"

Mathieu shrugged. "What happens when a sailor becomes ill in mid-ocean? We carry no physicians on board clipper ships. If it's a man's time to die, he will."

His visitor, the Governor thought, was beginning to sound like an Indian fatalist. Suddenly tired of the argument, he saw no reason to prolong it, but wanted to make certain he protected himself. His report would be studied with great care in Paris, and he had no desire to leave himself open to criticism. "I have just one more question. Suppose that in a year—or, more likely, six months—you grow weary of this hermit's life that appeals to you so much at present. Then what will you do? You'll have lost your ship, your vineyards, your title, everything! Where will you turn then?"

"I'm not as unrealistic or as scatter-brained as you think, Your Excellency. I've already considered the possibility that I may become disillusioned with a life that seems very attractive to me right now. I'm expert at several trades. And at the worst, I could work my passage back to France on a clipper."

That was what Charbert had wanted to hear. The imbecile was assuming full responsibility for his future, so the French government would have no financial burdens to bear.

"It would be almost worth seeing the expression on the face of

Victor's wife if I ever showed up again in Paris! How she'll crow when she becomes a countess. She's the kind who'll wear a coronet to bed."

Charbert could imagine precisely how the lucky woman would feel. Buttoning his collar, he stood saying solemnly, "I am prepared to hear you take the oath of renunciation. Think once again, my dear Count, before you take this step."

"I've made up my mind," Mathieu said, raising his right hand and placing his left on the Bible that the Governor pushed across the desk.

Mathieu knew he had been wrong to think that de Montaubans had been too short-sighted to realize that all men were murderers. As a small boy he had heard Grandpa admit it in so many words. A strange person, his grandfather, a silent, withdrawn man who had nursed a deep sorrow. Mathieu wished he had known Grandpa better. Now, of course, he would never find out why the first de Montauban to become an American had been so overwhelmed by grief.

The sun blazed in a cloudless sky, and the winds had vanished. The three-month monsoon season had come to an end at last, but the rains had been torrential. Mathieu, clad only in a pair of ragged trousers cut off at the knees, stood in calf-high water as he worked in the rice field. He had never realized that rice could suffer from too much water, and had been laboring from daybreak to sundown each day to save the crop. He had been eating breakfast before dawn, not touching food again until the coming of night sent him back up the gully to the pavilion. Every moment of daylight had been precious, and he had already discovered that a life of contemplation did not mean a life of ease.

His skin was as dark now as that of the natives in the village, some of whom had come to him out of curiosity and, at his invitation, had remained to share his evening rice, oil seeds and bamboo sprouts. Although illiterate, they were remarkably complex people, unknowingly reflecting both the wisdom and the crippling superstitions of their ancient civilization, and Mathieu enjoyed his talks with them. Oddly, he had been finding that their ignorance made him more humbly appreciative of the little learning he had managed to acquire in his lifetime.

Overall, he had no reason to regret his decision to retire to the Penner hills. His studies of Brahmanism still bewildered and irritated him, and some nights he was too tired to read by the light of the pavilion's only oil lamp. But he was learning patience, he was more alert both physically and mentally than he had even been, and he found he enjoyed living completely alone.

Only one unpleasant incident had marred his stay so far, and he should have known better. He was still a Westerner, and could not drink water as the Indians did, without boiling it. A violent illness that had incapacitated him for thirty-six hours had taught him a lesson he would not forget. Even though he was adopting some native ways, he would always bear in mind there were others he would be wise to avoid. And, he reminded himself, his mental conditioning had been that of a Frenchman, too. If he tried too completely to adopt the intellectual and moral attitudes of the Brahman, he might lose his way on the path he had chosen for himself.

It had already become evident to him that, although he had rejected the churches of Christianity, he still believed in the Holy Trinity of most Christian sects. His goal, therefore, was to utilize the techniques rather than the substance of Hinduism, to work toward a more perfect Christian understanding, faith and sense of union with God by way of the Hindu methods of detachment from the world and self-abnegation.

He realized, too, that, had he wished, he could have found ways to strive toward the same end within the varying frameworks of the Christian sects. But that would have been inconsistent with the rebelliousness in his own nature, his insistence on resisting any authority other than his own.

To an extent, he suspected, his revolt was childish. Since the age of eleven he had regarded Roman Catholicism as an oppressor, yet he had himself seen the compassionate, liberating work done by the Jesuits in Pondicherry. He had become contemptuous of Calvinism because of what he had interpreted as the weakness of the Huguenots when their church in Montauban had been closed. Yet he now knew that the tenacity of Huguenots throughout France had, in subsequent years, permitted Calvinism to survive and flourish.

What he enjoyed, perhaps, was the permissiveness of the Hindu faith. Every man was free to chart his own route to salvation, so the only rules the rebel was forced to obey were those of his own making, and if he found them uncomfortable, he could devise others. Was it possible, Mathieu wondered, that in retreating from Western society itself as well as from all of the obligations of organized Christianity, he was actually demonstrating a rather petulant weakness? He didn't know, but it was pleasant to realize he could take years to find out, even the rest of his life, if necessary.

Victor was an ass. If Mathieu suffered any one real regret, it was that the title had gone to a brother who substituted pomposity for dignity, and an unyieldingly rigid attitude toward humanity for true nobility.

487

Victor a count! In spite of his agony, Mathieu laughed, and thought it odd that he made no sound.

A signet ring bearing the "new" crest of the Counts of Montauban designed by Henry IV flashed on the finger of Victor de Montauban as he leafed through the daily *Journal des Débats*, pausing occasionally to sip his mid-morning coffee. His younger brother, Antoine, seated opposite him at a table in one of the sidewalk eating and drinking establishments that had become so popular in recent years, was equally engrossed in *La Presse*. Occasionally, when an attractive young woman walked past the table, Antoine looked up to catch a glimpse of her ankles beneath her skirts, but otherwise he did not move.

"The damned Socialists are godless," Victor muttered. "They reject the churches, the Crown—every institution worthy of preservation. They become louder in their demands for the vote, and it sickens me the way they hold out their hands for higher wages. There's an article here about a very dangerous radical named Louis Blanc, who not only admits he's an atheist, but actually believes the government should take over the ownership of all workshops. My God! I'd be expected to make a gift of the mill I bought two years ago—to the government, I suppose, or to my own employees. If Louis-Philippe and the churches don't stand firm against the Socialists, we're doomed."

Antoine grunted.

"Must you read that damned sensation-exploiting newspaper? It does you no credit as an aristocrat to be seen looking at it in public. You should read the *Journal*."

Antoine slowly lowered his newspaper, and looked scornfully at his older brother. "As it happens, I was reading something of concern to both of us. *La Presse* often reprints articles from London."

"The Socialists there are as impertinent as our own. I refuse to upset myself."

"This is about India. Moslems and Hindus rioted in Madras for three days, and nobody knows how many died before British troops and the East India's Company's mercenaries were able to restore order. The reports reaching London say that hundreds, perhaps thousands, were killed or wounded."

Victor poured himself more coffee, and added a liberal quantity of cream. "I have enough troubles right here at home to worry about. It will be another two years before my mill pays off the original investment and starts showing a profit."

"Madras isn't far from Pondicherry."

Victor wasn't listening.

"And we have only a token garrison in our colony. *La Presse* quotes someone at the Ministry of Colonial Affairs. He says we keep just enough troops in the town of Pondicherry to evacuate French citizens by sea if trouble develops there. The Moslems and Hindus of the East hate each other, so there's always the danger of an eruption anywhere."

"If the editors of *La Presse* are just becoming aware of the religious feuds in India," Victor said sarcastically, "they're even less well informed than I've always thought them."

Antoine carefully folded his newspaper and placed it on the far side of the table. "Apparently you've forgotten that Mathieu is living among Hindus somewhere in Pondicherry."

Victor's smile was very thin. "I've been told there are Hindus who torture themselves with metal instruments, but feel nothing. I trust that Mathieu has learned the art from them."

"My God!"

"Why should you be so shocked, Antoine? Mathieu elected to live his own life and accept its hazards."

"If it weren't for him—" Antoine tugged at his mustache. "You do call yourself a Christian, Victor?"

"I'm in no mood for one of your Catholic sermons this morning. The Socialist conspiracies in my mill need all my attention, so let Mathieu look after himself."

"Papa and Mama were Huguenots, and they had consciences. I know of nothing in Calvinism that rejects Christ's command to love your neighbor."

"If you insist on citing Scriptures, I am—literally—not my brother's keeper."

"Very witty, Victor. You're always clever. But your humor does nothing for Mathieu."

Thoroughly aroused, Victor de Montauban swung around in his chair to face his younger brother. "What can I do for Mathieu? What can anyone, including the Governor of Pondicherry, do for him? If you'll remember, Annette and I entertained that pompous old fool, Governor Charbert, when he came home from India after his retirement last year. You were right there at the dinner table, in my house."

"In what was once Mathieu's house," Antoine murmured.

Victor ignored the comment. "You heard Charbert say that no one is able to help Mathieu. For six years—seven, now—he's chosen to live like an Indian native. If he should ever come home, may the good Lord spare us the agony, it would be my duty to have him committed to an asylum."

Antoine laughed savagely. "Which you'd do immediately, for fear he might try to reclaim the title from you."

"I have friends in the judiciary." Victor spoke a little too quickly. "His renunciation is binding."

"Mathieu has no more interest in the title than I have, I'm certain. I'm relieved that I don't come to Paris often, Victor. It's enough that I rent the vineyards from you—and pay you an outrageous fee for the privilege."

"Buy some of your own, if that's the way you feel."

"That's exactly what I'm going to do when our agreement expires." Antoine tucked his newspaper under his arm, threw a coin onto the table and stood. "There, I've paid for the coffee. I don't like to be in your debt."

"You needn't be insulting."

"Mathieu is your brother as well as mine. I realize there's nothing either of us can do for him, and unless he's changed drastically, I'm sure he'd accept no help. But I feel desperately sorry for him, and I'm heartsick. He's an alien in a far place, caught between the hatreds of religious fanatics. Pretend he doesn't exist, if that makes it easier for you to sleep under the crest on the head of your bed. But I know what I'm going to do. I'm going to Notre-Dame, right now, to pray for his safety!"

Everyone in the family, no matter what his religion, recalled with pride the great Bishop de Montauban who had defied King Louis XIV. Until now, Mathieu had always been in awe of him, but now everything was different. How odd he had never understood that the bishop had not sought death, that he had probably loved life. Mathieu wanted to weep for him, but the tears refused to come.

There were two figures in the little shrine near the village water hole, both very old. One was a stone idol representing Śiva. It was chipped in places, but its face and ornate costume were repainted in pure white twice each year, the work being done with great care by residents whom a majority considered nimble and careful. Beside it stood a cylindrical block of stone, resting on a circular slab, neither of them carved or decorated. Everyone respected Śiva's reproductive power, and families who wanted children had placed token offerings on the slab, among them a few grains of rice, a bean or two, a perfectly formed oil-seed. Even the most ignorant and superstitious of the natives realized that Śiva was so powerful he needed no food, and that the offering was intended only as a sign of respect. It was essential that everyone grasp the principle, in fact, for the villagers themselves seldom had enough to eat.

Mathieu de Montauban squatted with some of the men in a semi-circle before the shrine. They were at ease, accepting him after seven and one-half years, and he was equally at home with them, aware that he was not one of them, but pleased that they no longer regarded him as a freak or an alien. The men said nothing, and he politely respected their silence, waiting for more than a quarter of an hour before he spoke.

"There are flowers, many flowers, at Śiva's feet today," he said.

No one contradicted the observation, and a few of the men nodded.

"I have never before seen flowers offered to Śiva." Mathieu knew he had to proceed cautiously, one small step at a time. He kept discovering traditions and customs of Hinduism that surprised him, but had learned he would be rebuffed if his questions were too blatant.

"We have made no offerings of flowers for many years," one of the elders said, after due consideration.

"They are white," Mathieu observed.

"Yes."

He tried again, patiently. "White is also the color of Śiva, for he is pure."

The elder thought for a time. "White is also the color of strength."

It was Mathieu's turn to nod. "There is no god stronger than Śiva."

One of the younger men stirred. "That strength is needed," he said in a deep voice.

Mathieu knew better than to say anything or look at the speaker inquiringly. The villagers soon would begin volunteering information.

"Śiva," another of the men declared, "will protect us."

It was the elder's turn. "Two days ago the Moslems attacked a village of our cousins." He pointed in the direction of the hills.

The assault, Mathieu realized, had taken place on the British side of the border, but that meant nothing. Only the Europeans recognized the boundaries they themselves had created; Indians knew no such lines of demarcation.

"Two girls and a boy-child who were working in the rice fields hid themselves and escaped," the man with the deep voice said. "All the others in the village were slaughtered."

"They had offered no white flowers to Śiva," another added.

Mathieu remembered that Krishna Mahishasura had told him, when they had last seen each other several months earlier, that a large band of Moslems had conducted a spectacularly successful raid on a British arsenal in Tiruchirappalli, the largest garrison town across the border of French Pondicherry. They had stolen several hundred rifles and bayonets, along with considerable supplies of ammunition and gunpowder. The British had braced for immediate trouble, but the thieves had vanished, apparently having decided it would be wise not to show themselves for a time. Now, it seemed, they had struck.

"Śiva," the elder said in a voice trembling with anger, "will destroy the Moslems!"

491

It would not be inappropriate, Mathieu decided, to ask one question. "What are you doing to protect yourselves?"

The men looked at him in surprise, their expressions indicating that he was an alien after all. "We have offered white flowers to Śiva," the deep-voiced man said patiently.

Mathieu knew that Hindu warriors were among the most ferocious fighting men on earth, but only the men of certain castes and sects were soldiers. The system was so maddeningly complex, so steeped in the ritualism of tradition that he found it difficult to understand, but he was impatient with the passivity of Indians who would not resort to physical violence in self-defense. "Śiva protects the warriors who fight in his name," he said pointedly.

The elder, a man who had never learned to write his name, who used methods thousands of years old to till his small plot of land and who had never traveled more than five miles from his village, looked at the Frenchman. "Those who have been marked by Śiva in this incarnation carry arms and fight for the *raj*." He spoke politely, without censure, and if there was condescension in his tone, he showed it by displaying a trace of pity.

Did a man need greater moral and physical courage to die for his beliefs, as Bishop de Montauban had done, or to go off into exile and create a totally new kind of life? Most people would undoubtedly say that dying required far greater courage, yet everyone died, sooner or later. It was far harder to break all of one's ties with the past. Mathieu had made that discovery himself. But the secret was his alone, and he wouldn't share it with anyone. He couldn't, and the knowledge made him hysterical, yet his inner core remained supremely, strangely calm.

The empty bowls were cleaned, and the two friends sat facing each other in the pavilion, ready at last for a conversation after their long months of separation.

"You look well, as always," Krishna said.

"So do you." Mathieu waited for the other to take the initiative, always remembering, when Krishna was present, that he was a guest in the man's home.

"You have made progress in your study of the Absolute?"

Mathieu had learned to observe the circumlocutious Indian amenities, but he had so much on his mind that he reverted to his old European ways. "Frankly, I've been too busy. I've spent several hours every day going up into the hills to keep watch for the enemy."

"Enemy?" Krishna looked pained.

"Surely you heard of the Moslem attack on the village eleven miles from here about eight months ago! If I'd thought you hadn't known of it, I'd have made the journey into Pondicherry to tell you."

"I knew. Everyone knew." Krishna's face remained impassive. "A battalion of East India Company mercenaries saw and chased them, so they have gone elsewhere to slaughter the innocent before they return here."

"How can you be so calm?" Mathieu demanded. "They murder Hindus with no feeling. A Frenchwoman in Pondicherry is at least annoyed when she kills mosquitos and flies, but from the descriptions the villagers have given me, Moslems cut down anyone—an old man, a little child—in cold blood."

"The hatred of Moslem for Hindu and Hindu for Moslem is very old."

"Why do they hate?"

"Why do the men of any two faiths hate? Not until Vishnu grants them enlightenment do they begin to find their way to Brahmā."

"I wish you'd be more specific, Krishna. I've grown fond of the people in the village, and I'd like to do what I can to help them."

"Siva will protect them."

"So they say," Mathieu replied with a trace of bitterness. "And they may die believing it."

"Have you forgotten what you have studied in the *Chhandogya Upanishad*, my friend? There is no evil in death, which leads to the next incarnation if one has striven——"

"No lectures this evening, Krishna. I still don't understand how the Moslems can be so fanatical—and yet so devoid of feeling."

"When a people has spent centuries killing those it hates, those murders are reduced to a symbolism, a ritual. Did the Greeks have feeling when they slaughtered sheep at the altars of their gods?"

"I imagine they felt a religious exaltation of sorts."

"That is what the Moslem feels, perhaps, when he rides through a Hindu village with his sword in his hand."

"Why do these feuds flare up?"

"Men who have not purged themselves of evil do evil. When I was a child, we lived for a time in Tanjore, where the population is mixed, the greater part Hindu, the lesser Moslem. One day mobs swept through the streets, burning the homes of the Moslems, and there was so much violence that my sisters and brothers and I were kept at home. Later we heard there had been a senseless argument in the market-place between a Hindu and a Moslem. No one could remember the real cause of the dispute, and my father heard twenty versions of the fight. My older brother, who was killed by the Moslems the very next year, came home with still more." Krishna spoke without rancor.

"I hadn't known you lost a brother that way." Mathieu looked at his friend. "You feel no bitterness?"

"When the smoke from his funeral pyre had ascended to the heavens, I put him out of my mind. If we meet again in another life on this earth, perhaps we will recognize each other." Krishna adjusted the wick of the oil lamp, turning it higher. "The Moslems were very angry after the burnings at Tanjore, and raided many villages in the vicinity. The Hindus of Tanjore have not forgotten, and some day there will be more riots. It may be, as the British believe, that the Hindus are responsible for the unrest in that area. In other places it is the Moslems. But it doesn't matter. Evil flourishes until man purges himself through an understanding of the Divine Spirit."

"I suppose," Mathieu said, "that there's no place on earth free of religious feuds. Any two men who hold different beliefs become suspicious of each other."

"If you assume that the differences in faith of the Hindu and Moslem separate one from the other, you may be wrong."

"I can't accept that."

"You still speak with the tongue of Europe, Mathieu. Hear me before you close your mind. As India measures time, Islam is new to this world. It was only twelve hundred years ago that Mohammed died. It may be true that when his first followers came to India, it was they who first attacked the Brahmans. You have visited the Ottomans in your travels, so you know their ways."

"There's no doubt," Mathieu said, "that the devout Moslem feels a fanatical hatred for those who don't believe as he does. All outsiders are infidels, and should be killed—or reduced to an inferior position, preferably that of slaves. Of all the major faiths I've encountered, I'd say Mohammedanism is the least civilized."

"That may be because it is so young. The faiths of the Hindu and the Buddhist are very old. Confucius lived only twenty-three hundred years ago, of course, but his followers have merely incorporated his beliefs into a far older tradition. You Christians are also young, but your heritage is the ancient one of the Jews. It may be that the older a faith, the more tolerant its members become."

"That's an interesting theory, but it would be hard to prove," Mathieu said, "and it certainly doesn't advance your claim that the feud of the Moslem and the Hindu isn't based on religion."

Krishna looked at him in surprise. "You have spent more than eight years in our midst, and yet you continue to hear with the ears of the West. Hatred breeds hatred, violence causes counter-violence. Perhaps the Moslem first killed the Hindu as a non-believer, but who can say for certain that this is so? It is enough that the man who has not yet found Brahmā and Vishnu is filled with the hates of this world. The Moslem kills the Hindu because it is his tradition. The

Hindu in the city riots against the Moslem because the presence of the alien has made him uneasy for generations."

"Then there's no real hope for the realization of Christ's vision of peace on earth, is there?"

"He who lives without hope lacks faith. At some other time, in a future life, it may be that he will gain it."

The infinite patience of the Brahman was still beyond Mathieu's ability to grasp.

"I know how you sometimes are ready to give in to despair, so I have brought you something that may help you to realize you are more advanced on the path to an understanding of the Divine Spirit than you know." Krishna reached inside his loose-fitting tunic and drew out a pamphlet, printed in English. "This was sent to me by my brother who lives in Madras. His opinion of the European is not high, and he wished to influence my thinking."

The pamphlet was called, *The Communist Manifesto*, and had been published in January of the same year, 1848. Mathieu glanced through it, and saw it was an invitation to battle. The closing paragraphs he found particularly strident:

> Communists disdain to conceal their views and aims.
> They openly declare that their ends can be attained only by the forcible overthrow of all existing social conditions. Let the ruling classes tremble at a Communistic revolution. The proletarians have nothing to lose but their chains.
> They have a world to win.
> Working-men of all countries, unite!

Mathieu handed the pamphlet to Krishna. "I'd be the last to deny there's hate in Europe. I'd hoped to find peace here."

"One man cannot create peace for another. Each must travel his own route."

"I'm still enough of a Christian to believe that men must work for it together."

The Indian was silent for a few moments. "You no longer have worldly resources of your own——"

"I don't need them."

"——and I sometimes feel I am responsible. Perhaps you would like to spend some time at my house in the city. My family and I would welcome you there."

"You've done more than enough for me, Krishna."

"But you would like to go to the city for a few months, a year, perhaps?"

Mathieu shook his head in surprise.

"It is wrong for one man to enter into the thoughts and heart of another. But I am wondering whether you would not find greater tranquility there until the British find the Moslem band that stole the arms, and defeat it in battle."

Mathieu grinned.

"Even those who are close to the gods in their understanding are sometimes prey to fear. Only Siva is lacking in the fears of mortals."

"Don't worry about me," Mathieu said. "I certainly don't look forward to a visit of Moslem horsemen to the village, but I'll be satisfied if we can work out some kind of warning system in time for people to scatter. I'm not afraid for myself."

"That might be imprudent."

"No, I'm willing to take my chances. I've had dealings with Moslems, and I can take care of myself."

For centuries the family had been preoccupied with the unholy disease of religious prejudice. What a waste! Never, in this world, would men stop hating each other, and it was as foolish to raise a hand to halt them as it was ridiculous to believe that such efforts could stem the spread of the plague. An intelligent man could do only one thing: withdraw from the world. But that, too, was a waste. Mathieu knew now that once one was committed to life, one was compelled to accept its problems. Bleakly, vaguely, he realized that the very knowledge was useless. If only the interminable pain would stop, he might share his discovery. But—with whom? He had no idea.

In 1848 a series of revolutions erupted, more or less simultaneously, all over Europe. From France to the Balkans, Scandinavia to the Mediterranean, men who clamored for the right to vote, for better working conditions and an end to serfdom resorted to physical violence in an attempt to attain the freedom they demanded.

Almost inevitably, churches were attacked, looted and burned. In blind fury mobs struck at Roman Catholic, Lutheran and Calvinist houses of worship. Protestant clergymen prudently vanished from Prague and Copenhagen, Budapest and Brussels. In Paris and Warsaw, Vienna and Palermo, Catholic priests went into hiding. So frenzied were the throngs that in Rome a cardinal who had been working for greater tolerance and liberty was murdered, and Pope Pius IX, the most liberal pontiff in many years, had to flee from Vatican Hill.

By 1849 the revolts had been smashed, the troops of established authorities had restored order and the rebels had been either scattered or punished. In most nations the voting franchise was extended and better working conditions were granted. But the gutted, charred remains of churches still stood as a reminder of the year of terror.

496

"We've been asked to contribute to a special church rebuilding fund," Victor de Montauban said, "but this time the Huguenot pastors are going too far. If they had taught their parishioners to respect God and man, the idiocy wouldn't have happened."

"Pope Pius has set up a fund, too," his brother, Antoine replied. "And I don't agree with you—as usual. I've given all I can afford. I believe Pius is right when he says the employer and laborer will come together through the churches."

"Rot! I've told our pastor he'll never get another sou from me until he bars the door to radicals. And if you ask me, Rome should excommunicate every rioter who claims to be a Catholic!"

Antoine knew it was useless to pursue the argument. There were prominent men of every faith who sought vengeance against the rebels, as Victor did, and people would continue to suffer until they realized that, as Thomas Jefferson had written in America three-quarters of a century earlier, all men had been created equal.

He was the last of the de Montaubans, and the realization made him panicky. There was so much still to be done. He had been wrong to think that the tide of hate could not be stemmed. The pain had robbed him of his reason, but now he was thinking with surprising clarity. It was essential that he continue the fight. Without him— well, there was Antoine, of course. He had almost forgotten Antoine. And it occurred to him that in every generation someone had clung to the hope that another would snatch up the sword and carry it into battle. But that wasn't the way to fight for peace and good will. To achieve that distant goal, swords had to be beaten into plowshares, he supposed.

The sky turned from blue-black to gray, dawn broke quickly, and soon the Penner Mountains were bathed in the glow of the rising sun. Mathieu had already eaten his breakfast and spent an hour meditating, but felt no relief from the depression in which he had been immersed for almost two years. The worst of his problem was that he had no concrete idea why he was so restless and gloomy.

He had no desire to return to his own people, nor would he accept the invitation of Krishna to spend some time in Pondicherry. After living alone for almost ten years, he had formed habits that would be hard to break, that he was reluctant to break. He reassured himself that he was not a hermit, thanks to his twice-weekly trips into the village, as well as the two months of each year that he and Krishna spent together. The mystery was one of many he could not understand.

He buckled on his belt, hitched up his sun-faded trousers and started out toward the rice field.

Before he reached the lip of the gully, the riders swept down toward the pavilion. Mathieu heard the thumping of their horses' hoofs, and turned just as a rifle cracked, spinning him around.

The pain in his side was excruciating, but he planted his feet apart and retained his balance. He had lived through just such a scene in his imagination, and had planned carefully for it. "*Salaam aleikum*," he called in Arabic. "Peace be unto you."

The roar of another rifle drowned his words, and he collapsed onto the ground as the galloping horses crushed him.

Mathieu's last thoughts were blurred. Why had this happened to him, who had done the Moslems no harm?

1868

Joseph Victor de Montauban was far younger than his one surviving uncle, Antoine, but he was the titular head of the family, so he led the procession from the comfortably furnished great hall of the castle to the graveyard that extended to the edge of the old moat. The gentlemen were dressed in black for the occasion, carrying their high hats in the crooks of their left arms, and there was no sound except the rustle of the ladies' dark taffeta skirts.

The pastor's graveside ceremony was mercifully brief, and his address was more of a summation than a funeral oration. Mathieu de Montauban had slept for eighteen years, he said, in a plot behind the Huguenot church in distant Pondicherry. God's will had prevented his cremation by the Hindu natives who had fled from their village, warned by the rifle shots that had killed him. He had been a strange, solitary man, and of all the members of the family who were present, only his brother, Antoine, had known him. To the others he had been only a myth.

But he had been a count of Montauban, and now he had come home at last.

The ladies kissed Antoine, lightly, and the gentlemen shook his hand before the entire family adjourned to the great hall for refreshments. Joseph Victor, ever conscious of the proprieties and of his own position, waited until the ladies retired before accepting a drink from one of the servants and lighting his cigar.

"This," he said heavily, his voice and manner like those of his late father, "has been a day we'll never forget."

Antoine, choked anew by long-buried griefs, looked at him in surprise. Earlier in the day he had attempted to explain to all the family that Mathieu had tried, in his own odd way, to come to terms with God, and that no one would ever know whether he had succeeded. Joseph Victor had appeared indifferent, and his sudden display of sensitivity was unusual.

"Mark it in black on your calendars," Joseph Victor said. "The world we've known is falling apart. In the United States the enemies of Andrew Johnson have placed him on trial. Think of it, impeaching the chief of state. That senile priest, Pius the Ninth, has called a General Council of ecclesiastics to discuss the issue of papal infallibility, and I can't for the life of me understand how a vote of his bishops will decide anything at all." He drew on his cigar. "And in England the House of Commons has given the Prime Ministership to Disraeli, a Jew."

EPILOGUE

"Hey, Viv!" a photographer shouted, and the crowd of newsmen waiting at the entrance to New York's West 48th Street pier surged forward.

Two lethargic groups of pickets came to life, and marched in solemn, ragged silence on either side of the busy entrance. The members of one were dressed in faded, striped concentration camp pajamas, with the Star of David prominently displayed on the left breast. Most were middle-aged and shuffled wearily, their faces devoid of expression as they held aloft their placards and signs:

VIV=NAZI
THERE IS NO ROOM IN AMERICA FOR RACIAL HATRED
VIVIENNE DE MONTAUBAN, GO HOME!

The other group was considerably younger, made up in the main of girls and boys in their teens, all neatly dressed, while two priests stood in the background, neither trying to make himself particularly inconspicuous. The signs carried by the youngsters were equally pungent:

C.Y.O. CONDEMNS "VIV"
BAN THE BIGOT
DE MONTAUBAN, A NAME OF SHAME

Other taxis and private cars were pulling to a halt before the huge covered-shed, and most of the people hurrying into the building paid scant attention to the pickets. Twenty or more uniformed policemen, the majority themselves Jewish or Irish Catholic, treated the pickets with gentle good humor. "Keep moving," they called.

The taxi door opened, and photographers' flashbulbs began to pop as a pair of long, shapely legs emerged beneath a very short skirt. A throng of reporters converged on the slender blonde in the chic traveling suit, making it difficult for two longshoremen to remove a huge mound of luggage from the automobile.

"What's your answer to these demonstrators, Viv?" a reporter called.

Another jostled for position. "In your last TV interview, night before last, you said the religious revival of the past twenty years is phoney. Then you claimed you were misquoted. Just exactly what did you mean?"

Vivienne de Montauban, looking young, helpless and naïve for a controversial French author of thirty, pushed back her hair, bracelets jangling. "Please," she said, "I must attend to my luggage."

"What do you say about all those sermons last Sunday, Viv?"

"What's your reaction to the boycott by the organized churches, temples and synagogues of the United States?"

"I'm delighted," the young woman said, her French accent slightly more pronounced because she was irritated. "The boycott makes a mockery of your supposed freedom of speech and the press, and will sell a great many more copies of my book."

A perspiring man in a topcoat had managed to shoulder his way through the crowd. "Miss de Montauban will hold a press conference in her suite on the ship!" he shouted. "She'll answer all your questions then. So give her a chance to go on board, will you?"

One of the longshoremen plowed through the throng of newspaper men and women, and vanished into the building.

Vivienne was disturbed. "He gave me no ticket for my baggage!"

"You won't need it," the public relations man in the topcoat replied as he took her arm and tried to clear a path for her.

A conservatively dressed couple were forced to make a detour around the knot of people. "Who's that?" the man demanded.

"I saw her on the Teddy Fuller show the other night," his wife said. She's the one who wrote, *If I Were God."*

The man made a wry face and turned away. "Just our luck to be sailing with her."

Vivienne caught sight of the picket lines and halted.

The publicity man tugged in vain at her arm. "Don't stop," he whispered. "Keep walking."

She planted her feet apart, tossed back her hair to reveal outrageously long earrings, and deliberately bestowed a scornful smile on the pickets, who returned her gaze stonily.

Again the photographers' cameras were busy.

The public relations man managed to propel her forward again, the reporters and photographers surrounding them.

"Why do you hate the Jews?" a woman reporter with a strong German accent called.

"I don't," Vivienne replied as they trooped into an elevator.

"In your book you renewed the charge that the Jews made no resistance when the Nazis hauled them off to extermination camps," the woman reporter said. "How do you explain Warsaw?"

In the confines of the elevator, there was no escape. "Later, please," the public relations man said.

Vivienne ignored him. "If you read *If I Were God,"* she said acidly, "you would see that I give the Jews full credit for the Battle of the Warsaw Ghetto. It was a show of great courage against impossible odds."

"But the others you hate, just like Hitler!" The woman was becoming overwrought. "They came for us, my husband and me, at two o'clock in the morning. What could we do against eight of those bullies?"

"Nothing," Vivienne replied quickly. "That wasn't the time for resistance. If it had been organized earlier, six million Jews might not have been slaughtered."

504

"My God!" the woman said, just as the elevator door opened and the entire party disgorged onto the concrete of the main floor of the pier.

"Are you sure my baggage is safe?" Vivienne asked the public relations man. "I bought a new typewriter, and a wig——"

"Stop worrying, honey," he assured her.

A reporter closed in on her other side. "Why do you call cardinals stupid old men?"

"You misquote me!" she retorted. "If you would only read, *If I Were God*, there wouldn't be all this silly fuss. I said they are stupidly short-sighted. The pill is a fact of life, the confessional is no solution to the bomb, and changing the Mass from Latin is five hundred years too late."

"Give her a breather," the publicity man begged. "Let her check in."

Two policemen halted the newspaper people, and Vivienne went alone to the booth where she surrendered her passage ticket and passport. But the photographers and reporters were waiting for her when she walked toward the gangplank.

"Bishop Smith of the Episcopalians says you're totally immoral," one of them said. "How about that?"

Only four or five of the newsmen were near enough to hear her reply as she made her way across the covered gangplank. "I've never gone to bed with him, so how would he know?"

The public relations man wiped his face with a handkerchief. Here was another of her flippant comments that would land on the front page of hundreds of newspapers, and would do her no good. He had been specifically warned by the American publisher of *If I Were God* not to allow her to indulge in off-the-cuff wisecracks, which invariably hurt the sale of her book, but she was incorrigible, and as nearly as he could judge, literally didn't care.

Personal luggage was piled high around the base of the first-class passengers' staircase, and Vivienne halted to search for her belongings.

Two sympathetic stewards in white coats came forward to help her, but the newspaper reporters and photographers swept them aside.

"Viv," a woman in the group said, "tell us straight out what you have against Baptists and Methodists."

Vivienne was hunting in vain for her luggage. "I neither like nor dislike them. I doubt if any of my friends are either." She turned and glared at the reporters, who were laughing. "That was not intended as humor. I've written in my book that I believe there is no place in the modern world for Protestant sects. The conditions that caused Luther and Knox and Calvin and Hus and Wycliffe and all the others to reject Catholicism no longer exist." She spoke very rapidly.

"Not so fast," called someone who was taking notes.

She continued to speak at the same clip. "There is no longer a Reformation in progress. Or a Counter-Reformation. Or a counter-counter-Reformation. Roman Catholicism, against which so many religious leaders—and the common people themselves—of the Renaissance were in revolt, has been impotent for several hundred years. And the Protestant churches have become forces of theological ultra-conservatism that fail in their attempts to reconcile God and man."

Longshoremen were heaping still more luggage on the pile, but were hampered by Vivienne and her escorts.

Assistant pursers on the S.S. France were trained to deal smoothly with any emergency. One of them, trim in his blue uniform, loomed at Vivienne's elbow. "You will find that your baggage has already been delivered to your cabins, Mademoiselle de Montauban."

Vivienne reluctantly turned away, and, with the public relations man still trying feebly to halt the running interview, started off down Main Deck.

"Why did you refuse the challenge of that panel of evangelists to a debate?" a reporter at the rear of the group shouted.

"I am an author, not a pseudo-clergyman."

"Are you saying that evangelists are fakes?"

"I'll stand by my original statement."

They had reached the suite, and the public relations man was relieved to see that his assistant was waiting at the bar that had been set up in the corner. "Drinks on us," he called jovially.

Vivienne hurried into the adjoining cabin, then beckoned him furiously. "Some of my things are here, but not my typewriter or wig case. If they are missing, I'll sue—"

"Relax, honey. I guarantee they'll show up. Now, get back out there and talk to those vultures. But lay off the wisecracks, will you? For everybody's sake?"

She hastily repaired her appearance with comb, powder and a pale lipstick. "I'll attend to my relations with journalists," she said coldly. "And you will serve a far more effective function if you find my missing baggage." She was smiling as she returned to the larger cabin.

Several photographers began to clamor for poses.

Masses of Vivienne's hair fell forward when she shook her head. "I'm not a cinema actress, gentlemen. You may take as many photographs as you please, while we talk, but I refuse to pose." She sat in a chair near the twin portholes, and the reporters scrambled for the remaining seats.

"Do you want to make a statement?" the public relations man's assistant asked.

Vivienne winked conspiringly at the reporters. "They think, these men who are hired to act as buffers between you and me, that all of us are cretins. Very well. My newest book, *Si j'étais Dieu, If I Were God*, has been published simultaneously in France and this country. It will soon be published also in England and elsewhere. It expresses my honest opinions and my firm convictions. Apparently no one ever tires of asking me the same questions repeatedly, but I can stand it if you can." She smiled broadly.

"Is it true," one reporter asked, "that you believe the translation into English was botched?"

"That's too harsh. I wish I had done the translation myself. Take, for example, the subtle difference in the opening sentence of the book. In French here is how it reads. *'Si j'étais Dieu, je m'en moquerais des chrétiens, je disrais aux juifs, Qui vous a mis en tête que je vous ai choisis?'* In the English edition, it reads, 'If I were God, I would laugh at the Christians, and would ask the Jews, What makes you think I chose you?' There is one discrepancy. God does not laugh at the Christians. As I wrote the line, he scoffs at them. There is a difference."

"Would you explain the subtlety, please?" someone called.

"If God were to laugh, it would be necessary for Him to be endowed with an extraordinary sense of humor. Of course, if we accept the thesis that He created man, He has already demonstrated His humor for all Eternity, but I believe it unlikely that Christians would amuse Him."

Several of the reporters noted that the cigarette Vivienne took from her handbag was French, as was her lighter.

"Do you consider yourself a disciple of the God-is-dead school of theology?"

"I am a disciple of no school. I have my own views, and the Protestant clergymen who advocate the God-is-dead philosophy are articulate men who need no help from me."

"Are you a follower of Sartre and Simone de Beauvoir?"

Vivienne stared coldly at the questioner. "I am a follower of no one. I believe myself sufficiently adult to have drawn my own metaphysical conclusions."

"Then you're an atheist—or an agnostic."

"Why must you Americans pin labels on everyone?"

The reporter gulped the rest of his highball and reddened. "Well, there's been a lot of talk that you're a Red."

"I am not a Communist, nor have been, nor will be," Vivienne said crisply. "If religion in Karl Marx' day was as stultifying as it is today, I can't blame him for calling it the opiate of the masses. I have no interest in politics, however."

Someone started to ask another question.

Vivienne held up her hand. "One moment. In my opinion the state-inspired atheism of the European Communist nations is only skin-deep. The superstitions and myths of centuries are not eliminated overnight, or even in decades. When you have nothing better to do, glance through the interviews and public addresses of Nikita Khrushchev during the years he was head of the Russian government and Communist party. You'll be astonished to see how often he invoked the name of God. And why do you think the Communists in China have been having such violent upheavals? The people there are reluctant to abandon their religions."

A young woman standing near the bar called, "What do you think of American men?"

"Really!" Vivienne jumped to her feet impatiently, and dashed out into the passageway to search for her missing baggage.

The reporters and photographers doggedly chased her, much to the dismay of the public relations assistant.

There was bedlam at the stairwell. Longshoremen were still carrying mountains of luggage on board the *S.S. France,* stewards were trying to whisk the baggage to staterooms, and clots of passengers, their relatives and friends were blocking the passages. Vivienne plunged into the maelstrom as an assistant purser made an attempt to head her off, while the newspaper people added to the confusion.

Vivienne snatched a portable typewriter, in its case, from a pile of luggage, and a steward made a valiant effort to retrieve it. They became involved in a bitter dispute, which ended only when the steward, after raising his voice, managed to prove that the machine belonged to a man from Chicago named Cook.

Vivienne accepted defeat with a show of temper, and retreated down the passageway, the reporters closing in around her. The air-conditioning vents hissed gently, there was a simultaneous babble of voices, and no one could understand what anyone else was saying. When they surged back into the suite, the public relations assistant was waiting with a fresh round of drinks, and a semblance of decorum was restored.

But Vivienne, still concerned about her typewriter, stood in the little corridor at the suite's entrance, peering out.

"You're called an anti-Christ," a young newsman said. "Do you accept the charge?"

She didn't bother to look around. "Could you be more specific?"

"Yes, I read in a magazine article last week that you're trying to block the spread of Christianity to the newly-emerging lands of Africa and Asia."

Vivienne spun around, laughing heartily. "Read my chapter on missionaries." Most of the faces were blank. "I wish I could take credit for this concept, but I have no objection to borrowing from others when an idea is good. The missionaries are wasting their time and the money of the faithful. Christianity can't and won't succeed in either Africa or Asia."

Some of the reporters were writing notes, scribbling furiously.

"In virtually all art work," she went on, "Christ is depicted as white. Historically, of course, I dare say he was, but the arrogance of the churches, both Protestant and Catholic, are beyond belief. People who have been subservient to the white man for generations and whose hatred for him is irrationally intense have no intention of worshipping a white God. The storm I created proves that the established authorities of the Christian churches are incapable of accepting good advice. I merely told them that if they wanted to succeed in equatorial Africa, they should show Christ in blackface and tribal dress. Isn't that sensible?"

The public relations man, collar wilted, arrived with the typewriter.

Vivienne snatched it from him, and carried it with her to the chair near the portholes.

A gong sounded in the distance, and a metallic voice on the ship's public address system requested visitors to leave.

The reporters ignored the warning. "You have a relative who's a cardinal," one of them began.

"He's my cousin, and he's a bishop."

"You have another cousin who is the president of some Protestant league of churches——"

"My uncle."

"What do they think of *If I Were God?*"

"I can say," Vivienne declared, "without fear of contradiction—that they haven't read it." She smiled, but those who were nearest to her saw no humor in her eyes.

"They don't agree with you?"

"We haven't discussed the subject, but I'm quite positive they don't."

"That winds us up," the public relations man called.

"Just one more question," a reporter said. "Miss de Montauban, what beneficial effects do you think the Vatican Council will have?"

"None," Vivienne replied flatly.

"Can you elaborate on that?"

"All the way across the Atlantic, and on a far slower ship than the *France*. To boil it down, the old men who met in Rome meant well, but what they did was too little and it comes too late. The other old men, the Protestants, have applauded politely. Now they're talking. They'll literally talk themselves to death. The world is sitting on an atomic time bomb, and all they can do is make pompous statements to each other. My generation is sick of talk. We need action! And if we don't get it in religion, we'll find our own substitutes for it!"

The Bishop poured coffee into two demi-tasse cups, and the Count, standing before the hearth in the library, measured pale cognac into bell glasses. "You're the theologian of the family, Charles. Do you think there's any chance of resolving our doctrinal differences?"

"Of course. If I didn't, if the Church didn't, the Council would have been an exercise in futility. I'm not saying we can achieve a reconciliation rapidly or easily, or that it will come in our lifetime. But it will come, because it must."

"I'm thinking of the positions taken by some Protestant sects, for example, on the Virgin Mary. Their stand and that of the Catholics would appear to be irreconcilable."

"Perhaps we won't be able to reconcile such differences," the Bishop said. "It will be enough, it seems to me, if we learn to respect one another's beliefs."

"Yes, that in itself will be a major step toward the achievement of universal tolerance. And that's the real goal, the paramount goal, regardless of whether a man is a Protestant, a Catholic, a Jew, a Mos——" He broke off as the door opened.

Vivienne stood in the frame, her mink stole over her shoulders. "I'm home, Uncle Philippe."

"So I see." The Count stood very stiffly.

"Marie is taking my cases up to my room. The boat train just got in, and I took a taxi straight home." She crossed the room and kissed him.

His return of the gesture was perfunctory.

"Well, Cousin Charles." She turned to the Bishop. "Shall I genuflect and kiss your ring?"

"If you've become a convert to Catholicism, if you know what you're doing—and mean it, I'd be very pleased." He, too, was reserved.

She kissed him lightly on the cheek. "That will have to do for the present." She picked up a bell glass and sniffed. "Am I invited to the party?"

"If you wish," Philippe de Montauban said, "please join us, provided you're civil."

Vivienne laughed.

Both men were looking at her sternly. "Was it necessary," the Count asked, "to make those viciously derogatory remarks about ecumenism just before you sailed from New York?"

"So that's what accounts for the chill. I haven't seen a newspaper for five days, but my publisher will have a complete set of clippings for me."

"No doubt you'll be pleased," Bishop de Montauban said, "to know you've appeared on the front pages again."

"Wonderful!"

"Is it?" The Count's disgust was tempered by his polite tone. "Since the days the first two tribes of pagans stoned each other for worshipping different gods, men of intelligence have yearned for a real brotherhood based on love and tolerance. That goal is finally within sight, but the self-publicity seekers—who can always attract a following of the shallow and unthinking—deliberately sabotage the most noble efforts ever made by civilized beings."

"I think," Vivienne said, "I'll go upstairs and start unpacking." She left quickly and closed the door behind her.

The two men sipped their cognac and coffee in silence, staring into the fire in the hearth. At last Philippe de Montauban stirred. "Why must people attack what they don't understand?"

author's note

It would be impossible, manifestly, to trace the history of bigotry or, conversely, man's struggle for religious freedom and tolerance, in a single work of fiction. Therefore what I have tried to do in these pages is illuminate some phases of these forces.

I am grateful to Dr. Georges C. Rodier, of Paris, for his assistance, and to my daughter, Noel-Anne Gerson, whose knowledge of past French customs was helpful. I deeply appreciate the guidance and advice of my editor, Herbert Katz, whose intellectual and intuitive judgments were responsible for the making of a cohesive whole. I am especially grateful to the Reverend Kenneth P. Flint, Pastor of St. Paul's Church, Waterford, Connecticut, who obtained for me, at considerable effort, all of the works, printed in English, of Pope John XXIII and Pope Paul VI; who offered me unstinting help in matters pertaining to Roman Catholicism; and who has checked the manuscript for technical details.

—N. B. G.